Waiting For A Girl Like You

Chloe I. Miller

Contents

For my readers.
Let's go home one last time.

ALSO BY CHLOE I. MILLER

<u>WELCOME TO HAVEN HOUSE</u>

THE SECRETS THAT YOU KEEP
PART ONE

OUR LIPS ARE SEALED
PART TWO

<u>RETURN TO HAVEN HOUSE</u>

SOMEBODY'S WATCHING ME
PART ONE

WAITING FOR A GIRL LIKE YOU
PART TWO

IF THE FATES ALLOW
A HAVEN HOUSE HISTORICAL NOVELLA

FAIRWEATHER
FAMILY TREE

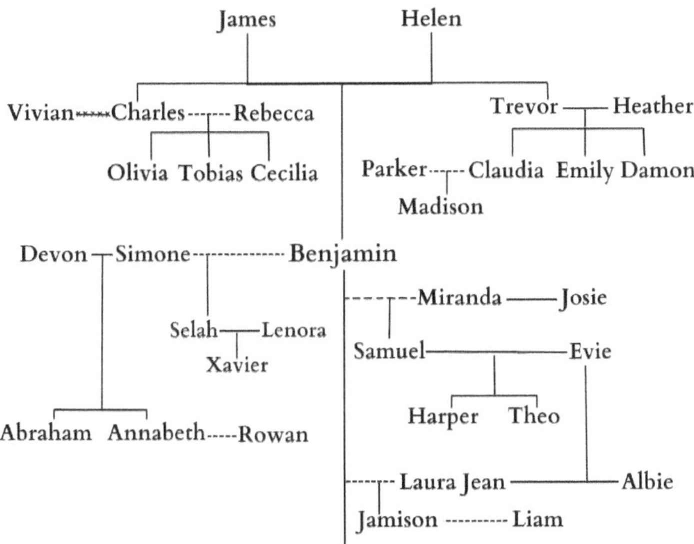

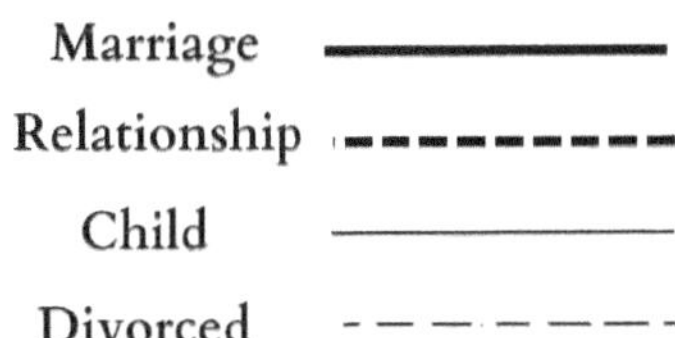

Marriage	————
Relationship	- - - - - -
Child	————
Divorced	– – – – –

MCINTYRE
FAMILY TREE

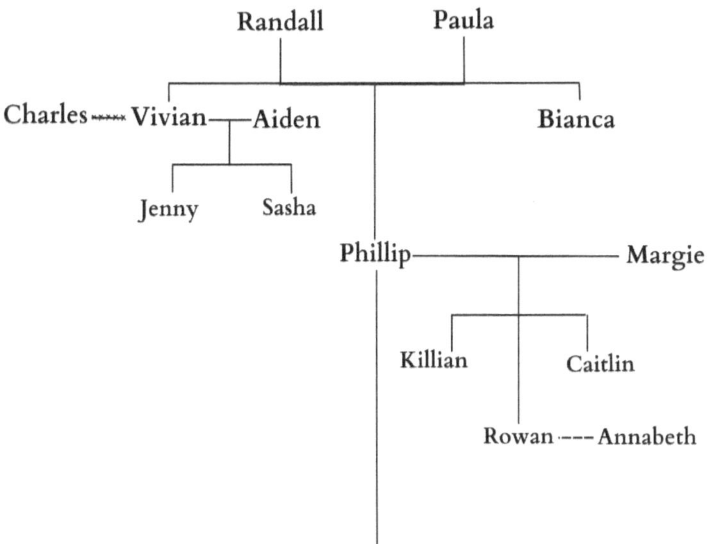

Marriage ———————

Relationship ----------

Child ———————

Divorced — — — — — —

Music plays a large role in this story, and to receive the most immersive experience possible, we invite you to explore the novel's soundtrack.

www.chloeimiller.com/playlists

WAITING FOR A GIRL LIKE YOU

SOUNDTRACK

Welcome to the final installment of the Haven House duets. If you're anything like me, you forget a book the moment it closes, and with this story, that unfortunate trait might leave you a little lost. Fear not, my friends. I won't allow you to return to Haven House without providing you with some sort of map. Below is a brief synopsis of the previous book in case you need a refresher.

<u>Somebody's Watching Me</u>:

We open in the past as we always do. Charlie Fairweather is preparing to marry Vivian McIntyre, and to everyone's surprise, they truly seem to love each other. The only problem is the McIntyre and Fairweather families don't exactly get along. As longtime business rivals, Vivian's mother and siblings are not thrilled with the marriage, and we get to see the Fairweather brothers work together to make the wedding happen, with Ben going the *extra mile* to win over Vivian's mother.

In the present, we enter the story five years after the arrest of Tobias Miller. Jamison Fairweather works in the Houston public relations department of Fairweather Holdings. Planning to go home for the weekend, she takes a Fairweather jet to Florida. Rowan McIntyre, the head of Fairweather IT, and Taylor, her father's flirty assistant, accompany her on the trip home.

Upon Jamison's return to Haven House, we learn that she and Liam parted ways six months prior to their wedding, which was scheduled to take place that very weekend. No one knows why they split, and Jamison makes a myriad of excuses even when Samuel, who is now a full-blown girl dad, calls her out for her behavior.

Another thing we discover during our entire reintroduction to this world is about Zanmi. Started by Tobias Miller's friends, the group has grown substantially over the last few years and operates much like a deranged serial killer fan club. They endlessly manipulate the public into thinking Toby is innocent and that the Fairweathers are the real villains. The organization holds several levels of 'membership' with everything from your average person who is overly obsessed with true crime, all the way up to the truly psychotic who think they've found like minded individuals.

Later that night, Rowan and Annabeth use the security system in a super fun way. Once they finish their game of *peek-a-boo, I see all of you*; Rowan spots an unfamiliar car driving up to Haven House. He sets off the alarms when three armed individuals approach the front door.

Passed out on a patio lounger by Haven's new pool, Jamison wakes to the screeching sounds of the alarm system. Before she can get inside, people wearing masks appear. Their leader's name is Michael Sinclair, and after his lovely introduction, the group drugs and kidnaps her, but not before one of the Zanmi cult members attacks Simone and Annabeth.

As the trio of Zanmi members flee with Jamison, they're forced to abandon their car thanks to a mysterious storm rolling in. A secondary escape plan is initiated, and the group attempts to make their way through the forest.

The haunted forest.

Raise your hand if, while reading, you thought this might not go very well.

The ghosts of Haven House make their presence known by attacking and killing the female Zanmi member. Michael Sinclair and the second man named Bruce hang back and allow it to happen, leaving Jamison behind as Liam rushes in to save the day.

Jamison wakes a few hours later and finds Liam in her room. She hasn't seen him since their breakup. We meet Theo and Harper, who are Evie and Samuel's daughters. They're adorable and will probably cause their father to have gray hair before he turns forty.

Downstairs, the FBI agent assigned to handle the Fairweathers has arrived. His name is Klausen, and several things are revealed during this meeting. The first is that Annabeth easily cracks under pressure when she confesses that she and Rowan were having sex via the security system. The second is that Liam has quit the FBI and is now officially running security for all of Fairweather Holdings. We also learn that Claudia and

Emily Fairweather, the daughters of Ben's brother Trevor, have both been kidnapped.

Oh, and we also learn that Michael Sinclair is a domestic terrorist. *Surprise!*

With this new, overwhelming information, the family hunkers down at Haven House, and over the course of the next twelve hours, dozens of Zanmi members are arrested. Emily Fairweather is retrieved in a raid executed by Izzy, the new secondary head of security at Fairweather. Claudia is dumped on the side of the road when her captors discover she's pregnant.

As things settle in the morning, and everyone utters a partial sigh of relief, Selah arrives and lectures Jamison about her treatment of Liam. She ignores him and stays hidden in her room, where she receives a phone call from Michael Sinclair. He worms his way into her head as the conversation progresses, and, from what I hear, far too many readers fell soundly under his spell.

Yes, I gave you all side-eye.

Liam and Rowan spend most of the day analyzing the call while Jamison mentally tries to process it. When she finally comes up for air, it's late at night. She and Liam share a quiet meal together in the kitchen, and Jamison confesses that she doesn't want to sleep alone. They finish dinner and head out to the cottages where Liam is staying. On the way there, the two of them have a *private moment* up against a tree. When phones begin to ring in the middle of their activities, Jamison slowly realizes Liam is using her to draw Michael Sinclair out.

The next day, Rowan talks with Annabeth at her bookshop on the beach. He convinces her to take a walk with him along the shore, where they share their first kiss.

Wanting revenge on Liam for using her, and ready to take Annabeth to her first real Halloween party at Firewater Beach, Jamison dresses as a sexy black cat to drive Liam crazy. It works, but the entire excursion out of the house ends up being a team effort, with Liam wanting to use the opportunity to draw Michael Sinclair out again so Rowan can track him.

While at the party, Jamison and Liam mingle with the crowd and run into a fellow member of the PR team at Fairweather Holdings. Her name is Jan, and Jamison has always enjoyed working with her. However, when

Jan introduces her new boyfriend, things begin to feel a little off, and the longer they chat, the more Jamison feels uneasy. Liam leaves her alone with Abe to see if Sinclair will call. As she waits, Jan returns with more off-the-wall commentary that steers into the topic of babies, which really freaks Jamison out.

A rainstorm blows in just as Michael calls. Jamison and Liam go home, but Annabeth and Rowan seek shelter in Annabeth's bookstore, where the two of them move furniture without their clothes on.

Back at Haven House, things are far less sexy. Liam and Jamison discuss the case in her room, running through it together. Zanmi has always been obsessed with building a family unit, and Liam reveals the FBI has uncovered something akin to a breeding plan within the group, yet they never took the chatter seriously. At the end of their discussion, Jamison realizes Liam is only explaining details to her because he feels that she's keeping something from him.

In the morning, Jamison and Liam head to Evie's ultrasound appointment, but not before dealing with Taylor. The woman pushes Jamison's limits, and Liam guides her away before she says something she might regret.

At the doctor's office, Liam waits in the car while Jamison goes in to be with her brother and sister. The baby isn't behaving, and the ultrasound tech tells Evie to take a stroll around the building. As the three of them walk outside, Jamison meets Holden, the new security guard assigned to Evie and Samuel.

After some shared giggles and a few jokes at Samuel's expense, Jamison returns with Evie to the ultrasound room. The baby cooperates this time, and everyone learns she is having a boy. With the ultrasound over, Evie desperately needs to use the restroom, so the tech permits her to use the employee one across the hall. Jamison insists that Samuel go and fill out the paperwork while she waits for Evie, but as she does, a ghostly visitor and a phone call from none other than Michael Sinclair alert her that something isn't right. Breaking into the bathroom, Jamison and Samuel find it empty and quickly search for Evie.

The ultrasound tech was a Zanmi member and attempted to take Evie. Holden and Liam stop her, and the woman dies in the process.

The next day, Liam tells Jamison he wants to test a theory and takes her to Evie and Samuel's house, where the power shuts off in all of Firewater.

Without explaining why, he rushes her out into the street and drags her down to the townhouses at the edge of the development.

Once there, Liam begins to *interrogate* her, and we all learn the reason she allowed things to end between them after a fight. A miscarriage. The traumatic event led her to have a breakdown, where she not only shut out everyone but also, in her depressed state, rationalized that it was a sign for her to let Liam go.

They reconcile... on the floor... on the kitchen table... until the next morning.

Back at Haven House, Dr. Cohen has arrived, bringing his new toy with him. A jammer, and not just a small one, but something that has a wide range and can block their discussions effectively. Once the jammer is activated, Liam reveals everything they've learned, including blueprints of a smaller version of Haven House drawn up by Michael Sinclair in 2019.

Upon turning off the jammer, Rowan announces that its use has annoyed Zanmi enough that they've left themselves exposed. He works through the information before running off with Liam as they lead a raid on Zamni members. Two days pass, and when the boys finally come home, Liam tells Jamison that they've nabbed the mastermind behind Zanmi's ability to spy on them. It's Michael Sinclair's sister, and they arrested her and her teenage son.

As everyone goes to bed that night, Jamison is plagued by a strange dream where the ghosts of Haven's past tell her that something is coming and not to be brave. She wakes up in time to see Jan from work walking across the lawn. They've had no contact with her since the Halloween party, and before she can sound an alarm, Jan slices her own throat.

Jamison's screams draw Rowan and Annabeth out onto the balcony. Jan is dead on the lawn, and more women dressed in white are exiting the forest, holding various weapons. The alarm system goes down, their phones won't work, and Liam fires a warning shot, which doesn't stop the women. They continue to come forward.

Even though Jamison says it's pointless, Ben keeps dialing various phone numbers, and (finally!) a call goes through to Taylor. They tell her to contact the police, just as everyone receives an ominous text from Michael Sinclair.

Over at Firewater Beach, Samuel's paranoia has doubled down, and he's forced the girls to sleep in the bed with him and Evie. No one is happy about it, especially when Evie's pregnancy cravings hit in the middle of the night. Being the perfect husband and father that we all knew he would be, Samuel goes downstairs to make her some food. As he does, we learn of his desperation for this Zanmi movement to end. They're literally ruining their lives and making every effort to get close to their daughters, including sending a member into Harper's old preschool.

On his way to the kitchen, Samuel finds Holden and Josie watching a documentary about Dr. Cohen. Holden tells him he's about to do a perimeter check, and Josie follows Samuel into the kitchen to help him make Evie's midnight snacks. They have a mother-son moment where Josie lectures him.

Once Samuel returns to the bedroom, he sees the girls are back asleep, but Evie is acting oddly, clawing at the window overlooking their moonlit beach. She's sleepwalking again, an unfortunate part of her pregnancy, and when he tries to lure her back to bed, Evie suddenly awakens.

"Miranda said, lock the door."

All hell breaks loose as their home's security system is activated when armed Zanmi women are attempting to break in. Everyone frantically barricades themselves into Samuel and Evie's bedroom, and Samuel calls (thanks to Harper & Theo's genius) Haven House.

A strange woman answers Haven's phone, and when Samuel demands to speak to Simone, he's told she's busy playing a game, and that he himself should prepare to play.

"Run, run, run as fast as you can."

*"Preserve your memories, keep them well,
what you forget you can never retell."*
-Louisa May Alcott

PROLOGUE

"**T**hat's for you to decide."

Throwing the ball into her court was the equivalent of a magic trick. Instantly, the woman sitting across from him lit up from somewhere deep inside. The Miami coffee shop was getting crowded, but at that moment, he could see nothing except her beautiful face scrunched tight as she laughed.

"What if I say I want to run away to Denmark?" Her eyes went wide as she thought of another possibility. "Or move to coastal Africa and open an elephant sanctuary?"

He smiled, enchanted by the shift in her demeanor. There had been an underlying sadness in her eyes for the past few days, and the difference he was now seeing left him amazed.

Which was a disturbing thought, considering this woman was a stranger. He didn't know her name. Her history. Nothing. And yet she was already past his defenses, settling into some buried part of him that had forgotten how to live, to laugh, and to love.

While trying not to cringe over the fact that he was thinking like one of those motivational signs his mother kept in the kitchen, he made a decision. Whoever put the sadness behind her eyes, whoever made her frightened enough that she felt the need to place her back to the wall and had her gaze darting to the door every so often, was as good as dead.

"Elephants don't live on the coast," he replied, hating to burst her bubble. "They're further inland."

She glanced down at his military fatigues. "Have you been to Africa?"

"Many times."

Taking a sip of the coffee he'd ordered for her, she sighed at the first taste. Iced white mocha with vanilla crème and caramel drizzle. "You've lived an interesting life, I bet."

"Not yet."

"Not yet?"

It was time to turn on the charm, and he hoped to hell he remembered how to do it. A good long while had passed since he'd last had a conversation with a woman, let alone attempted to sweep one off her feet. "As of today, my life has only just begun."

She giggled, tucking her long chestnut hair behind an ear. "Are you going to tell me your name?"

"Michael." He held out a hand, and she shook it. "Michael Sinclair."

"And just who is Michael Sinclair?"

Her voice held a flirty tone, and it was like a gentle caress down his body. "A small town boy who grew up to become a soldier."

"There's more to it. I can tell." She studied him with an adorable tilt of her head. "Where are you from originally?"

Talking about his family and life outside of work was easy. It was the simplest part of him. "My parents own an insurance firm that they thought their kids would one day run, but none of us are even remotely interested in doing so."

"How many siblings do you have?"

He forced himself to relax. Only fifteen minutes were left on the clock, and he didn't need to make this weird.

"Two. My little brother is about to graduate from high school, and my older sister is a stay-at-home mom who helps run her husband's cybersecurity firm."

She looked impressed. "Your sister runs a cybersecurity firm? That's pretty cool."

Most people would agree, as long as they didn't dig too deep into Kris's past. Her husband had no clue how lucky he was to have her handling the tough stuff.

"Wait, so that makes you," she arched an eyebrow and straightened as if in shock, "the middle child?"

"One hundred percent."

"Which means you're headstrong?" She raised a finger for each point. "Overly competitive? Highly independent?"

He couldn't deny any of it. "Guilty as charged."

"And openly admits it?" She tsked softly. "You, sir, are going to be trouble."

Leaning forward in his chair, he needed to be closer to her. "Since you know so much about being a middle child, I'm guessing you're one?"

There it was. That sadness creeping in again. "No. I'm the baby."

"How many siblings?"

"One sister and one brother."

"Same as me." She already mentioned how things with her family were complicated, and he wanted to know more. "Tell me about them."

"There's not much to tell." With a shrug, she avoided his gaze, choosing to stare out the café window instead. "It's just me and my brother now."

"Where's everyone else?"

The question was intrusive, but that mysterious sadness in her wasn't the only reason he asked it. The fear she radiated was just as loud, clinging to her actions and hiding beneath the melody of her voice.

"My mom died when I was little. I don't remember much about her," she said carefully. "Or my sister, really. They both passed away in the same accident."

He was on the verge of asking more questions, but then she sighed wistfully, the sound coming from a place deep in her heart. He couldn't help it and openly stared, completely transfixed.

"But I remember our home. It was big and white, with a library, beautiful gardens, and these giant oak trees. I thought I was going to spend forever in that house."

He would find it. She had obviously loved the place, and come hell or high water, he would rebuild it brick by brick to see her smile like this again. "A library? Are you a big reader?"

"I am, and I like to write," she replied. "I don't write stories or anything. I journal. Someone told me once I should write down my feelings when the world felt too big, and once I started, I never stopped."

"What about your dad?" he asked. "What's he like?

As swiftly as her happiness came, it melted into nothing once more, the melancholy she seemed to wear like a second skin returning. "My dad died in a boating accident when I was a teenager. We lived on a sailboat for a bit. That was fun—he was fun—and I honestly think he intended to be the best dad for us."

"It sounds like you loved him very much."

"I did in the beginning, but he changed and went back to his old ways."

Now he was getting somewhere.

"Drinking or drugs?"

"Both." She fiddled with her coffee cup. "Then, on one of his benders, he just went overboard and never came back."

The oddness of her explanation wasn't missed, but he didn't push. Now wasn't the time.

"So that leaves just me and my brother."

He took the opening. If the brother was the only one left, he was the complicated one. "What's he like?"

"A doctor." She wrinkled her nose. "Toby is a bit of an egomaniac."

"I know the type."

"I'm sure you do, but he's mine, and I have to be the one to deal with him." Her eyes rolled so high up in her head that he choked on his laughter. "And his girlfriend. She's an even bigger drama queen."

"A doctor's girlfriend, huh?" he mused. "Is she one of those who latches on for the money?"

"You would think, but no. She has her own money and has been chasing after my brother since he was a teenager. Toby hit a growth spurt when he was sixteen and totally changed. All the girls noticed."

"I mean, it happens." He smiled sheepishly. "It happened to me when I went into the military."

Her gaze dropped appreciatively, not missing any detail of his body. "You're going to have to show me pictures of pre-military you."

"When you meet my parents, ask my mom. She loves to dig out old photos."

The constant blush on her cheeks heated up a notch, and he reminded himself not to go too fast. "I'm sensing that you don't like your brother's girlfriend?"

"She's okay. I lived with her while I finished high school since our dad was dead, and Toby was off at college," she explained. "Brandy is crazy like Toby, but I'm used to her theatrics. She came with me when I moved here to start nursing school because Toby was interning at the University of Miami. Brandy can't handle being away from him for too long."

"So, what you're telling me is, you've got an egomaniac for a brother and a drama queen for a future sister-in-law."

"She's not my sister-in-law." Her mouth drew tight, obviously upset by his assumption. "Brandy likes to pretend that she is, and Toby goes along with it, but he doesn't love her."

"Then why is he with her?"

She floundered for a response and, when she couldn't find one, picked up her cup as if she were leaving. "This has been great, but I'm late for class." She scooted her chair back, the legs scraping across the floor. "Thank you for the coffee."

The bell above the shop door jingled at the exact moment of her retreat, and Bruce stuck his head inside. The man was punctual to a fault. "We're late," he said, not bothering to enter the small space fully. "Miami traffic."

Attempting to use his distracted state to slip off into the crowd, she tried to leave, but he caught her hand. "A name."

Chewing on her bottom lip, she hesitated.

"A name," he repeated, his thumb brushing over the softest skin he'd ever touched. When she still didn't answer, he stood and tried not to be too intimidating. She was scared enough and didn't need some man twice her size towering over her. "All I'm asking for is your name."

"CeCe. CeCe Miller." Inhaling deeply, she looked around as if half-expecting to find someone sneaking up on her. "But you can call me Cecilia."

Chapter 1

Devon

1998

"Now watch as air and water work together."

Releasing his grip on the balloon's neck, Devon let the air whoosh into the plastic bottle. CeCe and Annabeth clapped as water trickled from the straw sticking out of its side.

"The air pressure builds and forces water out." He waved the kids over. "What you're seeing is the applied theory of potential energy and atmospheric pressure."

Clamoring around the table he'd set up on the lawn, eight pairs of eyes squinted against the sunlight slanting through the oak branches. It was blazing hot, but with nothing except rain forecasted for the rest of the week, they needed this breath of fresh air before being cooped up indoors.

Simone glided in a rocking chair on the side porch while Laura Jean painted the scene with Jamison strapped to her front. Their argument over what to listen to on Laura Jean's coral pink portable CD player occasionally interrupted the lesson, but Devon didn't mind. It distracted the kids when things became a little too technical.

Catching him watching her, Simone's red lips curved. "Wrapping up soon?"

Devon shook his head and turned back to the kids. "As I was saying, air can move objects."

Swiping a brush across the canvas, Laura Jean shouted loud enough for everyone to hear, "Did you guys know the Greeks thought the wind and air were people? The entire sky had different gods that controlled it."

The crowd turned together.

Again.

"What kind of people?" Evie asked her mother.

"Fake people. Fairytale people," Samuel snickered. "The kind of people weirdos like you believe in."

Evie plowed her fist directly into Samuel's stomach, and Devon winced. You would think by now, the kid would have learned to keep his guard up. Sammy might be an only child running around Parkland Grounds, but at Haven House, you had to hold your own.

"Evangeline Renee Eddins!" Laura Jean hustled over to the side porch steps before Evie could land another blow. She marched across the yard, wagging her finger. "What did I say about hitting Samuel?"

"I'm fine." Bent in half and gasping, Samuel coughed through the pain. "She doesn't hit that hard."

Devon grinned at Selah, who was holding back his laughter. Come hell or high water, Samuel Fairweather was never going to let Evangeline Eddins get the better of him.

"I'm hot," CeCe whined while Laura Jean scolded Evie. "There's no air conditioning out here."

"Me, too," Annabeth chimed in. "I want to go inside."

The two leaned on one another, fanning their faces dramatically. "Can we be done?" they begged together. "Please."

And there went the lesson, which was fine. The temperature had reached hotter-than-hell levels, and Devon half expected the water he was using for the experiment to start boiling soon.

"Girls, come sit with me in the shade." Simone patted the rocking chair next to her. "We can listen from here."

Hand in hand, Annabeth and CeCe ran over. The girls were as close as sisters, forever together. Reaching the house, they bypassed the side steps and flopped onto the porch in an awkward belly-roll move.

Finished with lecturing her daughter, Laura Jean spun Evie around. "She's sorry for the disruption, Devon. Please continue."

"As I was saying, air can move objects." He silently counted those left. It was easy to lose a kid or two in this group. "Where's Abe?"

"Here." Abe's voice came from above, and all eyes rolled upward to the branches of the cypress tree. "Waiting was boring."

Wondering how in the hell his son got up there so fast, Devon schooled his features. He had to be stern with Abe, but it was hard. "Abraham, come down."

Abe continued to climb. "I think I can make it to the top."

The higher Abe climbed, the higher Devon's heart hitched in his throat. "I was about to break out the popsicles, but if you're up there, you won't get one."

Ruled by his love of sugar, Abe scurried down and was on the ground in seconds. "Can I have grape?"

Devon grinned. "Only if I can have the cherry."

"Mama!" Abe sprinted toward Simone. "Popsicles!"

Simone stood, ushering CeCe, Annabeth, and Abe inside to grab them for everyone.

"I want a blue one." Evie raised her hand, the squabble with Samuel forgotten. Taking Toby by the wrist, she raised his hand too. "And Toby wants a green one."

"Oh, I want a purple one," Livy said. "Or maybe green. Or maybe both?"

"I'm so hot. I want two." Selah wiped some sweat from his brow. "And I don't care what color they are."

"I want a blue one." Samuel sneered at Evie. "And I'm taller, so I can reach the box and eat them all first."

Evie took a step in Samuel's direction, but Jamison let out a blood-curdling scream, stopping her in her tracks.

"Oh, she's so hot in this thing." Laura Jean fumbled with the latches on the carrier. "Selah, will you help me get her out?"

Selah tried one side. Laura Jean, the other. When neither succeeded, Samuel stepped in and popped the carrier's latch, freeing Jamison from her baby prison.

"Thank you, Sammy." Laura Jean held Jamison high, making her youngest coo in delight. "Jamison is lucky to have big brothers like you two."

"Selah and I are definitely the superior older siblings here." Samuel propped an arm on Selah's shoulder. "Wouldn't you agree, Evie?"

"What are you doing?" Selah whispered out the side of his mouth. "Trying to get hit?"

Turning red, Evie stayed next to Toby while Livy diffused the situation. Haven House's own *little mama* knew how to handle every kid here. "Samuel, you might be the tallest, but I'm the fastest."

"Samuel is not the tallest!" Selah gasped at the insinuation. "I am."

Devon shook his head and flattened down his stepson's curls. The poor kid had yet to figure out how he wanted to wear it, and it stuck up in every direction. "Now, you're the same height."

"The fastest?" Samuel arched an eyebrow at Livy, unable to resist a challenge. "Ready?"

Smug like every other Fairweather out there, Livy stuck her chin in the air. "Set."

"Whoever makes it to the graveyard first wins," Samuel rushed out.

"The graveyard?" Livy scoffed, getting in position to sprint. "Afraid you can't make it as far as the mill?"

Samuel's eyes went wide directly before they narrowed on Livy. "Oh, you're on!"

"Go," Evie shouted, hoping to catch Samuel off guard.

Livy shot off toward the forest with Samuel right on her heels. The pair quickly disappeared beyond the trees, and Evie released a sinister giggle.

"What's so funny?" Devon asked, wrangling Selah into helping him clean up.

Evie shrugged and took Toby by the hand. "Livy will keep him busy while I eat all the blue popsicles."

Shoulders slumped, Laura Jean watched as Evie led Toby inside. "Is my daughter evil?"

"No more than Samuel is," Devon assured her. "They're a match made in... well, you know."

Jamison let out a shrieking giggle over some squirrels, fisting Laura Jean's shirt to bounce with excitement.

"What do you see, my baby?" Laura Jean pointed to the branches where the squirrels darted in a frenzied chase. "Do you see the squirrels?"

"Da! Da! Da!" Jamison whooped, arms outstretched, her chubby fingers opening and closing like she could catch them.

"That's not our dad, Jamison," Selah said as he dumped the leftover experiment water onto the grass. "He's not coming till tomorrow."

Laura Jean paused, her smile faltering.

"Da! Da! Da!" Jamison kept chanting and squealing the sound as if it meant something more.

Concerned by the distant look in Laura Jean's eyes, Devon stepped in front of her. "You okay?"

Laura Jean's small hand landed on his chest as if to steady herself. "Ben's here."

"Uh?" They were in the side yard and could partially see the front parking spots. Devon leaned around her to look, but Ben's car wasn't there. "Ben isn't her—"

A puff of dust lifted off the drive, and the sound of an engine could be heard. Seconds later, Ben's Rover appeared, sunlight glinting off the windshield like a signal flare.

"Well, alrighty then," Devon mumbled as Laura Jean took off with Jamison on her hip to greet Ben. "Weird."

There was no other word or explanation for that relationship. He would admit that Laura Jean was intuitive, but sometimes the bond between her and Ben could only be described as just plain odd.

And he meant that in a purely scientific way.

"Go see your dad," he told Selah, knowing how much coming home to his kids meant to Ben. "You haven't seen him in five days."

Selah placed the last beaker in the box and took off while Devon continued cleaning. Bringing all this crap outside had been a mistake, and next time, they would keep the experiments indoors where there was air conditioning.

He was almost finished when Simone's perfume hit his nostrils. "Here's your cherry popsicle."

Grinning, he turned to his wife, wondering if she'd ever figured out that he only liked cherry because it reminded him of the cherry red lipstick she always wore.

"Thank you." He took the popsicle and peeled back the wrapper. "Did you already eat one?"

Her slender shoulders shrugged, all innocent until you noticed that mischievous sparkle in her eyes. "Not yet, but I'm hoping you can feed me something bigger later."

Devon paused, the popsicle halfway to his mouth. "You are one dirty, dirty woman."

"Are you complaining?"

"No, ma'am."

She leaned in and dropped a kiss on his lips. "Didn't think so."

If someone were to ask him how much he loved his wife, Devon would readily confess he couldn't answer the question. He was a numbers man, so confessing there was no limit made his brain go crazy. The data gathered is what told the story. It laid out the details, giving him a path and plan that was easy for him to understand.

But Simone...she was an enigma. His enigma. Perfect in every imaginable way.

"So, ah, Ben's here." He stepped closer, snaking an arm around her waist as he ate his popsicle. "And last week, he bought a new grill for the back patio. Maybe we should let him handle dinner while you and I rearrange the furniture in our bedroom."

"That grill is enormous." She placed her hands on his chest. "And yes, I want some alone time with you, too, but Benjamin cannot grill. I don't know if he's ever even turned a grill on."

"I bought hamburgers." Devon gave the popsicle a long lick, hoping the move would seduce her. "He can't mess up hamburgers."

"Oh, yes he can." Simone pressed her lips together as she fought a smile. "He'll set the whole house on fire."

Squeezing her butt, he grinned when she giggled, but the sound was drowned out by the chorus of *ewws* and *yucks* coming from the side porch.

"Daddy, don't grab Mama's booty!" Hands on her hips, Annabeth shook her head at them. "That's dirty business."

Holding Annabeth's popsicle and her own, CeCe rocked vigorously in a side porch rocking chair. "Mama SiSi, you should spank him."

"Yeah, you should totally spank me," Devon whispered, finishing off the popsicle in one go. "And then I'll return the favor."

His beautiful wife rolled her eyes and elbowed him as if offended. He snatched her close, popping the ice to his lips to run it down the column of her neck. Simone shrieked, the girls gagged, and Devon realized that maybe enjoying this hot summer day wasn't so bad.

"No!" Livy's cry of denial echoed out of the forest, and two seconds later, Samuel appeared. The kid was hauling ass, long legs and arms pumping hard as he ran across the yard.

"Patio is base!" Samuel screamed, his foggy glasses half hanging off his face. "Victory is mine!"

Genetics dictated early on that Samuel would be tall like Ben. Once they were grown, he and Selah would be well over six feet, but Samuel would take top billing in the height department.

Livy shot out of the forest next, too far behind to have a chance of winning. "Someone stop him!"

Reaching the patio seconds later, Samuel collapsed. "I win," he panted up at the sky. Turning his head, he caught sight of Ben coming over. "Oh, hey. I won."

"I see that." Taking Jamison from Laura Jean and settling her on his hip, Ben arched an eyebrow at his son. "Don't you think it's a little hot to be running?"

Samuel lifted a finger in the air. "I had a point to make."

Livy gave up, taking her time as she walked over. "I need a popsicle."

"I got you one," Evie announced, striding out from the rear kitchen door. The screen slapped shut behind her with a satisfying pop. Crossing the patio, she stepped over Samuel like he was roadkill and casually dropped a popsicle onto his stomach. "And you. It's blue."

"I knew you loved me." Still on the ground, Samuel stripped the paper off the popsicle. "It was only a matter of time."

Evie turned to kill him with a death stare, but saw Ben standing with her mother, and she instantly turned on the charm. "Ben! You're home!"

"Hey, kid." Ben let out an *oof* when Evie tackled him with a hug. "I missed you, too."

"Are we grilling tonight?" Devon called over to Ben. "We can make you the chef."

Ben hesitated. "Um... Sure?"

For a man who ran a corporate empire, it always cracked Devon up how out of sorts Ben became with domesticated things.

"I ain't eating Ben's cooking." Ty rounded the corner from the opposite side of the patio. Dressed in his gardening overalls, he was covered in sweat and dirt. "I've worked hard today and don't want burnt meat as my reward."

Ben grinned at his friend. "Listen here, asshole."

"Swear jar," the kids shouted in unison while Jamison clapped her hands. As the collectors of the swear jar money, every child watched Ben like a hawk, knowing he was the one who provided a guaranteed payout.

"I sure as hell—"

"Swear jar!"

"Can cook a damn hamburger—"

"Swear jar!"

"And not fuck it up."

"Swear jar!" CeCe squealed, jotting it all down in her notebook. "That's five, Uncle Ben!"

"The beach arcade in Port Michaelson has a new go-kart track." Samuel sat up and took a huge bite of his popsicle, chewing the hunk of ice mercilessly. "If you keep talking, Dad, we're going to have enough money for all of us to race together."

Ben's eyes narrowed at the mini-version of himself. "Very funny."

"Fine, Ben can cook them." Ty wagged a finger at Devon. "But Devon has to season the meat and supervise the grilling."

"And there goes our alone time," Simone whispered under her breath. "Told you."

She gave him a parting kiss, leaving him for her shaded spot on the porch. Officially grumpy, Devon called Selah and Samuel over. "Finish cleaning up."

The boys whined but did the chore while Ben took Laura Jean and Jamison inside with Evie right behind them. Oddly enough, Toby remained outside, sitting next to his sisters and Annabeth. Once Selah and Samuel had the science experiment boxed up, Devon sent the boys into the house to put everything away while he went to join his wife in the rockers.

"Annabeth, go on and tell your brother to take his shower," Simone said when he approached. "Then get your things to go next."

With so many kids packed into one house, alphabetical shower order was the only thing keeping chaos at bay.

"Okay, Mama." Annabeth trotted off to do as she was told. Where Abe's head was firmly planted in the clouds, Annabeth was the grounding force between them, keeping her brother in check.

Most of the time, anyway.

Devon took the open chair beside Simone and laced his fingers with hers as they rocked slowly. CeCe and Toby swayed with them while Livy leaned against one of Haven's white columns, watching the sky's changing colors as sunset approached.

"Do you think we'll have enough money in the swear jar to go go-kart racing?" Livy asked.

Ty wandered over, leaning on the opposite column across from Livy. "Hell, yeah, we will."

The kids giggled, and Devon shared a grin with Simone.

"I don't know why the hell y'all are laughing," Ty went on, stoking the fire. "If you get me out on that track, I'm going to whoop all y'all's as—"

"That's enough," Simone warned her brother. "Go inside and make sure no one is causing problems."

Ty mumbled as he left, but stopped before completely disappearing around the corner. "Asses!"

The girls burst into loud laughter, with even Toby joining in.

"So bad." Simone acted shocked, her delicate fingers at her throat. "Someone should put him in a time-out."

"Or ground him," Toby replied, his voice a little louder. "Get it. Ty likes to garden, so we *ground* him."

CeCe and Livy laughed at their brother's joke, making him beam with pride. Devon caught Simone's eye, and she nodded. They had been told time and again how Toby's behavior was self-induced, and while Devon agreed, there was something else at play. Something that needed to be nurtured and not left alone to manifest into what might eventually become a problem.

He hated to say it, but they were already seeing such manifestations in his attachment to Evie. The fact that Toby was sitting outside without her was a feat in itself. Working as a teacher, he had seen similar behaviors in a few students, and attachment issues usually went one of two ways. The child grew out of it, or the attachment shifted to something darker, functioning almost like an addiction until a new fixation was found.

Off near the bayou, Rebecca exited her cottage, locking the door behind her. All at once, her children went to the edge of the porch, waving as she cut across the lawn to her car parked out front. "Hey, Mama!" they chorused.

"Uncle Ben is making hamburgers," Livy called out. "Do you want to eat dinner with us?"

Rebecca didn't even pause. "Not tonight, baby. I'm meeting Daddy at his friend's house."

"We're going go-kart racing!" CeCe shouted, wrapping her arms around a column so she didn't fall off the porch. "You wanna race me?"

"Maybe." Rebecca made it to her car, wiggling her fingers at her children. "I'll see you later."

Devon remained quiet, as did Simone, and they waited while Rebecca's children watched her drive off yet again without them. The older they got, the harder it was to make excuses. And once the dust settled from her departure, Simone cleared her throat.

"I believe we were discussing go-kart racing."

Livy plopped down in the rocking chair beside Toby while CeCe crawled into Simone's lap, the happy afternoon lost.

"Hey, none of that now," Devon said gently when CeCe started sucking her thumb. "There's no need to be sad."

A sniffle came from Livy. "I don't think she likes us."

"She loves you," Simone assured her. "It's just that your mama is in a... funk."

It was rare to see his wife struggle to find the right words, and Devon swooped in to save her. "Your mom does love you. She's your family."

"But why can't we be like your family?" Toby whispered. "What's wrong with us?"

"Like our family?" Simone placed her finger under Toby's chin, forcing him to meet her gaze. "You are our family, Tobias. All three of you are our family."

Livy shook her head. "But—"

"No, buts," Devon cut her off. "And I'm going to tell you something my mom told me when I was a kid. You see, we didn't have any blood relatives when I was growing up. It was just me, my mama, my mama's friends, and their kids."

"Like here?" CeCe's big brown eyes blinked in awe. "Just like us?"

"Well, the apartment complex I lived in wasn't as nice as Haven House, but the friends we made there were very similar to what we have here, and you know what, our time with them taught me a valuable lesson."

"And what was that, Mr. Howard?" Simone asked, rocking in her chair again as she cradled CeCe. Livy and Toby followed her lead, rocking as they settled in to listen.

"That sometimes the family God gives you isn't the one you're meant to keep. Sometimes, you've got to go out and make your own. Find your people. Find your place in the world with them." He gestured to the sweeping landscape. "And when you do, that's where you settle and make a home."

***

"Ah, hell."

Devon downed his beer in one go. "Dammit, man. I had faith in you."

Smoke poured from the grill, drowning them in a smog of burnt meat. Ben coughed. "I can fix this."

Ty leaned in to look, his own beer in hand. "How in the hell can you fix that?"

"Shut up." Ben stabbed at the meat until one patty broke completely apart. "Just shut the hell up."

"We're gettin' so much moolah for the swear jar," CeCe announced, head down as she scribbled in her notebook at the patio table behind them. "We're gonna go G-O-K-A-R-T-R-A-C-I-N-G."

"Capital T, CeCe," Devon reminded her. "And it's okay to make the tips curly."

Her handwriting continued to be inconsistent, even writing some letters backward. This journaling idea had come to him earlier in the summer. The process was meant to not only encourage CeCe to express her emotions when they got too big for her but also to allow her to write in a non-structured state, which gave him the opportunity to see what areas they needed to work on the most. He and Simone would review the entries at bedtime, discussing CeCe's feelings with her and noting any improvements or loss of skill in her handwriting.

"Everything okay out there?" Laura Jean appeared at the screen door. "How much longer before the food is ready?"

"About long enough for us to order pizza." Ty nudged Ben with his elbow. "You burnt it, so you have to be the one to tell them."

Shoving the tongs at Ty, Ben swiped a hand through his hair as he faced Laura Jean. His mouth opened and closed, his gaze sweeping over her as she cocked an eyebrow. "Since you look so nice, I think we should go out to dinner. How does pizza sound?"

Devon and Ty turned their heads so Laura Jean couldn't see them laughing.

Completely unfazed, Laura Jean shrugged, and Devon realized that she and the tornado of children behind her in the kitchen were dressed as if they already knew they would be going out.

"There's a pizza place that opened on the far side of Port Michaelson," Laura Jean said. "I read about it in the newspaper. It's family-owned, small, and perfect for us."

Ben and Laura Jean were still hiding their relationship. Normally, Miranda and Josie would've joined them, but the two were in North Carolina for their annual summer vacation while Samuel stayed at Haven House.

"Ben and I will take care of the mess out here," Devon said, already working on the grill. "Ty, take CeCe to get ready and help the troops prepare for pizza night."

After cleaning up what they could, he and Ben headed inside and found everyone waiting in the front foyer.

Everyone except Simone.

"Where's my woman?"

Laura Jean passed Jamison to Ben and went to adjust a loose strap on Livy's new summer tank top. "Simone said the spot cleaning job you did on the new grill isn't good enough, and she's staying behind to clean it."

"Cleaning a grill instead of getting dinner?" Devon frowned, not quite following. "What's that about?"

"This is what happens when you're too smart," Ty mumbled, bending down to tie Abe's shoelace. "You don't get subtle clues."

"Alone." Laura Jean rolled her eyes. "You and Simone will be cleaning the grill *alone* in the house."

Alone.

With Simone.

"Oh."

Laura Jean clapped her hands and put on her *mom* voice to address the crowd. "Okay, people, we're going two by two. Abe, there will be no running off. Evie, there will be no fighting with Samuel. Samuel, you will not tease Evie. Toby, stay with Evie. Annabeth and CeCe, you will not wander away to explore together. If Selah or Livy tells anyone to do something, you will do it. Does everyone understand?"

With a unified "*yes, ma'am*," the kids lined up at the front door in their proper order. Selah holding Abe's hand, Livy and Samuel side by side, Toby and Evie together as always, and finally, Annabeth and CeCe at the end.

Devon bent down to speak to Annabeth and CeCe. They were decked out in matching blue dresses and clutching twin Tickle Me Elmos tightly in their arms. The toys would drive the adults insane on the car ride, and since they were doing him and Simone a favor, the very least he could do was eliminate their time with the most annoying toys in existence.

"Let me have your Elmos. We don't want them to get lost."

The girls didn't argue—they never did—and kissed him on the cheek as they left.

"Thanks for getting rid of the Elmos," Ben said, carrying Jamison to the door. "Enjoy your night."

"Take as long as you want with your pizza."

"And go-kart racing," Laura Jean added, pushing Ben a little when he paused with a horrified expression on his face. "Oh, don't look at me like that, Ben. It'll be fun!"

The door closed, and in the unnatural quiet, Devon immediately headed to the rear of the house. He told himself not to run and to try at least to maintain some semblance of coolness. But when he reached the kitchen and found Simone pouring two glasses of wine, wearing the skimpiest nightgown he'd ever seen, the effort was lost.

Even the Tickle Me Elmos were impressed, giggling in his arms when he accidentally squeezed them too tightly.

Simone glanced over her shoulder and turned just the right way to show off the matching underwear. "Play some music. I want to dance with my husband."

"Dance?" Devon set the toys on the counter. "I was thinking of doing something else."

"Oh, we will." Simone sipped from her glass of wine, the red lipstick she wore staining the rim. "Several times over. Laura Jean promised that they wouldn't be back until midnight."

They had the entire house until midnight?

Devon almost giggled as loudly as the Elmos.

"How many rooms are in this house?" He should know this, but she was walking toward him, and his brain had turned into mush. "Twenty?"

"Something like that." She snagged the stereo remote and hit play, their favorite song filling the air. "Are we going to go exploring?"

Snatching her to him, Devon sprinkled kisses along her neck as they swayed to the music. "Yeah, we'll hit most of them. Not the attic, though. It's haunted."

Simone snorted, and he used his best move to catch her by surprise. A quick spin and then dip, holding her close. "But we can try if you'll protect me," he told her. "All the ghosts around here fear The Lady of Haven House."

"The Lady of Haven House?" Simone cracked the biggest smile. "Oh, I like that."

He kissed her soundly, straightening them to stand again. "Yeah, I thought you would."

Chapter 2

Rowan

2024

"I don't think I ever told you how he was screaming your name when he died."

The words echoed through Haven's cavernous dining hall, bouncing around the space. Shifting in his chair, Rowan focused on the laptop before him, remaining hidden from the monster taunting Benjamin Fairweather through a screen.

"He screamed for you to save him," Tobias Miller continued, amused by the lack of a reaction from his audience. "Begged for you to save him."

Rowan had to give Ben credit. The man was holding it together in a way he wasn't so sure he himself could do. The residual rage left over from the attack on Haven two weeks earlier continued to linger, and the McIntyre in him wanted swift retribution.

An eye for an eye and all that.

The women in white had made it into the house. Not many, but enough. Most died on the lawn, writhing in pain once overcome by the manchineel toxins. Sinclair had sent them on a suicide mission, and the women had complied without a second thought.

But the ones who made it inside Haven—two women with hunting knives—had every intention of killing them. Rowan firmly believed that. No matter what theories were floating around. No matter what Liam and his father thought. He refused to accept that this was merely a scare tactic.

"He called out for my mom, too." Toby shifted on his prison chair, folding his bound hands together as he lowered his gaze to the transport jail's table. Going quiet for a moment, he sighed wistfully, a sadistic killer reliving his father's murder in real time. "And Livy. Charlie wanted his little girl with him when he died. Hell, I think he even screamed for his ex-wife."

"Answer the question, Toby." Ben's jaw ticked as his patience reached its end. "What's your connection to Michael Sinclair?"

Flanked on either side of Ben was a Cohen. Father and son were observing and ready to leap in should something go awry. Klausen and another agent were also there, standing just enough in frame for Toby to see them.

Fighting a grin, Toby's savage gaze rolled up again. He was still handsome, even with the permanent scar left by Samuel five years ago. Rowan heard the women who followed him were obsessed with it and that some of the men in Zanmi had gone so far as to recreate the look, giving themselves a jagged slice over their left eye.

"Mike is family."

Rowan sat at the dining room table across from the group, watching the play-by-play on his laptop while they talked to Toby on another. Simone and Jamison were with him, leaning in to see the screen.

"Why did he send those women to Haven House?" The question came from Liam, his tone impassive and with zero inflection. "Was it to kill your real family?"

"How are you, Agent Cohen?" Toby did smile then, aiming his notorious charm at the prison's laptop camera. "Made an honest woman out of my cousin yet?"

A quick glance to his left showed Rowan that Jamison was reacting as expected. Poised and ready to leap across the table and through the screen to kill Tobias Miller with her own bare hands.

There was a pause. A flicker in Liam's dark eyes, and then, "Yes, I have."

None of them acknowledged the lie. Prepped and ready, they were testing one of Dr. Cohen's theories, and it was holding up.

"Ah, well, too bad I couldn't attend the wedding."

Klausen pushed his glasses further up his nose, his impatience showing. "Mr. Miller, I would suggest you ans—"

"Dr. Miller," Toby snapped, his pleasant demeanor morphing into annoyance. "I have nothing to say to you, Agent Klausen. I was told this visit would be with my family. My last one with them before you hide me away for good."

Dr. Cohen nodded slightly at Klausen and the other agent. "That's our cue, gentlemen."

Rising from the table, the two Cohens moved out of the laptop camera's range, taking the FBI agents with them. The four men came around to where Rowan was sitting to continue watching on one of the many monitors.

"Are you sure?" Liam mouthed to Jamison as he took a seat.

Determined as ever, Jamison rose from her chair. Extracting a diamond wedding ring from his pocket, he slid it onto her finger.

"Happily married," he whispered, not letting her hand go even once the ring was secured. "You know the rest?"

Jamison nodded, and with her chin held high, she went to sit with her father. Toby's reaction was instant, and a booming laugh of astonishment rang out, carrying all the way up to the dining room's vaulted ceilings.

"I ask this every time I see her, but how do you handle it, Ben?" Toby peered into his screen to get a better look at Jamison. The chains locking him to the table clanked, metal against metal rolling as he tried to get closer. "She looks so much like Laura Jean."

"Why does Sinclair want me?" Jamison asked, ignoring the comment about her mother. "What kind of bullshit insanity are you trying to pull?"

Toby's smile wavered as if he were confused. "You?"

"Babies," she hissed, color filling her face. "You want them to have Fairweather babies?"

Toby gave no outward reaction, only smirking in that eerie way of his. It reminded Rowan of Ben. Tobias Miller might not have the same dark features as Ben and Samuel, but that innate arrogance that lived in every Fairweather positively oozed from him.

"Did you know they come here all the time?" Jamison continued, well aware that Toby did. "They want a piece of you. They think we kept mementos of your life, and they're always disappointed when they find out we didn't."

Toby let out an annoyed huff. "Where's Evie? I said I'd do this, but only if she participated."

"You haven't answered our questions," Ben replied, remaining calm. "How do you know Michael Sinclair?"

"I told you."

"How is he involved with Zanmi?"

"He's not," Toby scoffed, this time appearing genuinely confused. "And why do you keep asking about Mike?"

The silence that followed Toby's question was deafening. He didn't know. Toby didn't know Michael Sinclair had taken over Zanmi.

Dr. Cohen was the first to recover and gestured for Ben to keep going.

"Why did you send those women?" Ben pressed. "Why did you tell them to kill us?"

Rowan zoomed in on Toby's face as something clicked in the good doctor's brain. "What's happening here?" Toby's eyes shifted back and forth between Ben and Jamison. "What women?"

Liam pointed at Jamison, and she stood, her turn in front of the camera over.

It was time to send in the big guns.

Rising from the dining room chair, Simone placed a hand on Liam's shoulder as she passed. The wounds from her attack were healing nicely, but some bruising remained, just enough to be seen on the camera.

Once Jamison was off screen, Simone came around Ben and took the vacant seat. She didn't say anything for a moment, and Rowan marveled at how an honest-to-God serial killer could squirm under the weight of this woman's stare.

The longer the silence stretched, the more Tobias Miller looked like he might cry. "Hello."

"Hello, boy."

"You never came to the trial."

"No, I did not."

Curiosity flared in Toby's eyes. "Why?"

"Because the man on that stand wasn't my Toby."

And with that, the monster returned. Hungry and desperate to inflict pain. "You're right. That Toby is dead. You killed him."

"And you killed CeCe." Folding her hands in front of her on the table, Simone stared straight at Toby. "So, I guess that means we're even."

"Do you ever feel guilty?" Toby smirked. "Have you ever once thought that if you hadn't thrown us away like garbage, none of this would have happened?"

"Every day," Ben answered without hesitation. "Is that what you needed to hear?"

"I think so." Toby released a long, trembling exhale. "Yes."

"Tell us why, Toby." Simone's tone changed, coming off as if she were scolding a child who had misbehaved. "Why did you send those women to the house to hurt us?"

"If they came to the house, they wouldn't have hurt you." Toby grinned, the evil darkness fading. "Like Jamison said, they wanted to find pieces of my life. They miss me and—"

"Look at me," Simone hissed, her demand shutting Toby right the hell up. She pulled the laptop closer, giving him a clear view of her facial bruising. "They beat me. They beat Annabeth. They tried to kidnap Jamison."

"What the fuck are you talking about?" Toby paled, his bewilderment growing. He glanced back at the guards standing stoically behind him. "What the hell happened?"

"Why don't you ask what they did to Evie?" Simone continued. "Why don't you ask what those women did to her and her little girls? Ask what they did when they broke into their home with machetes. Did you know they wanted to cut the baby she was carrying out of her? Did you tell them to do it?"

Just as they had practiced, Simone's voice rose with every question, higher and higher, until she sounded hysterical.

"Evie!" Toby tried to stand but didn't get far, thanks to the restraints. "Let me see you, Evie!"

They waited, allowing him to scream himself into a frenzy. The guards had been warned not to interfere, and the four men appeared to be upholding their end of the deal.

"She's not here," Ben said, watching impassively while Toby thrashed like a maniac in his chair. "You will never see Evie again. She's gone, Toby."

Something broke inside Tobias Miller. His screams splintered into wails and incoherent pleas. If it were any other man, Rowan would have said they were witnessing someone's soul shattering, but being that it was Toby, it was indescribable. There was no soul to shatter, no heart to break. The person raging on the other side of the camera was barely human, and comparing his response to that of a normal person wasn't possible.

"She suffered," Simone said, pretending to battle tears. "Evie suffered just like you wanted."

"No!" Toby screamed, heaving rough drags of air into his lungs. "She fucking promised not to hurt her."

The entire room went still.

She.

She promised not to hurt her.

Dr. Cohen and Liam had quietly been tossing theories back and forth between them. Rowan had overheard a few, and all held a similar theme—a woman. Babies and families tended to fall into the female's line of thinking, while males were merely the tools to acquire what they wanted.

Goosebumps skated down Rowan's forearms, and he double-checked his system to ensure they were recording without issues. The Cohens would likely watch this footage on repeat for days.

"Here we go," Liam whispered to the screen. "Give us something, you piece of shit."

Already versed on how to continue if Toby revealed anything, Ben and Simone showed no outward reaction.

"Who?" Ben asked gently. "Who promised?"

Dropping his head to the prison table, Toby slammed his forehead repeatedly on the hard surface. The prison laptop he was using jostled from the impact, causing the video to flicker, but Rowan wasn't worried. The feed would hold. His days of thinking Zanmi was a threat of the highest level to a home or business were gone. Thinking like that wasn't good enough. Since the night the women came, he had begun implementing security measures capable of protecting a small country. Humans weren't to be trusted. Outside flows of information were never permitted past his defenses. He had become paranoid, and he wasn't about to stop until they took every last one of them out.

"No! No! No!" With every scream of denial, Toby slammed his face against the table. Red sprayed across the linoleum, and when he lifted his head again, blood trickled from his nose in a heavy flow, covering his mouth and teeth as he screamed. "Say you're lying. She promised. Say you're lying!"

Behind him, the dining room door opened, and Rowan didn't need to turn to see who was silently slipping into the room. It had taken some pleading from Liam, but Samuel finally relented, agreeing to this scheme.

"Who promised?" Simone tried again, taking on a motherly tone. "Talk to us, boy. You know you can talk to us."

Toby wiped his nose, blood smearing across his face as he heaved. They were losing him, and this interview wouldn't last much longer. The guards stayed where they were, not offering Toby help. They were following their orders perfectly, but only because Fairweather money was lining their pockets.

"She hates Evie as much as I love her. Say you're lying." Toby rocked in the metal chair. "Say you're lying. Please. Say you're lying!"

With his unnatural rage building again, Ben turned the laptop to face only him, and Simone used the moment to sneak away, unable to watch any longer. She went to stand in the room's corner, keeping her back to them as her shoulders shook with silent tears.

"You keep saying *she*." Ben filled the screen, making himself the only thing Toby could see. "Are you talking about Kristina? Michael's sister? Is that who we're talking about?"

Michael Sinclair's sister and nephew had been captured during a raid executed directly before Zanmi sent their women. As Haven and Samuel's home had been surrounded, Sinclair had used the distraction to free his nephew, but had been unable to get to his sister. Kristina Scherer continued to sit in an undisclosed location, a place so secure even Liam and Dr. Cohen weren't privy to the information.

"Who is *she*, Toby?" Ben asked again, his tone one Rowan had heard a million times in boardrooms and negotiations. "Is it Kristina?"

"I don't know who that is," Toby whimpered. "Why do you keep asking me that?"

"We're losing him," Liam aimed the quiet assessment at his father. "It's time."

"Kristina is Michael Sinclair's sister," Ben explained to Toby while Liam went to speak quietly to Samuel. "She was arrested for—"

"What the fuck does Mike have to do with this?" Toby screamed, reaching a frantic state where the demon inside stood ready and prepared to decimate the enemy. Saliva and blood sputtered from his lips while his coloring seeped into an unnatural shade of purple. "Tell me what that bastard has done."

"How do you know Michael Sinclair?" Ben held his hand up, refusing to let anyone else over until he had his answer. "You want me to tell you about Evie? Tell me about Sinclair."

All at once, Toby quieted. Like a switch had been flipped, his head tilted to the side as he absorbed every angle and weakness, a predator preparing to strike. "You're a fucking liar."

Ben didn't bother to deny anything. "How do you know Michael Sinclair?"

"I already told you." Tobias Miller lunged forward, half lying on the table to hiss directly at the camera. "He's my family."

"No, he's not. I'm your family."

Maniacal laughter spilled out of Toby. Mouth wide and eyes wild, he roared with deranged glee. "Well, sometimes the family God gives you isn't the one you're meant to keep. Isn't that what we say?" Toby shouted as he tried to see past Ben. "Isn't that what Devon said, Mama SiSi? That we were your family? That you would always protect us and take care of us?"

In the corner, Simone covered her ears, tears streaming down her face. Jamison hurried over to wrap her in her arms, holding the woman who raised her as a sob tore loose.

"I was your family, Mama SiSi." Toby's smile only grew when he heard Simone's pain. Giving his bloody lips an exaggerated lick, he winked at Ben. "CeCe was your family."

"Samuel," Dr. Cohen whispered. "We need to get this back on track."

Remaining quiet the entire time, Samuel watched Rowan's screen. "This doesn't feel right."

Firmly pressed back against her husband's chest, Evie turned in his embrace to rest a hand on Samuel's cheek. Her pregnant belly hindered her from getting too close, and she teetered up on her tiptoes to look him in the eye. "I can do this. Trust me."

"Every ounce of trust I have is in you," Samuel whispered his reply, although a little louder than before. "But this is insane."

"Samuel, you know she can do it." Liam came over to lead Evie to the table, but Samuel refused to let go of his wife. Rowan couldn't blame him. He was a hair's breadth away from losing his shit entirely, and he couldn't imagine what Samuel was going through. "It's time."

Ben stood abruptly, which only made Toby laugh. Samuel's father was about as happy with this next part as Samuel was, yet understood it had to be done.

"Give me a fucking minute," Samuel snarled when Liam tried to take Evie by the hand again. He spoke at full volume, and the mic picked up his words. "This is probably a waste of time."

Hearing Samuel's voice, Toby's sadistic smile widened until it consumed his face. "Sammy?"

No one spoke, and the room waited to see what Samuel would do.

"Come on, Sammy," Toby taunted in a singsong voice. "Come talk to me."

Evie turned around, and with a calming breath, she tried to take a step, but Samuel stopped her. "No," she whispered. "This is for me to do."

"Sammy, Sammy, bo-bammy. Banana-fana fo-fammy." Toby slouched in his chair, dropping his head back as if bored. "Fee-fi-mo-mammy. Sammy."

With her brave face on, Evangeline Fairweather silently made her way to the seat across from the laptop. Toby remained oblivious to her arrival, his gaze locked on the ceiling. Once in front of the camera, she said nothing, allowing him to finish.

Laughing still when his head dropped, Toby nearly fell out of his chair when he saw the woman he loved. There was an immediate shift in his demeanor, and he straightened himself, trying to look presentable.

"Hey." Toby snuck in closer to get a better view, fixing his hair as best he could, even with the shackles limiting his movements. "Hey, Evie."

"Hello, Toby."

Liam moved to stand in front of Samuel, giving him his back in case he needed to block his friend from running over to his wife. Samuel couldn't handle having Evie upset or scared, and since the attack on their home and family, the paranoid state he lived in had only been amplified.

Surprising them all, Evie didn't show an ounce of fear. Rowan wasn't sure what he expected, but it sure as hell wasn't Evie being the brave one.

With an icy stare in place, the only hint of emotion coming off her was annoyance.

And the entire day was working out in their favor. None of them could have asked for a better setup. Behind Evie, the dining hall's high windows allowed the fall skies to roll past and serve as a backdrop to the oaks and floral gardens waving in the cool autumn breeze. It had been Liam's idea to position the interview here, with the grand finale being Evie. He had wanted Toby's last look at the outside world to be everything the man would never have again—the woman and home he'd left behind so many years ago.

"I knew they were lying," Toby spoke softly as if only he and Evie were in the room. "I would know if something happened to you. I would feel it."

Evie folded her hands on the table. "Women came to my home, Toby. They broke in with knives and had to be chased away by police."

"They would never hurt you."

"Scaring me is as good as hurting me."

"No. It's just sometimes…" Toby scooted forward, sinking into a childlike state. "Her selfishness gets in the way. These episodes never last long, and she'll snap out of it soon."

"Who is she?" Evie didn't falter, holding strong. "Are you talking about Michael Sinclair's sister?"

"What? No. I didn't even know Mike had a sister. And why does everyone keep asking about him?" Toby snickered as if she'd told him a joke. "I mean, he's a good guy and all that, but I hear he's become a little unhinged since I got put in here."

It was Evie's turn to snicker. "A little unhinged? Toby, he blows people up for fun and came here to hurt us."

Toby went so pale that the secondary laptop running a thermal scan registered the drop in body temperature. It was something Dr. Cohen wanted to do during the interview, but Rowan didn't know what good the data would be in a situation like this.

"Is this another lie?" Toby demanded, his eyes searching Evie's. "I didn't think he would go there without us."

"Oh, he came here." Evie's bottom lip trembled with outrage, her nose scrunching tight as she fought not to cry. "He came here, and he beat Simone and Annabeth. Then he tried to kidnap Jamison."

"Mike wouldn't do that."

"And then he sent women here to die, and more to my home to kill me and my little girls." A single tear fell, rolling down Evie's freckled cheeks. "They wanted my baby."

Toby's gaze dropped, finally landing on her pregnant belly peeking over the top of the table. He leaned back, all the excitement over seeing her dissolving into an empty stare. "Congratulations," he deadpanned. "Are you having a boy or a girl?"

Evie smiled at Samuel standing behind the laptop, looking dazzling and radiant in her maternal happiness. It was all an act, and after this was over, Rowan hoped someone had an Oscar to present to her.

"A boy or a girl? Hmm, I don't know yet." Evie sat up straight to speak in a condescending tone. "But what I can tell you is, I'm having my *husband's* child."

Toby's nostrils flared, and Evie smirked. "In our perfect home, where we live happily," she continued, packing each word with malice. "And where Samuel has me whenever he wants."

Ben lowered himself into a chair next to Dr. Cohen. "What the hell is she doing?"

Dr. Cohen glanced over the top of his glasses at Samuel and Liam. "I'm going to assume she's engaging in a plan those two concocted and didn't bother to let anyone else in on."

Rowan remained silent, also in on the plan, but not about to let Dr. Cohen know. The idea was to enrage Toby enough that he would slip and reveal details that would help them determine where to head next. The deadest of ends had been reached, with wall after wall rising to greet them at every turn. Nothing was panning out. None of their theories. None of the leads they gained from the raid. It was driving them insane, but none more so than Liam.

And the trail for Sinclair had grown cold, the man slipping off into silence after freeing his nephew.

Claudia and her family were also missing. In the aftermath of the women coming to Haven, Claudia's home was found empty, with no one knowing where she and her partner would have gone with their daughter. Before the raids, Damon had been enraged over Parker's lack of concern and threatened to snatch his older sister and niece to keep them safe. They could only hope that was the case, and that Damon had taken

Claudia and Madison to hide with him and Emily at an undisclosed location.

"Stop it," Toby snarled in disgust. "Samuel *can't* love you. He's not capable of the emotion."

Evie laid a hand on her belly, and Samuel tried to shove Liam aside. She had already been ordered to rest before all this bullshit with Sinclair, and from what Rowan had heard, things had gone from bad to worse in the baby department.

"He's very capable of it." Rubbing circles on her abdomen, Rowan could tell Evie was fighting the urge to wince. He recalibrated the feed, letting it freeze briefly so Toby wouldn't see her masking the pain. "I mean, at least I'm not just another woman in a harem."

She sounded disappointed and a tad jealous, which is exactly what Liam wanted.

By the time Rowan unfroze the feed, Toby was buying into it. Locked away for five years, his instincts had dulled, and while it was sick to watch this murderer dissolve into a puddle at the smallest hint of affection from Evie, it was playing into their plans perfectly.

"Don't say that." Toby licked his lips, thoughts of an impossible future with Evie likely rolling through his head. "I would have given her up. I would have given them all up. They were nothing."

"Her?" Evie's upper lip curled in jealous disgust. "Who are you talking about?"

Toby's eyes darted around the room, looking anywhere but Evie. "No one."

"Oh, so you're going to lie to me?" She slid her chair back, the legs scraping on the hardwood floors, giving the move just enough impact. "You know what? I don't have time for this. I will not sit here and listen to more lies. This whole time, you've said that you loved me. How can you love me if there's a *her*? And don't try to make excuses. Love—real love—doesn't require excuses."

Frantic over the idea of Evie leaving, Toby panicked. "Brandy!" he rushed out. "Oh, God, please don't hate me, but her name is Brandy."

Hitting the jackpot, Evie lowered herself into the chair again. "Tell me about this," she wrinkled her nose, "Brandy person."

"She's my wife."

CHAPTER 3

Jamison

Jamison's head nearly flew off her shoulders when it snapped around to see how everyone else was taking Toby's announcement. Silent chaos had ensued, and she and Simone hurried over to watch.

Klausen shook his head as he whispered to the second agent, and Will did the same while her father spoke to him. Rowan remained focused on the laptop, but his eyebrows were raised in shock.

Liam and Samuel shared a glance for a split second, then composed themselves, both signaling Evie to keep going with the charade.

"You are not married, Toby."

Evie rolled her eyes, acting her little heart out. Shocking statements aside, Jamison thought her sister was doing a fantastic job. Ever since the attack on her home, Evie had gone into what they were calling Monster Mama Mode. She had never been more ready—more willing—to do whatever it took to make this nightmare end. When Liam approached her with the idea of speaking directly to Toby before his transfer to Florence ADX, Samuel was wholeheartedly against it, but Evie had told him to get the hell over it.

"We would know if you were married."

There was no record of any marriage, either during his time in prison or while he was free. The investigative team had covered every facet of Toby's life, and once they were done, an obsessed public took over the task. If Toby had a wife tucked away somewhere, they would know.

"Oh God, I never wanted to tell you this." Toby covered his face with his hands. "But I was young and stupid, and in my defense, it wasn't legal."

Evie remained unimpressed. "Then she's not your wife."

"Do we have a record of a Brandy?" Jamison whispered to Will. "That name isn't sticking out to me."

Will shook his head. "He's playing with her after the Samuel comments."

A constant stream of names scrolled across one of the laptops in front of Rowan. He'd become a man on a mission these past two weeks.

"Not on any visitor list," Rowan confirmed, calling up a secondary scan. "No co-workers at the hospital here or—" He paused as the scan finished. "At the hospital, he worked at in Miami."

Toby's hands dropped, and fat tears rolled down his face. "I'm sorry, Evie. We just said some random vows on a beach."

Will's brows knitted together, and he grumbled to himself. "Beach," he whispered. "Go further back, Rowan. Anything we have on his time in the islands. St. Thomas and Grenada."

After leaving Haven House, Charlie had taken Toby and CeCe to Houston, where they stayed for a time before going to live in St. Thomas. Inheriting his mother's villa, Charlie enrolled the kids in school and seemed to live a normal life. But never one to stay out of trouble long, they learned he lost the villa in a poker game and had to live on a sailboat until his son murdered him.

Liam raised his hand to get Evie's attention. She didn't look directly at him, but tilted her head just enough to catch his signal.

"Beach," Liam mouthed. "Ask where."

"Random vows? On a beach?" Evie sneered at Toby. "How lovely."

Evie hated the beach. She would occasionally go watch Samuel surf or if their girls wanted to play in the sand, but spending time on a beach was probably her sister's least favorite thing in the world, and Toby knew this.

"I guess there's no time like the present to speak my truth, considering where they're sending me." Toby turned pensive, chewing on his bottom lip. "But it was nice. Our wedding. It was the first time I knew someone could love me for me. It made me think maybe you could love me like that, too."

"Nothing during his college years in Grenada." The screen to Rowan's left paused in its scrolling, highlighting a name. "Here we go. Brandy T. Carroll. Antilles Private School in St. Thomas. A couple of years behind Toby, but they would have overlapped." He ignored the laptop showing Toby and the group behind the screen gathered to watch Rowan engage in a search for the woman. "Daughter of Bryan Carroll. No mention of a mother in her transcripts."

Jamison crouched next to Rowan, her face wedged between his and Will's as they read. "Do we know anything about Bryan Carroll?"

"Yeah," her father said. "He's the man Charlie lost the villa to. Drug supplier to a few of the islands down there. When I found out who took the property, I decided Carroll was a big enough pain that even I didn't want to fuck with the guy to try and get it back."

"And that's saying something," Will mumbled, shifting in his chair to address Klausen and the other agent. "Bryan Carroll. St. Thomas. Drug runner. You know him?"

"Oh yeah. I know him," the other agent said. "He's still active. Operating out of St. Lucia these days, far as I know."

"Shit. This keeps getting better and better." Will turned back around. "Give me everything you can find on her, Rowan."

While Rowan continued to search, Evie continued working on Toby. She had spent the last two days rehearsing with Liam, learning how to act. Body position. Voice control. Emotional restraint. Liam had played devil's advocate to every worst-case scenario Toby might throw at her. He trained Evie to hold the line and to know when to let it drop.

It had been brutal to watch, but Jamison was sure it had been even harder for her brother. Samuel prowled around through the whole thing. He tried to focus on caring for the girls, but Josie took over that department, knowing it was for the best if he were involved.

"So let me get this straight." Evie looked pissed, pretending as if Toby had betrayed her. Off to the side, Liam grinned while Samuel scowled. "You married some woman on a *beach*, then came here and expected me to do what exactly? Play second best to your *wife*?"

"Equal," Toby replied, like he still had it all planned out. "You two will be equal in all things."

"And I'm sure she loves that idea."

Toby's face darkened. "She doesn't have a choice."

"She should have a choice," Evie snapped. "Marriage is a partnership."

"Oh, is that what you have? A partnership with Sammy?" Toby snorted and shook his head. "He has you so brainwashed. No offense, but it's pathetic. I guarantee he doesn't think of you as his equal."

"Because you know so much about us."

Toby remained unnaturally still for a moment, and Jamison checked the heat scan. The indicator showed his body temperature starting to rise, creeping higher and higher as he slid closer to the camera.

"I know everything about you." Toby blinked one eyelid at a time as he spoke. "I know how you like your coffee and the brand of wine you prefer. I know the type of books you read. I know how you sing along to every song on the radio and play music at a horrifically high volume."

Distracted by the shift in Toby's tone, everyone stopped what they were doing, returning their attention to the interview. Jamison moved around the table, already seeing the panic swelling behind Evie's eyes.

"I know how you sleep with the curtains open at night and how beautiful the moonlight looks on your skin," Toby went on, his lips twitching when he realized he was striking a nerve. "I remember standing behind that closet door, watching Sammy fuck you and memorizing every sweet sound you made. I know how the world laughs at you both. They call your marriage something straight out of a soap opera. Strangers worry over the welfare of your kids. What will happen when they enter school, Evie? Do you really think the other children will just let it go? You know they won't. They'll have the whispers of their parents in their little ears, and they'll repeat those vile things to Harper and Theodora."

Evie flinched. Her breathing had picked up, and the color in her cheeks was going from bad to worse.

And it was feeding Toby. The monster, who hadn't had a meal in years, was gobbling up the pain as if he were starving.

"When they're old enough, do you think your girls will abandon you?" Toby asked. "Will they leave their sicko parents behind, too embarrassed to have anything to do with you or Sammy? Trust me. No one wants to be known as a freak, and no one wants to know that their parents are basically step-siblings."

Evie rose from the chair, eyes wide and unfocused. "I think I'm done here," she whispered. "I'm so sorry, Cohen. I can't."

"Not yet." Realizing he had pushed her too far, Toby stood and knocked his chair over. Desperate and afraid, he screamed. "I might not ever see you again!"

Liam struggled to hold Samuel back, not wanting any engagement between the men, otherwise it might make the situation worse. Jamison was in motion immediately, ready to pull her sister away, but Evie appeared frozen, either by her panic or from seeing Toby decline into an animal-like state as he thrashed on screen. Railing against his chains, he roared in denial, begging her not to go.

Before Jamison could make it over, she watched as her father swooped in to guide Evie out of frame. "We're done," he shouted, loud enough for the guards in the room to hear. It was their signal to end the interview. "Turn it off."

All hell broke loose in the interview room. The guards went in simultaneously. It was a coordinated takedown, each handling a different part of Toby's body as he fought them.

"Evie, please!"

Samuel had Evie in his arms once she was out of the camera's view. Cradling her to his chest, he comforted his wife as she cried. "You are so fucking brave, Evangeline."

Toby's shouting halted when he heard Samuel's voice. Throughout what felt like endless days and weeks of his trial, the two men glared at each other, with Toby's lawyers vigilant about keeping their interactions limited, or else Toby would fall into a frenzied, nonsensical state.

Not that her brother needed to interact with Toby. Jamison didn't doubt Samuel would kill him if given the chance again. Witnessing her brother's own darkness come out that day in the graveyard would remain forever etched in her memory.

"Let me see you, Sammy!" Toby roared, straining as he battled the guards. "Let me see you."

Rubbing Evie's back, Samuel met Liam's gaze over her head. "It wouldn't matter. It's over, and you owe me this."

When Liam didn't move immediately, Jamison came over to take his hand. She understood the battle raging in his big brain. Good versus bad. Right versus wrong. He was weighing each outcome on how allowing Samuel to interact with Toby could play out.

"Hey." She tugged on his fingers, and his midnight brown gaze focused again, meeting hers. "If it were me."

That was all she needed to say. Since the night the women came, Liam had taken to overthinking everything. He was angry at himself for allowing it to happen or for missing something that could have prevented it. But to place him in Samuel's shoes, to make his mind accept that if things were reversed, he would want to send one last parting shot at the man actively ruining their lives and the lives of so many others.

"Go ahead," Liam said to Samuel, moving out of his way. "But make it count."

After handing off Evie to her, Samuel made his way to the laptop. Jamison held her sister tight as everyone waited to see what he would do.

Will stood suddenly when he realized Liam wasn't going to stop this. "Samuel—"

"Show your face, you bastard," Toby raged, his screams drowning out whatever Will was about to say. "You think you've won? You haven't won. She'll never be yours. Evie will always love me, and you can't erase that!"

The muscle in Samuel's jaw ticked, and the resolved look that came over him had Jamison holding her breath. He didn't move to stand in front of it, but instead leaned down so his face filled the prison's visitation room screen.

Seeing him for the first time in years, Toby went absolutely feral and fought the guards with a newfound strength. Kicking and biting, he struggled to get free, growling like a beast trapped in a cage.

Samuel watched it all with a sinister gleam in his eyes and a condescending smirk growing on his lips, especially when a guard struck Toby directly in the gut with a fist so the four of them could regain control.

Locked in tight, Toby wedged his head in a way that allowed him to see the prison laptop through the arms of the guards. "Listen to me," he snarled, aiming a finger at Samuel. "This isn't over. I'm coming for you, fucker."

Samuel rested a hand on the laptop, prepared to snap it shut, and cut the feed. "Not if I come for you first."

CHAPTER 4

Jamison

"Mr. Fairweather, perhaps next time you could refrain from antagonizing the serial killer on a live feed," Agent Klausen stated as they gathered in the media room. "That meeting took considerable effort to make happen, and far too many eyes were watching."

"Noted," Samuel replied, staring at the movie screen showing Evie and their girls in the parlor talking to Simone and Josie. Every room at Haven House stood on display, with Rowan leaving nothing to chance. Privacy wasn't something they could afford anymore, slipping right out the window with their sanity. "How long is this going to take?"

Jamison went to stand with her brother, wanting to offer comfort while everyone prepared for the post-Toby meeting. Samuel wasn't the touchy-feely type, and she wasn't quite sure how to help him. They had all been functioning in a haze for the last two weeks, putting one foot in front of the other as they tried to unravel this nightmare.

"The parlor door is engaged," she said, trying to keep him calm. "Holden is with them. You know he won't let anyone get past him."

Holden had made it his personal mission never to let the girls or Evie out of his sight. He went everywhere with them, not that they were allowed much freedom right now, and he was personally overseeing the installation of new security doors throughout Samuel's home. Every room would eventually have security doors like the one in their main bedroom, and a secondary panic room was being added to the first floor. Once that was done, Samuel wanted their new home in Georgia to be outfitted with identical measures, and wasn't moving the family up there until the work was complete.

Haven House was undergoing the same treatment. The hand-carved, heavy oak double doors welcoming people to Haven House? Gone. The kitchen rear entrance that used to be left open to allow for a cool afternoon breeze? Gone. All replaced with the best security doors money could buy.

"I know Holden will keep them safe," Samuel said. His trust was limited, but Holden had it in spades. "But I think he should be in here."

"I'm a big girl and can read the notes later." Izzy joined them at the screen, the noise level in the room rising behind them. "I can go be with your family while Holden comes in here, but only if you're okay with it?"

The reigning hero of Haven House could've asked to sit on the roof naked, and no one would object. They owed Izzy everything, even if she had ignored orders to stay put when the women made a run for the house. Strong-willed and capable, she'd come rushing to the rescue, and because of that, they could piece together what happened on the lawn while the rest of them were barricaded upstairs.

"They fell like dominoes," Izzy had told them. "One right after another, all of them clawing at their throats and convulsing."

Two women made it inside, but two more would have if Izzy hadn't intervened. One had a handheld sickle bought from a Home Depot on the Florida-Alabama border. She managed to slice Izzy's forearm before collapsing from the manchineel toxins.

The second woman, armed with a machete, had more fight in her. But, in the end, the manchineel fruit robbed the woman of strength. Izzy said the girl cried as she died, begging for help. Not knowing what else to do, and with the police handling the two that had broken in, Izzy sat on the ground and held her, whispering comforting words as the young woman took her final breaths.

"Thank you, Izzy," Samuel replied. "If you don't mind."

"I'll go with you." Abe rolled up, looking just as tired as everyone else. "I don't need to see or hear Toby. It'll just piss me off."

Abe wasn't one to hold on to anger, but after the attack, something had shifted in him. He prowled around Haven night and day, watching through the windows like the women might come again.

Izzy and Abe left, re-engaging the media room's security door behind them. Holden entered just as the lights dimmed, and the security feeds showing all the rooms in the house flicked off the movie screen and out onto various flat screens mounted on the walls. The media room was now a full-blown command center, with Rowan as its captain.

"You good?" Holden asked Samuel as they took their seats at one of the folding tables arranged in a U-shape. "We could hear Toby screaming through the walls."

The replay of Toby's interview fired up on the movie screen, opening with him shackled and shuffling his way to the interview table in chains.

"Yeah, I'm good. He looks like shit," Samuel answered, watching intently as Toby settled into his seat on the playback. "At least I know he's living in pain."

Jamison sat with them, watching the screen with Samuel as the others found their places. To her, Toby looked fine, even making jokes with the guards. "He doesn't look in pain to me."

Samuel smirked. "Watch his eyes when they tell him who's on the call."

Sure enough, when one of the guards informed Toby who was on the other side of the camera, his arrogance waned. The smile on his lips vanished, and what looked like tears gathered in his eyes.

"I didn't notice that before," Jamison murmured.

"Adrenaline makes you miss things," Liam said, coming over to kneel beside her. "You did great in there."

She didn't feel like she had done great. She'd felt sick the entire time, and when Liam slipped the ring on her finger, she'd nearly blacked out. It was hers. Theirs. The one he proposed with on a rainy day in Paris. It had been his first time in the city, and Liam, being Liam, had wanted to wander around on foot to get his bearings. During their little walking adventure, they passed an antique shop not far from the Champs-Élysées, and he'd swept her inside when something in the display window caught his eye.

That something had been a ring.

As they looked around the shop, Liam snuck off to purchase the ring while she was distracted by a pair of vintage Chanel boots. His plan had been to ask her on their last day in Paris, but he was so excited he couldn't wait and dropped to one knee later that afternoon while they toured the Luxembourg Gardens.

Even when she ended things, Jamison always kept the ring with her. She wore it around her apartment when no one was watching, and at work, she kept it tucked away in her purse or on a necklace.

Of course, she had packed it when it was time to come home. Liam must have gone rummaging through her bags, knowing her as he did, and found it. Now that it was on her finger again, it wasn't coming off. Ever. If she had to do the proposing this time, she would, and she would make it great. A moment that would knock his socks off and show him how much he meant to her.

But right now, she couldn't focus on life or the future. That would come later when the world wasn't against them.

"It's time to get started," Liam said, a spark of excitement in his eyes. "This lead could be it. We might finally get some progress."

Progress was something they sorely needed. "Well, get up there and explain," Jamison said. "I didn't catch half of what happened in there."

Liam gave her thigh a squeeze before moving to the center of the room, where Will was standing off to the side, flipping through a file.

"You want to take the lead, or me?" Liam asked his father as a hush fell over everyone.

"Go ahead," Will mumbled, shuffling through the batch of papers. "I'm working on something."

Stepping forward, Liam nodded at Klausen and the unfamiliar agent who had joined in on the call. There hadn't been enough time for formal introductions before Toby's feed went live, but Jamison thought she heard Will call the new arrival Agent Anderson. "That was productive. Thanks to the Bureau for making that call happen. I know it wasn't easy."

Klausen inclined his head. "It's always interesting joining a Fairweather family reunion."

Normally, Jamison would want to bite his head off for that remark, but Klausen was growing on her. He and his team were working their asses off to help, and she was learning not to snarl at every sarcastic remark that came out of his mouth.

"But the thanks should go to my colleague," Klausen continued. "Without Agent Anderson, that call wouldn't have been possible."

"You owe me one, Will." Anderson fixed Liam's father with a stare. "Actually, you owe me two if we count that crap that went down ten years ago."

Will continued reading. "The crap that went down ten years ago was a draw, but this," he looked up, waving the paperwork, "*this* I owe you for."

The lights dimmed further, allowing everyone to have a clear view of the movie screen and Toby. On the opposite side of the room from where she sat with Samuel and Holden, Jamison noticed how the three laptops aimed at Rowan glowed in the partial darkness, highlighting his sharp cheekbones. Tapping at the keyboard, he sent the video of Toby off to one side of the movie screen and ran a never-ending list of stats and details on the other side.

"He's out of the loop," Liam announced. "Toby has had no contact with the outside world for seven months. No visitors. No smuggled info."

"Why seven months?" Anderson asked. "How do you know such a specific time frame?"

Jamison held up her hand, wiggling the diamond on her finger. "He thinks we're married."

"We called off our engagement almost seven months ago, and Toby was unaware," Liam explained. "He likes to keep up with family gossip and pass it along to Zanmi so they can antagonize us with it. He wouldn't have missed a chance with something like that."

Agent Anderson's crystal blue eyes slid between Jamison and Liam, obviously not understanding. "But..."

"It's best not to get into it," Klausen whispered loudly to Anderson. "The whole family is..." He smiled apologetically at them. "It's just that I would leave it alone. They've been through enough."

Slouched low in his chair with his arms crossed, Samuel glared daggers at Klausen. "Careful, Klausen. You almost sound like you're protecting our privacy."

"It's not our job to protect your privacy, Mr. Fairweather," Agent Anderson replied evenly. "It's our job to stop the threat that's endangering your safety."

Jamison pressed her lips together to keep quiet. Her brother was strung so tight that he could snap at any moment, and no one was interested in being around Samuel when he did. Nor did they want to have to bury two FBI agents in the backyard should he decide to take out his frustrations on the very people who were trying to help.

"And Toby is no longer the threat," Liam cut in, deliberately moving to block Anderson from Samuel's view. "It looks like BOP and the Marshal's office were telling the truth. We tested several false scenarios, and Toby didn't recognize any of them."

"He could have been acting," Klausen pointed out. "This is Tobias Miller we're talking about. The man is a master at manipulation, so much so that you all allowed him into your lives again and didn't even realize it."

"He wasn't faking," her father said from the back of the room. Never the type to stay still for very long, he paced in the confined space. "When Toby thought Evie was hurt, he believed it. He was upset."

"How do you know, Ben?" Bernie asked as she reviewed documents with Annabeth. "This is only your second interaction with him since he's been incarcerated."

"Laura Jean and I took all the children go-kart racing one summer. While they were on the track, Toby tried to ram into the back of Samuel's car and knock him out, but the move backfired. Toby struck the railing, jamming his shoulder hard enough that we thought we might have to take him to the hospital. The whole time, he kept screaming the same thing."

"Say you're lying." Annabeth perked up a little when she gasped at the memory. "I remember that! He kept yelling it."

"Yeah, he sure as fuck did," Samuel mumbled softly where only Jamison could hear. "He would say it sometimes, but the day he tried to knock me out of the race because Evie brought me a popsicle, he just kept screaming it. After that, it became his crutch phrase when he was upset."

Jamison blinked. "He tried to hurt you over a popsicle?"

Samuel gave a half-shrug. "Evie was nice to me before we left to go to the track, and I guess Toby got pissed."

"Because she was nice to you?"

Turning his head to the monitor that showed his family, a hint of a smile softened her brother's face. "Back then, that was rare."

Will held up the papers in his hand. "And there are a dozen other indicators supporting Liam's claim. The biometric scans don't lie. His body temperature drops when he thinks Evie is hurt. It spikes when provoked." He looked over his glasses at Samuel. "And yes, that includes your little performance."

"Whoops." Samuel smirked, not at all remorseful. "What about this Brandy person? That had to be a lie. He had a horde of women at his disposal, and there's no way some 'wife' would allow him to kill and rape women unless she's as twisted as he is."

"And no woman would be okay with her man, or whatever, obsessing over someone else so much that he tries to kidnap her," Jamison added, agreeing with her brother. "I would think even psycho crazies have standards."

"I'm combing Toby's history for a Brandy," Rowan said. "Just the one so far. Brandy T. Carroll. I've got transcripts and a paper trail that ends in Kingston."

"As in Jamaica?" Agent Anderson quirked an eyebrow. "If she's Bryan Carroll's daughter, that would make sense. He hails from Boston but ended up in the Caribbean running drugs for his uncle and later built his own empire."

"Not Jamaica." Rowan switched out Brandy Carroll's school transcripts and brought up an island map. "St. Vincent and the Grenadines. Her dad bought her a house there as a high school graduation gift. She still owns it."

"St. Vincent and the Grenadines isn't far from Grenada, right?" Liam stepped closer to the screen as the map expanded, showing he was correct. "According to the transcripts, this Brandy Carroll is a couple of years younger than Toby, so when she graduated, he would have already been at college in Grenada."

"She's CeCe's age," Annabeth said, pointing to the school transcript for Rowan to bring it back up for them to view. "Maybe they were in the same classes together."

Liam rifled through a nearby stack of files. Jamison knew exactly what he was after. The single photo they had of a very young CeCe at school, happy and smiling with friends. "Got a visual yet, Rowan?"

Rowan's eyes didn't leave his laptop screen as CeCe's transcript popped up next to Brandy Carroll's, their years of attendance nearly identical. "Not yet, but give me an hour, and you'll have one."

"I'm sure CeCe Miller and Brandy Carroll had classes together." Agent Anderson said, studying the transcripts. "Look, I grew up in the Caribbean because of my mother's work. Schools are small, and while I'm sure things have changed in the last fifty years, the areas are not that big, so growth would be minimal. It's not a stretch to think Brandy and CeCe were in close proximity to one another during their time there. But do you really believe Miller? He's probably blowing smoke up your asses to try and divert attention from Sinclair."

"We follow every lead," Will replied with a shrug. "Even the weird ones. Like Liam chasing down a painting at a murder scene. If he hadn't followed that bizarre lead, Evangeline Fairweather might be dead and Miller still on the loose."

Samuel tensed, and Jamison risked a glance his way. The color had drained from her brother's face, and he was no longer paying attention to the conversation, but back to watching Evie on the TV.

Anderson gave a reluctant nod. "Fair. But Miller's case? It's never made sense. Ritualistic killings in both South Florida and Missouri that even you haven't been able to decipher."

"I have an idea," Will said evenly, not at all upset by Agent Anderson's words. "It's a far-fetched one, but it's possible."

"Far-fetched? This whole case is far-fetched." Anderson flipped open a file sitting on the table before him. "Miller kills those girls and then comes here to do what? Secretly seduce a woman he's been in love with, except, oh wait, he has a wife hidden away somewhere?"

"Don't forget, he also breaks into Haven House several times to steal stuff," Will added, the corners of his mouth lifting into a grin. "Paintings are just some of the items he took. Does anyone know the full list off the top of their head?"

"Ten plates, six Christmas ornaments, two boxes of family photos, a set of antique candlesticks, a wedding dress, a jewelry box, a wedding ring, a spare dining room chair, a mirror, fourteen crystal wine glasses, a chessboard, and twenty-six total paintings not including the ones recovered from the multiple crime scenes," Liam shot off the list without taking a breath. "The only thing we've recovered is the wedding dress.

Mathis found it when he raided the apartment Toby was staying in while pretending to be Lucas Fields."

Annabeth nodded. "My mom is still pissed about that dining room chair, and the crystal glasses were part of her wedding set."

"So, during the height of his active state, Miller was not only murdering women and trying to get Evangeline Fairweather to fall in love with him while he's *supposedly* married to someone else, but he's also dabbling in lifting random goods from his former residence to do what with exactly?" Anderson held up a photo of a candlestick. "Decorate his bachelor pad to make it homier for the misses?"

Jamison stared at Agent Anderson, as did everyone else in the room, all likely thinking the same thing. Who the hell was this guy? Older than both her dad and Liam's dad, he had a sharp edge to him. Anderson appeared capable and confident in what he was saying, even though no one in their right mind would ever challenge Will Cohen openly on a criminal evaluation.

Not that she regularly hung out with her—hopefully—future father-in-law during his brainstorming sessions with the FBI, but she liked to think she had gained enough experience to know Will's line of thinking was almost always right.

"Funny you should say that." Liam turned to face the main screen again. "Rowan, bring up the blueprints."

The movie screen was wiped clean of all data, and the blueprints of what they were calling the mini-Haven House filled every available inch.

Anderson stood and approached the screen to take a closer look. "This place?"

"Nope." Will excitedly smacked Anderson's shoulder with the folder he was holding. "Don't get mad that we kept this from you, but these are blueprints drawn up in 2018 by Michael Sinclair. A mini Haven House."

"What the hell, Will?" Anderson craned his neck, examining every corner of the drawing. "You hid this?"

"Klausen knew." Liam gave Klausen an apologetic smile for throwing him under the bus. "I'm sure he forgot since we showed him about five minutes before the raid."

"A raid executed by the Bureau, led by you." Anderson glanced back at Liam with an unamused expression. "You are aware you're no longer an agent?"

"Very aware."

"And if this leaks, Klausen's job could be at risk."

"Agent Klausen will always have a job, whether with the FBI or with Fairweather Holdings." Jamison nodded in agreement as her father sat beside Klausen in Anderson's empty seat. "If Will kept this quiet, he had a reason. Klausen and his *trusted* team executed a seamless raid, and best of all, they kept their mouths shut."

Klausen had pulled twelve agents in for the raids. One had been part of the security detail killed the night the women came. Two of the others who were shot and left in the pool to drown thankfully survived and were at home recuperating.

"With all due respect, Mr. Fairweather," Anderson said, his tone sharp, "I have a dead agent on my hands."

Anderson tossed the words over his shoulder, unaware of how seamlessly they struck their target. The world might think her father was an insensitive ass, but Jamison and everyone else in the room knew he wasn't. That agent's death had completely devastated him, and he was already making plans to care for the man's widow.

"The days of keeping things quiet are over," Anderson continued. "And that's why I'm here."

CHAPTER 5

Rowan

"Within reason," Will added to Agent Anderson's statement. "We're prepared to be more open within reason. I trust you, Ken, but I have a line I'm not willing to cross. Bureau or not."

Rowan's head jerked up when Anderson burst into laughter. The agent and Dr. Cohen were clearly friends, so if Will trusted him, Rowan would, too.

But, as stated, within reason.

"You really can't figure this out, can you?" Anderson studied Dr. Cohen. "I can't believe it."

Will lifted his glasses to rest on his forehead. "Even to me, the dots don't connect. I'm missing a single line that will make what I'm seeing more solid, and it's pissing me off that I can't chase it down."

"Sinclair," Agent Anderson said. "He's what's throwing you."

"*Mike*," Liam snarled softly under his breath. "Toby knows him, but the how and why is still in the air."

Rowan brought up Michael Sinclair's military headshot. The image took over most of the screen, and a split second of silence followed its arrival.

"There's no way Sinclair is down with this Zanmi bullshit," Anderson surmised, totally in agreement with the Cohens. "Zanmi is a disorganized hodgepodge of nutcases who has a few wealthy backers, and those backers were just giving the group money to shut them up."

"Always watch what you do in your college years, kids," Bernie said sarcastically. "It'll come back to bite you in the ass, especially if you engage in extremely taboo sexual experimentation."

"Zanmi *had* wealthy backers," Rowan said, so fucking tired of these people. His brain was raw from the information he'd consumed regarding Toby's friends. "Etienne is dead. Henderson is now dead, and all we have left is Gilbert."

"Gilbert has very little to do with the group," Klausen said. "But it doesn't matter. His hefty donations were for Toby's defense, and with Miller headed to Florence ADX, his funds are useless."

"Yes, while we can trace Gilbert's money to keep Toby's high-dollar lawyer on retainer, it also sustained Zanmi's way of life," Liam argued, and Rowan gladly tossed Sinclair's photo off the screen and brought up the intricate financial trail he had compiled. "Even in the trusts, each of Toby's college friends left large sums of money to the organization. It funded those who were heavily involved and left their lives behind."

Another line of money was coming in, matching the funds supplied by the doctors equally. With Etienne and Henderson's deaths, that income stream had grown until it covered most of what the group was missing from their steady money supply.

Liam had said that the flow of cash always existed, but when they explored its origins, they never found the source, and not being able to find it was yet another thing that weighed on his mind. He was failing at every turn, completely blocked and unable to navigate the chaos.

Jamison raised her hand. "Would Michael have that kind of money? I know he was just a soldier, but don't they get hazard pay or something?"

Rowan had thought the same. He knew exactly how much both foreign and domestic governments would pay someone else to do their dirty work. Sinclair seemed like a man who would readily dive into such ventures without hesitation.

"Not enough to cover what the group needs," Anderson replied. "Zanmi was bleeding those doctors dry, and it still wasn't enough." He walked over to the screen and tapped at the mysterious financial line. "And this right here? This isn't Sinclair."

"Tell me what you know about Bryan Carroll." Liam joined Anderson, and Rowan switched to the latest photo they had of Carroll. The image showed a man in his seventies lounging on a lanai, floral print shirt open and potbelly out as he enjoyed a cigar while talking on the phone.

"I'm going to play devil's advocate here and ask, what if Sinclair was working for someone like Carroll?" Bernie aimed her pen at the screen. "Not Carroll himself, but what if Sinclair is actually the one funding the group now? It would explain the dedication. Studies show that a high percentage of humans understand what it means to stay in line to maintain a certain way of life. Governments worldwide use the tactic to manage what would otherwise be unruly societies. Control the money, and you control the chaos. Sinclair would have picked up on this while in the service, so what if he gave up his bombing crusade to work for companies or governments that exploited their people with both brute strength and monetary abuse? What if he learned and, while he did, was paid well in the process?"

Rowan caught Liam's eye. He had only mentioned his occasional side job offers to Liam, not wanting the information widely known.

"Am I right, Rowan?" Bernie pressed. "They pay well, don't they?"

Liam's mother was downright scary, and Rowan bet Liam never got away with anything as a teenager. "Yes, ma'am. Very well."

Annabeth laid her hand on his thigh, relaxing him. She hadn't left his side these past two weeks. Rowan understood her desperate need to help was her way of coping, and he was fine with that, craving her nearness.

But they'd had no alone time. Cameras were everywhere, causing additional strain. The slightest brush of Annabeth's hand or a lingering look had him on edge. Five minutes—two, if he were honest—was all that would be needed for some relief.

"So, you agree it's plausible?" Bernie asked her son and husband. "Or is Sinclair just playing pretend?"

"Sinclair isn't the fake-it-till-you-make-it type," Liam replied. "Not with how meticulous he is."

"I agree." Anderson shook his head in dismay. "But it still doesn't explain why he's involved with Miller or their connection."

"It's personal," Samuel tore his eyes from the feed showing his family to address Agent Anderson. "This is personal to him. I don't know the why, but look at how he reacted when his sister and nephew were taken. Sinclair sent those women to my house—to Haven House—and for what? To kill his own group?"

"If anything, Sinclair was acting out during a psychotic break, which is common for his sort." Will tapped on the table, and Rowan switched the display to pictures of the women who died that night. Photos plucked from social media or provided by parents who didn't understand why their daughters would do such a thing, the images showed everyday women caught up in the fevered throes of a false community. "He needed those women for this Fairweather breeding plan," Will said. "Without them, it fails."

Samuel's brows snapped together. "I thought they needed Jamison and Trevor's daughters?"

Liam shared a glance with his father, and Rowan blew out a breath. It was something he and the three Cohens had already discussed, but none of them had worked up the nerve to say it in front of Samuel.

"They want Fairweather offspring," Liam told Samuel. "But they don't need just women. Males could achieve faster results if used multiple times with multiple women."

Samuel blinked at Liam and then sat up straight, his lips parting in shock. "What the fuck are you trying to say?"

"We don't think they were after Evie," Will replied plainly. "Perhaps the girls, but if you really stop and place yourself in their mindset, snatching themselves a viable Fairweather male to use over and over again on women of their choosing is a much more ideal outcome."

Zanmi had also gone to Selah's house, but things had been much less dramatic. Lenora's brother was protecting them around the clock, and when he fired gunshots into the air, the group dispersed with little fuss.

An unhinged laugh shot out of Samuel. "Ideal outcome? To have sex with me? If that were the case, they would also be after my dad."

The thought obviously hadn't crossed Ben's mind, and he paled slightly. "That's ridiculous."

"Not to be crass, Ben, but if everything is in working order..." Bernie shrugged. "It's a perfectly feasible idea for them to want to get it straight from the... *um*... Fairweather source?"

"I'm loving this," Jamison cackled softly. "From the source? Like farm to table, right?"

"This isn't funny," Samuel snarled at his sister.

"Oh, and my kidnapping was funny?" Jamison punched his shoulder. "Maybe now Michael will start calling you."

Sinclair hadn't called anyone since the raid, and he was no longer watching them either, giving Rowan zilch.

"I don't want him calling any of us," Ben snapped, shooting out of his chair again in a surge of anger. "I want this to be fucking over, so give me the breakdown from today, and then everyone needs to get to fucking work on solving the who, what, and why before they come at us again."

Rowan spoke quickly, knowing not to keep Ben waiting when he was like this. "Brandy T. Carroll. Daughter of Bryan Carroll. I'll find her, and we'll connect the dots from there."

"That familiarity in Toby's voice wasn't faked. He knows Mike. Not Michael Sinclair, but *Mike*," Liam continued. "And he's known him for years. The idea to build a smaller Haven House likely came from Toby."

Ben heaved out a pained sigh. "Sinclair doesn't care about them. Zanmi, I mean. Sinclair is using them and doesn't truly care about their well-being like Toby did," he said. "The friends who are like family. The idea of creating a large home where everyone can live. Toby was attempting to replicate what we once had here."

Ben had shared his theories before, but usually limited such conversations to Will and Liam. Or Bernie. Rowan noticed that Bernie often cornered Ben and Simone privately, compelling them to talk things through.

"The first several years of Toby's life were spent in an environment where everyone—whether related to him or not—loved him," Ben continued. "Simone raised Toby like he was her own. Devon mentored Toby as only a father would, and Ty taught him about the world in a way only he could. Abe shared a room with him, and Annabeth watched cartoons with him because no one else liked that weird Power Rangers show except them. They were his family, even though they didn't share a drop of blood with him."

"And we didn't know," Annabeth said softly, giving Ben a bittersweet smile. "We didn't know other families weren't like us. CeCe and I didn't fully understand we weren't real sisters for the longest time. I remember how it boggled our brains when someone pointed out we weren't physically related."

"We were a group of lost people who found a family together." Ben took a second to control himself, pressing his lips tight before turning to Annabeth. "Your mom? She's our foundation. Simone is, and always will be, the heart of this family." His gaze shifted to Jamison. "And your mom was the very air we breathed. Laura Jean kept us alive and happy, showing us how we could find the beauty in everyday things."

Finally, Ben turned his attention to his son, but Samuel shook his head. "Dad, I don't want to hear it. Not today. Today... it's too much."

Ben ignored him, continuing anyway. "And your mom was our center. Miranda was strong—so fucking strong—and a thousand times wiser than any of us. She could read people like a book and knew immediately when they were hurting or needed to admit things about themselves that they couldn't dare speak out loud. If you had a secret, Miranda would keep it safe."

In the years Rowan had known Benjamin Fairweather, he'd never seen him become emotional. And while he wasn't acting even close to what a normal person would deem emotional, this was different. Ben was devastated. It was like the past had rushed into the room, allowing all the years of pain and sadness to take the floor.

"Even Rebecca had a role in our family dynamic. She was so young, with so much potential, though I couldn't see it then. I was too self-centered, and me leaving that potential untapped opened her to being manipulated by my brother. That's not an excuse for what she did, by the way. I don't forgive her. I'm not a big enough man for that, and I never intend to be. Truth be told, I hope she's burning in the pits of hell. I hope she's in eternal pain for what she did to us." Ben cleared his throat, returning to sit beside Klausen. "But while I'm not big enough to forgive, I am smart enough to recognize her fall was because she wanted to belong. Like her son, Rebecca wanted to belong to someone, and I'm sure Toby was influenced by that. He was influenced by us and by the world here, trying to create his own twisted version. A world Sinclair isn't remotely familiar with, and those people are going to catch on soon enough if they haven't already."

No one spoke, with both Samuel and Annabeth shrinking a bit in their seats. Jamison was too young to remember three of the four women Ben was talking about, but Rowan was sure Samuel and Annabeth did. They probably remembered every moment. Every good time and every bad. There was such a thing as being bonded due to shared trauma, and when he first got to know the family after the whole truth came out, he had really thought that's what was happening here.

But it wasn't.

This family was bonded by their love for one another, and it happened long before July 4, 1999. That night might have irrevocably changed their lives forever, but it hadn't shaped them into a family.

"You're very right, Ben," Will said at last. "Sinclair isn't going to treat these people like whoever ran things before him, but he's put on a good enough front that they were willing to die for him."

"Izzy said the women were surprised." Liam went to sit at the table beside Jamison. "From the toxicology reports, we know they were heavily drugged, but she said they were surprised they were dying. I can't move past it."

"And that's significant," Agent Anderson agreed. "If they were surprised, I'm sure other members were too when the group didn't return. A suicide mission where your team isn't aware it's a suicide mission is the cruelest kind of betrayal, not easily forgiven."

In his research, Rowan had found that Zanmi had gone silent. The usual Tobias Miller social media chats were dead. Members who were once the loudest and most active hadn't even touched their phones in the last two weeks.

"They're either all dead, which seems unlikely," Rowan said, "or the rats are finally abandoning ship. The chat rooms and servers Zanmi used are now quiet or have just completely disappeared. The major players we didn't nab in the raid haven't been heard from in weeks."

"And we're checking to see if any of them have returned to their 'normal' lives," Will added, using air quotes around the word normal. "If they're no longer with Zanmi, they'll need to survive somehow. The newer ones should return to their jobs or their mom's basements soon, but the long-term members without Zanmi's support might begin applying for jobs or leases."

They could only hope. As much as he wanted to believe members were leaving the group, Rowan had found no evidence of that being true. It was as if they had all vanished.

"I've worked hard to keep this quiet and not to pat myself on the back, but I've done an outstanding job," Jamison said. "However, you're right. By now, Zanmi must know what went down."

Jamison truly had done a stellar job. They'd collaborated closely to spin the story just right. She provided measured comments to the press about the *mild* incident at the infamous Fairweather family property known as Haven House, claiming another attempted break-in by Toby's group. Meanwhile, Rowan planted false police reports for the media to discover and coordinated with Ben to keep the situation tightly under wraps.

"I don't think they're dead," Will said, excitement creeping into his voice, recognizing today as a victory. "But I do think the veil of Sinclair's leadership has lifted. Zanmi might finally see he doesn't have their best interests at heart, which could benefit us. The whole thing could implode from the inside out, and we won't have to do anything but watch it fall."

Chapter 6

Jamison

"Thanks for stepping in on this," Will said to Agent Anderson as they walked him to the front door. "Less than a month to go before you retire, and I dump this in your lap."

Hands in his pockets, Anderson grinned as he took in the paintings and décor lining Haven's central hallway. "You're giving me one last thrill before it's over." He paused to admire the grandfather clock that had been counting the minutes at Haven House since the day she was built. "And with Carter agreeing to come work for Liam, I couldn't help but throw my hat into the ring."

Trailing behind Will and her father, Jamison leaned over to whisper in Liam's ear. "Carter?"

"Carter is Agent Anderson's grandson. Our families were close when I was a kid, and once Samuel hired me, the first thing I did was try to bring Carter in," Liam told her. "But he wasn't interested. He thought private security would be boring after being in the Marines."

Jamison snorted. "He's obviously never met us."

They exchanged grins and continued arm in arm down the hallway once Anderson finally gave up his inspection of the grandfather clock. Simone waited at the front door, her posture perfect and that practiced smile of hers as sharp as ever.

"Ms. Howard." Agent Anderson gave Simone a curt nod. "Thank you for allowing me into your home."

"I'm sorry it wasn't under more pleasant circumstances," Simone replied, the crisp politeness not missed by Klausen, who hurried past to wait on the porch. "I understand we'll be seeing more of you?"

"You will," Anderson confirmed. "I've assembled a small team, but they're some of the best for handling this kind of situation."

Simone frowned. "Do you see many *situations* like this?"

Agent Anderson chuckled along with Will. "More than you'd think."

Jamison shot Liam a sideways glance, and he merely shrugged. "People are crazy."

"Ah, but it's the crazy ones who keep the job interesting," Anderson said, wandering over to examine the small cluster of paintings near the foyer mirror. "And if truth be told, I don't mind. I've always wanted to see this place. Haven House is something of an urban legend in my family, and when Tobias Miller was arrested, I realized my mom wasn't completely nuts."

"Come again?" The smile on Simone's lips dimmed. "What do you mean by 'legend' in your family?"

"My mom used to talk about this haunted house her grandmother grew up in and how she visited it once. My brother and I always thought it was just another one of her wild stories, but she swore it was real."

Jamison noticed her father was also frowning, almost mirroring the guarded look on Simone's face. "Only the Fairweathers have lived at Haven House. We've been here since the eighteenth century."

"My mom was Anne Anderson. She was a travel photographer, and we were always in the Caribbean or on some exotic adventure growing up." Anderson's gaze drifted up to the massive crystal chandelier hanging over their heads. "But this definitely is the place she talked about. Haven House. I think we even have a photo of that very chandelier stored in a box somewhere."

"Ben, wasn't there an Anderson family who once lived close to Haven?" Simone asked, relaxing a little, but not entirely. "I remember seeing the name on an old survey map when we added the gates."

"Yeah, but that place burned down over a century ago," he replied. "If that was your mother, it wouldn't be the same family."

Anderson shrugged. "My mother never married and kept her family name. The grandmother who supposedly lived here was from her father's side, so maybe those Andersons do belong to me."

"Any idea if—" Jamison started to speak, but was cut off by her father laughing.

Loudly.

Everyone turned to stare. It had been so long since Jamison had heard him do much besides snap or bark orders, and the sound of his laughter had her heart feeling light again.

"Your great-grandmother was Wilhelmina Fairweather," her father said, his laughter quieting when Simone gave him *a look* that meant he needed to get control of himself. "Haven House might be a legend in your family, Agent Anderson, but your great-grandmother is a legend in ours. The story, as I know it, is that she ran off with her doctor, and the pair supposedly killed her father during their escape. Shot him on the curve of the forest trail and then buried him in the family graveyard."

Jamison shivered. She knew exactly the spot he meant. The place had always given her the creeps, and whenever she passed it during a jog or while walking the paths, she used the unease everyone often felt as an incentive to move faster.

"Of course, there would be another murderer in your family tree," Liam teased with an exaggerated whisper. "What's one more at this point?"

"Well, I don't know about her being a murderer. The story we've heard went a little differently, but we've also heard of things like the conservatory," Agent Anderson said. "I was hoping to snap a photo for my brother. He's been obsessed with genealogy stuff, even more so since retiring, and would love to see it."

Ever the hostess, Simone gestured back down the hall. "Would you like to see it now?"

"Ah, thank you, but no. We've got a lot of work ahead of us, so I'll grab one next time."

Will escorted Anderson out to his car, leaving the four of them to watch as they maneuvered through the gauntlet of agents spread out on the lawn.

"That's the last of them?" Simone asked through a clenched smile, waving at the agents staring back at them. "Anderson is the last of them inside the house?"

"Yeah, that's it." Liam glanced back over his shoulder. "It's just family inside now."

Simone closed the new heavy front door, the clicks and whirls of it arming itself mixing with the sigh of relief that left her once it shut. "Thank God."

She kicked off her shoes right there in the hall. One pump. Then the other. They flipped and landed near the entryway table, the move being the most non-Simone thing Jamison had ever witnessed.

"Are you okay?" she asked, a little stunned.

Simone waved her off. "I want to change my clothes and take a nap." She gave Jamison her back and slid off her cardigan. "Unhook the top button of this dress for me."

Per Liam's request, they were wearing clothes that would remind Toby of the past and not the present. Her father was in a navy blue dress shirt and dark khaki slacks—his idea of casual—while Simone had chosen an old emerald green sheath dress she hadn't worn since the nineties.

Evie chose a purple blouse because she supposedly had always dressed in purple as a kid. For Jamison, it hadn't been so simple. She had been a baby when Toby left, so Liam had the idea of dressing her in her mother's clothes. There were trunks full of Laura Jean's things in the attic, but Simone also had a few pieces tucked away in her closet and pulled out a simple white tank top and green gingham broom skirt for her to wear.

"It's not even noon yet." Her dad watched Simone warily. "Are you sure you're okay?"

"I'm old, Benjamin." Simone smacked his arm with her cardigan. "As are you, you know?"

"Not old enough to nap before lunchtime."

Simone rolled her eyes and walked barefoot down the hall. "I'll be in my room."

"She's not sleeping at night," Jamison told her father once she was sure Simone was gone. "None of us are, but it's hitting her hardest."

"Yeah. I hear her shuffling around in the kitchen. She won't take anything to help her relax, so I don't even bother bringing it up, but something's got to give."

"My mom hears her, too," Liam said. "I'll ask her to talk to Simone. Maybe she'll listen."

Simone trusted Bernie. They were both survivors in their own way, and Simone had learned to lean on Bernie for support every so often, but none more than now.

Her father smirked at Liam. "That's pretty smart."

Liam shrugged. "I have my moments."

"What?" Jamison glanced between them. "What's smart?"

Her dad clapped Liam on the shoulder. "He'll tell you."

"Hey, hey, hey!" The front door opened, and Taylor stuck her head inside the foyer. "Are you all finished?"

Everyone fixed smiles on their faces. Jamison was well aware she would have to be nice to this woman for the rest of her life. Taylor had come through and saved all their asses by calling the police that night, and while Jamison still didn't care for the way she threw herself at her father, she was going to have to get over it.

"Yeah, we're done." Her father gestured for Taylor to come inside. "But our conference call with Johnson isn't until this afternoon. What are you doing here?"

Taylor popped through the door fully, waving two neatly folded paper bags with a logo that promised something sugary and delicious. "I know how you get in the mornings when you don't have a little caffeine and sugar in your system, and with that awful phone call happening at the crack of dawn, I figured you would need a pick-me-up before the afternoon."

"Thanks," her father mumbled, trying to look anywhere but at Taylor's prominently exposed décolletage. One wrong move on her part, and they would get an eyeful. "I probably do need to eat."

Jamison felt sorry for him. While she and Simone had made a vow to be forever kind to Taylor, it was her father who had to endure the brunt of the woman's *attention*. In the beginning, he made excuses for the behavior, but over the last week, Taylor had entered a kind of hyper-fixation mode, where she constantly chased after him with something he supposedly *needed*.

And always while wearing the shortest skirts imaginable.

Forever the hero, Liam snatched one of the bags out of Taylor's hand. "Who wants donuts?"

His shout was like a siren's call. Two sets of pounding footsteps hurried in their direction from the parlor. Harper and Theo appeared seconds later, still dressed in their footie pajamas.

"Unc, yous gots donuts?" Theo danced in place, her hair a mess and big eyes sparkling with hope. "Gonna gives to me?"

Liam held the bag high in the air while the girls tried to jump and grab it. "Ms. Taylor brought donuts for Papa, and I think he'll share them if you're good and hang out here for a little bit longer. Can you do that?"

The girls screamed, each latching on to one of their grandfather's hands so they could tug him down the hall toward the kitchen. "Come on, Papa!" Harper groaned as she pulled. "Before Daddy catches us!"

Evie's pregnancy had been fraught with complications, and somewhere during the second trimester, the doctors had warned her to adjust her diet. Samuel took that to mean everyone in the house had to eat healthier, including the girls who had been insisting their father was trying to kill them with a broccoli-based assassination plot.

"I'll pour the milk," Taylor chimed in, taking the bag back and sauntering ahead like she was on a catwalk. "Then maybe we'll watch cartoons. Papa needs a break after his busy morning."

The girls cheered. Her father groaned. The whole circus trooped away in a cyclone of noise, leaving Jamison alone with Liam.

Which was a rare thing these days.

Liam's midnight eyes slid over to her. "Blue."

"What?"

"Taylor's bra. She flashed it twice in under two minutes."

"Stop." She poked his chest. "That show wasn't for you."

"Oh, I know. And I know we're supposed to be eternally nice to her."

"Forever and ever, William."

His upper lip curled in disgust. "But this thing with your dad is getting old."

"I'm used to it."

"Liar."

"Okay, fine. I am a liar, and my pants are, in fact, on fire." She sighed. "You should totally take them off me."

Before she could register what was happening, he looped an arm around her waist and spun them into the library. A whoosh of air escaped her when he pinned her against the door as it closed.

Hands braced on his shoulders, she shivered when he buried his face in her neck.

"We're being watched," she whispered. Starved for privacy, she'd actually fantasized about dragging Liam into the woods to have her dirty way with him, but then Rowan ruined the idea with more security cameras out on the trails. "Like, right now. They're all probably in the media room, placing bets on how far we get before someone interrupts."

Liam's hips pressed into hers, and she groaned. "Ask me about my plan."

"Is it a dirty plan? Please say it's a dirty plan." Threading her fingers through his hair, she pulled him up to see his face. "Because the last time you said you had a plan, I was assigned to help Izzy stay organized while she did background checks. Not that I mind, but I would much rather be involved in a different kind of plan—a dirty plan—that involves you doing dirty things to me. Or me to you. Whatever."

"A dirty plan like the one you concocted the other night?" he teased. "You lost nine pairs of shoes, Jamison."

Simone wasn't the only one not sleeping. Rowan and Liam were up around the clock with Will, trying to sift through the wreckage of information coming in. But a few nights ago, Liam had snuck upstairs to *rest,* and when he slipped into bed with her, she'd suggested sneaking off to the walk-in closet to try to have some private time together.

And damn it, it had been a good plan. The closet had a camera, yes, but like the bathrooms, it had a code that would provide her with two-minute intervals of blackout so she could change in private.

Liam had thought she was crazy, and she should have listened. Wedging themselves behind the clothes in case the camera came back on before they were finished, she quickly learned that the shoe cabinet they tried to use for balance wasn't as sturdy as it looked.

"It was worth it," she said, even though they hadn't done anything. Just a little kissing and nothing more. "But Annabeth replaying the footage on repeat is getting old. How was I supposed to know the cameras have thermal and night vision?"

Rowan and Annabeth were suffering from the same lack of privacy as them and found the partial collapse of her closet and the reason behind it hilarious.

"Don't forget the facial recognition software." Liam grinned. Today really had been a good day, and seeing him happy was such a contrast to the cold and calculating man who had been prowling around Haven these last few weeks. "That's going to be a huge help if Zanmi ever shows their asses here again."

"We learned a bunch, didn't we?"

His smile grew until it took over his entire face. "If Toby is telling the truth, which there's a high probability that he's not, but if he is, this whole woman being the driving force behind their baby plan coincides with a theory my dad and I have been stuck on."

"Toby's group has never really had a high regard for women, but you think they're letting one run the show?"

He had her across the room and on the couch in another dizzying move. Flat on her back, she giggled when he laid on top of her. "William!" she whisper-shouted as he shooed away a cat who came over to investigate. "Everyone saw that!"

"And everyone has been lecturing me to rest, so I'm resting." Dropping all his body weight on her, he shifted his hips slightly, rubbing a very erect body part against her thigh. "To answer your question, yes. I think a woman might be running the show. Sinclair would never care about a plan to have Fairweather babies, but a woman—a woman who is obsessed with Toby—might be. Especially if he's led her to believe they had a relationship."

"Then how does Michael work into all of this?" she asked, but remembered what Bernie said. "He worked for him! You're thinking that if this Brandy person is real, and Sinclair gave up bombing to go private for someone, it would have to be for an individual who, like, I don't know, works in the shadows."

He chuckled at the description. "When you give Evie her Oscar for acting, make sure you give one to me and my dad. The whole Bryan Carroll thing checks all the boxes, but we had to be careful not to let on what we were thinking." Tracing her lips with his finger, he groaned when she nipped at it playfully. "Anderson has two new guys I don't know, and my trust... it's not there. Not yet."

"But you trust Anderson?"

The excitement in his eyes dimmed. "After my dad shot Mayhew, Anderson was the one who came in and took over. He protected my parents, so none of it touched them until it absolutely had to. He gave us time to heal, and I think my mom is doing as well as she is, partly because of how hard he fought to give her that peace. He also kept the whole media circus away."

Laying a hand on his cheek, she tried to get him to smile again. "Anderson sounds like a good man, which makes me doubt he's related to us, but if he is, then I guess we have more family."

The joke worked, and he smiled down at her. "Because that's something we needed. More family."

We.

She loved hearing him include himself again. "So, what's this dirty plan you were talking about?"

"I never said it was a dirty plan, but it's definitely not background checks." Shifting his hips again, he kissed the tip of her nose. "Thanks for helping Izzy stay organized, by the way. Not having enough people in our inner circle is hard."

Izzy had an almost insurmountable task ahead of her. Fairweather Holdings employed thousands, and background checks were an absolute requirement for them to one day return to the offices. A simple one was already performed upon hiring, but now they needed to go deeper. Izzy was starting with anyone hired in the last year and working her way back from there.

However, the sheer volume of people was overwhelming.

"She's not even close to finishing the first batch. I can keep her organized, but other than that, I feel useless." She tipped her head back so he could trace her jawline with his lips. "We need more help."

"We'll have it when Carter gets here. The man is part bloodhound."

Resisting the urge to wrap her legs around him, she tapped his shoulder. "Stop stalling and go over whatever plan you've concocted. What do I have to do?"

"That depends. Do you want to play the good cop or the bad cop?"

"I'll be either, but only if handcuffs are involved."

CHAPTER 7

Josie

JULY 5, 1999

"**I**s my mom okay?" Selah asked.

Keeping her face turned away, Josie squeezed her eyes shut because she didn't know. She didn't know what to say. She didn't know what to do. She didn't know anything.

"My mama?" Jamison's small voice shook as she spoke. "My mama red. Okay? Hurt with owie."

This...

This was a nightmare.

No.

This wasn't a nightmare.

This was hell.

This was hell, and they were paying for their sins. The lies. The secrets. The hiding.

Yes, this was hell.

And they were going to have to claw their way out of it.

Taking a deep breath, she turned to Selah. "Your mom is okay. I'm going to call the hospital in a minute."

"Will they answer?" Selah adjusted Jamison on his hip like it was second nature. "Cuz it's late and all?"

It had to be two or three in the morning. Josie tried to read the analog clock on the nightstand, but everything blurred when she attempted to focus.

"Selah, I want you to go sit with CeCe for a minute," Miranda said, entering the bedroom. "Everyone is in the gaming room."

Selah was such a good kid. He left without arguing, the only sound as he departed being Jamison's quiet pleas for her mama.

With a steady hand, Miranda closed the door. "We need to get them clean."

Everyone had blood on them. A splatter here, a drop there. Evie was the worst, with caked shades of red covering her body. When Josie managed to trap Samuel alone and ensure he was holding on, she learned a few details and how Evie had crawled to her mother.

As Laura Jean died on the cold ballroom floor, her daughter had crawled to her screaming.

"It was so bad, Jos." Samuel had broken then. Without an audience, he had broken down completely as they hid in the bathroom. He was a strong kid with thick skin and a smart mouth, but her brave boy fell apart when he told her everything that happened. The tears came first, and then he couldn't breathe, his skinny body shuddering as he tried to keep himself under control. "Livy. Her head, Jos. Her head... it wasn't where it was supposed to be."

He vomited as he went over it, and while embarrassed because he never liked to be seen as weak, he at least allowed her to help him clean up so he could get back to Evie. Pulling him away from the girl had been difficult, and Josie was smart enough not to keep him from her.

"Miranda, look at me."

"I'm fine, Josie." She wasn't. Miranda was pale and ready to collapse, but she squared her shoulders and, just like her hard-headed son, refused to be seen as weak. "I think if we get them clean, then we might be able to see if we can wrangle them into resting."

"We need to take Evie to the hospital."

"Tomorrow."

"Why tomorrow?"

Miranda lowered herself to sit on the edge of their bed, gripping its edge as if it could keep her steady. "If we take Evie to the hospital, we'll have to take them all. Toby will panic if we leave him behind, and part of me thinks Samuel will, too."

Josie didn't understand why that was an issue. "So, we take them all. We show up and drop the Fairweather name, and I guarantee you they'll—"

"Take one look at us and then go immediately out and spread gossip." Miranda shook her head. "I can't let that happen yet."

Dropping to kneel on the floor beside her, Josie forced Miranda to meet her gaze. "He can't hide this. No matter how powerful you think Ben is, he can't—he won't—hide this. The whole town will know what's happened before sunrise and the whole state by sunset."

"I called Trevor." Miranda pressed her lips together and inhaled deeply through her nose before continuing. "He already knew. I don't know how, but he was on his way. The plane should land in two hours. He's bringing Heather."

It made sense. Someone would have to deal with everything. They were busy with the kids, and Ben...Ben was lost to them. It had to be Trevor, and things would get done with Heather coming. The woman was a vicious snake, but that might be what they needed.

"Charlie is alive."

It was Josie's turn to go pale. The very least the son of a bitch could have done was die.

She immediately winced at her crude thoughts. They didn't need to wish death on anyone else tonight.

"He has several stab wounds, and some organs have been nicked," Miranda continued. "But Ty said they're pretty positive he's going to survive."

"Does Ben know?"

Thinking of Ben and Simone made her feel hollow, like her soul had shrunk a few inches. It was terror, pure and straight from the source, over realizing that one day she might know that pain. That one day, Miranda would be taken from her without warning.

"Ben is at the morgue with Ty." Miranda's grip on the bedspread tightened until her knuckles went white. "They're identifying the bodies."

Bodies?

They weren't bodies.

They were their friends.

They were their family.

A chill rolled through her as reality sank in, and unable to stay still any longer, Josie stood. "Have we heard from Simone?"

"Abe is being prepped for surgery now." A sob struck, and Miranda covered her mouth. "He's so small, and they're waiting for a pediatric surgeon to come and operate. The hospital is flying one in from Birmingham since there were none here who could do it."

"Jesus." Josie tipped her head up to the ceiling, blinking rapidly as if she could force her tears to stay back. "Annabeth?"

"With Simone."

A knock sounded on the door, and Josie hurried over to open it. They shouldn't have left the children alone. They didn't keep staff at Parkland, choosing to close up half the manor home since they never used it. The kids had likely become scared without an adult close by and had come looking for one of them.

Surprisingly, it was Samuel standing on the other side. "What's the plan?"

Miranda gave him a small smile. "We were just discussing that I think everyone needs to clean up and try to rest."

She didn't say sleep. Miranda would never suggest something so ludicrous. None of them would be sleeping anytime soon.

"How's Evie doing?" Josie asked him. "Is she talking yet?"

Samuel's dark brows pinched together. "Not yet, but I think you're right, Mom. Evie should be wearing clothes without... that stuff on it." He adjusted his glasses as he thought for a moment. "But we don't have any clothes for girls here, and Jamison needs her pull-ups because she still has accidents at night."

Josie caught Miranda's eye. "He's right."

"Toby is too big for my clothes. And we need toothbrushes for everyone," Samuel went on. "Selah needs his special cereal for breakfast tomorrow because if he tries to eat the cereal here, he'll get sick."

A piercing scream shot down the hall, and the three of them bolted from the bedroom, running as fast as they could toward Samuel's gaming room. It wasn't far, only a few doors down, but as they ran, it felt as if they would never get there. Door after door rushed past, and Josie pushed herself, wanting to get there before Miranda or Samuel.

Charging into the room, they found Evie curled into a ball on the floor and crying. Toby stood above her, pulling on her arm like he was trying to get her to sit up. CeCe was shoving at her brother, trying to get him to stop while Selah attempted to talk to him, having set Jamison down, which in turn was causing her to scream.

"Stop!" Samuel roared, sliding to a halt as he blew into the room. He was on his knees next to Evie in a second, knocking Toby back and away from her. "If she wants to be on the floor, let her be on the floor!"

Toby snarled, his big body too much for CeCe to hold back. He went to push Samuel away, but Selah was there, blocking him from doing so.

"No, Toby." Selah locked his hands on Toby's shoulders. "Not today. Leave her alone."

Toby fought him, but Miranda came up from behind. "Toby, we're going to take showers and then brush our teeth. I think you should go first."

"NO!" he screamed. "Evie needs me to hold her hand!"

Wedging herself between Toby and the children, Josie filled the boy's line of vision. "You can hold her hand after you clean up."

Toby glared at her with absolute hatred. "Samuel can go first. Or Selah. I'm not leaving Evie."

How were they going to deal with this? Handling him would take an army, and then they needed all the things Samuel mentioned from the store. She could run to the 24-hour Walmart, but she didn't want to leave Miranda alone for that long. Not with Toby in this state.

Then there was Evie. It was going to take at least two of them to get her clean. Miranda's lack of strength had become noticeable over the last month, and Josie had been nagging her to call the doctor.

Off in the corner, Jamison continued to screech, her face going purple. "Let CeCe go first," Selah said, picking Jamison up now that the adults were in the room. "You okay with that, Ce?"

CeCe's head bobbed in agreement, and she touched her brother's back. "I'm going to go first, Toby. You can sit next to Evie, but don't make her get up if she doesn't want to."

Toby dropped to the ground in a huff and forced everyone aside to scoot his butt over to Evie crumpled on the floor. "Move," he snapped at Samuel. "I'm sitting next to her."

Samuel wouldn't move at first, but finally gave up and went to Evie's other side, sitting beside where her head rested. "Happy now, freak?"

Josie's mouth opened to reprimand Samuel, but she quickly snapped it shut. If she did, it would only have led Toby to think he could get away with this behavior, and the less stress they had, the better.

The crying coming from Jamison continued, and it seemed to aggravate Evie. A trembling took over the girl's body as she lay on the floor.

"It's okay." Samuel leaned down to whisper, gently stroking her hair. He shifted his long legs out before him, working Evie's head up a little so it could be cushioned against his thigh. "Jamison is just tired and dirty."

"I have to pee," CeCe announced, looking nervous. "I can go before my bath, but I'm scared. Can someone come with me?"

Josie felt it then. The crash. It slammed into her like a million daggers slicing through her flesh. *Livy.* Livy would normally take her little sister to the bathroom in this situation. The brave little mama would always care for everyone if they needed help.

Two doors down, there was a pretty room with a pink canopy bed Miranda had found in a furniture store over in Pensacola. There was a giant pink inflatable chair and a desk that she and Miranda had spent a whole day putting together because the instructions were crap. They hadn't minded, though. Livy would need a place to study, and they had worked until nightfall, getting it right.

She had been so excited about her new school and excited that Samuel would be with her. The two always got along so well—a rare thing for their boy.

There was a closet full of clothes on the way. Going through that Deliah's catalog had been so much fun. The three of them had giggled and circled almost every outfit option available. Once they finished with that, they broke out the Macy's catalog to find more clothes and spent nearly a whole night placing orders.

Josie thought of the smaller sheet on the ballroom floor, and a cold sweat seized her. Sweet, perfect Livy was gone. Devon was gone. Laura Jean...*gone.*

And nothing would ever be the same.

The room around her spun, the faces of the children blurring. With a shake of her head, she stumbled off to the side, pulling Miranda with her.

"Toby and Samuel can't be left alone together, or someone will get hurt," Josie said in a hushed voice. "We need help, and I know where to get it."

Miranda's eyes searched hers, seeking an answer. When it came finally, her lips parted in shock. "Oh, I don't know about that, Josie."

"She's going to find out one way or another, and it's best if she hears it from one of us."

Not giving Miranda a chance to respond, Josie left, even though she understood that this probably wasn't the best way to deliver news. However, their options were limited. Actually, their options were non-existent. If Miranda wanted to keep this quiet, getting the help of someone who knew how to handle situations like this was their best chance.

Hurrying down the hall, Josie reached the back stairs in seconds, but almost lost her nerve when crossing the foyer. The marble floors were still wet from when they arrived, with big and small footprints tracking their way down the middle.

She hesitated before opening the front door. Hand on the knob, she told herself she could do this.

She *could* do this.

Couldn't she?

Miranda always said she was the brave one. It was bullshit. She might be opinionated and spoke her mind plainly, but in truth, she was a coward. She was scared all the time and of so many things. She was scared that the cancer would come back. She was scared that one day Samuel might look at them with disgust. She was scared that Miranda would push her away because "it was for the best" or because she couldn't take the pressure of hiding what they were to each other.

And in the middle of this horrific, nightmarish night, Josie was scared that what she was about to do was a grave mistake. There would be tears and screaming, but they needed help with the kids.

Taking the front stone steps two at a time, she hit the button at the end of the drive, allowing the security gates to swing open. She didn't need to get her car. Not when heading right next door. This request was best made in person, even though they might actually call the cops on her. They might also not believe her or be so furious that she had the nerve to ask for help. Especially once knowing the truth.

Mumbling to herself, she kept her head down as she walked the slick sidewalk. There were a few cars out on the road. Parkland Grounds sat directly off Main Street in Hollingsdale. It was a beautiful sight, and people would often make a special trip out to see how it looked lit up at night.

But right around the corner from Parkland Grounds was a smaller manor home, built not long after the main home came into existence. The property was always passed down to the firstborn Fairweather son, generation after generation, as he prepared to take over the business.

Yet, in this latest generation, the firstborn son didn't take over, and no longer lived here.

Only his wife remained.

The porch light was on, with gnats and moths flittering around in a fevered dance. Up the steps and spread around the enormous front yard, a kaleidoscope of colorful blooms greeted her, along with small whimsical touches the occupant had set up as she attempted to make it her own now that there was no Fairweather to suppress her.

Helen Fairweather would absolutely die if she saw it today.

Standing at the front door, Josie stared at the doorbell, wondering if she should knock instead. She chose to ring it and held her breath, aiming her finger at the button, the entire thing happening in slow motion until she connected with it. The chiming toll could be heard all the way outside, a tinkling ring to signal the start of a moment that would stay with them for a lifetime.

He was the one to come to the door.

Aiden.

Josie hadn't formally met him yet, only spying him once or twice through a pair of binoculars she and Miranda kept on the balcony. Whenever they caught a glimpse of the pair together, they would whisper how handsome he was and say things like *good for Viv,* or *I hope Viv is having the time of her life*. God knew she deserved a handsome, caring man after putting up with Charlie's crap for all these years. They had heard from Ben that Viv met him at a fundraiser and that he was involved with something medical.

Wearing nothing but sweatpants, Aiden stared at her in confusion. "Can I help you?"

He was even more gorgeous in person, with dark hair and light eyes. Usually, she wouldn't mind being greeted by a chiseled chest and pretty face, but it didn't even register tonight.

"I'm Josie."

An eyebrow went up. He obviously recognized the name.

"Is something wrong?"

The trembling that started on the way over deepened, striking her very bones to where she thought he surely must be able to hear them rattling. "Yes."

"What's happening?" Vivian's panicked voice approached, and she was out the door and standing in front of her before Josie could figure out what to say. "Is it Miranda? Is she okay?"

"Miranda's okay."

Josie swayed on her feet. What did she say to this woman? How much did she know?

"I need help."

Vivian cradled Josie's face, and it was then she realized she really was sweating. A whoosh of cold air came from the open front door, swirling around them in the sticky July heat. "Josie, everything is going to be okay. Is Samuel hurt? Are you?"

How could Charlie have ever strayed from this woman? She was stunning on all levels. Beautiful, for sure, but Viv was a decent human. She had kept their secret. They never told her outright, but she had to have known and never openly judged or said a bad word about it, as far as Josie knew.

"Is it Samuel?" Vivian tried again. "Josie, you're scaring me."

A light Texas drawl clung to her words, the sweet, hypnotic sound drawing Josie out of her stupor. "Can I come in?" She cringed over having the audacity to invite herself into someone's home in the middle of the night. "We need to talk, but I don't have much time."

"Oh, of course!" Viv acted as if it were all her fault for not inviting her inside in the first place. "Forgive me."

Aiden and Viv ushered her into the house, but Josie couldn't go far, standing frozen in the doorway of the dark manor. The floors were black and white checkerboard, while the rest of the home's décor was new, with all the latest styles and perfectly set to Viv's standards. The woman had impeccable taste and used it to make everything beautiful, including herself.

"Let's talk in the living room." Draped in a silky blue nightgown, the matching robe flowed around Vivian as she walked. "Aiden, can you turn on a lamp or something?"

"No," Josie whispered, not wanting any lights on. She didn't think she would be able to handle their shocked faces. "I can't stay. I can't leave Miranda alone with them."

Even in the dark, she could feel Aiden's eyes assessing her state. "I think you need to sit down."

"I'm fine." Giving Vivian her attention, Josie decided to deliver the first blow. "Simone Howard's husband was shot tonight. He's dead."

Vivian blinked a few times. "What?"

"Selah is over at Parkland Grounds."

"What?" Vivian's hand flew to her throat. "What are you saying? How could—"

"Simone's other son was also shot. I don't know if you're aware, but Simone and Devon have two other children. Twins." A ghost of a smile tugged at Josie's lips as she thought of Abe's adorable face. "Abe is in surgery now."

"Oh my God," Vivian whispered. "Who would do such a thing?"

There was no going back. It was like being stuck on the tracks with a train barreling toward her. Ready or not, Josie prepared herself to change this woman's life forever.

"Laura Jean Eddins was shot and killed." Images flashed in her mind. A heap on the ballroom floor. The bloody sheet. Ben in agony as he rocked next to it. She shut her eyes, as if she could block them. "Ben is at the morgue identifying her body as we speak."

Vivian's legs gave out. She wobbled in place, ready to drop to the cold floor, but Aiden caught her. "She was pregnant," Viv whispered to Aiden. "I ran into her and Ben at the new boardwalk in Port Michaelson two weeks ago. Laura Jean was so excited and so happy. Ben...h-h-he was happy. Ben is never happy. Aiden, he's never happy, but he was happy, and it was almost scary how normal he seemed."

Aiden whispered to Vivian for a moment before snapping at Josie. "What else? You said you came here for help. What the hell do you need help with?"

The nervous hum zipping through her body went silent, and Josie held Aiden's stare. The way he cradled Vivian to him… he loved her. Charlie would have probably let her fall to the floor and perhaps helped eventually, but only if someone told him to do it.

"She needs to sit down," Josie said, keeping her voice strong so they wouldn't argue. "This next part isn't going to be easy, and Viv needs to sit down."

The foyer held a single chair with a pair of men's running shoes next to it. Aiden looked like a runner. Lean and muscled, he looked like the type of guy that greeted the morning with a jog.

Viv continued to cry quietly as Aiden helped her to the chair. "It's Charlie," she mumbled to herself. "She's here to tell me Charlie is dead. He was living out at that house."

Well, that was a worry Josie could easily eliminate. "Charlie is alive."

The look of relief on Vivian's face was just one more heartbreaking thing to pile onto the millions of other soul destroying moments from tonight. "He's okay?"

"No, but he's alive," Josie spat out. "He's in the hospital, and the doctors say he's going to pull through just fin—"

"We need to go." Vivian was out of the chair and rushing for the door. "Is he at Hollingsdale General or the hospital over in Port Michaelson?"

Josie didn't move, and neither did Aiden. Viv had her a smart one this time around. "Come sit down, honey, and let her finish," Aiden said. "I think she has more to say."

He was a good guy. Any other man would have been pissed at how fast his woman was ready to ride to the rescue of her soon-to-be ex-husband.

Vivian's baby blue eyes flicked back and forth between them, realizing it wasn't over. "Say it, Josie."

"Do you know why he was living at Haven House?"

Returning to the chair, Viv nodded at her question. "Ben cut him off after he started having problems with drinking. Charlie wouldn't get help, and Ben cut off his allowance, even though it wasn't his fault. Charlie only started dabbling recently when I failed yet again to keep the baby to term."

Dear God. How much psychological damage had Vivian endured? They would be lucky if she walked away tonight without her mind completely snapping in half.

"Charlie has been dabbling in drugs for over a decade," Josie said flatly. "But do you know about the woman? I'm sure there were others, but do you know about the main one? Rebecca? He wasn't staying at Haven House only because Ben cut him off. He was staying there because that's where she lived. Charlie brought Rebecca to live at Haven House when she was barely seventeen years old. He was newly married to you, and he was sleeping with a seventeen-year-old child at the same time."

That had to be the cruelest thing she had ever spoken in her life, but it was the truth, and damn it, Vivian deserved to know. Fuck the Fairweathers and their *it's for the best if we keep things secret* motto. It destroyed people—real fucking people—who were just trying to live their lives.

The speech gained the expected reaction. Vivian looked ready to hurl her guts up all over the tile. Josie could relate, but now wasn't the time to wimp out. Miranda needed her back at Parkland as soon as possible.

"And he..." Vivian swallowed a few times. "He kept her out at that house? No. Charlie wouldn't do that."

"Why wouldn't he do that, Vivian?" Aiden hissed, already pushing through his shock. "You said that his brother hid a woman who he had gotten pregnant out there, so why wouldn't you expect Charlie to do the same?"

Yep, a smart man. Viv probably didn't know what to do with herself. "The first baby Charlie and Rebecca had together was a girl," Josie continued. "They named her Olivia, but everyone called her Livy."

Vivian quite simply lost control. It was like she was trying to rise, but didn't even make it a fraction of an inch before sliding right down to sit on the floor. "A baby? What do you mean, a baby?" she rambled, her head violently shaking in denial as the hysteria bubbled from her. "Charlie had a baby with her? A *baby*?"

"Three babies."

Aiden immediately dropped to hold Vivian when she screamed. Pain and shock ripped through the poor woman, the news shredding the last piece of her heart belonging to Charlie.

Holding her tenderly, Aiden cradled Viv as he settled them on the chair. She raged and cried in his arms, begging for someone to explain to her why. He didn't have the answer, of course. Josie didn't have an answer, either. But seeing her in such agony had the words spilling forth, and Josie revealed the plain truth through Viv's tortured sobs.

"Charlie and Rebecca had three children, and over the last... I don't know, year? Maybe two years? They've both kind of dropped off from being parents and started getting more into drugs and whatever else the fuck they do." Josie recognized that she was shouting, but there was no other way. "And then tonight, apparently, Rebecca snapped, stabbed Charlie, and then grabbed a gun. From what we can tell, she just started killing people, including her daughter and herself."

"Oh my God," Viv wailed, burying her face in Aiden's chest. "Oh my God!"

"I'm sorry!" Josie continued to shout through the woman's heartbreak. "I'm so sorry, and I would never have come here and told you all this in the middle of the night if I didn't need help."

Long minutes passed until, finally, Vivian's red-rimmed eyes, so full of contempt, met hers. "And why would I help you?"

"Not me. I don't deserve it. But they do. The children. They witnessed it happen and are over at Parkland Grounds with Miranda. They're covered in blood. There's so much blood, Viv, and they need to get clean, but we don't have clothes or toothbrushes or anything. I can't leave Miranda alone to go buy supplies, and I'm here for help." Josie wiped her cheeks. Her tears were worthless here. "Laura Jean's oldest isn't speaking. It's like she's in shock. The boys are fighting. Jamison needs pull-ups and—"

Vivian went utterly still, but then shook herself and launched into motion. "Aiden, can you grab us a change of clothes?" The brisk order had Josie's mouth falling open. This quick shift from pained shock to unwavering determination was too swift for her tired brain to comprehend. "We'll go over and help Miranda while you get the car ready and our clothes."

Aiden took off and jogged up the stairs. Once he disappeared, Vivian turned to Josie. "If Ben is at the morgue, who is handling damage control?"

"Damage control?"

Vivian sighed and rolled her eyes. "Who is handling what the public knows?"

Josie blinked stupidly at her. God, what was with these people?

"Trevor, I guess? He's on his way down here with Heather."

"Absolutely not." Vivian went to a side table just off the entryway and clicked on a lamp. She dug around in the table's single drawer until she found a small book. "Hillary should have been your first phone call."

Picking up the cordless phone, Vivian dialed a number she found in her little book. "Hillary? It's Vivian. Ben needs you here. Now. Laura Jean is dead… shot… stop screaming and listen to me… SiSi Howard's husband is also dead, and their little boy has been shot. No, Selah is fine. He's with Miranda at Parkland. I said stop screaming. Charlie has been stabbed and is in the hospital, and there are two more people dead. A little girl named Olivia and…"

"Rebecca," Josie said, filling in the blanks. "Her name was Rebecca Miller."

"Rebecca Miller," Vivian repeated. "Oh, stop crying out for God, Hillary. He can't help us now. It's only a two-hour flight from Houston. Take one of the jets and get here."

In a flourish of silk, Vivian slammed down the phone and marched again to the door. "Let's go."

Josie followed, numb and not knowing what else to do. "What about Aiden?"

"He'll know to follow."

Vivian swung open her front door and hurried down the steps. "You walked here?"

It had started to rain. A light misting, promising more in moments. "Yes."

"Well, then, come on."

They walked in silence. A car honked its horn in appreciation over Vivian's nightgown, and she kept her head turned away lest someone recognize her. Rounding the corner, Viv gasped when she saw that Parkland's gates had been left open and the twelve-foot-tall front door gaping wide, which permitted the lights to spill out onto the front steps.

"Vivian, let me go first."

She didn't listen. Hurrying through the front door, Vivian entered in a rush, but stopped short on the slippery marble floors when they heard a soft crying. It was coming from somewhere close, and after a quick search, they narrowed it down to a darkened sitting room off the foyer.

It was Toby. Hidden just beyond a small sofa, he sat on the floor with his knees pulled up to his chest.

Vivian didn't hesitate and kneeled to his level. "Hello, I'm Vivian. What's your name?"

Toby lifted his head, and instantly, his eyes went wide. He had probably never seen a woman like Vivian before. Beautiful beyond words, she looked picture-perfect even at three in the morning.

Vivian was also slightly taken aback. Toby might not be the spitting image of his father, but Charlie was there in the boy's features.

"Toby."

"I like that name." Delicately, Vivian touched Toby's shoulder. "And I like your hair too. Does it always curl like this when it's about to rain?"

Toby nodded earnestly, completely under Vivian's spell. "Yes, ma'am."

"Your father's hair does the same thing. I used to say he was my own personal weather station. We could always tell if it was going to be a rainy day by Charlie's hair." She ran her fingers through the tips of his curls. "Why are you crying down here?"

"Samuel's mean."

"Hmm, yes. He's like his father, so that's no surprise."

Toby giggled, obviously thinking he'd found a friend.

"Toby," Josie interrupted. "Go back upstairs. Vivian and I will be along in a minute. We'll get you some supplies to take a shower, and we need everyone together to make our list."

"Yes, ma'am."

Toby wiggled up from the ground to stand next to Vivian. "It was nice meeting you," he said before scampering off for the stairs.

"He's very polite," Viv remarked, watching him go. "I'm assuming SiSi had something to do with that."

"She practically raised them," Josie replied, wanting to make this easier, but there wasn't a way. Betrayal and pain were the foundations of tonight. "The youngest is named Cecilia, and we call her CeCe."

"Is she upstairs?"

"She is." Josie grabbed Vivian's arm when she tried to take off again. "Don't you need a minute to, like, I don't know, process all this?"

Vivian exhaled a humorless laugh. "Josie, it's going to take me a lifetime to process all of this, and I don't think we have time for that tonight."

Chapter 8

Jamison

"More lip liner." Liam rummaged through the makeup selections laid out on the vanity in front of her. "And apply it thick."

"Are you going to tell me what we're doing?" She wrinkled her nose when he picked a brownish shade and handed it to her. "You said to wear hot pink lipstick. This so does not go with hot pink lipstick."

He didn't answer, too busy looking for something on his phone. "Can you make your eyeliner go way out? Like way, way out?" Turning his phone around, he showed her a picture of a woman with exaggerated makeup and black wingtips. "Something like that?"

"And why would I want to?"

"Wait, scratch that." He disappeared into the walk-in closet. "Just pack the makeup. You can put it on when we're on the boat."

She turned on her stool to glare at him. "Why am I wearing makeup on a boat?"

"Because I need you to seduce a man."

"William, I love you, but you better start talking."

He reappeared shirtless, ruffled, and almost annoyingly perfect. His tousled hair gave him a boyish look, yet there was a hint of recklessness layered underneath. Her fingers itched to touch him, but she reminded herself to focus.

"Toby planned to take Evie using a small boat he'd beached near the mill ruins. Sinclair planned to do the same with you. The women came here the same way."

They had found the boats. Large inflatable rafts were left on the shore near the mill ruins, beached where the manchineel trees grow. As far as she knew, there hadn't been much evidence or clues left behind on them.

"Okay?" she said, begrudgingly tearing her gaze from his chest. "What does that mean?"

"Where did they launch from?" he asked, stepping out of his pants to stand in his boxer briefs. "Not a marina. Sinclair could have slipped by and not drawn attention, but a bunch of women in white taking off in the dead of night? That sure as hell would have alerted a harbor master."

He had been sorting through so many moving parts. Theory after theory, observation after observation. Every minor detail counted to Liam.

"So, you're thinking they launched from a private dock?"

"I know they did." He yanked open a dresser drawer. "Close enough to reach us fast, but remote enough to stay under the radar."

There were no private docks near Haven House. There were no homes or buildings whatsoever. The bayou behind the estate stretched east into a narrow river, eventually leading to another that fed into the Intracoastal. Most of the coastal uplands had long since been claimed by the swamp or eaten away by Mother Nature's violent storms.

Ty taught her to fish in those narrow inlets. She could remember how frightened she had been of the bald cypress and their exposed roots, which seemed to reach for them as they glided past. He would laugh and call her a scaredy cat, but then tell her stories of the mermaids who supposedly lived in the water around the trees and how they used the tree's root systems as underwater homes.

To the west of Haven House was a different story. A much wider pass opened directly off the shore, leading into a bay that eventually curved toward Port Michaelson or out into the Gulf of Mexico. The boats would have come from that direction, and Liam was right. Every time Zanmi arrived at Haven House, it should have drawn some attention, considering you had to travel under a major bridge to enter the bay that connected Port Michaelson to the land where Haven House was built.

"Have you found a private dock between here and the edge of Port Michaelson?" She frowned, trying to think of where one could possibly be. "There are some fishing spots, but I don't know about docks."

"Where are those cut-off shorts you drove me crazy with a couple of weeks ago?" Liam returned to the closet. "And wear a bathing suit. A cute one."

"A bathing suit?" She was off the stool and following after him. "It's November!"

October had come and gone, with the kids missing Halloween. Lenora and Selah held a spooky party for just the three of them, while Annabeth had done the same for Theo and Harper. Forced to participate for at least an hour, everyone was coerced into costumes and required to stand patiently behind closed doors so the girls could trick or treat. As a connoisseur of party planning, Annabeth made the night as magical as she could with decorations, handmade candy bags, and enough glitter to traumatize the vacuum.

It was the first time they'd all felt a flicker of normalcy since the attack.

And Samuel dressed as a vampire was something Jamison would never emotionally recover from. He'd insisted on biting Evie's neck every five seconds, and while it was weird coming from him, Jamison would admit it was also sweet.

In the closet, Liam was digging through another dresser. Behind him sat the wreckage of the destroyed shoe cabinet, and she took an elongated step to get around it.

"That cold snap's over, and it's back to being eighty degrees," he said, holding up a pair of dark blue board shorts. "Eighty-eight, to be exact, and that's warm enough for you to wear a bathing suit and a pair of shorts."

"It might be warm outside, but I'm not getting in the water. Neither are you without a wetsuit, so why are we dressing like we're going to the beach?"

He gave her ass a solid smack as he walked back into the bedroom. "Because I want to check something out from the water."

She groaned and dug through the same drawer he'd just ravaged. "So how does that tie into the 'seduce a man' part? Or are you the man I'm seducing? If so, I'm cool with that, but I didn't know you were into me wearing heavy makeup."

"I'll take you any way I can get you, woman."

Rolling her eyes, Jamison stuck her head out of the closet. "*William.*"

He grinned, tugging a T-shirt over his head. "I found a piece of property on the north side of the bay. It's just off a small inlet and literally has nothing on it but a shack. It's owned by a guy named Emmett Watson, who inherited the land ten years ago from his father."

"What do we know about him?"

"Thirty-eight. Caucasian. Lives alone. No job."

"That could describe the most boring man alive or a serial killer." She returned to her search for a bathing suit. "Give me the good stuff."

"He's local. Grew up here. Used to live in a nice place with his mom until she died in a car wreck when he was seventeen. Then the state handed him over to his dad, who was never around."

Recognizing this would be a long story, she took her time searching for a bathing suit. As she did, her fingers closed around a thin strap, and she lifted a bright orange thong from the options.

"Why doesn't he work?" she asked, stepping onto a stool to reach the security camera's access pad. She punched in the blackout code to give herself two minutes of privacy.

Or else Rowan would get quite a show.

The indicator light turned red, and she dropped to the ground, hustling out of her clothes and into the bikini, not wanting Liam to see what she was doing. Their first alone time in weeks called for a special surprise, and this bathing suit was perfect.

"He doesn't need to," Liam replied, moving around the bedroom. "Emmett sued the drunk driver who killed his mom and won. He's set for life."

The camera's light switched back to green just as she was zipping up her jean shorts. They were frayed at the ends and short enough that if Liam looked closely, he would be able to tell there wasn't much to her bikini bottoms.

She threw on an old T-shirt and stepped out. "But he lives in a shack?"

"Not just a shack. A fishing shack with a very nice dock," Liam said as she emerged from the closet. "The thing is basically a glorified tiny home where his dad kept their fishing and boating supplies. It doesn't have running water or electricity."

"But he doesn't *live* there."

"He does. He's a survivalist." Liam's dark gaze zeroed in on the orange strap peeking out from the T-shirt's large collar. "What bathing suit are you wearing?"

Knightly sat patiently on the bed, listening to their exchange, and she went over to give her best feline boy a proper scratch behind the ears. "What exactly is a survivalist?"

"Someone who lives off the land," Liam replied, his eyes now firmly glued to her ass. "And I asked you a question."

Pressing her lips together, she shrugged. She'd purchased the bikini for their honeymoon, and he had never seen it. "A new one."

"Let me see."

"No."

Knightly let out a low, annoyed meow, perfectly echoing Liam's growl of frustration.

"Fine." He turned away to grab a black backpack off the floor. The entire bedroom was an organized mess only the two of them could understand. It drove Simone crazy. "But you're showing me later."

She smirked at him. "When we get that alone time on the boat."

Liam grumbled something under his breath as he roughly unzipped the backpack.

"What was that?" She leaned in with a grin. "Didn't quite catch it."

"I said forty minutes."

She tilted her head. "Forty minutes for what?"

He finally stopped his aggressive packing to face her. "Between scouting Watson's place, maybe talking to the guy, and then getting the boat back to the marina before sunset, I estimate that we should have about forty minutes of *alone* time together."

She told herself not to giggle, clap, or fist-pump the air. "Forty minutes? That's it?"

Dropping the bag, he stepped in close. "It's enough time."

"For what?"

He hauled her tight against him, and this time, she did giggle—right up until his lips brushed her ear, and the giggle turned into a moan.

"To have you hard and fast," he whispered. "You won't mind, will you?"

Her head tilted, exposing her throat. The sharp inhale from him had her arms winding around his neck and pressing her body into every hard line of his. "No, sir," she breathed. "I won't mind."

They absolutely should not have been doing this with cameras on in the middle of the day. Anyone could walk into the media room and see this mini-makeout session playing on one of the screens.

But the second his lips met her neck, her concern was gone, and she arched up on her toes for more.

"God, I need to be inside you," he whispered, his grip coiling tight like he was afraid she'd vanish.

"But only for forty minutes?"

She felt him grin, and he pulled back to look at her. "Tell me something." He took her left hand from behind his neck and pressed it to his chest, right over the wild thrum of his heart. "Do you like that engagement ring being back where it belongs?"

Tears rushed forth. Silly and stupid and not at all needed right now. She bit down on her trembling bottom lip and nodded.

Liam chuckled softly, mimicking her awkward nod. "That a yes?"

"Yes. I'm sorry." She kissed him. Over and over again, she kissed him. "I am so sorry. Yes. I'm not taking it off."

She could never stop apologizing. And he never stopped listening, letting her release the guilt every time they were alone.

Each day, they carved out time for them. A quiet hour where they shared a meal or a cup of coffee and never discussed anything except their hope for the future. A future that involved a life they still believed in. A home. A family. Happiness.

Yet somehow, by the end of every quiet moment, the apology crept in. Like a reflex, she couldn't control. A scar that would never fully heal. Her *"I love you"* would inevitably always come with an *"I'm sorry"* attached.

"I want to keep my ring on forever." She finally stopped kissing him, not missing the unshed tears in his eyes. "I want to be yours forever."

He didn't speak right away and stared down at her while he worked out what he wanted to say.

It made her nervous. "What?"

"I had a long talk with Samuel the other day."

She wrinkled her nose. "I'm sure that was torture."

"Yeah. He's been more of an ass than usual with the stress." His smile returned. "But we were discussing how when Evie agreed to marry him, he didn't give her time to second guess it. It made me realize I've been screwing us up since the beginning. I should have insisted we get married sooner."

Again, something else that was her fault, yet he was taking the blame for it. She hadn't wanted a big wedding, just something special, but every time she got close to deciding exactly what that meant, life got in the way. They kept pushing it off, over and over, until the months rolled into years.

"I'm giving you a week."

Jamison's lips parted, quite positive that she hadn't heard him correctly. "I beg your *pardon*?"

"One week." Looking rather pleased with the idea, he gently pressed two fingers under her chin to close her gaping mouth. "One week from today, I want you to meet me under the Marriage Oak and become my wife."

Goosebumps rippled across her skin, and Jamison honestly thought she might pass out. "But... but the beach. The... everything."

"I'll give you a beach wedding later."

"Later?"

"A wedding isn't a marriage. We can do the big thing another day."

"But my dress." She sagged a little. "I had it made just for you."

"Then wear it just for me." He gazed out the window at the Marriage Oak. The massive tree had watched over their story and the stories of countless others through the years. "Right there, under that tree. Wear the dress you chose to become my wife in and marry me. Can you do that?"

This man was so perfect it hurt her brain sometimes.

"I can do anything you want me to do." Hell, she'd marry him right now if they could pull it off. "But are you okay with me adding a few touches? I know a wedding isn't a marriage, but can I include some of my plans?"

"I don't care if you ride down the lawn on an emu, Jamison. You can do whatever you want as long as it doesn't give me a heart attack." He turned back to her with a chuckle. "Just let me have you. Let me have you as my wife. That's all I've ever wanted."

His wife.

He still wanted her to be his wife.

Buried deep within her soul, that invisible string of destiny hummed with a melody she would know in any lifetime. It linked her to Liam and sang with such perfect happiness that it had her ears ringing. She was going to be his wife. Jamison Fairweather was about to disappear, and while that made her a little sad, it also brought forth an eerie sense of peace.

It felt right.

Perfect.

Exactly as it was meant to be.

"You really wouldn't care if I showed up on an emu?"

"Nah." He pressed his forehead against hers. "Just aim the thing at me and let it loose. I'll take it from there."

Dressed and ready, they stepped out onto the landing. Liam secured her bedroom door behind them, double-checking the locks. His new protocol required every second-floor room—occupied or not—to be locked down tight.

"You still haven't explained the makeup." She had placed everything he said she would need in the black backpack, along with his gun and their spare clothes. "Or the seduction part."

"Emmett Watson is a lonely man," Liam said, taking her hand as they descended the stairs. "And there's a certain type of woman he always pays attention to when he's on dating apps. They usually wear heavy makeup and favor skimpy clothes."

"Liam, did you stalk this man's dating profiles?"

"I had Rowan do it. He and Annabeth had a good laugh going through his matches."

Jamison halted halfway down the stairs, forcing Liam to do the same. "I have a feeling this isn't a good cop-bad cop situation, but more like you're using me for bait again."

"No, not at all." Eye to eye with her, thanks to being two steps lower, Liam flipped his baseball cap around to sneak a kiss. "Like I said, he's local, and since you're a Fairweather, you get to be the bad cop."

"Excuse me, the locals love us."

"They do. But *you* have… a certain reputation."

She looked down her nose at him, unimpressed. "Why is it that any woman with a spine and a voice automatically ends up with a *reputation*?"

Smart man that he was, Liam shrugged. "Because society is ridiculous."

"Good answer."

"I figured you'll either intimidate him or charm him."

"It's always one or the other with men," she muttered. "Never a middle ground."

They headed downstairs and into the parlor, finding Samuel sitting stretched out on the couch with Evie's head in his lap, fast asleep. Theo sat on her father's shoulders, braiding his hair, while Harper knelt on the floor, painting his toenails a vivid, unapologetic shade of pink.

"Are you almost done with Holden?" Samuel asked, not even glancing up from his phone. "We're ready to go home."

Without missing a beat, Liam extracted his phone to snap a photo of the entire situation. Samuel embraced every opportunity to make things normal for his girls, and allowing them to give him a makeover after the stressful morning they'd had was par for the course.

"He just sent a message saying he was almost here with the boat." Liam took two more pictures. "Hey, Harper, that's a nice color for your dad's toes, but you should go with blue for his fingernails."

Harper scrunched her nose in disapproval. "Blue is a summer color, Unc."

"Duh, everyone knows that." Samuel finally looked up to smirk at Liam. "How about you paint Unc's toes next, Harper? His troll-looking feet could use some color."

Liam gasped as if offended. "I have beautiful feet."

Hiding her laughter, Jamison looked around for Josie, who never strayed far from her granddaughters. "Did Josie already go back to your house?"

"No, she's in the kitchen with Bernie," Evie said, coming awake with a stretch. "They're having some tea. Josie said it calms her nerves."

Samuel set his phone aside and helped Evie sit up. "How are you feeling?"

"Surprisingly good, but hungry." After making it into a sitting position, Evie stroked her pregnant belly. "Girls, can you go check on Papa and grab me a snack?"

Theo rolled off Samuel's shoulders and bolted immediately from the room. Harper took her time finishing. "Daddy, don't move until I get back," she warned, packing up her supplies and following her sister.

The moment the girls were gone, the serene smile on Evie's lips faded, and the stress of the day showed. "Explain to me where this dock is. I know you two want some private time while you're out. I get that. I'm not stupid. But I don't want Jamison out of the house for too long and want to know that you'll be back before dark. Got it?"

"The dock is on a small plot of land just outside Port Michaelson. It sits way back off in a swampy inlet and is pretty well hidden," Liam told her. "There are no property records indicating a building is onsite, but there's definitely a structure along with the dock. I had Izzy look into it earlier this week, and she said it was a single room dwelling about the size of a large shed. Rowan's been watching via satellite over the past few days. Not much has been happening, but two cars came and went yesterday."

As he spoke, Liam subtly pulled Jamison to his side, lifting her hand just enough for the diamond ring to catch the light.

"And yes," she added, grinning at her sister, "my eternal love will have me back here under lock and key before sunset."

Samuel and Evie's eyes narrowed on them simultaneously. "Why did you say it like that?" Evie asked.

"Like what?" Jamison replied innocently.

"Like a fucking weirdo," Samuel said and then focused on Liam. "My eternal love? I thought we were living in a Lifetime Movie, not a Hallmark special."

Samuel was many things, but never—in a million years—would he ever be subtle.

And her siblings still didn't know the truth behind the breakup. Jamison wanted to keep it that way for now. There hadn't been a good moment, and maybe there never would be, but with all the stress weighing on Evie and the complications with her pregnancy, the last thing she and Liam wanted to do was give her yet another thing to be upset over.

Liam lifted her hand and kissed the back of it. "She has one week."

"One week?" Evie was already wrestling her way off the couch to stand. "What happens in a week?"

"We're getting married," Liam replied, physically bracing himself. "No exceptions."

"What?" Evie shrieked, struggling to get upright. Samuel was trying his best to help, but she was flailing so much that it was hard for him to get a handle on her. "What do you mean in a week?"

Liam waited patiently for Evie to come marching over. "We're getting married here, under the Marriage Oak."

Evie pointed a finger in his face, her mouth opening and closing. "You can't give us just one week to plan!"

"I'm not waiting. We don't know what's coming next, and we sure as hell don't know when you're giving birth." Liam nodded at her baby bump. "Still having those Toni Braxton contractions?"

Evie jabbed a finger into his chest. "They're called Braxton Hicks, and yes, but that doesn't mean anything." She swung her finger at Jamison, who straightened under its power. Her sister was terrifying on a good day, but add in pregnancy hormones, and things could get crazy real quick. "Is this what you want? What about the beach wedding? With the lanterns, and the fairy lights, and the bonfire, and the girls in their pretty dresses?!"

Jamison struggled with what to say because if she were honest, none of it mattered anymore. They could have a big beach ceremony for their one-year anniversary when life settled down, but in the meantime, she was prepared to admit Liam was right. All she needed was him.

And her dress.

She wasn't giving up that dress.

"We can still incorporate most of the details. We'll just be walking on grass instead of sand. Also, let's be for real here. You're not upset we're skipping the beach wedding, Evie. On the inside, you're completely fine with this."

"Oh, she's not upset." Samuel came up behind Evie, wrapping his arms around her so he could lift and massage her lower stomach. "If you guys want to get married in a week, do it. We'll support you no matter what."

A sarcastic smile twisted the corners of Evie's mouth. "Have you told Annabeth?"

"No, I have not yet spoken to my wedding planner," Jamison replied primly. Annabeth hadn't been thrilled with a beach wedding either, worried that she would miss out on the whole thing if she panicked. "This is all pretty fresh."

"We're going to need a new dress for Harper," Evie rattled off, already ten steps ahead. "She had that growth spurt over the summer. The menu's easy because it will just be us, but then Rowan needs to set up a screen for Selah and Lenora. It should feel like they're here and not just watching through someone's phone."

Samuel rested his chin on her shoulder, rubbing slow, calming circles as she sped on. "And flowers. What are we going to do about the flowers? Oh! I know." Evie squealed, suddenly excited. "We can make bouquets from the flowers in Ty's rainbow garden. Yes, that'll be lovely and appropriate."

"Don't forget music," Liam said, tossing fuel onto the wedding planning fire. "We'll need someone to play DJ."

"Holden can do it." Completely lost in her thoughts, Evie headed for the door. "Abe's notary license is still valid, I think. Annabeth and I will figure out the photography. Ugh, then there's videography..."

And she was gone. Samuel watched her retreat with a small smile. "Nice distraction. You're pretty smart, Cohen."

"That makes you the second Fairweather to say that today," Liam said with a nod toward Samuel's new hairstyle. "Speaking of pretty, those braids are really working for you."

"Shut up." Samuel tilted his head at Jamison. "Can you get this clip out?"

Jamison smirked at the glittery butterfly holding Theo's braided masterpiece together. "Won't Theo be mad?"

"She's already forgotten." Samuel worked his fingers through his hair once all his accessories were out. "Okay. Give me the real details on this dock."

Liam showed Samuel something on his phone. "Watson's dad was ex-military. Emmett, though? Total recluse. Rowan dug through his last three years. The guy basically lives online. Dating apps, conspiracy forums, anime boards, even the server Zanmi uses for public announcements."

The public server for Zanmi mainly consisted of Toby's basic bio and a call to action to help free him. During the years when the public was obsessed with their new favorite serial killer, Rowan said it wasn't uncommon to see close to eighty thousand unique users. These days, there were barely a hundred, with a few more who only trickled in when Zanmi did a press conference.

Samuel's face darkened. "Do you think Watson is one of them?"

"No. He hasn't even searched for Toby or Zanmi in over a year. When he did visit the forum, it was brief and more out of curiosity than anything else."

Jamison stood off to the side, listening quietly. But before Liam could dive deeper, both men's phones buzzed, and the distinct, high-pitched sound that followed alerted them that someone was at the gate.

"Who's here?" Jamison leaned to see Liam's screen. The security feed clicked on, showing a blacked-out luxury SUV. "Are we expecting anyone new?"

The SUV's window lowered to reveal a stunning woman with cropped blonde hair. She wore enormous sunglasses, so it was hard to gauge her exact age when she tipped her head up to the camera.

"Open the gates, Rowan," the woman ordered, her demand ringing loud and clear through Liam's phones. "Or so help me, God, I will drive right through them."

CHAPTER 9

Jamison

T he gates opened.

"This is a me problem." Rowan's voice boomed down the hall, each of his heavy, measured footsteps pounding closer. "I'll handle it."

They made it to the parlor door just in time to see Rowan shoot past. Annabeth wasn't far behind, but instead of following him out onto the porch, she veered sharply, squeezing past Liam to get to the parlor's large front windows.

Evie and the girls hustled in behind Annabeth, with Abe right on their heels.

"What the hell is happening?" Jamison stumbled toward the window to watch with everyone else. "Rowan sounded upset."

The SUV pulled up fast, parking right beside Simone's bright red sports car.

"All he said was, *you've got to be fucking kidding me*, then took off when the buzzer hit," Annabeth said, hiding partially behind a curtain as she tried to see what was happening out front. "Could anyone tell who was driving?"

Being the tallest, Samuel and Liam had a clear view. Harper and Theo attempted to climb up their legs until the men each grabbed one of them to sit on their shoulders.

"If I didn't know better," Samuel said, adjusting Harper into position. "I'd say it looks like—"

"Make a hole." Their father stalked into the room with a mob of women trailing in his wake. "Is it who I think it is?"

Simone and Josie darted around him to get to the front of the window, practically pressing their noses to the glass.

"Who?" Izzy asked, bouncing on her toes. "Who does he think it is?"

Taylor's slender shoulders shrugged as she tried to peek around Evie. "I have no idea."

On the path, Rowan stood frozen, his fists clenched at his sides like he was preparing for a standoff. The driver's door of the SUV opened, and Jamison let out a low whistle when a woman stepped out wearing a flawlessly tailored cream suit and four inch heels. Adjusting the jacket with practiced ease, the woman smoothed away imaginary wrinkles with the kind of detached elegance that only came from living far too many years in luxury.

"Hell," her father growled. "It is her."

"She's purdy," Theo said. "I likes hers shoes."

"She's not just pretty. She's gorgeous," Jamison agreed. The security feed hadn't done the woman justice. She was older, close to her father's age, but it didn't matter. Even with the sunglasses covering most of her face, it was easy to tell she was beautiful. "Dad, who is she?"

"Hot damn, she does look good." Josie nudged Simone with an elbow. "Bet me. How many surgeries do you think it's taken to look like that this late in the game? I say seven."

Simone clucked her tongue, but as the stunning woman started to walk up the front path, she pursed her lips like she was thinking. "Five," she replied, placing a hand on the glass. "Yeah, I'm going to go with five. The second husband is a plastic surgeon, right?"

"Not when she married him, but I heard he became one later." Josie reached blindly behind her to shove Samuel. "Go say hi to your aunt."

"Yeah, that's a hard no. And she's not my aunt anymore," Samuel said, moving out of the way so Izzy could get a better look. "She's Rowan's aunt. Let him deal with her."

"Wait, wait." Izzy scooched in next to Simone. "You and Rowan share an aunt? What am I missing here?"

"Jeez, Izzy, I figured you had this family tree memorized by now," Liam teased as Theo removed his baseball cap to place on her head.

"Charlie Fairweather's wife was Vivian McIntyre, and I'm guessing that's her."

Vivian McIntyre—the woman Charlie cheated on. Hearing that it might be her, Jamison rose on tiptoes.

Her father went pale. "Oh God. It's Bianca and... *is that a fucking parrot on her shoulder*?"

"Who's Bianca?" Bernie asked, popping into the crowd. "Ooh! That's not just a parrot. That's a green macaw."

A tiny woman close to Vivian's age had hopped out of the SUV's passenger side. Two more exited from the back, looking to be in their early twenties and equally appalled by the parrot sitting proudly on the smaller woman's shoulder.

"Bianca is Rowan's other aunt. He told me she raised parrots in Costa Rica," Annabeth said, sounding legitimately afraid. "I thought he was joking."

"That thing is not coming into my house, Benjamin," Simone hissed when Vivian reached Rowan on the front path. "I mean it."

Aunt and nephew didn't speak, with Vivian simply patting Rowan's cheek lovingly before moving on toward the house. He allowed her to pass, waiting for the others.

"Should I do something?" Taylor asked, wisely hovering near the back. "I can go greet them and say, you know, welcome to our home or whatever."

Jamison shared a look with Liam *Our home*? She told herself not to say anything, but good God, Taylor was pushing all her buttons today.

Vivian walked unhurried, allowing the security detail in the front yard to stare. She paid them no mind, completely comfortable with the attention.

"I'll get the door." Simone shoved her way through the crowd. "Everyone be nice. It can't be easy for Vivian to be here."

"I think I'm going to throw up," Annabeth whispered with a hand on her stomach as everyone else hurried off to the hallway. "Why is Rowan's family here?"

Jamison took her hand and pulled Annabeth out from behind the curtains. She couldn't hide in the parlor, not with half the women in Rowan's family about to walk through the front door. "It's going to be okay," she assured her. "They're probably just here to check on Rowan."

Evie joined them, the room clearing out entirely. "Yeah, but how would they even know something's wrong? All the public knows is that we had some skirmish with Zanmi, and it was played off like it was no big deal. No, they must be here for Annabeth. Rowan's probably been talking about the relationship, and if those women are anything like the women in our family…" She waved a hand erratically. "They're nosy as hell and want to meet you."

Leading Annabeth to the hall, Jamison shot Evie a glare. "We'll stay right next to you."

"No, you won't. You're going on the boat with Liam," Annabeth whispered. "Going to check out some dock, my ass. You're going to check out his dick."

Jamison didn't think there was any point in lying. "Well, it hasn't been used in a while, and I need to make sure it's in proper working order."

Evie waddled behind them, her blonde ponytail swaying in time with her hips. "I tried to check out Samuel's dick on a boat once. It didn't work out."

"You're about to pop with his third kid, Evie," Annabeth snickered once they entered the hall to stand with everyone else. "At some point, I think it worked out just fine."

Simone swung open the front door just as Vivian climbed the final step, her heels clicking smartly across the porch.

"Vivian."

"SiSi." Vivian paused at the threshold like a vampire waiting for an invitation. "Am I intruding?"

"Not at all." Simone swept her hand in a grand gesture, ushering Vivian inside. "Welcome to Haven House."

Crossing into the foyer, Vivian removed her sunglasses with a practiced flourish. Up close, she was even more stunning, and Jamison caught Annabeth's eye. If this was the aunt, what the hell was Rowan's mother like?

Josie stepped forward with a cautious smile. "Viv."

"Jos." Vivian leaned in, and the two women dropped air kisses on each other's cheeks. "Long time. Where's your boy?"

"He's the giant in the back."

"Hey, Aunt Vivian." Samuel gave a half-hearted wave, keeping one hand on Harper, who was still on his shoulders. "This is my oldest daughter, Harper. The one turning Liam into a jungle gym is my youngest, Theodora." His arm slid protectively around Evie. "And you've met my wife, Evangeline. Once."

"Yes, we did meet, but that was a lifetime ago," Vivian said, her approving gaze lingering on Evie before pivoting back to Josie. "Your boy looks like *him*, but thank God, I see Miranda in there too."

A new voice cut in, flat and utterly unimpressed with their guest. "Hello, Vivian."

Jamison tensed at her father's brusque greeting. He stood off in the shadows of the foyer, arms crossed and shoulder propped against the wall.

Ever so slowly, Vivian turned to face him. When their gazes connected, she raised her chin defiantly, an exhale of disappointment crossing her lips.

"Hello, Benjamin. Not dead yet, I see."

"Afraid not."

"Pity."

Jamison's eyes went round, but her father remained unfazed. "Why are you here, Vivian?" he asked.

"Why are *you* here, Benjamin? Shouldn't you be in Texas? Or holed up in one of your countless other offices?" Vivian sounded amused, as if she were toying with him. "Oh, wait. That's right. Fairweather Holdings has closed their offices for a... what was that bullshit lie you put out there? A fire and safety inspection?"

"Whatever the reasons are for closing *my* company's offices are *my* reasons," he replied smoothly. "And has nothing to do with the McIntyres."

"It does when you're holding one hostage."

"No one is holding Rowan hostage."

Vivian smiled, but it didn't reach her eyes, and Jamison felt the pressure shift in the room. Beside her, Annabeth sensed it too and had gone rigid, eyes locked on the floor. Instinctively, Jamison eased them both back, not wanting to be caught in this woman's crosshairs.

But shiny, beautiful things were Jamison's downfall, and the broach securing the silk scarf draped across Vivian's shoulder caught the light in just the right way and had her speaking without her brain first alerting her that might not be the best idea. "That's a lovely ruby broach."

Yep. A mistake. A total and utter mistake. Vivian's attention zeroed in like a sniper sighting her next shot, and Jamison braced for snarky comments. She'd gone up against worse, but this woman looked like she knew how to make every hit count.

"I've seen your picture many times, Ms. Fairweather, but I have to say, it doesn't do you justice. You're unique in your beauty, just like your mother," Vivian said, giving Jamison a thorough inspection. "However, like your brother, you've got that dark edge. A true Fairweather down to the bone."

Jamison had no idea if the observation was meant to be a compliment. "Thank you?"

And then the McIntyre chaos arrived.

The second older woman came marching in, the squawking parrot on her shoulder flapping its wings. She wore an oversized buttoned-up Hawaiian print shirt and hot pink leggings. Her long gray hair hung past her shoulders in braided pigtails with streaks of purple at their tips.

"Oh my God," Simone hissed when the parrot screamed. "We have cats."

This was it. Jamison was so sure this would be the moment Simone lost her ever-loving shit. It was a long time coming, and she was thankful that she wasn't to blame.

"Monty eats cats," the woman replied cheerfully to Simone before heading straight toward the corner. "Hey, *mother*fucker."

Jamison's soul briefly left her body. She was fairly certain no one in recorded history had ever called Benjamin Fairweather a *motherfucker* to his face. Her dad was tough, never taking crap from anyone.

And yet, here he stood—utterly unmoved. "That joke is getting old, Bianca."

"Not to me." The bird's screeching reached a deafening level, and Bianca cooed at the thing. "Now, where is she?"

"Where's who?" Josie asked warily.

"No. No, no, and no." Rowan bounded through the front door with the two younger women right behind him. "This is not okay."

Seeing the other new arrivals up close, Jamison could easily tell they were Vivian's daughters. The two women shared the same delicate bone structure along with the same high cheekbones, full lips, and flawless skin as their mother.

But that's where the similarities ended. They were much more casual than their mother, decked out in leggings and college sweatshirts. Both had dark chestnut hair and dark eyes to match, a total contrast to Vivian.

"What's not okay is you avoiding our calls for two weeks," Vivian shot back. "Your mother is worried sick, and you're lucky I didn't bring your sister."

Rowan's face went red—deep red, with some purple mixed in. A good foot taller than his aunts, he loomed over the women but still managed to look like a teenager caught sneaking in after curfew.

"I am a grown man."

"Then act like it. Call your mother. Poor Margie is going out of her mind," Bianca scolded, with her hands on her hips. "No one knows what's happening with you. Not even Killian, and we interrogated him for three hours."

"Poor Kill," one of the younger women said. "I think Aunt B made him cry."

"You can understand, can't you, ladies?" Vivian asked, addressing the mothers in the room. "If one of your children went missing and couldn't be bothered to text, wouldn't you send an army to track them down?"

"Yous been bad, Row-lo," Theo whispered, positively aghast. "Yous might gets a spank."

"No one is getting spanked, Theo." Rowan spun around to face Simone, who was still holding the front door open like she might shove someone back through it. "I am so terribly sorry for this."

"Call your mother next time." Simone pushed the door shut with a little more force than necessary. "Now. Can I interest anyone in some coffee?"

Chapter 10

Rowan

"I'm sorry we're a little off today," Simone said as she set a steaming mug of coffee in front of Vivian. "We had an unpleasant phone call earlier."

"It was Tobias," Ben snapped as he hovered impatiently on the other side of the kitchen. He was supposed to be in his meeting, but had canceled it. "And the word unpleasant doesn't quite cover what we went through before you and your horde arrived."

Rowan winced. There was no love lost between his Aunt Vivian and Ben. The sad thing was that Ben understood he was the villain in her story, and while remorseful, he knew damn well he couldn't change the past. His aunt knew this also, but whenever the topic of Ben came up, she couldn't help but release a venomous quip or two.

It was for the best that everyone kept their distance, and that's exactly what he and Annabeth were doing. Izzy and Abe had retreated to the media room, along with Bernie and Will, so that they could have privacy in the kitchen. Once Holden got there, Samuel had taken his crew home, save for Josie, who had wanted to stay for whatever reason.

Liam and Jamison were out the door the second Holden brought one of the Fairweather boats alongside Haven's dock. Rowan had been a little pissed when he saw the make and model, knowing that particular class had a small single cabin.

With a bed.

Bastards.

"I knew you were up to no good, Ben," Vivian said, sipping her coffee. "But even I'm surprised to hear you were up at dawn conversing with serial killers."

Bianca adjusted her oversized glasses and pinned Rowan with a glare. "Care to elaborate, Randall?"

Randall?

Ouch.

It was a little early to be throwing out government names.

"Listen, Aunt B, things around here are complicated, and I'm doing my job."

Bianca leaned sideways, peering around him at Annabeth. "Hello, *Job*. Lovely to meet you."

"He-hello." Annabeth bravely met each set of appraising eyes. "I'm Annabeth. It's lovely to meet you all."

Bianca opened her mouth to reply with some off-the-wall remark but was poked in the shoulder by Vivian's oldest daughter. Jenny excelled at keeping their aunt's crazy in check. "Calm down," she ordered Bianca. "We came to make sure Rowan is okay, and now that we see that he is, we can leave."

"Yeah, fat chance of that," Sasha mumbled from her spot on the wall. Unlike her sister, Sasha had no patience for their family's particular flavor of crazy. She thrived in high-stress situations, but had her limits when it came to Bianca. "You've awakened the beasts, Row."

Vivian placed her cup down and kept her gaze trained on Ben. "I don't believe you've met my daughters," she spoke smugly, always proud of her children. "Jenny is my eldest and has recently finished nursing school. Then we have Sasha over by Rowan. She's in her second year of college but is still undecided on her future path in life."

"Oh, I've decided, but according to my mother, seeing the world isn't a valid life path," Sasha whispered loudly to Annabeth. "And let's be for real. She shouldn't be surprised that I don't care about college and want to wander instead. It's in my DNA. McIntyres can't sit still for very long, or we'll go insane."

Sasha was a good kid and only trying to be friendly, but the way Annabeth edged further along the wall had Rowan going on alert. He was positive that Killian had briefed every McIntyre woman in this room on what Annabeth meant to him and the challenges she faced. Knowing his weak ass brother, Kill probably folded the second they closed ranks and spilled all the details, including what went down here.

"Children do what they want in the end," Josie said, standing by the kitchen island where Simone had retreated. "Look at Selah. He was supposed to be head of Fairweather, and now he's off changing the world for the better."

"How is Selah?" Vivian asked Simone. "He had the best smile when he was a little boy and was always so kind." Her gaze drifted toward Ben. "So much so, it was hard to believe he was your child."

"Selah is fine." Ben crossed his arms, jaw ticking. "Cut the shit, Viv. What do you know?"

Vivian hesitated for a moment. "Simone, would you mind if my girls peeked at the conservatory? I think they'd enjoy it."

Understanding immediately, Simone nodded. "It's lovely this time of day, and all the new kittens should be out basking in the sun."

"I'll go with them," Bianca said, rising from the table. The damn parrot flapped wildly as she stood, its wings knocking poor Jenny in the head. "Easy, Monty. And no terrorizing kittens."

Simone led the McIntyre women out while Vivian remained engaged in her endless glaring contest with Ben.

"I know everything," she said once the others were gone. "But I don't want them to know. I don't want them to even come close to understanding how evil and awful the Fairweathers can be or of what I had to endure before their father came into my life."

The lines around Ben's eyes softened a fraction. He looked tired. More tired than Rowan had seen him through this entire ordeal. "Goddamn it, Viv," Ben said in a low voice. "Why did you have to show up today of all days?"

Rowan moved to intervene, but Josie beat him to it, seating herself next to Vivian. "How is Aiden?" she asked. "Is he doing well?"

It was the perfect pivot. Aiden and Vivian had the kind of relationship other couples could only dream of having. They adored each other and did everything together with their girls.

"He's good." Vivian was immensely proud of not only her daughters, but also of her husband. She gave Josie a bittersweet smile. "I was very sorry to hear about Miranda. She was such a brave soul."

Both Josie and Ben stiffened. "Thank you," Josie said finally. "She often said the same thing about you."

Vivian gave a small laugh. "I still remember how Helen would throw those dreadful Christmas parties. Miranda and I would pretend Samuel was a fussy baby just so we could sneak off and hide from those insufferable assholes James and Helen called friends."

Ben looked like he might actually smile. "You two disappeared so often at those things, I started wondering if my son had some kind of allergy to people."

Josie snorted. "Samuel is kind of allergic to people, Ben."

"You can blame me and Miranda for that," Vivian replied. "We probably ruined him early on."

A rare hush settled over the table until Rowan cleared his throat. "Aunt Viv, I don't want my mom to worry—"

"Too late for that," she interrupted.

"But I'm not leaving," Rowan continued, taking Annabeth's hand. "Ever."

Vivian's sharp gaze dropped to their joined hands. "I see."

Josie looked impressed, while Ben let out one of those sighs that said he really didn't want to be involved with this discussion.

"You know what?" Annabeth squeaked, wiggling her hand free of his grasp. "I think I'll go check on the others. No offense, but I don't trust that parrot around the cats."

"No offense taken." Vivian drummed her manicured nails against the ceramic coffee mug. "You're right to be worried. Monty is a monster."

Annabeth made a quick exit with Ben not far behind her. "Come on, Josie," he said. "Let's go check on the cats."

Josie didn't move. "Why me?"

Ben let out another one of his sighs. "Because Simone is probably in a full-blown panic over that damn bird, and she'll expect me to do something about it, and I have no idea what the hell to do with a parrot. Just... come be my backup."

Grumbling under her breath, Josie followed, patting Rowan's shoulder on her way out.

Alone with this aunt, Rowan sat at the table. "Go ahead and say your piece."

That was all the leeway Viv needed. "This is absurd. We were against you taking the job in the first place, thinking it was simply you being your usual rebel self, but you have no business being involved with these people."

"These people were once your family."

"They were once my family when I was a young fool." Vivian's spine snapped straight. "Back when I was so in love, I couldn't see Charlie for what he really was."

He shouldn't say it. He should keep his damn mouth shut because his aunt had suffered enough, but he wasn't about to sit here and listen to a bullshit comparison. "Annabeth isn't Charlie. Hell, she's not even a Fairweather."

"It doesn't matter that she's not a Fairweather by blood. That girl is one of them."

"And what if she is?" He leaned forward to drive his next words home. "Fairweather or not, she's mine."

Vivian's mouth slammed shut, her nostrils flaring.

"Yeah, you heard me. This is the end of the line for me. I want nothing else in life but her," he continued. "I love Annabeth. I've loved her for years. Years, Aunt Viv. I've bided my time until I couldn't wait anymore."

"You do realize you'll likely never leave Haven House?"

He was so damn tired of hearing this argument. "So what if I live and die in the same spot? If I'm with her, it doesn't matter."

Vivian relaxed, settling back into the kitchen chair. "My, oh my. You sound just like your father."

He loved his father, but they were nothing alike. Phillip McIntyre was a serious man who had dedicated his entire life to running McIntyre Industries until his health no longer permitted it. Rowan would never call his father uptight, but yeah, that was as close of a description as possible and the exact opposite of himself.

No, he was more like his mother. Margie McIntyre was a free spirit who could hold her own with Bianca. His mom always wanted everything to be fun and beautiful for their family, even coaxing her husband to engage in a few of her more eccentric ideas.

"I don't know how I could possibly sound like my dad."

"When Phillip brought Margie home, our parents hated her and thought she was just a passing phase," Vivian explained. "Then, when he said he wanted to marry her, I honestly thought The McIntyre might disown him."

Well aware that the man he shared a name with had been an evil son of a bitch, Rowan wasn't surprised. His grandfather was always tough on everyone, but none more so than his own son.

"And your dad told him to fuck right the hell off." Vivian chuckled at the memory. "Phillip was prepared to leave it all behind for your mom, and he gave this big speech in front of the whole family. It was probably the most romantic thing I've ever seen."

Rowan tried to picture his father as romantic but couldn't. "I'll take your word for it."

"I know Margie draws everyone to her, but have you ever stopped and noticed your father whenever they're together? How he watches her?"

"Uh, no?"

"You should." Vivian rose to take her coffee mug to the sink. "He's so in awe of her and the love she stirs in him. McIntyre men aren't known to show their emotions very much. Take your brother, for example. I don't know that Killian will ever settle down."

Killian would never marry. That was a given. A house with a white picket fence and two and a half kids would never be in the cards for him. There was absolutely nothing wrong with that, either. His brother enjoyed life and was happy having a constant parade of women rotating in and out of his bed.

"I once thought the same of you," Vivian said, returning to her seat. "But here you are. Battling armies of psychotics and serial killers, all in the name of love."

He rubbed a hand down his face. "How much did Killian tell you?"

"Enough."

"And how much did you tell my parents?"

"Not a damn bit of it," she replied. "I might not be a Fairweather anymore, but I remember the rules. McIntyres live by the same ones. The less everyone knows, the better."

Rowan hesitated to tell her what he'd heard during the phone call, but ended up blurting it out anyway. "Toby talked about Charlie this morning. He talked about how Charlie was screaming when he died and what he said."

Vivian stilled. Whatever bravado she'd clung to deflated in a breath. "Tell me."

He shouldn't. It was wrong on so many levels, but he wanted her to understand how fucked up this all was.

"Toby said Charlie was screaming for people to help him. CeCe. Ben." Rowan met his aunt's steely gaze. "You."

Her bottom lip trembled. She turned away, staring through the kitchen window. "Charlie deserved so much, but not that. Never that." She wiped a wayward tear, and a small sob slipped past her lips. "God dammit. That man can still make me cry."

Rowan checked the hall. Later, he'd erase this conversation from the security recordings. "Killian agreed," he said.

Vivian's tears vanished, her expression turning cold. "Then let it begin. Give Samuel what he wants and end this."

"Ben is completely unaware of the whole thing."

"Benjamin has enough sins on his scorecard and doesn't need more, but I can tell you right now he isn't totally unaware," she stated plainly. "He'll ignore it. The man sitting here just now wasn't the ruthless bastard I once knew. Laura Jean changed him, but her death... it brought that old darkness back, twisting it into something even I can't recognize."

Yeah, Rowan could get that. The stories he'd heard about Ben back in the day were almost unbelievable now. "Samuel wrestled with this decision for a long time. But after everything that's happened, he's ready to pull the trigger."

"Then allow your brother to pull it, Rowan."

Guilt over what to do wasn't the cause of his hesitation. He had been taught early in life that there was a distinct difference between doing what was right and what was necessary. Samuel was the same, and they were both keenly aware his plan wasn't the plan of a good man. It was the plan of a desperate one.

And while he felt that same desperation, Rowan didn't want the McIntyres involved. He wanted time to find another way, but time was something they didn't have.

"I worry about Killian," he admitted. "This isn't our fight. If it goes wrong—"

"Is it your fight, Rowan?" Vivian's head tilted to the side. "Is this Fairweather problem yours?"

He knew what she was asking and told the truth. "I would marry her tomorrow if she would have me."

"Then this is our fight," Vivian said. "But I don't want you anywhere near it. Samuel, that ex-FBI security person, even your brother, can run, but you can't."

Annabeth.

He couldn't run if things went sideways because of Annabeth. Samuel and Liam had the means to restart their lives elsewhere if they were caught. It would break hearts, sure—but their people would understand. Their women and Samuel's girls would, of course, go with them. Ben would continue to run Fairweather, with Damon likely taking it on after him. It would be the same for Killian. If his brother needed to flee, McIntyre Industries would survive with Caitlin at the wheel once she figured out where and how to steer it.

But Annabeth? She could never disappear if their plans were discovered. Haven House remained her prison. A beautiful cage that refused to release her from its clutches.

And because of that, he would stand down. He would allow Liam and his brother to decide how to move forward without him. He would let Samuel shoulder the guilt of giving the order.

"I hate the Fairweathers," Vivian whispered, as if Haven House might strike her down for saying such a thing. "They've used me, poisoned me, and broken me in ways I will never allow anyone else to see."

"Aunt Viv—"

She laid her hand on top of his, effectively silencing him. "But I love you and will stand by you. I will stand by your brother. We'll greet this end together because it's time." A shudder ran through her, the old ghosts of the past making their presence known. "It's time for Charlie's son to die."

✦ ✦ ✦

Standing on the front porch, Rowan tucked Annabeth against his chest as his family pulled away down the drive.

"How long are they staying?" she asked.

Rowan rubbed his chin along the top of her head. "Viv said they're flying back to Texas today."

As the SUV disappeared around the bend, Annabeth turned in his arms. "She's nothing like I expected. Everyone always said Vivian was a pushover."

"A pushover? Well, I guess that depends on who's telling the story," Rowan said. "But when she kicked Charlie out, and Aiden swept in? That changed everything. My uncle worships her. And I think having someone love you like that allows a person to start loving themselves."

"It's amazing how that works." She stretched on her toes to kiss him. "Loving the right person makes you feel powerful."

She hadn't said it out loud yet. The *I love you* that would, in essence, seal her to him forever.

But it was coming.

He could feel it.

Their lips connected, the kiss sweet and simple since cameras were on them. "I am so pissed at Jamison for leaving me," Annabeth muttered against his lips. "That heifer is probably out on the water having the time of her life while we're stuck researching another dead-end lead."

"I have an idea." He waggled his eyebrows. "A naughty, unbelievably good idea."

She laughed, her eyes dancing. It was good to see that glimmer of happiness in them again. The bookstore had been closed since the Firewater Halloween party—quietly shuttered for the off-season. No one questioned it. The tourists were gone, leaving only the locals meandering around Firewater until the quickly approaching holidays. By now, Annabeth should be lost in the throes of prepping for the upcoming shopping chaos.

But this year, it wasn't possible. Not with everything happening. The loss of routine had left Annabeth mourning her little store, and Rowan was actively trying to figure out ways to get them over there for a visit.

"I like naughty ideas from you," she purred. "They usually involve me being naked and sweaty."

God, he loved this woman.

"I can block the security system for about twenty minutes. It won't be able to read anything. No visuals, no biometrics. Nothing. We can go for a *walk* in the forest."

Her finger traced the shamrock tattoo on his neck. "And what can you do to me in twenty minutes, Mr. McIntyre?"

The shiver started in his spine and shot straight to his dick. No longer caring that there were eyes on them, he grabbed two handfuls of her perfect ass and pulled her hard against him. "You're gonna find out exactly what I can fucking do."

Annabeth's giggle mixed with the tinkling of wind chimes blowing about in the midday wind. Rowan often wondered if she ever realized how enchanting she could be. Her smile quite literally knocked the breath out of his lungs. And her laugh? Her laugh could linger in his mind for days.

"Fucking being the key word?"

"Yes, ma'am." He dropped into his full Texan drawl. "It'll be one of those save a horse, ride a Rowan kind of things."

They were both grinning when she kissed him again.

"Tell me what your aunt said," she murmured, nipping his bottom lip. "It looked serious in there."

The color drained from his face, and he released his hold on her. "You were listening?"

She could do it. Annabeth knew his passwords. They were a team, and she had access to all points of the security system.

"I wasn't. Not really." She frowned at the sudden change in him. "But I did peek in once or twice."

"She knows what happened," he said quietly. "And is... concerned."

Annabeth stepped back, arms crossing as if to block out a sudden chill in the eighty plus degree weather. "There's more."

"I thought you weren't listening."

Her eyes narrowed. "I wasn't."

He believed her. But fear still clawed at his throat. Vivian knew a plan was in place, but she had no idea its full scope. Killian would never have told the whole truth, even under interrogation. That wasn't how it worked.

Vivian was a McIntyre that had once walked among the Fairweathers. As she said in the kitchen, she knew the rules. She knew the power of secrecy. Annabeth didn't, and she wouldn't like being left in the dark. She'd push for the whole truth when really, the less she knew, the better.

Hell, the less he knew, the better.

"They didn't like me, is that it?" Annabeth turned away from him, stalking down the porch toward the curve of the railing. "She thinks I'm a waste of your time. That being with me is ridiculous, and that I'm trying to trap you here with me."

He couldn't help the surge of relief. Thank God she had her back to him, or she really would get angry at the smile on his face.

"No, sweetheart. Viv doesn't think that at all. And if she did, I wouldn't give a shit."

"But I bet your mother thinks that."

"My mom believes in doing whatever the hell makes you happy." He tugged playfully on the back of her shirt. "And you make me happy, Annabeth."

She let out a dismissive little *hmpf,* and moved to walk inside, but he spun her around before she could escape. Out on the lawn, the agents were drifting back into view after finishing a perimeter sweep. If he didn't wrap this up soon, their little spat might end up in someone's incident report.

"I love you." He gripped her chin, holding her gaze. "I love you here or there, or any–fucking–where."

She jerked free of his hold. "You sound like Dr. Seuss."

"And you sound like a brat who needs her ass spanked."

He walked her backward, pressing her against the exposed brick exterior of one of Haven's many fireplaces. Bracing his hands on each side of her head, he caged her in soundly.

"This doubting us crap? Yeah, it needs to end."

He kept his tone soft, not wanting her to hear the exasperated anger that came every time she started this kind of talk. It hadn't happened much since the night of the attack, but as each day passed and normalcy came closer, it had begun to creep into their conversations once more.

A haunted look filled her beautiful brown eyes, cutting him like a knife. "But I don't ever move forward, Rowan. Not really."

"Selling your achievements short just because of something you *think* my aunt said is a shitty move, Annabeth."

The sadness that was there a second ago flashed to anger. Quick and swift, she struck him in the chest. One good punch that he hardly felt. "I love you, you big asshole. And it scares me."

Another punch. This time to the heart.

"I'm allowed to have doubts. I'm allowed to be scared." Another strike. "I am allowed to voice my fears in any snarky, sarcastic way I want because you're mine. And because you love me."

Another hit, softer now. Almost tender.

"If you want me, you have to put up with my crazy."

He was grinning like a fucking idiot when he kissed her. Seizing her face with two hands, he nearly crumbled to the floor when she let out a muted growl that vibrated against his lips. But with a skilled swipe of his tongue, she calmed, almost crawling up his body as she sought more.

They ended the kiss right as the security detail rounded the corner. "You love me," he whispered, slightly out of breath and refusing to move no matter who was watching. "You. Love. Me."

In the shadow of his arms, she rolled her eyes. "Don't be weird about it."

"You're weird. I'm weird." He chuckled over how good it felt to hear her say it finally. "We're going to be a weird family one day."

The growing smile on her lips faltered. "Rowan..."

Shit.

Too much, too fast. She was skittish as a wild colt, fresh on the ranch. Straightening, he reeled himself back in.

"Come on. Let's go inside. We've got work to do."

Taking her hand, he tried to lead her to the front door, but she wouldn't budge. "Rowan, we need to talk."

Stubborn woman.

"Look, I know you have doubts, and you're scared. But, baby, let me have this. Just for a minute. Let me hold on to this perfect moment where I'm floating because you said you love me."

"I wouldn't call this a perfect moment. A perfect moment would be me screaming *I love you* mid-orgasm." She glanced at the security personnel nearby as the men and women pretended not to watch them. "Just saying, you know?"

"Soon," he groaned. "I swear. We just need to find a place."

It was her turn to shiver, and she wrapped her arms around his midsection. "Jamison and Liam are planning to bring the boat back here. Someone still has to return it to the marina."

"Okay?"

"I've never been on a boat," she said, looking up at him. "And while I don't think I could sail on one, I wouldn't mind sitting on it with you tonight. Maybe we could take a break after sunset—have dinner on it, watch the stars? From what I heard, it has a small dinette?"

"Annabeth Howard, you're a genius." He kissed her forehead. "It does have a dinette, and I'd be honored to have dinner with you on it tonight."

"I would be the dinner, Rowan."

Holy hell. Had he really missed that? He should've caught what she was hinting at a mile away. But his brain had been too busy conjuring up all the ways they could sneak around on a boat together, and in that process, another image hit—one he definitely didn't need.

"Uh, maybe. We don't know what kind of condition it'll be in when Liam and Jamison get back."

Annabeth snickered. "They're only supposed to check out the dock and come right back. But yeah, if I had a chance to have you alone on a boat right now, we'd spend about five seconds looking for some stupid dock before things got dirty."

"Oh, really? And what exactly would you do?" Draping his arm around her shoulder, Rowan squeezed her close as they headed back inside. "Be specific. Don't leave anything out."

Chapter 11

Jamison

"That's where CeCe died."

They were coasting away from the house, the boat gliding down the dark waters of the bayou. Liam stood at the helm, guiding them along the winding channel that stretched from Haven's dock to the distant bay, roughly three miles out. According to the map beside him in the pilot's chair, their route would hug the swampy shoreline, weaving through inlets in search of hidden launch sites before reaching Watson's place.

"We estimated it was right about there." Liam pointed to a sandy patch surrounded by reeds swaying in the breeze. "They found a few manchineels in that spot and nowhere else."

Neither of them spoke as they drifted past the place where CeCe had spent her final moments. Jamison left the pilot house, stepping out to stand on the padded bow bench. She couldn't remember the last time they'd taken a boat directly from Haven's dock, certainly not since CeCe's murder.

"How did he get her out there?" she asked, returning to Liam's side after they passed the small barrier island. Dropping into the co-pilot's chair, she propped her feet up. "Toby said he drugged her, but someone at a marina would've noticed a guy carrying an unconscious woman."

"It's one of those details I didn't follow up on." The muscle in Liam's ticked jaw with annoyance. "Too many moving parts back then. Not an excuse, but now look where we are."

She gave his bicep a light punch. "Stop blaming yourself."

"Who else should I blame?" He smirked as she shook her hand, trying to get the feeling back into her fingers. "This is on me, and I take full responsibility."

"Well, you shouldn't."

Liam focused on steering, keeping a low wake as they passed the old mill and its remaining pilings protruding from the water. Through a thinning patch of trees, the graveyard could be seen. Just beyond it, the manchineels waited, their twisted branches claiming more of the shoreline every year.

"Your dad contacted a company out of South Florida," Liam said, eyes still forward. "They specialize in removing manchineels. The plan is to start the extraction process sometime next year."

They rode in silence for a long stretch, the forest unspooling endlessly beside them. High in the sky, the sun shone down on them once they hit the widening pass, and knowing they were nearing Watson's place, Jamison decided it was the perfect time to reveal her bathing suit.

At the back of the boat, the bench seating offered the best view and the most sun. She strolled over, peeled off her T-shirt, and casually tossed it aside. The top of her suit was little more than string and two tiny triangles that barely covered anything. She wasn't overly endowed in the breast department, but the minuscule coverage gave her shape a nice definition.

Liam glanced back and did a double take. "What the fuck?"

Even over the whine of the motor, she heard him loud and clear, but refused to smile. Discarding the jean cut-offs, she adjusted the thong bikini bottom high on her hips and turned to give him the full view.

"Where the hell did you get that?" he shouted, the boat suddenly losing speed. "Come here."

Running her hands over her hips, she crawled onto the white leather bench, deliberately angling her ass in his direction. "Do you like it?"

The engine dipped into a low hum, and Liam ripped off his sunglasses, no longer paying attention to where they were going. "Are you seriously asking if I like seeing my woman in a thong bathing suit?"

The boat veered sharply, cutting across the gleaming water toward a narrow inlet ahead. It wasn't deep, but it curved just enough to keep them out of sight.

"What are you doing?" she asked, feigning innocence as she settled onto the bench and spread her legs ever so strategically. "I thought we were supposed to be looking for docks."

He didn't answer, slowing the boat to a crawl. The silence stretched as he worked the anchor, every second fueling the anticipation sparking in her chest.

"Liam?"

"Get in here." His voice was tight, the small remaining shred of his sanity reaching its end. "The cabin bed is big enough for both of us."

"No." She leaned back, resting her arms on the bench as she stretched across the cushions. "I like it out here."

He stopped what he was doing and arched an eyebrow at her. "We're doing this in the open?"

"Oh yeah." She tapped the bench between her thighs, spreading wider as she tipped her head back to soak in the sun. "Right. Here."

The engine cut off completely, leaving only the sound of the forest rustling around them and Liam's hurried footsteps as he left the pilot house.

"You're keeping that damn bathing suit on the whole time."

Eyes still closed, she smirked. "I was worried you wouldn't like it. I know orange isn't your favorite."

"Orange? I don't know what you're talking about. I'm colorblind at the moment." His hands wrapped around her ankles, lifting them so her feet rested on the bench.

Her eyes popped open to see him kneeling in front of her—hat turned backward, chest bare in the sunlight, lips parted as he took her in.

"Are you sure you want to do this out here?" he asked, his head already lost between her thighs. A groan left him as he nuzzled her softly, his breath hot against her skin. "Someone could see us."

Knocking his hat aside, she threaded her fingers through his longer-than-usual hair. Like when they were changing earlier, it was tousled and boyish, a dangerously charming combination. The entire look and attitude made him hard to resist, but she was more than ready to embrace this new non-Bureau Liam with open arms.

And open legs, apparently.

Pushing at her thighs, he spread her further, settling in.

"I don't mind if someone sees us," she whispered, her breath catching as he slid the thin fabric of her bikini bottoms aside. "It's kind of exhilarating."

His mouth hovered for a beat, and then he pressed a soft, deliberate kiss against her center. "Dirty girl," he murmured. Another kiss followed, featherlight. "*My* dirty girl."

With the flat of his tongue, he tasted her leisurely, and she nearly came right then. That was the thing with Liam. Sex was always incredible, but the man knew how to give the most divine pleasure with just his tongue. And he enjoyed it. *Loved it.* He could spend hours with his head nestled right between her thighs, worshipping every inch of her like it was a calling.

The sun glinted off her ring, and she clutched his hair tighter, hips rolling to draw him deeper. He responded with a growl that shot heat straight through her, and somewhere off in the forest, a bird squawked in horror, positively appalled by the carnal scene playing out in its private sanctuary.

Man. Animal. She didn't care.

Let them all see.

With light suction and steady flicks of his tongue, he easily had her body trembling as she climbed, whimpering from the pleasure building fast and wild.

"Oh no, you don't." Liam lifted his head to tug at the strings of his shorts. "We're doing this together."

Positively ravenous to have him in her mouth again, she all but fell off the seat. On her knees and gripping his base the second his cock was free, she took him into her mouth until he was hitting the back of her throat.

"Fuck, that's good." He let out the most satisfying groan, his head falling back. With one hand knotted in her hair, he met her rhythm, matching the bob of her head with a roughness that made her want more. "God... this mouth."

She thought about how they must look. Her in a neon thong bathing suit, greedy, on her knees, and getting her mouth properly fucked by a beautiful man.

And Liam. If someone did come across them, she didn't think he would stop. Too far lost, she honestly thought he would keep right on thrusting, slamming his cock into her throat like nothing else mattered.

The more she pictured the scene, the more crazed with need she became. When she finally pulled back with a deliberate swipe of her tongue, her smile was pure sin. "Ready?"

He didn't let go of her hair, forcing her head up so she could look at him. "On your back. Brace your arms."

She crawled onto the cushions, flashing him another wicked grin over her shoulder as she wiggled her ass. "Are you sure you don't want me like this?"

"I said, on your back." He gave her a sharp smack, following it with a rough squeeze. "Now."

Curving her spine, she gave him one last look at her position on all fours, and the muscles in his abdomen shuddered. "Yeah, but I think I might frame this bathing suit." His tongue darted out to wet his lips. "It's a work of art on your body."

"I'm glad you like it," she started to say, but the rest of her sentence dissolved into a gasp. For the most part, Liam Cohen was a patient man. Calm, level-headed. He never allowed much to get him riled up.

Except when it came to sex.

In one swift move, he flipped her over. "Are we not in a listening mood today, Jamison?"

"Never." She instinctively wrapped her legs around his waist when he covered her body with his own. "You know, I was worried you wouldn't like the color...*oh, God, who cares*."

Lined up and ready, Liam thrust his hips forward, sliding into her with ease, thanks to their frantic foreplay. Given his size, he paused for a beat, letting her adjust—but after a few hard pumps, she was clawing at the cushion, breath hitching with every stroke.

"Arms up and hands braced against the back of the seat," he warned.

She placed her palms flat against the seatback and locked her arms as he gave up any pretense of restraint. Pounding into her, he set a relentless pace until her body clenched around him.

"Give it up, Jamison." Liam's cocky, open-mouth smirk grew as her whimpers turned to punctuated moans. "I can feel you squeezing me, baby. You're so ready to let go."

He grabbed the metal bar at the top of the seat, using it as leverage to fuck harder and drive himself as deep as possible. With his other hand, he yanked her top aside to watch her breast bounce from the impact. "Need them in my mouth."

Bending low, he took one nipple between his lips, sucking hard while his hand worked the other. The rhythm of his thrusts never faltered, and when Jamison bucked her hips to meet him, her orgasm hit like a lightning bolt—shattering and raw, her cries echoing across the inlet.

"Come on, baby. Be my good girl and breathe through it." Liam lifted his head to watch, his arrogant smile blurring when her vision blacked out for a second. "Yeah, there you go. That's it."

She did as she was told, allowing the pleasure to consume her. The veins in his forearm popped as he continued to use his grip on the bar as an anchor, and with a guttural curse, he increased his speed, hammering into her as the wet slap of skin on skin drove them into a frenzied high.

Having him this deep, pounding this hard, threatened to send her spiraling over the edge again. And only when his hand locked around her throat, his heavy ramming turning erratic, did she lose herself once more.

They rode out their release together. She took every last thrust, the tension in his body making her own quake. He shouted as he came, the sound alone increasing her pleasure.

"I fucking love you, woman." Impossibly thick and purely masculine, he spilled into her completely, shuddering from the intensity. "This... *you*...belong to *me*."

Their lips met in a searing kiss, and when he finally let go of the seat, he wrapped her up tight. His mouth wandered, nipping at her neck, tongue tracing a lazy pattern over her collarbone before dipping back to her breasts, unable to get enough.

"Can we go for round two?" she panted, the scent of sweaty, hot sex filling her as she fought for air. "Like... now?"

A shrill ring interrupted their moment, and Liam sighed into her skin. "Can't they give me a little peace?"

He reluctantly pulled away, her body instantly protesting the loss. "Did we not drop enough clues about what we were doing out here?" Her phone started to ring, too, and she sighed. "Obviously not."

Liam answered his first, gloriously naked and entirely unbothered. "Do you remember how you used to call at the worst possible times when

I was in college?" he grumbled into the phone. "Yeah. Your streak lives on."

Jamison grabbed her own phone, huffing when she saw Rowan's name flash on the screen. "What?"

"Let me talk to Liam."

"He's talking to…" Her eyes went wide when she saw Liam staring down at her as he stroked himself. Biting his bottom lip, his dark eyes roamed, and when he jerked his chin, gesturing for her to spread her legs so he could see the remains of their fucking… she didn't hesitate.

He *had* told her to be a good girl, after all.

Rowan's call disconnected, and she tossed her phone aside, more than ready to give Liam a show. Time was limited, and they needed to make the most of it.

Sliding her fingers down her belly and between her legs, she rubbed circles as she waited impatiently. And when he watched, yet still continued to talk, she rolled to her front to lift up on all fours. At this angle, he could see everything, including the absolute mess he'd made of her.

"God damn," she heard him exhale, which he quickly covered with a hasty throat clear. "No, not you. Right. There's no way to tell who? Got it. Yeah. We'll head out now."

Ending the call, he bent down and sank his teeth into the curve of her ass.

"I'm sorry," he said, mouth still against her skin.

"For the bite or because we're going back?"

"We're not going back, and I'm sure as hell not sorry for the bite." He kissed the red mark his teeth had left. "But Rowan spotted Watson at the shack. He's got people with him, which apparently never happens. Dad wants us to make contact and see what we can dig up."

She really needed to find out how Rowan always seemed to know these things. But, then again, he'd probably never tell her.

"So, what you're saying," she rolled over to pout, "is that our time is over, and I have to put on makeup."

"Our time is over for now." He bent down, and, sliding his hand beneath her hair, he tugged her closer by the nape. "Once we're done at Watson's place, we're coming back here."

"For round two?"

"And three." He grinned and kissed her. "And four."

"Do not paddle," Liam growled. "Just relax."

"I can paddle," she hissed over her shoulder, trying not to tip the kayak. "I am perfectly capable of handling myself."

The grunt he gave said otherwise, but she wasn't giving in. They'd always been *the couple* to beat in any group activity—until it came down to kayaking, their one weakness. Liam expected her to just let him do all the work, but that wasn't going to happen.

It wasn't her fault they could never get their paddling in sync.

And really, she should surrender. The inflatable kayak stashed on the boat had been a last-minute call, and she could admit that it was the right one. When they'd passed the inlet near Watson's shack, Liam switched course, guiding the boat out of sight. Now, with the kayak, they could sneak up along the water's edge undetected, weaving through the marsh and tall trees growing directly off the shore.

Jamison's paddle dipped too hard, sending a spray of water over the bow. The dark, sluggish waves slapped against the side of the kayak, bouncing them a little too close to the knotted cypress roots.

She sucked a sharp breath as Liam corrected their course. "I could have done that. Why don't you let me lead for a second?"

Liam's paddle tapped her shoulder playfully, cold water dripping onto her shirt. "Not gonna happen."

"Fine." Resting her paddle across her lap, she gave in, glancing back to find Liam grinning over his victory. "Happy?"

"Delirious."

They drifted closer, inching along the edge of the swamp until the shack came into full view. *Shack* really was the perfect word for the place. Leaning slightly, the structure looked one strong wind away from collapse. In contrast, the dock appeared to be in perfect shape. Nice and stable, it was ideal for most mid-sized vessels.

"How the hell did I miss this?" Liam whispered, keeping his voice low to avoid it carrying over the water. "I swear this wasn't here when CeCe died, but now, I honestly can't remember if we swept this far out from the scene."

Jamison scanned the shoreline, nodding toward the dock. "Look at the wood on the house versus the dock. It's new. That means it either wasn't here when CeCe died, or it was in such bad shape back then that no one paid attention to it."

"Which means someone recently constructed it."

Just then, the shack's back door creaked open, and a man stepped out. Even from this distance, it was obvious he was on the short side. Jamison sat up and squinted as if it would help her see better.

"Is that Watson?"

Liam extracted a compact pair of binoculars from the pocket of his board shorts and handed them to her. "That's him, but I don't see anyone else."

Peering through the lens, she stared at the man pacing slowly across the lawn with his hands in his pockets. He had dark hair and a scraggly mustache that needed some attention. Even in the warm weather, he wore a flannel shirt and jeans.

"Why is he dressed like a mountain man?" She passed the binoculars back to Liam. "A flannel shirt and jeans in this weather? Seriously?"

Placing the binoculars on the kayak floor, Liam studied the area as he thought through his plan. "Watson has scars on his arms, and he doesn't like for people to see them."

Jamison found the man's insecurity intriguing and thought about how she could use it to their advantage. "When we head over there, how am I playing this?"

Liam no longer wanted her to be Jamison Fairweather. Instead, they were going to pretend to be tourists on the hunt for rainbow swamps. Natural reflections where oil-slicked water and refracted sunlight appeared to capture the colors of a rainbow, tourists were known to lose their damn minds over them.

"Be cute," Liam said, still scanning the shoreline. "Bubbly, maybe?"

"Sweet Jesus," she grumbled. "I have never in my life been bubbly."

He chuckled softly. "Flirt with him. Like Taylor does with your dad."

She recoiled, almost tipping the kayak. "Now you're pushing it."

"You can punish me later." Using his paddle, he nudged them free of the tangled roots they'd been using for cover. "You ready?"

Jamison pressed her lips together, trying to smooth out the electric pink coating them. Her makeup felt like stage prosthetics, heavy and unnatural. "I guess so."

Winding through the trees, Liam's paddling turned erratic as he pretended to be an amateur on the water. When they emerged from the swamp into open water, he let out a loud, forced laugh to draw Emmett's attention.

"Hey!" Jamison waved enthusiastically at Emmett, feeling like an absolute moron as she spoke in a country accent. "Excuse me, sir! Can you help us?"

"Nice acting," Liam whispered. "But give it more of a twang."

She would not roll her eyes.

Continuing to wave, she gave a toothy grin and hoped to hell the hot pink lipstick wasn't covering a random tooth here or there. Whatever she looked like, Emmett Watson seemed to like it. Quirking an eyebrow, he meandered down the dock as Liam brought them alongside the structure.

"Off." Behind her, Liam gave the hem of her shirt a tug. "Quick."

He could not be serious.

"I'm going to kill you," she said, slipping the T-shirt over her head. For good measure, she shook her hair back and forth, fanning herself as if it were too hot. "Your days are numbered, William."

"Hey, can you give us directions?" Liam shifted his tone to sound younger, a trick that never failed to amaze her. "We're looking for a rainbow swamp."

"A what now?" Emmett called out as he neared. "Hold up. I can't hear you."

Reaching the edge of the dock, Emmett Watson stood above them, and Jamison felt Liam's toe nudge her thigh, meaning he wanted her to take the lead.

Wonderful.

"Hi! I'm McKenzie, and this is my boyfriend, Rick," she chirped. "We're lookin' for the rainbow swamps I saw online?" She tossed her shoulders in a casual shrug that conveniently jiggled her breasts. "And, like... we're totally lost."

Emmett took his time to answer, enjoying the show she was putting on. "Don't think I've ever heard of a rainbow swamp."

"We read about them before coming down here on vacation," Liam said, pulling her back into his lap so she was stretched out against his chest. It was a calculated move—one that displayed her torso and bikini top in full glory. Emmett visibly paled, his tongue darting out to swipe the corner of his mouth.

"They're really pretty," Jamison purred. "At least in the pictures."

"She's been dying to see one," Liam added. "And what this woman wants, she always gets."

On cue, Jamison giggled like a moron. While they inflated the kayak, Liam had explained that Emmett was big into porn and loved to watch it all day long.

And the guy was definitely watching now. Playing into the moment, she opened her legs a little while Liam's hand stroked her stomach, his fingers dipping dangerously low. "Don't you, baby?"

Jamison let out another sugar-coated giggle. "Always."

"Mother of God," Emmett exhaled, his chest rising and falling a little too fast, his eyes locked on the popped top button of her denim shorts. "I might, *uh*, have some maps in the house. Miss, you can come inside and take a look while your friend waits in this here, *uh*... floatie thing."

There was no way in hell she was walking into the Little Shack of Probable Horrors. Judging by the way Emmett was hard-eye-fucking her from ten feet up, Jamison would've bet her left ovary that fish weren't the only thing he filleted in there. The guy had unhinged written all over him in Comic Sans, and her gaze swept the yard, half expecting to spot fresh mounds of dirt from where he buried his victims.

"We'd love to, but we only have a few minutes to explore." Jamison bit down on her bottom lip. "Our guide boat is parked just around the bend."

"It won't take but a minute." Emmett adjusted himself—right there in her face—and she tried not to gag. "You look like you've been cooped up in that little dingy for too long and need a good stretch."

Calling on every ounce of acting ability she had, Jamison held Emmett's stare. "Is it just you back here?" she asked, dialing her accent up to an eleven and adding a sultry back arch for good measure. "In this little slice of quiet paradise?"

"Yeah, just me." Emmett puffed his chest with pride. "Ain't nobody else out here for miles."

"You mean you're the only one with a spot on the water?" She gestured west toward Port Michaelson with an exaggerated flourish. "All the way to that city over yonder? Nobody else has a house and a dock like this?"

"That's right. Ain't another dock 'til the marina in Port Michaelson."

Jamison batted her lashes like a Disney princess. Simone had taught her years ago that appealing to a man's ego would get you almost anything. She had called them simple creatures with simple needs, who would roll over and tell you all their secrets, but only if you discovered exactly which part of their self-confidence to stroke.

"Oh, my." She sat up off Liam's chest with a breathy gasp. "Secluded waterfront property? I can't *even* imagine. We live in a boring ol' apartment up in Tennessee. It's so cold this time of year, and there's not much to do."

Emmett sneered at Liam over her shoulder, and Jamison would've paid good money to see his expression right then. He was playing his role like a pro, but the man had a temper and he was armed. If Emmett didn't dial it down, this little field trip could easily turn into a justifiable homicide.

"I take you places," Liam said in a convincingly annoyed grumble. "I brought you on this vacation, didn't I?"

Emmett's attention slid right back to her, and Jamison hit him with another big, shiny smile. "I guess."

"Sometimes a woman needs more than a vacation," Emmett drawled in a low voice that was about as seductive as a clogged garbage disposal. "Sometimes she needs the heat all year long."

Dear God, make it stop. Drawing in a breath, she pretended to look around, focusing on the patch of forest leading east and straight to Haven House. "What's down there?"

The flirtatious glint in Emmett's eyes dimmed. "Don't go down there."

"Are there alligators?" Jamison clutched her imaginary pearls. "Are there alligators around *here*?"

"Oh, come on now. Gators don't hurt nobody." The darkness in Emmett's gaze faded at her question, his smirk deepening as he directed his words at Liam. "Except maybe dumb fuckers who bring their girls out in a stupid inflatable floatie 'cause they can't afford no real kayak."

Oh, yeah. This man was just looking to get shot.

"You know, we should get going. That guide boat will leave us." Liam shifted behind her, preparing to shove away from the dock. "And we wouldn't want to interrupt your company."

Jamison hadn't noticed the truck pulling up to the shack, and by the way Emmett's head whirled around to watch it arrive, he was just as surprised. The old thing looked half-rusted like someone had almost driven it out of the swamp, and when it stopped in front of the shack, the brakes whined in protest.

"Yeah, we better go. Come on... *Rick*." She winced, realizing she'd forgotten the fake names they had decided on. "I don't want to be left."

Liam gave the dock a sharp push with his paddle, sending them drifting back into the water. They weren't far from the main boat, but she doubted they'd be returning to it yet. Knowing Liam, they were heading right back to their hiding spot to watch.

"Give him a goodbye wave," Liam murmured, "and try to see who's in that truck."

Twisting in her seat, Jamison mustered another cheery wave and scanned the scene. "Goodbye! Thank you for your time!" she called, smiling too hard and too wide. "Maybe we'll meet again once I finally get to see those rainbow swamps!"

Emmett cupped a hand to his mouth. "Hey, man! Ain't you gonna find her that rainbow swamp? A woman like that deserves better!"

"Please don't shoot him," Jamison hissed as she faced forward, her posture tight with unease. "*Rick* is a pacifist, and shooting him would really mess with *McKenzie*'s moral code."

"Rick and McKenzie need to get the fuck over it, and Emmett needs one of these paddles jammed straight up his ass," Liam snarled, his strokes quick and rough as they glided out of sight. "Could you see who was in the truck?"

"Two men." She wanted to look again, but couldn't risk it. "They parked in a shaded spot, so I can't see their faces through the windshield."

"I'm going to take us out and then double back so we can watch safely from the trees."

She perked up. "Does that mean I can paddle now?"

"Hell, no."

CHAPTER 12

Jamison

The stillness in the swamp reminded her too much of the dread often felt on the forest trails back at Haven House. She could run them fine, even enjoy a stroll if Liam was with her. But walk them alone? Never. Not since Toby. Not with that heaviness lingering in the air that made her feel like she was being watched. It had always been around, but since Toby, the sensation had felt more palpable and *alive*.

Like if she stared too long into the darkness beyond the path, she would find someone—or something—staring back.

The kayak floated slowly past the cypress, Liam guiding them deeper into the trees until they were swallowed by the marsh. Too close to the shore now, he didn't speak, and she didn't either.

Emmett still lingered outside, standing in the yard like he was waiting. The rusted old truck remained out front, but its cab was empty. Liam watched it all through the binoculars while Jamison kept her perch at the bow. When he tucked them away to reposition, he whispered that they would pull out soon if the mystery guests didn't show.

To her left, a group of white cranes tiptoed through the water, soundless in their hunt. One by one, they slipped from view into the shadows, leaving them behind.

With afternoon giving way to dusk, the swamp had cooled thanks to an autumn bite creeping into the air. Liam wrapped an arm around her shoulders, pulling her back to rest against his chest. "Grab your phone," he whispered. "If anyone steps out, snap a shot. Don't zoom in too much. Rowan will handle all that."

She did as he asked, waiting patiently for something to happen. Once or twice, she had to swat at a lost mosquito buzzing around them, not wanting them to take a bite out of Liam when they had no Benadryl. He was impervious to most things, but mosquito bites always did him in.

"I can see someone in the doorway." Liam leaned forward, pushing her slightly with him. "These guys are starting to piss me off."

Jamison smacked another unnaturally big mosquito and nearly dropped her phone into the water. "Let's give it five more minutes."

"Agreed," he replied, lowering the binoculars. "I said we'd be back before sunset, and I still need time with you."

"Exactly." She shifted just enough to catch his eye. "I'm not done modeling this bathing suit."

A low groan rumbled against her skin as he dipped his head to kiss her neck. "Oh, the things I'm going to do to you while you're wearing it."

The shiver she felt had nothing to do with the cold. Sighing, she tilted her head back, letting him trail kisses toward her ear. "What if we run away? Just disappear into a hotel room for the weekend before anyone tells us no."

His teeth scraped her skin, deliberate and slow. "You know we can't."

She pouted, only half joking. "But think about how *refreshed* you'll be after a naked, sweaty, orgasmically good weekend, where neither of us are walking straight afterward."

"I don't think orgasmically is a real word."

"It is," she insisted. "And you know damn well you'd come back with a clearer head if you just sat still long enough for me to have my way with you." She wiggled back until she was snug between his thighs. "Hell, we could be extra adventurous and try something in this kayak."

He fought not to grin and lost. "Jamison, you're a strong, capable woman who eats weak men for breakfast."

"Only after I've had my coffee."

"And you can do anything you set your mind to."

"Such compliments, Mr. Cohen." She batted her lashes like she had done back at the dock with Emmett. "You're definitely trying to get lucky."

Liam's lips twitched. "But, babe, you're loud. All. The. Time. When you talk, when you sleep, and *definitely* during sex."

"I am not!" she whisper-shouted, knowing it was a lie, especially about the sex part. Her motto was the louder, the better. "I'm the epitome of a lady."

"Yeah. A lady who screams for hours. Surveillance sex is out, I'm afraid."

She tried to hold in the giggle, but it cracked out of her in wheezing bursts. He clamped his hand over her mouth, covering half her face in the process. "See?" he whispered, shaking with silent laughter. "Freaking loud."

"Maybe I wouldn't scream so much if you weren't so handsome and annoyingly good in bed." She squirmed free to kiss him. "And while you're at it, stop being so charming, and maybe I won't laugh as loud as I do."

"Not gonna happen. You're stuck with my handsome, great-in-bed, charmingly hilarious self." He kissed her again, nipping at her bottom lip. "And don't worry, I won't let your compliments go to my head. I know none of them are true because if they were, you wouldn't have left me."

The smile on her face vanished.

"Liam..."

He was making a joke, but the residual pain hung on, chipping away at this happy little moment.

"Forget what I said," Liam rushed out, digging his fingers in the hair on the back of her head as they held each other nose to nose. "I'm sorry. It's done and over with, and I shouldn't have said that."

"I know, but—"

"No. Just no. Let's make that time apart one of those stories we don't tell. Not until we're ready." The kayak teetered as he pulled her as close as possible. "You know the ones I mean, right? Like the time you thought you could build that IKEA bookshelf by yourself, but ended up having a breakdown because the instructions sucked."

"Thank you for setting those instructions on fire. It made me feel better to watch them burn."

"Jamison, I would set the whole fucking world on fire for you."

He always knew the right thing to say, and her smile wobbled back into place. "You really were reading romance novels while we were separated."

"Several," he confessed with zero shame. "But I was depressed, and reading them made me feel close to you."

"Do you remember Aruba?" she asked softly. "We didn't do anything but read romance books together on the beach."

"We also had mind-blowing sex all week, but that's beside the point."

"Amazing sex should never be beside the point, but I get what you're saying. A story for later. Something we can talk about once the sting's gone. Like when you got us epically lost going to that Fairweather Christmas party, and we had that awful fight."

"Or the time at that other Fairweather party when you farted and blamed it on poor Cathy from advertising?"

Her mouth dropped open. "You swore, William. Asparagus doesn't agree with me, and you *swore* you would never bring up that fart again."

Placing a hand over his heart, he turned solemn. "And I never have. Until now. In this kayak. In the presence of God and all the swamp things listening."

Silence settled between them again, but it was a comfortable silence as they both watched Emmett continue to shuffle around his yard by himself.

"These people are robbing us of premium sexy time," she complained. "And this thong? Not exactly comfortable. I can't wait for you to rip it off."

Not taking his eyes off Emmett, he brushed a kiss on the top of her head while slipping one hand beneath her shirt to palm a breast. "I've already said I'm fucking you in that thing again. So, you're going to have to get over it."

"We could do it now." Half turning, she braced her hands on the kayak's sides. "I'll be quiet."

"We'd flip the kayak."

"We'll go slow."

"No, Jamison."

"Yes, Liam." Shifting her position before he could stop her, she tried to straddle him. "Just hold still. I'll do all the work."

The kayak immediately pitched hard to the side.

Slamming a hand against a tree trunk, he righted them before they were tossed into the water. "Baby, I know you want to rock my world, but maybe don't do it *literally*."

She snorted. "Incredibly hot men aren't supposed to be this goofy."

"Says who?" He turned her back around, adjusting their balance. "One day, I won't be hot anymore. One day, I'm going to look like my dad. Then my goofiness will be all that's left, and you'll be grateful."

"Don't sell your dad short. He's still attract—"

Movement caught her eye, and she fell silent, already knowing Liam had raised the binoculars. Someone was emerging from the back of the shack.

Scrambling for her phone, which had fallen to the bottom of the kayak, Jamison quickly lifted it and started snapping photos in rapid succession. Too worried about getting the shot, it took her a moment to focus on the man chatting casually with Emmett.

"Bruce."

She nearly dropped the phone when she recognized Bruce. Much taller than Emmett, with a bulky frame and buzzed hair, the man had haunted her nightmares.

"That's him," she hissed, the need to flee hitting so insanely fast that she almost tipped the kayak again. "That's the man who tried to take me. The one who was with Sinclair."

Liam didn't lower the binoculars. He just wrapped his arm tight around her, anchoring her trembling body back against his chest. "I'm here. Nothing is going to happen to you, okay? I'm right here. But I need you to breathe. Quietly. Breathe through it."

"Breathe through it," she echoed as she continued to take pictures. "Breathe."

She focused on the screen, watching Emmett and Bruce while they talked before turning to face east. Bruce moved his hand about, pointing at the channel leading directly to Haven House.

"I'm going over there." Liam dropped the binoculars into her lap. "Call Rowan and tell him to get people here."

Phone and binoculars forgotten, she flung herself on top of him. "You are absolutely not going."

"I'm armed."

"That doesn't mean anything!" she spat out, close to becoming hysterical. "Not a damn thing!"

Extracting himself from her death hold, the kayak sloshed about under them. "It means I can arrest him."

"How? You're not a fucking agent anymore," she snapped. "And how are you going to get over there? Swim? If your gun gets wet, it won't work."

"Yes, it will." He went for the side, arching up on his feet to slip right off into the water. "Now, call Rowan."

He would do it, and she wouldn't be able to stop him. Always the hero, the drive to do what was right would override any argument, and Liam would swim right over there and try to capture both men.

But in her mind, the entire scenario showed him failing and dying for his efforts. It showed her how he would sneak onto the shore to ambush Emmett and Bruce, but at the same time expose himself and essentially lose the upper hand.

"No, I will not!"

Her shout bounced around the silence, sending all manner of birds catapulting into the sky. The cranes fishing near them fluttered past with the rest of the avian army, ghosts hovering low over the green foam until hitting the tree line to rise higher.

With wide eyes, Liam froze, half in and half out of the boat, his head snapping toward Bruce and Emmett.

"Do not move," he breathed.

Never one to listen, Jamison turned her head at an achingly slow pace, heart pounding as she peeked at the shore.

Emmett was watching the cranes scatter into the sky, but Bruce... Bruce had a hand up to shield his eyes from the sun and was staring straight at the batch of cypress trees they were hiding behind.

She pressed her lips together, holding her breath as if he could hear it. The way sound carried over the water, even a whisper might betray them.

They stayed in their positions for what felt like an eternity, and then, surprising them, Bruce broke out into a wide grin. "Come here," he shouted, glancing back at the shack. "You've got to see this."

For one horrible second, Jamison thought he was speaking to them. But Bruce turned to shout in the opposite direction, waving an arm.

"Look at these birds. There are hundreds of them."

A third man emerged from the shack. Tall and lean, he had sandy brown hair and a face that could be described as handsome. On his shoulders sat a little girl. She pointed at the birds flying overhead, her expression sweet and happy.

Jamison's blood turned to ice, her lungs collapsing inward. Madison.

Bubbly, beautiful, and the apple of Claudia's eye, Madison.

Liam dropped into a sitting position in the kayak as if the air had been knocked from his chest. "Oh my God."

Her hand searched blindly for his and squeezed it with white-knuckled urgency. "Why is Claudia's fiancé—and her daughter—with Bruce?"

"I don't..." Liam's face lost all its color. "I don't know."

Her heart pounded with such force she thought it might burst. The roar in her ears drowned out everything else, and dark spots freckled her vision.

And then came the whispering.

Carried on the wind, it warned her not to linger, and the closer it came, the more she felt as if she might truly vomit. It was just like the night Michael Sinclair came to Haven House. The night he tried to take her, and the shadows in the forest whispered their warnings.

But then it got so much worse.

The whispering grew louder, telling her they shouldn't be here. Demanding that they *go. Leave. Don't look back.*

Unable to tear her eyes from the shore, she watched Madison squeal with laughter, pointing to the sky as Parker played along, naming the birds. He looked relaxed and obviously not threatened by Bruce and Emmett.

The whispering grew sharper. Louder. A shriek in her mind, clawing at her sanity.

This is wrong.

This is dangerous.

So distracted by the voices in her head, she didn't even feel Liam slip into the water. Didn't notice the kayak tilt slightly with his weight until she turned and saw him already waist-deep with one hand on the bow.

"No!" She lunged forward to grab his arm, her fingers digging into his skin. "Please, Liam, don't—"

He easily broke free of her hold and mouthed one word. "Rowan."

And he was gone. Moving fast, his body disappeared into the murky green sludge of the swamp. The urge to jump in after him had her partially rising from her seat, but common sense kicked in. She first needed to call for help.

Her fingers shook as she scrambled for her phone, quickly turning the volume down before tapping the screen.

Rowan answered on the first ring.

"Bruce is here." She made sure to enunciate, so every whispered word was clear. "And Parker is here with Madison. They're with Bruce at Emmett Watson's place."

Realizing he should keep his voice low, Rowan whispered back to her. "Parker and Madison? As in Claudia's Parker and Madison?"

"Yes."

In the background, she could hear so much action. There were shouts and the sound of chairs scraping. Cupping the phone's speaker, she attempted to muffle the noise. Like the cranes before, Liam had vanished into the dark depths of the swamp, and a fear like she had never known had tears spilling from her eyes.

"Rowan, hurry," she begged. "Liam went to confront them."

There was a beat of silence.

"Alone?"

"*Yes.*"

Rowan hung up without saying goodbye, and the phone fell into her lap, its weight too heavy for her trembling hands. On the shore, Parker had taken Madison off his shoulders, and with Emmett, the two men watched as the little girl picked flowering weeds around their feet. Bruce had moved away from them, his attention continuing to zero in on where she sat. But then abruptly, his gaze moved on, creeping steadily along the trees until it looped to the shore.

"Alright, playtime's over," Bruce said loud enough that it almost sounded like he was standing beside her. "Let's get this stuff loaded."

Parker took Madison's hand and led her back toward the shack. Emmett followed close behind.

But Bruce lingered for a second more, his gaze locked on where she sat frozen. It was like he was waiting for something, but when whatever it was didn't show, he returned to the shack, shutting the door firmly behind him. The moment it latched, Liam broke from the trees.

He ran low and silent, making his way along the shore toward the shack. She nearly shouted when she saw him, both in relief that an alligator hadn't eaten him, and in absolute mind-numbing fury that he was being reckless enough to try this.

Rowan or whoever might come to the rescue had to be at least twenty minutes away since they would have to take the long way around by road instead of boat. There was no way they would arrive before Liam made his move.

She debated on what to do for a split second and ended up grabbing a paddle to shove the kayak away from the cypress that held it steady. Liam could handle himself. She *knew* he could handle himself, but that didn't mean she couldn't help.

And if something happened to him or he was hurt, she would never forgive herself for sitting idly by when she could have stopped it. Paddling like crazy, she collided more than once with a tree or an exposed root that threatened to deflate the kayak then and there.

As she advanced through the swamp, Liam made his way from tree to bush, getting closer and closer to the shack. He had his gun drawn and ready, the sight causing her fear to grow tenfold.

"Wait for me," she huffed, jabbing the paddle again and again into the water. "Make him wait for me."

The wind was in her favor, pushing the kayak along when she hit a batch of open water. The strain on her biceps burned, and she was pretty sure her back teeth were going to crack with how hard she was grinding them, but the desperate need to get to Liam strangled her with determination even when all she wanted to do was scream.

Bruce and the others could be seen through the shack's single window a few feet from the back door, right as Liam neared the structure. Placing his back against the wall, he gripped his gun with two hands, keeping just out of sight.

It didn't make sense why she was crying by the time she reached the shore, watching helplessly as Liam charged through the door, gun raised and commanding voice ringing loudly through the air. It didn't make sense why she was listening to the whispers on the wind that were telling her to run and save him, allowing the strange voices to fuel her fear.

There was no logic, only instinct, and it roared inside her. No one else could stop this. No one else could *save* him, but her.

The awful terror pushed her from the kayak, sending her falling onto the muddy sand. Shoving herself upright, she fought her way over the shore with its slick roots and jagged branches as they tore at her skin. The steep embankment loomed ahead, her muscles threatening to lock up before she even attempted the climb.

But digging her fingers into the earth, she clawed her way up. The dirt packed under her nails made her skin crawl, and in those last few feet, she thought she would fall and have to start over.

But she didn't. Cresting the top, she rolled onto the flat ground, finding her footing immediately. She ran as fast as she could, never stopping. Not even when Parker burst from around the front of the shack, dragging a crying Madison to the truck with Emmett behind them. She didn't stop when the truck's engine roared, its tires squealing as it vanished down the road.

She didn't stop when voices erupted from inside the shack. Liam and Bruce's shouts overlapped, both issuing commands neither seemed willing to obey.

She didn't stop when her heart screamed, *you're too late*. A lie she refused to believe. It wasn't too late. It would never be too late. She and Liam had a life to live. A destiny to fulfill. A story to see to its end.

But then—

A gunshot.

One. Single. Shot.

The sound cracked across the inlet, and her knees buckled. She hit the ground hard, her raw, animalistic screams ripping through the air.

And just like that...

Jamison Fairweather's world stopped.

Chapter 13

Charlie

2000

*Y*ou are my sunshine, my only sunshine.

"Charles, are you listening to me?"

You make me happy when skies are gray.

"Charles?"

He should answer his mother. He should talk. He should try. For Tobias. For Cecilia. He should pretend.

But really, he just wanted to listen to his Livy sing.

The fire popped and crackled as if it were devouring real wood with its heat. But it wasn't. A cheap imitation made of plastic, the logs in the fireplace at his mother's home weren't real, and neither was most of the shit crowding the space.

The sitting room right off the foyer was a poor replacement for the one at Parkland Grounds, and he hoped she hated it. He hoped she rotted here, remembering her glory days of being the Fairweather Viper Queen to all those venomous bitches who loved to hate the world as much as she did.

But, oh baby, look at her now.

Helen Fairweather did not wear the distinction of middle class well. Sure, she had more money than the average person, but it wasn't enough. Not for her. The small amount left to her by her husband and her family's investments would never be enough for this woman's lavish taste.

"Charles!"

"Yes, Mother?"

The high-back chairs they sat in squeaked every time either of them moved. Furniture of the lowest quality filled the ground level, all of it—much like Helen—on full display as it pretended to be something it wasn't. Wealthy and worthy enough to grace a place grander than this three-story monstrosity built on the outskirts of Houston.

Toeing the rug likely purchased from some mass-market home interior store, Charlie fought not to snicker at the idea of his mother wandering a showroom with other shoppers as she searched for decor that resembled her previous life. Nothing in the house matched. Not the outlandish floral rugs nor the couches and chairs with their horrible geometric patterns. At least there was a decent formal dining set with a side cabinet and hutch. However, it held a piss-poor set of cheap china Helen would probably never use because who in the hell would come here to visit?

Oh, yes, how the mighty had fallen. He was glad for it. Even if she were his only savior in this hell, he was glad he had the chance to witness Helen's fall. He knew Ben paid her a visit, as did Miranda. They came begging for his kids while he was in that facility getting better, and God, he wished he could have seen their faces when they walked through the door.

Helen took a sip from the elegant crystal glass in her hand. Proper to a fault, she drank slowly, as if the red wine sloshing around inside the goblet hadn't come from a box.

"You can no longer stay here," she said, not bothering to meet his gaze while announcing his time was up. "You're fine now and need to get on with your life."

You'll never know, dear, how much I love you.

Toby and CeCe were in bed already. They didn't like their grandmother, and she felt the same way in return. He hated to leave them with her while he'd been in that place, but there hadn't been much of a choice. Trevor wouldn't take them, thanks to Heather's nagging. His brother's wife didn't want their brats to mix with his, as if Toby and CeCe were beneath their cousins.

And he couldn't allow them to return to Haven House. Not even for a second. If either of them ever stepped foot in that house again, they would refuse to leave, and he would be alone.

Forever.

Please don't take my sunshine away.

His girl had a beautiful voice, and she sang to him every day. It started on the night she left him. The night Rebecca murdered her. As he lay there bleeding out in that goddamn cottage, it was Livy's singing that startled him awake once help arrived. If he hadn't called out, the police likely would never have found him in time.

And since then, Livy kept right on singing.

They left him heavily sedated in the hospital, and when he was awakened again by his precious girl singing, it was to see Viv. She had brought Livy's ashes. Becca's, too.

But all he'd been able to focus on was the small black box that now held his baby girl.

Viv watched him cry, remaining quiet as he screamed in denial. It was her way of torturing him. Cold revenge served in the form of silence. When he finished, she gave her condolences. Polite and proper, just as he always demanded she be.

But it was when she claimed she only brought the boxes so he could decide what to do with his woman and child that he lost his temper. Becca had never been his woman. She was a tool, a necessity in his life that helped cull the dark parts he didn't want to touch Vivian.

She should have thanked him for keeping Rebecca close. Vivian should have appreciated the efforts that went into the entire ruse because it had all been for her. She would never have been able to handle him in those moments when he showed his true self or when he needed to make someone feel as much pain as he did.

And Vivian sure as hell hadn't been able to give him babies. The babies he deserved. The perfect family *he* created. Why didn't she understand that? Why did she just stand there, no longer the woman he loved, and listen as he raged?

That son of a bitch she was fucking was there too. Standing in the corner like a true bastard. Aiden. The walking dead man. Viv might never love him again, but Charlie would be damned if that piece of trash would be the one to take his place. He didn't know how he would do it. His connections to the people who handled such matters were lost when Ben cut him off, but if what Vivian said was true —that she wanted to marry that loser —there would be no choice. He would end him. For her, he would do it and save his Viv from a miserable life.

It had taken everything in him not to jump out of the hospital bed and stop her from leaving, broken and alone, with nothing except two boxes of ashes to keep him company.

But Vivian left him, even when he asked her to stay. She left and never looked back.

Trevor visited the next day, saying he would take him to the condo he and Heather used when in the area. The hospital was done with him, and so he had no choice but to go. Gathering his boxes of ashes, Charlie allowed a random stranger in scrubs to push him out in a wheelchair while he clutched his girls close.

And through it all, Livy sang to him. She wanted to rest. She wanted her peace. Trapped in a box, she sang her little song and haunted him with the memory of his sins. She reminded him that his life was pointless without her, making him understand that all the suffering he was feeling was solely because she was gone.

Perhaps it had been a mistake. Perhaps he shouldn't have forced Trevor to drive him to that godforsaken house, but his baby wanted to go home. He could feel it. Deep in his bones, he could feel her begging to return. That was the peace she sought. Born and raised there, Haven House would always belong to Livy—their little mama.

But not Rebecca. The bitch deserved nothing.

When he dragged himself down the forest path, balancing a shovel and his boxes, he paused to look out over the bayou and listen. He listened to the voices. To the whispers. They were forever there in the woods, but never loud. Not like they were that day. That day, the voices had been enough to drown out Livy's song. Some shouted for him to continue to the graveyard, while others urged him to leave Becca's ashes right there on the forest path as if she were garbage.

There had even been a sweet one beckoning him to the bayou. It sang a song that promised relief if he would only join her in the water. He thought about it. He listened, and he thought about how he could end it all.

But in the end, he decided against becoming the offering it claimed to want. Instead, he gave it someone else, pouring Rebecca's ashes into the swirling black bayou. He couldn't believe he'd done it, but sitting Livy's little box aside, he dumped his lover's remains in a place no one would ever find them.

The Fairweather in him was pleased with his actions. Rebecca Miller had been nothing in life and would be even less in death. Fish food floating out to sea.

Worthless.

Meaningless.

Insignificant.

That would be her legacy.

Her soul would never know peace, never rest with her daughter in the graveyard. The world would forget her, just as it should be.

His brother could pretend to be some moral ass all he wanted, but Charlie knew Ben didn't care about Rebecca's final resting place, either. He wouldn't care about any of them, and a part of Charlie had wanted Ben to kill him on the lawn. He'd wanted that extra pound of guilt sitting on his brother's shoulders as he nearly beat him to death.

But then Evie stopped it from happening. Standing next to them as they rolled across the grass, trying to rip each other apart, she stopped their battle when she spoke in that eerie way that sounded like Laura Jean. Ben picked up on it immediately and nearly collapsed when he heard what sounded like the woman he loved speaking.

"I'll need to get a job first," he spoke evenly, not wanting his mother to hear the panic in his voice. "Can you give me some time?"

"A month." She polished off the remainder of her wine faster than she gobbled up those little cakes she ate every afternoon. No longer concerned about keeping up with appearances, Helen had chosen to wallow in every indulgence possible. "That should give you time to secure something."

"Yeah, but I'll need to find a place to live, and there are deposits to pay for apartments."

He nearly puffed his chest with pride at knowing the odds and ends of what went into him and the kids making it in the world on their own. He had investigated it when Vivian asked for a divorce.

"One month, Charles."

A few things in life would never change. The sky would always be blue, water would always be wet, and Helen Fairweather would always and forever be a heartless hag.

Charlie knew the monster well, having been the sole one of his siblings to be "loved" by her. She hated Ben since he first began growing in her womb, and Trevor's arrival only made the whole motherhood situation worse. However, once they got out of diapers and Helen realized she could use her sons to her advantage, all bets were off. Pawns in her game of life, none of them were ever safe.

For himself, she dangled him in front of debutantes, promising them marriage to the Fairweather golden boy while she whored Ben out to their mothers or grandmothers, all in the name of connections. With Trevor, she forced him to serve as her ears, listening to the gossip from the shadows since no one paid him attention.

Helen never pretended to love them, and he truly didn't think she was capable of it. Being tolerated by her was the best one could hope for, and it would seem he was failing yet again in that department.

"I'll start looking for a job in the morning."

With her gaze locked on the flames, Helen chuckled. "You could always ask Ben for a job."

The joke missed its mark by a long shot. Charlie would never speak to his brother again for the remainder of his life. The day he buried Livy left no doubt in his mind that Ben would kill him if given the chance.

"That won't be necessary," he replied. "I was actually thinking of approaching your brother and seeing if he might have a position for me."

Helen nearly dropped her wine goblet, the chair squeaking double time when she flopped around to face him. "You will do no such thing," she hissed, the wrinkles covering every inch of her face deepening in their outrage. "You will not embarrass me."

Before becoming a Fairweather, his mother had been a Powell. While not as wealthy and powerful as the Fairweathers, the Powells held a tight grip on the Dallas real estate market.

"Me?" he scoffed, leaning across the arm of his chair. "Are you kidding?"

She didn't scare him anymore. This pathetic woman next to him wasn't the she-devil that raised him. Helen was a caricature of her former self, wasting away to the sounds of the Home Shopping Network blaring on the TV.

Lumbering to her feet, she tugged at her polyester top to ensure it covered the protruding belly permanently hanging around her midsection. Every piece of clothing she owned was two sizes too small since she refused to acknowledge that the shit ton of food she ate to combat depression might not be a great idea.

"You will stay away from them." Helen pointed a finger in his face. "I mean it, Charles."

He was half tempted to pop the gaudy fake press-on nail off the finger aimed between his eyes. "Or what?"

Blinking rapidly, Helen choked on her next words. "You wouldn't dare."

Is this what power felt like? This absolute rush of energy punching its way through your veins? If it was, he liked it.

"It won't be pretty if you back me into a corner."

Rising to stand, he marveled at how small and frail she seemed. When did this happen? When did this viper shrivel up into nothing more than a garden lizard?

"Does your family know where you live?" he asked. "How you live?"

"Charles—"

"Yeah, I didn't think so."

"Listen to me. I have plans for you that don't need to involve them. When I go, this house will be yours." Placing her hands on his chest, Helen smoothed the wrinkles building on the cheap fabric of his shirt. "The villa in St. Thomas is also yours. I have it all laid out in a trust. It's not much, but the properties will be worth something to you one day."

No, they wouldn't. He could maybe pull a couple hundred thousand out of this place, perhaps a little more, but not enough to do anything with. The upkeep on the villa would eat any income he could garner from it, making the property virtually worthless.

And she expected him to fend for himself in the meantime. The bitch. This place might be a hollow palace of cheap shit, but it had plenty of room for him and the kids. Sure, if they stayed, it would come with the requirement to tolerate her and all her vicious eccentricities, but it would be a stable roof over their heads.

You are my sunshine, my only sunshine.

"How do you expect us to survive? You tell me to get a job, but I would have to save for a long time to afford a decent place," he yelled, hoping the kids were already fast asleep. These walls were thin and allowed little privacy. "What am I supposed to do with the kids? They've been locked up in that house their whole life, and you just expect me to dump them in a school or a daycare?"

"You cannot live here, Charles." An evil glint entered Helen's eyes. "Not unless you help me go after your brother."

Ben.

It was always about the son she could never bring to heel. There was a point in their lives when she and their father could make Ben dance their dance, but now she held no power over him, and maybe she never really did. Maybe Ben had been playing the long game this entire time. Maybe he was as smart as he pretended to be.

"You will leave Ben alone."

Helen scoffed in disappointment. "I expected more from you."

You'll never know, dear, how much I love you.

"Then you're an idiot."

The look of horror on his mother's face... oh, he was going to hold on to that sight for a lifetime.

"How dare you speak to me like that," Helen seethed, her lips peeling back from her teeth. "I am your mother. I took you in when no one else would, and I will not listen to you belittle me and my hospitality."

Charlie tilted his head. "I'm sorry, but didn't you just say that the only way for me and the kids to have a home was either if you were dead or if I helped you go after Ben? I don't know why you hate him, but he's hurting. From what Trevor says, there's not much of our old Ben left, so pat yourself on the back. He's already defeated, and you didn't even have to lift a finger."

He might hate Ben, but God, he couldn't stand that self-satisfied smirk on their mother's face. She was loving this. The suffering. *Their* suffering. She loved being the one he was forced to run to and how Ben was so broken he'd left the remaining board members at Fairweather Holdings without their fearless leader.

"It's not enough—"

A scuffle in the hall cut her off, and their heads turned toward the sound in time to see Tobias and Cecilia running off.

"Great," Charlie mumbled. He didn't want them to be scared about their future, and hearing his mother spouting off her insanity wasn't going to help. "I need to deal with them."

Helen shoved her wine goblet at him. "You'll deal with cleaning up first," she said, using the distraction to exit their conversation. "We'll talk more in the morning."

All he could do was stand there, wearing borrowed clothes and holding two cheap glasses that weren't even worth the effort to smash against the fake fireplace. He was sleeping in here anyway, and didn't need a mess. Ever since he returned from the facility, Helen had made it clear that she didn't want him in any of her beds, too afraid he might be carrying some sort of disease after staying in rehab.

So, the couch in the living room was his only choice, and it wasn't that bad. The bed at the facility had been far worse. Made of the firmest plastic covering in the known universe, it caused many sleepless nights long after his withdrawal episodes ceased.

He placed the glasses on a side table and reminded himself he needed to be kinder to Helen. She paid for the center, which wasn't cheap, and cared for his kids while he was in. Maybe her attitude was just tough love—if she even knew what love was—and he should be thankful that she had done so, allowing them a chance at a life together.

Please don't take my sunshine away.

But fucking hell, the pain. His baby. He missed his baby so much. Livy had been his sunshine. She had been his whole world.

When the house went quiet late at night, he could hear her singing louder than usual. The pain it caused stole his breath and robbed him of the heartbeat he no longer wanted. Livy had taught him that love was real, and he had never fallen so deeply—not even with Vivian.

"I'm so sorry," he whispered. "I'll do better next time, baby. I promise."

There would be a next time. He was sure of it. They would be together once more, but next time, they would work hard to be better. While in the facility, he met a man—a holy man—who taught him about things like karmic principles. Monads. Soul families. Things that made sense. To live through what he had, to feel these deep connections, a soul family made sense.

A stifled scream sounded through the house, followed by a rush of banging that ended in a grotesque thud. Dropping the glasses, he ran into the hall, nearly tripping over Helen's body, lying sprawled face down at the foot of the stairs.

She didn't move, and he froze, listening to her struggle for air.

"Dad?"

Charlie's head snapped up at the sound of Toby's voice. He and CeCe were coming down the stairs in their pajamas. Toby's eyes grew wider and wider the closer they came, and CeCe was already sucking furiously on her thumb.

"Don't come closer. Your grandmother is hurt."

Kneeling next to her, Charlie tried to turn Helen over, but she began to convulse, and the children rushed forward to the bottom step.

"Guys!" Charlie shouted. "I said stay back. She's hurt."

"We know."

They clamored around him, peering over his shoulder. He shouldn't allow them to see, but he didn't know what else to do. "We need to call 911," he said weakly once Helen went still. "Someone find a phone."

"Why?"

The question came from Toby, and it didn't surprise Charlie. The boy lacked empathy on all levels, and while in group therapy, he listened to others, immediately recognizing the traits of those gathered around in the circle. They were just like Toby, and they all said the same thing. Their addiction was someone else's fault. Their problems were always someone else's fault. In the beginning, he'd felt the same way. It was Rebecca's fault. It was Ben's fault. It was Vivian's fault. They had made him into this weak man who couldn't hold his own without help.

Over the course of six weeks, the facility changed his mind. Six weeks. That was all it had taken. In six weeks, he learned to be held culpable for his own actions. He learned how to thrive in a non-toxic world made up of caring counselors and staff who wanted you to be a better person. Yes, the others were just as complicit in his downfall, but he could now admit he was responsible for his own path in life, and for the choices he made.

Helen's ragged breathing returned, high and shrill. Leaning down, Charlie swiped the hair from her face. "Mom?"

She didn't answer, her lids half-closed with only the whites of her eyes showing. Smacking her cheek lightly with his palm, Charlie winced when, on the third slap, the high-pitched wheezing from her lips halted completely.

"Is she dead?" Toby whispered. "Did we win?"

"What the hell do you mean, did we win?" Charlie hissed, unable to peel his eyes off Helen. "Fuck. We need to call an ambulance."

There was no rise and fall of Helen's chest, or any movement. The slits of her eyes had opened more, and her mouth hung wide with the tip of her tongue protruding through the gap.

Charlie released a shuddering breath, not in grief or shock at seeing his mother this way, but for his kids. Death didn't need to revisit them so soon yet.

"Tobias, take your sister upstairs and wait for me."

Latching on to CeCe's hand, Toby led her to the stairs. "But did we win?" he asked again. "Can we have a home now?"

"What are you talking about?"

Toby lifted his chin bravely. "She said that we couldn't live here until she was dead, and we needed a home, right? So did we win it?"

Shit. They had been listening.

"I don't know what to say to that, Tobias."

"Well, she's dead, right?" Toby pressed. "She told you that once she's dead, we would have a house here and another one, so we pushed her extra hard to make sure."

You are my sunshine, my only sunshine.

Every drop of blood drained from Charlie's face. Rising to stand, he stared at his children. "What did you do?"

CeCe whimpered around her thumb and hid her small body behind Toby, who kept a firm hold on her hand. It took the boy a minute to gather enough courage to reply, his bottom lip trembling as he spoke. "We won."

You make me happy when skies are gray.

"What did you win?"

Charlie tried to keep his voice even and not let his churning gut get the better of him. He couldn't very well tell the police that his two small kids had shoved their grandmother down the stairs, hoping they would kill her so they wouldn't be homeless.

"A house," Toby answered. "We can make a Haven House here!"

You'll never know dear, how much I love you.

Charlie's gaze lowered to his dead mother at his feet. Once the word got out about her death, he wondered how many people would cheer over Helen Fairweather's demise. He almost laughed. Everyone. The answer was everyone. His mother had no friends and no family she spoke to except for him and Trevor. She was alone.

With no one to mourn her.

And like she had said, the house and the villa were now theirs. Helen was a bitch, but she wasn't a liar when it came to things like money and trusts, so all Charlie probably had to do was make a phone call, and everything would be moved to his name.

Please don't take my sunshine away.

"A Haven House? Here?" Charlie stepped over his mother to take the kids upstairs while he called the police. They had to make the scene look just right, and the less interaction cops had with Toby and CeCe, the better. "Nah, I've got a better idea."

Charlie had once considered the sunsets at his family's beach house to be some of the best in the world, but this? Nothing compared to this.

"Run, run, run as fast as you can!"

Toby's gleeful shout carried over the wind and was followed immediately by CeCe's squeal of delight as her brother chased her down the beach of Magens Bay. They had been playing all day in the surf, and while the sand here wasn't as nice as the stuff back home, the kids had managed to build an entire sandcastle village along the shore.

His kids were happy.

He was happy.

And they were home.

Sitting on his beach lounger, Charlie swiped the sunglasses off his face. His mother's villa—his villa—rose up high behind him on the cliff. A small place with six bedrooms and four bathrooms, it was just enough for them to live out a great life. Maybe not the kind of life he had thought he would live, but that dream was as dead as the old him. This was the new Charlie Fairweather. A man with a new life and new dreams.

A man who would never allow himself to sink so low again.

"That's a nice place you've got there."

With one eye on the kids, Charlie half turned to greet the man walking over from the section of beach next door. "Thanks."

"Bryan Carroll."

Charlie shook the guy's hand. "Charles Fairweather."

Bryan stared up at the villa behind them. "I thought the Powells owned this place?"

Giving him a once over, Charlie determined that Bryan wasn't a local by the expensive clothes and the way he held himself. The Bostonian accent was also a dead giveaway. Neat and tidy, with a belly hanging past the waistline of his shorts, Bryan looked like he knew how to eat and drink well.

"My mother was a Powell," Charlie replied, unwilling to give him more information. Trust wasn't something he would have here. "She's passed on, and now the villa is mine."

"I've always been interested in the property, but the Powells never entertained the idea of selling." Bryan sat uninvited on the lounger next to him, knocking CeCe's beach towel off and into the sand to make room for his large body. "My place is next door, and I already bought the lot on the other side. I like my privacy, you know."

"I'm not interested in selling."

Bryan chuckled. "For sure, not yet. You just got here! Take your time to enjoy island life." He took a puff on the cigar clenched tight between his knuckles and focused on CeCe and Toby, continuing their game of tag. "But maybe one day you'll figure out island life ain't for you. So, if that day comes, you make sure you call your buddy Bryan first."

Past where they sat on the beach, in the direction of the villa Bryan claimed to own, three men stood positioned not far off. Their gazes never stayed on one thing or another for very long, obviously security of some sort.

"Ignore them," Bryan grumbled. "They're necessary, but not the prettiest sight on this beach."

Charlie took a good look at the man, trying to determine if he was famous. "Necessary?"

"They're mainly for my daughter. I'm one of those over-protective fathers," Bryan continued, grinning when CeCe whooped excitedly as she chased off a flock of birds resting in her path. "Fathers and daughters. You know how it is. We share a special bond."

You are my sunshine, my only sunshine.

"Yeah."

"With sons, you have to mold them and guide them. They're so much fucking effort." Bryan waved a hand at Toby stomping in the waves. "But our girls, they don't need us. They're almost as smart as we are, and they can make their way in the world without our help, you know?"

You make me happy when skies are gray.

Livy would have loved it here. She would have been the final touch to making this place perfect. "Yeah, I know."

"My daughter is the same age as your kids. She's taking a nap right now, but maybe I'll bring her by tomorrow so she can meet the new neighbors," Bryan said, whipping a second cigar from his pocket and handing it to him. "Brandy doesn't have many friends because I don't trust nobody."

You'll never know dear, how much I love you.

Leaning over, Charlie allowed Bryan to light his cigar. "I get it. I'm one of those overprotective fathers, too."

Nudging him with an elbow, Bryan grinned when CeCe kicked at the lapping waves. "And it looks like our girls will get along. Brandy can be wild, but that's good for girls. It's good for them to have a little spunk early on. That way, when some dirtbag man tries to pull one over on them later in life, they can handle it."

That was a problem he didn't want to think about just yet. CeCe looked almost identical to Rebecca, which was dangerous enough, and he could only hope she wouldn't grow up to act like her mother.

"I think you're wrong. I think our girls need us to help mold them." Charlie puffed on his cigar appreciatively and pointed at CeCe. "I don't want that one turning out like her mother."

Bryan coughed as he laughed. "I hear ya. My ex was a Cabot, and if you ain't from Boston, then you don't know that means spoiled rich bitch. Not mother material, you know? Anyway, I cut her loose, and now it's just me and my little girl."

"Probably for the best."

Toby joined CeCe, the two of them finding absolute joy together without the noise of Haven House and the other children getting in their way. It hit Charlie then just how close they had become. A family unit. A real one and all their own.

"We're going to be okay." He hadn't meant to speak, but Charlie couldn't hold it in with the sun setting in the background and the sounds of his children's joy in his ears. "This is all going to be okay."

"Of course, you're going to be okay." Bryan nudged him again, a little harder this time, and gestured to the expansive beach. "You're in paradise, where nothing bad ever happens."

Please don't take my sunshine away.

"You know what, Bryan? I think you're right. Nothing bad could ever happen here."

Chapter 14

Rowan

The small home of Emmett Watson stood solitary in the night, flashing red and blue lights washing over the dilapidated structure. Federal agents had roped off the area with police tape, the extra layer only amplifying the home's macabre aesthetic. Between the ambulance, firetruck, and various police vehicles, Emmett's driveway had likely never seen so many visitors. The clay road leading to this strip of land hadn't been easy to traverse on his bike, and Rowan had given up about halfway down, catching a ride with Ben in his Rover.

"They have a half-hour jump on us," Agent Klausen told the assembled group of law enforcement. "Maybe more, depending on how well he knows these woods."

Toward the back of the group, a Hollingsdale detective held up a large photograph so everyone could see the man who shot Liam.

"The suspect's name is Bruce Hughes, and he is a known domestic terrorist. Big guy, approximately six foot seven with brown hair..."

Rowan turned away, heading toward the ambulance. He didn't need to listen to stats he'd already read a thousand times. It would only piss him off. They should have found these people by now. *He* should have found them.

And his failure had led to this.

"Sir, if you don't hold still, I'll have to take you to the hospital and finish."

Holly, the paramedic, returned to stitching Liam's arm after the warning. She'd agreed to treat him in the rear of the ambulance instead of making him go to the hospital and was probably regretting the offer.

"I'm sorry. I'll do better." Shirtless and grinning, Liam watched intently as Holly worked at the wound. The bullet had grazed his upper bicep, tearing the flesh wide enough to need a heap of stitches. "As much as I would love to ride in the whoo-whoo van, I would rather get this taken care of here.".

Not only did Liam have a hole in his upper arm, but he was also heavily drugged. Poor paramedic Holly might have been willing to go above and beyond by stitching him up on the side of the road, but that didn't mean she wasn't going to give him something to relax.

And they were thankful for the sedatives. It was the only thing keeping Liam from tearing off into the night after Bruce. When Rowan arrived at the shack, he'd found Jamison sobbing while trying to restrain a bleeding, manic Liam.

"The whoo-whoo van?" Dr. Cohen shook his head. "Holly here must have given you the good stuff."

"Yep," Liam said, popping the *p*. He glanced around the crowd, eyes landing on Ben. "I'm sorry I suck at my job."

The serious edge in Ben's features softened slightly. "You don't suck at your job."

"Yes, I do." Liam slouched in defeat, earning himself a dirty look from Holly. "I got shot, and now you're probably not going to let me marry your daughter. I asked her again, and she said yes, but I don't want to wait."

The pitiful tone in Liam's voice had Ben pressing his lips together for a second. "You can marry her if she says yes."

At the moment, Jamison didn't look like she'd say yes to anything. Standing off behind Liam while Holly worked, she was not at all pleased after having been put through the scare of a lifetime.

"She did say yes!" Liam beamed, then leaned down and whispered to Holly. "She said yes."

"Wonderful," Holly mumbled, intently sewing the wound together. "Can you hold still and tell me about the big day?"

"We're getting married in a week." Liam turned toward Simone, giving her a sheepish smile. "At your place? Under that big tree? Can we get married there? I think that would be nice. Evie and the girls could come then, and I guess they could bring Samuel. They kind of have to, since he's my best man."

Simone looked about as happy with Liam as Jamison did, but nodded. "Yes, you can get married at my place, but I don't know about us doing it in a week."

"Awesome, and yeah, we can do it in a week, or I'm hauling Jamison's beautiful butt to the courthouse." Liam sighed, clearly pleased with his own plan. "Jamison has a great butt."

"I'm glad she has a nice butt," Holly replied dryly. "Now, can you relax that arm for me?"

Liam complied but jerked back up seconds later, causing Holly to groan in frustration.

"Wait, is Samuel my best man? Oh shit, I hope not. He's so fucking mean and tries to tell me how to handle my board all the time. I know how to handle my board. It's my board."

"My son is referring to his surfboard," Bernie explained, watching Holly's hands closely. "And may I ask what type of medication you gave him?"

"Ketamine," Holly said, holding Liam's arm steady while rifling through her bag. "And before you say anything, that was all I had. This isn't exactly a fully stocked rig. It's used to transport risky L and D cases from Hollingsdale General to Port Michaelson, and I was en route back when the shooting call came in. Since I used to work trauma before labor and delivery, we decided to respond."

"You're not a fully trained paramedic?" Liam's voice slurred with disbelief. "Are you sure you can do this?"

"Relax, buddy. She's a nurse," Rowan cut in, suppressing the urge to pull out his phone and record everything for Annabeth. "Let her work so we can get back."

Liam's eyes lit up when they landed on Rowan. "Oh, Rowan is my friend! See, I don't just have Samuel. I can get Rowan to be my best man, so I won't have to listen to Samuel telling me I don't know how to surf while saying my vows. Yeah, that's better since I can't have my real best friend be my best man."

Holly didn't pause. "Why can't your real best friend be your best man?"

"Because it's Jamison. My wife is my best friend." Liam realized what he said and laughed at himself, swaying slightly. "I mean, my *future* wife is my best friend. She's fucking amazing. You should meet her, Holly. I know she's around here somewhere. You can't miss her. She's so pretty it makes your heart hurt. I have no idea why she chose me."

A smile tipped the edge of Holly's lips, and her gaze flicked briefly to Jamison standing just out of sight. "She sounds lovely."

Liam groaned in total ecstasy. "It's unreal how beautiful she is, but you know what? That's not even the best part. Nope. She's smart as hell. Brilliant. Totally brilliant, and she puts up with my shit. Oops—sorry. Crap. *Shit*. I mean, crap. She's so pretty and likes my crap."

"Easy, son," Dr. Cohen said, trying hard not to laugh. "You've had a little too much fun juice."

"I like the juice, and the juice likes me." Liam hummed a little tune before rambling on. "But Jamison does put up with my bullshit. Let me tell you something, Holly. I am not an easy man to handle. I got all these thoughts rolling around in my head, but Jamison can take it. She listens and works through the shit ton of messy ideas I have and gets all of it. She gets me. I missed her. I missed us. But we're gonna be us again, and I'm so *happy*."

Jamison finally stepped forward, resting her hand on Liam's head. "Hey, you."

"Oh my God, we were just talking about you!" Liam arched toward her, jostling Holly as she finished. "Holly, this is my Jamison. Jamison, this is my Holly. Well, not my Holly. I don't need another woman, and I'm sure she has a husband at home."

"Actually, my husband is a firefighter, and he's right over there." Holly leaned back and examined her work. "Okay, here are the rules..."

While Holly gave aftercare instructions, Rowan drifted closer to Ben. "Do you have any idea how pissed he's going to be when he finds out we drugged him?"

"He'll get over it," Ben replied. "But are we sure the bullet didn't hit something serious? He's covered in blood."

"Nah. I've been shot before. It bled like that."

Ben turned his head slowly. "Who the fuck shot you?"

"My sister. She tried to shoot me in the ass once but missed." Rowan grinned, thinking of Cait. "The bullet grazed my hip and bled pretty good. Hurt like hell, too."

Ben snorted. "Yet everyone thinks we're the weird family."

Rowan's expression sobered. "Speaking of family..."

He struggled with how to tell Ben the news. No one had delivered the full details to him regarding Parker, and Ben was going to be furious when he found out that his niece's partner might be involved.

Then again, there wasn't really a "*might*." Parker was involved. There was no other explanation for why he'd been with Bruce.

Emmett Watson was clearly in bed with Zanmi, and the weapons cache inside the shack made that abundantly clear. The guy seemed like he would fit in perfectly with the cult crowd.

But they couldn't afford to focus on that right now.

"We need to find Claudia," Rowan said, pulling a stunned Ben away from the crowd after he relayed the information he knew. "Jamison said Madison was with Parker, but Claudia wasn't."

"Claudia is not involved with Zanmi." Ben halted abruptly. "I know the Fairweathers are dysfunctional, but this? Even Claudia, during her bitchiest of days, would never get wrapped up in Zanmi's bullshit."

"What about Parker?"

Thinking for a minute, the steady sureness Ben held seconds ago disappeared. "I've only met the guy a few times. All I know is that my sister-in-law loves him, which isn't saying much. Heather's got a... unique personality, and that's me being polite."

"She's horrid."

Simone joined them, shivering in the crisp night air. Wrapping her arms around herself, she wrinkled her nose at the buzzing activity. The canine unit had arrived, and teams were preparing to search the swamp for Bruce. It was a waste of time in Rowan's mind. A man like that would be long gone or so well hidden, local cops wouldn't see anything even if they were standing right on top of him.

"Why are y'all talking about Heather?" she asked. "Did Damon show up with Emily and Claudia?"

"Not exactly."

Rowan filled her in while Ben stayed silent. With every new detail, Simone's horror grew over what she was hearing. "I don't care for

Claudia. I know she and Evie have struck up this odd acquaintance, but I haven't quite decided how I feel about it. That said, she would never become one of those people. That's just not who she is."

"I hope not, and I plan to operate as if Claudia is in imminent danger and not an associate of the group. Klausen is chasing down Bruce, while Anderson leads the team going after Emmett and Parker, and, from my understanding, we're all tackling this development the same way. The focus is to retrieve Madison and find Claudia," Rowan replied before turning to Ben. "You need to talk to your brother."

"There's no service out here." Ben frowned at an officer approaching, and the woman promptly turned and went the other way. "I know he'll want to stay, but Liam needs to rest. I'll call Trevor once we get him back to the house."

Rowan agreed, not liking them exposed like this. "We all need to get back to the house and let Klausen and Anderson follow up on things here. I would stay, but honestly, there's not much I can do, and I want to focus on tracking down Damon. He and Emily haven't been in communication since before the raid."

Over at the ambulance, Liam attempted to stand on shaky legs. With his good arm slung across Jamison's shoulders, they tried to stumble their way over. Bernie followed with her hands out as if she could catch Liam if he fell. Dr. Cohen had disappeared into the chaos of the search, the best out of everyone to handle the feds and police.

"Do you have any idea where Damon might have gone?" Simone asked.

Rowan had a few places in mind, but he wanted to be sure before saying anything. "Damon would never try to hide somewhere he hadn't been before. I'll take a deep dive into his travel records to see what pops up."

"That's going to take forever," Ben said, helping Jamison keep Liam upright when they reached them. "Damon travels constantly."

"Passport. He wouldn't ping it. He'd stay stateside," Liam said, struggling to get the words out and have them make sense. "Stick to the dirt. *Ground!* Travel by car. Not air. Train. No ticket. No trace. Forty-eight."

Ben glanced at Rowan. "Forty-eight states?"

"Yeah." Rowan rolled his shoulders, easing the tension as he mentally organized the search. "Are we ready? They won't find Bruce, and I can do more damage at home."

Dr. Cohen came up behind them, leaving the group of cops disappearing into the forest. "Anderson says it's a dead chase, but he's following through just to confirm. I'm with Rowan. Let's get back. We'll monitor the situation from Haven."

"Then let's get the hell out of here," Ben grumbled as he went over to relieve Jamison of Liam while Dr. Cohen braced his son's injured arm.

Liam's head started to dip as if he were falling asleep, but he caught himself in time, the usual sharp edge in his gaze returning for a nanosecond. "I don't like this."

If he was already becoming aware of his drugged state, that meant the Special-K gift from Holly had been a small dose. Then again, Rowan had learned Liam was too stubborn to let something as minor as a drugging get in his way.

"We have to find those fu...ck...ers," Liam growled. "Why am I talking like this?"

"You'll be okay in about two hours," Dr. Cohen grunted as they turned Liam around. "A nice long nap is what you need. Then we can hunt the fuckers down."

"That's what I just said," Liam insisted as Bernie led the way to where they had parked the cars. "Isn't that what I said?"

Jamison tried to follow as her father and Liam's parents led Liam away, but Simone grabbed her arm, stopping her in place.

"Not so fast."

Holding Jamison by the shoulders, Simone attempted to level her with a motherly stare. It reminded Rowan of how Annabeth would try to do the same with him, but instead of being adorable, Simone remained her usual terrifying self.

"Are you okay?"

Jamison's bottom lip trembled, and she nodded, making Simone cluck her tongue. It amazed Rowan how she could always convey the smallest of messages by the mere clucking of her tongue. That little sound held a variety of emotions, from issuing a warning to casting judgment, depending on the situation.

"You can tell us," Simone pressed. "It's better to fall apart with Rowan and me than to do it in front of Liam when he's so out of his head. Seeing you upset would set him off."

Rowan schooled his features, keeping a straight face as he waited to hear what Jamison had to say. However, on the inside, he was flying. Simone was including him in this private moment, like she trusted him.

Like he was part of the family.

Convincing Annabeth to trust in the strength of their relationship was one thing. But winning over Simone? That was a different beast entirely.

Jamison sniffed, watching the canine units wrestle with their leashes. "He scared me."

"Men tend to do that," Simone said, pulling her into a hug. "It's so aggravating."

Rowan remained silent, knowing he wasn't meant to comment. Tears streamed down Jamison's cheeks as she rested her head on Simone's shoulder, and he gave her a quiet, sympathetic smile. She rarely showed her vulnerable side—no Fairweather ever did—and seeing her break open not only in front of him but also in front of at least fifty other people meant that what had gone down had done much more than scare her.

"I told him not to go. I begged him, and he went anyway," Jamison babbled. "Why does he always have to just jump headfirst into the fray? Why does he always have to act like Superman?"

"Because Liam is Superman." Simone smoothed her hand across Jamison's back. "He's not like us. He's brave, and he does what's right. I remember that first day he walked through our door and how you could just tell he was the type that would be good for us. You and Annabeth were too busy checking him out to notice, but I did. I noticed. That's when I decided to shove him in your path."

Jamison let out a watery laugh. "I love that you always take credit for us being together."

"It's true, isn't it?" Simone lifted her chin, daring her to deny it. "Are you questioning my genius?"

"Never."

Ahead, Liam's legs wobbled again, and Ben and Dr. Cohen did an awkward little dance to keep him upright without yanking the stitches. Bernie trailed after them, flapping her hands in mild panic.

"Oh shit," Jamison hissed and released Simone. "I better go help."

They watched as she ran off, and after a beat, Rowan spoke. "You're a good mom."

It was maybe a weird thing to say, especially since Jamison wasn't Simone's daughter by blood. But it felt like something she needed to hear.

"I've had plenty of practice." Simone hooked her arm around his as they started toward the cars together. "I'll be a good mother-in-law, too."

Rowan nearly tripped but caught himself.

If she was giving him an opening, he wasn't about to let it pass. "That's because you're not just a good mom. You're a fierce one."

Simone leaned on him as they crossed the uneven ground. "You don't have to be so grandiose when flattering me, Rowan."

"Oh, but I *do*," he teased her with a grin. "I'm a man of style. Being grandiose is kind of my thing."

She snorted. "That's why my baby loves you. You do everything with your whole heart."

"When it comes to Annabeth? Always and forever." He looked down at her with full sincerity, not wanting to miss his mark. "And I mean forever, Simone."

"You scare her."

"I know."

"You scare me, too," she admitted, eyes ahead. "A big man with a motorcycle, tattoos, and piercings isn't exactly what I expected for my daughter."

"I only have one piercing left. You made me take out the rest," he joked. "And what kind of man did you expect?"

"I thought she'd end up with a man like her father."

"What was he like?"

"Perfect," she said simply. "My Devon was perfect."

Even in the dark, the aching sorrow in Simone's expression struck Rowan. It had been nearly twenty-five years, but when she spoke of Devon Howard, it was with fresh grief and unshakeable love.

"Devon was calm and kind. I was forever running after the kids, and he carried the weight of our family right alongside me." Her voice turned wistful. "But he always made time for us. We'd sneak off to watch the sunset on the porch or slow dance in the kitchen before bed. He made the little moments count."

"I like that." Rowan held her steady as they walked up the small hill leading to the road. "Slow dancing before bed sounds like the perfect end to a day."

The unmistakable sound of her clucking her tongue carried through the darkness. "Just keep your dancing out of my kitchen."

"Yes, ma'am."

CHAPTER 15

Jamison

"*That was a close one.*"

Standing on Haven's porch, Jamison glared at CeCe drifting through Ty's gardens. "A close one?"

CeCe plucked a bloom, twirling it beneath her nose with an impish smile. "Everything turned out fine."

Could she punch a dream? Jamison sure as hell wanted to try, but her mother was watching.

"I wouldn't say fine, CeCe," Laura Jean said from the lower porch step. "I thought Jamison was about to have a heart attack. I usually back your ideas, but this wasn't your best."

"It worked, didn't it? Message received and all that." CeCe dropped the flower. "We had to sell it, or else the others wouldn't believe."

"What message? What are you talking about?" Jamison's voice climbed with each word. "What the hell are either of you talking about?"

"Princess, calm down." Her mother climbed the steps, glancing nervously at the haint porch ceilings. "Sometimes we have to let certain things happen—

"He was shot!" Hands fisted at her side, Jamison screamed at her mother. "Those women came here and tried to kill us, and then Liam was shot, but yet you want to tell me I have to let certain things happen? Are you kidding? What part of this are you okay with? Me watching the man I love almost die the same way you died? Or are you just good with people breaking into Haven House so they can hack us to death with machetes?"

"None of it." Her mother tried to rush another step, but the flesh on her arm sizzled as soon as the shade hit. *"I hate all of this, and we're working to keep you safe. We'll be with you every step of the way, Jamison. Have faith in us. Have faith in me."*

In the soft glow of sunrise, Jamison's eyes opened to find Liam staring at her. "You drugged me."

And she would do it again.

The sound of the gunshot as it echoed through the air had yanked at her connection to Liam, snapping that invisible string tight in her chest. It had her dropping to her knees, forcing her to crawl through the muddy mix of sand and grass to get to him.

She had been so sure he was dead.

But when Bruce burst out of the cabin, reality returned. Smiling and giving her a salute, the bastard had run off into the forest. A part of her had gone immediately feral, demanding that she give chase and hurt him as much as he'd hurt her.

But she didn't. Getting to Liam had been too important, and inside the shack, she found him crouched on the floor and bleeding. He wanted to go after Madi, and when she tried to reason with him, his blood soaking them both, he wouldn't listen and actually ran down the lane after the old pickup speeding away.

"Holly drugged you." She scooted closer until their legs tangled beneath the blankets. "Blame her, not me."

How he'd convinced a nurse to stitch him in the back of her ambulance remained a mystery. By the time the fire trucks, police, and every other agency arrived, she'd gone numb and couldn't remember much.

As she snuggled closer, he tried to arrange them so his injured arm wouldn't be in the way, but failed, wincing in pain when he moved. "I did not need this right now."

"And I didn't need the heart attack."

"I'm sorry." He shifted so they could share one pillow and lay nose to nose. "When I saw Madison, reasoning went right the hell out of my head."

Jamison's heart lurched. "They still haven't found them. Rowan's been up all night digging into Parker."

"Has he discovered anything?"

"Nothing."

The guilt each of them felt—especially her father—hung heavy through the house this morning. Parker Monroe, Claudia Fairweather's boyfriend for the last three years, was a member of Zanmi, and none of them had ever picked up on it. If they were honest, none of them had cared enough to pay attention.

Claudia and Evie had a friendly relationship, their burned bridge mending in the aftermath of Toby. Samuel dealt with Damon several times a month, but Jamison doubted the two cousins shared intimate details about their lives. Her dad never said much more than a hello to any of his extended family, except when discussing a deal or venture that Fairweather Holdings was pursuing.

And she was just as much to blame. She worked with Emily one-on-one for at least a few months out of the year, yet neither ever pushed beyond those easy surface-level conversations reserved for the workspace.

They didn't *know* that side of the family. Once upon a time, Trevor and her father had kept things cordial, going through the motions of what a family was supposed to act like in public. Sometimes, they would even invite each other to private family events, but more often than not, the other brother would decline the offer unless there was no other way to avoid it.

Mainly because Trevor's wife made things awkward.

A vicious beast, Heather Fairweather held high expectations in life. She wanted to rule everything and everyone, and God forbid her husband or her children didn't assist in those plans for world domination. On the rare occasion she interacted with Heather, even Jamison struggled with keeping up with the woman's carefully concealed insults.

"My dad talked to Trevor last night." Coasting her fingertips across his brow, she smoothed his hair back to see his eyes. "It turns out he and Heather have never met Parker's family. They only know what Claudia or Parker have told them."

She'd caught snippets of the conversation. There had definitely been panic in her uncle's voice. The heartbreaking kind any father would display in this type of situation.

But then Heather took over the conversation.

"Heather basically hung up on him."

Untangling himself from her hold, Liam rolled to his back with a groan, wincing again when he shifted his arm. "Heather makes our side of the family look sane."

Our side of the family.

She grinned. "You can't marry me with a hurt arm."

"The hell I can't." His head snapped to the side, and she noticed how well-rested he looked. Last night was probably the longest he'd slept in weeks. "One week, Jamison. You get one week."

"Actually, it's six days now." Snuggling at his side, she rested her chin on his chest. "And you're sure you want to do this with all the crazy?"

"Crazy or not, you are marrying me. I don't care if Michael Sinclair himself is in attendance." He lifted his head to kiss her, snaking his good arm around her waist to haul them closer. "And I'm sorry about the boat."

"You owe me a few more rounds." She kissed him again. "But first, you need to have those stitches looked at. Holly said you have to go get them checked out today."

"I need to send her some flowers or something, although the entire point of convincing her to patch me up on the side of the road was so I could keep working. What the hell did she give me?"

"Ketamine?" She ran her hand down his chest and abs. "I think Rowan called it Special-K?"

"Holy hell," he mumbled. "Maybe I'm not going to send her flowers after all."

***

Rowan snored softly in the corner chair. They had moved two recliners back into the media room so he or Liam could catch cat naps, and that was exactly what the overly exhausted man was doing.

"He's working himself to death." Annabeth sat at one of the folding tables, her gaze locked onto the laptop screen. She'd been searching for information on Parker alongside Rowan, determined to be helpful. "Stubborn man."

"You haven't slept either," Jamison pointed out, scrolling through her laptop search results. This felt like they were trying to find a needle in a haystack. They weren't stupid. They knew a simple internet search wouldn't yield anything of value, but had to give it their best shot. "Or Izzy. I'm surprised she was coherent enough to drive Liam to get his stitches looked at."

And she was surprised Liam wouldn't let her go with them.

"I made her sleep." Across from them, doing his own research, Abe let out an exhausted sigh from behind his laptop. "She fought me, but I won, and she got about three hours of rest. Then a shower and some food. I made her a full meal to make sure she had some fuel."

Jamison lifted her head, ignoring her screen just as Annabeth did. They glanced at each other before turning on Abe.

"You cooked?" Annabeth asked. "Actual food?"

Abe looked up, his eyes darting back and forth between them. "Yes, I cooked her food."

Tilting her head to the side, Annabeth studied him. "Like a… microwave meal?"

"No." Unamused over what she was implying, Abe's face darkened. "I am capable, Annabeth."

"Oh, I know you're capable, you just never do it," his twin shot back. "And don't you snap at me as if I think you're not capable of something. You're the one all up in your head."

Abe's hard gaze dropped back to his screen. "I don't know what you're talking about."

"Oh, that's some bullshit." Folding her hands neatly on the table, Annabeth's spine shot ramrod straight. She was about to lecture her brother, and Jamison braced herself. Annabeth could be as scary as her mother when in a bad mood. "Get your head out of your ass. You like her."

Typing furiously, Abe sneered at the keyboard. "So?"

"So, don't screw this up by pushing Izzy away because you think you're not good enough." Annabeth leaned forward. "We watch you do it all the time, and now you have one that could really be something. No, it's not the ideal time to be romancing a person, but none of us want to see you get in your head—"

"Hold up." Abe flopped back in his wheelchair. "*You* are lecturing *me* about getting in my head. Are you for real right now?"

One of Annabeth's hands lifted in the air, and with a grand flourish, she gestured in Jamison's direction. "Tell him."

Jamison shrank a little in her folding chair. "You're dragging me into this?"

"I am." Annabeth spared her a sideways glance. "Now, tell him."

Closing her laptop, Jamison took a deep inhale. "I love you, Abe. You're like my brother. In fact, I like you better than my brothers. Samuel is an ass, and Selah can lecture too much."

Abe nodded in agreement. "All of this is true."

"But you go through women, Abe. Like, a lot of women. Izzy isn't that type, and I think you should tread carefully with her."

"What are you talking about?" Annabeth whispered out the side of her mouth. "This isn't about Izzy."

"It isn't?"

"No. Not really."

"Then what is this about?"

Annabeth rolled her eyes. "It's about how he goes through all these women because he doesn't think he's good enough. He thinks that chair limits him when we know it doesn't." She tapped a finger against her temple. "Those limitations are in here."

Eyes going wide, Jamison floundered on what to say but could only come up with, "Oh."

"He's been scared," Annabeth continued. "So, he loves them and leaves them."

"Or maybe I like Izzy and don't want to mess this up." Abe grinned at his sister when she huffed. "Okay, fine. Maybe I do want to prove to her that this chair doesn't limit me. I already know that it doesn't, but sometimes I feel the need to prove it to people. Just like I'm sure Izzy feels she has to prove herself as a woman while working in the field that's dominated by men."

"It's not the same thing," Annabeth grumbled. "But whatever."

"And just like you have to prove to yourself and everyone else how capable you can be in the world," Abe said, arching forward with a grin. "We're all fucked up, Annabeth, but thanks for being a brat and calling me out on my bullshit that doesn't exist."

"Oh, shut up."

They continued their search, three little fish in a very big pond. A half-hour went by, and Jamison checked the time, expecting Liam soon.

Taylor popped her head inside the media room. "Hard at work?"

Why did she always have to sound so condescending? Sure, Taylor's annoying voice was something Jamison was learning to live with, but it still grated and made her want to punch the woman in the nose.

Annabeth and Abe kept quiet, and Jamison kicked both of them in the shins. "We're good," she told Taylor. "Just keeping busy while Liam is out having his stitches checked."

Taylor cooed and entered the room a little further. She had been asked—politely—on several occasions to stay out, but continued to find excuses to come in and take a look around.

"How's Liam feeling?" Taylor strolled, her progression through the doorway timed with the measured clicks of her heels. Today, she was dressed as if she were heading into the office, even though Fairweather's buildings remained closed. The grey high-waisted slacks tailored to fit her narrow hips and long legs looked good, as did the white blouse. The open neckline showcased her cleavage, giving the entire outfit a feminine look. "He should practice running away more. We wouldn't want him to actually take a bullet next time."

Abe's fingers halted their typing, his hands hovering over the keyboard. "I'm going to check on my mom," he murmured. "She's taking a nap and wants me to wake her after about an hour."

Rolling his chair back swiftly from the table, he turned and sped from the room, almost colliding with Taylor, who had paused to review the information regarding Bryan and Brandy Carroll tacked to a giant display board.

"What's this?" Taylor asked.

Jamison closed her search window. They were being much more open with Taylor, so she supposed it didn't hurt to explain.

"Toby mentioned a woman named Brandy during our phone call with him yesterday, and Rowan tracked her down. We think her name is Brandy Carroll."

Reading the data on the sheet, Taylor's head tilted. Jamison couldn't see her face, but she imagined that heavily freckled nose of hers was wrinkling in distaste as it usually did when Toby was discussed. "What do you know about her?"

Annabeth stretched in her folding chair, closing her laptop. "She's the daughter of a drug runner in St. Thomas, and her time on the island coincides with Toby and CeCe's. They even went to the same school."

Taylor glanced back at them, her strawberry blonde hair sweeping over her shoulder. She really was beautiful, and while her father wasn't interested, Jamison wondered how Taylor hadn't snagged herself another rich man. In her mid-thirties, with a fantastic body, beautiful face, and an obviously shrewd mind—otherwise, she would never have survived working with Benjamin Fairweather—the woman was an ideal candidate for a corporate executive's wife.

On the recliner, Rowan's snoring picked up, and the three of them grinned. "Rowan was on the phone with his brother and just dozed off," Annabeth said, smiling at him. "I took the phone and told Killian he would call him back."

"Have you ever talked to his brother before?" Jamison asked, getting an idea. Killian McIntyre might be an eternal bachelor, but maybe all he needed was to meet someone who could match his notoriously bad attitude. Someone like Taylor. "I've seen him at events, but have never spoken directly to him."

Annabeth shrugged. "Not really. He seemed nice."

"He's not." Giving them her attention, Taylor turned slowly and shoved her hands in the pockets of her slacks. "He's conceited, and rude, and an arrogant jerk."

"He's also hot," Jamison added, liking that fiery glint in Taylor's eyes. "I'll wholeheartedly admit that I stopped and stared."

Taylor took a seat across from them and rested her elbow on the table. "Dangerous people often hide behind pretty faces, Jamison. You need to remember that," she said, propping her chin on the palm of her hand. "Killian McIntyre gives me the creeps. I get that he's ruthless and evil, but does he have to be so charming while doing it? It's gross behavior."

"My dad sort of operates the same way." Jamison searched her memory for an example. "He can be charming while—"

"Your dad isn't like that," Taylor interrupted. "He and Samuel are both unapologetically themselves, and I find that much more trustworthy. Fairweather men are superior to McIntyre men in every possible way."

"I beg to differ, but I'm too hungry for this argument." Annabeth stood to leave. "And Rowan is going to wake up soon, so I'm going to make us some lunch."

Jamison batted her eyes. "Can you make me some lunch, too?"

"Have Abe make it," Annabeth said with an evil giggle as she left. "Apparently, he's a cook now."

"Abe can cook?" Taylor asked when they were alone with nothing but Rowan's snoring filling the silence. "That's new."

Jamison awkwardly fiddled with her keyboard, hoping Taylor would leave if she kept her reply short. "I guess."

It wasn't that they hadn't been alone together before, but it was all business during those times, with one or two snarky comments tossed in for fun. Taylor usually kicked things off with a random off-the-wall observation, and waiting for the first one to come out was annoying Jamison.

"What was it like?" Taylor asked, crossing her legs to settle in. "Yesterday, I mean."

"Are you asking me what it was like thinking the man I love had died?" Jamison sneered at the audacity. "It suc—"

"I wasn't asking that. I'm very familiar with the feeling," Taylor cut her off bluntly. "Or did you forget I lost my husband?"

The sting of embarrassment singed her cheeks. She had forgotten. Taylor's deceased husband had never been more than a whisper around the office. Jamison knew there had been a mourning period, but that was about the extent of the information she had.

"I'm sorry." She would own her horrible misstep. Forgetting something like a dead husband was unacceptable, even if it was Taylor. "I know firsthand what losing a loved one can do to a person, and I didn't mean to be so insensitive."

The lines in Taylor's face softened. "It's okay. I don't talk about him much, so you're not the only person who forgets."

"What was he like?" Being around her family, she had learned a thing or two about grief. Most people tried to avoid conversations regarding those who had passed, but that wasn't necessarily the right way to handle things. Sometimes, those left behind were internally begging to have the chance to speak about their loved ones. "He was so young when he died."

Taylor nodded, and as if she were uncomfortable maintaining eye contact, her gaze drifted to the movie screen where Toby's information was on a constantly rotating cycle of pictures, reports, and video interviews. "It was tough in the beginning. We did everything together and had since we were kids. He was my first love, my first everything, and when he died, my world just stopped," she said quietly. "We were in the process of buying a house and starting a family. I even had baby names picked out. Rachel for a girl and Dane for a boy. Cute, right?"

Her stomach twisted in knots. She knew the hope and the pain that came with its loss well. "Those are very cute baby names."

"But then our happy life ended because he made a stupid mistake."

The anger in Taylor's voice spoke volumes. She wasn't over the loss, and her emotions were hanging soundly behind the many shades of grief. Like everyone else in the world, Taylor was allowed to process her pain in whatever way helped her cope, so if anger and resentment over her husband's death were what got her through, then it was best to leave it alone.

But curious to a fault, Jamison couldn't stop her questions. "A mistake?"

"Yeah." The word slid past Taylor's lips with a heartbreaking sigh. She continued to stare at the screen, squinting at the small square in the corner broadcasting Toby's interview from the day before. "He kept overindulging himself all the time, and finally, it was that *just one more* attitude that put him down for good."

"I don't know what else to say other than I'm sorry."

Continuing to stare at the interview, Taylor stiffened, and Jamison understood the feeling. Seeing Toby was like watching a car wreck happen in real time.

"He really looks bad, doesn't he?" Taylor whispered.

Jamison glanced over. The sound was muted so Rowan could sleep, but the adoration shining in Toby's eyes said the video was in the section of playback where he and Evie were speaking. "Prison will do that to you."

"I remember how handsome he was when he was arrested and thinking, how could a gorgeous, articulate doctor be considered a monster?" Taylor's lip curled in revulsion. "But like I said a second ago, dangerous people hide behind pretty faces."

"Toby's pretty face once had an army of people willing to do anything for it."

"Not anymore." Shaking her head, Taylor turned away from the screen. "At first, I thought those people who wanted to get involved did so because they were going through some phase, depending on where they were in life, but no. It really grew, didn't it? Almost overnight, there were legions of people proclaiming his innocence regardless of what the evidence showed."

"That kind of crap happens every day. Humans love to live in denial as long as they're accepted," Jamison replied, and smiled sheepishly when Taylor arched an eyebrow. "Sorry, being around Liam and his dad so much, I've listened to their discussions, and I guess some of it has rubbed off on me."

"No, I think you're absolutely right. Acceptance is incredibly powerful and can be an excellent manipulation tool if handled correctly."

It was Jamison's turn to arch an eyebrow, and Taylor grinned. "Hey, I can be insightful. I watch Dr. Cohen's documentaries all the time. Don't tell him because it'll make it weird, but I'm a huge fan and geek out every time I see him."

Jamison chuckled. "I won't tell him."

"Speaking of Dr. Cohen," Taylor began coyly. "What's this I hear about you and Liam getting married in a week?"

"Six days."

Snatching up the water bottle next to her laptop, Jamison took a giant gulp. This might be the first non-hostile conversation she'd had with Taylor, and it was nice and all, but a piece of her wanted to keep things quiet.

"We're doing it here," she said, knowing Taylor wouldn't leave it alone until she had more information. "Something small with only us."

"Let me know when you go to get the license so that I can brief your department. The second a county clerk sees the name Fairweather on a marriage certificate, they'll be running to the press."

Realizing she had a point, Jamison felt relieved that Taylor was willing to handle things. While her father worked to keep his stress levels even during all this, she was the opposite. Her job had been the furthest thing on her mind since stepping back through the doors of Haven House.

"I'll draft a statement for Tammy to have on file and then copy you on it," Jamison said, thinking she was long overdue for a gossip session with her assistant. Tammy would have questions about what was happening, and while she couldn't answer most of them, she could at least check in on her friend. "You should have the email by this afternoon."

"Perfect." Taylor shot her a smile, her face blooming into something beautiful as she stood. "I hope everything goes well with the wedding. If you need me to do anything, don't hesitate to ask. Liam doesn't want you off the property without him, but we can wrangle up an FBI agent or two if you need to get out and pick something up personally."

Jamison checked the time on her phone. "I wish he would hurry. How long does it take to have stitches looked at?"

"He went to Samuel's house first."

The polite smile on Jamison's lips faltered. Samuel's house? That didn't make any sense. Liam knew she wanted to see Evie, and he had promised to take her the first chance he had, so why go there without her?

A sharp knock sounded on the doorframe as her father passed. "Taylor, we're starting. Let's go."

"He never takes a break." Taylor rolled her shoulders while heaving out an annoyed puff of air. "I can't wait to get back to the office. I mean, I love Haven House. It's beautiful, and honestly, I would *kill* to live here, but being in such close quarters with your dad is intense sometimes. When he gets going, there's no stopping him."

Jamison fired off a text to Liam, asking for an ETA, and tried not to grin at Taylor's comment. It would appear that the honeymoon phase of being her father's assistant was officially over. "My dad is interesting."

"That's one way to put it." Taylor wrinkled her nose. "Do you think he's going to freak out when I ask for time off next week?"

"I doubt it, and if he needs an assistant, I can fill in." Jamison laughed at the idea of taking orders from her father. The two of them would butt heads like crazy. "And I don't blame you for needing a break from all this."

"It's not that. I'm going to visit some family and help them move into their home, and well..." Taylor bit her full bottom lip and looked everywhere but directly at Jamison. "There's someone I want to see again. He's in the area, and I thought it might be a good time to reconnect."

"Yeah?" Jamison refused to fist pump the air at hearing Taylor was interested in someone who was not a Fairweather. "That's cool."

"I don't want to jinx it. He's incredibly attractive, but also the corporate type who might not have time for anything long term."

The handsome corporate type could easily translate into being the Taylor-type. This was perfect.

"But it doesn't hurt to have a little fun," Jamison pointed out. "Especially if he's going to be in the same area."

"Oh, I plan to have fun with him." Taylor sighed wistfully. "So much fun."

Chapter 16

Jamison

Glaring at her phone, Jamison resisted the urge to text Liam again once Taylor took off to do her father's bidding. It had been twenty minutes, and he had yet to respond, making her more frustrated with each passing second.

No, screw that. She wasn't frustrated.

She was pissed.

Mainly because she was worried, but still pissed.

Why would he go to Samuel and Evie's place and not tell her? She was sure there was a reason. There was always a reason with Liam, but it annoyed her that she was being left out.

Again.

"Why are you giving your phone a death glare?" Rowan asked with a yawn. Stretching his arms overhead, he rose from the couch. "And where's Annabeth?"

"She's making you food."

Rowan grinned stupidly. "Really?"

"Stop looking so happy, you Neanderthal. She's just as tired as you, but is in there cooking."

The goofy smile on his face dropped mid-stretch. "Oh, shit."

Would she ever get used to seeing Rowan like this? Probably not. Annabeth had him soundly wrapped around her dainty finger, and Jamison was pretty sure he was in it for the long haul.

"Care to tell me why Liam went to my brother and sister's house and didn't tell me?"

"You know, it's weird when you refer to a married couple as '*my brother and sister*,' right?"

Jamison didn't miss a beat. "You know it's weird that you watched Annabeth use her masturbation station through our security cameras instead of asking her out like a normal person, right? Now stop avoiding the question."

Rowan dropped into a folding chair in front of his many laptops, the thing nearly buckling under his weight. "I didn't know he was going, let alone why he went."

With her eyes narrowing into slits, she tried to mimic Simone's expression when she thought someone wasn't telling the truth. "You're lying."

"Shit, this scan finished thirty minutes ago," Rowan mumbled, his fingers flying deftly over the keyboard. "Did you text Liam?"

"Like a bazillion times, but he hasn't responded."

"He'll answer."

"But he hasn't."

Rowan rolled his eyes. "Probably because they had to go to the hospital. You know how shitty the cell service is there."

"That's a crap excuse." She slouched in her chair with her arms crossed. "I could've taken him."

"You're a target. He's injured. If something went down, he'd throw himself at it even if he's half-functioning."

"I'm texting him again." She sent another message and waited while her foot tapped rapidly on the hardwood. Five minutes in, Rowan's left eye started to twitch.

"That is super fucking annoying. Don't you have something to do? Elsewhere? On the other side of the house?"

"I just need to know he's okay."

That last line cracked something in her voice. Getting over what happened at Emmett's cottage would take time, and not having him near made her feel as if she were choking on the *what-ifs*. What if they came after Liam again? What if this was another ambush?

"Hey. Look at me." Rowan turned his laptop toward her. A map glowed on the screen, two tiny dots moving along a road. "That's the road from Samuel's place. That's Liam. And Izzy."

Phone in hand, she texted Liam again. This time, putting a little less crazy in her language. "Thanks, Rowan." Hitting send, she set the phone down. "I didn't mean to go all psycho there."

"You're pretty psycho all the time, but good for you on becoming self-aware." He spun the laptop back around with a smirk. "And it looks like he's almost here."

Her phone rang, and she snatched the phone back up. "Are you okay?"

Liam's laugh rumbled through the speaker. "I missed you too."

"What's taking so long?"

"I had to talk to Holden."

"About what?"

"We were discussing next weekend."

His tone suggested that whatever he and Holden had talked about was a not-on-the-phone topic, and she let it go.

"Are you sure we should be doing this?" she asked. "With Madison still out there and Claudia MIA."

"We'll talk when I get there. We're pulling onto the drive now."

She hung up, the adrenaline still buzzing in her limbs.

"Feel better?" Rowan asked, watching her.

"Yes." Her hands shook, a sign of the adrenaline attempting to even out. It happened so much these days that she hardly noticed anymore. "I'm just on edge."

"We all are." Rowan rose and shut the media room door. "Can I ask you something?"

Frowning over how he suddenly seemed nervous, Jamison's eyes slid between Rowan and the closed door. "Uh, yeah?"

"It's kind of personal."

"Dear God, what?"

Rubbing a hand on the back of his neck, he spoke to the floor. "If I give you and Liam twenty minutes, will you return the favor?"

"I'm not following, Rowan."

"We all need to focus, but we're so high strung that we can't." He winced over what he was saying, confusing her even more. "Izzy and Abe are supposed to bring the boat back here this afternoon, and there's a little cabin in it."

"What does that have to do with twenty minutes?"

Rowan didn't reply, merely staring at her as if she were an idiot, and when the realization of what he was asking finally struck, she snorted. "Only twenty minutes? Poor Annabeth. That's so sad."

It was sad for all of them, actually. Twenty minutes here. Thirty minutes there. Moments together reduced to small increments of time.

"Shut up."

An honest to God blush covered his face, and Jamison couldn't hold in her laughter. "You could've at least asked for a half hour."

Returning to his laptop, Rowan hunched over the keyboard like he wanted to disappear into it. "Forget I asked."

"Why?" Jamison folded her legs under her, settling into the chair. "We're in the middle of this insane crap, but you're focused on getting laid. Why? That's not like you."

"I'm sorry, but what were you two doing when Will called to tell you guys Watson was at his shack?" Rowan held up his hand to stop her from answering. "That was a rhetorical question. A response is not needed."

"Our party was just getting started," she grumbled. "But then Liam had to go rush off and almost die."

"That's my point. I'm not the only one with their mind in the gutter."

But there was more to it. She could see it in the way he moved and how tense he was over this discussion. "Spill it, Rowan," she pushed. "Why is getting Annabeth naked on your mind?"

It was his turn to snort. "A naked Annabeth is always on my mind."

"Okay, that's fair, but what else is going on in that head of yours?"

He didn't answer at first, his fingers tapping at the keys. But then he stopped, refusing to look at her when he spoke. "I think Annabeth is getting skittish about us. My family scared her yesterday. McIntyre women are a bit much—"

"A bit much?" Jamison echoed, scoffing. "I was at an event where your sister was in attendance. I'm not a pushover, but Caitlin McIntyre gives even me pause."

A genuine smile spread across Rowan's face. "Cait's not one to mess with."

"Yeah, the guy who grabbed her ass learned that the hard way."

"Did she break his hand?"

"I heard it was two fingers."

"That's my girl." Rowan's grin grew. "Killian and I taught her not to take shit from any man."

"I can assure you, no shit was being taken. And yeah, that little flex your Aunt Vivian pulled yesterday was over the top, but Annabeth can hold her own."

"My aunt didn't flex anything."

Jamison cocked her head to the side. "She sounded disappointed my dad was still alive."

"She wasn't disappointed," he said flatly. "Viv already knew Ben was alive. She was just being..."

"Insane? Over the top?" She sneered at him, knowing she was right. "Pick an adjective, Rowan."

Propping his hands on top of his head, he studied her for a second. "What do you know about it?"

"About what?"

"Charlie and Vivian."

The truth was not much. No one talked about it. Selah told her a little, but even he was tight-lipped over the entire thing. "They were married. He cheated. And in doing so, destroyed lives."

"That's a very Fairweather way of putting it."

"What the hell is that supposed to mean?"

"It means that's not the meat of it. That explanation leaves a shit ton of wiggle room for the blame to be shifted." His hands dropped to the keyboard, typing harder than before. "Your uncle—"

"Whom I've never met," she interrupted.

"—swept Vivian off her feet, making her believe he truly loved her. My mom and Bianca said it was like a damn fairytale."

Jamison stiffened at the word. *Fairytale*. People had said that her relationship with Liam had been like a fairytale and that she had ruined it. She knew the day would come when their time apart would have to be addressed in depth. They had touched on the subject, but she needed to sit and listen to what he had to say. Liam deserved that from her. He deserved to be able to tell her how much she hurt him.

Maybe Rowan was right, and a little private time was needed. Not only to connect, but also to talk and not have to whisper so the security cameras wouldn't hear. Liam wanted to marry her in less than a week, and she knew why he was rushing. They were both afraid. Her fear was simple. She was scared he might never truly forgive her, and marrying her so quickly was his way of reassuring her that he would.

His fears were just as simple. Liam was afraid she would change her mind. She could see it in his eyes. That undercurrent of unsureness that had never been there before. It broke her heart, shattering it into a thousand pieces whenever the slightest hint of doubt came over him. And while she wanted nothing more than to be his wife, she needed him to want this for the right reasons and not just to make her happy.

Rowan's voice cut through her thoughts. "A year after Viv married Charlie, he started an affair with a child. A child, Jamison. Rebecca Miller was seventeen. And not only did Charlie hide it, but your dad did, too. Ben is just as guilty, and he knows it."

Pressing her lips together, she stayed silent. They might not discuss Rebecca Miller often, but Jamison's morbid curiosity had gotten the better of her on more than one occasion. Countless documentaries were out there, all circulating with variations of the truth. They usually centered their reporting around Tobias, but a few covered Rebecca's background and what the media liked to call *The Women of Haven House.*

The tales spun by the public always made Haven House sound like a low-key brothel. It was one of the main reasons people flocked to Toby. They thought he never stood a chance and couldn't help but become a monster. They believed he only needed a little love to fix him.

"Ben and I made peace a long time ago," Rowan said. "He understands how his role in the whole thing hurt so many, and he understands it quite well. I can't begin to imagine his guilt over it."

"That's why you took the job at Fairweather Holdings?"

"Nah, I took it because you guys had shitty security, and I was pissed at my own family for my own reasons. None of which I'll be elaborating on," Rowan replied. "And I happen to get along with Samuel, which not many people can claim to do."

The whole being pissed at his family part was intriguing, but she didn't want to pry. Not with him, at least. She would corner Annabeth later to see what she knew, or maybe Liam. He would know. Her man knew everything.

"But my point is," Rowan continued, "I want time with Annabeth to remind her that even if my family is a little extreme, it shouldn't matter. Not when it comes to her."

"Why not when it comes to her?"

"Because eventually, she's going to be my family."

He said the statement with such conviction that goosebumps tickled down her arms, making Jamison grin. "What are you getting at, Rowan?"

"You're not an idiot," he sighed. "You know what I'm getting at."

Jamison giggled, unable to hold it in. "We should do a double wedding."

"Hell, no."

"Why?"

"Because my woman deserves her own day." Rowan's voice sharpened. "Annabeth gets the whole wedding experience and is not about to share it with another bride. I want her to have it all. The dress. The tiara. The attention. Everyone serving her like she's royalty."

Jamison could already see it. Annabeth would definitely want a tiara and all the extravagance of a formal wedding. There would need to be caterers and flowers—lots of flowers—in the right shade to compliment whatever theme she wanted. They might do it on the lawn or something unique. Annabeth adored the conservatory, so maybe they could make it work there.

"You do realize that just a few weeks ago, you were having sex with her through a camera. And now you want to drag her down the aisle wearing a tiara?"

Rowan relaxed at the thought. "I'm aware, but I don't care. If she wants a tiara, she gets a tiara."

"Who gets a tiara?"

Dressed in a dark blue T-shirt and jeans that had seen better days, Liam popped his head through the door. One sleeve of his shirt was rolled up, exposing a white bandage on his muscled bicep. His hair was askew like he'd run a hand through it a million times. The entire look had her doing a double take.

"Are you okay?"

He gave her a thin smile. "I'm good. What are you two talking about?"

Patting the seat next to her, Jamison crooked a finger. "Rowan's saying he wants to marry Annabeth in a tiara."

Liam smirked as he crossed the room and dropped beside her, tugging her legs across his lap like it was second nature. "Are we doing a double ceremony? Because if so, we need to order a tiara by, like, yesterday."

"He hasn't even asked her yet," Jamison whispered. "He's just planning the tiara logistics."

Liam kissed her quickly. "Annabeth would rock a tiara. So would you. Want one?"

"Nah, I wear an invisible one twenty-four-seven." She poked his chest. "And this whole conversation started because Rowan wants twenty minutes of alone time with Annabeth. Twenty. Not even a full half hour."

"Twenty minutes?" Liam raised a brow, all faux-serious. "We can make it happen, but you better return the favor. And no security camera footage, please. I don't need Ben seeing anything."

Rowan looked like he wanted to sink into the floor.

Jamison didn't care. She was back where she belonged. Her legs in Liam's lap. His hand on her knee. The storm of everything else fading into the background.

"Yeah," Rowan grumbled. "That was what I was getting at. And I'm done talking about this."

"I'm not," Liam said, his hand drifting higher. "When are we doing this? Better yet, when do Jamison and I get to collect our twenty minutes?"

"He originally wanted to take her on the boat," Jamison said. "But not, like, on the water, right?"

"We were going to have dinner under the stars," Rowan said. "But someone had to go and get himself shot."

"You have my sincerest apologies," Liam replied sarcastically. "I'll never let it happen again."

"You better not," Jamison mumbled.

Liam's hand reached her thigh and squeezed. Not enough to tickle, but just to comfort. He could handle her tears and her pain, yet when it came to her being scared, it drove him insane. Being the protector was ingrained in him.

"Have you talked to Simone?" Liam asked Rowan. "You know how this works. She and Abe need to be in the loop before you drop this on Annabeth."

Rowan waved a vague hand at the room. "I've been a bit busy."

"That's such an old-school take," Jamison huffed. "Annabeth can make her own decisions."

This time, Liam squeezed her thigh hard enough to make her squeak. "I talked to your dad."

"No, you didn't. That proposal was spontaneous."

He just smiled. "Wouldn't dream of contradicting you."

"So, what? You talked to him *before* proposing?"

"Something like that."

"Explain, William."

With Rowan occupied, he leaned in. "I talked to your dad. And Samuel. But first, I went to Simone. I'm not an idiot."

"They would've told me."

"For once, this family's inability to communicate like normal people worked to my advantage. No one told you. Not your dad, your brothers, Simone, the twins, and definitely not your sister. Evie was the most excited out of everyone." He bit down on his bottom lip to suppress a smile. "And Tammy—"

"Not my Tammy."

"Oh yeah. Tammy helped. Hillary did, too. The two of them got together and made a global spreadsheet of proposal locations."

Jamison stared. "And you picked Paris."

"I picked us."

She pressed her lips to his, cradling the back of his head with one hand. "I love you."

There it was. The hint of sadness in his eyes. It struck her like a knife because she knew exactly what was going on in his head. If she loved him, how could she have left? How could she have thrown them away and hidden what happened?

Pathetically enough, she didn't have an answer. She hated herself and what she had done. Liam was the better man—the best man—for the forgiveness he'd shown, but she wasn't so sure she deserved it.

"When you two are finished making out, I've got something you need to see," Rowan said, his war on the keyboard over. "Looks like we're barking up the right tree after all."

CHAPTER 17

Rowan

T he media room was packed again, everyone pressing in to see the screen. Rowan could toss the image up on the wall, but he suspected it might be too much for Simone. She sat to his left—Annabeth to his right—their hands intertwined across his lap.

"This picture of Bryan Carroll was taken at a casino in San Juan," Agent Anderson began. He had provided the Bureau's file on Carroll, including the photos. It wasn't exactly protocol, but Rowan hadn't questioned it, and Anderson hadn't offered an explanation. "The men around him are his guards. And the young woman behind him—"

"CeCe," Annabeth breathed. "That's CeCe."

The footage was grainy and dated, and the FBI had tried to clear it up, but they didn't have his tools. Slowly, the image came more into focus and showed Bryan Carroll in a tailored suit and, with a smug grin, leading a procession through the casino's glittering maze of slot machines. The crowd parted in their path, the photographs following the party as they exited the building. CeCe walked a few paces behind, no older than sixteen, her dress flashy, her smile bright.

"Since when do they allow kids into casinos?" Ben snapped.

"Carroll does what he wants," Will said flatly. "That photo was taken during the peak of his operations. No one would have dared stop him."

"Can you zoom in on the woman next to CeCe?" Bernie leaned forward, her hand resting on Simone's shoulder for balance. "She has to be Brandy Carroll."

A big, burly guard blocked the second young woman, and nothing but a slender arm could be seen in the front view. The next photo showed the group from behind as they were leaving, which was much of the same. All they could see was a sliver of the girl's dress and the sweep of her long hair.

"Can we get this in color?" Liam asked. He already had the print pinned to the board in the corner, where he and Jamison stood studying it. "The time stamp's missing. Is this before or after Charlie died? If CeCe's with Bryan here, where is Toby? College?"

"Makes sense," Will said, joining his son at the board. "Toby heads for college and leaves CeCe in the care of his girlfriend's family. Who also happens to be cartel royalty."

"Yeah, that tracks," Jamison sighed. "CeCe never caught a break, trading one psychopath for another. Poor thing went from Charlie to Toby to this guy."

"My brother wasn't a psychopath."

Silence fell, and everyone turned to Ben. He never defended Charlie Fairweather. Ever. As far as Rowan knew, the brothers weren't close growing up or as adults, learning to hate one another more and more until their lives exploded into devastation.

"Charlie was a narcissist. He used people," Ben continued. "But Toby got his twisted mind from our father, not Charlie."

"Charlie loved his children," Simone said, her eyes still on the photo. "He loved Rebecca. He loved Vivian in his own way." She let go of Annabeth's hand to reach for Ben's. "We might have been kidding ourselves, but both Benjamin and I believe that when they first went to that island, Charlie probably tried to give the kids a good life."

"You would be correct, Simone." Will nodded over his shoulder at Anderson. "Tell them."

Anderson pulled a file from his bag. "We went digging into Brandy Carroll's school records, and while no one currently at the school was there during the years she and the Fairweather children attended, they were able to put us in touch with a teacher who taught all three of them in a science class." Anderson handed the file to Liam. "The teacher wasn't much help, but did say how involved Charlie was with Toby and CeCe. He was at every school event and every award ceremony, never missing any of it until Toby reached the high school years."

Simone's eyes dropped from the screen to her lap, tears welling. "Thank you, Agent Anderson. I needed that."

"Was the teacher able to identify this Brandy person?" Taylor stood off to the side with her arms crossed and head tilted as she studied the photo of CeCe with everyone else. "Could she give you any idea of what she looks like?"

Rowan hadn't volunteered information to Taylor about their investigation, leaving that completely at Ben's discretion. But if asked, he wouldn't lie and say he cared for her having access to certain details, like the connection between Brandy Carroll to Toby.

And judging by the way Anderson was studying her, the agent shared Rowan's reservations.

"No, ma'am," Anderson said coolly. "Not as an adult. But we did get a school photo."

Rowan popped the photo onto the movie screen, and a little girl with reddish brown hair and a toothless smile stared back at them. She looked to be around six, with freckles dusting her chubby cheeks and nose.

Taylor sneered at the photo as her cell went off. "She's not very cute," she said as she checked her messages. "Ben, we've got the Fire Marshal meeting in five. They're buzzing to confirm you'll be there."

"Damn." Ben pushed to his feet. "Let's go."

Ben and Taylor left in a hurry. The Fire Marshal meeting wasn't going to bring good news. They had been willing to cover for them once, but the charade couldn't last forever. Ben was already planning to return to the office, even if it put him at risk, but he refused to bring back the staff. With so many Fairweather employees working remotely and Thanksgiving looming, they could use the holidays as an excuse to push a full staff recall until the New Year.

But there was no guarantee Sinclair would be captured by then.

Samuel would likely never return, not with Zanmi still being active. Rowan would even go so far as to say his friend would leave his job altogether if necessary. Taking things to the extreme was the Fairweather way, and Samuel wasn't playing any games with his family.

"Carter will be here in the next day or so?" Liam asked Agent Anderson, who nodded in confirmation. "If the plan to return to the Fairweather offices is solid, I'd like him placed with Samuel so I can bring Holden here."

"Yeah, no one's better at logistics than Holden," Izzy agreed, sitting across the table in front of her own laptop. "But can Carter handle Samuel and his... *um*... personality?"

"You mean his shitty attitude?" Abe's lips twisted so he wouldn't smile. "It's okay. You can say it."

"Carter can handle him," Liam replied. "That's why I had you swing me by their place this morning. I walked Samuel through the changeover."

"Then I'm glad I stayed behind," Jamison said, settling into a chair beside Annabeth. "That must've been fun."

Combing through the remaining information from his scan on Brandy Carroll and the fresh details Anderson and his team provided, Rowan tried not to wince. He'd already received a text from Samuel wanting a breakdown of Carter Anderson's credentials. Samuel trusted Liam completely, but he was the type of man who needed to see everything for himself.

"It was not," Liam assured her. "Got anything else for us on Carroll?"

"Not yet," Anderson said. "We're raiding every known residence, every family member's known residence, and we're already getting answers."

Rowan shifted Brandy Carroll's picture off-screen and brought up Parker Monroe's driver's license photo. With dark blonde hair, blue eyes, and a chiseled jaw, Parker looked like one of those frat boys Rowan hated in college. Women could always spot them a mile away and were careful never to leave their drinks unattended when those assholes were nearby.

"Mother is Abigail. Father is John. Mom is a housewife, while Dad owns a construction company down in Dania Beach."

"Dania Beach?" Annabeth squinted at the map presented. "Oh, I see. Fort Lauderdale."

"Parker started at NSU, then transferred to the University of Miami," Anderson added. "Same time CeCe was there."

"Oh, CeCe," Simone whispered. "What did you do, baby?"

Ben had left the door open when he departed, and his snappish orders carried in from across the hall. He didn't like what the Fire Marshal was telling him, and the conversation lulled as they listened to the head of Fairweather Holdings express his displeasure. Loudly.

Simone rose from her seat with a weary sigh. "I'm going to lie down. Y'all can fill me in later."

"Have you eaten today?" Abe grabbed his mother's arm when she passed him. "And coffee doesn't count."

"Not yet."

"Let me cook you something." Abe rolled behind her. "I make a killer omelet."

Simone didn't reply, and the two of them left the room with Annabeth shaking her head. "He's taking this cooking thing to the next level," she whispered. "I think I should go supervise."

Rowan nodded absently as she hurried out, trying to listen while Liam and Will continued to run down the specs on Parker. He'd already reviewed the information, but the two of them interpreting the details would be where they discovered what the rest of them couldn't see.

"Rowan, can you print the file on Parker with your notes?" Bernie asked him quietly so as not to interrupt. "I want to see everything in hard copy."

"Sure thing." He sent the information she wanted to the printer and handed it to her, trying to keep his attention on the conversation happening at the board.

"We've got location proximity, but it doesn't prove Parker's linked to Zanmi," Will said. "There is such a thing as a coincidence."

"Not likely." Liam tapped his tablet, swapping the screen to bring up Parker's school transcripts and juvenile records. The guy had quite a long history of being an abuser. "From even his elementary years, the school counselor's notes are telling, with several mentions of unrepentant aggressive behavior. Combine that with the constant arrests for destruction of property and assault during his teens, and we have a nice, pliable Zanmi member."

Anderson frowned. "I didn't give you those juvie records."

"We have a child in danger." Liam swiped the data and reports away. "We're not leaving any avenue unexplored and will obtain information any way we can."

Ready to take the fall for Parker's information being illegally obtained, Rowan joined the group. The feds didn't scare him. Not many organizations did.

But as he opened his mouth to speak, Anderson raised a hand to stop him. "Don't tell me. It's better that I don't know."

Deciding that was fair enough, Will began to drill Anderson with questions regarding the search for Madison. "What about Madison?"

"I've got nine members of CARD plus two dozen agents working in teams out there," Anderson replied. "I'm not holding anyone back."

Bernie let out a soft laugh. "Well, hello. Parker's got mommy issues."

"Don't we all?" Liam remarked sarcastically.

"Cute." Bernie used a pencil to circle something on the paper she was reading. "It seems Mr. Monroe did not get along with his mother and found her *oppressive*."

One of Dr. Cohen's eyebrows lifted. "Oppressive? That's a big word for a child."

"I'm sure the guidance counselor was leading him. But as you say, the devil doesn't just live in the details. He hides there, too." Bernie rose from her seat to bring them the information. "When he would speak to anyone with authority, a young Parker would go into great detail about how horrible his mother was and how he wished she could be like his grandmother, who lived in Maine."

Rowan hurried over to his computer, gaining every last detail he could on Parker's grandmother while Izzy organized the information. Holden might be great at logistics, but Izzy kept everything orderly so they could recall their research without having to hunt for it.

"The grandmother's dead. Left him the house and the land." Rowan scanned the expansive map. "Lots of land. Jesus. It's acres and acres of forest."

"Perfect hideout for a cult." Anderson pulled out his phone. "Rowan, send me everything you have. I'll redirect the team."

He did as Anderson asked, openly breaking into systems to gather as much information as possible. Anderson said nothing, at least not regarding his methods. The agent took it all in, shooting off messages to his colleagues.

"We need to assume that Parker is involved with Zanmi," Will said once Rowan's data stream on the grandmother slowed. "And that Madison might be the first of their Fairweather children."

Rowan agreed as much as he didn't want to, but for Madison's safety, there was really no other way they could operate. Claudia had been with Parker for years. If he was involved, she might have had some inclination.

"But did Claudia Fairweather know?" Anderson asked, voicing what they were all thinking. "That's the question."

"I don't think so," Jamison said. "She's been so kind since Madison was born. I can't see her being this way."

"Kind to whom?" Liam pointed at the photo of Samuel and Evie's house tacked to a board. "Evie. What if she was trying to get close to Evie?"

The suggestion struck Jamison, and she paled, laying a hand on her stomach. "I need to call my sister. If we're thinking Claudia might be involved... I need to be the one to tell her."

Jamison rushed out the door. Evie's pregnancy was nearing the finish line, and the last thing they needed was for her to become so upset that it sent her into labor early. The birth plan was already in place. Not for Evie, although Rowan was fairly certain Samuel had the entire thing planned down to the second, but for security. Every agent and family member understood what was required of them to make the delivery go smoothly.

"Do you think that's possible?" Rowan asked, debating on whether to call Samuel. It might be best to prepare him while Jamison talked to Evie. "That Claudia might be in with these people?"

Liam turned back to the board, his mouth set in a grim line. "Right now, anything is possible, but if she is, Madison's not in immediate danger."

"On the other side of that, if Claudia isn't involved." Will pulled a family photo of Claudia, Parker, and Madison from his file and tacked it on the board. "Then we're in even deeper shit than we thought."

His eyeballs were going to fall out of his skull.

So tired.

He was so fucking tired.

Liam looked just as bad. The two of them were bleary-eyed and hollowed out from working nine hours straight with no real break. The women had pushed food and coffee in their faces every so often, but at this point, they were running on fumes.

"I napped this afternoon, so you need to get one. Go to bed," Rowan groaned as he stretched. "You're a wounded baby, and sleep will do you good."

"Fuck you." Liam shuffled through folders, his frustration mounting. "Where's Sinclair's family file?"

There was no known connection between Sinclair and Carroll. No thread linking them to Parker, either. Three dangerous men from three separate paths.

And none of them connected to CeCe except for Carroll. Anderson was still chasing down Sinclair's military history. They had details from the bombings, but for nearly a year, there was nothing. No paper trail. No record.

"Nurse Jamison is here," Jamison announced, stepping into the media room with a shoebox in her arms. The house was quiet at almost midnight, and hearing her voice startled them both. "I read that we're supposed to clean your stitches twice a day."

She sat in the chair next to Liam, meticulously unpacking her supplies. "I think I've got everything."

Liam watched her intently, a ghost of a smile on his lips. "Going to patch me up?"

"*Clean* up the patch." She pushed his sleeve higher. "Your girlfriend, Holly, did great work."

Rowan rolled his neck, his body stiff. He needed a breather. Maybe a fresh hit of caffeine.

And Annabeth.

She'd disappeared over an hour ago. Hopefully sleeping in her own bed, safe and warm.

"Is Annabeth awake?" he asked.

Not looking away from Liam's stitches, Jamison snickered. "Ready for your twenty minutes?"

God, she was never going to let him live that conversation down. "I told you to forget about that."

"Mm-hmm." She didn't sound convinced. "Too bad because I told her about it, and she was very interested."

Rowan was standing before he realized it.

"She's in the kitchen," Jamison continued sweetly, "with a bottle of wine and the idea that you two are going to look at the stars."

He was on his feet before she finished speaking. "Seriously?"

Jamison smirked. "Everyone's asleep, and a fresh guard rotation just started. You couldn't ask for better timing."

He needed to stay focused. There were still leads to follow and threats to assess. But thinking about Annabeth naked and bouncing under him as he fucked the hell out of her had his cock hardening to the point where he couldn't see straight.

"I've got to set the security system to run a maintenance check."

Rowan fumbled with his laptop. Where the hell was the override code? It had to be changed every twelve hours. Annabeth. He remembered using her name as the anchor.

Annabeth and... numbers?

"Fuck. I forgot the passcode."

No—wait.

He had changed it before his nap.

The screen blinked, cursor waiting.

Annabeth McIntyre.

He would not smile. It was stupid and soft and borderline embarrassing, but for a split second, it made him feel human again. Like something inside him had clicked into place.

Gaining access, the security system accepted the code, and he adjusted the parameters to queue the run. "It'll start shortly and should run for twenty-two minutes."

"Twenty-*two* minutes?" Liam fought not to squirm when Jamison dabbed his stitches with a washcloth. "Pushing your stamina there."

Stamina had nothing to do with it. He just needed his woman. To breathe her in. To remind himself that the world wasn't all blood and chaos.

"I owe you." Rowan was already halfway across the room. "And we're just going to look at the stars."

"Next weekend," Liam said as Rowan passed. "I get to stargaze with my wife."

His wife.

Jamison stilled at the *my wife* comment, her eyes ticking upward to meet Liam's gaze. "Helluva honeymoon," she whispered.

"It's not what I had in mind, but it'll do for now." Liam kissed her forehead. "And I don't want to brag or anything, but Rowan's going to have to give me a whole thirty minutes to get the job done this time."

Rowan grinned as he hit the hallway. He'd give them their thirty. Hell, he'd lock down the entire property as a wedding gift so that they could have a moment of peace.

Tonight, though, that peace belonged to him and Annabeth.

CHAPTER 18

Rowan

He found her in the kitchen.

The entire lower level stood quiet, with only the light in the media room spilling into the hall. Walking as softly as he could, Rowan found Annabeth standing with her back to him by the fridge.

Sensing his presence, she raised a half-empty bottle of wine by the neck with one hand and two red solo cups in another. "I have our drinks ready."

Before she could turn around, he was on her. Rushing up from behind, his arms circled around her. "Mine," he whispered, roughly palming both breasts. "All fucking mine."

She gasped as his thumbs rolled over her nipples, a moan slipping past her lips when he bit gently at her neck. Her perfect ass rocked back against his hard-on, and he nearly lost his balance. Every part of him burned for her. The feel and taste of her again had his brain clicking off and into full static mode, knocking common sense out the door.

He thought about shoving her forward to fuck right on the countertop. It would take only a second. The pretty yellow dress she was wearing would be so easy to lift, allowing him to get them both off with a few quick pumps.

"Are the cameras doing the security thing?" she whispered.

"Not yet. We've got time to make it to the boat before it shuts down." He sucked her earlobe between his teeth, breath hot against her skin.

"But when it does… do you have any idea how hard I'm going to fuck you?"

She twisted in his hold, her mouth slamming against his lips. The kiss was nothing but tongue and desperation, the two of them nearly devouring each other. Her arms wound around his neck as she sought more, completely lost to this burn of insatiable—

"Shit. I'm sorry."

Ben's apology had Annabeth jumping a good three feet in the air.

Not out of shame, but because Ben had scared her.

And him.

Standing there with a raging hard-on and half of Annabeth's lip gloss painted across his face, Rowan stared at his boss, who looked just as uncomfortable over finding himself in this situation.

"Uh. Hey, Ben."

Ben tried to smile, but it came out looking weird since the man didn't smile much. Coupled with the fact that he was wearing a pair of pajama pants and a rumpled black T-shirt, he looked even more un-Ben-like, pushing the moment to a level ten on the embarrassment scale.

"I didn't mean to interrupt. I got an alert about the security system and wanted to make sure everything was okay."

"Yeah," Rowan mumbled. He would not cover his dick. He would not do it. He would maintain eye contact. "We're good."

Annabeth slinked in front of him as if she could hide the evidence of his arousal, and while it was a poorly executed move, he had to give his woman props for trying.

Ben ignored her, keeping his gaze pinned on the cabinets behind Rowan's head. "Then why did I get an alert?"

"The cameras are down for a few minutes since I'm running a security check. The guards outside know. Klausen knows. Anderson knows. Samuel knows. Liam and Izzy know. Holden knows."

Holy hell, he was rambling like a fucking moron.

"The system texts everyone, so everyone—"

"Knows. I get it," Ben cut him off, his left cheek muscle twitching. "Next time, keep me in the loop."

"Yes, sir."

The three of them stood there with nothing but the hum of the refrigerator packing the long, mortifying silence. A solid thirty seconds passed, and it was Annabeth who broke first.

"We were just going to look at the stars," she said, weakly waving the wine bottle. "I mean, the cameras are always on, and it just gets to be a lot. We needed… a moment."

"I think we all do." Liam hurried into the kitchen, his shirt still off and stitches on his upper arm glistening with Vaseline. "Jamison finished cleaning my wound, and we were going to have a glass of wine. Did you want to join us, Ben?"

"Should you really be drinking while the cameras are down?"

"It's not totally down," Rowan said quickly. "It's just the cameras recalibrating. The doors and windows are secure."

Ben didn't seem very impressed with the response. "But yet, you two were going to go outside and look at the stars?"

Jamison darted into the kitchen with her box of medical supplies in hand. She skidded to a stop behind Liam. "Daddy, what are you doing up?"

"I suppose I'm having wine with you four while the cameras recalibrate." Ben headed for the pantry. "There should be a decent bottle of red in here. Simone used to hide the good stuff behind those enormous bags of cat food she insists on buying."

Once Ben disappeared into the cavernous pantry, Liam leaned on the counter. Propping his good arm's elbow on the granite, he rested his chin on his hand and covered his mouth with his fingers. "I'm sorry, man."

Rowan glared at him. "You suck."

"What kind of wingman crap is this?" Annabeth hissed at Jamison. "You said it was all planned out."

"It was!" Jamison hissed back. "You were supposed to be naked on the boat by now."

"Well, we got distracted."

Liam straightened, motioning toward the back door. "Just go. We'll stall."

"Yeah, no go," Rowan whispered. "If I take her outside, Ben will flip the fuck out."

From the pantry, something crashed, and Ben let out a string of curses. "Why does she have to store this much cat food?"

Summoned by all the noise, Simone's bedroom door snapped open. "What's going on?"

Realizing their perfectly planned idea was well and truly ruined, Liam's shoulders drooped. "We're running a security camera check, and while we wait for the cameras to calibrate, we thought we would have a glass of wine. Ben woke and wanted to join us, but I think the cat food might have attacked him."

Never missing a damn thing and able to smell a lie—even a partial one—Simone took them all in. One. At. A. Time. Rowan would never get used to her. Five, ten, twenty years from now, she would continue to unnerve him in a way no one else could.

"Why aren't you two in bed?" Simone asked, zeroing in on Annabeth and Jamison. "And Annabeth, why are you in that dress? It's almost one in the morning."

"I was cleaning Liam's wound," Jamison rushed out. "And Annabeth was taking Rowan outside for fresh air."

The sounds of dry cat food spilling across the floor broke the tension building, and they all moved out of the way when a dozen or so felines slinked from out of nowhere to see what Ben was doing.

"Damn it, Simone," Ben shouted from the pantry. "Where the hell are you hiding the good red these days?"

"Third shelf," she replied, not taking her sharp gaze off the four of them.

"No, the stuff there is crap," Ben snapped. "I'm looking for the wine you make me ship in by the case from France."

Ignoring Ben for a moment, Simone pointed at Liam. "You will take care of yourself. If that wound gets infected, I will make you regret it."

"Yes, ma'am." Liam was a smart man and knew not to argue. "It won't happen again."

"See that it doesn't." Simone's finger swung in Rowan's direction. "And you. Get some fresh air with Annabeth. Do not wander far and keep a tight hold on her."

"Won't Ben freak if we leave the house?" Rowan whispered as they slipped toward the door. "He was already pissed about the recalibration."

"I'll handle Benjamin."

And just like that, Annabeth yanked him into the cool night air, and they grinned at each other. All the stress and worry melted, giving them a single silent minute of peace.

"Is it off yet?" Annabeth whispered, her voice low so the security detail scattered across the rear patio wouldn't overhear.

Rowan shook his head. "We've got a few minutes. I don't want to say we should run, but we should definitely walk fast if we want to make the most of it."

"Then let's go." She grabbed his hand and tugged him off the patio, her short legs hustling with determined urgency. "We're not going to the boat."

"No?" He let her lead, amused as hell. "Where are we going, then?"

"Guest cottage."

His grin spread like wildfire. "Ms. Howard, are you saying you would like to seduce me in private?"

"Hell yeah, I do."

"I am shocked."

She threw a wicked smile over her shoulder. "I'm not wearing any underwear. I don't have a bra on. I want to be naked and riding you in less than three seconds after the camera feed is cut."

Rowan's steps faltered, but he regained his footing easily. "Anything else?"

"I'm going to need two orgasms." The smirk disappeared, her demands turning serious. "At a minimum."

"I've always been an overachiever."

"Speaking of which, this dress has pockets, and I have a handful of condoms stuffed into each. We're not stopping until the cameras come back on."

They were passing the large oak in the center of the yard, far enough away that the security team could no longer notice what he was doing. Cameras were still tracking their movement, so he kept his voice low. "We'll use as many as we can, but I want you riding my face before you ride my cock, understand?"

"No promises."

They made it to the cottages, hurrying up the porch of the one set aside for guests. The seconds on his phone counted down. "Key?"

She extracted a key from her pocket and a condom, handing the latter to him. "Get it on."

Unlocking the door, she yanked him inside right as his phone buzzed with an alert that all cameras were off. The blue lights on the internal cottage cameras switched to red right as the door shut behind them, and Rowan swiped the lock into position.

"Bedroom," he said, voice ragged.

Annabeth slipped off her shoes and walked backward away from him. In one swoop, she had her dress over her head and on the floor, her naked form illuminated by the moonlight streaming through the windows facing the bayou.

He followed her down the hall, his own shirt lost and his pants undone. In all his life, he had never been this hard. He had never wanted a woman like he did Annabeth. When they reached the main bedroom doorway, he tore open the condom with his teeth and slid it on.

"My tongue first." Moving past her, he stretched out on the bed and tapped the wood headboard above him. "You're going to want to hold on."

She didn't hesitate. Crawling up his body, she kissed and licked her way to his mouth before climbing higher, positioning her knees on either side of his head.

When she lowered onto his tongue, she let out a low, shuddering moan.

Giving her ass a sharp smack, he gripped her hips to coax her into a slow grind. Tongue deep and mouth relentless, he used his nose to nuzzle her clit with each pass. Her rhythm built gradually until she was frantically riding his face, her moans echoing off the cottage walls.

It only took a few more strokes before an orgasm tore through her, and groans turned to begging. Dragging her down by the hips, he adjusted her above his cock. She was wet and ready, her hands firmly gripping the headboard as she lowered herself onto him. Inch by inch, she took him inside until she was fully seated with a broken gasp.

"Don't let go of that headboard."

And that was the only warning she was going to get. Mercilessly. Brutally. He fucked, the heavy pounding of his cock robbing him of all thoughts. There were screams and moans, some his and some hers. Like the good girl that she was, Annabeth held on to the headboard for dear life, taking everything he gave while whimpering for more.

"Is this what you wanted?" he growled, no longer recognizing his own voice. Releasing the hold on her hips, he looped his arms around her back to hold her suspended above him as his cock slammed in and out. "Is this how my woman wants to be fucked?"

"Y-yes," she sobbed. "Yes—*God*—yes."

Another orgasm hit, and her guttural cries were the sound his entire body craved. Forever. He would want this forever. The feel of her holding him so tight, the pulse of her pleasure working his length. He would crave this every day for the rest of eternity.

"You're so fucking beautiful." He bounced her harder, grinning when her eyes rolled back. "You take me so good."

She cried out her agreement, grinding on his dick as if she were riding for her life. The trembling of her small frame intensified, and she let go of the headboard, wrapping her arms around his head when he began to suck and lavish her breasts with his tongue.

Not wanting her orgasm to end, he flipped them around and laid her on her back. "My turn."

Securing one hand on the headboard and another on her chest, Rowan thrust into her without control. His girl moved with him, the slap of their bodies driving him to fuck faster when her nails scraped his shoulders, and her punctuated cries ripped through the room.

When her next orgasm hit, she clamped down so tight he saw stars. He arched higher, positioning himself so he could watch her tight body pulse around his cock.

"Fuck, Annabeth. Look at you." He couldn't tear his eyes from the sight. Never. Not in a million years would he ever stop this. "Look at my good girl."

Ruined.

Annabeth Howard, with her wicked smile and terrifying brilliance, had ruined him in the most perfect way, and he would never recover.

"I love you," he choked out, spine bowing as his orgasm hit. "I love you."

Goosebumps covered him, and he collapsed, yet still unable to stop rocking into her until every last drop filled the condom. Latching onto her throat, he dragged her lips to his, softening her cries with his kiss.

"How much time do we have?" she whispered when they came up for air. "I want that again."

A quick check of his watch had him grinning. "That was only six minutes. We've got time."

He managed to have her once more, thinking he could last a little longer, but nope. Not even close to possible. They were deep in the third act when the countdown buzzed again.

"No!" she cried beneath him, her hips rocking as he pounded into her with desperate force. "Don't stop. Please—"

"I have to," he groaned, not slowing in the slightest and even increasing the strength of his thrusting. "But we're going to figure out how to finish. I can't—*fuck*—I can't live without this."

Another buzz. Two minutes left.

Bracing his hands under her thighs, he spread her wide. "Come for me. One more time."

She was already there, crying out as her orgasm hit. It was all he needed, and he followed her in a surge of heat, his groans of pleasure drowning out the second warning ping.

"One minute."

He pulled out in a rush, lightheaded and stumbling into the bathroom like a drunk man. "Get your clothes on," he shouted as he worked the condom off and into the wastebasket. "The cameras are about to go live, and everyone will get an eyeful if we're not dressed."

Falling off the bed when she struggled to rise, Annabeth's footsteps thundered down the hall as she searched for her dress in the dark. He came busting out of the bathroom after her, snagging his pants and shirt off the floor.

The high-pitched beeping from his phone reached a dizzying speed until it silenced right as he zipped his pants close. They stood frozen in the hallway, breathing hard and laughing at each other's disheveled state.

"Is it back on?" she panted.

Rowan's heart continued to hammer in his chest, and he glanced up at the single camera above Annabeth's head. The light clicked to blue. "We're live."

The shrill calibration tone echoed through the cottage, demanding a manual passcode reset. He hadn't realized she'd grabbed the phone in their hurry to get dressed.

He reached to take the phone. "I need to put in my password."

"I've got it."

Rowan winced. She knew the old password. "Let me do it."

Typing rapidly, she waved him off. "I said, I've got it."

The phone let out a rumbling buzz, the security lights immediately flashing at the incorrect entry. "Annabeth, give me the phone."

"Did you change the password?" She ignored him, walking into the living room. "Or maybe I typed it in wrong."

"I changed it."

"To what?"

"Give me the phone."

Her head snapped up, and she stared at him as if he were insane. "What's the new password?"

Running a hand through his hair, he gave up. "Annabeth."

"Yeah, Annabeth1992, right?"

"McIntyre."

She blinked at him, her big brown eyes going round. "What?"

"Annabeth space McIntyre is the password."

Already ruined by her, the woman he loved broke him wholly with her next words. "Oh, Rowan. No."

That was all it took.

The world inside him crashed down in a raging ball of fire. He snatched the phone from her and punched in the code, ending the calibration and plunging the house into silence.

"Rowan—"

He turned to the front door, giving her his back. "Let's get back to the house."

"Rowan, we need to talk."

"There's nothing to talk about."

Fuck. He sounded like a goddamn child. They did need to talk, but all eyes were on them again, and he didn't want every single person to witness his soul being stripped into nothing. That absolute clear denial ringing in her words told him she meant it.

No.

Her answer to forever was *no*.

"Look at me," she whispered.

This was his own fault. This was always going to be the way they ended. He thought he could fight it. He *had* been fighting it. Every second of every day, he had thought he could make her see that he was worth it. That he was worth the fear and the uncertainty that plagued her, but he was wrong. So very fucking wrong.

Turning around, he gave her a half-hearted smile and tried to make a joke. "I'm sorry I was rough," he said, his tone quieter now. "Want me to carry you?"

She stepped in close, chin lifted. "I love you. I will love you for the rest of my life."

The truth was there again, and while he should have been swooping her up in his arms to kiss, he just couldn't. He didn't have it in him. "But," he replied gruffly, tired of the fight. "There's always a *but*."

"But I'm never going to marry you, Rowan. You should know this. I would never be so selfish."

"How the fuck is marrying me selfish?"

"Tying you to me legally?" Her expression grew dark, and she swung away from him to sit in one of the recliners. "That's selfish. Loving you and being with you is one thing. But I'd always want you to have an out."

"Watch what you say next." He moved before he could stop himself, caging her in with his hands on the arms of the chair. "If you're about to tell me that you won't marry me because you think I'll *need* a way out—then this is over."

The stubborn glare in her gaze slipped, and while it was cruel of him, he relished the fear replacing it. "You don't mean that."

"The hell I don't," he snarled, keeping his voice low. "I am sick of the buts. Sick of thinking we're getting somewhere, only to end up in another goddamn loop."

"You've never wanted marriage. Or did you forget that I was your best friend before we became this? That I was the one you spent countless hours talking to about life and how marriage and kids were never something you would want."

"We didn't become this. We've always been *this*." He held her by the chin. "I've never wanted another woman the way I want you. I have never—in my whole fucking life—been in love. Never once. Not until Annabeth Howard strutted out the back door of Haven House and straight into my worthless fucking heart. So watch what the hell you say about giving me a way out. There is no fucking way out, not for me."

She jerked free of his hold, but he wasn't done. Not by a long shot.

"And to listen to you continue to insult me by thinking I would ever want to be anywhere except at your side as your *husband* is taking it too far." He pushed off the recliner to loom over her. "What's worse is I haven't even asked you. I haven't even started the conversation, yet you've already decided."

Christ. He was shouting and suspected that this entire conversation was playing out in the media room. The elevated noise would have the main camera monitor focusing on them, and if anyone were paying attention, they were now getting a show.

But he no longer cared.

"I love you, Annabeth. I wanted a life with you. A long, happy fucking life as your husband. One. Day. Not tomorrow, but one day. Kids. No kids. Whatever. As long as you and me were doing the whole 'til death do us part thing, I would have been happy."

Having said what he wanted, Rowan headed for the front door, but Annabeth shot out of the chair and was across the room to block his way. "Don't you dare speak in past tense to me!" she shouted. "*Wanted* a life? *Would have been* happy? Just because I said no to a piece of paper doesn't mean you get to stop loving me, you stubborn jackass!"

Jackass? Did she really just call him a stubborn jackass?

Catching her by surprise, he pressed her back against the wall. The entryway to the cottage was small, and when he placed a hand on either side of her head, he felt as if he were taking up every inch of space.

"I could never stop loving you," he breathed, the exhaustion and pain mingling together to where his raw emotions could no longer remain bottled up. "Where you go, I go. If you stay, I stay. That will never change. You're the other half of me, Annabeth."

Snatching her hand, he rested it against the thundering heart in his chest. "I'm not going to lie and say that it doesn't hurt that you won't even consider a life with me as your husband. It does hurt."

"Row—"

"No, fuck that. It feels like I'm bleeding out." He pushed off the wall and wrenched open the cottage door to get some fresh air. "I haven't even asked, and you're already saying no. I haven't even begged—because I would do exactly that—to make you mine."

He stood in the cottage doorway, his chest heaving while he stared out over the lawn and directly at Haven House. He would spend his life here. In this prison, he would dedicate every day to her and be perfectly happy doing so.

Yet it wasn't enough.

"Can I speak now?"

Ah, but she was pissed. Good. Let her be pissed. Let her be angry and hurt and frustrated. Then, he wouldn't be the only one in misery.

The corner of his mouth flicked upward. "Go for it."

She shoved past to stand on the porch directly in front of him. "You will stop this right now. I love you. You love me." Her finger jabbed at his chest like a weapon. "We're going to have a good life. I'll even let you get that damn dog you won't shut up about."

Staring down at her, it took every ounce of power he possessed to remain steady when her tears started. Not many things in his life were absolute. Frankly, thinking in absolutes gained you nothing. It made you lose perspective.

But his love for Annabeth was an absolute truth. There was no middle ground. There was no stopping it. It allowed him to see things that others couldn't. Like now, and how the terror over what they were discussing was eating away at her. How there was guilt for wanting exactly what he was promising but thinking she didn't deserve it.

"You have too much damn faith in me," she whispered, her bottom lip trembling. "I don't want to slip off into my mind again. If I spiral... I can't doom you to that fate."

And just like that, it hit him. He was never going to change her mind. Not today. Not tomorrow. Maybe not ever. To be with her, he had to accept that Annabeth wasn't afraid of becoming his wife. She was afraid of hurting him, thinking that if she fell apart again, she would take him down with her.

But the thing of it was, he would gladly fall if it meant falling through life with her.

"Okay."

She blinked. "Okay?"

He stepped forward and cupped her face, his thumb swiping away the tear that finally spilled over. "If you don't want to marry me someday, I'll get over it and accept your choice."

Confused by the shift in his tone, she glanced around as if expecting another version of him to manifest and say something else. "You can?"

"I can." Leaning down, he brushed his lips across hers. "But that doesn't mean I won't ask. When I'm ready, of course."

She let out a sharp huff, her lips twitching. "I said I'd say no."

"Say no. It's fine." He kissed her deeply and held her close as a light, misting rain began to fall. "I'm still going to ask. All the time, in fact. I'm going to ask and ask and ask."

"I'll still say no and no and no."

"Will you? Okay, that's fine. I can keep asking until either you give in, or I accept defeat."

She snuggled against his chest. "It's not a defeat. I love you, and we have something…"

"Special," he finished for her. "Put your big girl panties on and say it, Annabeth. We have something special."

"First of all," she mumbled into his shirt, "I'm not wearing panties."

He smirked, squeezing her bare ass. "And I thank you for that."

"Second… we *do* have something special. But—"

He growled playfully. "There you are with your buts again. Just because you have a nice butt doesn't mean you get to always throw the word at me."

"Very funny." She traced a finger over his bicep tattoo. "Lots of people have something special, and they never get married. They live together happily and don't feel the need to define their love by what's considered normal. A marriage is only a piece of paper with two signatures."

"If it's only a piece of paper, then sign and be done with it."

"You're missing the point."

"No, I'm not." He tipped his head back so she could see his smug expression. "I'm being thickheaded on purpose, and this is what you'll have to live with."

She made a face. "Wonderful."

Walking right into his trap, he kissed her once more. "You've had your buts, *but* now I have mine. I'm okay with never signing a piece of paper… *but* only if you give me something in return."

"And what's that?"

"Your vows."

"Come again?"

"I want you, one day, to stand under that old Marriage Oak and vow that you'll spend your life loving me, for better or worse, and listen to me do the same. I want you to wear my ring, and I want to wear yours. I want us to be a family with our house full of cats and the dog you'll eventually let me get."

She sniffled and kept her face buried in his black T-shirt. "That isn't fair."

"I'm not here to play fair, and, by your request, I'm not asking for a piece of paper. I'm only asking for you." He shrugged, attempting to keep things light. "And maybe, when it's just you and me in the quiet of our life, you'll let me call you my wife."

Lifting her head, she aimed her big brown eyes at him. Annabeth's beauty held him in amazement every day, but at this moment, it nearly tore him in half. He had to have her promise of forever, or else he might go insane.

"If you want to do all that, me being afraid of a piece of paper seems pretty silly."

He nodded as he pretended to think it over. "It does, but we're not about to downplay your fears."

With her arms wrapped tightly around his waist, she squeezed, catching him off guard. "Well, I guess I'll have to think about it."

"You do that," he replied, slightly winded. "But remember, I haven't asked you anything yet, so you still have time to change your mind."

Chapter 19

Josie

2004

"Can you see him?"

Josie stood to the side of the open window in their bedroom, the sheer curtains billowing around her in the coastal breeze. "He's fine."

From her place on the bed, Miranda could only see a strip of the overcast North Carolina sky, and Josie wished they could figure out a way to get her into a more upright position, but nothing had worked.

"The waves might be too rough," Miranda replied. "It looks stormy out there."

"You worry too much."

"It's my job."

Still hidden behind the curtain, Josie tracked the slow return of their son. "He's on his way back, but it might take a minute. That pack of girls who've been eyeing him finally worked up the nerve to say hello."

"Does he look interested?"

"He's a teenage boy." Josie chuckled as Samuel balanced the surfboard with one arm, trying to look cool in front of the girls. "Of course, he's interested."

Chuckling, Miranda's thin fingers absently smoothed the thick pile of blankets piled on top of her. She'd been complaining of the cold lately, and when she asked to have some fresh air, Josie had wanted to make sure her wife was warm.

Her wife.

Never in a hundred years—never in a thousand—did Josie think she ever would have the chance to stand on a mountaintop and claim Miranda as her own. It wasn't legal, but it didn't matter. The vows were made, and the pact eternally sealed. With their boy at their side, she and Miranda had seized their chance at happiness.

Back in March, the doctors had told them to hurry. They gave their *I'm sorrys* and *make-the-most-of*-it platitudes, but the message was clear. None of it would halt the inevitable from coming. Miranda's body wouldn't hold for one last battle, and if there was something she wanted to do, it needed to happen before April ended.

And so they lived.

Pulling Samuel from school, they lived. Every second, every day, with a kind of reckless joy. Small adventures stitched together into something beautiful—a winding trail hike through the mountains, a quick trip to New York so Miranda could show her son the sights of her childhood. They packed every moment they could into those first fragile weeks after the news.

But the grand finale had been so stunningly spectacular that nothing else could compare. Josie would owe Benjamin Fairweather until the end of time. And not just for that day, but for everything. He had made their lives possible. He had given them their boy. He had made them financially secure. He had accepted what she and Miranda were to each other long before anyone else dared.

And then, he threw them a wedding.

A real, honest-to-God wedding. For Samuel, more than anyone. He would need these moments to hold on to once Miranda was gone.

Samuel had been so awkward that day. He tried hard to get everything right, even though a recent growth spurt meant his suit no longer fit. His ankles showed, and his sleeves rode comically up his forearms. He hadn't cared, too focused on making sure things went smoothly for his mom.

With his father's help, of course. Ben arranged the whole thing. A female officiant so that they would feel comfortable. Miranda's favorite flowers in the bouquets they carried. A helicopter—Samuel's favorite part—to take them to the mid-point before they transferred to an off-road vehicle that would bring them to the mountaintop where they would say their vows.

Just as Miranda wanted.

Ben had given them a place to speak openly of their love, leaving only God and the vast surrounding peaks to bear witness.

There had been just a single hitch in their plans. The weather. A cold front swept in the night before, and their extravagant wedding gowns weren't made for wind chill. But wrapped in flannel blankets, they had their ceremony anyway, shivering and smiling.

Showing up at the last minute, as only a true Fairweather would, Ben came swooping in with a professional photographer in tow. Miranda had been nervous at first, already unsettled by having an officiant present, but Josie had thanked him for thinking ahead. Deep down, she knew Ben had done it for Samuel. Their boy would need evidence of the day because time was the cruelest of thieves. It made quick work of stealing precious memories, erasing them from the mind in the most merciless of ways.

After that impossibly perfect day was over, Josie took them to the North Carolina coast. Parkland Grounds, while a huge part of their lives, was theirs no longer. They said goodbye to the manor home, trading it for the small beach house she and Miranda loved so much.

A cozy, quiet place to say goodbye.

In the beginning, they continued to have fun, albeit on a smaller scale. The summer days were spent doing everything and nothing at all. Movie marathons and lazy afternoons ruled. A board game here. A puzzle there. But their favorite pastime, without question, was people-watching from the back deck.

Well, Samuel was girl-watching, but close enough.

"I wonder what kind of woman he'll end up with," Miranda had mused one evening as they sat cuddled under a blanket, watching Samuel surfing his final wave. "Or *how many women* if he turns out to be anything like his father."

Josie nudged her shoulder. "Remember that Christmas LJ said she thought Evie and Samuel would end up together someday? That was hilarious."

Miranda had smiled at the memory, but it faltered a beat later. "That was our last good Christmas. We were all so hopeful."

"Life changes in an instant." Josie had nothing more to say, no other words to give. They'd hashed it out a thousand times, talking through the pain so that they could live their days and not waste them. "But here we are, still talking about LJ and her crazy ideas. We'll always love and remember her."

"Yeah, we will." Miranda wiped away a tear just as she burst into laughter when a wave took Samuel down hard. "He needs someone like her. Not Evie exactly, but someone who won't back down. Someone just as stubborn as he is."

She wasn't wrong. Samuel was at that messy midpoint of adolescence—bullheaded and sensitive in equal measure. He had time for fun now, time to surf and flirt and stumble through these last bits of childhood, but there would come a day when he'd need someone to help him find his footing.

They would have to help guide him.

No.

Not *they*.

There would be no more *they*.

This was the end.

Their time was up.

It would only be her from now on. She would have to do it alone, without Miranda's calming nature to keep them steady.

Ben would be there. That was a given. Ben was always there for his son, but it wasn't the same. Samuel wanted nothing more than to impress his father, and never truly permitted his vulnerability to show.

"Josie?"

"He stopped to talk to the girls." Leaning against the balcony door frame, Josie smiled at Samuel's attempts to act smooth and flirt. "Oh, goodness. He's nervous. I can see that rash on his neck blooming from here."

Miranda's laughter floated through the air, warm and raspy. Josie stepped away from the door and returned to the bed, reaching for her hand.

"Go ahead and rest a little. He'll be inside soon," Josie told her as Miranda's eyes drifted closed. "Then I'll make him lunch."

Samuel was the only one eating these days. Josie's stomach stayed tied in knots, and Miranda... well, eating was something only the living did, or so the hospice nurse said. The dying, if they chose to partake, only did so to make those around them feel more comfortable.

There was a crash on the first floor. Samuel had yet to learn how to do things gently and always managed to knock a few things over whenever he slammed the back door.

"Mom!"

His size fourteen feet thundered on the stairs. He never liked leaving Miranda for long, only surfing when she forced him to take a break.

"I caught a barrel wave!" Soaked and still in his wetsuit, Samuel skidded to a halt at their bedroom entrance. "And I didn't wipe out!"

Miranda's eyes stayed closed, her voice thin as she smiled. "That's so wonderful."

The overcast skies shifted, allowing a hint of sun to peek through, slanting across the room in warm bands of gold. It illuminated the pieces of their life scattered about. All the things Miranda had wanted near her as she prepared to depart. Photos and trinkets, the little nothings that would soon be all that was left.

A gull cried from somewhere nearby, mixing with the waves greeting the shore and Miranda's ragged breathing.

"Mom?" Samuel crossed the room to his usual chair on the far side of the bed. He would spend hours in it reading to Miranda or just talking to her about nothing at all. "Did you hear me?"

"I did." The shallow rise and fall of his mother's chest stalled momentarily, and Miranda opened her eyes to look at her son. "I love you."

Those three little words were uttered every day in this house. But today, it was different. Today, the *I love you* falling from Miranda's lips wasn't a normal one. It wasn't the *I love you* mothers said to their children in the hurried rush of life. It wasn't the kind that was uttered with pride when they'd achieved a goal, or the kind that was whispered when trying to console their broken hearts.

This time—this *I love you*—was the final one.

The one reserved for the end. The goodbye. The promise to always watch over him.

Samuel's face drained of color, and he clutched his mother's hand, recognizing the power behind the words. "I love you, too."

"Look after your father and Josie," Miranda whispered, her voice barely audible. "Look after them all, my darling boy. They're yours now."

Samuel nodded through his tears. "I will."

For an aching fraction of a second, Josie thought Miranda was gone, but then—as she always did—Miranda surprised her.

"I love you, Josie."

Josie took her wife's other hand and squeezed. "I'll love you forever, Miranda."

"I don't need to tell you to take care of Samuel. I know you will." Miranda's head sank into the pillow, her eyes drifting closed once more. "He's yours, as much as he's mine and Ben's."

"Samuel's stuck with me." A sob threatened to tear right out of her, but Josie covered it. "Right, boy?"

"I'll take care of them, Mama." Samuel leaned down, pressing his face to his mother's shoulder, his arm draped protectively over her. "Always."

The room went still.

And they listened.

To the waves. To the gulls crying in the air. To the precious sounds of Miranda's final breaths.

"Josie?"

Josie startled and released a tearful laugh. Her girl really was always full of surprises. "Yes?"

"Don't be sad," Miranda exhaled, her muscles relaxing. "My friends are here, and I'm not afraid anymore."

It might have been silly, but Josie had felt them this whole time. Their past. Their friends. They had been there, waiting to take Miranda. She wasn't one to believe in such things, but she would make an exception this time. Laura Jean and Devon weren't the type to let their friend down. She knew they would walk with Miranda as she journeyed into the unknown.

"Okay."

That was all she could say. Her tears ate away at the words she wanted to speak, drowning them out while she counted Miranda's breaths. One. Two. Three.

And then...

Nothing.

Samuel's shoulders shook violently as he cried. Burying his face in his mother's neck, he screamed, his heart shattering on what should have been a simple September morning.

Josie gathered her in from the other side, wrapping her arms around her wife's body and her son's grief.

The anger would come later—she could already feel it rising—but now wasn't the time. Now was for sorrow. For the weight of absence. For falling into the void Miranda left behind.

But she couldn't let Samuel drown in it.

After one minute more, just one, Josie pulled back and ran her fingers through Samuel's hair. "Do you want to call your dad, or do you want me to?"

He lifted his head, red eyes staring at her. "I'll do it."

Swallowing hard, he released Miranda and came to where Josie sat next to the nightstand that held the house phone.

"Should I call his office or his cell?"

Normally, Josie would've said his cell. But not today. Today, she wanted the call to route through Hillary first. She would soften the blow before it hit Ben.

"The office."

Samuel dialed and put the call on speaker. Hillary answered on the first ring.

"Mr. Fairweather's office."

"Can I talk to my dad?"

Samuel sounded so small. Too small. Josie had to turn away so he wouldn't see her tears return.

Hillary didn't ask who was calling or what was wrong. She didn't need to. Everyone knew they'd been playing the waiting game. "Oh, sweetheart. I'm so sorry. Let me get him."

It took less than a minute. Ben had fought hard against leaving North Carolina earlier in the week. He hadn't wanted Josie and Samuel to go through this alone. But even from afar, he was there when they needed him.

"Samuel?"

Samuel didn't speak. He just simply broke all over again when he heard his father's voice.

"Samuel, listen to me," Ben said, clearly trying to keep it together but failing. "I want you to take care of Josie. I'll be there in less than two hours."

Samuel nodded as if Ben could see and hung up. Josie pulled him immediately into her arms, swaying back and forth with her boy until he calmed again.

"What do we do now?" Samuel asked.

"We call the hospice nurse."

Picking up the phone, Josie dialed the number. Nurse Kelly had been so helpful in answering all her questions and taking wonderful care of them. "I'm close," Kelly said after giving her condolences. "I can be there in a few minutes. We'll take care of everything when I arrive."

Josie hung up, reality setting in. It was time to begin the business of death. There would be paperwork to fill out and procedures to follow. All of it designed to box up a life into files and forms. It was beginning already.

The process of packing Miranda away.

"Samuel, can you go downstairs and let Nurse Kelly in? She said she's close."

"Okay."

His footsteps, once loud and unsteady, were quiet now as he left.

Josie took a moment to look down at Miranda's beautiful face, half expecting her to stir and say her name again.

But she didn't.

It was over.

Their story had well and truly ended.

Some part of Josie had believed it wouldn't happen. That Miranda would somehow keep going just to spite the odds. But the silence in the room said otherwise.

Her hands shaking, Josie picked up the phone and dialed a number she hadn't used in what felt like forever. Ben would understand this pain, and she could talk to him about it eventually, but for now, she needed someone else. Someone who knew what it meant to live with this quiet rage of unfairness.

The line picked up.

"Hello?"

God, it really had been too long.

Miranda had wanted to go back one last time. They had planned to. But life—and dying—had other plans. They'd said goodbye to that chapter and to the people who filled it.

"SiSi? It's Jos."

Her voice broke, and she cleared her throat, but it was useless. Simone was already crying, her screams of losing yet another friend carrying through the phone.

"Miranda's gone."

Chapter 20

Jamison

"I'm not taking the melatonin gummies, so why does this keep happening every time I close my eyes?"

"Beats the hell out of me," Miranda replied, walking up the front path. "Haven House has always held a little magic, but I think it has more to do with—"

"My mother."

"As much as I'd love to feed that romantic notion, my darling, I cannot," Miranda said with a hint of regret in her tone. "It's the Fairweathers. It's the land. It's the curse. The amalgamation of those three damns us all."

Jamison tried not to let her disappointment show. "Oh."

"I'm sorry, but it's true." Miranda paused to examine Ty's rainbow garden. "You forget that I lived at Parkland Grounds. It was built with the blood of others and, much like Haven House, has a few things that go bump in the night."

It was hard to believe this woman had been so sick at the end of her life. Here, Miranda looked radiant. Healthy. Dressed in fitted trousers and a rather chic hunter green jacket, she tossed her long brown hair over her shoulders.

"In most of the pictures I've seen, your hair was short," Jamison said, feeling the odd need to make small talk. "But I like it long."

Miranda beamed. "Josie likes it long, too."

Ah, there was some common ground. Jamison grinned. "Josie is awesome. She puts Samuel in his place."

"Someone has to." Miranda laughed. "My son isn't like anyone else. I'm thankful for Josie. And I'm thankful for your sister."

Jamison figured if she was going to talk to imaginary Miranda, she might as well ask the hard questions. "You don't think it's weird?"

"Samuel and Evie?" Miranda quirked an eyebrow. "God, no. Can't you see how their souls are bound together? Destiny is a fickle creature, but she always strikes true."

It wasn't the answer she expected, and Jamison glanced at the side yard, searching for her mother.

"She's not here," Miranda said, her face softening. "Laura Jean and CeCe are busy preparing."

"Preparing for what?"

"The end."

Jamison swallowed, not caring for the way Miranda's words felt like a punch to the gut. "The end of what?"

Hands in her pockets, Miranda strolled slowly down the path. "I was so young when I first came to Haven House. I thought I knew everything about life back then. I thought I was strong. Hell, I knew I was strong after going up against your grandmother and not backing down from the old dragon."

She stopped to grin at something in the distance, pointing at a maple tree close to the dock. "Your father proposed to me right over there. We went for a walk with Selah and chased squirrels."

"Did you know you were in love with Josie when you married him?"

"Oh, yes. Josie is mine, and I'm hers, and that's all there is to it." Miranda turned to face her again, and the smile on her lips made her appear positively radiant in the morning sun. "But you see, the societal norms and expectations of me during that time left me in denial. I had obligations. Marriage. Home. Children. There was an order to maintain without deviation or resistance. I was to be the perfect wife, mother, and counterpart to an empire crafted by the Fairweathers."

"That's a very... traditional way of thinking." Jamison folded her arms and leaned against a column. "Thank God we're moving past it, and women who want something different aren't looked down upon. By the time Harper and Theo grow up, maybe it won't be such a big deal."

"Aren't they amazing?" Miranda whispered, giddy with excitement. "I am in complete awe of my granddaughters and of my new grandson on the *way. Those three will become a force to be reckoned with, and I can't wait to see it all play out."*

Jamison opened her mouth to tell her new imaginary friend that she had no idea what the baby would be like, but Miranda cut her off. "All children need to be loved, Jamison. Every one of them. And it's up to the right people to provide that love, even when society expects something else from you."

The soft click of her bedroom door opening had her waking in a terrified rush. Miranda's smiling face vanished, and Jamison sat up in a panic.

"It's me," Liam whispered. "You okay?"

"Dream." She flopped back onto the mattress. "Nightmare? Christ, I don't even know anymore."

The faintest hint of morning peeked through the curtains, giving her enough light to watch as Liam stripped off his clothes. His lean body, packed with its usual definition and those new muscles, made the whole no-touch rule extremely hard.

"Why do you have to look so good?"

He grinned, focused on removing his pants. "It's both a gift and a curse."

"Do you want pain meds?"

"I'm okay." Down to his boxers, he slid into bed and reached for her immediately. "My arm is stiff from sitting in the same position for so long."

"What did I miss?"

"Circles." On his back, holding her hand under the sheets and blankets, he fixed his tired gaze on the ceiling. "Circles and circles and circles."

His frustration was so palpable that she could feel it oozing into her skin and merging with her own. "But there is no endpoint."

"Why can't I find him? Sinclair tries to kidnap you. He orchestrates Emily and Claudia's kidnappings. But why? What does he gain?" His voice dropped to a whisper, knowing that neither of them had the answers. "Why is this happening? Why babies? Is the Brandy thing real? And if what Toby says about her is the truth, is she—this woman we've had no contact with nor knew existed—the mastermind behind it all?"

"Top to bottom?" she offered.

Eyes closing, he nodded. "Go."

"Sinclair targets Fairweather women for Zanmi," she started. "Three of us. Me, Emily, and Claudia."

"But why Claudia if she's involved?" he countered. "Kidnap her and *then* let her go? Was it for show, or was it for another reason? It could be that Parker found out Sinclair's people grabbed her and ordered them to let her go. If that's true, then Zanmi's fractured with one hand, not knowing what the other's doing."

"You sound happy."

"I love chaos. That bitch is my best friend." He turned his head to wiggle his eyebrows at her. "Chaos exposes cracks. Makes people sloppy."

"You really should have followed in your father's footsteps."

"Don't start."

But he would notice the small things no one else did. She propped up on her elbow. "What mistakes are you seeing?"

"The women."

"The ones who came here?"

"They died scared," he said, empathy sneaking into the words. "The whole thing was nothing but theatrics, yet when it came down to it, I don't think they knew they were going to die."

She thought back to how Izzy had described the woman who died in her arms, young and frightened with her whole life ahead of her. If Liam was right, then those women were pawns, murdered by the family they thought they had found in Zanmi.

"That makes it worse." She laid a hand on his chest, careful to avoid his wound. "What would be the point?"

"Punishment. Performance. Maybe both. Sinclair used them—of that, we're sure."

She studied his profile. The long slope of his nose, the fullness of his lips, the sharp cut of cheekbone and jaw.

Five years later, this man still gave her butterflies. "I can't wait to be your wife."

The strained lines on his handsome face lessened. "We need to wait."

She released a humorless laugh, thinking the same as him. "With Madison still out there..."

"It makes me sick to think of her with them." He pulled her close, kissing her forehead. "We have no right to take a moment for ourselves.

Not a real one. A quick break is one thing, but celebrating a wedding... we just can't."

"I agree." She nestled her face in the crook of his neck, breathing him in. He smelled like home, and she never wanted to leave. "I'll wear that damn dress one day."

"You will. Sooner than you think."

That got her attention, and she pulled back. "What?"

"Before you say no, hear me out."

Ugh. She knew that tone. He had some genius idea that would probably work, but that she wasn't going to like. "Spill it."

"We'll keep pretending we're getting married this weekend."

"...Okay?"

"I know someone's talking to Sinclair."

"How?"

"Because I'm me." He smirked down at her. "And I know everything."

She kissed his neck, nipping playfully with her teeth. Under the sheets, he hardened, his long length brushing against her hand still splayed on his stomach.

"Tell me your plan," she whispered, her fingers wrapping one by one around his cock. They had done this only once before, with neither of them able to focus enough to finish, too concerned with the cameras watching. "And relax. No one can see us."

The muscles in his entire body tightened on the first slow pump, his breath hitching in his throat. "Someone's talking to him... and I want them to *keep... doing that.*" He shifted slightly to block the camera's view, letting her work him with a slow, steady rhythm. "I want Sinclair to think this wedding's real. He's been quiet too long. It'll piss him off."

"You know what I want?" She pressed her thumb to his tip, smearing the moisture. "You in my mouth until I gag. Then fucking me so hard—"

"Evie's coming tomorrow," he said loudly for the camera. His eyes shuttered closed as she worked, and using his bad arm, reached behind him to grab the T-shirt left half hanging off the bed from where he'd undressed in a hurry. "Samuel wants to review what we've gathered so far while you and Evie do wedding stuff. Try on your dress."

She giggled into his neck. "I want to be fucked in that dress," she whispered. "It's so short, and I don't plan to wear any underwear when I walk down the aisle."

He shoved the T-shirt under the covers and handed it to her, panting. "Rowan's dropping the security block on your phone, so keep... *uh*...it with you as you try on... *shoes*. Shoes? Dresses. The dress." Goosebumps broke out across his body as he shifted, pretending to be repositioning himself on the bed when, in reality, he was using the move as an opportunity to thrust against her palm. "Did you *want* that tiara? I can buy you a tiara."

"Get me a tiara, and I'll wear it while I ride you." She flicked her tongue along his jaw as he rambled, tasting his skin while carefully keeping her face hidden from the camera. "Can't you just picture it? Me bouncing hard on your cock with your hand around my throat like a collar and that pretty little tiara sparkling as I come?"

"*Yes.*" He shivered, sucking in air through his nostrils as he tried to keep himself under control. "*Yes.*"

Fisting her hair, he yanked her up to kiss, moaning into her mouth as he came. For the cameras, they kept it as a lingering kiss goodnight—or good morning as it were—with barely a brush of tongue, all while she wrung every last pulse from him.

Once it was over, he took the shirt from her and balled it up with one hand under the blanket. "You're so going to get it for that."

"Get what? A prize?" She flopped onto her back as he discarded the shirt in the laundry basket. "It can be the tiara. I'll wear it proudly."

Returning to bed, he pulled her up against his side again. "And I didn't even need twenty minutes."

She snuggled against him, secure in his hold. "Babe, you didn't even need two."

"Fuck me. Don't tell anyone."

A giggle teased its way out of her, spreading across them both until, before long, they were laughing like a couple of idiots. After what went down at the cottage between Rowan and Annabeth, she knew how much sound the security system could pick up.

And she honestly didn't understand Annabeth's thought process. She, her father, Liam, and Simone had stood around the screen, sipping their wine and watching the whole thing. Of course, they pretended not to have heard a peep when Rowan and Annabeth returned.

But her father had a horrible poker face when it came to these types of things and nearly gave them away, stumbling over his words as he awkwardly walked back to his room.

Jamison shielded her face from the camera with a flattened hand. "Did Rowan say anything?" she mouthed. "About Annabeth?"

Liam rolled to his side, mirroring her position. "When we were finally alone, I asked if he was okay. He just shrugged and said he'd wear her down, eventually."

"You should have asked more questions!" she whisper-shouted. "If Samuel and Evie had gotten into a big argument like that, you would have been all up in his business."

"That's different."

"How is that different?"

"Because I'm comfortable telling Samuel to fuck off when he's being an idiot. Rowan's a nice guy, and we're working closely together." He yawned, his eyelids growing heavy. "I don't want to make things weird."

She understood. If someone pried into their lives, she'd shut it down in a heartbeat. So would Liam. But that didn't mean they couldn't gossip for a second.

"What about Abe and Izzy?"

That had his eyes reopening. "Something's happening there."

"He cooked for her."

"I thought that's what I heard, but I didn't believe it. Does he even know how to do that?"

"Apparently."

Liam grinned. "Honestly, I did think this was how it'd play out."

"Abe being smitten and Izzy being responsible for it?"

"Something like that."

She lifted her head and pressed her lips to his. How had she survived without him for those six months?

In truth, she hadn't survived. Not really. She'd been a shell, with surviving being the last thing she was doing. Liam was her entire world. Her best friend. Her lover. Her confidant.

Her forever.

"I love you," she whispered. "And I think I need therapy."

"I love you too." The grin on his lips dimmed into something bittersweet and infused with love. "Can we also have sessions together?"

God, he was perfect. Not just because he supported her unconditionally, but because he was also willing to admit when he needed support, too. Always ready to stand beside her, no matter how messy it got.

"Yes."

"I don't want to use the same therapist, though. I've got mine. We can find someone you're comfortable with, but I'd like us to find a totally separate person from those two for couples counseling."

"What an interesting strategy." It was her turn to grin. "It almost sounds like a plan your mother would devise."

"God, don't tell her."

"All these secrets you want me to keep." She squealed when he tickled her under the sheets. "Fine! Fine! My lips are sealed."

"Is that what's wrong with us?" Settling beside her again, he laced their fingers together. "We have mommy issues?"

She snorted. "Duh."

"And daddy issues."

"Oh, hell yeah."

"And in two totally opposite ways." He blew out an exhausted exhale. "Mine was always there, pushing me as I was growing up, while yours was pushing himself and never around."

"Don't forget the trauma," she added. "We've got lots and lots of trauma."

"Heaping amounts of trauma." He went quiet, minutes passing as the sun rose, its light catching in the chandelier and scattering prisms across the ceiling. "I need to be out there."

A part of her knew this was coming. Trapped at Haven House, unable to get his feet on the ground and be in the thick of the hunt, was killing him. Liam craved control. He was a strategist. And this threat to their family was personal.

"Before the women came, I heard snippets of your conversations," she said, keeping her voice low. "With Samuel."

His hand squeezed hers. "Don't ask me about it."

A tear slid free, but she didn't let him see. She was a Fairweather and understood that sometimes, the less you knew, the better. Even if the unknown was terrifying.

"Promise that you won't do anything that could take you away from me."

Silence.

"William?"

"I can't promise that."

The finality in his tone told her not to push. Whatever he and Samuel had in their heads was firmly planted, and that was okay. She would work on breaking down the idea little by little. If she couldn't, that was also fine because she had a secret weapon.

Evie.

Her sister would handle Samuel and end whatever he and Liam were planning with just a look. Samuel could take almost anything except his wife being upset. It was the ultimate chink in his armor.

"Yes, you can," she said. "Or else I won't marry you."

And there it was.

Liam's weak spot.

He was on top of her instantly, bracing himself above her with an arched brow. "I'm too tired to argue."

"And I'm too tired to hear that you won't promise not to die." She bucked her hips. "I thought Bruce had killed you. I thought you were dead."

He rolled off, grimacing. "You have to trust me."

"That's the problem. I do trust you." She let him tug her close again, curling into his side. "But I also trust that you'll run straight into danger and call it a solution."

"I'm well aware of the cost. So is Samuel."

Ah. So her brother was in on it.

"If you won't tell me, maybe Evie will. Samuel doesn't hide anything from her."

She would swear she saw his eye tick in annoyance. "Leave Evie out of this. We're ready for the birth, but we're not ready-ready. Don't upset her."

"Fine." In a grand huff, she rolled away. "Try to get some sleep."

"*We* will. Together." Not about to let her get away, he followed, securing her back against his chest with his wounded arm. "Close your eyes and go the hell to sleep."

Smirking, she wiggled her hips, the curve of her butt fitting perfectly between his thighs. "Yes, sir."

"Damn it," he hissed as his body responded. "Stop torturing me."

"Then stop planning something dangerous."

He bit down on the soft spot beneath her ear, making her shiver. His hand slid under her camisole, cupping her breast and teasing her nipple into a peak.

"I'll do my best."

"Your best?" She tried to look at him over her shoulder. "Are you kidding?"

"Jamison, I want you to listen to me," he said roughly. "There's nothing on this earth I want more than you. Nothing I want more than to grow old beside *you*. You're it. You're my reason. My purpose. And I would never put myself in a position where I couldn't come back to you."

"But—"

"But I'm a selfish man." Barely above a whisper, he snarled directly in her ear. "And I will burn this whole fucking world to the ground to keep you safe. Samuel would do the same for Evie. We didn't make this decision lightly, but we're done playing by the rules. We're done giving a damn. We'll protect our family, no matter the cost."

She melted into him. "That's why you left the Bureau. It had nothing to do with me. You just couldn't play by their rules anymore."

"It had everything to do with you."

She turned to face him, smoothing her hand along his cheek. "I can't live without you. I won't."

"You'll never have to. But you will have to trust me."

She would forever trust him, and while not knowing what he and her brother were planning was unbelievably hard, she would get over it.

"Okay."

Dipping his head, he kissed her, the promise in it unable to be ignored. "Evie is coming at noon with the girls, and Rowan's going to drop all barriers to our system. Anyone who wants to listen, watch, or even call into our phones... they'll be able to."

"And we haven't done that since the night the women came," she said, realizing exactly how important today would be. "Mighty tempting bait."

"Yes, you are." He rubbed his nose against hers. "Super fucking tempting."

"Are you going to track him?"

"Of course."

"And then go running off to play the hero?"

He kissed her, nipping at her bottom lip. "Let me worry about that. You just focus on keeping him entertained while Rowan works."

Jamison hated the cameras more than ever. They'd stolen their privacy, their intimacy, and now they were being turned into weapons—not just to protect them, but to provoke.

"If Michael even tries to make contact."

"He will."

CHAPTER 21

Jamison

"**D**ear God, your butt is as big as the Grand Canyon." Evie's voice rang out from the landing as Jamison climbed the attic ladder. "I don't know how you're going to fit into that wedding dress, but *oooh*... maybe we can play Sir Mix-A-Lot when you walk down the aisle."

On the floor, Harper and Theo immediately launched into humming the baseline of *Baby Got Back*, their tiny shoulders bouncing in rhythm.

"What kind of mother teaches their kids that song?" Jamison asked, thinking she might drop her shoe directly on Evie's head.

With a shoulder propped against the wall, Josie grinned as she waited with Evie. "I taught them."

"Why am I not surprised?" Jamison sighed. "We'll be back in a minute."

"Take as long as you want." With a plate full of food in one hand, Evie smacked on her third mouthful of casserole. "Who knew Abe could cook? Am I right?"

Above her on the ladder, Annabeth *hmpfed*. "He could've said something sooner and helped out."

"He's my son," Simone replied from farther up the ladder. "And I still don't know if I'd try his food first."

"I wouldn't have," Jamison admitted. "Food poisoning is my least favorite thing."

"Hey, hey," her father barked, already in the attic and steadying Simone at the top. "Eyes forward. Watch your step. I don't want anyone falling."

"We're fine, Benjamin." Simone brushed off her leggings with a huff. "Who do you think put all the wedding stuff up here to begin with?"

He helped Annabeth up next, then reached down for Jamison's arm. "Why is my wedding stuff even up here?" she asked as she climbed into the attic. "Why not just shove it in one of the unused guest rooms?"

"Because I knew it would hurt you to see it." Simone wrinkled her nose at the dusty air, already eyeing the clutter with disdain. "So I put it somewhere you wouldn't have to."

The front section of the attic was filled mainly with holiday decorations, all of which were left close to the entry point so they could be removed easily every year. But behind those stacks were layers and layers of Fairweather history crowding the space. A few things belonged to Ty and Simone from when they first arrived, but most were incredibly old pieces belonging to the various Fairweathers who lived at Haven House once upon a time.

Wandering his way through the jumbled chaos, Jamison caught sight of her father directly before he disappeared behind a wall of boxes containing Annabeth's Nutcracker collection. "Dad, where are you going?"

She followed, leaving Simone and Annabeth to debate whether to bring the Thanksgiving decorations down this year.

"Dad?" Popping out to the other side, she found him in the larger section of the attic where the ceilings rose high above their heads. "What's that?"

Smiling in a way that tugged on her heartstrings, her father held up a small pink CD player. "This was your mom's. Laura Jean took it everywhere."

"Oh, yeah?" She hit the button on the top, making the CD lid open. "I wonder if it'll play anything."

"I don't know, but maybe we can give it to Harper and see if she can get it to work." He nodded at a box with the words *LJ's music* written on it. "Those are her CDs. Grab them, and we'll take it all with us."

Gathering the small box, Jamison tucked it under one arm, but when turning back around, she accidentally bumped into a candelabra.

"Oh, crap."

The gothic looking thing tilted in what felt like slow motion until it finally gave up the fight. It crashed into several pieces of Victorian-era furniture, clanging loudly as it collided.

"What are y'all doing?" Simone hurried through the box maze with Annabeth right behind her. "Don't make a mess up here."

"Whoa," Annabeth breathed, pointing to a now-exposed painting. "Who's that?"

The ornately framed picture was of a young woman, and setting the box of her mother's CDs down, Jamison tilted it forward to see the inscription. "*Margaret Fairweather. Wedding Portrait*," she read aloud from the plaque. "She must be some great-great-grand-whatever."

"She looks like Charlie, so I guess so." Her father scooted a velvet chaise lounge to reveal a massive family tree framed in the same extravagant way as Margaret Fairweather's painting. "Yeah, here we go." He tapped at the glass. "She was the mother of Calvin Fairweather, who was my father's grandfather. They were the last Fairweathers to live here before they built Parkland Grounds."

"She doesn't look very nice," Jamison said, eyeing Margaret's painting. "But then again, she also looks sad for this being a wedding portrait."

"Forget Margaret, check this out." Squatting to get a better look at the family tree, her father grinned. "Here she is. The infamous Wilhelmina Fairweather." He pointed to the name sitting on the same line as Calvin's. "She's the one who murdered their father. His death is what forced the mill to close and why the Fairweathers moved to Hollingsdale."

"But why did she kill him?" Annabeth asked. "That's what I've always wanted to know."

"The way the story was told to me was that she wanted to marry her doctor, but her father wouldn't allow it, so she killed him and ran off."

"Agent Anderson says otherwise," Jamison noted.

Staring at the family tree, Simone wrapped her arms around herself as if cold. Admittedly, it was a bit drafty in the attic, but she was wearing Devon's college sweatshirt and should have been warm enough. "If a Fairweather is telling the story, you better believe it's probably only half true." She nodded at Wilhelmina's name. "I hope that poor girl ended up with her doctor and had a good life."

"I guess we'll never know. Now she's just a name on a family tree." Jamison studied Simone for a second. "Are you okay?"

Simone's gaze darted around the space, landing on the massive array of boxes with their various markings on them. *R.M. clothes. Classroom supplies. Livy. Evie toys. Devon shoes. LJ's painting supplies.* A lifetime of memories crammed into a corner with nothing but the cobwebs to keep them company.

"Oh my God." Annabeth pointed toward a dusty bin. "Is that Dad's old science experiment stuff?"

Snapping out of her staring contest with the past, Simone followed Annabeth's line of sight. "Yes, but be careful. I think we cleared out the chemicals, so it should just be beakers and whatnot in there, but I'm not sure."

"We should take it down to the girls," Annabeth said, wedging the box from beneath an oversized case marked *Devon's Tuba.* "Or save it for when Xavier visits. He's all about science now."

"Hey, is the old record player still in the conservatory?" her father asked. "The one your mom always used?"

Kneeling next to her as she flipped through a stack of records, Jamison laughed when her father slipped one from her fingers. "Here, take these two," he said. "Those were her favorites."

"The record player is still there," Simone sighed, rubbing her temples. "And bring down the *Chipmunk Christmas* album while you're at it. We'll send it home with Samuel and Evie."

Annabeth let out a cackle. "Samuel hated that album, and Evie tortured him with it every December." Leaning down the attic hatch, she hollered, "Hey, Evie! We found the Chipmunk Christmas album!"

Evil laughter floated up to them. "Bring it to me," Evie ordered. "I think it's time to introduce our girls to the classics."

Annabeth's phone rang, and she answered on video. "What?"

"Why you gotta be so mean all the time?" Selah asked with an eye roll. "That man of yours not treating you right?"

Annabeth frowned at her brother. "Mind your business."

"Oooh, someone's touchy," Selah teased. "There's a story there. I *better* get the scoop later."

"I thought Lenora was calling," Annabeth grumbled. "Not you."

"I'm here!" Lenora's face squished in next to Selah's on screen. "And so is Xavier."

Hearing that Xavier was on the call, his Papa and GiGi hurried over, practically snatching the phone out of Annabeth's hands as they launched into rapid-fire questions. Jamison rushed to get out of the way, knowing it was best not to get between them and their grandchildren.

"How's the guitar?" her father asked.

"How's school?" Simone interjected. "Are you doing okay learning at home?"

"Is your dad driving you crazy yet?"

"We found a science kit in the attic you can play with when you come visit."

Xavier handled the interrogation like a pro while Jamison and Annabeth slipped away to a quieter corner of the attic, navigating past stacks that seemed to have multiplied.

"The wedding stuff should be over here," Annabeth said, brushing dust from a bin. "I know the lanterns are."

"Should I still do the lanterns?" Jamison asked. "Or is it too much?"

"I already said yes." Annabeth held up one of the small white lanterns Harper would carry instead of a bouquet. "You can do the ceremony directly after sunset, and it'll look awesome."

Half-listening, Jamison ventured deeper into the wedding clutter. It wasn't just her ceremony things up there. A display box holding Simone's wedding dress, sealed and labeled with the date, stood off to the side. Nearby, Evie's gown—the one Laura Jean had worn for her first marriage to Evie's father—hung in a plastic garment bag.

"These should be downstairs," she murmured. "Why are the dresses hidden up here?"

Annabeth glanced up. "Mama was worried those people would come back and steal them again, so she stashed everything up here for safekeeping."

Jamison stepped past the others, her eyes landing on a dress she hadn't expected to see. The one her mother was meant to wear when she married her father. They were going to have a beach ceremony, just like the one she had planned with Liam.

"I bet I could fit into it."

"It'll be short on you." Annabeth gave the gown a once-over. "But yeah. I think it'll fit."

⚘⚘⚘⚘⚘ ⚘⚘⚘⚘⚘

Annabeth knocked lightly on Jamison's bedroom door. "Let me in. I want to see!"

"Let me in. I want to pee!" Evie's voice was significantly less graceful as she thumped her fist on the door. "Ugh—never mind. I'm using Annabeth's bathroom. Don't show anyone anything until I get back!"

Jamison stood alone in front of her floor-length mirror, her breath caught somewhere in her throat. The dress was too short. It hit just above her ankle, leaving her painted toes exposed.

But that's about where the problems with the dress ended.

The satin skirt floated around her hips like it had been made for her. The bodice hugged her curves, and the halter tie secured firmly behind her neck helped to show off her cleavage perfectly. As she spun, the fabric fanned around her in a sweeping arc of white, and the image she caught at every turn made her immensely happy.

She would still wear the dress she designed for Liam, but at this moment, wearing her mother's gown in the quiet of her room felt so right. To her, Laura Jean Eddins was something akin to a fairytale. A myth more than a memory. And while it often felt like she was living in the shadow of a legend, it allowed her to observe how everyone processed the loss of Laura Jean in their own way. Her father told his stories. Simone would always stop and admire a painting or visit a new art exhibition that might roll through town. Evie would dance at the oddest of times, making Samuel and their girls join in.

For Jamison, it was a little more surreal. She had her dreams. Those weirdly fantastic fantasies her brain concocted to show mother-daughter conversations never to be had.

Yet, in this dress, the woman she would never know felt very much real. A ghost at her side. A memory that might not have been hers to have but was still hers, nevertheless.

The door opened and shut, scaring the shit out of her. "Jesus!"

Liam flipped the lock to keep a shouting Annabeth out. "Wow," he exhaled as his gaze roamed over her. "You look...I don't have the words."

She swished her skirts at him, making the hemline creep upward to her knees. "Tell me I'm pretty."

He took a slow step closer. "You're beautiful."

She twirled for him, letting the skirt swirl higher. "Tell me you love me."

"I'll love you always and forever."

"Well then, Mr. Cohen, if you think this looks good…" She bit her bottom lip, eyes dancing. "Just wait until you see me in my real dress."

Liam glanced up at the camera. The indicator light glowed blue, which meant sound only. Rowan was giving them privacy.

"He said I have two minutes."

"Two minutes to what?"

Her question was answered with a kiss.

One heartbeat, then another, and Liam had crossed the room. His mouth crashed into hers like a man starved. "To have a moment alone with my future wife."

She clung to him, pretending for a moment—just one—that the world outside didn't exist. No Sinclair. No Zanmi. No surveillance. Just them in this room, on the brink of forever.

"Easy." Liam chuckled when she moaned. "They can still hear."

"I can be quiet," she whispered, dropping kisses against his throat. "We could slip into the closet and—"

Her phone on the vanity buzzed with a text, and she glanced at it, rolling her eyes when she saw it was from Samuel.

Stop being fucking gross and tell Liam to come down.

Liam sighed, pressing a final kiss to her lips before pulling back. "We were in the middle of going over everything when I snuck out to see you in this."

"Samuel can wait." She pouted. "I don't care if he hears us."

He winced. "Actually…it's not just Samuel. It's Samuel, Holden, my parents, Klausen, Anderson, Izzy, Abe—oh, and Carter just got here."

Her mouth opened. Then closed. "Wonderful."

"Don't be embarrassed." He gave her a final squeeze. "You look amazing."

She caught his hand before he could go. "Anything yet? Any pings or whatever?"

A shake of his head was the only reply she got.

"Do I have to keep this up?"

She asked because the whole thing was depressing. Of course, they couldn't get married right now, but that didn't mean the urgency they both felt had gone away. She wanted to be his wife. Today. Not tomorrow. Not this weekend. Not when the time was right. She wanted it now.

Liam nodded and walked backward to the door. "I love you."

"I love you, too."

He opened the door, slipping out just as Annabeth rushed in with Evie waddling behind her. The girls were holding their mother's hands, both gasping when they caught sight of Jamison.

Annabeth skidded to a stop. "Oh, wow."

"Turn me around!" Selah's voice boomed from the phone in her hand. When Annabeth flipped the screen, his jaw dropped. "Holy crap. I remember the day your mom tried that dress on and stood right in the same spot. Do you remember, Evie?"

Evie didn't answer. She stood still and stared wide-eyed, with one hand clutching her baby bump while the other covered her mouth. Her cheeks were flushed, the glow from earlier now eclipsed by something else.

"That's a super sparkly dress," Harper said from her mother's side. "Can I have one like it?"

"Yous so so so verys pretty, Auntie!" Theo bounced excitedly, tugging on her mom's arm. "Isn't she, Mama?"

Evie promptly burst into tears, and not just a trickle. This was full-blown sobbing, shoulders shaking, breath hitching, kind of crying that left you breathless. She turned her face away, trying to muffle the sound behind her hands, but it only made it worse. "She sure is, baby," she gasped between sobs. "Auntie is always beautiful, but today she looks extra special."

"What's going on up here?" Jamison heard her father's question seconds before he appeared in the doorway. "Who's crying? Kid, answer m—"

Jamison froze as her father stared at her, the concern on his face crumbling into shock. "Holy shit."

Behind him, Simone and Josie hurried in, both women colliding with one another when they came to a full stop. "Girls, come with us. Let's get some lunch," Simone said, sounding like the wind had been knocked out of her. "I'll make your favorite."

Theo and Harper went with their grandmothers, and Annabeth followed, taking Selah on the phone with her.

And then the room was quiet again, except for the sound of Evie trying to breathe through her tears.

Swiping his hand over his mouth, her father approached slowly as if she were a wild animal. "The resemblance is uncanny."

Evie's tears went into full waterfall mode, and Jamison shifted uncomfortably. She didn't realize how much this would upset them. "I should change."

"No, I want a picture!" Evie rummaged through her maternity dress pockets but came up empty, which only brought on more crying. "I don't have my phone!"

Heavy footsteps pounded down the hall, bringing a charging Samuel into the room. "What happened?" He went straight to Evie, placing one hand on her belly, the other smoothing over her lower spine. "Hey. Deep breaths. You're okay."

Samuel hadn't noticed her yet, and when his eye flashed her way, he paled as deeply as their father had. "Holy fucking shit."

Jamison looked at each of them—her father, her brother, her sister—and tried to make sense of the emotional hurricane stirring around her. "What is wrong with you people?"

"You look like her," her father began, then let out a small laugh, shaking his head. "Of course, she does."

Evie sniffled. "We knew that, but seeing you in that dress is like... well, it's like she's standing right in front of us."

Feeling helpless about how to make this easier, Jamison swished the skirt like she had with Liam. "I'm too tall."

Her father grinned, his two dimples popping out. "Yeah, you are. That's on me, I'm afraid. Sorry, princess."

Evie hiccupped and calmed a little. "Mom would have loved how tall you are. She adored comparing you to Ben. She loved you both so much and how alike you two are."

Samuel's expression softened, freaking Jamison out even more. "You're a Fairweather for sure, but sometimes—"

"Yeah, sometimes, the way you move or the way you say something in just the right way catches me off guard because it's her," Evie cut in, wiping her cheeks. "You act like Ben, but you act like her too, and on the outside—other than your height—it's all Mama."

Taking Jamison by the shoulders, her father turned her to face the mirror. "Your mom was really into this kind of stuff. Laura Jean loved wedding dresses the most."

"Ben?" Taylor's voice carried in from the hall. "Where are you?"

"It's Sunday," Jamison whispered. "What is she doing here?"

"Hell, if I know," he replied, starting for the door. "In here, Taylor."

"Oh, hey!" Taylor popped into the room before anyone could stop her. "Wow, Jamison. You look... great? That dress is a little old-fashioned but works with your figure."

Getting herself under control, Evie leaned on Samuel for support. "It was our mother's wedding dress."

"The wedding dress she wore when she married your father?" Taylor pointed at Evie before swinging her index finger in Jamison's direction. "Or the one she was *supposed* to wear with your father? Sorry, but I get confused."

If it weren't for everyone being used to Taylor's obliviousness and total lack of filter, she would have been thrown out on her ass for such a stupid question. But after their talk, Jamison had come to the conclusion that this was just Taylor. The stark bluntness likely got her ahead at the office because, as they all knew, the head of Fairweather Holdings appreciated loyalty and honesty above all else.

Jamison would also bet that the behavior was a defense mechanism. After losing her husband and dreams of the future, Taylor probably didn't want to get close to anyone and just let any random thought that entered her brain fly right out of her mouth.

"It's the dress Laura Jean was going to wear when she married me," her father said, taking over the conversation. "And not to be rude, but why are you here, Taylor?"

"The Fire Marshal has been trying to get in touch with you. He thinks he has a solution to the recall and wants to run the plan past you before he signs off on it." Taylor held up her ringing cell phone, answering the call with a sharp jab to the screen. "Taylor Cabot, assistant to Mr. Benjamin Fairweather, speaking. Yes, sir. I have him right here."

Jamison watched as her father attempted to corral Taylor out of the room and downstairs, careful not to touch her as he did. The door closed behind them, and Evie nudged Samuel to follow, making him frown at his wife. "Why can't I stay?"

"Because she needs to change," Evie told him. "I haven't seen her actual wedding dress on her yet, and I want to have a moment alone with my sister when she tries it on."

He smirked down at her. "Technically, she's my sister too."

"This argument will not get you anywhere, Samuel."

"I don't know what you're talking about. My arguments get me everywhere, Evangeline." He kissed her temple, patting her ass on the way out. "I'll be right on the landing."

Once he was gone, Evie sighed dreamily. "I love my husband."

Jamison wrinkled her nose. "I'm surprised he even let you out of his sight for the fifteen minutes we were in the attic."

"Izzy was on the stairs." Evie joined her at the mirror, fiddling with the halter strap to get it smoothed down just right. "He thinks he's sneaky and sent her."

"At least he seems to be in a playful mood today. That's new."

"He's sex-starved, so he's trying to get on my good side for the next time you guys shut the security system down," Evie explained. "We missed this last one because Harper had an upset stomach."

Jamison shushed her. "The security cameras are still transmitting our conversation into the room where *everyone* is getting an update."

"Do you think the people in that room don't know Samuel and I have sex?" Evie waved a hand at her stomach. "I think the cat is out of the bag."

"Gross."

"Whatever," Evie shot back, ready to defend her marriage. She did it so much initially that it was second nature to her now. "Go try on your dress for me."

She would since it was Evie asking, but really, Jamison wanted the next time she put on her wedding dress to be when she walked down the aisle to Liam. "Fine."

Grabbing her phone, she slipped off into the walk-in closet and checked to make sure she hadn't missed anything. No missed calls—thank God—but there was a new message from Liam.

You look lovely today, Mrs. Cohen.

She grinned like a complete idiot and texted back:

I'm not Mrs. Cohen yet.

The phone pinged with a response.

Just testing it out. I like the way it rolls off my tongue.

With an evil cackle, she began typing a rapid-fire response. He had left himself wide open with that text.

I like the way you fuck me with said ton—

Her phone rang immediately, and the screen displayed Liam's name. She answered it with a giggle. "I was just typing back and saying I love the way you fuck me with your tongue."

Silence.

But then a chuckle, rich and deep, tickled her ear.

Michael Sinclair.

"I haven't fucked you with my tongue yet, but I hear I'm pretty good at it."

CHAPTER 22

Jamison

S he told herself to remain calm. They were expecting this, and she had to keep him on the phone. "Why do you have Liam's phone?"

Another huff of laughter had every hair on her body standing on end. "I don't. We cloned his number."

"We?"

Michael didn't reply, and she searched her brain for what to say. Liam had rehearsed a few options with her, but now that the moment was here, she was drawing a blank.

"Why are you calling?"

"Because I missed you."

"Fuck you," she hissed, unable to hold back. "If you come near us again—"

"Easy there. I don't want you to say something you'll regret." He tossed another laugh in her ear. "And to answer the question you really want to know, I'm doing fine. How are you?"

No one had to tell Rowan that Michael was on the line. The camera in the closet clicked from blue to green, transmitting not only sound but video to those below. An army of footsteps rattled the floors, making it sound like the entire household was charging into her room.

"Hey, what's going on?" Evie asked, her voice muffled through the partially closed closet door. "Samuel?"

Jamison heard Samuel shushing her as Liam silently slipped into the closet and closed them in.

"You know, I hear your sister is doing fine too," she said to Michael, struggling to keep her tone even and not pant in total terror. "Rotting in a jail cell because of her brother."

"Kris can hold her own for now."

"For now? She'd better get used to it. They're not going to let her go."

"Of course they aren't. But where's the fun in that?" Michael whispered. "I do love a challenge."

"You don't even know where she is."

"If you say so. But that's not why I'm calling," Michael replied. "I wanted to check on you. Bruce told me how you had a meltdown the other day."

"If I ever see Bruce again, he's a dead man."

"That's a shame. He thinks very highly of you."

"He's lucky Liam didn't kill him."

"That is something, isn't it? Two armed men, both excellent marksmen, facing off in a single room, and yet no one is dead?" Michael made a noise as if he were thinking. "Sounds suspicious. You should really question things more, Jamison."

She didn't know how to process what he was implying. Bruce was ex-military—more than comfortable with weapons—and Liam definitely was. So why had only one of them walked away with a minor injury?

Meeting Liam's hard stare, she searched for a sign that what Michael was suggesting couldn't possibly be true.

"Did Liam tell you what Bruce said?" Michael asked.

"No, he didn't. But how about you and I discuss something?"

"I'm all ears, baby. What do you want to know?"

"Where are Madison and Claudia?"

That sick chuckle of his scraped across her nerves. "You only want to know about Madison and Claudia? Jeez, I bet poor Emily and Damon will be pissed to hear their cousin wasn't at all concerned about them."

Jamison's eyes went wide. She flapped a hand at Liam, who moved closer to listen.

"Madison is safe," Michael said, his tone turning less casual as Liam joined. "Hello, Mr. Cohen. It's nice to talk to you finally."

Liam grabbed the phone, switching it to speaker. "Where's Madison?"

There was shuffling on the line, and Michael's tone turned soft again. "Hey, Mads, can you say hi?"

"Hi," Madison's sweet voice came through the speaker. "Mama?"

Time stopped. Jamison forgot how to breathe. Michael Sinclair had Madison. Right there. Right next to him, he had Claudia's little girl.

Vomit burned in her throat, and she swallowed a few times so she wouldn't spew it all over the floor. "Don't you dare hurt her."

"Madi, am I going to hurt you?"

Madison let out a high-pitched squeal, as if being tickled. "No!"

"That's my girl," Michael said. "Now go play."

Liam stayed silent, his head lowered as he listened and gathered information. The only background noise coming through now was the occasional whisper of wind, which meant Michael was walking around outside.

Or he could be standing by an open window. Or perhaps playing decoy ambient noises to throw them off.

Frustrated by all the possibilities, Jamison spouted off the first thing that came to mind. "You're a monster."

She could hear the bastard grinning. "I'm not a monster."

"Yes, you are."

"Eh, yeah. Maybe I am. However, I won't hurt her."

Breathing in through her mouth and out through her nose, Jamison forced herself to ask the unthinkable. "Is Claudia dead?"

"Nah. She's too mean to die. I've got her locked in a cage, so she can't hurt anyone. Same for Damon, though his cage has more cushion," Michael said, amused. "Those two are surprisingly vicious. Damon nearly bit one of my guy's ears off."

"Good."

"Yeah, I figured you'd be proud."

"Where's Emily?"

"Ah, but where is our Emily?" he purred. "Emily's a good girl. Beautiful, but not like you and Claudia. No, with you two, your beauty runs hot and can burn a man alive. Am I right, Liam?"

Remaining utterly still, Liam didn't acknowledge the question, too intent on listening.

"Emily's beauty is cold," Michael went on. "Lethal. An ice queen with a frozen heart."

Holden chose that moment to enter the closet, the three of them cringing when Evie shouted his name and demanded to know what was happening.

"What the hell is going on?" Evie yelled, and as the door to the closet started to close again, Jamison shook her head, trying to communicate to her sister to stay out. "Oh, hell no. You guys better tell me what you're doing in there."

With the door closed once more, Holden held up a sticky note that had one word written on it.

Arkansas.

Goosebumps prickled along Jamison's arms. Rowan was making progress.

Liam caught her gaze. She had to keep going.

"What are you doing with Emily?"

"Me? Nothing," Michael replied. "She's not mine."

"Yours?" Her stomach turned. "What the hell does that mean?"

A faint sound echoed through the phone. It was a bird crooning or cawing or making whatever the hell noise birds make. Liam heard it, as did Holden, who leaned in.

"Emily belongs to Emmett. You remember him, right?"

The bird called out again, louder and longer than before, but Jamison was too disgusted over the thought of Emmett Watson touching her cousin to pay attention. "You son of a bitch."

"It was love at first sight and—" Michael paused. "What is it, Madison?"

Madison's cries could be heard through the speaker. "I fell down on the rocks."

"Come here, sweetie." Fabric rustled against the phone. "It's just a scratch. Let's go back to the house and get it fixed up, okay?"

"Okay," Madison whimpered. "I want my mommy."

Madison's plea for her mother had Liam yanking the phone close to him. "If you touch them, if you hurt them, I swear I'll put a bullet in your head."

"There he is," Michael said. "Remember, you've got to catch me first, Cohen."

"Catch you? By the time I'm done, you'll be crawling to me." Taking the phone from her completely, Liam seethed in his rage, letting the weeks of exhaustion out in a string of venomous threats. "You love your family, and if any of our people are hurt, I'm going to make them pay for your crimes. Those grandparents in assisted living? Consider them homeless. Mom and Dad and their insurance firm? Consider them bankrupt. The baby brother? I hear he's doing well in both his professional and personal life. New wife, new house, new baby. Consider them gone, gone, gone."

"Empty threats."

"Where's your sister, Sinclair? Do you know? Have you learned her fate?" Liam snarled. "No? Well, let me tell you. When she was arrested, it was on the Florida border, and we dragged her across the state line into Alabama so local officials could handle the initial arrest. Do you know what that means? It means she's eligible for Wetumpka. Wetumpka, Sinclair. I know you know what that is. Oh, and your nephew? When we find him, that little boy is on the line to be sent to Holman. You've sentenced them to the worst prisons in the country, you piece of shit."

There was a pause on Michael's side. "You don't want to back me into a corner."

"I already did, so what will it be now? Send more murderous lackeys to the house to kill us—"

"You think that's the worst I can do?" Michael snapped. "That was just a preview."

Liam laughed, and Jamison's heart stuttered. She'd never seen him like this. Never. Not even when he confronted her at the townhouse.

"You know, you're quite the adversary, Sinclair. I'll give you that. Being a coward, you've learned how to hide and do it well, but I think my time hunting you has ended," Liam said loud and clear into the phone. "And since I can't have you, I'm going for the next best thing. Your family. From here on out, all the effort and money we're investing in a manhunt for you will be redirected to them. Every fucking move I make will be to drag them down."

"Oh, that's hilarious," Michael shot back, sounding slightly winded as if he were jogging. "You've become what you hate the most. *Me*. Desperate to destroy anyone—even innocent people—who might threaten to harm the woman you love."

"You don't love Jamison."

"I wasn't talking about Jamison."

Liam straightened, the manic smirk on his face blooming into a terrifying smile. "I know. But thanks for confirming."

In the background, Madison's scream pierced the line. "I want my mommy! Please let me have my mommy!"

The desperation in Madison's voice resonated deep in Jamison, and she covered her mouth to hold back a sob. If she could crawl through the phone to get to her, she would.

And unfortunately, as Madison's screaming continued, the growing sound carried through the closet door to those standing just beyond it.

"Is that him?" Evie burst into the small space to savagely manhandle the phone from Liam, who gave it up without much of a fight. "Is this the sick son of a bitch that came after my babies?"

Madison cried out again, a little further away this time, as if she were fleeing from Michael. "Madi?" Evie screamed, turning a deathly shade of white. "Madison!"

Appearing behind his wife, Samuel plucked the phone out of her hand. "Listen to me, Sinclair, because I'm only going to say this once." He kept his tone even, that lethal calm of his saturating every word. "You came to our homes. You tried to take my wife. You tried to hurt my girls. All of which makes you a dead man walking, but I want you to understand one very important thing."

Holden jerked his chin at Liam, gesturing for him to shut Samuel up, but Liam remained where he was, nodding in agreement as Samuel kept talking.

"I plan to teach you what it means to suffer. I plan to see your band of freaks suffer, and most of all, I plan to see your family suffer," Samuel spat out. "Fairweathers excel at inflicting as much pain as possible, and I'll not only play witness and construct your demise, but I will have your screams before we're done. I will hear you beg. I will hear you beg for those you love, and then I'll pull the trigger, anyway."

Madison's crying tapered off into whimpers, with Michael shushing her soothingly. "Madison, tell them you're okay."

"I'm okay." Madison's sniffles echoed around them. "Can I go see my mommy now?"

"Yeah, I think you've earned some time with her."

There was more shuffling, with Madison's laughter growing distant.

"I won't ask you to show mercy to my family," Michael said after a lengthy pause. "I've seen the way you treat your own and how much damage you can do, so why would I think you'd be capable of something so basically human as showing mercy to strangers."

Samuel sneered at the phone. "I don't know what the fuck you mean."

"I do," Liam said. "But I can't figure out the Arkansas connection. Parker, maybe? He was a plant the whole time, or did you guys lure him after he and Claudia hooked up?"

"Put that big brain to work, Cohen, and figure it out," Michael replied. "I'll be waiting."

The line went dead.

"What did he mean?" Jamison asked.

She didn't get an answer. Will shoved his way inside, making the closet well and truly cramped. Her father had it remodeled while living at Haven House with her mother, needing the extra room for all his suits. But even with it being as large as it was, she had gone out of her way to fill it and regretted that fact when Holden backed into her wedding gown, nearly knocking it from where it hung.

"Are we right?" Will whispered to Liam.

Liam held a finger to his lips and nodded. The reply didn't seem to be what his father wanted to hear if Jamison was judging his facial expression correctly.

Will gave a curt nod. "I'll go get the jammer fired up so we can tell Anderson and Klausen."

"Try to convince them not to speak to their teams until we say so."

"They're going to want a time frame," Holden said. "You can't just drop a bomb and expect them not to move on it."

Liam thought for a minute. "Ask for an hour."

Will left without another word, and they waited, expecting Liam to tell them what was happening. Or at least Jamison did. She was completely lost and didn't understand what was going on.

"Give my dad a minute to clear the room."

Samuel clutched Evie tightly against him. "And then you're going to explain what's going on?"

"As best I can." Liam pulled out his phone to make a call. "Rowan, kill the closet. I need five minutes."

"Take all electronics out," Rowan instructed. "And even then, you need to keep your voices low."

"Got it."

After grabbing all their phones, Liam swung open the closet door and hurried out to hand them off to the lone man left behind.

"And you thought private security would be boring," Liam mumbled, shoving the phones at the new arrival. "Carter, the beautiful woman in the wedding dress, is my future wife. Jamison, this is Agent Anderson's grandson."

Carter Anderson was a younger version of his grandfather, distinguished and classically handsome, with chiseled features and crystal-blue eyes that stood out against his tanned skin. He was also tall—taller than even her brothers and father—with the top of his head skimming the crystals dangling from her chandelier.

Jamison gave him a weak wave. "Hello."

"Hello." Carter Anderson smiled half-heartedly. "Nice dress."

"We'll do formal intros for everyone else in a minute, but don't let anyone in." Liam rushed back to the closet and, snapping the door closed, glanced at the security camera. There was no blue light, nor green, or even a red one. The camera sat dead, Rowan not taking any chances.

Holden leaned his head to the side so his hair wouldn't catch on one of her cashmere sweaters. "Before we start this, can I just say well freaking done. You two managed to antagonize not one but two mass murderers this week, and Evie? I have never been prouder. I think you scared Sinclair the most."

Evie looked ready to cry, hunched and nearly wrapped entirely around Samuel. "I've never wished death on another human, but with that man, I want to see him burn from the inside out."

Dropping a kiss on his wife's head, Samuel's hold on her tightened. "Don't upset yourself."

"I'm not." She tilted her head all the way back to look at him. "I'm doing okay."

"Give me that sticky note," Liam said to Holden. "Jamison, can you get me something to write with? I need to jot down my thoughts."

It wasn't easy, but she finally squished herself behind Samuel to retrieve a pen from her top dresser drawer. "Here."

Taking the pen, Liam pressed the paper to the wall so he could write. After jotting down a few lines, he reread it to himself. "It's her. This whole time, it's always been about her."

Jamison tried to look over his shoulder, but couldn't make out anything. "Who?"

He held up the note containing his scribbles so they could read it. Most of it was illegible, but the two words at the bottom were clear.

CeCe Miller.

Chapter 23

Jamison

E vie blinked back tears as she read CeCe's name. "I think I'm going to vomit."

"I have theories on the why." Liam balled the sticky note up and shoved it into his pocket. "But nothing conclusive."

"So, give us the how." Samuel gathered Evie's hair into a ponytail in case she did actually throw up. "As much as I don't want to believe she's involved, I know you. You wouldn't say something like that without proof."

"Too many coincidences."

"And you don't believe in coincidences," Jamison said, searching for a hair tie to give to Samuel. Her sister looked awful. "But which one convinced you?"

Liam's gaze cut to Holden. "Come on, man. You're my logistics guy. You didn't see it?"

The frown on Holden's lips deepened as he thought it through. "Locational proximity to one another. Fort Leonard. Sinclair taught at the base before he was discharged, and she was right there."

"Teaching nursing in St. Louis," Samuel said, taking the offered hair tie and securing Evie's hair away from her face. "We always thought that was such an obscure place for her to move to."

"Then he's deployed on his final mission overseas," Liam added. "Which was when she died."

"You mean when she was murdered," Evie heaved, puffing her cheeks to keep her airflow even and steady. "Toby killed her, so why would Sinclair help them?"

St. Louis. The marsh. The manchineel. Around Jamison, the closet spun as the entire thing came together in one dizzying second. "Toby didn't kill her."

Liam grinned. "No, he didn't."

"What are you talking about?" Evie snapped, guiding Samuel's hands to massage her belly. "Toby killed her on the marsh."

"No, Toby didn't kill her." Holding Liam's stare, Jamison smiled back at him. "CeCe killed herself."

"That's bullshit," Evie snarled. "Complete and utter bullshit."

"But that's the story Zanmi has maintained." Samuel worked his hands lower to massage Evie's hips. "There's not a single record where Toby admits to killing CeCe. He claims, and continues to claim, that she killed herself."

"He brought her home." Holden's brows pinched together as he watched Evie with concern. "I remember that clearly from the court transcripts and all those damn interviews. He's always said he had brought her home to try and convince her that it was time to return."

"Toby drugged her and dumped her in the marsh. He wasn't trying to convince her of anything." Evie clutched Samuel's shirt with clawed hands, twisting the material tight. "She chose to kill herself instead of facing what he'd do to her."

"And Toby tried to stop it from happening," Liam countered. "I'm sorry, Evie, but I have to play devil's advocate. The physical evidence showed he tried to pull the fruit from her mouth."

"Before he beat her!" Evie shouted. "What is wrong with you, Cohen? How could you even—"

Everyone stared in shock as Evie bent at the waist and let out a scream. "Oh, my God!"

Samuel dropped to his knees to see his wife's face. "Evangeline, I think we need to go home."

"I'm fine!" she roared as she panted. "I just don't want to listen to him defending Toby!"

Jamison put a hand on Liam's chest, ready to shove him behind her if her sister went crazy. These pregnancy hormones were insane. "No, really. You need to rest."

"Oh, fuck. Fuck. *Fuck*," Evie screeched, holding Samuel's shoulders, or else she would tip over. "I think the baby's coming."

Holden's cheeks drained of color. "No. Just no. The baby's got to cook for three more weeks." The panic in his voice rose with each word. "Tell him to go back inside and take a nap or something."

Liam grimaced when Evie let out another cry. "Holden, I don't think it works like that."

"This isn't just a set of fake contractions?" Cradling Evie's face in his big hands, Samuel sounded terrified. "You've been having a lot of those."

"I don't know," Evie whimpered. "There's so much pressure and... *ahhh...* I think he's about to fall out."

It was Samuel's turn to go an extreme shade of white. "Dear fucking God, don't say that."

Liquid trickled down Evie's leg, and then a sudden gush drenched her lower half, splashing onto Samuel's pants and all over the shoes strewn about on the floor. Everyone gasped, and without taking his eyes off the scene, Liam reached high above him to press the button on the security camera. "Baby on the way. We're going with Plan A until I say otherwise."

The light on the camera clicked on, and Rowan's shout came through the speaker. "Shit."

Flinging the door open, Samuel led Evie out. "Sorry about the shoes, Jamison," Evie mumbled as she hobbled away. "We'll get you another pair."

Staring at her soaked wedding shoes, Jamison's lips parted. Shoes were the farthest thing from her mind now. "O-okay."

"This is what we're doing," Liam ordered as he snapped out of his shocked state, and they all entered the bedroom together. "Carter, you're with me and the girls. Holden and Izzy are going with Samuel and Evie."

"And me. I'm going with them." Josie rushed in, nearly colliding with Carter. "Who the hell are you?"

Carter dipped his chin, handing back everyone's phones. "I'm Carter, ma'am."

Simone appeared next with Theo and Harper, who ran to their mother. "Ben will drive them," Simone said. "Evie, is your hospital bag in the car?"

"No," Evie wailed, the tears coming as Samuel lifted her into his arms. "I just finished packing it but haven't put it in the car. It's still at the house."

"I can get it!" Taylor stuck her head in the room when Annabeth hurried in. "I just need the security passcode, and I can bring it to the hospital."

"Ben and Will are getting the cars," Bernie shouted, running in next. "Klausen's got the escort covered—"

Evie screamed. A blood curdling, heartbreaking scream.

"Move!" Samuel bellowed, pushing through the crowd. "Girls, stay with Unc."

Harper and Theo rushed to Liam, who scooped up Theo and handed Harper off to Carter. "Okay, people. Let's go have a baby."

❧❧❧❧❧ ❧❧❧❧❧

"It sounds like someone's singing in the forest." Carter kept a trained eye on the line of pine beyond the oaks as he waited for Jamison and Liam to secure the girls into their car seats. "You guys hear that, right?"

"What is he talking about?" Jamison's gaze connected with Liam's as they tried to figure out the harnesses of the car seats. "This guy's not crazy, is he? We don't need crazies, Liam. We have plenty already."

"I hears hers. She sings all da times, but she's not Mama's Mama." Theo swung her feet back and forth when they finally got her buckled in. "Mama's Mama don't sings. She funny doh. She laughs lots."

"The song is loud today." Harper arched upward to help Liam adjust her straps. "She must like you, Mr. Anderson."

Carter grunted and got in, taking the front passenger seat. "This place is weird."

Once the girls were ready to go, Liam slid behind the wheel while Jamison crawled into the back to squish herself between the car seats. "I likes yous dress," Theo whispered. "Fancies."

There had been no time to change, and honestly, she hadn't even noticed she was still in her mother's wedding gown until Theo's comment. The dress was surprisingly comfortable to wear.

Simone's red sports car shot off in a hurry, carrying her and Josie. Rowan and Annabeth had already left on his motorcycle while Abe was in his van, following them to the Port Michaelson hospital. It would take thirty minutes to get there, but probably under twenty for her father, who was driving Evie, Samuel, Izzy, and Holden in his Rover with a whole police escort.

"Okay, listen up," Liam said, looking at the girls in the rearview mirror as he drove down Haven's oak tunneled drive leading to the highway. "Say hello to Mr. Carter. He's here to protect you."

"Hello."

"Hiya."

Carter raised a hand, his attention on the passing forest. "Hello, ladies."

Theo leaned across Jamison to whisper to Harper. "Hims calls us ladies. Bees a lady, Harper. No farting."

Harper rolled her eyes. "Do you have a gun, Mr. Carter?"

"A few."

Harper sat forward with a look on her face that said she didn't exactly believe him. "I don't see them."

"I know how to keep them hidden."

"Unc usually carries four weapons on him, but today he only has two." Harper wrinkled her pert nose. "I find that most unfortunate."

"Most unfortunate?" Carter turned halfway around. "How old are you? "

"Our Harper has a vast vocabulary, and when you get to know her father more, you'll understand why," Liam replied before raising his voice to direct his next statement at the girls. "You will each hold either my hand or Carter's hand. You will never let it go. You will not go to the bathroom, not even with GiGi. If we tell you to do something, you will do it and not question us."

Theo puffed her chest. "I dos my bestest, Unc."

"Who's gonna look after Auntie?" Harper asked. "That bad man tried to take her, too."

Harper's concern caused an ache in her chest, and Jamison laid a hand on her niece's leg. "I'll be fine."

"You and me, Harper. We'll watch over her." Liam turned onto the main road, catching up with Simone in no time. "Think you can handle that?"

"I might need a weapon, then." Craning her neck, Harper peered at Carter. "You can let me borrow one of yours. My hands are small, so whatever you give me needs to be lightweight."

With a stunned expression, Carter turned back around to face forward. "Liam. Man, I know we haven't hung out much since that thing with your mom, but I need you to be honest with me. I reviewed the files last week. I've watched the documentaries. I've had Tobias Miller's interview on loop for the last forty-eight hours." He spoke in a low voice, as if he honestly thought the three of them in the back couldn't hear. "But seriously, what the hell have you dragged me into?"

"I told you this job wouldn't be boring." Liam gunned the engine, shooting them down the long stretch of highway. "Welcome to the family, my friend."

CHAPTER 24

Rowan

"**Y**ou're not bringing a gun into an operating room."

Samuel's jaw ticked. Standing in the hallway outside Evie's hospital room, he glared down at the small woman in navy blue scrubs. When they arrived, Rowan thought it had been lucky that the nurse who stitched up Liam was the head labor and delivery nurse on duty.

Turns out he was so very wrong.

"My wife has to be under constant protection."

Hands on her hips, Nurse Holly shook her head. "I know who you are, and I know what happened. Hell, everyone in this county knows what happened, but I can assure you that it won't happen here."

"Samuel!" Evie shouted from inside the laboring suite. "Where are you?"

"Go in there with her," Rowan whispered to Annabeth, who was already turning to head into the room. "She's probably scared."

Annabeth was scared, too. As they hiked up the stairs because she was too terrified to take the elevator to the second floor, he could tell the rush and excitement were getting to her. She had been to the hospital before and was comfortable with the maternity wing since Evie had given birth to both Harper and Theo there. Still, that hint of the unknown lingered, and he was hoping they could find a quiet spot for her if she needed it.

"We're here."

Hustling down the hall with Josie behind her, Simone sailed past them and into the birthing suite, but Josie hung back when she caught sight of Samuel's expression. "What's wrong?"

"They need to do a C-section," Ben explained. Leaning on the wall behind Holly, he frowned at the nurse, mirroring Samuel's expression. "But they won't allow guards in the room."

Holly held her ground, unflinching against the Fairweathers. "We need to move her quick—"

"Holly! How are you? Are you Evie's nurse?" Liam swept around the corner with the new guy, Samuel's girls, and Jamison, still in a wedding dress, at his side. "If so, that's fantastic. I'll feel better knowing she's in your capable hands."

"I... uh... Mr. Cohen, how are you?" Holly cleared her throat. "I was just explaining that we can't have armed guards here."

"But you can help us out, right?" All smiles for the nurse, the rest stared in disbelief as Liam proceeded to charm the woman. "Mrs. Fairweather needs a guard."

Holly fidgeted in place. "Well, we have rules."

Liam's smile widened, and he stepped closer, holding Holly's gaze. "Yeah, but sometimes we have to bend the rules."

"What in the hell is this?" Abe whispered to Rowan. They had taken up a spot in the hallway to stay out of the way. "Is he... flirting?"

Rowan adjusted the laptop bag hanging from his shoulder, equally confused. "I have no idea."

Overhearing their conversation, Izzy smirked. Flanking the entrance to Evie's room, she and Holden were decked out in tactical gear with various weapons strapped to their bodies. "This is Liam in the wild."

"Or at least, the Liam we knew back in the day." Holden struggled to keep a straight face. "The man was notorious."

Throwing her hands up, Holly growled. "There's no time for this. We need to get her to the OR."

"Wait, did you say OR?" Jamison nearly shouted. "Is she having a c-section?"

"The baby isn't in position," Samuel said, the explanation sending his sister and Josie straight into the room.

"And she can't have this many visitors." Holly released an annoyed sigh. "I'm about to kick every last one of you out."

"Okay, so no armed guards," Liam said, drawing Holly's attention back to him. "How many entry points does the OR have?"

"Two."

"And can we have a guard stationed at each entry point?"

The nurse hesitated, but Liam added a "please," which finally did the trick. "Outside the doors," Holly agreed. "And they have to stay out of the way."

"Your staff has had background checks?"

Holly's eyes narrowed. "My people would never associate with that insanity."

"I bet the ultrasound tech's office thought the same thing about her, so please forgive my lack of trust. We just finished navigating a threat less than an hour ago, and we're all on edge," Liam replied smoothly, careful to keep his smile in place. "One guard at each entry point, Samuel in the OR, and us in the hall."

Holly pointed to the glass-encased room at the end of the corridor. "I'll accept the guards and the husband, but the rest of you can wait in the OR waiting room."

"Feds and cops in the hall," Liam countered. "The family will stay in the waiting room."

"Fine, but get those visitors out of the birthing suite so we can transport her." Holly walked off in a huff. "You have less than two minutes."

"Holden, you're at one door, and Izzy, you're at the other. Follow Holly and find out where you need to go. Text me if there's an issue," Liam ordered. "Samuel, get everyone out of there so you can focus on Evie. And where the hell are my parents?"

"They're coordinating with the men Klausen and Anderson sent," Ben replied. "Will wants to know exactly where everyone is going to be positioned."

Holden and Izzy ran after Holly while Samuel went into Evie's hospital room. Seconds later, everyone—including Simone—exited.

"Rude!" Jamison huffed, marching out into the hall. "Those nurses need to give Samuel a sedative or something."

"Ben, can you take Theo?" Perched on Liam's hip, Theo held her hands out so her grandfather could grab her. "Rowan, keep Jamison close while I see if I can do a quick sweep of that OR."

The new guy, Carter, glanced between the group and those coming and going down the hall, maintaining a firm grip on Harper. "You need me with you or them?"

"Them." Liam snatched Jamison and gave her a quick kiss. "Behave."

Jamison pretended to be offended. "I always behave."

Liam jogged away, and Rowan took Annabeth's hand as she exited Evie's room. "Okay, everyone. Let's try to be good boys and girls and go to the waiting room."

"I don't see why we can't wait outside the OR with Izzy and Holden," Josie mumbled, her arm hooked into the crook of Simone's arm. "We wouldn't be in the way."

"She needs us. Samuel needs us. This is serious." Simone turned to Ben. "Can't you do something?"

"Yeah, I can corral you two into the damn waiting room," Ben replied dryly, which made Theo giggle. "So, let's go."

"Swear jar, Papa." Theo laid her head on his shoulder. "I tired."

"We're all tired, Theo." Abe rolled his wheelchair down to the waiting room and pointed inside. "Hey, at least it'll be just us in here."

They all started to turn and leave when Evie's bed emerged from her room, pushed by two nurses, with Samuel right beside her.

"Wait!" Simone and Josie nearly fell all over themselves to get to her. "Evie!"

Annabeth and Jamison ran off, too, as did Ben with Theo. Harper tugged on Carter's hand until he scooped her up. "Come on," he muttered. "But don't touch my gun."

Rowan hung back with Abe, giving space while the women hugged Evie, and Ben spoke quietly to Samuel.

"Sammy is barely holding it together," Abe said. They were far enough away that no one could hear him. "Everyone always thinks he's the strong one between him and Evie, but they're wrong."

Samuel did look ready to pass out, and Rowan imagined he'd feel the same in that situation. "I get it."

And he truly did. If Annabeth didn't want to marry him, it would suck, and it would hurt, but in the end, it didn't matter. He needed her. If something horrible happened between them or to one of them, she would be the strong one who could continue on with life. But him? Not a chance. His life would be nothing if she weren't in it, and if that made him weak, so be it.

The nurses shooed the group away, and Annabeth returned to his side as they headed toward the waiting room. "Doing okay?"

She shrugged lightly. "Just nervous, like everyone else."

They reached the waiting room, and the group spread out. Ben guided Josie and Simone to the rear corner so the three of them could entertain the girls with Abe. Carter positioned himself at the door, nearly filling the frame. His presence relaxed Rowan enough that he thought he might be able to focus on hacking into the hospital's security cameras.

Grabbing seats near the door, he pulled out his laptop. "Let's keep an eye on them," he said as Annabeth sat beside him. "And here they are."

On the screen, Evie was being wheeled into the OR with Samuel at her side, holding her hand tightly.

"My mom had a c-section with Cait, and it didn't take long." Rowan clicked through to check the OR entry points. Holden guarded one, Izzy the other. "Let's find Liam."

"What about Liam?" Jamison came and sat on the other side of him to peek at the laptop. "Hacked into the security system already?"

"Yeah, just snooping around."

He clicked through each section under surveillance until he found Liam talking with some federal agents. Bernie appeared to be heading to the waiting room while Will stayed with Liam.

"Nothing looks out of sorts. Maybe we're okay." Annabeth placed a hand on his thigh, the spot instantly warming under her touch. "That phone call was awful."

It had been more than awful, and Rowan was doing his best to remain calm when, really, he wanted to be back at the house with Anderson and Klausen as they coordinated efforts to track down Sinclair.

And there was something about that call. Sinclair had left himself wide open as if to say, come and find me. It had been easy to track his origins in Arkansas and even easier to zero in on the state's northern section.

Yet, there hadn't been enough time for him to pinpoint exact coordinates before the call was disconnected. The data would be there when they returned to the house, and maybe one of the various federal teams would utilize the information and make some progress while they were at the hospital. Maybe by the time they returned, there would be a fresh lead established.

A lead Liam would want to personally chase.

It was no secret between the two of them that he was dying to get out there, and staying trapped in the house was driving him insane. He needed to be in the thick of it, and Rowan understood. Working on the ground during the raids had been a hella good time, and he wouldn't mind getting out there with Liam again.

"Hey there, pretty lady," Carter rumbled as Bernie approached. "Good to see you."

Bernie kissed Carter's cheek. "I'm sorry I didn't get to say hello earlier. Things have been crazy."

Carter glanced back over his shoulder at all of them. "I kind of noticed."

"He's cute," Annabeth whispered to Jamison. "In a follow-the-rules kind of way."

Most men would have been jealous, but Rowan kept scanning the hospital's camera feed as he tried not to grin. He wasn't worried about losing Annabeth, and her comment only solidified her comfort level with him.

"I'm not going to say he's hot because, apparently, we're related." To get a better look, Jamison dipped her head lower so Carter wouldn't catch her staring. "But I will say he's attractive."

On the screen, Taylor hustled down a hallway with Evie's hospital bag. "Taylor's here," Rowan told them. "She's got Evie's bag."

"Taylor?" Jamison's eyes lit up with mischief. "Perfect."

Annabeth seemed concerned, and quite frankly, so was Rowan. They both knew you should hold on tight if a Fairweather ever appeared to be up to something.

"Hey, Carter. There's a pretty woman headed our way with a suitcase," Jamison called out. "Her name is Taylor, and she's my dad's assistant. You can let her pass."

"I see her." Carter raised a hand, signaling Taylor. "She's coming."

An evil smirk stretched across Jamison's mouth, and Annabeth smacked her arm. "Stop."

"What?" Jamison feigned innocence as Taylor approached the waiting room door. "I didn't even describe her. I just said she was pretty."

Annabeth pinched the bridge of her nose. "So?"

"So, he thinks she's pretty, and my job is halfway done." Jamison shrugged. "If Taylor is still on a crusade to land a Fairweather, maybe we can throw her a watered-down version."

Rowan looked up from his screen to stare at Jamison. "An hour ago, you were talking to a terrorist. Like a real fucking terrorist was on your phone."

"And now your sister is about to have surgery while under guard," Annabeth chastised in a low voice.

"What's your point?" Jamison continued to observe Taylor and Carter interacting. "Look, if I can unload the pain in my ass that is Taylor on Mr. Diet Fairweather over there, it'll be worth coming off like I'm insensitive. Besides, watching this will keep me distracted."

Annabeth chewed on her bottom lip. "She has a point."

Jamison stood, smoothing the wedding dress. "Better than the alternative."

Rowan was almost too scared to ask, but did, anyway. "What's the alternative?"

"Picture me on the floor, hyperventilating until I pass out."

Jamison hurried off to greet Taylor and fill her in on the developments with Evie. While they chatted, Rowan tilted his head, watching as Jamison strategically included Carter in the conversation.

"You know, I've realized something," Rowan mumbled. "Jamison is insane."

Annabeth snuggled against him. "Oh, yeah. That's my favorite thing about her."

He chuckled softly, kissing her forehead before refocusing on the camera feeds.

"And you better get used to it."

He didn't look away from the screen. "What do you mean?"

"You better get used to being around Jamison's crazy." Annabeth looped her arm in his, the warmth of her body giving him a break from the arctic level of air conditioning blasting its way through the waiting room. "You'll have to deal with it for the rest of your life."

His face almost collided with hers when he turned his head. "What are you saying?"

"Nothing you don't already know."

Thump. Thump. Thump. His heart slammed against his rib cage. *Thump. Thump. Thump.* Jesus, was he going to have a heart attack? *Thump. Thump. Thump.* Fuck. Maybe he was having a heart attack.

"Did you change your mind?"

"No." She smiled sweetly. "But I'm not letting you go either."

His heart crashed abruptly and in the most painful way. It was his own fault for thinking she'd change her mind overnight. Still, he wouldn't make it easy for her.

"If you keep me around, expect me to keep asking," he told her. "After I finally do ask, that is. It could be decades before I'm ready to settle down."

"That's fine."

She rested her head on his shoulder, and they checked in on the OR entrances. Liam had joined Holden and was discussing something with Nurse Holly.

"I bet she's giving him baby news," Rowan guessed when Liam broke into a huge smile. "Yep, here he comes."

Moments later, Liam jogged into the waiting room. "Boy. Ten pounds, ten ounces. Healthy. Evie's great, and Samuel nearly fainted."

"Ten pounds?" Abe's mouth dropped open. "I don't know much about babies, but that's pretty freaking big, right?"

"A name?" Annabeth asked, before anyone could answer Abe. "They were keeping it a secret, but did you hear what it is?"

"Albie." Liam's gaze landed on Ben. "Albert Benjamin Fairweather."

Simone started to cry and reached for Ben's hand, who was also wiping away his tears. "That's a good name." Ben cleared his throat, regaining control as Josie dropped into the seat next to him to pull Theo onto her lap. "A very good name."

Witnessing Ben become emotional continued to be the weirdest thing. Hanging around Haven House for nearly a month, Rowan was getting used to it. But still, this was a private moment where Ben could have easily hidden his vulnerability, yet didn't, and Rowan's respect for him grew tenfold. McIntyres never showed weakness. Their grandfather hadn't allowed it. Things began to thaw only once he was dead, and then it still took some time for everyone to feel good about being open and free with who they truly were as individuals.

"Albie was Evie's dad?" he whispered to Annabeth.

"And Ben's best friend." She wiped her nose, sniffling a little as she tried to hold herself together. "They were like brothers, and Ben swore he would care for Laura Jean after his death."

"So, he married her?"

"No, that's how the media spins it." Annabeth released a laugh, a tear or two rolling down her cheeks. "But there's much more to the story. I'll tell it to you one day."

Chapter 25

Jamison

"I'm going to the nursery." Liam gave her a kiss. "That kid isn't leaving my sight."

Albie.

Albert Benjamin.

Jamison loved the name as much as she loved her new nephew, and she hadn't even met him yet. Her sister was sentimental, and so was Samuel—whether he wanted to admit it or not—and choosing such a perfect name to honor their fathers was very much on par for their little family.

"If you hang around him too much, you might end up changing diapers."

The comment earned her another kiss. "I'm good with that."

She waited until he headed out, covertly signaling for him not to interrupt Carter and Taylor's conversation. They were really chatting it up now, with Taylor giving him her infamous pouty lip look as she grilled him about his military background.

Thinking she would text Liam and explain her genius plan, she went for her phone and realized it was back at the house. When Carter returned them, she had set hers on the vanity and, too concerned for Evie, never picked it up again.

"Well, crap." Catching her father's eye, she grinned at him across the waiting room. "You good over there?"

"I'm good, princess." He rose from his seat and came over to hug her. "How are you holding up?"

She laid her cheek against his chest, relaxing into the embrace. "Keeping myself distracted."

"How so?"

She angled them slightly so he could see Taylor and Carter, and a deep chuckle rumbled from his chest. "You're clever as hell. Did you know that?"

"Got my smarts from my dad."

"As much as I'd like to take credit, I'm afraid I can't. That brain of yours comes from a mixture of your mother's DNA and Simone's upbringing."

Taylor's breathy giggle reached them, and Jamison buried her face in her father's shirt to hide her grin. She couldn't have planned this better. Earlier, she hadn't noticed Taylor's outfit, but the sleek green pencil skirt and tight white bodysuit were providing Carter quite the show.

"I really am a genius, but this genius needs the restroom."

Hearing her say she had to use the bathroom, Carter paused the conversation with Taylor. "If you go, you know I'm going with you."

She did know and wasn't particularly excited about having the new guy listen to her pee. Nor did she want Rowan in on the action. Sensing her unease, Carter tried to negotiate. "I'll wait outside."

"Yeah, no. I'm not good with that idea," her father said. "Someone could be in the restroom and grab her."

"I'll go with them," Taylor offered, setting Evie's bag down. "Carter can clear the bathroom first, and then we girls can handle business while he waits outside. Jamison will need help with that dress, anyway."

God, she hated that Taylor was right. Her mother's wedding gown might be easy to move around in, but positioning herself over a toilet and not getting something gross on the skirt would be impossible on her own.

Harper appeared next to them. "I can protect her if Mr. Carter gives me a weapon."

"That's a big fat no, Harper," her Papa quickly replied. "No weapons before ten. We've discussed this. Repeatedly."

Harper huffed and crossed her arms. "I think we need to reevaluate."

Jamison hid her smile when her father's eye twitched. "And I think you're starting to act too much like your dad," he said. "Way too much like him."

"Is that bad?" Harper asked innocently. "What's wrong with how my daddy acts?"

"That's a loaded question, Harper." Jamison sidestepped toward Carter and Taylor, leaving her father to manage the mini-female version of himself and Samuel. "We'll be back."

"There's a bathroom at the end of this corridor," Taylor said, sending a quick text as they exited the waiting room and veered left. "It's through those double doors over there."

Carter led the way, the hall growing darker the further they traveled. "The lights are low for the newborns," Taylor explained as they passed several open doors where families quietly celebrated their new arrivals. "The nurses keep the doors open this time of day since they're doing rounds for shift change."

Try as she might, Jamison couldn't help but peek inside, feeling like a voyeur violating people's privacy. Everyone looked so happy. Nothing but smiles and joy poured out of each and every room. "How do you know that?"

"My best friend became a nurse, and my husband was a doctor, though he practiced internal medicine," Taylor replied, pointing ahead. "The bathroom's right through there."

A shirtless father stood in the entryway to one of the rooms, a bundle cradled against his chest as he spoke with a nurse. "I didn't know your husband was a doctor," Jamison said, attempting to keep up with the conversation while her mind switched the new father out with an image of Liam holding their baby. The vision hurt as much as it gave hope, and already so tired of hurting, she chose to hold on to the hope and store it away for when she needed it. "I'm surprised you didn't enter the medical field."

"Not my thing." Taylor flashed Carter a beauty queen smile as he opened the double doors. "Growing up as I did, you learn the importance of proper medical care, and I wouldn't want to mess things up."

"Growing up like you did?"

Stepping through the double doors, Taylor shrugged. "It was hard to get medical care in certain parts."

Another long, darkened corridor stretched on the other side of the double doors. About halfway down, on the left, there was an empty nurses' station, and on the right, more patient rooms; however, unlike the previous hall, these were empty.

"The bathroom is just past the nurses' station." Taylor pointed to the sign hanging from the ceiling. "Right next to the vending machine."

Carter slowed his pace. "Where the hell is everyone?"

Not a soul was in sight, and the only sound was the squeak of the flip-flops Jamison had hurriedly put on when they left Haven House.

"This wing is for hospital overflow," Taylor explained. "They used it a lot during the pandemic."

Carter kept a trained eye on every hospital room doorway, sweeping Jamison behind him to secure her at his back. "We're turning around."

"No, look, it's right here." Taylor strode ahead confidently, passing the nurses' station, which then turned off to another long, poorly lit hallway. She stopped in front of twin vending machines. "See, all clear."

From the corner of her eye, Jamison would have sworn she saw a vague figure in the patient rooms. A woman in white with long, dark hair and pale skin. She was in one room, and then in the next, and then the next, her figure flashing as they passed. With a finger pressed to her lips, she shook her head, appearing and disappearing in a blink.

"I don't like this." Jamison buried herself deeper into Carter's massive back. "Carter?"

"Yeah, I hear you." He tightened his hold. "Let's go, Taylor."

"You two are being silly." Jamison couldn't see Taylor since she was sheltered behind Carter, but it sounded like she was continuing to walk ahead. "Okay, fine, but let me grab a water from the vending machine."

"No, Taylor." Carter's voice took on an annoyed, commanding tone. He halted at the nurse's station. "We're leaving."

"And I said I wanted water."

Jamison peered around Carter so she could glare at Taylor. There might have been a consensus that they were all supposed to be nice, but the woman's audacity sometimes ventured into levels of stupidity she couldn't even begin to comprehend. "Taylor, no one cares about your water. You're putting us in danger."

Taylor rummaged in her purse, mocking Jamison's tone. "You're putting us in danger," she whined. "God. If Mike wanted you, he'd have taken you already, so chill out."

Carter didn't hesitate.

"Go!" Spinning her around, Carter shoved Jamison into motion, catapulting her back the way they came. "Run!"

An enormous shadow—no, a man—emerged from behind the nurses' station. With a syringe in hand, he crawled onto the counter and leaped high into the air to tackle Carter.

The syringe's needle plunged directly into Carter's muscled neck on impact, and Jamison stumbled back in shock, time inching to a stop as her brain attempted to comprehend what she was seeing.

The shadow man lowering Carter to the floor.

A second syringe appearing, the wielder giggling with maniacal laughter as they waved it about in the air with glee.

And the reflection of a young woman in the vending machine glass. Wearing a white nightgown, her jaw unhinging and mouth gaping wide as she screamed.

Run.

Run.

Run.

As fast as you can.

CHAPTER 26

Charlie

2007

You are my sunshine...

He didn't deserve this.

My only sunshine...

Life shouldn't be this hard.

You make me happy...

This wasn't how it was supposed to be.

When skies are gray...

Why did Rebecca do it?

You'll never know, dear...

She ruined everything.

How much I love you...

And now he was in hell.

Please don't take my sunshine away.

Sprawled in the sailboat's hammock, Charlie's eyes fluttered open, and, for a moment, he thought he'd gone blind. "What the fuck?"

His mind slowly woke from its drunken slumber, and he realized he wasn't blind. The inability to see was the moon's fault, annoyingly hiding from the night sky as if it couldn't be bothered to do its job.

"Goddammit."

He tried to sit up, but his surroundings spun in a whirl of stars and the inky blue-black water of the Caribbean Sea. Landing on his hands and knees, Charlie hissed when he connected with the hard deck.

"Cecilia!"

In the distance, the lights of St. Thomas twinkled brighter than any star in the sky, and he cursed each one. He cursed his mother, the hag. He cursed his brother, the son of a bitch. He cursed Viv, the heartless woman who stole the best years of his life.

"Cecilia!"

Wherever she was, she better not be crying. He couldn't stand it when she cried. She looked like Rebecca when she did, pouty and covered in crocodile tears. It fucking annoyed him.

"Cecilia, come here."

He winced at the loudness of his voice, throwing a curse at Bryan Carroll for good measure. He'd learned long ago not to run with that man, let alone drink with him. But when Bryan sauntered into Latitude 18 as if he owned the place, Charlie didn't argue when his former friend sat at the bar next to him. And he didn't stop Bryan from inquiring about how life was going, as if he hadn't been the one to ruin it.

Everything they ever said about the man was true. Bryan Carroll was a thief. There was the whole drug thing, too, but at his core, the guy was nothing but a common thief who stole from everyone.

And Charlie was one of his favorite targets.

His money. His home. His son. His daughter. Bryan held them all in the palm of his hand. Charlie was preparing for a fight, first to break the man's influence over his kids, and then he was going after his villa. He would call Trevor—hell, he would call Ben if he had to—and they would fight with him. A common enemy. That's what he and his brothers needed, and Bryan Carroll was about to fit the bill.

Feeling like he might vomit when a larger wave struck the sailboat and sent it pitching sharply to one side, Charlie roared for his daughter a final time. She was likely hiding below deck, sulking because he hadn't allowed her to stay the night in their old villa. The villa Bryan now owned, thanks to one stupid round of poker.

Brandy had invited her for a sleepover, doing so out of spite, since that was the only way the Carroll family knew how to operate. Oh, wait. They couldn't call her Brandy anymore. No, the brat wouldn't allow it, and neither did Bryan, because whatever his little girl wanted, she got.

People could call her what she liked; she was still a whore. Charlie couldn't even begin to count the times he had caught the slut with his son. The two of them went at it like rabbits, fucking each other all over this cursed island.

Bryan was tired of his daughter's whoring behavior, too, and brought it up while they drank together. "I swear, I'm going to get her fixed. It's a sorry thing to say, but she's not just fucking your son. She's fucking everyone's son."

Toby was an idiot. That kid was perfectly fine with his girlfriend spreading her legs for whoever she wanted. There were rumors on the island that he liked to watch, and at first, Charlie refused to believe it. Fairweather men didn't share. It was ingrained in their DNA. No one could touch what belonged to them.

But then he caught a glimpse of it himself.

A week—maybe two—ago, he'd spotted his son and Bryan's daughter in the back of a club he frequented. The place was mainly for tourists, and while he might be older, Charlie knew he was still attractive, and that night he'd been on the hunt for a warm body to fuck. Right from the get-go, he packed himself with tequila shots while wedging between a couple of college girls at the bar. The pair had sized him up like they had daddy issues for days, and it wasn't long before he was licking salt off their perfect tits.

Until he went to take a piss.

The rear of the club was always kept dark, allowing for private moments if couples should need them. Charlie never hung out there much, not caring for the thick cigarette smoke clinging to the air or the heavy vibration of the bass brought on by the massive speakers near the bathroom.

And that night, he came across Bryan Carroll's daughter riding some college boy who was most definitely not Tobias.

Even worse, Tobias was there. Standing right next to the guy getting ridden to holy hell, his teenage son had been aggressively fucking the face of some poor girl who appeared to be unable to breathe, thanks to the dick in her throat.

Charlie had never left a building so fast. He hardly saw his kids anymore since they spent so much time with Bryan. But whatever was happening had to stop, and he immediately called for CeCe to come home to their sailboat.

Toby refused to return, but eventually showed up to check in with CeCe. He stayed for a day or two and then disappeared again, jetting off on one of Bryan's many luxury speedboats.

"CeCe!"

Forcing himself to stand, Charlie squinted into the night. He could tell they were off the Buck Island lagoon, and why the hell he had anchored them so far out was lost in the haze of booze occupying his brain. Lapses in memory were an unfortunate side effect of drinking, but as every level in his life seemed to want to drop him deeper and deeper into hell, alcohol had turned into a necessity for him to function.

Stumbling over to the entrance leading below, he tripped but caught himself on something soft before hitting the ground. Whatever it was groaned, and as his eyesight adjusted, Charlie dropped to his knees when he realized it was a body.

"Toby? That you, boy?"

With his back against a wall, Toby lay slouched and moaning as if in pain. His skin had dark splotches, like bruises mixed with dried blood. Crouching lower for a closer look, Charlie could see the kid's lip was busted and his left eye swollen nearly shut.

"What the hell did that little bitch drag you into?"

No other boat was tied to theirs, which meant Brandy must have gotten them into trouble and dumped Toby out here for him to deal with. It wouldn't be the first damn time and probably wouldn't be the last.

"Stay here," he ordered, as if Toby could hear him. Half falling down the short set of stairs to their living quarters, Charlie felt around for the light switch. "CeCe, where the hell are you?"

He clicked on the low lights, hissing as his pupils dilated. She wasn't in her normal chair, the one she virtually lived in while watching TV. CeCe loved movies. The big sweeping romances that drove him insane. He hated that she watched them. They built unrealistic expectations and ideas about men.

Unsteady on his feet, he lumbered to the aft bedrooms. They had two, with CeCe getting one all to herself. Sliding open the cabin door, he snapped on her light and found her in bed, curled into a ball and crying quietly.

"Come help me with your brother."

She didn't move, her trembling only increasing the closer he came. Lying on one of the quilts he'd had made for her, he figured she must be in the middle of a nightmare again. CeCe often dreamed of the night her mother died. She didn't see it happen since she was upstairs with SiSi, but she had run right into the aftermath. Slipping and sliding on the blood and gore, Charlie had been told she tried to wake Livy, sitting with her sister's body until they forced her to leave.

"Cecilia, can you hear me?" He didn't shout this time. It wouldn't do any good pulling her out of the nightmare too fast. "I said, come help me with your brother."

His brain was slow to catch up, but standing at the foot of her mattress, it felt as if he were watching an abstract painting pull together to create a new and terrifying truth. CeCe was hurt. Like Tobias, blood splotches covered her clothes. There were bruises on her arms, and the shorts she wore showed even more on her legs.

"Oh my God, baby." He reached for her, dying a little at seeing her hurt. "What happened? Did Toby do this?"

CeCe hadn't left the boat. He might not remember how he got back from the bar or why he had brought them out to Buck Island, but he knew CeCe was his obedient one. If he had told her to stay, she would have stayed.

The sound of a speedboat approaching carried through the air, and he recognized the whine of the craft's engine immediately. It was one of Bryan's. "Did Brandy do this to you?"

He laid a hand on her shoulder, and it was like she was electrocuted. CeCe screeched in terror and, scurrying away from him, cowered at the top of the mattress.

"Cecilia, tell me right now who did this." A sick thought hit him. It was possible. James Fairweather had once gotten off on the pain of others, and Toby was turning into a sadist, just like him. "Was it Tobias?"

She shook harder, covering her head with her skinny arms. "Don't hurt me."

"I won't hurt you." He placed a knee on the mattress and tried to crawl over to her. "Let me see your face."

CeCe lowered her arms. Broken. His little girl was broken. Bruises littered her tear-stained face, her bottom lip was split open, and there were gashes covered with dried blood near her temple.

"I'm going to kill him."

"No!" CeCe launched herself at him, clawing and fighting as if he were the enemy. "Leave him alone!"

Tobias thundered into the room. Off balance and catching his shoulder on the doorframe, he screamed like an insane person. "Don't touch her!"

"What the hell is wrong with you two?" Easily pulling CeCe off him, Charlie dropped her as gently as he could on the bed. "Someone better start talking."

"What's wrong with us?" Toby's face turned purple as he continued to scream, the veins in his neck straining against the flesh. "How could you do this to her?"

CeCe resumed her position into a ball, the wailing coming from her lips feeling like a knife to the skull. "I didn't do anything," Charlie yelled, not quite sure if he was telling the truth. "Now start fucking talking."

His reflexes were off. Charlie didn't know what in the hell was wrong with him, but he didn't react in time, and Toby's fist struck his cheek with enough force that he went flying into CeCe's small computer desk.

Before he could clear his head, Toby was hauling him up by his shirt. His son had always been a big kid, but the older he got and the more his looks carried weight in the world, the more Toby began to pay attention. Working out was part of his regular day now, and not only had it toned his muscles, but it had also provided the boy with a newfound strength.

Charlie found himself flying again, smacking into a polished wooden wall on the opposite side of the cabin. When his body hit with a sickening thud, it knocked some of his brain awake, and he held up his arms to block the next blow.

"Don't talk about her that way." Spit flung from Toby's lips, his eyes wild as he lost himself to another one of his raging episodes. "Don't you ever talk about Taylor that way."

Brandy materialized in the doorway, a sleek black mini-dress hugging her curves. Tossing her strawberry-blonde braid over one shoulder, she cooed, "Yeah—don't talk about me like that."

"Brandy," CeCe sobbed, "help me."

CeCe had always looked up to Bryan Carroll's daughter, and in the beginning, when Charlie thought the Carrolls were decent people, he'd encouraged their friendship. But after that night at the poker tables—after he lost their home in a single round of luck—he'd reversed course, wanting his daughter to have nothing to do with any of them.

"Oh, no, CeCe. That's not right, and the last time I checked, you weren't an idiot," Brandy admonished, wagging her finger in disapproval. "What did we say? People with the name Brandy don't become famous. We're using my middle name. I'm Taylor now. T-A-Y-L-O-R."

"I'm sorry." CeCe cried harder. "I just forgot."

Charlie opened his mouth to call Brandy something off the long list of derogatory names he kept in his head to use on her, but Toby slammed his fist into his face before he could get anything out.

"What the fuck, Tobias." Charlie spat out a string of saliva and blood. "Stop and talk to me."

Toby burst into tears, choking on his sobs as he went over to hold his sister. "You did this to us."

Lifting a hand, Charlie wiped his mouth, wincing at the pain in his swollen knuckles. With a confused frown, he extended his fingers to examine them. Blood. Dried and caked on his skin, streaks of blood littered his hands.

No.

No, he wouldn't.

He couldn't.

Once upon a time, perhaps, but he had changed. He wasn't a monster anymore. He wasn't that man. Sure, he drank and did a few lines every now and then, but not like before. Never like before.

Racking his brain, Charlie tried to think back to the last thing he could remember. The bar. He had been drinking at the bar when Bryan appeared with his goons in tow and sat uninvited to discuss the kids and the villa. The asshole had thought he could talk him out of getting his brothers involved.

He had held firm and wasn't about to let Bryan strong-arm him. Not again. What could he do? Kill him? Bryan was ballsy, but not that ballsy. Everyone on the damn island knew him and knew he and Charlie had a tenuous relationship.

So, with one parting smartass comment, Charlie had left Bryan at the bar to take a piss, and the bastard was gone by the time he returned, having ordered a fresh round for him to finish on his own.

After that...

Charlie frowned at his kids cowering on the bed. After that, things got confusing. He didn't even finish his drink before the liquor hit like a tidal wave. One of the goons Bryan had brought must have stayed behind because when he'd nearly fallen off his stool, it had been that ugly motherfucker who helped him leave. Charlie knew the guy's face but not his name, and he didn't think it mattered. He was a lackey there to serve, and that's what he did when he dropped him off at his sailboat docked at Crown Bay.

There was a vague recollection of Tobias being onboard when he arrived, claiming he was leaving to meet Brandy for dinner at her place. They were going to discuss plans to visit Florida, with Brandy wanting to see Haven House and meet the family. For whatever reason, an unnatural rush of anger had struck at the idea, but beyond that, Charlie had nothing. There was no memory, only darkness.

While Toby consoled his sister, Charlie glared at Brandy—*Taylor*—sneering down at him. "What did he do?"

Brandy batted her eyes. "What do you mean?"

Bryan had given him something. At the bar, he must have slipped something into his drink. Charlie broke eye contact with Brandy to stare in bewilderment at his hands. "What did he do to me?"

CeCe gagged, completely overtaken by her hysterical tears, and with Toby distracted as he whispered to her, Brandy bent down to speak directly in Charlie's face. "If you would've just fallen off the boat and drowned, this would have been easier."

Charlie's head snapped so he could speak to this evil bitch face-to-face. "What did you say?"

"Daddy always gives me what I want, and I want them."

This level of anger hadn't filled him in years, if ever. The entire world always wanted him to give up everything he had. It wanted to rob and steal away what was rightfully his. Toby wasn't lost. He believed in his boy. Those odd behaviors took life experience and age to iron out, and while Charlie would admit he might be kidding himself, he had to hold on to the fact that a change might be possible.

But Brandy didn't want that. She was always single-minded in her actions, never taking no for an answer. If she had an idea in her head, she wouldn't let it go, and she wanted Tobias to be dark and twisted, a sadistically sick bastard to do her bidding.

"Both of them."

What she was saying finally penetrated his brain.

CeCe.

The bitch wanted CeCe, too.

The cabin was cramped, but Charlie needed only a heartbeat to gauge the distance. He clamped a hand around Brandy's ankle and yanked—*hard.*

She came crashing to the ground with a scream, her head cracking on the floor as she hit. The sound only fueled his anger, and he craved to hear her cry out in pain again.

"They're my kids. My family." He hauled her beneath him, trapping her. One hand crushed her jaw so tightly he half-expected it to snap. "You and your father can't have them. They're mi—"

It was over when CeCe's scream pierced the air. Charlie would readily admit he didn't know a whole lot of things, but he knew that sound. His little girl's scream wasn't over what he was doing to Brandy, but because she was scared.

Her brother. His demon. It was here.

And it wanted Charlie's blood.

He laid there and took it. Every hit. Every strike. Charlie took on his son's demon and its wrath. Ripped off Brandy, he was tossed onto his back while Tobias pummeled him. Hit after hit, he waited it out, knowing it would end soon. This was something Toby needed, and Charlie had been the punching bag plenty of times before.

"He tried to kill me!" Brandy screeched as she scrambled out of the way. "He wants me dead because he doesn't want us to be together."

One feeding the darkness in the other. That's all Brandy and Tobias were to each other. Like called to like, and the pair were twin flames in their depravity.

Yet Charlie still thought he could save his son. He shouted Toby's name. Pleading with him to see what he was doing and to stop and ask himself why. "Bryan drugged me. You know I would never hurt you two."

"Yes, you would."

The hits continued to rain down on him, the world blinking in and out. CeCe sat unmoving on the bed, cradling her favorite teddy bear to her chest. She shouldn't see this. She should be safe in her bed at Haven House. SiSi should have raised her. What a fool he had been.

Tobias sat on his chest, the endless beating gaining new steam as the boy grunted with every slam of his fist. Charlie's head whipped back and forth, and he thought he might be drowning from the blood gathering in his throat and mouth.

"Stop, Toby," CeCe's small voice pleaded. "That's enough."

Brandy hovered above them, her sick smile slicing across her face in the dim light. "It'll never be enough. Not until he's gone."

With a roar, Tobias flipped him to his front, and so badly beaten, Charlie had no strength to rise. Not that he could with a six-foot teenager on his back. There was shuffling as if Tobias searched for something at CeCe's computer desk. He tried to lift his head, but all he could see was the cabin doorway and the narrow hall leading to his bedroom. Two people were standing there. Two sets of bare feet. A woman and a child. Waiting. They looked as if they were waiting for something to happen.

The cold cord was the first thing he felt. The second was CeCe's wail of denial, piercing his heart with the truest aim. She fell to the floor, rushing over to him on her hands and knees.

"Don't, Toby." CeCe's beautiful face filled Charlie's vision, blocking the bare feet of the woman and child in the hall. "Please don't. We can leave. We're old enough."

"But you'll never be free of him." Brandy crouched next to CeCe, the fevered glee in her eyes full of crazed malice. "You can leave him, but he'll always turn up. A bum with no one. He'll be a thorn in your side forever, CeCe."

The cord pulled tight, silencing any protest Charlie might have. CeCe screamed once more, but it was no use. When she tried to shove at her brother, Brandy was there, seizing his little girl by the hair on the back of her head.

"Watch." Brandy shoved CeCe forward and directly into Charlie's face. "You love him so much. You need to be the one to look him in the eyes when he goes."

And that was it.

A simple thing, really.

His life.

Not that long, but long enough for him to realize that the pain would never end. It would forever be his burden. A haunting past that left no room for anything else.

It was better this way, maybe. As the pinpricks of light popped in and out of his vision, Charlie thought that perhaps it was better this way. CeCe was smart. She would escape and live a full life. He had to believe that. Ben would find her and bring her home. He would bring her home to Haven House, where she could live out her days in the one place she belonged.

"Toby, please," CeCe begged as the darkness beckoned. "For me. Don't do this for me."

There was hesitation. Charlie got one ragged breath in when the cord's pressure went lax.

But all it took for it to go tight again was for Brandy to want it. "For me, Toby. Get rid of him for *me*."

Whoever was out in the hall was coming closer to watch. He could see them clearly now—a woman and a little girl. The woman was shrouded in darkness, with a pulsing red heartbeat at her center, the weight of her sins a constant companion for all eternity.

And the other—the little girl as bright as the sun—sang for him. Louder and louder until he could focus on nothing but her voice. His end would come at the hands of his son while his youngest daughter screamed for his life, but his oldest child... she would be the one to sing him to sleep.

He would leave this world as he lived in it, with nothing to show and no one to mourn him. Yet, that didn't matter. Because in the end, Charlie Fairweather remembered everything.

You are my sunshine...

Viv and her baby blue eyes on their wedding day.

My only sunshine...

Ben and Trevor. His safe harbor when he was young, his enemies as they grew old.

You make me happy...

Rebecca aiming her sly smile at him from behind the bar of the Blue 42.

When skies are gray...

Those four damn women. Laughing on the patio while children played in the yard.

You'll never know, dear...

Toby and CeCe squealing in delight when he brought them to the island. A family. They had been a real family that day.

How much I love you...

And his Livy. His beautiful Livy walking with him along the bayou at Haven House. Forever young and forever his to love.

Please don't take my sunshine away.

Chapter 27

Jamison

Time regained its momentum, propelling Jamison into motion as Taylor's shrill laughter chased her down the dark hospital hall. The vile sound reached a crescendo just as another shadow barreled out of an empty room, tackling her before she could escape.

But, of course, it wasn't a shadow. It was a man dressed in clothing so dark he was nearly invisible. Her eyes adjusted quickly, and her fight instinct took over. Growling in rage, she punched his masked face, and while her aim might have been off, she landed the hit.

"Bitch."

Parker.

Understanding his involvement was one thing, seeing him with Bruce and Emmett another, but hearing his voice and recognizing his build sent Jamison into a rage. She clawed at his face. "I will kill you!"

Tossing his head back and forth to avoid her nails, Parker slammed a fist into her stomach. She doubled over, gasping as she crashed into the wall.

A few feet away, Carter continued to struggle with the larger shadow man on top of him, but he was losing more and more strength as whatever they injected into him did its job.

"Poor baby. He was so cute." Taylor stepped primly over Carter's legs, moving toward Jamison, who was still fighting for breath. "You guys always hire the hottest bodyguards."

"We trusted you!" Raw instinct surged, and Jamison lunged, but Parker caught her around the waist before she could reach Taylor. "Samuel trusted you! My dad trusted you!"

"Uh, yeah, but they wouldn't fuck me." Taylor waved a second syringe about in the air. "I tried for years. First, with your brother, but Samuel gets weirdly focused on projects, and he can't even notice a pair of great tits and a firm ass right there in front of him. It was so frustrating."

"Because my brother is a decent human."

"Whatever. No, he's not. Samuel's a total dick. A hot dick, but still a dick," Taylor scoffed. "On the inside, he's just like my man. Every Fairweather male is. Some hide it better, while the others—the best ones—let it all out."

"Your man? Is this about Toby? You're one of them? Those losers, Taylor?" Halting her struggle against Parker, Jamison edged her laughter with ridicule. "That's disappointing, even for you."

Twisting the syringe between her fingers, Taylor jabbed it menacingly toward Jamison's face. "They're not losers, you entitled cow. They're my friends, and if you keep saying horrible things about them, I'll stick this needle right in your eye."

Taylor stepped closer as she made her threat, and Jamison tried to break free, but when she couldn't, she jerked her head back to crash her skull directly into Parker's face. The solid crunch of his nose felt good, and a tiny flare of satisfaction came from knowing she'd done a little damage.

"And then I'll jam this into Evie's eye," Taylor seethed, the insanity in her tone growing wilder. "Stupid, stupid Evie. Ugh, I hate her. What makes her so special, huh? She's not that pretty, and she ruins *everything*. She sent my husband to prison. *My husband, Jamison.* Your bitch sister basically killed him, and all he did was respect her and want to bring her into our family."

Parker continued to groan behind Jamison, swaying slightly. She tried to squirm away again, but still had no luck. "He wanted to kill Evie."

"No, he didn't!" Taking a cleansing breath, Taylor calmed a minuscule amount. "Toby likes to play, so I let him play whenever we make new friends, but really, with Evie, he was taking her for me."

"Why you?"

"It's complicated." Taylor's lips wobbled. "I wanted to be an actress."

Jamison knew her limits, and Taylor's confession pushed her solidly past them. Even with her life hanging in the balance, she couldn't stop herself from snickering. "An actress? You wanted to be an actress?"

Taylor's mouth dropped open as if no one had ever questioned her career choice. "Yes, I wanted to be an actress! I'm great at it! I taught Toby how to behave around your family so no one would figure out who he was, and then look at how many years I've fooled you. I fooled you all!"

She truly had. Taylor had woven herself so deeply into their lives that they hadn't even stopped to entertain the possibility that she could be part of Toby's insane group. Ever since she was hired as a secondary assistant for Samuel, they had trusted her. For years, they had trusted her to keep their secrets and lives safe.

Shaking her head, Jamison told herself not to focus on the betrayal and try to gain more information. "How does that lead to Toby taking Evie?"

"Ambition makes you do tough things."

"What the hell does that even mean?"

At their feet, Carter tried to push himself up, but the man on his back held him down until he went limp again. Craning her neck, Jamison watched for the measured rise and fall of Carter's breathing, hoping to God he wasn't dead.

"Daddy had my tubes tied when I was younger," Taylor continued. "Those extra organs take up space in your bits and make you fat. Fat women can't act."

Jamison's attention snapped back to Taylor. "Your bits?"

"The tube parts. It's wasted space, anyway. Daddy said they were easily removed to make you thinner, so he had them do the surgery when I was seventeen," Taylor explained with an air of annoyance. "But I reversed the whole thing when Toby and I were ready for a family. If we had babies, I wouldn't mind getting chubby."

"That's not how it works. Having your tubes tied… Taylor, that's not how it works!" Jamison's eye twitched, her frustration over what she was hearing causing her to lose her mind. "You cannot be this stupid and have pulled all this off."

"I'm not stupid." Taylor tilted her head to the side. "Stupid women don't—"

"We need to go."

The attacker on Carter stood, and Jamison recognized him immediately. "Bruce."

"Good to see you again, Ms. Fairweather." Removing his mask and hood, Bruce grinned. "Mike's going to love that dress."

At the mention of Michael, terror replaced her irritation. Jamison's head whipped around, scanning the hallway. Was Michael here? Were they planning to blow up the hospital?

Taylor stomped her foot, the heel of her shoe cracking against the vinyl flooring in outrage over being interrupted. "Bruce, I was in the middle of my monologue."

"You'll have to finish in the car." Bruce took the syringe from Taylor, his smile turning apologetic. "Hold still, Ms. Fairweather, or you know how much this will hurt."

Parker's grip on her tightened, with one arm wrapped around her chest and the other around her head. Yanking hard, he exposed her neck to Bruce, who jabbed the needle into her flesh.

Jamison squeezed her eyes shut as if she could make it all go away. "Michael likes his women responsive," she blabbered. "Don't give me too much."

"Oh, sweet girl, Michael's not here. It's just you and me this time," Bruce said, pushing the drug into her veins, igniting a familiar burn she thought she would never feel again. "I don't need you responsive."

Every muscle in her body—every nerve—every ounce of her being right down to the bone trembled. As Bruce gripped her face, he squeezed hard, and the rush of fear struck anew. The literal light at the end of the tunnel shone ahead, the glow of fluorescents coming through the paned window on the double doors. Her family was on the other side. Her dad.

Liam.

The drugs hit, but not like before. There was no slow flow through her system, allowing her to remain upright yet woozy. This time, it hit within seconds, giving almost immediate results.

She would have struck the floor if not for Parker.

"This will leave you pretty much paralyzed for around three hours," Bruce explained, taking her limp body from Parker so he could be the one to carry her out. "If we aren't at our destination by then, you'll get another dose. Understand?"

Nodding was impossible, and he knew it.

"Wait, so she'll be awake, and I can keep talking?" Taylor asked, retrieving the used syringe from Carter's body. "I've got a lot to say to this bitch and might not have another chance."

"Yes, ma'am." Bruce headed toward the stairwell door. "Talk her head off, but she can't respond. She can only listen."

Taylor giggled in absolute delight. "Oh, Bruce, you're so my new favorite henchman."

CHAPTER 28

Jamison

*"*T*aylor breaks all her toys. Don't let her play with you."*

Bruce hadn't been entirely truthful. The drugs did knock her out, albeit only briefly. She woke to strange whispers, which were quickly drowned out by Taylor's incessant rambling.

"So where was I? We took the sailboat further out, went choppy-choppy to Charlie's body, and tossed him." Sitting in the front passenger seat, Taylor tapped her chin thoughtfully. "Then we grabbed my boat and went ashore. Buck Island is a nature preserve and is so beautiful. Toby and I said our vows on the beach right at sunrise. It was amazing. Much prettier than what your stupid beach wedding would have been. Ours was spontaneous and fun."

A laundry list of responses rolled through Jamison's head. So many smartass things she could say that would tear a hole right through Taylor's ridiculously over inflated ego.

Trapped in her body, she imagined this must be what hell felt like. She had no control of her movements, and the only thing she could hear was Taylor's yapping as it mixed with the erratic thumps of her own heart. Fast and slow. *Fast* and *slow*. Like her body was fighting a war to regain control, shooting adrenaline through her veins, but the drugs, being as potent as they were, gave the chemical no purpose and nowhere to go.

"Anyway, Toby had a way with the human body, right? He knew how to fuck, and he could... disassemble? Yeah, let's go with that. No need to get into all the gore of Charlie's transition into shark food."

Taylor wrinkled her nose. "And I told him, babe, you should totally be a doctor."

Driving the van, Parker mumbled something. Jamison couldn't hear clearly, but Taylor punched his shoulder. "Not cool, Parker. Toby isn't here to defend himself."

One of the only things Jamison held partial control over was her eyes. Rolling them as far up as she could, she stared at Bruce, who appeared both bored and annoyed by what he was hearing. With her head in his lap, she glared—or tried to glare—at him. Beyond his head, there was only sky through the window with the soft glow of night descending, but there was no way she could properly gauge time in this state.

"At first, Toby wasn't into being a doctor, but when he changed his mind, he refused to take my dad's money for school. That pissed me off, but Toby wanted to prove he had the financial status to be worthy of someone like me. My dad said he had a point. We didn't know who the fuck the Fairweathers were. All we had to go off of was Charlie, which wasn't saying much. Toby and CeCe always talked about Haven House. They would say how beautiful and majestic it was. Toby always promised to take me there."

There were others in the van. Two women sitting on the third row, and try as she might, Jamison couldn't see them clearly. The only thing she could make out were a few features, like how one woman had a head of long, dark hair and wore white. The second one also wore white but had much lighter hair, almost platinum blonde, and very similar to her own. There was something shiny and green at the base of the second one's throat. Jamison stared at the color, hypnotized by how the dying light danced over it. Bruce never acknowledged them, nor did Parker or Taylor, which meant they were probably Zanmi "sisters" only here to do the dirty work if needed.

"You see, I don't do poor. It's a bad look for me," Taylor jabbered on. "Toby understood that. When you can talk again, I want you to explain what you were thinking with Liam. FBI agents make no money, at least not enough for your high-dollar ass. I mean, he's got the body, the face, the brains, but Jamison, babe, there's no money. You fuck those types of guys. You don't marry them."

The GPS informed Parker he needed to make a left, and Taylor danced in her seat, excited over something. The car turned, and Jamison felt as if she were going to slide right off onto the van's floor, but Bruce held her in place, grunting at Parker to take it easy on the turns.

"Yay! It's here!" Taylor clapped like a seal. "Bruce, I told you they'd come through. My daddy's friends have connections you could only dream of. Remember, you and Mike aren't the only ones with private planes."

Parker hit the brakes abruptly, and Jamison fully expected her body to go flying, but Bruce came to her rescue again, keeping a firm enough hold on her that she remained in place. Once they parked, Taylor rushed out of the van, with Parker right behind her, both slamming their car doors hard enough to rattle her teeth.

Jamison thought Bruce and the women would follow, but they stayed in the van. "When your next dose comes due, I'm not going to give you as much, but I need you to keep calm," Bruce whispered, turning his head to the side so those outside the car couldn't see he was speaking. "No stunts, got me? I don't want them catching on."

Pumping air in and out of her nose, Jamison attempted to blink a few times and was excited to find that her eyelids worked once more. She tried to communicate her thanks with her gaze, but he wouldn't look at her directly.

"Taylor doesn't need you long-term. Behave, and she might let you live," Bruce continued softly. "But remember, what she wants doesn't require consciousness. If you make trouble, she'll keep you knocked out for the whole nine months."

Nine months.

Nine.

Months.

The air thinned, panic constricting her chest. Nine months. Nine fucking months. This wasn't new information, but at their mercy, and hearing it spoken aloud had the fear clawing its way through her.

The women in the back leaned forward, their faces sandwiched around Bruce's head. Even this close, Jamison couldn't see them clearly, nor could she hear what they were saying in his ear.

"Damon has to be kept fully sedated. Your cousin is one big motherfucker with some fight in him. Taylor wants him first, but then she has a list of others she's approved to have him." Bruce frowned, his eyes sliding to the side where the dark-haired woman continued to whisper. "And she's about to knock Claudia out for the duration of her pregnancy. That woman is fucking terrifying, and when paired with Emily, the two have already maimed a few Zanmi sisters. Taylor is tired of it."

Jamison's eyelids fluttered, and Bruce noticed, the corner of his lips curved upward. "Oh, you like that, huh? Figures. Taylor thinking she can handle kids with your family's DNA is ridiculous."

She began to blink rapidly, urging him to keep talking. He was giving her information she could tell Liam if she saw him again.

When.

When she saw him again.

Liam would come for her. Now and forever, he would never rest until she was found, and scared out of her mind, she had to hold on to that.

She thought of her father. He didn't deserve this. Living with as much pain as he did, he didn't deserve to go through the kidnapping of his daughter. It would break him. A final straw that would put in him an early grave.

The smaller woman—the one with the lighter colored hair—slipped her hand over the top of the seat to wrap her fingers around Jamison's ankle. Her touch was a mixture of ice and fire, searing the flesh as each digit made contact.

Either out of terror or anticipation of what was to come, Jamison's heart thundered in her chest. Faster and faster, it beat until her ears roared with the sound of blood flowing through her veins.

Bruce spared her a glance, but shook his head in warning when she continued to blink. "I don't know why, but that shit is running through your system faster than normal, and you need to chill. I don't want them to force another dose on you until we're in the air."

In the air? She blinked double time, making Bruce heave out a sigh. "You can't see it, but we're on a private airstrip. Decoys will drive this car while we fly north."

She didn't stop blinking, and his enormous shoulders slumped. Bruce might have served with Michael, but he was older, not by much, but enough to make it noticeable.

"Mike will be at the house," Bruce told her as the sound of voices outside the car came closer again. "No one is going to hurt you once we're with him, not even Taylor. She's a dangerous idiot, but she's smart enough not to do anything stupid when he's around."

Whether it be from the blinking or the finite terror, a tear gathered in the corner of her eye. Spilling over, it landed on Bruce's hand, and he finally lowered his gaze to meet hers. "I want you to listen to me. Mike Sinclair is a good man—one of the best. He finishes what he starts, and before he goes down, he will end the game for good. That family—your family—has a shadow hanging over it. A challenge between Destiny and the Grim Reaper. A never-ending battle for the fate of the Fairweathers. It's all there if you're paying attention."

Bruce's eyes softened a fraction. "I don't say all that with an outsider's perspective. I'm not some asshole who makes judgments about people over what he sees on television. Well, not totally. I watched some of the movies. I find your dad to be the most interesting. The empire and the emotional crash. The balance he'll never know."

The blonde woman laid a hand on Bruce's shoulder, and the drugs in her system made Jamison think that a shimmering glow came from the touch. She began to whisper in his ear, her face completely obscured by the light.

"I bet he really did love her. Your dad. I bet he really loved your mom. I don't think she was a homewrecker. I heard she was actually very nice," Bruce said, his gaze returning to the activity happening outside the car. "But ol' Grim won that round. He always wins eventually. Destiny might have saved you and those girls in the graveyard when Toby came calling, but Grim doesn't take losing well, and honey, I'm afraid he's going to make it hurt when you're back on the playing table."

The darker woman's whispering picked up in Bruce's free ear while the blonde continued doing the same. Their lips moved in a blur, and Jamison wished she could reach out and touch one of them, if only to reassure herself that what she was seeing wasn't a hallucination.

"And I don't like that graveyard. I don't know what your people did, but that place isn't right. Never has been. Something is out there. Watching and waiting like a damn animal, ready to pounce and drag you to hell. It was there the night we tried to take you. What was that? What was that... *thing*?" Bruce went pale as the women's whispers grew louder. "She didn't deserve to be tied to that place. She needed her own home, her own family. Destiny. She needed her destiny, and he was it."

The dark-haired woman seized Bruce by the face, squeezing his cheeks with her long, spindly fingers. She held him still as she hissed into his ear with a fevered frenzy. "No, don't say that. We won't let this go too far. He loves you," Bruce said in a hushed voice, as if talking to himself. "He loves you more than any man has ever loved a woman. It'll be over soon. I promise."

The voices outside the car grew louder, the groups sounding like old friends as they approached the vehicle. Feeling a tingling sensation in her limbs, Jamison attempted to wiggle her fingers and nearly cried with relief when she found that she could.

"Mike has blamed himself for so long," Bruce continued to speak to the darker woman as a sheen of sweat popped out across his brow. "Oh, sweet girl, you know what he's going to do."

The darker woman released Bruce's face to slink back into her seat while the lighter one did the same, their whispers halting.

"It's done. Grim will win the round." Bruce swiped a hand down his face as he panted. "Death will win big, and every last one of them will pay for their sins."

CHAPTER 29

Rowan

He couldn't listen to them.

The chatter. The noise. Annabeth's crying. Ben's rage. Rowan couldn't listen to them. He needed to be in his own head, deciphering the information on his screen.

They'd let their guard down. Caught up in the excitement, they had let their guard down, and now they were paying the price. He should have stayed at the house to track Madison. That should've been his top priority, but he stupidly believed the feds could handle it for a few hours.

There would be time to hate himself later. Right now, they had to find Jamison.

"We have a visual on the van," Klausen was telling Ben. "It's heading west and into Louisiana."

West.

No.

That's not what the data said. He'd traced the call. He wasn't wrong. Arkansas. Sinclair had been in northern Arkansas. A red herring, maybe, but Rowan trusted the information.

Setting his laptop aside, he moved to the corner of the waiting room to call Liam. "They're saying the van is headed west."

"Tell them about the airstrip."

Rowan had given Jamison and the others five minutes to reach the bathroom, use it, and return. He watched them on the security feed as they crossed through the double doors. The cameras in that particular hall had been dead and not in use, so by the time he hacked into the system and activated them, it was too late.

And it was his fault.

Once the camera feed powered up to reveal Carter face down on the floor, it took less than a second for the image to register, but when it did, Rowan sounded the alarm, running as fast as he could while shouting for Liam.

After that, it was a blur of insanity. Trusting someone else would help Carter, he and Liam had searched for Jamison on the abandoned hospital floor and, in the process, caught sight of her through a long panel of exterior windows as she was being hauled into a van with three other people.

One of which was a laughing Taylor.

Taylor was one of them. Zanmi. And she was as good as dead now. Ben would see to it. Her family. Her friends. No one connected to her would ever know peace. Once Jamison was found, Rowan wouldn't be surprised if Ben himself didn't murder the woman with his bare hands.

Assuming he didn't take out a federal agent or two first.

"A visual on the van?" Ben snarled. "Then get my daughter the fuck out of it."

Klausen glanced around at the other agents. "It's not that simple."

"Why the hell is it not that simple?"

Guns.

Bombs.

A hostage situation.

Klausen ran through the possibilities. Ben had already been forced both physically by agents and verbally by Simone to stay put at the hospital, but hearing how a rescue could go down had him heading for the door again.

This time, it was Bernie who blocked him from leaving. "Wait for Will. Let him go with you."

No one would be able to keep Ben from going after his daughter. The fact that Simone had persuaded him to wait was a miracle, but with each passing minute, Ben's need to find her ripped away at his rational thought. He wasn't nearly as calm and collected as Liam.

"Rowan," Liam shouted his name through the phone. "Did you fucking tell them about the airstrip?"

So maybe Liam wasn't exactly calm. When he saw Jamison limp in Bruce's arms, he lost his shit. Finding the first set of stairs, they stormed down to the ground floor and out into the parking lot just as the van carrying Jamison sped away.

Liam had already pulled his gun out to commandeer the first passing car, scaring the shit out of the woman who was now in the hall screaming at anyone she thought might have the authority to get her vehicle back.

"I told Klausen."

While tracking Liam as he chased after Jamison, an abandoned landing strip on the Florida-Alabama line caught Rowan's attention. Liam had been close to it when he'd lost visual on the van, and, for whatever reason, something told Rowan to guide Liam to the landing strip. The place had been empty, but the fresh tire tracks on the single dirt road leading to it hadn't sat right with either of them.

"Eureka."

Rowan frowned. "What?"

"Bruce said Eureka." Liam paused for a handful of seconds. "In the cabin. Right before he winged me, he said Eureka."

Turning around, Rowan faced the wall to focus, leaving the room's chaos at his back. "I'm not following."

There was a sigh and a muttered curse from Liam. "I promised Killian I wouldn't drag you deeper into this, so I didn't tell anyone but my dad."

"Still not following."

"When Sinclair called, you tracked him to northern Arkansas."

Rowan had been so close to finding the fucker, probably closer than he'd ever been, and was again cursing himself for not staying behind at the house to finish the job. "Okay?"

Liam let out a distorted laugh. "There's a haunted hotel in northern Arkansas. Jamison's wanted to go for years, but I always said that if she wanted to stay somewhere haunted, she should just pitch a tent in Haven's woods."

Oh, fuck. Liam was freaking out. Even when things were at their worst, Liam Cohen held his shit together. When Zanmi first tried to kidnap Jamison, and they thought she might be in some way connected to Sinclair, he kept calm. When those women charged into the house, he never allowed his emotions to get the better of him.

But now he was choking on them. Panic and strain clung to his words, and were the roles reversed, Rowan didn't think he would be doing much better.

"The hotel is in a town called Eureka Springs. It's crazy, but it makes fucking sense, doesn't it?" Liam cleared his throat, trying to keep his voice steady. "Sinclair warned us about Evie, and if it really is CeCe that connects him to this, I think... I think Bruce was giving us a clue."

It was a stretch. A massive Grand Canyon of a stretch. "Are you sure you're thinking clearly? That theory is a gamble. If you're not going after that van and heading north to follow a hunch, you could be putting Jamison at risk."

"Anderson and Klausen already have a dozen agents on that van, and my dad will handle that." Liam cursed as horns blared in the background. "I was distracted, Rowan. Madison distracted me when I entered Emmett's shack, and Bruce could have easily dropped me, but he didn't. He said Eureka and grazed my arm."

"Liam—"

"No, dammit, listen!" Liam shouted. "My woman is not in that van. I feel it in my fucking bones. She's not there. She's in Arkansas, or she will be. I'm not wasting time on a lead someone else can chase while I ignore what my gut is screaming."

Ben came around to see what was happening, glaring at Rowan as Simone crowded his other side.

"Okay," Rowan spoke evenly so as not to scare Ben or Simone. "Tell me what you need."

"Private airstrips," Liam exhaled. "I want a full list of all the private airstrips in northern Arkansas, starting with those closest to Eureka Springs."

"You'll have it in ten minutes."

He hung up, moving around Simone to sit with his laptop while he waited for the barrage of questions to hit.

Simone was first. "What will he have in ten minutes?"

Ben didn't give him a chance to answer. "Is he going after the van?"

"Sweetheart, I want you to write this information down for me," Rowan addressed Annabeth first. She needed something to do. A quietness had come over her, and he had to keep her focused. "Do you have something to write with?"

"Um, yes." Annabeth snatched a scrap of paper and a pen from her purse with a small tremor in her hands. "What is it?"

Will swept into the room, cutting through cops and agents. "They've got the van in sight and are on approach. I'll call Liam, and he can meet us."

"Liam isn't going after the van." Rowan began pulling everything he could. Commercial, private, and even the airstrips hidden from the public. Long patches of grass that were kept maintained for a variety of reasons. "Annabeth, I'm going to give you the names of possible landing spots, and I need you to write them down for Liam."

Will dropped into a chair across from him. "Talk, Rowan."

"When Liam lost visual on the van, he was north of here." Rowan cracked his knuckles as the list began to populate. There were so many possibilities. "Past the Florida-Alabama border and in a rural area with a private landing strip. It wasn't much, but enough to land a small passenger plane."

Will grumbled, working through his thoughts. "But then the van shows up west of where he's searching."

"Silver Wings Field," Rowan told Annabeth. "Trigger Gap Airstrip. Circle Farms Airstrip."

Annabeth wrote as fast as she could. "How long does it take to drive to Arkansas?"

Sparing a glance at the GPS in the corner of his screen, he noted Liam's location. Hauling ass through the state of Alabama, he was already nearing Birmingham. "About nine hours."

"Let me recall the jets to get him there." Ben sat next to Will. "The plane can meet him at a halfway point."

"That would eat up more time." Rowan shook his head. "Taking a plane should be faster, but if we calculate how long it takes to recall the jets, fuel up, get the pilots in... we'd be wasting hours."

Holden pushed through the crowd of agents. "Evie is in a room. She's good. Albie's good. Samuel's calming down. Josie and the girls are with them. Izzy's at the door with agents and Abe. Carter is being seen by a nurse. He's coming around and shouting for Liam. He heard some of what went down before they knocked him out."

Having been locked in with the Fairweathers these last few weeks, Holden had learned how important it was to get as much concise information out in one go. "Evie and Samuel don't know what's happening. I told them that no one is in there seeing Albie because you guys wanted to give them a private moment with the girls and Josie."

"Thank you, Holden." Ben ran a hand through this hair, musing it even more. "So, which way do we go? North or west?"

"Eureka," Will whispered. "Son of a bitch."

"Lost Bridge Airstrip," Rowan said to Annabeth before addressing Will. "Liam thinks she's in Eureka Springs."

"She could still be in the van." Will puffed out an exhale. "Okay, this is what we're going to do. Rowan, you stay on Liam's theory. Guide him as best you can until we get back. Ben and I will handle the van. Anderson has a damn army chasing it, but I'm going to have Klausen begin coordinating with the teams in the Arkansas area."

With a plan in place, Will and Ben rushed out, leaving Simone and Bernie holding each other in their wake. "Come with me to meet my new grandson, Bernie?" Simone was trembling so hard she could barely get the question out. "I can say my tears are because I'm happy, but I'll slip. I know I'll slip up and say something."

"Of course, I'll come." Bernie rubbed Simone's shoulder, leading her through the maze of agents and police. "We'll do this together."

"Eigsti Field," Rowan read off. "It's not technically an airstrip, but a small plane could land there."

Annabeth scribbled down the name. "How will Liam find them? Is he just going to drive around aimlessly?"

"The bird was a loon." Holden took the seat Will vacated. "Can you play Sinclair's phone call back, Rowan?"

Recalling the recording, Sinclair's voice came through Rowan's laptop speakers. "*I don't, babe. We just cloned his number.*"

"Fast forward to the part where he's talking about Emily." Holden's brow furrowed as he listened, making Rowan reverse twice more so he could hear the bird calling out. "Yeah, that's a waterfowl. Sinclair is on a lake or river."

Holden pulled out his phone and made a call, placing it on speaker when a woman answered. "Where can I find a loon in northwest Arkansas?"

There was a pause, and then a woman with a heavy Southern accent spoke sarcastically. "And a good evening to you too, son."

"Mama, I love you, but right now, I'm in the middle of something, and I need you to get into Dad's avian database so I can figure out where to find a common loon in northwestern Arkansas during this exact time of year." Holden held the phone between him and Rowan. "My friend is listening, so don't say anything untoward."

Rowan paused in his airstrip search, slowly rolling his head in Holden's direction as if truly seeing the man for the first time. Annabeth did the same, obviously just as surprised when Holden slipped into an accent much like the woman on the phone. And it wasn't something mild, like Rowan's own Texan drawl, but deep and total backcountry.

"Are you from Alabama?" A stupidly pointless question at the moment, but Rowan had to ask.

"God, no." Holden's face twisted in horror. "Go Dawgs."

Georgia. Yeah, Rowan could hear it now. Holden's rolling twang positively oozed with the sounds of rural Georgia.

"Who's that?" the woman on the phone asked. "Holden, where are you?"

Not answering the question, Holden kept on pushing for the information. "I need the info, Mama. It's super important that I know about these loons."

"Specifically, near Eureka Springs," Rowan added, leaning closer to make sure he was heard. "Please. *Ma'am.*"

"Are y'all playing trivia or something?"

"No, ma'am," Rowan began. "We're in the middle of a manhun—"

Holden immediately swooped the phone away from Rowan. "Yes, Mama. We're playing trivia, and the clock is ticking. Can you fire up Dad's old computer and look for me?"

"That man better not have been about to say what I think he was going to say," the woman on the line huffed. "You promised you would take it easy."

Holden glared at Rowan, sending a clear signal that he needed to watch what he said. "I'm taking it easy, Mama. I promise, I'm sitting here calmly while my friend and I toss questions around."

"What's happening?" Annabeth whispered.

Rowan didn't look away from Holden. "I have no idea."

"Elijah Ezra Holden, you better not be lying to me, or I will find you and take a switch to your butt, grown man or not." The woman sighed. "You need a break after what happened. Mentally and physically."

"And I'm getting one," Holden assured her, lying his ass off as an agent came running into the waiting room to speak to Klausen. "Crisscross over my heart."

"I'm going to crisscross over your ass if you're lying to me," his mother shot back. "Okay, the laptop is turning on. Ugh, this thing needs a good overhaul. I would hate to lose all your dad's data if it dies. Marsha Fitzsimmon's teenage son does computer repair. You remember her, don't you? She lives down the street. Anyway, maybe I can get that boy to come over—"

Holden placed his phone against his chest, silencing his mother as she continued to talk. "My dad was an amateur ornithologist. Birds were his passion, but he loved waterfowl the most and created an extremely detailed map of their migratory patterns. I'm talking like, this is shit you can't find on Google. People all over the world would contact him about it."

Neither Rowan nor Annabeth said anything, unsure of how to take this new information.

"With it being November, migration will be in full swing," Holden told them. "And if we can narrow down where the loons rest during migration, we can narrow our search."

Annabeth's mouth opened and closed a few times while Rowan's brain processed what Holden was saying. Birds. Holden thought they could find Sinclair by using birds. It was insanity. True insanity.

But that didn't matter anymore. Sanity was for the weak, and while he didn't even know what the hell a loon was, if this bird could give them a clue on where to direct Liam, then cock-a-fucking-doodle do. They would chase a damn bird and its migration patterns halfway across the country.

Rowan snatched the phone from Holden. "Ma'am? Hi, it's me again. My name's Rowan, and I'm pretty good with computers. If you can help us, I'll gladly transfer all your husband's data to a new computer and set up a cloud that you can access from any device. But can you please hurry?"

"Hello, Rowan. I'm Chasity, and it's lovely to meet you. Wait, is that what we're doing? Meeting over the phone?" Chasity asked with a chuckle. "Do you work for the Geek Squad? Holden, turn on the camera so I can see this man."

Before Holden could grab the phone, Rowan clicked on the forward-facing camera and switched the call to video. On the screen, a blonde woman adjusted her glasses to get a better look, her eyes going wide once she did.

"Oh, lord," Holden's mother exhaled. She sat in a plush, black leather chair, surrounded by dark, plaid walls, holding various photos of birds in flight. "Uh, hello. You said your name was Rowan?"

"Yes, ma'am." Smile in place, Rowan turned on the charm. "Is the program working?"

Chasity's lips parted. "You have a very deep voice."

"Yes, ma'am. I do."

"It's very soothing." Chasity squinted at him. "Matches the face. You could do a lot with that face. The girls like it, I bet."

"A fair share. Can you give me your IP address or even your home address so I can look at the information myself?"

"My home address?" Chasity set the phone down, propping it against something as she typed on a laptop's keyboard. "Are you guys close? Are y'all coming over for supper?"

"No, ma'am."

When he didn't elaborate, Chastity took the hint and got to work. "Holden, there are four types of loons in northern Arkansas. Which one do you want?"

Holden struggled. "I want the one that sounds like a bird howling."

Diverting her gaze from the laptop screen, Chasity tossed an eye roll at her son. "They all sound like that."

The next thing Rowan knew, the wailing calls of various loons were shooting through the phone. Several federal agents turned to stare, and Klausen paused his conversation on the phone, giving them a confused frown.

"Which one is it?" Chasity asked, running the bird's calls on a loop. "If it's northwestern, my guess would be the Common or the Red-Throated."

"Play them one at a time." Holden closed his eyes to concentrate. "And slow it down as you do."

Chasity did as he asked, and Holden's eyes popped open on the third bird. "It's that one."

"I was right. The Common Loon." Chasity reclined in the chair that nearly swallowed her small body whole. "According to your father's map and the tracks he has laid out for their migratory pattern, which can vary, the answer should be Beaver Lake."

"Thanks, Mama. Love you." Holden ended the call so fast that his mother didn't have time to respond. "Okay, get me up there. Taking a Fairweather jet might slow Liam down, but not me. If we start the process in the next few minutes, I can meet him and coordinate with locals while he searches."

Klausen swore and everyone went silent as he chucked his phone clear across the room in frustration. "They got her."

"Jamison?" Annabeth surged out of her seat. "She's okay?"

"Kristina Scherer," Klausen spat out the name of Michael Sinclair's sister. "She's escaped from the holding center."

Rowan set his laptop aside to hold Annabeth as she processed her disappointment. "How the fuck did that happen?"

"I don't have the full details yet." Klausen stared helplessly at his phone on the floor. "But she was our main bargaining chip in getting Jamison Fairweather back."

CHAPTER 30

Jamison

Taylor didn't order her to be injected again once they boarded the plane. In fact, she all but ignored Jamison, leaving Bruce to handle her while she went off to sit with Parker.

About an hour into the flight, Jamison found she could sit up and form words. Proud of herself, she took in her surroundings. The aircraft resembled one of the smaller jets owned by Fairweather Holdings, with four rows of double seating. Taylor and Parker were in the back row, far enough away that Jamison could speak without being overheard.

"Explain them."

Bruce took her by the shoulders to straighten her in the seat. "I told you to behave."

"Everyone tells me to behave, and I'm just not good at it," she slurred. "Tell me."

Taylor giggled obnoxiously, and Jamison arched an eyebrow at Bruce, who looked equally annoyed by the sound. "Parker hung with them in Miami. He was in the outer circle, always wanting more, but Toby wouldn't allow it. Your cousin had this philosophy he lives by. Something about weak links should never be tolerated. He saw Parker as weak and wouldn't let him into their inner circle."

"Sounds like he's in now." Taylor's giggling slipped into a moan, and Jamison winced. "Literally."

Bruce snorted, then masked it. "When Toby said it was time to come home, Taylor took a job at Fairweather. She wanted to see if it was worth their time. Her first thoughts are always about monetary gain, followed closely by her more...carnal needs." The moaning continued, and he didn't bother hiding his disgust. "Taylor started by applying in the Fort Lauderdale offices and worked her way up to Samuel after a few months before he moved back to north Florida. It surprised everyone that she could do the job. Taylor has always thought she was destined to be famous and never bothered to work a day in her life, yet somehow fooled your brother into thinking she was dedicated to the position."

"Maybe she is a good actress, after all," Jamison mumbled sarcastically. "But what does that have to do with Parker?"

"When Samuel opened applications to join him up north, it was around the time baby fever really struck Taylor. She'd already had her tubes untied, but nothing happened. Toby blamed her. She blamed him. That's when he started ending his 'girlfriend' sessions with flair. Staging it and torturing them more."

"You mean when he started cutting their legs off and removing their eyes?" she asked, not missing the way Bruce shifted uncomfortably as she spoke. "Or when he would force them to drag themselves across the floor as they bled out?"

"Toby prefers pain. He likes to inflict it on his partners, and he loves to prolong their deaths. Taylor enjoys watching, but for her sexual kicks, she has to get them elsewhere." Bruce glanced over his shoulder at where Taylor and Parker sat. "Parker is just one of many submissive dogs she keeps on a short leash."

Her foggy brain attempted to grasp the information. "And they wanted to bring a baby into that?"

"One way or another, Taylor always gets what she wants. She wanted a baby, and she wanted it with Toby. But they weren't having any luck even though the tests for these kinds of things showed they were both fine," Bruce replied, noticeably not giving her a straight answer. "When they reached the end of their rope, Toby agreed that they should try another way and spread their options around. Use other people to see if they could make it happen. The only rule was that she wasn't allowed to get pregnant by one of her side pieces in their little friend group. The baby—a baby Toby would be willing to raise—had to be a Fairweather. From what I've been told, he's always hated your brother. He liked the idea of Taylor fucking Samuel Fairweather so she could get pregnant, only for the baby to be raised by Toby."

A wave of nausea struck, washing over Jamison and forcing her eyes to roll up in her head. But she wasn't about to give up. Even though it was never a good sign when the bad guy was willing to part with so many secrets, she wasn't about to halt this information train. "What about my sister?"

"Toby wanted her and no one else. Taylor knew there was some mild obsession there, but I don't think even she realized how deep it went." Using a finger, Bruce tipped her upright when she started to slide off to the side. "He would have killed you to have her. I meant what I said about that day in the graveyard, and I honestly can't believe it went down the way it did. The idea of finally having your sister got under his skin, and Toby refused to let it go. He was going to have her, and Taylor would give him his revenge on Samuel."

Not far off from where she and Bruce sat, the two women from the van stood just out of sight. Neither had sat for the entire flight. Even during takeoff, they remained standing, holding hands and watching.

"And Parker?"

Bruce huffed when Taylor's cries for more grew louder. "He's moved to the top of the food chain. Taylor was ecstatic when Madison was born and ramped up Zanmi's activities to free Toby. Again, it was luck on your side. If her father had approved of this shit, she would have the muscle, the money, and the power to disappear with Madison already.

"So, Bryan Carroll isn't okay with his daughter leading some bizarre cult?"

"All this Zanmi crap? Bryan washed his hands of it long ago. He'll get her fake IDs and passports to live and work for Fairweather or visit Toby without being easily detected, but he's curbed her funds significantly. Don't get me wrong. She has enough to run, but it would be tough, and it sure as hell wouldn't provide the lifestyle she thinks she deserves."

The activity between Taylor and Parker reached its end, with Taylor howling as she finished. Bruce rolled his eyes. "And, of course, what she really wants is a boy. She's been fixated on getting herself a Fairweather boy since the beginning."

The plane lurched violently, catching some turbulence. Jamison's stomach pitched, feeling like it had gone flying up to the cabin's ceiling while her body remained strapped to the seat. "Oh, that's not good."

Bruce didn't so much as flinch when the plane dropped again. "Won't be much longer. I've told Mike we're inbound, and he's hustling back to the house to meet us."

"The little," she paused to swallow vomit, "Haven House?"

The entire jet vibrated, and Bruce let out a yawn. "That's what she wanted."

"Taylor?"

Something that resembled a chuckle came from Bruce. "Honey, I know you're woozy from the drugs, but that doesn't make you stupid."

Jamison waited for a heartbeat, listening to make sure Taylor remained occupied. "CeCe."

"Cecilia was a good person." Folding his hands across his chest, Bruce closed his eyes as if he were going to take a nap. "Nothing like her brother."

The thundering heart in her chest felt as if it had dislodged from behind her ribs, floating up into her throat and then her head until it beat steadily in her ears. Michael and CeCe. He was right. Liam was always right.

"Thank you for telling me all this," she said quietly. "I understand that you don't have to explain, but it's nice to finally know the truth."

"It doesn't matter what you know and what you don't. When this is over, no one will be left to care."

⊱⊱⊱⊱ ⊰⊰⊰⊰

She was definitely going to vomit.

They had landed roughly an hour earlier, the plane touching down in some dark field that turned out to be a landing strip. Another van met them, driven by a woman in her mid-thirties who looked like a regular functioning human. Her name was Krystal, and she smiled with her mouth closed, her lips thinning in disapproval as they exited the plane.

"You're late," Krystal chided when she got behind the wheel of the transport van. "Mike got back an hour ago, and when he heard what you did, he was pissed. I thought you'd beat him so I wouldn't get yelled at."

"He'll get the hell over it," Taylor snapped as she buckled into the front passenger seat. "He's basically family and all, but Jesus Christ and Hail Mary, he's so fucking full of himself."

Krystal said nothing, adjusting her glasses as she drove through the pitch black dark. Jamison tried to make sense of her surroundings, but she couldn't see much, not with Parker's tall frame on her right and Bruce's bulky one on her left. Some roads they went down were paved, and some were nothing but dirt or clay. The last road was rocky, full of dips and big rocks that shook the van like a rag doll.

"How's my baby?" Taylor asked. "I can't wait to see her."

"She's doing good." Krystal smiled. "She's been reading and sounding out the words like a big girl. She takes her nap on time and has never fought me about eating her vegetables. The juice, on the other hand, well, we're still battling that."

"Madi loves apple juice," Parker said. "It helps her—"

"I don't give a shit, Parker. I have told you this." Taylor twisted around to snarl at him. "Madison will not be one of those fatties who eats nothing but sugar. I will hold my daughter to a higher standard."

"Claudia's daughter." Feeling brave, Jamison raised her chin. "Madison is Claudia's daughter."

Holy hell. The backhanded slap from Parker stung like a son of a bitch, and Jamison's head went flying. He'd struck her cheek and nose, causing blood to squirt from her nostrils.

"Easy," Bruce barked. "Calm him the fuck down, Taylor."

"Calm down? *Calm down*? I think not," Taylor shrieked as Parker shoved Jamison's head forward. "Madison belongs to me now. She's my little angel, you worthless skank."

"Skank?" Jamison laughed directly in Taylor's face. "What are you, twelve?"

Parker smashed her face into the back of Taylor's seat, and Jamison's vision swam with swirls and pops of color. The one good thing about the drugs was that they had left her slightly numb.

Yanking on her arm, Bruce locked her swaying body at his side. "That's enough."

"That's enough," Taylor parroted before returning her attention to Krystal. "And how is our favorite boy?"

Krystal glanced sideways at Taylor, her smile grotesque in the dashboard lights. "Sleeping."

"A sleeping beauty, I bet."

"He really is," Krystal replied with a sigh. "I'm serious, Taylor. I don't know why you've been wasting your time going after that crusty old Ben Fairweather or his son when Damon's prime piece of ass is ripe and ready to go. I have never seen a more gorgeous man."

Taylor squealed. "Just think of all the beautiful babies we're going to get from him."

"And the fun we're going to have making them," Krystal added. "Now that we have Jamison, we can start. I called everyone to come home. Most were already on their way, but the others should arrive by morning."

The two women high-fived, and Jamison opened her mouth to say something, but Bruce squeezed tight enough to knock the air from her lungs. "Nope. Keep that comment to yourself."

Hitting a large hole in the road, the van's tires bounced hard, and just when Jamison thought she was going to hurl all over Bruce's shoes, the ground evened out. She sat up straight, trying to see where they were going. Thanks to the headlights, she could make out the large twelve-foot-high barbed wire fencing up ahead. There were gates and guards, two men dressed in black with guns holstered at their waists.

"Hey, boys!" Taylor waved at the guards, who half-heartedly waved back. "I'm here for more than just a quick visit this time."

The road's curves became sharper the further they traveled, the van climbing higher and higher until it plateaued onto a gravel drive. A thick forest encased their path, and on the final turn, the glimmer of light building in front of them gave way to an astonishing sight.

Haven House.

Jamison nearly fell off her seat, trying to get a clear view. It wasn't as big as Haven, but it stole her breath for a second when she thought they had brought her home. The closer they came, the more she could see the differences. A single gable instead of two. Four columns in front instead of eight. The upper level's porch didn't appear to wrap all the way around, nor did the lower level's porch. There were no gardens. No oaks. No vast side yard one could run around in. It was like a large home with hints of Haven House, making it a miniature version of the estate.

And it would seem that every light in the house had been left on.

Simone would've had a fit.

The windows were uncovered, allowing some of the interior to show, and the oddly whimsical lamp posts sitting off the front path revealed a group of people waiting.

At the forefront of the growing crowd, a man stood. Hands behind his back and head forward, Michael Sinclair watched their approach. The black pants and T-shirt he wore hugged every muscle like a second skin, and once they parked, he aimed his furious gaze at Taylor.

"Honey, I'm home," Taylor sang, exiting the van. Michael didn't move as she sashayed over to him, nor did he acknowledge the kiss pressed to his cheek when she passed. "Oh, lighten up, Mikey. I brought you someone to play with."

Bruce kept a firm grip on her arm when he pulled Jamison from the van and over to Michael. She held his mismatched stare, and the defiance he must have seen had his jaw ticking.

Parker went ahead, chatting with Krystal as they walked around Michael, neither of them acknowledging the other. The crowd dispersed, following Taylor inside through the front door. Jamison wasn't sure, but she thought she counted about eight people, mainly men of various ages.

Emmett Watson had been one of them. Standing in the open front door, he held Madison's hand as the little girl cheered when she saw Parker.

"Who wants Daddy when I'm here?" Taylor lifted the girl into her arms. As far as Jamison could tell, Madison looked healthy and unharmed. "How have you been, my beautiful girl?"

With the crowd gone, Bruce stopped directly before Michael, holding her out to him. Breaking from her gaze for a second, he dipped his head toward the guards at the gate, signaling them to shut it.

"How?"

Michael's question wasn't for her, and she pressed her lips together. The drugs were clearing her brain finally, and if she had to pull the eyeballs out of every single one of these Zanmi freaks to get out of here, she would and take all the info she'd gathered with her.

"Parker got the call," Bruce said. "Taylor pitched a fit that you were going after Kris, saying it was the perfect opportunity to snag Jamison. I told them I would tag along in case they needed help, since I stayed behind when we sent Emmett back here."

"How did you get here so fast?" Michael clarified as he looked her over from top to bottom, not missing anything. "Nice dress, by the way."

"Plane," Bruce answered. "Taylor called in a favor."

"Tracked?"

"Don't think so."

Michael's lips twitched with a smirk when he caught sight of the flip-flops peeking out from under the wedding gown. Jamison scrunched her toes, slightly embarrassed.

The move had Michael's smirk turning into a grin. "If it belonged to Bryan, it wasn't tracked."

"It belonged to a friend of Bryan, from what I was told," Bruce said. "You know Taylor. She ignores the details and just does shit, yet it somehow works out."

The two women who had been with them the entire time slid past, pausing right beyond Michael to stare at the house. The dark-haired one laid a hand on his shoulder.

"Not for much longer," Michael murmured to the woman and then addressed Bruce. "Casualties in the grab?"

"None." Bruce shrugged. "Maybe. Her guard was a big son of a bitch and wouldn't go down, so I had to juice him up pretty good."

"Who was the guard?"

"New boy. Didn't know him."

"Carter." Jamison supplied the answer in a small voice. "His name was Carter. It was his first day."

"And probably his last," Michael said as the noise inside kicked up a notch. Taylor was speaking, and once or twice, a cheer or clapping could be heard. "If not, then this Carter might deserve to be dead. Anyone stupid enough to stay around the Fairweathers for too long gets what's coming to them. A smart person would run."

Fighting the urge to stomp on his steel-toed boot, Jamison sneered instead. "Run, run, run as fast as you can. Isn't that what you weirdos say all the time?"

"It's a stupid phrase to latch on to, don't you think?" The tiny hint of amusement over her attire disappeared from Michael's eyes, replaced by a deep cynicism one would expect from a man like him. "Run, run, run as fast as you can. Do you know the origin of the phrase? Why Toby said it?"

Of course she did. It was a trick question. Toby would chant the phrase when he hunted his victims. He admitted to using it in his initial confession, and Zanmi continued to taunt them with it throughout the years. Everyone knew this.

"The day your mother died." Michael nodded at Bruce, who released his hold so she could stand on her own. "On the morning of July 4, 1999, the kids—including you—played tag on the side lawn. Selah opened the game as he always did by shouting *run, run, run as fast as you can*. It was the last normal moment your family shared before the end."

"Toby told you that?"

Michael shook his head slowly, a measured back-and-forth movement. "No, Toby didn't tell me that."

The dark-haired woman removed her hand from Michael's shoulder and walked with her smaller counterpart toward the house. Jamison gritted her teeth, annoyed that the double vision wouldn't permit her to see their faces. The hold the drugs had on her was wearing thin, but not enough where she could see those two.

Michael heaved out a sigh when the gates at her back were shut with a loud clang. "When's the last time she had a dose?"

"Hospital. Evangeline Fairweather had her baby. A boy. Named it Albert or something. I took a peek at the thing before we went in for the grab. Cute kid. Lots of hair. A screamer." From the corner of her eye, Jamison could see Bruce fiddling with a small pouch secured at his waist. "I thought Taylor would want us to snatch him, but I guess common sense took over finally."

Michael snorted. "That woman has no common sense."

When another syringe emerged from Bruce's pouch, she tried to bolt, but Michael caught her easily. Securing her against his chest, his strong arms wrapped around her like a vice. "Don't fight. This one won't fully paralyze you," he said calmly as Bruce speared her upper arm with the needle. "Trust me. It's better this way. Less trauma to digest when your head's clear."

"Please, don't. Please." Unable to be brave any longer and realizing he was about to take her into the house, tears spilled down Jamison's cheeks. "I can't handle not being in control."

The sympathy on Michael's handsome face dissolved into a look of disgust. "*You* can't handle not being in control? Imagine living your entire life that way."

The darkness pulsed around them. The laughter and the lights from inside the house swirled before her eyes. The two obscure women stood on the porch now, looking around as if seeing the smaller version of Haven for the first time.

She slumped against Michael, the meds hitting their mark fast. "You chose to go into the military, so it's your fault you allowed them to control your life."

"How adorable. You still think this is about me." Michael leaned down to whisper in her ear. "It's not. Now be my good girl in there, and I'll tell you everything."

Selah had once said that insubordination was a key personality trait of hers, and as she stared up at the twinkling stars overhead, Jamison thought it was time to use what she once thought of as a stubborn defect to her advantage. It was the only way she could mentally cope with this. "You mean you'll tell me about CeCe."

"No one called her CeCe except Toby and that psychotic whore of his." Michael's lips brushed her ear as he grinned. "Her name was Cecilia, and she was mine."

"Yet, you're helping them?" Jamison panted up at the sky, her head heavy on her neck. "The people who celebrate the man responsible for murdering her?"

A few Zanmi members stumbled out onto the porch. Loud and obnoxious, the men's voices were slurred from drinking.

"Bruce, get inside. Move the girls into the room with Damon and put Mark on the door. Warn him not to let any of those fuckers in there." Michael lifted his head to issue the order in a low voice. "Emmett already tried to get to Emily again tonight, and I arrived just in time."

"Got it," Bruce said, stuffing the used syringe back into his pouch. "Is Claudia still in the dog crate?"

"Yeah, but there's no fight in her tonight," Michael replied. "Well, there's enough in case Taylor or one of those tweaked out Zanmi sisters tries to get to Damon. We can let her lose on them."

The one thing we can rely on is Emily and Claudia protecting their brother." Bruce paused. "What about Kris?"

"Third room in the main hall."

Jamison's legs went out from under her as she listened, and Michael didn't hesitate, swooping her up to carry like a bride. At the same time, Taylor marched outside, her heels banging loudly on the wood as she talked on the phone.

"It was just a plane!" she screeched. "Why are you so upset?"

Bruce moved on, carefully avoiding Taylor as he traveled up the steps and into the house.

"Wait, you're where? No, I'm not in Florida. I'm... um... north of Florida." Taylor's loud pacing halted, and terror filled her voice. "Daddy... what? Ugh, fine. I'm near... Tulsa. Huh? What do you mean tomorrow? No! I can't meet you for brunch tomorrow. Oh, you're coming to Tulsa. Tonight. You're coming to Tulsa tonight?"

Jamison shivered in Michael's arms when he nuzzled her neck in an almost playful manner. "Not a word out of you," he whispered. "Understand?"

Taylor disconnected the call and let out a frustrated yowl, chucking the phone across the porch. "This cannot be happening! Why should I meet him, anyway? He reduced my fucking allowance, basically leaving me to *die* in poverty."

"Tulsa is almost a three-hour drive." Michael walked down the path, and Jamison turned her face into his chest, not wanting Taylor to see her crying. "Are you going tonight or first thing in the morning?"

Taylor didn't answer, the click-clacking of her heels telling Jamison she was coming down the steps towards them. "Isn't this cute? The dress. The house. The handsome groom. Too bad it's the wrong bride."

The grip on her body hardened, Michael's fingers digging into her muscles. Jamison refused to squirm, knowing it was best if she didn't draw Taylor's attention.

"Don't fuck with me tonight, Taylor," Michael snapped.

"Oh, get over yourself. You're enjoying this. Fucking her as a fuck you to the Fairweathers? It's the perfect revenge." Taylor released a huff. "And I guess I'll go early in the morning, but you have to promise not to have sex with her until I get back. I want it to hurt and have some fun ways we can really make this bitch suffer."

"I can do that." Michael adjusted his hold. "Besides, I need to take her upstairs for a family reunion. I know her cousins will be *so* happy to see her."

Chapter 31

Jamison

"**H**ow long?"

She asked the question as Michael carried her up the stairs. On the second floor, he made a quick right, leading into a narrow hall. The upper level didn't have a landing like Haven House, coming off as more of a suburban home than a grand estate.

Or maybe that was the drugs talking. Her senses were overloaded the second they entered the house. Someone had been blaring music, the bass shaking her brain while Michael carried her through the insanity.

"Damon tried to take Claudia and Madison with him when he ran off with Emily," Michael explained. "Parker told Taylor where they were going, and when you guys thought you would be cute and snatch Kris, I returned the favor. Taylor was ecstatic to begin her bullshit plan."

He turned down another hall, taking them deeper into the house. "Honestly, I expected more effort from you guys to find them."

"We didn't know they..." Her head fell back, dangling mid-air when she could no longer hold it upright. "...were gone."

"And that's something you need to take up with your family," Michael said, slowing as they neared the end of the hall. "I made sure their parents knew they had been taken."

A door closed in the distance. "I've got them all together," Bruce said as he approached. "Claudia's calm. I gave her something that will help her relax, and that's safe for the baby."

"The next time they lock her up, make sure they don't do it for more than an hour," Michael ordered as he paused to speak. "We can handle most things, but a feral Claudia will take off more than someone's ear next time, and keeping her crated for long periods only makes it worse."

Jamison gasped, which made both Michael and Bruce chuckle.

"Relax, Jamison. Bruce and I know never to fuck with a Fairweather woman," Michael said. "But Claudia is a whole different kind of demon."

"I told her she could have time with Madison tomorrow if she behaves," Bruce added. "That took the fight out of her, and she sat on her mattress without much prompting."

"How could...lock...pregnant...cage?" Her mouth didn't work again, and she stiffened her body in protest. "Hurt."

"It's to protect her more than anything. She could hurt the baby, and we don't have proper medical care here. Not yet, anyway." Michael jerked his chin at Bruce. "Taylor's father wants to see her in Tulsa tomorrow."

"Tulsa?" Bruce frowned. "Why the hell in Tulsa?"

"Sounds like he was chewing her ass out about that plane, and she blanked when he asked where she was."

"Does Taylor even know where she is?"

"Probably not," Michael sighed. "My guess would be that she just went with the first big city she could think of that might be near here."

It was Bruce's turn to sigh while Jamison dangled helplessly. Those two freaky women were back again and listening to the conversation. One stood at her head, the scent of vanilla and patchouli overtaking her as it floated in the air. Jamison knew the scent because it was the same smell that drifted on the wind at Haven House. She always assumed it came from a bloom in Ty's garden, but never figured out which one. It was strongest whenever it rained or when a full moon shone bright in the sky. Once, when she was a little girl, she asked Simone which flower held the smell, and all Simone would say was that no flower in the garden produced that particular scent.

Tears pricked her eyes at the thought of Simone, and she moaned. A knowing—a cruel realization—hit with acute clarity. This house. No matter how strong she convinced herself to be, she had to accept that she might never leave it. These people were going to use her and then kill her.

They couldn't very well let her go. Perhaps Claudia, Emily, and Damon had been unconscious when they arrived, but she hadn't.

And Michael knew this. He would know she had paid attention. She belonged to Liam and would have noted the dips in the road, counted the seconds between turns, and memorized the small details down to the emblem on the outhouse looking building at the end of the rural airstrip where they landed.

Michael would understand that if she were free, she would relay the information to the authorities, and this house would be found.

"Kill me," she breathed. "You kill me."

Michael shushed her with a grin. "We'll get to the fun stuff soon. Promise."

"Are you done with me for tonight?" Bruce asked.

Michael grunted with a nod. "Go see Kris."

A surge of adrenaline hit, and Jamison swung her legs violently. "How?"

"How did I get Kris? Don't worry about the details. Just know that I have loyal friends anywhere and everywhere I go." Michael tilted his head to the right. "She's in there, Bruce."

Bruce knocked softly on a closed door. It opened a fraction of an inch, and the angry, pale face of a boy on the cusp of becoming a man appeared. When he saw it was Bruce, he opened the door more, revealing a woman sitting on the bed in the room.

The look of relief on Bruce's face spoke volumes. "Hey, Kris."

The woman pushed off the bed and flew directly into Bruce's waiting arms. "You're so stupid. So, so stupid," she blubbered. "Both of you. You are both so unforgivably stupid."

Bruce buried his face in Kristina's hair, his hug lingering long enough to solidify the fact that this was more than a simple friendship. After a second or two, Michael's sister saw her in his arms and released Bruce.

"This is her?" she asked, adjusting her glasses as she peered at Jamison's slack face. "Well, now what?"

"I have it under control."

Jamison didn't care for Michael's tone, and neither did his sister. "And just how do you have it under control?" Kris asked through gritted teeth. "Because what's happening here is anything but *under control*."

"Trust me." Michael grinned, looking almost human instead of the monster that he actually was. "Go back inside and lock the door. Bruce will be in soon to talk."

With one final glare at her brother, Kris returned to the room while the men waited for her to close and lock the door. "What exactly do you want to talk about with Kris?" Bruce whispered. "There's nothing to discuss. She and Colton are getting out of here."

"Yeah, but I need you to prepare her a little more," Michael whispered in return. "Taylor knows how valuable Kris is, and that if we truly wanted this all to work, I wouldn't allow her to vanish. We've come this far. I can't trip things up now."

"So, what do you suggest?" Bruce all but growled. "I don't want them here, Mike."

Michael went quiet, and the dark-haired woman moved closer. Threading her fingers through the hair on the nape of his neck, she whispered in his ear, and the longer she spoke, the more Michael regained focus. "I have an idea. God knows we've laid enough breadcrumbs for the fucker. Get Kris back out here."

Bruce knocked on the door again, and this time, Kris opened it. "I need you to track lover boy's phone," Michael said, lifting Jamison higher. "Taylor arranged a van decoy, but I guarantee you that smart bastard didn't fall for it."

Kris disappeared into the small bedroom, returning with a tablet in hand. "Mississippi."

"North or south?"

"North."

"Just as I thought. He's coming to us," Michael said, sounding pleased. "I'm guessing it'll be Parker taking Taylor to see her dad since she refuses to drive that far alone."

Bruce shrugged. "That would make sense."

"Whatever car Taylor takes, we need to be able to track it. She's known to shut off her location, and if she's meeting with Bryan, he could have a block that'll wipe any cell transmission. The main point is, I want to know when she's headed back here."

"What the hell does that have to do with William Cohen?" Kris asked. "Damn it, I told you we should never have gone up against these people, Mike. You should have ended this months ag—"

"I want you to track Cohen and give the coordinates to Bruce," Michael cut her off with a whisper. "When he takes the car Taylor is driving out to get gas—"

"Why the hell would I do that?" Bruce interrupted.

"Because you're a good little soldier doing something nice," Michael replied. "While you have access to the car, you can set a tracker on it *and* magically appear in front of Cohen, who will then follow you all the way here. Boom. Two birds. One stone."

Bruce and Kris gaped at him, and Jamison used all her energy to thump Michael's chest. She didn't want Liam here. Zanmi would kill him on sight. She understood her purpose, but Liam was a liability the group wouldn't risk, and he would be murdered outright if he came anywhere near the house.

"Why on earth would you want that man here?" Kris asked, echoing Jamison's thoughts. "And don't tell me to trust you. I do trust you. I trust both of you, but you have to tell me what is happening."

Michael adjusted his grip. "William Cohen is your ticket out of here without attracting attention. He won't wait for anyone. Not where Jamison Fairweather is concerned. He'll march in here alone. I know I would."

"So?" Kris hissed. "He'll come here alone, and he'll die here alone."

"That's not the point." Bruce grinned with a nod. "He'll have a car. An unmarked one. I watched as we sped off. That fucker yanked an old woman out of her Honda to chase after us."

Kris rolled her eyes. "There are a dozen cars and vans here already. Why take his?"

"Those cars would be noticed if one went missing and if someone realizes I've rescued you, but then let you run off without helping their cause first?" Michael shrugged. "These people are stupid, but not that stupid, Kris."

"It'll work." Bruce wrapped an arm around the woman, staring down at her with genuine affection. "I'll make it work."

"On the edge of the property, way out on the other side of the lake, there's an access road." Michael signaled for his sister to go back inside the room. "Tomorrow, Bruce will lead Cohen down it, and I'll take over from there."

CHAPTER 32

Jamison

Michael proceeded down the hall after Kristina returned safely to her room, and the further they went, the more the man he'd been in her presence—the brother, the protector—faded. What remained was the cold villain Jamison had come to expect.

Bruce went ahead when two men intercepted them in the hallway, both dressed in similar attire to Michael. "If you've no further need for us, we'd like to head out," the stockier one said in a low voice. "My hands are dirty enough, and these people feel like grit under the nails."

"Gentlemen, you have my thanks," Michael replied sincerely. "Please be discreet when you leave. Smitty and Paul are at the gate. They'll let you out, but know that it's a ten-mile hike before you reach any town. A second option would be to bypass the gate altogether and take the two miles to the other side of the lake. There's a small road there. Head west, and you'll reach civilization in about eighteen miles."

"Is there a back door here?" the second man asked. "The less interactions, the better."

The men didn't acknowledge her, making Jamison wonder how many defenseless women they had seen Michael Sinclair carry around during their service to him.

"There's one in the kitchen and another in the lower study that leads to a patio."

"Got it." The men moved around them to leave. "And when can we expect you at the rendezvous point?"

She felt it. Something in Michael Sinclair shifted, squeezing him tight on the inside. "Bruce, Kris, and Colton should be on their way in less than twenty-four hours," he replied with his back to his men. "Smitty and Paul, not long after. I'll follow when I can."

"And then onward to the point of no return?"

Michael continued walking. "That's the plan."

He couldn't even look them in the eye. Jamison grappled with the information. Those two men were individuals who served his dark deeds, and Michael Sinclair couldn't even look them in the eye as they left.

She thumped him again, and he finally glanced at her. "I said I'd explain, and I will."

The words came out on an exhale, surprising her even more. He was tired. Michael Sinclair was tired, and squinting at him, she could see the lines of strain stamped upon his face.

But any exhaustion that had been there was erased as they came to a stop. "Emmett, I told you that you didn't need to station yourself outside the door."

"I want to help," Emmett whined. "I don't want those freaks near Emily."

"Just because Taylor said you could have her first doesn't mean you'll be the only one," Michael informed him. "You need to accept that fact."

Jamison tried to roll her head to see Emmett's response but could only make out his hazy shape standing with the two women who were following them everywhere. More than the others, they were the most annoying. Silent and eerily still, Jamison wanted to scream at them to speak.

"Once she has me, she won't want anyone else, and will get pregnant without a problem."

Michael pressed his lips together before responding. "Yeah, that's not how biology works, Emmett."

"It will with me," Emmett snapped. "Emily is meant to be mine."

"Watch your fucking tone."

Emmett's head dropped, his gaze lowering to the floor. "Yes, sir."

"I don't have time to sit here and explain the female reproduction system to you, so get the fuck out of my way and go downstairs," Michael spat out. "If you want to make yourself useful, see that Madison makes it to bed, and tell those assholes down there to turn the music off."

"Yes, sir." Emmett stalled, risking a glance at Michael. "But can I see her for a second?"

Michael's lips curved. "You know what? That sounds like a plan. You go first."

Shifting to the side, Michael let Bruce slide by as he joined them while Emmett unlocked the door.

"Juice kick in yet?" Michael asked Bruce under his breath.

Bruce shook his head. "Nope, and she's loose. So is Emily."

"Did you give Emily anything?"

"Negative."

"Good." Michael grinned. "Let her get a few licks in before breaking it up."

An animalistic screech rang out as the door opened, and when Emmett entered the bedroom, it sounded like he was being tackled up against a wall. "Baby, please don't be like this," he cried. "I just want to talk!"

Bruce and Michael hung back, listening to the sound of flesh pounding flesh and Emmett's grunts of pain. The screeching turned into a rage fueled feminine cry, with Jamison recognizing Emily's voice as she screamed. "I will fucking kill you!"

A handful of heartbeats passed, each thump of Emily's fists driving her panic higher. Jamison squirmed or tried to, wanting to get inside the room to see her cousin.

"That's enough," Michael ordered, and Bruce immediately entered. Following him, Michael carried her through the door and straight into a nightmare. "Easy, Em. We're just bringing your cousin in for a visit."

Dizzy from being spun around, Jamison attempted to absorb the details of the room. There was a double-sized bed against the wall with a large man strapped to it. His dark head was turned away from them, but on the opposite side of the room, two twin mattresses were on the ground, and an animal crate was in the far corner.

The only other thing she could see was a dresser and mirror set next to a small bathroom with the light left on. Various pillows and blankets were strewn about like Emily had been wrapped in them before she attacked Emmett.

Not acknowledging Michael or anyone else, Emily continued pummeling Emmett. Claudia stood off to the side, her arms crossed and

a smile on her face. She watched with glee as her sister unleashed a fury
so savage that it echoed through the halls of the wannabe Haven House.

But just when the beating had gone on for suspiciously too long,
Emmett gained control of the situation. Lunging at Emily, he flipped her
onto the hardwood. Her head hit with a sickening crack, and she went
quiet.

"I told you to behave, Claudia," Bruce shouted when Claudia jumped
in to help. "God dammit."

Emily could be considered vicious on a good day. Around the office,
most employees kept their distance, terrified of her sharp tongue and
explosive temper. But for all her rage, she was still a tiny woman. Small
and lean, she didn't have much in the way of physical power.

Claudia was another story.

She had the height that came with the Fairweather bloodline.
Taller than even Jamison, she stood at nearly six feet and possessed
a powerhouse punch matching her bad attitude. Coming up behind
Emmett, Claudia plowed her fist into his neck and head, a rapid
succession of strikes that had the man squealing like a stuck pig.

Bruce waited nearly a full minute while Claudia wailed on the small
man, and in Jamison's confused state, she began to grasp that Bruce and
Michael wanted Emmett to get hurt.

"Come on now," Bruce said softly to a crying Claudia after she had
Emmett off her sister. Taking her by the shoulders, he gently guided her
to one of the twin mattresses. "Calm down."

From her angle, Jamison couldn't see Claudia's face, but she could
hear the raw panic in her voice. "I'm sorry. I'm sorry. I'm sorry. Please
don't hurt Madison. Let me see her. Please."

"Easy, Mama Bear. Sit on your mattress." Bruce continued to talk in
a kind voice. "Emily, off the floor and onto your mattress. You know the
rules."

Jamison heard Emily crawling heavily across the floor as Emmett rose
to stand. "Why do you hate me, Em? I just want to love you."

"Don't push your luck," Michael warned, then swung around and
dropped Jamison unceremoniously on the bed next to the person
strapped to its frame. "We'll take it from here."

Jamison flopped to her side, immediately recognizing the man chained
to the bedpost. He had the same dark hair and jawline as her father, a trait

she'd heard annoyed his parents. Trevor and Heather hated that their only son looked so much like the man who not only held their purse strings, but also the future of Fairweather Holdings.

"Damon?"

His name came out slower than normal, almost as if her tongue was too big for her mouth. She could tell he was breathing since he was lying flat on his back, but there was no recognition or any other movement.

The two silent women came up behind her, placing their hands on her shoulder and hip. Their touch burned like it had in the van, making the blood in her veins boil in a heated rush. Whoever they were, Jamison wasn't going to give them the satisfaction of knowing they were hurting her.

"Damon, can you hear me?" She didn't sound so drunk anymore and spoke louder. "It's me, Jamison. I'm here with you."

The women leaned over her to touch Damon next, his eyes fluttering at the first contact. Their hands massaged his chest in tandem, pressing over his heart as he started to thrash.

"Bruce, he's coming out of it." The women's hands were replaced by Michael's, and he moved to hold Damon down when his large body strained to break free of the restraints. "Those idiots probably forgot his nightly dose while we were busy."

"He needs to wake up a little," Emily said. "They didn't feed him either."

"These fucking idiots," Michael muttered and then spoke a little louder to Damon. "Hey, big guy. Calm down. Emily and Claudia are safe. Madison's safe. You'll all be together tomorrow."

Damon's eyes flew open, and the absolute volcanic rage in them locked onto Michael. His cheeks puffed while he tried to control his breathing, and he bared his teeth.

"I know you're mad, but we're okay now," Michael said, keeping his tone steady. "Look, Jamison is here to see you."

Damon turned his head. When his eyes found hers, the breath in his lungs caught. "No," he rasped. "No."

"Yeah," Michael said, patting his chest. "It's about that time, big guy. I'm going to bring your girls in for dinner and a bath. Don't fight them, okay? Bruce will hang out here while they work. Is that good?"

From the doorway, Emmett piped up, "Are you sure you want me to leave? If he gets loose—"

"You're dead, Emmett," Michael said flatly. "If Damon Fairweather gets loose, you die. This fucker might not like me, but you? Touching his sister the way you do? You're a dead man, and I bet he'll make it hurt. I know you think these Fairweathers are just corporate types, but look at Tobias. He was a doctor—sworn to help and heal. Look what he did to those women. Did you see the photos? The way he took their eyes? Taylor said she saw him do it with nothing but his bare fingers and a pair of pliers."

A flicker of fear touched Emmett's features. "Damon Fairweather is nothing like Tobias Miller."

"Don't think so? You weren't with us when we brought him in. He's got that same kind of crazy." Michael chuckled softly. "Honestly, they all do. Take your little hellcat down there. I bet Emily would love to remove your eyeballs with only her fingers if we gave her the chance."

"Already planning worse," Emily snarled as she moved to crouch on the mattress. "But thanks for the idea."

"You're most welcome." Michael sneered as Emmett stumbled to the door. "Now, go tell Krystal and Jessica to bring Damon's dinner."

The door slammed shut behind Emmett, and Michael huffed in exasperation. "I know I've said this before, but these are the dumbest fuckers we have ever encountered."

Bruce shook his head and sat on the floor. "Come on, girls. Backs against the wall. I've got to cuff you before Krystal and Jessica get here."

"No biting, Claudia," Michael ordered as he reached over Jamison to loosen Damon's restraints. "Same goes for you, big guy. Don't hurt the ladies."

At the first hint of slack, Damon tried to lunge for Michael, which only made the sadistic bastard laugh. "I'm going to tell you what I told your sisters. Be good."

"Madi," Damon choked. "Where's Madi?"

Michael turned serious. "Safe. I promise."

"I get to see her tomorrow, D." Claudia's labored breathing sounded like she was still upset and close to losing it again, especially when the clatter of her chains scraped across the floor. "I get to see my Madi. So please... don't hurt anyone."

Damon settled, his deadened stare fixed on the ceiling, while Bruce secured Claudia and Emily. Thinking she was next to get the chain treatment, Jamison braced herself, but Bruce nor Michael made any move to do so.

Noticing how her gaze had begun to frantically volley between Bruce and himself, Michael leaned down to whisper directly in her ear. "You should have enough juice to keep you docile, but if you act up, I'll restrain you, too. Got me?"

She nodded, her insides shrinking in terror. A few more agonizing minutes passed, and the food arrived, except the person delivering it wasn't who they expected.

"Mama's here," Taylor sang, balancing a tray in one hand as she swung the door open. "I'm ready to serve my man his dinner."

Damon's eyes closed, a tear slipping from one corner. His chest rose and fell with the pull of oxygen in and out of his flared nostrils. Jamison inched closer, as if she could use her body to shield him from Taylor.

"Oh, don't be like that," Taylor cooed, setting the tray on the dresser. "Why is *she* next to him?"

Before Jamison could react, Michael scooped her up and held her out of the way as Taylor climbed onto the bed to straddle Damon's thighs. Her short skirt hiked high, revealing the curve of her ass as she ran her hands over his chest.

"He's so freaking pretty!" Taylor squealed. "Especially like this. Around the office, you're this impenetrable dickhead that just snaps at people. It's hot, for sure, but seeing you like this? Oh, baby, you are just wrapped up in a pretty bow all for me."

The woman named Krystal, along with another woman, stood in the doorway, watching. They craned their necks to see the action, eagerly taking in the scene. Jamison fisted her hands, fighting the urge to drag Taylor off Damon by her hair. However, even though the drugs in her system were dissipating at a rapid rate, she couldn't risk it and stayed cradled against Michael's chest.

Taylor leaned down and kissed Damon's mouth, slowly shifting her weight until she was grinding against his hips. "I can feel that," she whispered. "Is it for me? Should we move your sisters out so we can have a little privacy?"

Jamison would swear Damon was turning multiple shades of green under Taylor, and she hoped he vomited right into the bitch's mouth.

"Come on, Taylor. He's half-drugged and doesn't know where he is or who you are," Michael said, trying to reason with her. "And he looks like he's about to throw up."

That got Taylor moving.

"Eww, gross," Taylor screeched, stumbling backward off the bed. Her heels slid out from under her, and she flailed about. "This skirt is vintage!"

"We'll take care of him," Krystal said, rushing in with the other woman to help Taylor stand. "You've had a long day and should rest."

Taylor pouted between the two. "I do feel like I need a good hydration mask and a bath," she sighed. "Think you can handle him?"

"We've been handling him," the second one said. "Damon is our little pussy cat."

Taylor's lip curled at the snarky tone. "Well, thank you so much, *Jessica*. Since he's such a pussy cat for you, maybe I'll bump your name to the bottom of the list. Everyone knows men like a challenge, and if he's already comfortable being around you, it might be hard for Damon to muster up the effort to even want to impregnate you."

A shade of green, similar to Damon's coloring, tinged Jessica's face. "Please don't make me go after Barb. She smells, Taylor."

Taylor snatched the tray off the dresser and shoved it into Jessica's stomach. "Then serve my man properly and never call him a fucking pussy cat again."

Head down, Jessica spoke to the floor. "Yes, Taylor."

Bruce cleared his throat, wisely staying back with Claudia and Emily. "What time are you heading out in the morning?"

In the most exaggerated huff of disgust, Taylor tossed her long, luxurious hair over one shoulder. "Parker said at six, but that's *so* uncivilized."

"Agreed. So how about I gas up the car for you in the morning?" Bruce offered. "That way, you can leave around seven and give yourself time to rest."

Taylor eyed him suspiciously. "And why would you do that?"

"Because you did well today, and I was impressed with the execution of the grab." Bruce shoved his hands in his pockets and rocked on his heels. "Hell, it was so flawless, you might've been able to run with our team back in the day."

It was as if a light bulb had been switched on inside Taylor. Already possessing some unhinged need for praise, Bruce's compliment sent the psychopath soaring. "I did well? Really?" she squeaked. "That means so much coming from you!"

Michael kept his expression blank, but Jamison couldn't, and the next thing she knew, he was tossing her over his shoulder. "Ladies, when you're done with Damon, bring some food to my room for Jamison."

"Wait, you said you wouldn't do it until I could watch." Taylor stomped her foot, and Jamison thought she might snap if she heard that sound one more time. "And I wanted to relax tonight."

"I already told you I wasn't starting tonight." Michael smacked her ass hard, gripping it roughly when she squirmed. "Not that I don't want to."

"Okay, so no fucking," Taylor ordered, lifting her pinkie. "Swear?"

Michael snagged Taylor's pinkie with his own. "Swear."

CHAPTER 33

Jamison

M ichael's boots pounded on the hardwood floors as he carried her down the hall. "I know you're not as out of it as you're pretending."

"Fuck you."

"That's the plan, isn't it?"

She couldn't see anything but the floor while he hauled her across the upper level, but she could hear the laughter in his voice.

"You'll have to kill me first."

"That can be arranged. It would make all this easier."

She punched his back. "I can walk, you know."

"But can you shut up?"

Down another long hall, they came to the last room, and Michael swung open the door. It was dark inside, lit only by the moonlight streaming through a wall of windows. She barely had time to register any details before being tossed onto a bed.

With her limbs fully functional again, she scrambled to the headboard. "Do not touch me."

Michael clicked on a lamp, illuminating his chiseled features and the hint of auburn in his dark brown hair. "Not a problem."

As her eyes adjusted, Jamison scanned the space. It was a world apart from the room her cousins were trapped in. This one was much larger with a king-sized bed, twin dressers, and a sitting area that featured not only the most comfortable-looking reading chair she had ever seen but also wall-to-wall bookshelves.

"Where are we?"

Moving to stand in front of the glass double balcony doors on her right, Michael stretched his arms overhead, his shirt riding up slightly to reveal a muscled torso. "My bedroom."

She figured as much. The room was simple and masculine but not without taste—clean lines, warm tones, unassuming elegance. It fit him.

"Take your shoes off the bed."

When she didn't move, he sighed and pinched the bridge of his nose. "Take your shoes off the bed, or I'll rip every piece of clothing off you and parade you around the house naked."

She kicked her shoes off and let them fall to the floor one at a time.

"Thought so." He kept his gaze fixed on the night beyond the windows. "I picked this room for the view. In the morning, you'll see why. The lake's beautiful, and the balcony is the perfect place to have coffee."

Michael's massive shoulders sank a little at the mention of coffee. "She loved iced coffee. Even on cold mornings. Always a mocha with vanilla crème and caramel drizzle. I tried to drink it with her a few times, but it was just too damn sweet."

Jamison shook her head, trying to clear the lingering fog from her vision. But no matter how she focused, she couldn't make the shadowed figure circling Michael go away. Her brain told her it was one of the women who kept following them, but it was impossible, even when the dark silhouette trailed its fingers along Michael's shoulders while it swayed in the full moonlight.

"Why are you doing this?"

"Taylor wants a baby." He smirked at the beautifully etched glass. "You understand that feeling, don't you?"

She shifted, bracing herself on her knees. "That lunatic doesn't deserve a baby."

Glancing back over his shoulder, Michael Sinclair had the audacity to wink. "Agreed."

Positive she hadn't heard him correctly, Jamison opened her mouth to voice one of the many questions sprinting through her thoughts, but a knock at the door silenced them all, and she clung to the rustic wooden bed frame.

"Come in."

The door opened, and Jessica appeared, cradling a tray with two bowls of steaming hot soup and sandwiches on it. "I have your dinner."

"Set it on the dresser." Michael turned, crossing his arms. "Damon?"

Jessica placed the tray down carefully, then stood with her hands folded in front of her. "Fed."

"Were you respectful, Jessica?"

"We only washed his chest and face. But… I think he needs to use the bathroom."

"Bruce will handle it."

"Do you want anything else from me?" Shuffling her feet, Jessica's gaze flicked down Michael's body. "I can help with her if you need me to. Or I can help in other ways. Taylor said you can't have Jamison Fairweather tonight, but that doesn't mean you should be alone."

Michael took slow, deliberate steps toward the woman who looked so much like her partner in crime. With glasses and dark hair, Jessica and Krystal could be sisters, and maybe they were, which made their presence here all the more disturbing.

"Are you offering to have sex with me?" Michael asked, stopping just in front of her. "Answer me, Jessica."

"I'll do anything." Jessica's lips parted, her tongue darting out to lick them. "Anything."

"Anything?" Michael sighed. "Great. Then get the fuck out."

"But—"

Jamison's eyes widened when Michael grabbed Jessica by the upper arm and shoved her toward the door. "Did I stutter? You said you'd do anything, so leave and stop sniffing around me, thinking I'm going to pity fuck you."

Behind Michael, the not-quite-there shadow moved again, trailing its ghostly fingers down his spine when Jessica wouldn't budge. "Taylor said we would have free rein over this place, and once we arrived with you still here, we assumed it meant you were finally ready to play. And I, for one, was excited. You're lonely and so fucking gorgeous. There's not a woman here who wouldn't let you have them, me included."

Michael ran a hand through his hair, switching on the charm. "I'm sorry, Jessica. I'm tired and still have to deal with the problem currently gaping at me from my bed."

Snapping her mouth shut, Jamison squared her shoulders. "I'll be happy to leave if you two want to be alone."

"That won't be necessary." Michael opened the door, giving Jessica a roguish smile. "I'll see you later."

Jessica left without comment, a blush painting her cheeks, and Michael locked the door this time. "You need to take a shower."

The man really was insane if he thought she was going to remove any of her clothing in this house. "Uh, no."

Michael's charming smile disappeared, and he looked tired again. "The dress is ruined. Your feet and shins are covered in dirt, your food is too hot to eat right now, and I need to check if it's been drugged."

"Don't you decide who gets drugged?"

The shadow playing tricks on the wall appeared to almost hug Michael from behind, resting its head on the center of his back. Jamison decided right then that the drugs must be driving her insane, especially when it looked like Michael leaned into the thing's touch.

"Tomorrow is a big day for us both." He wouldn't meet her gaze as he spoke, instead staring at the reading nook in the corner. "You need to rest, and the best way to do that is to get clean and have a full stomach. There are clothes in the bathroom cabinet you can wear."

The constant chill in the air worked its way into her bones, and a shiver crawled through her body. "I said no."

"Whatever."

In one smooth motion, Michael reached behind his neck and pulled his shirt off. She gasped and lifted her hand as if she could block the sight of his naked chest. "I don't need to see that."

"But you don't mind."

Stupid bastard. She snatched one of the many throw pillows on the bed and launched it at him. Dipping his head casually to the side, Michael avoided the projectile as it sailed past his ear.

"Your aim sucks. Now go shower, or you'll be subjected to a lot more than just me shirtless."

He arched an eyebrow when she didn't move, his fingers going for the button on his pants next.

The moment the zipper lowered, she was on her feet and staggering to the bathroom. "Asshole."

Slamming the door shut, she was momentarily taken aback by the sight of the massive bathroom. Black marble tile flooring with beautifully textured smokey black walls stretched outward, ending at a muted gray stone soaking tub set beneath ten-foot balcony doors. To the left, a long dark-wood cabinet ran the length of the space with twin glass vessel sinks sitting on top. Various potted plants were scattered throughout the space, and thanks to Abe, she recognized a few.

"What the hell is this?" she whispered.

Like the bedroom, the bathroom held the same understated elegance. Crafted and constructed with care and love. Taking hesitant steps forward, she found towels and women's clothing stored in the cabinet, just as Michael said.

And tucked away on the very top shelf, neatly folded and still in pristine condition, was a stack of navy-blue nurse scrubs.

Jamison ran a hand over the dark material. "CeCe."

Something rustled in one of the plants behind her, and she fought the urge to squeal. Whatever else was in this bathroom, she didn't need any more surprises, even if it was just a wayward lizard. "Go away."

The shower was around the corner from the soaking tub, and after she figured out which of the many buttons to press, she lurched back when water came from all directions.

Narrowly missing the streams, she peeked through the windows in the shower's alcove while waiting for the water to heat up. This balcony was more concealed than the one in the bedroom, with trees standing tall and close, like they'd grown to protect the room inside.

"Okay. Let's get this over with."

It was a struggle to remove her mother's ruined wedding dress, and she ended up ripping off a button or two to get the halter off. When her growl of frustration echoed through the bathroom, a light knock at the door sounded.

"I can help," Michael's deep voice offered through the door.

"No, thank you!"

No, thank you? Had she just said *no thank you* to the terrorist? She silently blamed Simone for instilling good manners in her, and thinking of Simone again made Jamison burst into tears instantly.

Not wanting Michael to hear her sobbing, she entered the shower. The water pelting her from the various showerheads made enough noise to cover the sound. She had never felt so helpless. Never. She wanted to pay attention and had tried to notice the details so she could tell Liam later, but there were too many moving parts working against her.

She nearly collapsed when she thought of Liam coming here. Her mind was starting to clear, and now running wild, showing her all the horrible things these people would do to him.

"No, no, no." She scrubbed her skin raw, her bottom lip trembling. "I won't let it happen."

Getting control of herself, she finished cleaning up and got out. From the choices of clothing available, she picked an oversized T-shirt—clearly one of Michael's—and a pair of women's sweatpants to wear. Leaving her feet bare, she noted the pair of women's tennis shoes at the bottom of the closet. They looked like they would fit, and if she had the chance to run, she would need them.

Back in the bedroom, she found more lamps ablaze, revealing further details about the room. In the corner, close to the reading nook, there was a table with chairs for two where Michael stood waiting. He had also changed, wearing dark sweatpants and a T-shirt similar to the one she had on.

"Come and eat."

Warily, she took the offered chair, eyeballing the gun tucked into the waistband of his pants. "Do you always wear a weapon in your own home?"

He took the seat across from her. "No, I do not."

That was it. No elaboration. No explanation. He just started eating, so she did the same. The soup had reached a decent temperature, and she paced herself, even though she was starving.

The silence dragged. Needing to distract herself, Jamison peered past him to the rows of books on the shelves. She expected war memoirs or thrillers, but was surprised when she recognized row after row of romances.

"She liked to read," Michael said, his eyes still on his soup. "Rom-coms. After a long day with patients and dealing with her family, she always needed something light."

Jamison set her spoon down. "Did you live here with her?"

"No."

"But you built this for her."

Michael's green and brown eyes ticked upward to meet hers. "We designed it together. She loved her childhood home. When we talked about settling down, we started sketching out this place. I had the plans drawn up in 2018 after we found this area. In fact, I proposed to her here when we signed the papers to purchase the land." He glanced at the balcony windows. "Right out there, on the edge of the lake."

His mouth curved slightly at the memory, softening his features. Michael Sinclair was already handsome, but like this, it was quite a shocking difference.

"She didn't know I'd had the plans completed when she died," he went on. "Didn't know I was already working with contractors to bring it to life. Down the hall, there's a huge library. Her library. I filled it with every romantic comedy book I could find. After I saw the one at Haven, I even considered adding a conservatory."

Ice trickled through her bloodstream. "You were at Haven House before the night you tried to take me?"

The easy smile on Michael's lips slid into a thin line. "I've walked those trails for years and watched your family for just as long. Sometimes with Cecilia. Sometimes without her. I kept trying to figure out what made you all so special. What did you have that she thought was worth protecting?"

"Did you ever find the answer?"

"No." He returned to his food. "None of you were worth her."

Now she was getting somewhere. "Is that why you joined Zanmi? Because you blame us for CeCe's death?"

"Cecilia." Michael clenched his jaw as he stared at his soup. "Her name was Cecilia."

Jamison shifted gears. She wouldn't get anywhere with him if she acted contradictory. "I'm sorry. I don't remember her. The only name I know is CeCe."

"She remembered you," he said quietly. "She remembered every single one of you, even after everyone forgot her."

Forgot her?

CeCe Miller?

That was a comment she couldn't let slide.

"Simone didn't forget her. Neither did Annabeth. I may not remember Cecilia, but they do. They mourn her. We all do. I don't think any of us knows how to exist without the weight of grief sitting heavy on our shoulders. Mourning is our thing, and mourning CeCe is at the forefront," she said, her voice rising as her anger snapped. "You know, maybe instead of lurking outside Haven House and kidnapping people, you should have introduced yourself like a normal damn person. Simone would've welcomed you. She would've asked about CeCe until your ears bled. And she would've shown you the photos. They hang everywhere now. We don't have many, but each one Liam found hangs proudly in the main hall and library."

"Fine. They mourned her. But no one fought for her."

"Yes, they did!"

He dropped his spoon into the bowl, the full force of his menacing glare striking her. "If they did, she never knew it. Cecilia lived her whole life thinking she was the one not worth saving."

Jamison mimicked his move, her metal spoon clanging loudly against the ceramic. "My dad and Simone honestly thought Charlie had gotten his shit together and was giving them a good life."

"He tried. Charlie did giv—"

Michael sucked in a sharp breath, wincing as he closed his eyes and rubbed his left temple. The look of pain on his face had goosebumps breaking out across her arms, and she lowered them from the table so he wouldn't see.

There was more going on here.

"Charlie did give them a good life in the beginning," Michael said, regaining control of whatever pain had seized him. "They were happy."

"So, what happened?"

"Bryan," he bit out. "He's one of those individuals who can't stand not to own everything. Land. People. He needled his way into their lives and used his daughter to gain the upper hand. The villa Charlie lived in with the kids was next door to Bryan Carroll's place, and being greedy, he wanted to expand."

Since he was willing to talk, she pushed. "Toby said Cecilia helped him kill Charlie."

"Not true." Michael leaned back in his chair, his expression now devoid of pain. "But by the end, Charlie had it coming. He was using again. Drinking himself into oblivion after losing everything to Bryan. It made him violent."

"Did Cecilia help Toby kill the others?"

"Some she did." His voice dropped lower. "But not how you're thinking. She wasn't there when the murders happened, but she cleaned up after him."

Jamison tried to mask her revulsion. "Where do you come in?"

Michael paused, then turned toward one of the bookshelves, staring at the spines like they held the answer. "Miami. I met her at a coffee shop. And I just... knew."

"You just knew what?"

She expected him to say he just knew he wanted her because she was beautiful or that he just knew she would accept his work because he could sense something in her. Or perhaps that he knew Cecilia Miller held the same warped sense of life and death as he did.

But Michael Sinclair didn't say any of that.

"I knew she was the other half of my soul," he exhaled. "Just standing there in front of me in a coffee shop line. It was the strangest thing. Like a scene in a movie playing out." He released a short laugh. "And once I saw her, I did the most bizarre things to gain her attention. I played the part of a lovesick fool, but it wasn't an act. It was real. I would've done anything to have her."

Jamison kept silent. The first thing Liam ever taught her was that it was easy to gain information when a person was left to wander through their thoughts and memories. Half the time, the world was too loud, and humans—the selfish beings that they are—were forever too concerned with themselves to stop and listen.

"I didn't know about Toby at first. But when I met him..." Michael shook his head. "I felt it. Evil. He's evil as hell, and Taylor's worse. It took me forever to convince Cecilia to leave them."

"Why wouldn't she leave them?"

"She thought she was protecting your family." Michael's face scrunched in pain once more, but only for a second. "Toby wanted to go back to Haven House right after college. But Cecilia and Taylor talked him into doing the Miami internship with his friends. Cecilia did it to keep him away from all of you. Taylor did it because she was tired of the islands and thought Miami would be the place where she might finally be *discovered*."

Jamison snorted. "Taylor thinks very highly of herself."

He shared a small smile with her. "That she does."

There was a knock at the door, and Michael rose to answer. He cracked it an inch, but it was enough for Jamison to hear Bruce speaking, although she couldn't make out what was being said.

"Eugene and the last six arrive tomorrow," Michael said. "So, it'll work. And if it doesn't, we'll leave the hard way. Tell Smitty and Paul, then get back to Kris. I don't want one of these assholes trying to wander into her room tonight."

The door clicked closed, and Jamison folded her hands into her lap, waiting patiently. The information he'd been willing to share was invaluable, and she needed him to continue. It would matter one day.

As he turned back to her, Michael paused, the color draining from his face. Staring past her for a long minute, his throat worked as he swallowed.

"Are you..." Jamison didn't exactly care, but reflex had her asking anyway, "okay?"

"Sometimes I see her."

Oh, shit. The ice already seizing her internal organs crystallized into a hard freeze, stopping her heart. Not only was Michael Sinclair a raging terrorist who was currently holding her hostage, but he also had some sort of misfiring happening in his brain.

"Do you see her now?" she asked cautiously.

He blinked a few times, the moisture gathering in his eyes receding. "Not anymore."

"Do you see Cecilia often?" She kept her voice soft, trying to find her inner Bernie. "Does she talk to you?"

"Yeah." Michael went to one of the bedside tables. "Give me a sec."

He rummaged through a drawer, pulling out a prescription bottle to pop two pills into his mouth before returning to the table to gulp them down with his water. "Finish eating."

Taking a bite of her sandwich, she chewed slowly. With food in her system, she could stay more alert, but the nausea was still right there, riding her stomach as it threatened to revolt.

"You're worried Zanmi might try something with Kris," she said. "But what about Claudia and Emily? Shouldn't you be worried about them, too?"

"I'd be more worried about Damon than his sisters," Michael replied before swiping up his own sandwich. "He's got all those sickos in heat."

Michael clearly hated Zanmi. He hated Taylor. Hated Toby. And yet, here he was.

It didn't add up.

Jamison studied the man across from her. "Why are you doing this?"

Chewing his sandwich, Michael Sinclair kept his eyes averted. "Cecilia and I had a fight before my last deployment. It was time to start our life together, and I told her she had to cut ties with Toby and Taylor. I'd been working hard to transition her out of that relationship. It was working, with Toby only showing up now and then."

"Transitioning her out of a relationship? So before that, you were just sitting back while your girlfriend's brother was torturing and murdering women?"

Michael's gaze snapped to her face. "Our fight was about Toby. He had killed those girls in Missouri, and we had agreed that she wouldn't get involved, but he convinced her to help. Then he went after her student. Her fucking student, and yet she still wouldn't cut ties with him, too afraid of what he would do. By then, he was planning to move back to Hollingsdale and had planted Taylor pretty deep at Fairweather."

She almost asked why he hadn't just gone to the police, but the answer was obvious. If he had, CeCe would have been arrested. Locked away and left to rot.

But she would've still been alive.

"Why didn't you just kill him?" Giving up on her food, she was ready to ask the big questions. Her emotional and physical state couldn't get much worse, so she figured, why not go for the gold? "You were a soldier. A hero. Heroes don't let the bad guys win."

Michael found her reasoning funny. "Bad guys always win, Jamison. War is not comprised of good versus evil because they're all evil. It's just one monster battling another for supremacy."

"I can't believe that."

"Doesn't matter. It's still true. And Toby?" He gave a humorless laugh. "Toby's nothing new, nor even the worst monster I've come across."

She tilted her head to the side, noting how his pupils dilated. The pills he'd taken were for pain, and likely why he was willing to talk. "Is that why you bombed those buildings?"

"All my targets deserved what they got." Michael sobered, and he lifted his shirt, showing the tattooed names of the children who died. Right over his heart, just as he said. "Except them. I carry them here. Like I carry Cecilia. The innocent victims of violent men."

Now or never, she chose to use his statement as an opening. "Cecilia killed herself. She wasn't a victim. She killed herself. She ate that manchineel willingly."

The entire atmosphere went still. There was no air, no sound, nothing but the staccato of her heart as it hammered with the knowledge that Michael Sinclair was about to kill her. The fire in him—the absolute hate and pain he carried—shone through, etched in every line on his face and tightening muscle of his body.

Michael tilted his head, observing her as if she were the prey and he the predator. "As I previously stated, Cecilia and I got into a fight the night before I deployed. I told her we couldn't move forward with our lives if she were still involved with Toby. She got upset and said it was over. She chose you and your family—a family that abandoned her—over me. It cut deep, so I left and slept my last night stateside at Bruce's place before flying out a few hours later."

"What does that—"

"I didn't say goodbye. On Christmas. *Fucking Christmas*. It was her favorite holiday. She never got to really celebrate it growing up, so I always made it special for her. And then I left. I ruined it. I ruined her." His massive chest pumped rapidly with a mixture of loss and desperation to be understood. "I got on that plane thinking we'd work it out. But Toby beat me to her. He showed up at our place and tried one more time to pull her back. She refused and said she wanted to wait for me, so he drugged her. He drugged her and dragged her back to Florida. That's what they were doing on that inlet across from Haven House. He was trying to show her their old home, thinking it would convince her to return."

The story was exactly what Toby had told the authorities. He had taken CeCe from her home in Missouri without her permission, not to hurt her, but to convince her that it was time to come home so he could be with Evie.

"Can we backtrack for a second?" Michael might not answer the question that kept nagging her, but it didn't hurt to ask. "One thing is completely confusing me. If Toby is so devoted to Taylor and wants her to have a baby, why is he obsessed with my sister? The things he said in that graveyard...they were sick and disgusting, but we believed that he held some sort of deranged love for Evie. Are you trying to tell me it was fake?"

"It wasn't fake," Michael said. "Toby loves Evie. He always has. Taylor will never compare to your sister. Not in his heart."

Frustrated with his answer, Jamison waved a hand in exasperation. "Then why is Taylor doing all this for a man who loves another woman?"

Michael shrugged. "I don't know if you've noticed, but Taylor is what we call a narcissist. She can't accept that *anyone*—especially poor Toby—could love someone other than *her*. She gaslights herself almost as much as she gaslights other people."

"Did you say poor Toby? That's a fucked up way to describe a serial killer."

"I've often wondered what Toby would've become without Taylor. He likes pain. He likes to inflict it, but killing? Mutilating the women? Removing their eyeballs, sawing off their legs?" Michael shook his head. "Would he have done it without Taylor pressing him to go further for the thrill?"

An image of Toby in his jail uniform, writhing on the table and screaming, appeared in her mind. "Yes, I think so. He's insane. I mean, mass murder aside, why would he come in and steal random things from Haven House? That behavior—"

"Was for Taylor."

"What do you mean, *was for Taylor*?" Her gaze narrowed on him. "Taylor put him up to all that crap?"

Michael smirked. "You think the rest of the world has become obsessed with your family and their insane story? Well, guess what? Taylor was the Fairweather's first Super Fan."

Jamison didn't think this could get much worse. Obviously, she was wrong. "You're telling me that Taylor told him to steal our stuff?"

"Taylor loves your mother's paintings the most and has them hanging at several of her properties," he replied. "Toby would talk about Haven House and the massacre all the time, and I guess through their years together, Taylor became just as obsessed. She wanted souvenirs. Trophies. Hell, she even encouraged him to act out that night when he killed women."

She slouched in her chair. "I don't... I don't get it, Michael."

"It's simple. Taylor was raised in a world where the lives of others were considered insignificant. She loves wielding power over Toby, over anyone really, and when he killed, it was only when she was with him. Even while in college. Her father bought a villa near Grenada so Taylor could easily zip on and off the island because she demanded to stay close to him." Michael's green and brown gaze stared at her, unwavering and filled with suppressed rage. "Cecilia was well aware that Taylor was Toby's pressure point, and when Taylor appeared out in that swamp, chasing her through the brush and edging Toby into a frenzy, she fucking knew what was going to happen."

From the beginning, Liam had always thought that was the case. His very first theory during the investigation was that CeCe had chosen to end her life rather than face what her brother might do.

"Wait." Jamison leaned forward. "Taylor was there that night?"

"Yes."

"How do you know?"

"Because Taylor told me."

Jamison gave herself a second to let that information settle in her mind. "When?"

"Not long after I finished building this place." His expression turned to dark amusement. "I was done with my... public service work and planned to live a quiet life. But I went to see Taylor during one of my visits to Haven House."

"Whoa, what?"

"Cecilia is buried there. Even in death, I can't stay away." He stood to clear their plates, chuckling. "By the way, that forest? I don't know what the Fairweathers did, but it's haunted as shit."

She watched him as he moved about the room. "How is it that we've found nothing on your relationship with CeCe?"

"Because I'm careful with my life. I've made too many enemies to count, and Cecilia was a liability that could be used against me."

Out of everything she'd learned, that was the one thing that made sense. Years in PR had taught her how dangerous exposure could be—how social media could ruin or weaponize a life in seconds.

"But now you're helping Taylor?"

"That's what she thinks."

"So, the phone calls? The stalking? All of it was a ruse?" Jamison shot to her feet and marched across the room. "You've been pretending this whole time? You don't really want to—" she flapped her hands wildly, "—rape me and make some sicko baby for Zanmi?"

Michael looked down his nose at her, unimpressed. "I don't give two shits about you, Jamison Fairweather. Sorry to disappoint."

She punched him in the chest.

Hard.

And the man didn't even flinch. "Feel better?"

"Yes! No!" She surged up on her toes to shout in his face. "Why am I here? Why did you let them take us? Why are you doing this?"

"Because I needed Fairweathers," he said calmly, "to draw them in. Taylor is making this whole baby mission into a free-for-all. She's calling in her friends to come and play. The psycho wants her Fairweather baby, but she wants a boy. A mini-Toby. And you guys didn't have any boys for her to take. Well, until today when your sister gave birth."

"What about Xavier?"

"Oh, did I forget to mention that Taylor is also a raging racist? Xavier has always been safe. I only sent Zanmi men there to get their asses shot or arrested. Just like that first night I tried to kidnap you. The men I sent after Emily were completely incompetent, and one of my guys accompanied them to ensure they were taken care of by the police. Same thing with Claudia. As soon as Smitty discovered she was pregnant, he dumped her. She could be carrying a boy, and we weren't about to give Taylor what she wanted."

Jamison stumbled back a step, horror curling in her stomach. "The women. At Haven House and Samuel's house? You sent those women to—"

"Those *fertile* women who would have been used on Damon or your brother or even your dad? Yes, I sent them. To. Their. Deaths. Eugene gave me the list of who was the most viable to carry a child, and those are the ones I sent."

For the briefest of seconds, hope had flared inside her. For a single moment, she thought Michael might not be the monster he pretended to be.

But she was so wrong.

Those poor, misguided women had been murdered by him.

"Eugene Gilbert?" she whispered. "Toby's friend from college who started Zanmi?"

"Eugene didn't start Zanmi. Taylor dragged him into it. He wants the group dead as much as I do. They're bleeding him dry with their blackmail."

"They could have killed us." She went to the bed and sat on its edge. "Those women wanted to kill us."

"But they didn't, did they? They stupidly ate the fruit I told them were decoys. They never even questioned me."

"And Taylor didn't know you were doing it. That's why she sounded so surprised on the phone."

"Yeah, that took some smoothing over. Unfortunately, I lost focus during the whole thing and allowed my ego to take control. Something in me needed Taylor to know her people were about to die, so I let your dad's call to her go through. It was a mistake, and she almost caught on that I wasn't completely on her side, but her narcissism won. She couldn't fathom anyone not wanting to be dedicated to her needs." He inhaled deeply, rubbing an eye that had begun to spasm. "In the end, it was a win. I was able to eradicate a round of future rapists and use it as a distraction to get my nephew from the feds."

Staring at her hands folded in her lap, she replayed everything he'd just said. "Are you going to let us go before you do whatever you have planned?"

Michael crossed over to where she sat and knelt in front of her. "Grief twists people into unrecognizable things. I was already standing at the tipping point, but I completely lost my soul when I lost Cecilia."

That strange shadow returned, merging with Michael's on the wall. It crouched beside him as if it, too, were listening.

"That's not a yes." She shook her head, overwhelmed but somehow clearer in her thinking. One's impending death did that to a person. "You're going to let us die here."

"That depends."

"On what?"

"On how fast you run."

CHAPTER 34

Ben

2008

E verything.

Laura Jean.

The air he breathed, the heart hammering in his chest, the blood in his veins—every bit of it belonged to her.

Laura Jean was everything.

The other half of his soul, she filled the blank spaces in him. Spaces created by the careful chipping away of his own doing. Dark deeds and dirty deals hollowing him into a shell that wasn't worth anything.

A machine no one could love.

But she loved him.

She made him whole, the missing piece of his puzzle. Click. Perfection personified with the union.

It would hold him. For an eternity, the love he held for her would seal their destiny together. Tied tight like a string, knotted with one end in him and the other in her.

Forever.

"What are you thinking about?"

With her back to him and little Jamison on her hip, Laura Jean stood a few feet away on a dune's peak. The wind whipped about, coming off the waves and sending her beautiful blonde hair flying around her in a tornado of silky tresses. Their other children played on the shore. Three *small figures looking for shells while he examined the remains of his family's old beach house lying in ruins on the sand.*

No.

This wasn't right.

Jamison shouldn't be here. The skeleton of his old beach house was long gone by the time their princess was born. The structure had been peeled from the earth when they renourished the beach to make it strong again. Strong enough to build their home here.

A castle.

He had built Laura Jean a castle among the dunes, rising high in the sky so she could see the entire expanse of white and the spectacular emerald shade of the water that matched her eyes.

"Laura Jean?"

The laughter of their children ceased, dying abruptly on a gust of salty sea air. In a panic, he scanned the beach but saw nothing. No Selah, nor Samuel, nor Evie. No Jamison on Laura Jean's hip.

Above them, the sky turned over on itself, too fast for his eyes to track. Night entered and erased the multicolored sunset, leaving a sea of stars to carve out a place in the darkness.

Laura Jean raised her arms high, her hands clawed. "Find him."

She whispered the demand, the night and earth pulsing with her will. The scene should scare him or, at the very least, set him on edge.

But it didn't.

It never did.

These whispers of what the world deemed unnatural were completely natural with Laura Jean. Loving her had only made it easier to accept.

"Find him."

Her repeated order shot through his chest, pulling at his heart with enough force that he thought the organ might shoot out the back of his body.

"Who?" He couldn't breathe; oxygen ripped right from him. "Who do I need to find?"

Laura Jean's clawed hands slammed down to her sides. She spun in a dizzying whirl and faced him as the wind went silent, leaving nothing but his ragged breathing. Wild emerald eyes overfilling with pain met his, and the woman he loved above all others glared at him with absolute rage.

The sight shocked him. Seeing her this way shocked him to his very core, and when another slice of her anger seared through him, it nearly knocked him to his knees.

"Talk to me," he begged. The stars continued to twinkle, battling with the rotation of night. Comets and other celestial objects joined in on the dance, weaving through the sky as they worked to craft a screaming kaleidoscope of space. "Laura Jean?"

"Find him." She took heavy steps down the dune, a crackle of lightning shooting out along the beach. Strike after strike, bolts of electricity rained down upon the shore, sending sand exploding into the air. "Samuel! Find your father!"

Laura Jean stopped directly before him, as heartbreakingly beautiful as the day they met. His soul sighed at her nearness, a feeling he'd never quite become used to. Maybe in a thousand years, he might, but for now, he would never get used to how his entire being sang in her presence.

Tears streamed down her cheeks, and she shuddered as her anger melted into agony. "You have to stay."

"With you?" He cupped her face, wanting nothing more. "Forever. I'll stay with you forever. You know that. We have a deal."

"No." Her bottom lip trembled. "Not with me. With them. This is a new deal. You have to stay."

They struck then. The memories. The sound of the gunshots. The feel of Laura Jean taking her last breath in his arms. The vacant look in her eyes when she left him.

And the pain. He remembered the pain. The soul devouring pain. The nightmare of loss he lived day after day. He was only now learning how to hide it, but that seemed to be making it worse.

Until it became too much.

They thought he was strong, but he was nothing. Laura Jean was everything, and he was nothing. Without her, he was nothing.

The notes. The tears. The bottle of medication on his desk. The way the pills felt as he meticulously swallowed them down one at a time.

"I'm sorry." He cried with her. "I'm so sorry."

Way down at the edge of the beach where the forest met the sand, a pinprick of light erupted in the darkness. A cry of relief burst from Laura Jean's lips, and she laughed through her sorrow.

"He found you. Samuel found you." She reached for his hand, cradling it in her palms. The size difference between them had always been amusing, but seeing it again made Ben feel her loss all over again. "Ben, we have to make a new deal."

"I don't understand."

"Stay."

"Where?"

"Stay for them." Licking her lips, she glanced over her shoulder as if expecting something to rush upon them. "Give our kids a good life. Stay for our babies."

Miranda and Devon appeared to his left, materializing out of thin air. Neither spoke nor came any closer, giving them privacy. Devon had a soft smile for him, the gentle kind Ben had never been able to master.

But Miranda.

It had been so long since he'd seen her this way. Beautiful. Healthy. Glowing. There was no smile for him. Only bittersweet sadness. She missed Josie. Devon missed Simone. He could feel their pain as much as he could feel his own.

God, how selfish he had been. Swallowing those damn pills. A fool. Throwing it all away, and squandering what he still had.

"Make this deal with me," Laura Jean pleaded, the swirl of light in the distance growing. "I'll wait for you. You know I'll wait for you, but you have to stay behind. It hurts. I understand. But you have to live for as long as you can. Live to be a hundred."

Time was a beast. A monster ticking away the seconds without her in his head. It played with his thoughts, driving him into madness and making him think she was still near. A shadow on the wall that resembled her shape, a whisper on the wind carrying her voice. Idle time and empty memories were nothing but torture devices created by an unforgiving universe.

"I'm sorry I did it." He allowed his tears to fall. They came so easily now whenever he was alone. "I'm drowning in this fucking hell without you, and then my mind...it tricks me into thinking I see you. Everywhere. I fucking see you everywhere."

He placed his hand against her cheek, and she leaned into his touch, her eyes closing. "It is me. I wanted to remind you that I'm still here. I'm waiting for you to come home at the end of it all. To me. I'm your home, Ben, but so are they. Our kids are your home and your responsibility."

"I'm so scared." Who better to confess his fears to than her? Whether they were ridiculous or not, who better to hear the inner workings of his mind? "I'm scared I'll lose my memories of you. Time passes, and the years are eating away at the little things. Sometimes, I forget the exact shade of emerald in your eyes or the way you sing off-key in the shower."

Laura Jean's lips parted in shock, her eyes opening to stare at him in disbelief. "I'm an excellent singer."

"Oh, baby, no, you're not." He laughed through tears. His Laura Jean could always make him smile. "I just never had the heart to tell you."

"Well, that's your opinion." Planting her hands on her hips, she stuck her nose in the air. "Opinions are like buttholes—"

Wrong or right, he couldn't stop himself. Whether they were in heaven or hell, he couldn't stop himself from snatching her to him for a kiss and groaning when the feel and taste of her brought as much pain as it did pleasure.

"Don't leave me."

Begging. He was begging.

And he wasn't at all ashamed.

"I'll stay," he whispered. "I'll give them a good life. I'll make sure everyone is taken care of, but in the end, I want to find you waiting. I want to find my girl waiting for me so we can watch eternity go by together."

She kissed him again, clinging to him as much as he was to her, both desperate for a second more together. "Deal."

Pain flared through his body. With a groan, Ben jerked awake. The dream was always the same, coming to him night after night since *the night* he made the stupidest mistake of his life.

Suicide?

What the fuck?

Shifting slightly, he fought against the sheets. Josie had tucked him into his old suite at Parkland Grounds, the room acting as a time capsule of the years he'd spent living a lie here.

Josie and the boys had brought him home from the hospital days ago, keeping vigil in shifts as though he were going to break again. The pills had fucked him up pretty good, but he was finally regaining some semblance of strength.

He absolutely hated this. The inability to care for himself was one thing, but seeing those haunted looks in Selah and Samuel's eyes had the power to make his heart stop all over again. What he'd done wasn't fair, and while he might not be much of a father anymore, he loved them with every ounce of his being.

Blinking against the afternoon light, the room came into focus. He'd nearly slept the day away, and another wave of self-loathing surged. This had to stop. He had to get his shit together. Josie was mumbling about him returning to that family shrink she'd forced him to, but he didn't want that. He wanted to find someone else. Someone who specialized in grief. He needed out of his head because he'd made a deal.

And dream or not, he would honor it.

Movement in the corner caught his attention, and he rolled to his side to see who was there. That section of the room had a small bookcase and chair for reading, which was never used except by Samuel whenever it was his turn to watch over him.

But it wasn't Samuel sitting in the chair. Not today. Today it was someone else entirely, and he knew without a doubt he was about to pay for his sins tenfold.

"Benjamin."

"Simone."

The lump in his throat refused to go down. SiSi looked about as rough as he felt. Not on the outside, of course. On the outside, SiSi Howard would remain an immaculately beautiful woman, the construct of a curated image she used to her advantage. She wore one of her sheath dresses that showcased her figure. Her hair was longer than he'd last noticed, and her makeup subtle, yet still with her signature red lipstick.

But he knew her as well as he knew himself.

The ghosts of their past hung heavily in her gaze, and he hated himself a little more. Laura Jean was the other half of his soul, but SiSi would forever hold a small chunk of it. She was his family. His real family. Not the Fairweathers, but her. From the first moment Ms. Maudie brought her little niece into the Parkland's playroom, and SiSi had proceeded to boss him and his brothers around in that high-handed way of hers, she had become his.

And she would forever be his, no matter what she thought. No matter how much she hated him. No matter how much of that hate he deserved. She was his responsibility to care for in life.

Even if she didn't want him near herself or the children.

"What are you doing here?" The boys had sworn never to breathe a word of what happened. He had listened as they worked it out. Two fully grown men, hashing out their plan to stay away from Haven House and her prying ears.

Two men.

His boys were men.

The realization had hit hard while he listened to them talk quietly at the foot of his bed. His boys were gone, and responsible men stood in their place. Selah's goofy grin and easy way had begun to disappear years ago, as had Samuel's awkwardness, but to see the transformation so vividly when he was at his lowest had really driven the fact home.

It broke his already damaged heart.

"You look good," he lied. A stupid thing to do when SiSi was involved. "I wasn't expecting you."

"I would imagine not." She remained perfectly still, glaring daggers at him. "Josie sent the boys to the grocery store, and since neither of them has any inclination as to what that involves, I would imagine we have time to talk."

He refused to do this lying in a damn bed. Shucking the one too many blankets and sheets aside, he tried to swing his legs over the edge to sit up. Big mistake. The whole room spun as he let out a curse.

And damn it, he was in pajamas. Striped, navy blue pajamas. Selah. This had to be Selah's doing.

Fuck, he really must have been out of it.

SiSi made no move to help as he attempted to gain his bearings. "Let me know when you're ready," she said. "I want your head clear when I say what I have to say."

They had hardly spoken in all these years. Occasionally, she would watch as he and Jamison talked on the porch, but if there was something he needed to know about the kids, about life, she usually sent the message through Hillary so he could show up when needed.

Or show up when wanted. Half the time, he knew they didn't want him around.

"If you're here to tell me I'm a horrible person, and that I suck at being a father, you can go ahead and get it out of your system," he snapped. "A clear head isn't needed to hear things I already know."

"Don't you take that tone with me, Benjamin." Pushing off the chair, she sailed across the room to stand before him. "I go first."

"What?"

"I. Go. First." She spoke the words through clenched teeth, vibrating with every punctuated hiss of breath that escaped her. Pointing a finger directly in his face, she bent at the waist to meet his gaze and hammer the point home. "You don't get to be with them before me. I go first. They were mine before they were ever yours, and I get to go to them first."

"SiSi—"

"And don't call me that! Don't you dare call me that! The woman you knew as SiSi is gone," she screamed. "She died out on the bayou, right next to her husband. She died on the ballroom floor as her best friend took her final breath. She died watching those children she helped raise gather around their sister as she left this world, and then she died once more when they were ripped from her arms to be tossed into the unknown."

He tried to reach for her when she burst into angry tears, but his efforts were swatted away. "And she died on that September day when cancer won and ate her dear friend whole."

Tears blurred his vision. "I'm sorry."

With her pain on full display, Simone prowled around the room, pacing as she worked through her rage. "My name is Simone, and Simone is a new breed of woman. She cares for her family. She loves them and lives each day to see that they get the most out of life." Her red lips twisted into a disgusted sneer. "She's not some weak coward of a man who hides from what he's done. I don't hide from my mistakes."

"I don't hide."

That had her halting to a screeching stop. "Bull—fucking—shit."

Her roar ricocheted off the walls, making him flinch.

"They don't want me, Simone. The kids don't want me around. I'm broken, and seeing me as this pathetic mess is a reminder of what we went through."

"Your absence is a reminder. Your absence shows them they were never worth anything," she shot back. "Laura Jean is gone, and now you just can't be bothered to deal with them. That's what they think."

"If they think that, it's because you planted the idea in their heads."

He saw it coming. Unlike the day he sent Toby and CeCe away, he saw this slap coming a mile away. Launching herself at him, she struck with a powerfully precise hit, and he took it, the strike being the first thing he'd felt in years.

"I would never do anything like that." She moved to slap him again, but he caught her wrist, stopping the blow before it connected with his cheek. "Your damnation is your own doing."

She was right, of course. This tiny woman who knew how to put him in his place was always right. "I want to get better."

The simple declaration had her anger deflating. "Then make yourself better."

"I can't."

How could he explain? Simone was a force; the world bent to her will. If she wanted to make herself carry on, she would. If she wanted to get her head on straight, she would. She was strong—a certifiable superwoman—while he was exactly as she claimed. A coward.

"I went to someone. A family therapist. Josie made me."

Simone's eyes narrowed into slits. "You don't like them."

"Not really." He released her wrist. "The doctor is good with relationships and family things, but not loss. At least, not the depth of this loss."

"Then we'll find someone new."

We.

We'll find someone new. The two of them. Together.

God, that felt good to hear.

"I was thinking of looking around Houston for a new doctor."

She sat on the bed next to him. "That's better than what you have around here," she conceded, lost in thought. "Houston will have more options."

They went quiet, the emptiness of Parkland Grounds surrounding them. Once, this house had been full of staff, a person assigned to every whim of the Fairweathers. Now it was nowhere near the grand home it had been. Lost to time and neglect, Parkland had become a haunted house, holding all the Fairweather secrets.

Or was that Haven House? God knows his family had enough skeletons to fill more than one home's closets.

"If I go, then you need to find someone as well."

Simone bristled at the idea. "I think not."

"Why the hell not?"

"As we just said, the doctors around here aren't worth anything, and besides, nobody needs to know my business."

"Why do you have to be so stubborn all the damn time?" He heaved out an exhale, knowing he'd already lost the battle. "But that's your personal choice, and I'll respect it."

"You've never respected anyone's personal choice."

"Neither have you, so let's accept that lie and move on."

She pressed her lips together while staring at the bank of windows along the eastern wall. The view overlooked the gardens, a place that was once his mother's cruel joke. "You're making a deal with me. You make deals with everyone else, and now I've come to collect mine."

It almost made him smile. "Let's hear it."

"I go first," she whispered, the rays of afternoon light tracing the tears rolling down her cheeks. "You have to be the one who stays behind. That's my deal. You *stay* and take care of yourself and them. You stay until Father Time drags you off."

"You're not going anywhere, Simone." He seized her hand, not giving a damn if she didn't want him touching her. "You're stronger than me."

"Oh, I know that." She laughed, wiping her tears with her free hand. "But I want you to take care of yourself, and I'll do the same, but when the day comes—when something happens, and they say it could be the end of the road for either of us—I want you to continue to fight to *stay* but if it's me, let me go in peace."

"What you're talking about won't happen for years."

"Be that as it may, I want your word."

"You have it," he promised. "We have a deal, but I have a counteroffer for you to consider."

"I'm listening."

"I want more time with them."

It would probably sound ridiculous to anyone else in the world, a man negotiating to have more time with his children, but they weren't normal and never had been.

"Evie is getting ready to start college. She still has her moments, but they come few and far between now." A wistful smile tugged at the corner of Simone's mouth. "And with Samuel having just been at the house, she's all up in her feelings."

"Why the hell do they have to fight all the damn time?"

"Oh, is that what they're doing?"

He didn't know what that was supposed to mean. The battle of Samuel and Evie had raged since they came into existence, and it would never change. They entered this world snarling at each other and would continue to do so until the day they left it.

Not that his two cents mattered on the subject, but he wanted Simone to understand that he did pay attention to what was happening with the kids. The big and little things that made up their lives. "I know Evie has come out of her shell more, and with high school over, I thought it was a great idea that she chose to stay close to home to go to the state college's satellite campus."

Of all people, it had been Samuel who argued against the decision. He wanted Evie with him and Selah up at Georgia Tech, telling anyone who would listen how Evie's mathematical brilliance was being wasted.

"But Jamison... I want to know her, Simone," he continued. "I want to get better and know my daughter. I can't make up for all the wasted time, but can you help me with this? Can you give me a chance to put my head on straight and find my way back to her?"

Simone remained quiet for a long minute. "She is so much like you. Stubborn and with a damn temper that's hard to tamp down when it gets going. We're heading into the tough middle school years. She has no real friends. All the kids keep their distance because of her last name. I even offered to let her have a slumber party at the house." She shuddered at the thought. "She invited twelve little girls, and none of them showed up."

He remembered those years. Without Albie and Ty, he would have been miserable. "Kids are assholes."

"They are, and yes, your little girl is growing up. It's time to move on. Get yourself together and come be part of her life."

It was a goal. One he could hold close and work towards. To see his boys enter the world as men, to help Evie as she navigated this new phase in life, and to be there for Jamison. For every moment, good or bad, he would be there and become the father his little girl deserved.

But first, he had to get better.

"I need time. A few months."

"Take it," she said, rising to stand. "But remember, life is passing us by, Benjamin."

He watched as she headed for the door, calling out to her before she could disappear from his sight completely. "Are we okay? You and me?"

"One day we might be," she replied, as honest as ever. "But pull another stunt like this, and I will follow you down to the depths of hell, where you will have to live in eternal damnation with me right at your side."

He liked that idea and crawled back under the covers, thinking he might rest until the boys got home. When they did, he would help them unload, help them cook a meal, and just be with them as a father should.

Then, in the future, Jamison would join them. Maybe even Evie, too. If she could handle listening to Samuel's smartass mouth.

Reclining back on the pillows, he smirked. "You're a little dramatic sometimes."

Simone's big brown eyes went wide, sweeping over him in a wholly judgmental way. "Says the man wearing striped pajamas."

"This has to be Selah's doing."

"Don't tell the boys I was here." Hand on the doorknob, Simone hesitated before leaving. "Josie has agreed not to, and I want you to do the same."

He cocked an eyebrow at her. "Why?"

"Let them think they've got a secret to keep. It's good for them."

"You just want to see how long they'll be able to hide it from you before cracking."

And there it was. Her smile. "Oh, absolutely."

CHAPTER 35

Rowan

"Holden will be there soon."

Liam didn't reply, and Rowan shot Ben a worried look. They were back at Haven House, having left Izzy and the feds to protect Evie. Josie stayed behind at the hospital with Simone and Abe, but Annabeth and the Cohens had returned with them. Will said he needed quiet to think, and Rowan couldn't agree more.

"Liam, check in with the authorities when you arrive," Rowan told him, holding the phone out so everyone could hear him. "Anderson has two teams en route to Eureka Springs."

"He's not in Eureka Springs." Will studied the map spread across the folding table in front of them. "Holden said Beaver Dam."

"Western side," Liam mumbled. "I'm starting there and working my way around."

Bernie came up behind her husband. "Local officials can help."

"Then someone can call them because I'm not stopping for a chat." Liam blew out a lengthy exhale. Rowan had no idea how he was still going after driving straight through the night. "Ben, when are you coming?"

"My jet is ready. The FBO landing field is on the lake's western side, and I'll have a car waiting."

"Does Holden have a car waiting?"

Ben was at his breaking point. He and Will hadn't gotten far when the call came that Jamison wasn't in the van. "He does."

"Good, we can spread out and search."

"Where do you want me?" Will asked his son. "Coordinating here or in the field?"

"I don't know." They heard what sounded like Liam's hand smacking the steering wheel. "I don't fucking know."

"Go with Ben," Annabeth said, thumbing through her phone as she did her best to help by scouring the internet for details on the area. "If they took Jamison to Arkansas, that's where you need to be."

"But keep the planes on standby," Liam added. "We might need to move fast elsewh..."

He trailed off, and Rowan's brows snapped together. "Liam?"

"I swear to God I just saw Bruce," Liam hissed. "He pulled out of a gas station in front of me."

The screech of tires tore through the speaker, and Will snatched up the phone. "Son, you're functioning off very little sleep. The likelihood of you seeing Bruce right away is insane."

"The fucker shot me," Liam snarled. "I know what he looks like."

The call disconnected, and Rowan split the screen on his laptop, tossing Liam's GPS onto the media room projector while pulling up satellite imaging. "Shortstop Conoco, Marshall Street in Garfield, Arkansas. Heading southeast on Highway 127."

Will called someone and relayed the info. "No, he won't do anything but search for Jamison Fairweather, so please stop asking for my son to check-in. Get your people out there."

The dot showing Liam's signal increased its speed. The satellite feed wasn't live, holding a short delay, but could catch up in a matter of thirty to ninety seconds.

"He really thinks he's after something," Bernie said quietly.

"The sun's up," Ben said, leaning over his shoulder as Rowan made his way into another satellite to try for a better signal. "We can't chalk this up to Liam mistaking someone for Bruce because it's dark."

Annabeth darted across the room to a stack of files. Rowan tried to stay focused, but she'd become shaky in the last few hours, and he wanted to make sure he stayed on top of anything she might need.

"Babe, what are you doing?"

Digging through a file, she waved away his concern. "Looking for something."

"He's turned off the highway," Bernie said, redirecting his attention. "County Road 917."

Will tried to call Liam, but he didn't answer. "Are all sons this stubborn?"

"Yes," Ben replied grimly. "Yes, they are."

Rowan started sorting through property records in the area. There weren't many, and the further Liam drove, the fewer options there were to search.

"Okay, so County Road 917 becomes Hayden Road, and then Hayden Lane?" Rowan hated rural areas like this. The service was always shitty, and the old maps weren't worth crap. The satellite would never sync to a truly live view, and there was a slim possibility of losing sight of Liam.

Annabeth returned with a sheet of paper she'd extracted from a file, typing on her phone one-handed. "Seligman, Missouri," she said and continued to type. "Seligman is just north of Beaver Lake."

Rowan expanded the map, and sure enough, there was a Seligman, Missouri. "Yeah?"

"Give me a minute."

Liam's tracker dot stopped, reaching the end of the road. Will stood from his chair, walking toward the screen. "Something's wrong. Rowan, how much longer until satellite catches up?"

"It's never going to be live-live. This one is about a ninety-second delay, but it's the best option considering the area and provides us a better lay of the land than the tracker software, which uses an older map system."

"My God, this woman posts everything," Annabeth muttered, her finger swiping across her screen repeatedly. "No one cares about your casseroles, Janice. Ah, here we go. Photos from 2017. At least she's organized."

Bernie swooped around the table to see what Annabeth was doing. "Who is Janice?"

Annabeth flipped the phone around to show an elderly woman and Bruce standing together at what looked like a barbeque. "Bruce grew up in Seligman. It didn't click until I saw the map because it's in Missouri, right over the Arkansas border. I found his mom's social media account with no problem."

"I've already checked that," Rowan said. "I've checked every relative of every person connected to Sinclair."

"But did you check his mother's great-aunt's hairdresser's page? The one who comes to their family parties and is tagged in a few photos?" Annabeth shrieked and dropped her phone on the table. "CeCe!"

Will dove for the phone and, checking the screen, went pale. "We were right."

Rowan rushed over to see what Will was looking at, and right there, mixed in with photos of casserole recipes and cats, was a photo of Cecilia Miller snuggled up next to Michael Sinclair. The pair smiled at the camera, happy and carefree with Bruce beside them. The caption read, *Bruce taking his friends Mike and Cecilia to see property for their forever home. #lakelife.*

"It's always the most random people in your life that will give away your most private details." Will tossed the phone back at Annabeth. "Annabeth, keep digging. Rowan, see if you can find any other satellite to give us a more up-to-date lay of the land."

He was already in one, and while Liam's tracker map showed nothing but forest surrounding him, the new satellite feed revealed a different story. "Bingo."

Everyone froze as he merged the satellite with Liam's tracker dot, a collective gasp filling the room. Nestled in the burnt oranges of the Ozarks, just off Hoot Owl Hollow, was a structure. It wasn't in the older aerial snapshots, and held two entrance roads. A main one cutting through a thick forest before ending at what looked like a gate, and then a side road that traveled closer to the water and rear of the property where Liam was currently located.

Haven House.

Smaller.

Hidden.

A near perfect replica.

"Will, call Anderson," Bernie's voice shook as they realized the full scope of what they were seeing. People. Dozens of people were moving around the property. A full army against Liam. An army with a terrorist at its helm. "Will?"

Will shook his head, his gaze locked on the dot representing their son. "We need to get up there."

Unbeknownst to anyone else, Rowan was already keeping an eye on the teams Anderson and Klausen dispatched from Little Rock. They were taking their time and not yet close.

"Holden is about forty minutes from reaching Liam." Rowan switched the screen and pinged the plane carrying Holden and some of Anderson's men. Carter had wanted to go with them, but was still feeling the effects of the sedative. "At least, that's what I'm calculating based on where he is in the air, car retrieval, and the eighteen-minute drive."

"It'll take us a little more than two hours to fly there." Ben was already going for the door. "Will, let's get in the air now."

The two men were gone before anyone could get a word out, and Bernie collapsed into a chair, her mouth moving as she whispered to herself. "Two hours, and then driving time is approximately an hour total without a variation in traffic patterns." She met Rowan's gaze. "They're too far away."

Keeping his phone on speaker to help calm Bernie, Rowan called Holden and relayed what they knew. "And now Liam's not answering his phone."

"Can you send me a feed of the satellite?" Holden asked.

"Yeah, I can."

Sending him what he had, they watched together as Liam's indicator dot moved onto the property. "He's not answering because he's not waiting for backup," Holden said after a long pause. "But one thing is for sure."

"What?"

"They know he's there."

CHAPTER 36

Jamison

"D id I ever tell you what that body of water is called?" Michael pointed to the deep, almost black lake in the distance. "They call that Hoot Owl Hollow. Isn't that silly?"

Walking with her mother in the chilly early morning air, Madison flapped her arms. "Hoot. Hoot."

Jamison's foot slipped on the wet leaves scattered across the ground, and she held on to Emily as they followed behind Michael, Claudia, and Madison. Her legs ached, her head throbbed, and she hadn't slept. Not really. Not with Michael beside her.

He never touched her. Not once. Rolling to his side, he dozed on and off, waking a handful of times throughout the night with gasping breaths and clenched fists. In the gray morning light, stripped of adrenaline, Jamison could see the weariness now, as if Michael were pushing himself to function.

Claudia looked just as bad as Michael, but for another reason. Her high cheekbones were more sunken than usual, and her tall frame was noticeably thinner. She clutched Madison's hand tightly, fighting tears while they walked.

"Is Claudia okay?" Jamison whispered to Emily.

With a slight tremor, whether from fear or the drugs, Emily's head slowly turned to give her a deadpan stare. "What do you think?"

At daybreak, Michael had risen and ordered Jamison to do the same. "We're going to get some fresh air," he explained after strapping more weapons than she could count across his chest. "Go grab one of Cecilia's coats from the closet and get two more. We're taking Emily and Claudia with us."

She had done as he requested but asked, "Aren't you worried I'll tell someone what you're up to? That this is all fake?"

"Why do you think they'll allow you to live if you ruin my plans?"

"But are you going to let me live?"

Michael had chuckled. "I told you, that depends on how fast you can run."

They left his room to head to the one holding her cousins, and found Jessica and Krystal curled up asleep on the bed with Damon. Claudia and Emily were on the floor, their hands bound and mouths gagged.

"Did they leave him alone?" Michael whispered.

The sisters nodded, indicating that Damon had been safe through the night. Michael had then snapped his fingers at the two Zanmi women, and they bolted awake with a start.

"I'm taking Claudia to see Madison," Michael told them once Jessica and Krystal scrambled off the bed. "Feed Damon, but no meds today."

Even with it being the crack of dawn, the statement had elicited excitement from the Zanmi women. They hopped about squealing, and when they left the room to get Damon some food, Jamison risked another question. "Why are they so excited?"

"Damon is heavily sedated, and he can't perform as they would like," Michael told her as he untied Emily and Claudia. "It'll take about twelve hours, but he should be fairly conscious and able to function slightly by this afternoon."

He then proceeded to lecture Emily and Claudia on how they had to behave. Once they agreed, the four of them headed down the quiet hallway, stopping next at the room holding Michael's sister and nephew. The door opened without a sound, and Kristina, along with her son, emerged to walk downstairs with them.

The house was completely silent, a total contrast from the night before. They didn't take the main stairs to the lower level, but rather a back staircase that brought them directly to the kitchen exit, where Bruce waited with Madison.

The moment Claudia saw her daughter, she choked on a sob but carefully held it together when Michael pressed a finger to his lips.

"There are enough people up and moving about on the grounds, but we don't need anyone else joining us. Got me?"

They departed the house then, with Michael speaking quietly to his nephew while the rest of the group trailed behind. Claudia remained engaged with Madison, listening as her daughter jabbered endlessly about the pretty fall colors on the trees.

Jamison stayed close to Emily, with Bruce and Kristina functioning as their shadows. Emmett Watson caught sight of them when they left the house and started to follow. That was when Jamison latched onto Emily's arm, refusing to let her cousin near the disgusting man. Michael eventually shooed him off and told Claudia to have Madison run ahead and get some exercise.

Madison was a curious child. With a sweet face, and an even sweeter disposition, she was comfortable with Michael, darting back and forth between him and her mother. Jamison felt awful that she wasn't sure exactly how old Madi was. She knew that the girl was younger than Harper but maybe only a few months older than Theo.

Not too far in the distance, the fencing broke at the drop off. Jamison didn't know what was on the other side. It could have been more land, or the edge of the lake, or even a road that led to civilization.

Bruce drifted closer as they walked. "Still planning that beach wedding?"

Stunned, Jamison gaped at him. "Do you mean if I *survive* Camp Psycho, will I still get married on a beach?"

Keeping Michael's sister close, Bruce shrugged. "Same thing."

Eyeballing Michael's right-hand man as he tucked Kristina at his side, Jamison scoffed at them. "Looks like you two are the ones who need a beach wedding."

"Yeah. That does sound kind of nice." Bruce squeezed Kristina closer. "What do you think?"

Kristina's lips transformed into a genuine smile. "I think that does sound nice."

"Don't you have two kids?" Emily asked, her question full of snarky sarcasm. "Or are you just going to abandon that second one to run off into the sunset with Bruce?"

"My son is waiting for us." Kristina's smile fell. "Not that it's any of your concern."

"You're right. It's not," Emily shot back, leaning across Jamison and Bruce to hiss in Kristina's face. "But you see, we're being held against our will and your business just became my business due to that fact, so unless you don't want to hear my very loud opinions on the matter, tell your boyfriend here to stop making fucking filler talk and leave us alone."

Bruce chuckled. "Emily, you're like this little black kitten I had when I was a kid. It was adorable but had a crazy, mean bite. Its cuteness was all a disguise."

Emily didn't find his observation at all funny. "Call me cute again and see what happens."

Up ahead, Kristina's son fell back from Michael's steady trek forward. Wiping his face, the kid rejoined his mother. "Your turn," he said solemnly. "He's ready."

Kristina's expression went blank. She quickened her pace and caught up to her brother. They walked side by side through the trees, with Kristina resting her head briefly on Michael's shoulder. It made for a lovely image. A handsome brother and beautiful sister taking an early morning stroll through the autumn foliage.

Jamison had an uneasy feeling as she watched them. The blanket of leaves on the ground grew thicker the further they walked, as did the forest. Soon, they could hardly see the house and were winding their way down a worn path, closer and closer to the water.

"What's that about?" Jamison asked Bruce, nodding at Michael and Kristina talking.

Bruce stared at the back of Michael's head. "Goodbyes aren't easy."

With her mind unhindered from the drugs, she recalled the conversation between them about Liam. At first, she had been terrified, but now, she realized how ludicrous of a plan it was to think that Liam would already be here, ready to rush in. If anyone on this earth was calm, level-headed, and able to get them out of this mess, it was Liam. He would have a plan and wouldn't rush headfirst into this without a care for safety.

"You can't seriously think Liam has made it here already." She shook her head at the ridiculous notion. "I know he'll come. I *know* he'll save us and make you all pay, but—"

"Sinclair."

The sound of Liam's voice struck her like lightning. Liam hadn't shouted or made any type of noise other than speaking Michael's name. He had simply slipped silently out from behind a tree with his focus and gun trained on his target.

Everyone except Madi came to an immediate stop, but before Jamison could shout her relief at seeing him, she felt the unmistakable press of a gun to her temple.

"Next time, have a little faith in your man," Bruce whispered, steadily holding a gun to her head. "He's the kind that always comes through."

Michael already had his gun in hand and half poised in Madison's direction as she skipped ahead, singing *Ring Around The Rosie*. "Cohen."

Ready to make a run for her daughter, Claudia moved to go after her, but Bruce's sharp order had her stopping. "Let her go, Mama Bear. If our friend here plays it cool, then Madi is safe."

Scrunched on one side of her body, Emily vibrated with hope while on the other side, Bruce firmly held Jamison by the arm.

Liam wouldn't look at her, too focused on Michael. "Let them go."

"You know that's not going to happen," Michael replied, his tone far too relaxed for the situation. "Is your car parked on the lane around back?"

Liam kept his gun steady. "It is."

"Keys in it?"

"They are."

Michael spread his free hand wide in a welcoming gesture. "Then please come in so we can talk. You have a lot to hear, and I have a lot to say."

Shocking her, Liam clicked the safety on, lowered his weapon, and took cautious steps forward. "Where's Taylor?"

"All in good time." Michael took Liam's gun, his knives, and even his wallet, tossing them aside like they were nothing. "First, we walk."

"Have a good life, Jamison Fairweather," Bruce murmured as he released his hold. Resting a hand on Colton's back, he guided the boy ahead, the two of them following Kristina, who was already in motion.

But before leaving them all behind, Bruce paused and gave Michael one last nod. "An honor, brother."

"An honor," Michael echoed back, handing over Liam's phone. "Dump it ten miles out and snag yourself new transport."

Bruce's big hand closed around Liam's cell, and he opened his mouth as if he wanted to say something, but Sinclair shook his head. "Go, man," Michael said quietly. "Take care of my people."

Without another word, Bruce left them, and Michael whistled to get Madison's attention. The little girl had wandered off, too busy dancing and playing in the morning fog. "Claudia, go get your daughter. Emily, go with her, and if either of you are inclined to run off, remember I have your brother upstairs."

The two sisters jogged toward Madison, weak and not moving very fast. Michael ignored them, his gaze fixed on the fog where Bruce was disappearing with his family. "I almost didn't have to involve Jamison."

"Part of you is glad she's here," Liam said, hands still laced behind his head, exactly where Michael had left them after the search. "Revenge takes no prisoners and carries no empathy."

"Your father said that," Michael pointed out almost fondly. "In that book about the guy who went on a murder spree after his daughter was raped in Minnesota. He killed everyone. The gang. Their families. Their pets." He grinned. "I'm a big fan of Dr. Cohen and was pleased to discover that he was the one who worked up my profile during those domestic jobs."

"Jobs," Liam repeated, daring to step in her direction. Michael didn't stop him, and he risked another. "Interesting word."

"Hell, man. I don't do anything for free. Sure, killing those fuckers was the right thing to do, but I've got to pay the bills like everyone else and needed funds to build this place." Michael turned to face the house. "She's gorgeous, isn't she? Cecilia wanted something like Haven but more rustic, like a mountain home. When we talked about it in front of Bruce, he suggested the area, and it was perfect."

Jamison couldn't hold still. The need to touch Liam and know he was real was too strong. Her body trembled so violently that she bent at the waist, struggling to breathe.

"Go to her, but make it quick," Michael ordered, even though Liam wasn't waiting for permission. Already there, he caught her before she dropped to the ground.

"I'm here," Liam whispered, wrapping her in his arms. "I'm here, baby."

She pressed her face to his neck, inhaling deeply as if her body knew only his scent would calm her. "I love you. I love you," she kept repeating, unable to stop. "I love you. I knew you would come. I knew it. I never doubted."

He didn't hush her. He just held on while she broke—shattered entirely in his embrace.

"That's enough," Michael said once Madison, along with Claudia and Emily, rejoined them. "It's time to get this show started."

⚘⚘⚘⚘⚘ ⚘⚘⚘⚘⚘

"Comfortable?"

Handcuffed to a bedpost and sitting on the floor of Michael's room, Liam rested back on the mattress. "No."

"Excellent." Michael pointed at Jamison. "You need to eat, and Liam, do you want anything?"

"I'm not eating any fucking food here."

Forced to sit on the reading chair in the corner, her handcuff securing her to its arm, Jamison tried to find a comfortable position. She was only a few feet from Liam, but it felt like miles.

"Yes, please get him some food," she said.

Michael burst out laughing. "Trust me, Cohen. You're gonna need your strength. But don't worry. I'll make sure whatever I bring is pre-packaged, so you know it's not tampered with."

Liam's eyes didn't leave him. "Why are we not being kept with Emily and Claudia? And why is Damon chained to a bed?"

Madison had been taken from them when they reentered the house, ushered away by the women preparing breakfast. Claudia tried to follow, only to be blocked by Emmett. Michael handed the man a gun and ordered him to take rear guard.

As they crossed through the lower level, people stared. Most wore next to nothing, and several of the men had reached out to pet Emily or Claudia's hair. Liam had smacked one hand away from Claudia and nearly caused a full riot. Yet, all it took to calm the crowd was a sharp order from Michael to disperse.

Once things were settled, Emily and Claudia were herded back to their room. Michael told Emmett to stand guard at the door, but made it clear that he was to remain outside in the hall.

"I guess you've never noticed how damn big Damon is," Michael answered Liam, pausing in the doorway as he left. "It takes both me and Bruce to handle him. Restraint is a must. So is sedation."

"I get it, but totally knocking him out? That's pathetic," Liam taunted, his gaze roaming around the room. He hadn't stopped absorbing details since they started back for the house. "I thought you were some kind of super soldier."

Michael's mouth twitched. "Sedation keeps his muscles relaxed. That thing downstairs, with the crowd trying to touch the women? That wasn't normal. The men are usually on a short leash, so I'm guessing word got out that I said we were tapering Damon off his meds. The women think their chance is coming, and the men probably think the same thing."

Jamison's brows furrowed in confusion. "Their chance for what?"

"I'll let Liam explain exactly which one of Damon's muscles those women and Taylor want to use."

And with that, Michael left them.

Immediately, Liam was twisting around to work on getting free. "Top to bottom, Jamison. Give me everything."

It all came spilling out. Every observation. Every overheard conversation. The weird shadows. The strange women. Parker appearing from nowhere. Taylor's unhinged confession. Bruce keeping her safe. Michael's connection to CeCe. His hate for Zanmi. His nightly medication routine.

Liam froze at the mention of the medicine. "Where are these pills?"

"In the nightstand next to you."

Stretching over to reach the nightstand, Liam yanked the drawer open to rummage through it until he found the pills. His mouth opened and closed as he scanned the label in stunned horror. "Fuck."

She had never seen Liam scared. Not once. Upset? Sure. She had seen him upset. She had seen him heartbreakingly devastated, cracked open by grief so profound it left nothing but rage. But this?

This was absolute panic. And that wasn't Liam. He never panicked.

But she could physically feel it. His fear was alive, and it slammed into her without warning. She started crying the moment he collapsed backward, hurling the bottle against the wall to cause an explosion of pills in the air.

"Jamison, look at me. If given the chance, I want you to escape. Don't try to save anyone." Liam's voice shook, his dark, bottomless brown eyes staring directly into her soul. "Not your cousins. Not Madison. Not me. Just go and don't look back."

Leave him? Leave Madison to these people? Leave her cousins? As if she could do that. As if she would ever do that. "Tell me."

Liam exhaled hard, jaw flexing as he wrestled to stay calm. "If he really is working Zanmi from the inside out, and if he really hates your family as much as he says, it's over. Sinclair has nothing to lose, and any promises he's made about allowing you and the others to leave are worthless."

"Why are you saying this?"

"Because Michael Sinclair is dying."

CHAPTER 37

Jamison

"**Y**ou didn't have to throw them." Michael sat forward, forearms braced on his thighs as he and Liam stared each other down. The pills lay scattered across the floor or crunched under Michael's boots. "I might lose my nerve and need them tonight."

"You and I both know you won't lose your nerve." Liam's nostrils flared as he leaned back against the bedpost. "Tell me your plan. What exactly are you going to do?"

"What I do best," Michael replied, his voice soft and packed with arrogance. "I need one go, and it'll be over. No more pain. No more suffering."

"And take down innocent people with you."

"You think those people downstairs are innocent? No, of course, you don't. You don't give a shit about what happens to them."

Liam didn't deny it. "Taylor can get them to stop you."

"Taylor is a certifiable idiot, but she knows how dangerous her people are. No weapons except mine are permitted on the property, especially since that batch of medical fetish enthusiasts arrived," Michael countered. "Etienne ran the show in the beginning, and after I killed him—"

Jamison raised a hand. "Etienne died of a... *oh*. A heart attack. Just like Richard Henderson."

"Bruce's specialty." Michael grinned with pride. "He's on his way to Tulsa now."

"Taylor?" Jamison thought she should be outraged. She wasn't. Let the bitch die. "He's going to kill Taylor?"

"No. Taylor will die how and when I want her to die," Michael said, with cold malice lacing his words. "But as you know, Bryan Carroll is in town."

"You're killing Bryan because you're concerned about retaliation?" Liam's head tilted as he studied Michael. "Oh, I get it. You're a walking corpse with nothing to lose, but the folks back home are a different story."

Annoyed by Liam's statement, Michael's jaw flexed as if he were clenching it too tight. "My family doesn't deserve to pay for my sins."

"Bit late to worry about that. You've already condemned your sister and her son by involving them."

"If Bryan is dead, it won't matter. He doesn't belong to a larger syndicate, and his successor won't come knocking. No honor among thieves and all that. Hell, the new guy will probably send a thank you note for getting rid of Bryan." An evil sneer tugged at Michael's lips. "And who are you to judge me for condemning people I care about to gain retribution? What the hell do you think you and Samuel are doing? You're damning your women, Samuel's kids, and screwing Killian McIntyre over while you're at it."

"That's our business."

"No, fucker. Tobias Miller's death is my business and my kill," Michael snapped. "Have you told Jamison your plan? Or were you just going to drag her into exile when the authorities catch on?"

Jamison listened quietly as they talked about killing Toby, the two men fighting over who would get to play a role in his death. The idea of Liam orchestrating some murder plot had come to her a million times, but deep in her heart, she knew he would never follow through. Liam and her brother were good men who would never—

"It's already in motion," Liam said evenly. "Tobias Miller will be dead within the week. Our women—our families—might hate us for it, but Samuel and I have made peace with it. We're willing to be hated if it means protecting them."

Jamison stared at the man she thought she knew better than anyone, not understanding how she could have been so wrong about this. "Liam?"

Liam's eyes slipped closed, and he rested his head back on the bed. "I'm sorry."

But he wasn't sorry. There wasn't a single ounce of regret in him over making this choice. Her shock gave way to pricks of anger that stabbed viciously at her nervous system. The feeling made her want to rip off Cecilia's tennis shoes Michael had given her to wear and chuck one at each of their damn heads.

"You're sorry? Man, I thought I sucked at being a partner, but even I would have told Cecilia." Michael reclined casually in his chair. "And what about Killian McIntyre? What does he gain from helping?"

"The McIntyres have reach the Fairweathers don't," Liam answered. "Killian loves his brother. Rowan was involved, but with Annabeth... he would never leave her behind, so we pulled him out. He knows next to nothing now."

"A clean conscience and a clean life for Rowan McIntyre so he can care for Annabeth? Jesus, Cohen. You really are some golden boy hero." Michael's eyes narrowed as if he were seeing Liam for the first time. "Cecilia loved Annabeth and talked about her often. When I lost her, I would visit her grave at Haven House. That's a nice marker she has, a creepy place to be buried, but it's a nice memorial in her small section. I understand that Simone Howard is the one who picked out the headstone?"

"And my father chose the engraving on it," Jamison said softly, attempting to build a connection. "Annabeth sees that it's decorated for every holiday or family event and chooses the flowering bushes for Abe to plant around it. She makes him change out the potted plants for each season."

Liam's eyes cracked open, realizing what she was doing. "Selah helps clean the grave when he's home, and Samuel sits with Evie when she visits. I've caught him talking to CeCe on more than one occasion, bringing her flowers to add to Annabeth's offerings."

"Cecilia is our family, whether you want us dead or not," Jamison continued. "She was ours before she was yours, but the difference is, she's still ours. We care for her now, and had we known what was happening, we would've cared for her then, too."

Michael averted his gaze, his attention drifting to an empty patch of wall. For a moment—just a moment—Jamison would've sworn he nodded.

"I knew I was sick in that graveyard," Michael said, his tone turning almost gentle. "I saw her in the pines, walking with me on the trails. I came back the next day, and she was still there. In the pines. Always wandering in the pines, like she was part of the forest."

"Brain tumors cause hallucinations." Liam inclined his head toward the pills on the floor. "Do those help?"

"No, those are for the pain they said I would only have at the end." Michael blinked a few times and rubbed his temples as he chuckled. "I would never take drugs to stop seeing Cecilia. I want to see her. I want my girl. If Jamison were dead and you had lost her forever, would you willingly take medication to stop seeing her, or would you allow yourself to go insane while getting to live your last days with her at your side?"

Liam didn't hesitate. "Insanity. I would choose insanity."

"Ben Fairweather goes through episodes of seeing his woman." Giving her a sideways glance when she gasped, Michael grinned. "I told you. Your dad's therapy notes are interesting as hell, and reading them might make you feel better. They certainly made me feel better. Who the hell sees dead people? Apparently, grieving men. I couldn't get my head around it at first, and I know you probably couldn't either, but that doesn't change the fact that you saw Cecilia the night I almost had you. Bruce won't admit he saw anything kill Denise, but I know you will. You saw her."

Michael's voice had become strained as he was—in his way—begging for her to confirm what he'd been seeing was real. And if admitting such a thing would help them, she would do it.

"Yes, I did see something that night."

"You saw Cecilia." Michael Sinclair's damaged mind was leaving no room for doubt, and his unfocused eyes shifted back to the room's empty corner. "Can you see her now?"

Jamison followed his gaze. The mid-morning sun streamed through the balcony curtains, painting jagged shadows across the walls. The branches outside swayed in the breeze, casting movement over the corner in question.

However, there was no one there.

No CeCe.

No ghost.

But...

Jamison squinted, and the longer she stared at the shadows on the wall, the more they formed a shape. A human shape. A female human shape.

"Um... I..." She couldn't say no. She couldn't lie and say there was nothing there because when she tried, it felt like something was holding her tongue between its fingers. "I'm not sure."

"Don't encourage him, Jamison." Liam had arched up to look over the bed. Dropping back down to a sitting position, he massaged his cuffed wrist. "Listen, if I lost Jamison, I would do anything to see her again, but you've got to know that seeing what is essentially a ghost is just the tumor messing with you."

"I know, but God, it's so hard living without her." Michael didn't glance away from the shadows on the wall. "I don't care that I'm going crazy. It's her. It's Cecilia with me."

"Simone would have liked you," Liam said out of the blue. "You know, if you weren't a terrorist. She would've liked how devoted you are to CeCe. She's a very particular woman, and I think you would have impressed her."

Michael Sinclair's throat worked as he swallowed, finally breaking his stare off with the empty corner. "Wouldn't that have been something? We could have been normal. Me, Cecilia, and whatever small family we made merging with the Fairweathers and the Howards? Cecilia didn't think she would be accepted back into the fold, but I knew better. Who wouldn't want her in their life? She was good and kind, never allowing any of that darkness to touch her."

A sharp knock rattled the bedroom door, and Michael stood to answer it. "You're early."

The man who entered wasn't what Jamison expected. Eugene Gilbert, the college roommate of Tobias Miller, came to an abrupt halt when he saw them handcuffed to the furniture.

"Mike, we agreed I wouldn't be involved in this part."

"Things change." Michael returned to his seat. "Taylor left for Tulsa at dawn. She's meeting Bryan for brunch."

"I just spoke with Taylor," Dr. Gilbert said, adjusting his too-tight bowtie. The man was downright unattractive, in Jamison's opinion, looking very much like a nervous rodent in his perfectly pressed khakis and pink polo shirt. His nose was too big for his face, and his lips were chapped, which was probably why his tongue continued to dart out to moisten them. "She said her father never showed for their brunch date and isn't answering his phone, so she's headed back."

"Then I guess we need to hurry. Are you prepared?"

Eugene fidgeted, his shiny loafers squeaking as they touched. "I'll administer the neurosteroids to the men via an intravenous transfusion. That will take me about an hour. The women will continue the bremelanotide injections. I'll handle those last, since they've already been on the regimen for a month."

Michael nodded once. "And how long until we see the effects?"

"Thirty minutes to an hour."

Liking the answer, Michael told Dr. Gilbert he could begin. "Oh, but please speak with Jamison and Mr. Cohen here before you leave. I think they have a right to know what you've learned."

Dr. Eugene Gilbert winced, his large rat-like nose scrunching in distaste. "I want to start by saying that I mean you no harm nor harbor any ill will toward you or your family," he said in a clipped, professional manner. "But I have reviewed your medical records thoroughly, and I'm sorry to say that children are not possible."

It hit like an ax, severing something deep inside her. Jamison blinked, barely able to form her one word reply. "Okay."

Eugene Gilbert was a respected fertility doctor. He would know. He would *know*.

And there was no reason to lie to her, not now, anyway.

"Okay." She couldn't say anything else. There were just too many emotions strangling her. "Okay."

Dr. Gilbert continued, flustered. "Don't let other medical professionals give you false hope. It's a cruel game, and some in my field play it to keep profit margins high. But you've been through enough. Live your life. Enjoy what you have." He turned to flee, hustling for the door as fast as he could. "Good luck."

"Thank you, Gene." Michael motioned for him to leave. "By the way, were there two men at the gate when you arrived?"

"No one was at the main gate." Eugene bowed his head respectfully. "It would appear you are the last of your men here."

Eugene Gilbert left them then, and Michael unlocked her handcuffs before she knew what was happening. Flying across the room, she stumbled straight over to Liam, collapsing into his lap.

She sobbed openly, her grief cracking through every barrier. "They said maybe," she whispered. "They said maybe."

Liam held her like he could shield her from Eugene Gilbert's words, his own tears falling. "Why her?" he rasped. "Why would Taylor want her if she can't..."

He was searching for the lie. Not wanting to believe the news could be true. But he wasn't with her that day in the doctor's office. He didn't see their faces as they explained the *maybes* and the *possibilities*. They wanted to give her hope, but even then, the options had been limited.

"Taylor doesn't know," Michael said from across the room. "Gene lied to her and said Jamison was fine, but he told me the truth a few days ago when I explained what I needed him to do to make this work. That's why I took the risk and went for Kris as fast as I could. If Taylor found out Jamison truly can't have kids, she would have accepted the win of having Damon, Emily, and a pregnant Claudia."

Liam gritted his teeth. "So why hasn't she started yet? If you've had the three of them this long, what's she waiting for?"

"Because Taylor loves theatrics. She wants one big, giant extravaganza. Sure, I'm supposed to have Jamison, and Emmett is supposed to have Emily, but she's going to let every man down there have their chance with them," Michael said, as casually as if he were describing the weather. "And Damon? There's going to be a fucking line a mile long. Taylor will get the most time, but the rest will gladly wait as long as they need to for him."

"Giving Taylor all the Fairweather babies she wants," Liam concluded grimly with a hiss. "You're all a bunch of sick fucks."

Michael had the nerve to laugh. "Don't lump me into that group."

Jamison gagged, barely choking down the images Michael's words were placing in her head. "Why?" she screamed, her sanity no longer intact. "Why would those people do this?"

"Because those people are nothing." The sound of Michael's heavy footsteps approached, and he squatted on the floor next to Liam so he could see her face. "They're sheep looking for a purpose. Followers who have no mind of their own. They do as they are told and accept things at face value. Look how long I've existed with them, barely hiding my contempt, and they accept it. They turned the other way when I weeded out the most fanatical, the problem ones, and those that could create issues once I prepared to finish them off."

Liam anchored her to his chest as she shoved at Michael, ready to claw his eyes out. "If you wanted just to eradicate them, you could have done it. You didn't have to drag us into this hell with you!"

Michael dodged her swing easily, dropping to his knees but remaining just out of reach. "I dragged you into this hell because I wanted you to suffer. A part of me wanted all of your family to suffer for abandoning her. You left Cecilia in the care of that monster, and you never once fought for her. None of you! I don't care what you say. I don't care how much you claim Simone or Annabeth loved her. When I met Cecilia, she thought she was worthless. And if I was going to take down this entire nightmare your family created, I was going to make it hurt as much as possi—"

Michael's words cut off as his body seized, his eyes rolling upward. Convulsing violently, he fell to his side on the hard floor, limbs twitching while choked gasps crossed his lips.

"Shit." Liam shoved her off him and moved Michael to his side using his free arm. "Help me. I can't do it one-handed."

Jamison scrambled over and held Michael up by his shoulders. His body convulsed for seconds—eternal, gut-churning seconds—before going still.

When it was over, Liam dragged her back into his lap. "Sinclair?"

Michael groaned faintly. "Still here."

"Let us go." Liam kept his voice even and calm. "Let all of us go. End it. Don't fucking go through the pain of waiting for your body to fail. You wanted Cecilia's family to suffer, and they have. Over and over again, the Fairweathers have suffered, and the last thing CeCe would have wanted was for the man she loves to cause them more pain."

"I know that." Michael continued to lie on the floor, the rise and fall of his massive chest being the only movement. "I was just talking to her, and she told me the same thing."

Jamison's eyes went wide and slid to Liam, who gave no indication that the *I was just talking to my dead girlfriend* comment was out of the ordinary.

"Then listen to her," Liam pushed. "Get us out of here and finish what you started with Zanmi."

Michael groaned, dragging himself upright and wiping drool from his cheek. "I was going to let Jamison and the others go before I set off the timer. I wasn't going to see them safely out, but let them try to run for it. If they made it, great. If not, oh well."

"CeCe would want you to do more to save them."

"Yeah, she just said as much." Michael pressed his palm to his forehead as if checking his temperature. "And she wants Taylor dead. By my hand, she wants that bitch to die. She wants them all to die."

The pitch of his voice climbed, a laugh bubbling out of him like a geyser. But just as suddenly as it started, it stopped, and Michael's wide eyes snapped to Liam.

"What the hell was that?"

"Jamison, go to the chair." Liam shifted into a squat. He couldn't stand fully, not with the cuffs still attached to the bedpost, but he positioned himself between her and Michael as best he could. "That tumor is pressing on something it shouldn't, and I'm guessing the seizure didn't help. When things like that happen, you can have uncontrollable swings in mood and act violently."

"So, you're saying I'm going to lose control of myself." Planting his hands on the floor, Michael pushed himself to stand. "How do you know so much?"

"My friend in college had a brain tumor, but they were able to remove it." Liam watched Michael rise, risking a glance at her to make sure she was back in her chair, away from them. "I'm guessing removal is either not possible for you, or did you just not want to fight it?"

"Didn't want to fight it. I don't believe in heaven or hell, but I believe in Cecilia. She'll be there waiting for me once it's over." Michael ran a shaky hand through his hair, the seizure, and its aftereffects clearly unnerving him. "I'll finish this, and I'll help you, but you have to agree to something first. It's a two-parter."

Jamison wanted to blurt out that they would do whatever he wanted, but Liam held his hand up for her to keep quiet the second she opened her mouth. "What did you have in mind?"

"Tobias Miller is my kill."

"How?"

"I have my ways." Michael shrugged and, extracting a key from his pocket, unlocked Liam's handcuffs. "People owe me. The job will be done before he's transferred to ADX. Hell, it could happen while he's in ADX. My reach is not limited to a supermax prison."

"Before he's transferred," Liam countered, standing immediately and placing himself between her and Michael. "I want the world to know and any of his remaining followers to have the full details. ADX will sweep it under the rug."

"Agreed. I get Tobias, and you get to eliminate not only the threat of him from your lives, but also the threat of being caught." Michael held out his hand to Liam. "So, the second you get out of here, you have to make the call to Killian McIntyre so he can stop whomever he has ready to strike."

Liam grasped Michael's hand and shook it. "I can agree to that, but you have to make it hurt. Samuel's stipulation. He regrets not ending Toby that day in the graveyard and wants that son of a bitch to know nothing but pain in the end."

"I excel at being ostentatious so that I can do."

"And Taylor?"

"Same goes." Michael's lips curved into an evil grin. "I have something special planned for our friend."

Satisfied, Liam released Michael's hand. "Then let's do this."

Michael tried to move around him but was blocked. "I said my deal has two parts," he told Liam. "And the next part doesn't involve you. It involves Jamison."

Liam allowed Michael to pass, yet didn't go far, remaining at her side. "Go on."

Grabbing one of the chairs, Michael dragged it over to sit. "This isn't your decision to make, but you'll have to swear you'll never stop trying to convince Simone Howard to do it."

Jamison reached for Liam's hand, needing the grounding touch of his skin against hers. "Convince her to do what?"

"Convince her to bury me with Cecilia."

Chapter 38

Jamison

S quished between Emily and Claudia on a thin mattress, Jamison kept her back pressed to the wall. Michael had re-cuffed her and Liam to transfer rooms, not wanting anyone to catch on. It worked since he was apparently supposed to move her, anyway. According to Michael, Taylor's plan was for all the Fairweather women to be confined to one room while the men came in one after another to take turns using them however they wanted.

Jamison fiddled with the cuffs, her skin irritated under the metal. "I'll explain everything once we're out of here."

"I don't trust him," Claudia whispered. Her long, matted hair partially obstructed her face and muffled her voice to the point that Jamison had to lean close to hear her speak. "If we were really leaving, Madi would be here."

"Grabbing her now would raise suspicion," Emily reasoned, pulling her knees tight to her chest. "And you know I don't have faith in anyone, but I have to believe this will work. If I don't, I'll go insane."

Emily wasn't a weak woman. She was a problem solver, never wavering when there was an impossible task to be done. Where Claudia was all fire, her sister was the complete opposite. An Ice Queen right down to the bone. Both were notorious for their resting bitch faces and destroying anyone who got in their way without a second thought.

But to see them now, beaten and afraid in the light of day, had Jamison second-guessing this entire thing. Was she insane for trusting

Michael? Was this all a trap to make them look like idiots before they were murdered? One last humiliating strike to the Fairweathers?

"We're getting Madison and getting the hell out of here," she promised, "or we'll die trying."

Neither of her cousins said anything, but then Claudia scrambled to stand. "What can we do to help?"

Working on Liam's cuffs, Michael jerked his chin at Damon. "You and Emily come over here and help me with Damon. We should see some improvement by now. Has he come to at all yet?"

"Yes." Damon's bloodshot eyes opened. "Not long. In. Out."

Liam leaned over Damon to speak. "Hey, man."

"Holy fuck. You're here." Damon blinked rapidly, losing the ability to keep his eyes focused. "What's happening?"

"We're getting out," Liam told him. He caught the keys Michael tossed over and freed Damon's ankles. "Don't try to stand. You've been restrained with your arms above your head for who knows how long, so your blood flow is fucked to hell and—"

The second Liam popped the cuff loose, Damon surged upward, lunging straight for Michael. He made it off the bed, but lost momentum quickly and collapsed into a heap on the floor.

His sisters gasped when Damon tried to rise again, his dark features set with determination. Yet, when he realized he was going under once more, he let out a guttural snarl and passed out.

"Goddammit," Michael hissed, standing on one side of Damon's unmoving form while Liam stood on the other. "Fucking Fairweathers."

"We'll have to carry him." Liam stared down at Damon with Michael, the two men gauging their task. "The only question is, you or me?"

"You," Michael said flatly. "If things go sideways, I'll give better cover. Hopefully, that scratch Bruce gave you won't reopen and bleed everywhere."

Liam nodded. "Speaking of which, give me a gun."

Michael pulled a Glock from his waistband and handed it to Liam. "Don't shoot me."

"Don't tempt me."

A soft ping echoed from Michael's phone. "Shit. That's the alert letting me know Taylor and Parker are back."

Emmett knocked on the door. He was in the hall when they arrived, never leaving his post. Keeping with appearances, Michael had called him a good soldier, saying Emmett was a far superior partner for Emily than any of the others.

"Is everything okay in there?" Emmett asked through the closed door.

"We're good," Michael replied, loud enough for Emmett to hear. "The girls are just feisty today."

"Want me to come in and help with Emily?"

"Oh, please let that bastard in," Emily growled, tucking her dark hair behind her ears. "I'll show him exactly how feisty I am."

Michael's phone rang. "Hold that thought," he said before answering. "Smitty? You're clear? In Garfield? Good. Wait, they're staging already? I need them further back, or we're going to have a bunch of barbequed feds and cops. Yeah, I know, but plans have changed. No, don't call Bruce. You and Paul, get your asses out of here. I fucking know. Give me a second."

Lowering the phone, Michael addressed Liam. "Your father is here with all his FBI buddies, and they're having a pow-wow at the diner one town over. My guys overheard they're staging on Hayden Lane, which is too close."

The countdown started before they left Michael's bedroom. Jamison had clung to Liam as they watched him calculate how long it would take. Thirty-three minutes. Michael had decided on thirty-three minutes because he said CeCe was whispering the number in his ear.

And for once in her life, Jamison hoped ghosts were real. She hoped those whacky dreams were totally freaking real, and that CeCe knew what the hell she was talking about.

Liam bent down to grab Damon's arm and check the time on his watch. "It's two o'clock in the afternoon already?"

Michael had told them they couldn't move until Eugene finished administering the drugs. The group downstairs thought they were receiving medication to enhance their sexual performances for later tonight, and they were, but with a heavy sedative added in.

Eugene had returned an hour ago to say goodbye to Michael. "Keep your hands off little girls, Eugene," Michael threatened. "I might be dead soon, but someone will always be watching you."

To his credit, Dr. Gilbert hadn't balked, but instead held his head high. "Taylor should be arriving any minute. I've been ordered to stay until she can speak with me."

"Then I suggest you get the hell out of here."

"For what it's worth, Mike, I am sorry," Eugene said as he took his leave. "Cecilia was a lovely woman, and what you're about to do, while barbaric, is necessary and very much warranted."

Michael remained quiet until Eugene left, only snickering when the door was closed. "It's necessary because once this is over, he thinks not a soul in the world will know how much of a monster he is."

"I'll take care of Gilbert," Liam promised. "Get us out of here, and we'll make sure he's prosecuted to the fullest extent."

"Prosecuted? Don't disappoint me, Cohen." Michael had shaken his head. "Have someone cut the guy's dick off and let him bleed out. Eugene Gilbert likes them ten and under if you catch my meaning."

Cutting off the man's dick had sounded like a great idea to Jamison, and now, as she listened to Michael and Liam hash out what to do with the incoming raid, she wished she could start castrating every sick bastard in the house.

And she wasn't the only one.

"If Taylor and Parker are already here, shouldn't we go?" Emily rose to stand next to her sister. "And if someone gets in our way, just shoot them. Or give me something sharp. I can stab people."

Michael ignored Emily's escape plan idea. "Is there someone out there my men can pass a note to? Someone who'll take it seriously? Your dad?"

Liam shook his head. "He'll be surrounded by agents."

"Then who?"

"I'm locked in here with you, remember?" Liam snapped. "I have no idea who's out there."

"All this trouble better be worth it." Michael placed the phone to his ear again. "Smitty, do you recognize anyone else?" He listened for a second. "Ben Fairweather is there."

Jamison scrambled to her feet. "My dad is here?"

"Yeah, but he's surrounded by cops, too," Michael told her. "Smitty says there's another guy. He's with your two dads, but keeps wandering off on his own, and he sure as hell isn't obeying when the feds or the cops tell him to stay back."

Liam glanced at her, and they both shrugged. It could be anyone.

"Big guy. Blondish." Michael's brows snapped together. "Smitty says he looks like Thor from the Avengers?"

"Holden," Jamison said at the same time as Liam.

Michael's annoyed gaze flicked between them. "Can he be trusted?"

Liam swiped the handcuff keys off the bed and started unlocking everyone. "If your guy can approach Holden when no one is around, he'll take the note. But have Smitty tell Holden it's from Beetlejuice, drop the note, and then get the hell out of there. Holden will shoot first and ask questions later."

Michael relayed the information and gave the Smitty person a time frame while Liam worked on Claudia's handcuffs and then Emily's. Saving Jamison for last, he snuck a kiss as he snapped her cuffs off. "I love you."

"I love you too."

Her bottom lip trembled, but she refused to cry. Now was the time to remain strong. Breaking into a million pieces would have to come later.

"Hey, guess what we're doing tonight?" Liam gave her a bittersweet smile as he stroked her hair. "We're going to have a nice dinner and a couple of bottles of wine. Maybe get naked for a few hours. Then I'll tell you all about the night Holden and I got completely wasted in our early training days and how when we showed up for hostage training the next morning, I was so hungover I thought it would be a great idea to act like Beetlejuice during mock negotiations."

Ah, hell. So much for not crying. He was trying to distract her, which meant that he knew something bad was about to happen.

When the first tear fell, Liam cradled her cheeks in his palms, brushing his thumbs under her eyes. "No tears. I won't lie and say this is going to be easy. This is probably going to be the hardest moment of our lives and screw us up mentally for years, but it's not going to screw *us* up. It's you and me. Okay? It's always been just you and me. We're getting out of here, and we're going to live a long life. We're going to grow old together and be so fucking happy." His voice broke, but he kept talking as fast as he could to help her remain calm. "You and me. Always has been. Always will be."

She couldn't control her breathing. Seeing him terrified earlier and then hearing his words now had panic gripping her firmly by the throat. "D-d-don't leave me."

Without another word, Liam grabbed her hand and dragged her across the room and into the bathroom. "We need a minute."

"We don't have—"

Michael's voice cut off as the door slammed shut. Her breathing had turned shallow, her lungs simply unable to get a full gulp of air as the weight of what was about to go down sunk in. Pressing her back against the door, Liam held her by the shoulders.

"Let it out, Jamison. No one can see or hear you but me. Give me your fears."

Her brain tried to articulate what to say, so she didn't sound like a horrible person, but she couldn't, and he was right. They were the only ones in the bathroom, and no one else would hear. "I don't need you to be a hero today," she blabbered through tears. "I need you to be mine. I need you to promise you won't do something that could get you killed. Like if you see someone down there begging for help or saying they didn't mean any of this and to please get them out. I know you. You're a good man. You'll want to try to save them."

"I'm not a good man, Jamison. Not anymore," he rasped, dragging her into his arms like he needed the reassurance as much as she did. "And maybe I never was because I don't give a damn what happens to those people. I don't care what happens to Tobias Miller. Samuel should have killed him in the graveyard. We... *no*, not we. *I* failed that day. I should have finished the job. I should have shot Toby. I failed to protect you and everyone else. Now dozens of people are about to pay for that failure, and yet... I still don't care. I'm going to walk away and allow Sinclair to have his vengeance."

Pressed against his chest, she shook her head. "How did he do it? How did he stay around these people and pretend for so long?"

"Because he's ambivalent to life. The man handed out death to hundreds during his career, and when the world finally gave him something to cherish and love, these people ripped it away," Liam whispered into her hair. "Sinclair is a man who has lost everything, and when there's nothing left—"

Liam didn't finish his sentence. Going instantly on alert, he slammed one hand against her mouth while readying the Glock in his other.

"It's not time to start," came a shrill voice through the bathroom door. "So why is he on the floor, Michael?"

Taylor.

"Don't just stand there," Taylor screeched. "Answer me!"

As slowly as possible to minimize any noise they might make, Liam moved Jamison behind him to listen.

"I leave for a few hours, and this is what happens. I get wanting to rest for the party tonight, but did everyone need a nap all at the same time?" Taylor whined. "And where the hell is Jamison? Did you leave her in your room? I want to talk to her."

Something big hit the wall, rattling the medicine cabinet. "And why are these bitches out of their chains?" Parker bellowed with a grunt. "Stop biting me, Emily!"

"Oh my God, Michael. Get them under control." Even through the bathroom door, Jamison could hear Taylor stomping her foot. "I don't have time for this. And Parker, don't step on my Damon!"

Liam swung open the door, his Glock aimed at someone Jamison couldn't see. She balled her hands into fists, fighting the urge to pull him back.

"Taylor." Liam stepped out of the bathroom. "Move away from Damon."

A snorting round of giggles rolled out of Taylor. "How the hell did you get in here?"

Careful to keep out of sight, Jamison peeked around the corner, her breath catching in her throat at the scene.

Michael stood back while Taylor squared off against Liam. On the wall next to the bathroom, Parker was getting absolutely wrecked by her cousins. Claudia was pummeling him with her fist, giving his face a rapid succession of strikes while Emily had him pinned around the waist against the wall as if she had tackled him like a linebacker.

But before the beating could continue, Parker regained control and tossed Emily aside to go after Claudia. With a backhanded hit, he knocked the mother of his child flat onto her back.

"What is wrong with you, Parker?" Taylor yelled. "She's pregnant."

Parker shook off Taylor's warning to stalk Claudia as she crab-crawled away. On the ground, Emily sat dazed from hitting her head against the hardwood floor. Michael moved to intervene, and, keeping his gun trained on Taylor, Liam rushed up behind Parker to stop him.

But a small voice had everyone halting instantly.

"Daddy?"

Wearing a pretty floral dress with a matching ribbon woven into her braid, Madison clutched her teddy tightly to her chest as she watched them from the doorway. "Why's Mama crying?"

Parker didn't look away from Claudia. "Go back downstairs so Ms. Jessica can take care of you."

Madison stuck her chin in the air. "No, Daddy."

Baring his teeth, Parker turned to Madison, and Claudia used the distraction to her benefit. Popping to her feet, she got one good punch to Parker's nose, but paid for it dearly. As if swatting a fly, Parker knocked her into the wall, where she went crashing back down to the floor.

Madison screamed and tried to run to her mother, but Emmett caught her from behind.

"Take her to the stairs, Emmett," Michael ordered. "But don't go down until I join you."

"Yes, sir."

With a kicking and screaming Madison secured in his arms, Emmett left as Parker went for Claudia again. Out of instinct, Jamison shouted for him to stop, but Liam let off a shot right above Parker's head. The bullet struck high on the ceiling, cracking the plaster and freezing the entire room.

"If you touch her again, I'm going to paint the walls with your brains," Liam said in an eerily calm voice. "Now, get the hell back."

Hands in the air, Parker stepped back and waited.

"Why is he even alive?" Taylor pointed at Liam as she rounded on Michael. "Can't you do anything right?"

Taylor stopped short when she came face to face with Michael's gun inches from her nose. "Yeah, I can do a lot of things right," he told her softly.

Jamison was sure Taylor was about to get a bullet point blank to the face, and she squeezed her eyes shut, not wanting the gruesome image stuck in her head. But when no shot went off, she risked a look and saw

Liam moving closer to Parker while Michael smirked at Taylor, who was turning purple.

"You son of a bitch," Taylor hissed. "I knew you weren't totally down with my plan, but I never thought you would turn to their side. They hated Cecilia, and she hated them!"

"No, she didn't." Michael wagged his gun toward the room's empty corner. "Now, wait over there while we discuss what to do with your pet."

Surprisingly, Taylor obeyed, storming to the far side of the room to sulk like an angry child. "When I tell my father about this, that'll be it for your men. You might be dead soon, but it'll be Bruce, and the rest of them he'll hunt down."

"Sorry, Taylor, but Daddy Dearest is dead." Michael shrugged with a hint of a smug grin on his lips. "Or should I call you Brandy? Your dad always hated how you used the name Taylor, and it just feels wrong not to honor his preference now that he's rotting away in his own shit and piss on some hotel floor in Tulsa."

Taylor's hand flew to her mouth. "What are you talking about?"

"The shit and piss? That's what happens when you die," Liam said casually, pressing the barrel of his gun to Parker's temple when he again tried to advance closer to Claudia. "So, what are we doing with this one?"

"Claudia?" Michael didn't look in her direction when he said her name, keeping his focus on Taylor. "It's your choice."

Cowering on the floor with her sister, Claudia stuttered as she spoke, barely able to get the words out. "My choice?"

"Parker is dead either way, but you're the one he used," Michael explained gently. "The only question is whether you want to pull the trigger or do you want me to do it?"

Claudia's tears overwhelmed her, and she held onto Emily. "I can't. I just want my daughter. Just give me Madison, and let us leave."

"You're so fucking weak. Manipulating you was probably the easiest part of all this." Parker sneered at Claudia. "Poor, lonely Claudia Fairweather. I expected a challenge, but you're so emotionally starved for affection that it took less than a month to convince you to have my kid. No ring, no questions asked. You just wanted someone to love you."

Emily tensed beside her sister, but Claudia didn't even flinch. Parker's words seemed to be doing the opposite of what he wanted, building her strength instead of tearing it down. She openly glared at him, looking like she might want to be the one to have Parker's kill shot instead of Michael.

"How many times did we laugh and ask ourselves, is Claudia blind or just stupid? Turns out, it's both." Taylor tossed the insult down at Claudia, laughing wildly as she continued. "News flash, bitch. No one will ever love you, and you will ruin that beautiful little girl. Madison will one day hate you the way you hate your own mother."

Standing on shaking legs, Claudia dragged Emily to stand with her. "Michael, you can be the one who kills Parker. But I have one request."

Michael spared her a glance. "What's that, Mama Bear?"

"Make it hurt."

A glimmer of satisfaction crossed Michael's face. "That's a very Fairweather type of request. But yeah, Claudia. I plan on it."

"Good." Claudia nodded once, then pulled Emily toward the door, keeping her head held high. "I look forward to hearing his screams."

"Jamison, go with them," Liam ordered once Claudia and Emily had cleared the room. "But stay right outside the door and wait for us."

She hesitated, rooted in fear. Her instincts screamed that this could all still be an act. Michael switching sides, Bryan being dead, Taylor quietly biding her time in the corner. It could all be a show. If she left Liam alone...

"Go, baby," Liam said quietly, his focus and gun steady on Parker. "You don't need to see this."

Choosing to trust his judgment, she took a tentative step toward the door. In her mind, there had never been a more deserving person to meet their end with violence. Parker had used Claudia, wormed his way into her heart, and had a child with her. All for Taylor, who probably didn't care about him at all.

She couldn't meet Parker's hate filled gaze as she left, keeping her eyes lowered while she moved around him to step over Damon, still sprawled on the floor.

And that's when things got a bit fuzzy.

She was stepping over Damon when the world turned upside down. One second, she was upright, and in the next, Parker's elbow was coming directly at her face. It connected with her nose, the crunch of pain shooting her backward into the wall. The dull smack of her skull against the wood vibrated loudly in her ears, mixing perfectly with the echo of a gunshot. She tried to scream, but the darkness was too much. It claimed her immediately, swallowing her consciousness and wiping away the chaos as it descended upon the room.

CHAPTER 39

Rowan

Annabeth gnawed at her fingernails while Rowan watched both his semi-live satellite streams, one eye on the map, the other tracking the cell signals of their people. Liam's phone was long gone—tossed or dumped, and the GPS in the car he'd stolen had been disabled not long after he parked it close to the little Haven House estate. Rowan would eventually trace it, but right now, all that mattered was the raid.

Will and Ben wove constantly through the crowd of feds and local cops. Holden did the same, but often went off on his own, hiking as far as he could through the dense forest until he reached the far edge of the property. He would stay there for a few minutes, hanging back in the line of trees at the rear end of the fence, directly next to a body of water.

Rowan fired off a text to Holden. *Anything?*

His phone rang immediately.

"It's too quiet," Holden said.

The satellite feed showed the same thing. One car had come and gone this morning, followed by a second one not long after. The first car had been Eugene Gilbert, and the cops had hung back, wanting him to cross state lines so the feds could take over.

The second car held Taylor and Parker. There was a debate when she entered the property. A massive one where Benjamin Fairweather nearly lost his shit on Dr. Cohen when he directed the feds and the cops to stand down and not approach.

Not yet.

The number of men and women preparing to raid the property they now knew belonged to Michael Sinclair was staggering, but everything was in place and ready to begin.

Rowan watched Holden's tracker dot on the movie screen as he navigated the forest. "What do you mean, it's too quiet?"

"Earlier, there were people everywhere, but once Eugene left, the traffic outside tapered off into nothing."

"They could have gotten wind of what's about to happen and are in there preparing."

Holden's breathing picked up as he started to jog, his tracking dot heading back to the staging zone. "And no Liam."

Rowan pushed away from the desk, forcing his expression to stay neutral for the sake of the room. Bernie and Simone sat on the sofa in the corner, hunched together as they talked. Simone hadn't stayed at the hospital for long, too concerned about what was happening with Jamison. She and Bernie wanted to go to Arkansas, but Will and Ben had told them no. None of them knew what was going to happen in the coming hours, and they didn't want the women stuck in the middle of the insanity.

Rowan slipped into the hall and kept his voice low. "Holden, this isn't good. If Liam made it inside and we've heard nothing—"

He couldn't finish. He knew better than to think with a defeatist attitude. It wasn't his style because when you did, you never got out of your head to find a solution. But even as he gave himself internal pep talks, there was no way he could shake the unease.

"Liam Cohen is one of the most capable men I know," Holden huffed as he ran. "If he made it in, I guarantee you, he's talked circles around everyone until they figured out what to do with him."

Rowan leaned his forehead against the cool plaster wall. "I should've gone. I need to get on a plane."

"Has anyone told Samuel?"

"Simone thought it was best if Selah was the one who handled him."

"And?"

"Samuel isn't telling Evie, but she's been asking for her sister. He lied and said Jamison caught the stomach flu."

Holden's breathing slowed. "I get it. I've learned there's nothing more important to Samuel than keeping his girls happy and safe... *Whoa, whoa, whoa*—stand down!"

There was rustling on the other end and a loud thud, as if Holden had dropped the phone.

"Who the fuck are you?" Holden snarled. "Hell, no. I'm not taking shit from you. Drop the paper and put your hands where I can see them."

An unfamiliar voice responded, "My name is Marco Smith. But you can call me Smitty. I have a message from Beetlejuice."

Rowan hurried back into the media room to see where Holden was on the satellite view. With the delay, it didn't do him much good, but then, as if out of nowhere, two men approached Holden in the woods.

Marco Smith. Marco. Smith.

Rowan knew that name. "Annabeth, grab the file with Sinclair's people. The one with all the men who followed him after he left the military."

Hearing the urgency in his voice, Annabeth snatched up the folder and ran it over. "What's happening?"

Rowan dug through the file and found Marco Smith almost immediately. "Shit."

Placing the call on speaker, everyone listened as Holden spoke. "Let me hear it. And don't come any closer unless you want to lose part of your face."

"Hold on the raid. The place is about to blow," the voice of Marco Smith replied. "By this point, you've probably got less than twenty minutes."

"Are they alive?" Holden snapped. "The Fairweathers? Liam Cohen?"

"They were a few minutes ago, and if they make it out, they'll probably be coming from the far western side of the property." Marco Smith paused. "If you can get a car there fast enough, you *should* be able to get to them in time."

"I can do that," Holden replied, his voice growing louder, like he had picked up his phone again. "How far is the blast zone?"

"The last bend in the road is the safety point. If they make it there, they'll live."

Chapter 40

Jamison

Someone was singing.

A mixture of humming and words floated through the fog, telling the story of a girl being led to her death by a man. A man who wanted to bury her deep down in the earth so her soul wouldn't make a sound.

Cecilia.

Someone was singing about Cecilia, and how Tobias killed her, and all the other women.

But then, the song changed, telling those who listened that Toby would be the next to die.

One at a time, Jamison's eyes opened and connected with the two women traveling next to her. She was being carried yet again, and while the women's faces were upside down as she hung in someone's arms, she still knew exactly who they were.

Her mama was so pretty.

Laura Jean must have been something to see in life because even in death, Jamison was left speechless by her beauty. Her mother smiled down at her, a soft, silver light surrounding her body.

"You're going to be okay, my princess."

Beside her mother was CeCe. She was the one singing the words to the song Claudia hummed. Two steps ahead, with Madison wrapped firmly around her and Emily at her side, Jamison tried to focus on her cousin's melody, but it continued to evade, drifting in and out of her brain's reach.

Claudia was humming to soothe Madi. That much was clear. But it didn't make sense. Why hum at all? They were running for their lives, and keeping calm should be impossible.

Another wave of dizziness slammed into her, and her mind tilted toward unconsciousness again.

But it was okay.

She was in Liam's arms.

Safe.

He would always keep her safe.

Snuggling close, she curled against his chest, liking the way his heartbeat sounded. The organ pounded as he carried her, drumming in time to his hurried footsteps.

"That's enough, my sleepy princess," Laura Jean crooned, brushing the hair back from Jamison's eyes. "It's time to wake up now."

As it had been this entire time, her mother's touch lit her veins, burning through the haze caused by Parker. He was dead. That she knew with absolute certainty. Directly before she was knocked out, Liam's gun had gone off, and Jamison was pretty sure she had seen Parker's head half explode when the bullet hit.

Blinking a few times, the fire and ice touch of her mother disappeared, and she tried to straighten. Liam's heavy breathing penetrated her brain first, and lifting her head to see him better, Jamison realized the fog wasn't only in her mind, but everywhere.

"Where are we?" she rasped.

"Almost to the property line," Liam told her. "Can you walk?"

Reality returned in a rush, pouncing on her like a wolf in the mist as she tried to comprehend what she was seeing. Liam was bringing up the rear, carrying her with long, swift strides. Ahead, Claudia held Madison draped around her, stroking her daughter's head as she hummed, the tune losing steam the faster they jogged. Emily was at her side, the women working together to keep Madison calm. Leading the group—barely upright—was Michael, dragging Damon along with Emmett Watson bracing the other side.

Wait.

Michael wasn't in the lead.

With one hand, Michael held a gun aimed squarely at the back of Taylor's head as she stumbled forward. Hands cuffed behind her back, she struggled to walk, her tight skirt and heels hindering her progress.

Jamison tapped Liam's chest. "Let me down."

He set her down without pause, urgency tightening every movement. Behind them, the house loomed tall and proud, yet hardly discernible through the dense wall of white.

Already breathless, she fell into step beside him. "How long do we have?"

"Twelve minutes. Give or take."

Movement flared at the edge of her vision. Phantom flickers that had her whipping her head around, only to see that nothing was there. "What about the people inside?"

From somewhere behind them, a shrill alarm wailed, echoing across the compound.

"Pick up the pace," Liam shouted the order so the others could hear him over the sound. "Sinclair, is that the ten-minute alarm?"

"It is." Michael stopped and turned his head to address Damon, slumped between him and Emmett. "You'll have to go the rest of the way alone."

Damon nodded, but when released by both Michael and Emmett, he collapsed forward onto his hands and knees.

"I've got it," he wheezed as his sisters tried to help him. "Get Madi out of here."

Emily tugged on Damon's arm, her hysterical state causing her to scream. "We are not leaving you, you big asshole. Now get up!"

Emmett helped haul Damon upright, but Emily pushed the man away when he tried to follow. "Leave us alone!"

"I'm coming with you. You're mine, Emily," Emmett yelled in her face, his pot belly pumping hard after all the effort he'd put in to carry Damon. "That was what we said."

Michael didn't even look at Emmett, his attention solely on Taylor as he spoke. "I said if you helped me get them out, I'd let you go. And I meant it, Emmett. Now go, or I'll change my mind."

Emmett's gaze bounced from Michael to Emily, then onward, striking each of them until his gaze landed on Taylor, who swayed where she stood. Hair disheveled, her clothing clinging to her sweaty skin, she stared at him with open contempt.

"Go or stay, Emmett. I don't care." Taylor jerked her head back, attempting to knock her hair from her face as if appearances still mattered. "You were never worth anything to me."

He only hesitated for a second, but finally, Emmett turned and darted into the fog, leaving them for good.

Michael gave a short nod toward the trees ahead. "This is where we part ways. The fence line is just there, running adjacent to a side road. When you reach it, take a left, and it'll take you into town, but you're going to have to haul ass."

Not waiting any longer, Claudia shifted Madison to her back and helped Emily with Damon. The three siblings hustled through the mist, never looking back.

"Let's go," Damon's booming voice called as their forms disappeared. "We don't have time."

Michael dug into his pocket and produced a folded slip of paper. He held it out for Jamison to take. "When it's over, this is where you can find me."

Glancing at the paper, she didn't know if it was the hit to her head or the adrenaline roaring through her, but she had no idea what she was looking at. The scribbles appeared to be just a bunch of numbers.

"It's where I proposed to Cecilia," Michael told her. "Right down by the lake."

Liam took the paper from her. "We'll see what we can do."

But neither of them moved.

Despite everything—the countdown, the danger—Jamison couldn't leave without knowing what was going to happen to Taylor. And from the stillness that had come over Liam, she knew he needed to hear it, too.

Understanding, Michael lowered his gun, and Taylor took a stumbling step back, nearly falling without the use of her arms to balance her.

"Tell me about Cecilia's final moments."

The raw desperation in Michael's demand saturated the air, covering the very mist surrounding them with his anguish. There was no need to hide from the pain, not here at the end, and to hear him release his torment with a few simple words brought tears to Jamison's eyes.

"What do you want to know? *Hmm*?" Taylor's face twisted in macabre delight. Mascara ran in black rivers down her cheeks, her body shaking with excitement over the idea of inflicting more pain. "Do you want to hear how, when we arrived at your place, she really thought it was over between you two? How she was so sure she would never see you again, because who would ever want her? Who could ever want boring, dull *CeCe*?"

"You and Toby knew otherwise." Michael slid the small backpack he was carrying around to his front. Jamison hadn't noticed he was wearing it until now, and she glanced at Liam, who shook his head for her to remain silent. "You two knew I would never leave her."

"Yeah, but you were off playing soldier." Taylor popped her bottom lip out. "And poor CeCe. All alone in the world with only her brother to love her. She was so pathetically lost without you that she listened to whatever nonsense we put in her head."

"She was your friend."

Taylor threw her head back and cackled up at the treetops. "She was my toy."

Hand poised to retrieve something from inside the backpack, Michael stilled as a second alarm—this time coming from the main house—wailed louder than the first.

Taylor took a step forward to hiss directly in his face. "Why don't I tell you about how when we were out there playing in the swamp, CeCe thought she might be able to escape? And how, when she saw me, she ran like a frightened animal, going straight for the shore and directly to Toby. They usually try to fight, but not CeCe. She was dead the moment she woke up in that swamp, and she knew it."

Jamison gasped, and Liam tugged her arm, knocking her out of her trance. "We need to go."

She shook her head. She had to hear this. A part of her needed to hear it. Simone would want to know. Annabeth would need the truth. Will would dissect the moment for years.

And it was up to them to listen. It was up to them to play witness to the end of the story for themselves and everyone else.

"But then she killed herself, ruining all the fun." Defiant even now, Taylor held Michael's icy stare. "Toby had been so easy to work up that night that I almost got bored with the whole thing."

Michael tucked his gun in the waist of his pants and extracted a roll of duct tape from the backpack. He ripped a piece off with his teeth, his stare never wavering. "Keep talking, Taylor."

Eyes wild and entire body trembling, Taylor braved another step forward. "Oh, I know what you want to hear. You want to know how CeCe never once believed you would come to save her? How she ate that manchineel fruit because her Michael was always the hero for others, but *never* for her?"

"We need to go, baby," Liam whispered in Jamison's ear. "Time is running out."

Jamison almost shook her head again, but quickly changed her mind when Michael's hand shot out to seize Taylor by the throat.

"Yes, that's exactly what I wanted to hear, and now that you've had your fun, I'm ready to have mine," Michael seethed, drawing Taylor's terrified face toward his. "We're going to play a little game, Taylor. I know how much you love them."

"Move, Jamison." Liam's hand latched onto hers as they shot off in the direction of the road, the two of them running blindly through the fog. "We have seven minutes."

The sounds of Taylor's anguished cries cut through the air, joining Michael Sinclair's manic shouts as he found his revenge. "Come on, Taylor! Open wide for me!"

Jamison turned back in time to see Michael shoving something into Taylor's mouth. She couldn't tell exactly what it was, but the bulky thing protruded past Taylor's lips as she flailed about, struggling to get free of Michael's hold without the use of her hands.

"Holy fuck." Liam was watching with her, his speed increasing when Michael sealed Taylor's mouth with a long strand of duct tape. Holding her by the throat, he wrapped it all the way around her entire head. "Don't look back, Jamison."

She faced forward again. "What's he doing?"

A single gunshot rang out, followed by Michael's laughter cutting across the landscape. "Oh, come on, Taylor. You can do better than that. Go! *Run, run, run as fast as you can.*"

Jamison risked another glance but could only make out Michael's silhouette.

And the silhouette of a woman standing next to him.

A woman who was not Taylor and was as transparent as the fog itself. She had her hand on Michael's shoulder, and when she turned to meet Jamison's stare, her smile was one Jamison had only ever seen in her dreams.

"CeCe?"

CeCe wiggled her fingers at them, the fog swallowing her and Michael in the next second.

"I said don't look." Liam yanked her forward, forcing Jamison to run faster. "You don't need to see what's about to happen."

They reached the split-rail fence, the only stretch not enclosed in twelve feet of wire. Liam lifted her easily and tossed her over before leaping effortlessly to the other side.

The fog was starting to thin, a good indication that they were moving farther away from the lake. Turning left, they sprinted down the road until they caught up with Claudia, Emily, and Damon. More alert now, Damon was trying to run on his own but was moving too slowly, and Liam rushed over, throwing an arm around his waist to support him.

Another crack split the air.

"What was that?" Damon pushed to the front as if he could shield the group with his body, even as he stumbled. "Do you guys hear it?"

Madison whimpered and buried her face in Claudia's neck.

"It's one sicko killing the other sicko," Emily snarled, covering Madi's head with her hand. "All down on the psycho farm."

"No, not the gunshot." Damon glanced over at Liam, who was also listening. "You hear it?"

Everyone stopped talking, and a second round of alarms began to wail, but as Jamison listened, she could hear something else.

An engine.

"Car." Liam turned to Damon, half dragging him to the side of the road. "A big one. Let's go. Everyone, take cover in the forest. Claudia, get on the ground with Madi and cover her with your body."

Headlights broke through the fog just when they reached the trees, the twin beams of light bouncing as they headed in their direction. Liam dropped Damon on the edge of the brush and crouched low.

"We don't know who this is and if it's a Zanmi," Liam began, but catching sight of the big red truck's driver, he rushed from the safety of the woods, waving his arms in the air.

The double-cab truck skidded to a stop, and Holden shot out of the driver's side. Not asking any questions, he bolted over to help Liam haul Damon into the front cab while Jamison led the rest of them out from hiding.

They all worked together, everyone hustling as fast as they could. Emily crawled across the driver's side to assist Holden and Liam in maneuvering her brother's heavy body further into the passenger seat. At the same time, Jamison secured Claudia and Madison in the rear cab before getting in herself. They positioned Madi on both their laps, holding her tight as the little girl sobbed.

Yet another bang went off, sounding more powerful than a gunshot, and a plume of smoke and fire lifted into the air.

"Daddy?!" Madison screamed over the alarms that seemed to be growing louder. "Is Daddy coming?"

Claudia pressed her face into her daughter's hair and shook her head. "No, Daddy's busy right now."

Holden sprinted around to the driver's seat as Liam shut Damon up in front with Emily. "Go, go, go," Liam yelled, hustling to get into the back with Jamison. The truck lurched forward before his door even closed. "Three minutes. Tops."

Expertly maneuvering the big truck on the narrow dirt lane, Holden didn't waste time. He took out a few bushes and a small tree, but once they were aimed in the right direction, he hit the gas. The truck flew blindly down the road, holding up against the endless number of dips and potholes like a tank. No one spoke, everyone silenced by their fear.

"That was the point of no return." Holden made a sharp left, and the truck fishtailed, but he regained control without much effort. "Sinclair's guy said we should be clear."

"Clear of the blast, but not the shockwave or debris." Liam held onto the back of the driver's seat, leaning forward to watch their progression down the road. "And where did you get the truck?"

Holden caught his eye in the rearview mirror and grinned. "Stole it."

Sliding back into his seat, Liam turned to look out the rear cab window. Jamison turned as well, unable to see anything except the truck's bed and the fog descending on them again.

"Was that a bomb a second ago?" she asked him quietly. "When we were on the road?"

Liam nodded. "A small one."

"How small?"

"Small enough to fit into someone's mouth."

"Oh," she exhaled. "Are they all going to be that small?"

"No, they're going to be much bigger," Liam said, locking eyes with her. "And we're too close. The shockwave... baby, we're way too close."

As always, he was correct.

An earthquake struck. Or it was what Jamison thought an earthquake might feel like. The ground shook, rumbling like thunder beneath the truck's tires. Thick vibrations tossed them about violently, and Madison shrieked in terror.

Holden drove faster, shoving Emily at Damon. "Get down!"

The truck's back end lifted when a blast of energy hit, causing Holden to swerve as soon as it released them, and the tires slammed back to the ground. The vehicle rattled as if it were about to fall apart right there on the road.

Liam pushed Jamison and Claudia to the floorboard, covering them—and Madison—with his body right as the truck's windows exploded inward. Glass rained down on the truck's interior, the sharp shards spraying everywhere.

A coughing fit overtook Emily when debris and smoke flooded the cab. It covered them like a blanket, sticking to their bodies and clothing.

"That was the first round and not even the biggest charge!" Liam shouted over the roar of destruction. "Get us the hell out of here!"

Never letting off the gas, Holden plowed the truck ahead, fishtailing again as he made a sharp turn.

And that was when the second explosion hit.

This time, it was bigger. Brutal, with a shockwave ten times more powerful. Screams erupted as the whole truck lifted and slammed down again, rocking side to side as it came to a full stop.

Past Liam's shoulder, Jamison saw it. The end rising, its hungry flames clawing at the sky, the cloud of destruction blooming upward like a mushroom of fire and death.

"Oh my God."

CHAPTER 41

Rowan

T hey had to hold Ben back.

More than seven cops, each thinking they could get between a father and his possibly dying daughter, scrambled to contain Ben behind the barrier set up by officials. Will wasn't much better. From what Rowan could see via the security cameras scattered around the buildings near the staging area, both men were sure the worst had happened.

Bernie was curled up on the couch, Simone holding her as she wept. Annabeth sat on the floor, having lost the ability to stand when the second explosion hit. The delayed satellite feed was only now catching up with the action, revealing the main building going up in a spectacular ball of fire.

They sat stunned, helplessly watching it all go down. First, there was Holden running through the woods and back to the staging area, where he broke into an extremely large red truck to steal. He nearly drove over a few people when he sped away, only pausing briefly to speak to Will before barreling straight through the barricade.

Then they watched the truck pop in and out of the fog, all of them shouting in relief when Holden stopped about halfway down the road to pick up a group of people running out of the woods. But not just any group of people. Jamison's platinum hair was a dead giveaway that it was *their* people.

And then...

Then they watched the end.

When the first explosion rocked the security camera transmission, Rowan switched the feed to Will and Ben. Unlike the satellite, those cameras were live, and when their aerial feed caught up, Rowan could only assume it had been one of the outer buildings on the property to go. The fog made the house nearly impossible to see, but he expected a much larger spectacle for the main building.

It was.

The footage rolling on the media room's screen caught up with the truck as it dealt with the first small detonation right as the second explosion shook the live feed at the staging area. Once they could see the second blast from the sky, there were screams as the bright red truck disappeared in the wave of smoke. The unbelievably powerful debris field shot far and wide, covering the entire area.

They waited. Hoping. Praying. They waited, but as some of the smoke cleared, and the forest surrounding the blast burned in the growing inferno, Rowan attempted to run a thermal scan to check for signs of life. With this much heat coverage, it would be near impossible to obtain any data, but he had to try.

"No movement on the ground," he announced. "Nothing."

"Get Ben on the phone," Simone cried as she pointed a trembling finger at him. "Right this minute."

The man screaming on the split screen while he fought off the dog pile of police wouldn't hear his phone. Benjamin Fairweather was lost in his pain and calling him would be useless, but Rowan did it anyway. A ringing pulse poured from the speakers in the media room. As expected, the call went to voicemail, and before Bernie asked, Rowan called Will next, receiving the same results.

Empty minutes ticked in his brain, syncing to the erratic beat of his heart, and without thinking or holding onto his obligations of monitoring the system, he came up behind Annabeth to sit on the floor with her. No one in the room was unfamiliar with this foreboding sense of shocking loss. Each of them had a close relationship with pain.

Each of them, except him.

He was the only one here who had never experienced this uncertain tennis match between hoping for the best or moving forward to accept an insurmountable loss. Dragging Annabeth back between his legs and into his arms, he held her tight while they watched the satellite feed, both unable to look away.

"Come on," Annabeth whispered through the onslaught of tears. "Don't you die on me, Jamison. I'll never forgive you."

Nothing.

Still nothing.

The only movement being the black smoke billowing in the air.

Shoving up from the floor, Annabeth stood and yelled at the satellite feed. "Stop messing around, Jamison. Get the hell out of there!"

"Sweetheart." He didn't know what to say or how to act. Moving to stand, Rowan tried to hold her, but she wouldn't let him. "I'm so sorry."

Simone rushed over, but Annabeth shook her head and spun around to shout and point at the screen. "She'll drive the damn truck out of there herself. *It's Jamison*. She'll do it. I know she'll do—"

Rowan didn't know who screamed first. It could've been Annabeth. Maybe Bernie. Might've even been him.

But it didn't matter.

All that mattered was the sight of that big red truck racing out of the smoke and destruction.

It hauled ass down the dirt road, the outline of it becoming clearer the more distance it gained from the destruction. The driver didn't have much control, and the satellite's gauge measuring speed showed distinct acceleration patterns on the straightaways and hard braking on the curves, which almost sent the thing flying more than once.

"This is a delayed view!" Stumbling over to his laptop, Rowan switched out the satellite view for the cameras at the staging area, expanding the live shot just as the truck came to a skidding, steaming stop behind the barricade. "Holy Mother of God. They made it."

He zoomed in as far as possible to try and get a look at the truck's occupants. Emily Fairweather sat behind the wheel. Eyes wide and scared shitless, she promptly burst into tears when the police surrounded them.

Damon was in the passenger seat, his face and upper body covered in ash. With one swift kick, he had his door open to haul himself out. The shocked crowd didn't know what to do as he staggered around the front of the truck, shouting for someone to get help.

The rear cab doors flew open, and Liam and Jamison exited next. They were followed by Claudia, clutching a terrified Madison. Yanking open the driver's side door, Liam pulled Emily out to reveal an unconscious Holden slumped in the seat behind her. Rowan thought he could make out a gash on Holden's forehead that seemed to be bleeding pretty good, and Liam pulled off his shirt to staunch the flow while they waited for medical personnel to join the party.

Ben was shoving people out of his way. Being as tall as he was, it was easy to follow him through the crowd. Jamison launched herself into his arms when they connected, hysterically crying against her father's chest.

So many things were happening at once, and Rowan didn't know exactly where to look. Will directed medics to the truck while Liam and Damon pulled Holden out. But then, once they had Holden on the ground, Damon lost consciousness and dropped next to Holden. His sisters and niece clamored around him but were moved aside by another set of paramedics who began chest compressions.

"They must have given him something," Rowan murmured. "A guy as big as Damon, they would have either had to lock him up or keep him drugged."

Simone laid a hand against her throat. "That poor baby," she whispered, watching Madison sob as she clung to Claudia. "What on earth did they go through in that house?"

"Hell." Bernie joined them. She hadn't taken her eyes off her son, tracking him as he moved through the crowd. "They've been through hell."

Seeing what was happening on the ground, Ben hurried to where they worked on Damon and Holden. He and Jamison spoke to what appeared to be the medical team leader, with Ben pointing off in the distance while shaking his head.

"Ben's already telling everybody what to do, and… oh, my." Annabeth's mouth dropped open. "Is Damon really trying to get up?"

Damon was indeed trying to rise, pushing away the poor paramedic attempting to place an oxygen mask on him.

"That would be how he is," Rowan replied when Damon broke free to trap his sisters and Madison in a hug. "Does anyone know if Trevor has been notified?"

"Will said he called him earlier." Bernie grabbed her phone from the couch. "But I'm not sure what he looks like. Have you seen him? Did he make it?"

"He's not there," Simone said solemnly as she searched the crowd. Rowan flipped through several camera views to double-check, but Simone was right. There was no sign of Trevor or Heather Fairweather.

"Ben will handle it," Annabeth assured them. "He'll take care of everything. He always does."

Bernie's phone rang with a call from Will, and she and Simone huddled in a corner so they could hear.

While they were distracted, Rowan pulled Annabeth into the hall, and the second she was out of view of her mother, the tears started. He kept walking, dragging her straight into the library. Once they were inside the room, he closed the door to hold her so she could let her emotions free without an audience.

"I thought she was dead." Annabeth covered her face with her hands. Finding a spot on the small sofa, Rowan plopped down and hauled her into his lap. "I thought Liam was dead. After that explosion, I thought we lost them."

He tucked her head under his chin. "But we didn't. They made it out, and you helped make it happen. You were amazing."

"I loved helping," she cried. "And I know it's stupid, but I liked how well we worked as a team."

Rowan groaned at his stubborn woman. "We are a team. We're the best team. Team McIntyre."

Annabeth Howard's laugh was the most beautiful sound in the world. When she was truly happy, it always came out as a cross between a giggle and a sigh. Hearing it mixed with her tears of relief made it somehow more beautiful, and when she moved to straddle him, he damn near fell in love all over again.

"I'm not a McIntyre."

Lifting his back off the couch, he cupped her cheek and moved in for a kiss. "Yet."

"Yes."

The kiss forgotten, his half-closed eyes flew open as his heart bounced right up into his throat. "Wait, what?"

"I said, yet." Her smile turned mischievous. "I just repeated what you said."

"No, you didn't."

He was shouting.

He realized this.

He did not care.

"You. Said. *Yes.*"

Annabeth shrugged her slender shoulders and tried to rise off him. "If I did, I misspoke. It's not like you actually asked me a question or anything."

If he hadn't been so tired, he would have shouted a victory cry, but as it was, he was nearly dead on his feet and settled for pouncing on her instead. Flipping them to where she was spread out under him on the couch, he kissed her. And it wasn't just a regular kiss. It was a kiss for the ages, one that he poured every ounce of love into.

"Promise me something," she said, breathless when he finally pulled back. "Promise me that you'll kiss me like that every day."

She was his. All his. She could fight him however she wanted, but Annabeth Howard would be on the losing side of the battle. He would win her over, and one day, he would marry her standing under the Marriage Oak. Haven House would become their home. He would give her an amazing life under this old roof. A million adventures in the backyard. Kids. Cats. Dogs. The world. Whatever she wanted, it would be hers.

"I'll kiss you like that every morning."

To prove his point, he did it again.

"Every night." And again, but this time deepening the stroke of his tongue, until he had her moaning.

"Every chance I get." And one more kiss for good measure.

"Forever." He cleared his throat, refusing to let his emotions ruin the moment. "I am forever yours, Annabeth Howard."

The saucy minx beneath him had the gall to grin. "Annabeth McIntyre sounds better. I mean, it is already your password."

Maybe he was going to get a little emotional after all. "I one hundred percent agree."

CHAPTER 42

Ben

2010

"You're doing it wrong!"

Ben sat grinning on the villa's long leather couch, watching as Jamison attempted to teach Samuel and Selah some dance that involved Single Ladies.

"Jamison, I know I'm pretty like Beyoncé," Selah huffed, bent in half with his hands braced on his knees. "But I've fully accepted that I cannot dance like the woman."

Red-faced and soaked in sweat, Samuel collapsed onto the floor. "I'm out. I can't '*oh, oh, oh*' anymore."

"It's not that hard," Jamison huffed with exasperation. "You guys just need to practice."

An evening breeze floated in through the open patio doors. Cool and crisp, it brought the scent of flowers into the room. "We can always switch to a movie, but your sister gets to pick which one," Ben said as the wind ruffled his hair. The floral scent was familiar, but it disappeared before his brain could fully recognize it. "Although I will say, I'm fine watching this all night."

Jamison beamed excitedly, a mouth full of braces nearly overtaking her entire face. "Twilight?"

The boys groaned in unison. Even Ben winced. He'd avoided this moment for as long as he could, and it was finally catching up with him.

"Haven't you seen that one a few times?"

The smile on his daughter's face dimmed, her eyes narrowing on him. "I've seen Twilight seventy-seven times and New Moon sixty-two times. Why is that important?"

Selah flopped down onto the floor to lie next to Samuel. "I've seen it once. That was enough."

"When?" Samuel lifted his head to look at his brother. "And with who?"

Selah grinned. "No clue when, but it was with Marcie Colson."

"The cute blonde from Alpha Delta Pi?" Samuel's head dropped again. "So, you didn't actually watch it."

"All I'm gonna say is that Twilight was on, but my eyes were occupied with something far more attractive. And nude."

"Ewwwww." Jamison plopped down onto the couch, nudging Selah's head with her bare foot. "Stop talking about naked girls."

Ben had thought the age difference might be a problem. This whole trip had been a spur-of-the-moment thing, and he'd initially been worried that two college boys and a middle school girl wouldn't have much in common. But his kids surprised him. Selah and Samuel managed to keep things PG-rated for the most part and indulged Jamison every chance they could.

Including doing highly intricate choreography to her favorite songs.

However, he secretly hoped they would draw the line at a vampire-werewolf movie marathon.

The phone on the end table rang, and Ben resisted the urge to roll his eyes. The call was either Simone or Josie checking in. Or Hillary. Again.

Jamison crawled over and picked it up. "Hi, Simone! Yes! We went to the market today and bought food for Consuela to cook. And I went shopping! I got you a purse. It's leather and green. You'll love it."

She paused to inhale more oxygen. "Who's Consuela? She's the cook Daddy hired. She comes three times a day and cleans up after... no, ma'am. We're not making a mess for her. Tomorrow? Oh! The boys are going to teach me how to surf. Yes, ma'am. I'll listen. I won't go too far. Yes, ma'am. I know I don't know everything. Lifeguards? Um... I think so? Yes, ma'am. Selah? He's right here."

"Tell her I'm asleep," Selah mouthed, eyes closed.

Jamison covered the receiver. "She says she can hear you, and it's rude to lie to your mother."

"Amateur," Ben whispered. Simone could hear a pin drop three counties over. Selah should have known to keep his mouth shut. "I thought I taught you better than that."

"Hi, Evie!" Jamison squealed. "Oh my God, this place is so cool!"

Hearing that Evie was on the phone had Samuel going weirdly still, and Ben fought the urge to say something. He continued to hope they'd outgrow their animosity toward each other, but maybe he was asking for the impossible.

"I wish you were here," Jamison said, still rattling off at top speed. "There are so many cute guys. If you had come and worn that hot pink bikini from last summer, they would have been all over you."

Midway through lifting himself off the floor, Samuel face-planted into a throw pillow. "I need a beer."

Selah patted him on the back. "I'll get it."

"No, I got it." Samuel pushed up to stand. "Who wants one?"

"Me." Ben raised a hand. "And make sure we have plenty in the fridge. I feel like we're in for a long night of vampires and werewolves."

The boys were halfway to the kitchen when Jamison shrieked, "You went on a date?! Three dates?! *Eeek!* We've only been gone for a week! What's his name?!"

Since Evie never mentioned guys, Ben was intrigued and slid down the couch to learn more. Life had been tough on the kid, and he was glad to hear she was finding her footing at college.

But before he could reach Jamison, the boys were there. Flying over the back of the couch, Selah landed with a hard bounce onto the spot next to his sister. Samuel was no better. Tripping over himself, he nearly took out a lamp rushing around the edge of the couch to loom over Jamison.

"Where'd she meet him? Does he have a job? Is he ugly? I bet he's ugly," Samuel whispered, looking strangely blotchy. "Get his name."

"First and last." Selah snatched a piece of paper off the coffee table. "And the proper spelling."

Samuel nodded solemnly. "And his date of birth. We'll need that for a background check."

"Social security number," Selah added, nudging Jamison. "And his mother's maiden name."

Jamison scrunched her nose at their behavior. "His name is Brett?"

"Brett?" Samuel snarled, the rash on his neck gaining speed. "What kind of stupid name is Brett?"

"You have classes with him?" Jamison shoved Selah away when he leaned over to eavesdrop. "Oh, he's a political science major? That sounds cool."

"That sounds boring." Samuel kneeled before Jamison and spoke clearly so Evie could hear him. "People who major in Political Science are losers."

"Evie said you're the loser," Jamison told him. "Now go away."

Samuel didn't move. Neither did Selah.

"Dad!" Jamison whined. "Make them leave me alone."

Rising from the couch, Ben stretched and made his way to the kitchen. "Come on, guys. Let's get our drinks."

Selah followed immediately, but Samuel took his sweet time. Popping the caps off their first round, Ben handed his middle child a beer when he finally joined them. "What's going on with you?"

Instead of answering, Samuel chugged the entire beer.

"Nothing."

Ben wanted to call bullshit, but Samuel had a prickly temper, much like his own, and it was best to let it go. "So, how are we getting out of Twilight?"

"We could go somewhere," Selah suggested. "There's a quiet bar down the street with smoking hot waitresses."

Samuel snagged another beer from the fridge. "I'm good with that. Definitely in the mood for hard liquor tonight."

Ben heaved out a sigh at his two short-sighted sons. "We are not taking Jamison into a bar."

"Then let's take her shopping," Samuel said. "Nothing makes Jamison happier than trying to spend several thousand dollars in a single night."

Selah smirked. "And it makes her tired. So tired, she won't want to have a movie marathon."

"Shopping it is." Tapping the neck of his bottle against his sons' bottles, Ben raised a toast to them. "We have a plan."

A loud boom of thunder came directly after his statement, followed promptly by torrential rain pounding on the villa's roof. "Never mind." Ben took a long pull from his beer. "Any other ideas?"

"Okay," Jamison shouted from the living room. "I'm off the phone and putting on my pajamas. You guys have to put yours on, too. That way, we can watch the movies in a row and straight until dawn."

Selah groaned. "When did this become a slumber party?"

"Do we have food?" Samuel went for the fridge. "I'm getting drunk if I'm watching teenage vampires, and food will be mandatory."

"Consuela left a bunch of stuff," Ben said, bending down to peer into the fridge with Samuel. "There are dips, beef for nachos with all the fixings, and she pre-made empanadas."

"God bless Consuela." Selah finished off his beer and smacked the bottle on the granite countertop. "Let's put on our pajamas and start this vampire slumber party. Sammy, do I get to braid your hair?"

Samuel shut the fridge door without looking at him. "If you touch me, I will break your hand."

"If you do, I'll tell Evie, and she'll come here to defend my honor."

"You're so not funny." Samuel looked almost serious, like the threat of Evie coming to Mexico was worse than a vampire slumber party. "At all."

Selah blew his brother a kiss as he left the kitchen, and Ben eyeballed his broodiest kid. Not that he faulted Samuel for the bad attitude. He could remember behaving the same way at his age.

"You sure you're okay?"

"I'm fine." Samuel opened his third beer, somehow having already downed the second one before anyone realized it. "Hearing about Evie—"

Ben wanted to roll his eyes but wouldn't, sparing them yet another battle regarding Evie. "I know you hate her."

"I don't." The words came out in a rush, and Samuel focused on opening the bottle. "I don't hate her. I worry about her."

Samuel stumbled over the last part, revealing the piece of himself people were never allowed to see. Miranda would say that their son was a sensitive soul, and Ben would forever agree with that fact. Samuel's tough attitude stemmed from learning that, as a Fairweather, it was best to harden one's heart, because when you allowed it to show, the world wasn't always kind.

"She's doing well at school, and you were right. I had no idea Evie was a mathematical genius. I'm proud that she's majoring in accounting," Ben told him, knowing damn well Samuel was aware of Evie's major since he kept close tabs on her. "A boyfriend—a first boyfriend—going into Political Science is a good meshing of the minds for her to explore."

"Meshing of the minds." Samuel looked appropriately disgusted by the term, and Ben couldn't blame him. The whole meshing of the minds comment came off as pretentious, reminding him of something his shrink might say. "You sound like an asshole, Dad."

"Yeah, I do." With a sigh, Ben finished off his first beer of the night. "Now, let's go. I want to get my vampire watching over with."

Samuel smirked at him. "You know these things sparkle, right?"

"What things?"

"The vampires."

Ben blinked at his son, who usually made more sense. "We're watching a movie with sparkling vampires?"

"Not *a* movie, Dad. There are two movies, and she brought them both." Samuel returned to the fridge to grab yet another beer to hand him. "That means we're looking at about four and a half hours of sparkly vampires."

"Sweet mother of Jesus."

Jamison came bouncing in, her high ponytail swishing side to side. She'd already changed into her light pink satin pajamas with black piping—a Christmas gift from the year before. According to Simone, she wore the matching set all the time. Ben had picked it out himself, thinking the bubblegum pink color would suit her style. He'd bought Evie a light blue set and Annabeth one in purple because those three always did everything together.

"Why are you not in your pajamas?" Jamison whipped open the fridge and began piling up all the food Consuela had left. "Let's go, people. Edward awaits."

Ben arched an eyebrow. "Who is Edward?"

"My future husband," Jamison said seriously. "He's so—oh my God—perfect."

Samuel snorted, and Ben gave him a light punch to the arm. "Edward is perfect, huh? We'll see about that."

Thirty minutes later, they were all piled on the couch as Jamison danced along to the opening credits. Her hands and arms flowed above her head in a move that oddly reminded Ben of her mother.

Thinking of Laura Jean had that familiar ache thumping around in his chest. She didn't appear to him much anymore. Those initial, quick glimpses in his dreams transformed into daytime chats and then full waking conversations through the years. She would walk with him through life during the day, and then they would stay up all night talking about the past and how much they loved each other. Yet, when the visions began to taper off into nothing, part of him was relieved, but the other part, the part that learned long ago to accept the magic of Laura Jean, was terrified that one day, his brain would erase her forever.

"When I marry my Edward, I want this song played as I walk down the aisle," Jamison said, pausing her swaying to stick a finger in Samuel's face. "Promise me."

Eyes wide and beer halfway to his mouth, Samuel nodded. "Promise."

"Jamison, if you bring home a sparkly vampire, we're going to kick his ass," Selah said with his eyes glued to the movie. "Just saying."

Ben propped his arm on the back of the couch and settled in to watch. "Simone will take him down long before you do."

"But you'll protect him." Jamison cuddled against his side. "Won't you, Daddy?"

"Of course, princess."

They focused on the movie, and surprisingly, Ben wasn't bored. If anything, he was annoyed.

"What the hell is wrong with him?" Ben asked as Edward squirmed dramatically in biology class. "That guy's a dick. I'm not protecting him."

"Edward is mysterious and dreamy," Selah scoffed. "How could you call him a dick?"

"Because he's a dick."

Jamison said nothing, utterly transfixed by the emo ginger vampire. No one spoke for the remainder of the movie, and by the time the credits rolled, all the snacks were gone.

"New Moon is next!" Jamison jumped up and crawled over to swap the DVDs. "This one is so depressing. I love it."

Sitting on the floor for the entire movie, Samuel rolled to his feet. "I'm changing my clothes and putting another twelve-pack in the fridge."

"I told you to put on your pajamas already," Jamison said as she waited for the DVD tray to pop out. "You don't have to be cool all the time. We're your family. It's okay to act normal."

"That boy ain't never been normal," Selah mumbled and got punched in the arm as Samuel passed him on the way to the out. "He's abusive, yes. But never normal."

Samuel returned wearing sweatpants and a plain white T-shirt. He handed out another round of cold beers and a Dr. Pepper for Jamison. "Is this normal enough for you, brat?"

The second movie started, and everyone watched as Edward broke Bella's heart. "Dang, check out my boy Jacob." Selah pointed at the TV. "He's looking as good as me with my shirt off."

"I'm sorry, but who in this room actually has a six-pack?" Samuel raised his hand. "That's right. Me. Not you."

Ben chuckled to himself. Both his sons had the biggest egos, and deservedly so. While he only passed along his height and maybe a few other fragments of his DNA, the remainder of their genetics—the pretty parts, if you asked Simone—were all their mothers' doing. Selah's smile and kind eyes belonged to Simone. The slope of Samuel's nose and the way his brows knitted together when he was thinking was all Miranda.

Females flocked to them everywhere they went, and while Selah handled women with ease, Samuel kept them at arm's length. Ben thought it was because, at the heart of it, Samuel remained that awkward boy who never had friends growing up. The one who would much rather sit quietly and fish with Abe, surf alone on a clear morning, or even argue with Evie over a chess game.

Selah lifted his shirt to roll his stomach in Samuel's face. "I'm working on it."

Jamison shushed her brothers. "We're getting to the part where we find out Jacob is a werewolf. Be quiet!"

And God help him, but Ben knew Jamison would give him the most trouble. Headstrong, fearless, and developing a level of sarcasm even he had trouble keeping up with, Ben knew his daughter's upcoming teenage years would turn him into an old man.

"You don't want a guy like Jacob?" he asked. "He's tough and dependable—"

"It sounds like you're describing a truck, Daddy."

"I'm just saying. Don't ignore the good guys. Not every boy you fall for needs to be mysterious and…" He waved vaguely at Edward. "Five hundred years old and full of angst."

Jamison reared back in outrage. "Edward is one hundred and four."

"Not the point, princess."

She rolled her eyes so hard he thought they might get stuck. "I want popcorn."

"Not it." Samuel swung his head around to look at Selah. "I got her a drink."

"And I paid for the place," Ben added, propping his feet on the coffee table. "So, you're up, Selah."

Selah half fell off the couch, sliding to the floor as if he'd been asked to do something that could possibly kill him. "Fine, but I'm making it cheddar flavored."

A round of boos went up, and as Selah evil-laughed his way to the kitchen, something through the open patio doors caught his attention. "Who is that?"

"Consuela said her nieces might stop by with fresh linens." Ben yawned and wondered what time it was. He'd never been on vacation where he relaxed enough to stop looking at the clock, which was a bit disorienting. "They're using the entrance on the south side of the complex."

"Hola!" Selah called out. "Tienes un buen culo!"

"For the love of God, Selah. Stop saying that." Ben whacked a snickering Samuel on the back of the head for lying to his brother. "It does not mean, *how are you doing*? Do not disrespect those girls."

"Those *fine* girls," Selah whispered. "Sammy, come look."

Samuel didn't appear even remotely interested. "No."

Selah flapped his hand behind the curtain so the girls outside wouldn't see. "Come here," he hissed through clenched teeth as he smiled. "Now!"

The phone rang, and Jamison crawled over to answer it. "Evie! You're back from your date? No way! Shut up!" She giggled and flopped down to talk. "Tell me everything."

"Yeah, I'm not listening to this." Samuel peeled himself off the couch to join Selah at the balcony door. "Good evening, ladies."

A string of rapid Spanish answered them, followed by feminine laughter. Ben watched his sons step through the patio doors, disappearing down the sloping yard toward one of the outer buildings.

"I hope they realize they're still in their pajamas," Ben grumbled once they vanished around the corner. "Not that they're thinking with their brains right now."

He finished the last of his beer and waited for Jamison to wrap up her call. But when Annabeth got on the phone, too, and the three of them started chatting together, he gave up.

"I think we lost the boys, so I'll make the popcorn."

Jamison gave him a thumbs-up and flashed her mouthful-of-metal smile, which made the heart in his chest go tight. He would do anything for his kids. Anything at all to make them happy. They could ask for a T-Rex, and he'd figure out how to get one, even if he had to open a Jurassic Park.

Not bothering with the lights, he allowed the full moon's glow to guide him to the pantry. The balcony doors were open, and that floral night breeze had the sheer panels billowing about into the kitchen.

Finding the popcorn easily, he stuck the bag in the microwave and started it up. The second it was done, he poured it into a bowl, burning his fingers in the process. "Shit."

Jamison would want to finish the movie, and since there was no way out of it, he went for the fridge next. Sticking his head in, he searched for a beer, knowing it would be his last one for the night. He was getting older, and alcohol wasn't as kind to him as it used to be.

"You're so handsome when you're relaxed and happy like this."

He nearly hit his head on the fridge shelf when he heard her voice. Keeping calm, he snagged the beer and straightened to shut the door. "No, I'm not."

Laura Jean stood next to him, looking as beautiful as the day she left him.

"Don't argue with me," she huffed. "You know I'm right."

She was never fully solid during these encounters and always wore the same thing. A white tank top and matching broom skirt. Her emerald necklace dangled around her neck when, in truth, it actually sat in a jewelry box back at Haven House, as did the engagement ring twinkling on her pale finger.

"You don't come to me as much anymore," he mumbled, feeling like he'd reached a new low by whining to a hallucination. "It pisses me off."

"You don't need me to," she replied in that way of hers that made everything sound so simple. "You're getting stronger, Ben."

He didn't even bother with a bottle opener, wanting the sharp prick of the cap to keep him grounded. "Stronger?" He popped off the beer's top in one go. "Sure as hell doesn't feel like I'm stronger."

Taking a step forward, she laid a hand on his cheek. There was no heat. No pressure. Just the sense of cold air. But he still leaned into her touch, seeking contact with something he knew wasn't truly there.

"You are stronger, and with that strength, you can be present to live life." Her gaze held a hint of mischief in it. "Look how happy you're making our kids. Look at the life you're giving them. It all matters in the end, Ben."

Good and drunk, he couldn't stop staring. She was barefoot, as usual, with her wavy blonde hair hanging loose around her shoulders. "Your eyes sparkle like Edward Cullen's skin."

"The vampire?"

"The very one."

Laura Jean burst into laughter, and it wasn't the laugh of some small woman. Not when it came from her. It always started in the belly, rolling upward through her body until she was gasping and heaving like some sort of deranged hyena. God, how he missed that sound. It had once been as vital to him as oxygen. And it still was, except now, it existed only in his pathetic mind.

"I think you're drunk, Ben."

He took another huge swig of his beer. "I think I know that, Laura Jean."

His sarcasm made her laugh harder, and he grinned in the darkness.

"The movie isn't bad, and I get why Jamison likes Edward. He's handsome with a sharp jawline and has that forbidden nature all girls find attractive," she explained. The hand on his cheek dropped to his chest, and if he concentrated hard enough, he could almost feel the pressure of her fingertips. "You know, Edward kind of reminds me of someone."

"I do not sparkle."

"If I rolled you naked in glitter, you might."

It was his turn to bark out a laugh, but he sucked it in just as fast as it burst out of him, afraid Jamison might hear and wonder why her father was standing in a dark kitchen talking to himself.

"You've been watching the movie with us?"

"Not exactly," she exhaled, tipping her head to see past him and into the living room. "I like to watch her. She has so many expressions, and I'm trying to memorize them all, but she changes so quickly. Time... I can't keep up with it here."

"Where?" he asked, as if he could jump through space and infinite levels of existence to find her. "Where are you?"

From the other room, Jamison squealed at something Evie said on the phone, and Laura Jean's unwavering stare filled with tears. "My Evie is growing up. She gets so sad sometimes, and while this boy is not her end, he is a beginning. A real start to her learning how to live."

"So, you're saying," he reached out and toyed with a strand of her wavy hair, "that I need to be nice to this guy."

She grinned. "Yes, be nice to him. And make Simone be nice, too."

"Now you're pushing your luck." He leaned his hip against the counter, marveling at how she mirrored the motion. Their bodies tucking together perfectly as they talked. "That's like asking me to get Samuel to be nice to Evie."

She found his comment humorous. "Samuel loves Evie very much."

"He would've been a good brother to her."

Laura Jean's lips parted, her eyebrows shooting upward. "Brother? *Uh*... okay."

"Why do you say it like that?"

"You need to pay attention more, Ben."

"Pay attention to what?"

"Nothing," she sighed in exasperation and wiggled her fingers at the small radio beside the fridge. The thing popped on with a click, cycling through static and fuzz until it landed on something they both instantly recognized.

Their song.

The one they were supposed to dance to on their wedding day.

"Dance with me?"

Could he dance with a figment of his imagination? He figured why not and set the beer aside to take her in his arms. "I'll never pass up a chance to dance with you."

"I'm the only one you better be dancing with," she said, trying to be serious as her cold arms wrapped around his neck. "I would hate to haunt some poor innocent woman you might try to date."

He smiled bigger than he had in years. The idea of being with someone else was ludicrous, and as they swayed, Laura Jean felt a little more solid, and so—on impulse—he dipped her low in a sweeping motion. "I'll keep that in mind."

"Don't test me, Benjamin." She nuzzled his nose with hers. "I will scare—"

He kissed her.

Insanity and cheap beer had dragged him to the brink, and tumbling off the cliff sounded like a great idea. She was here. The woman he would love for all eternity was in his arms exactly where she belonged. He wasn't about to waste a second of it.

And of all the torturous things, she kissed him back. Burying her fingers in his hair, she didn't feel quite so cold anymore. The touch broke his heart, but it also multiplied his desperation by a thousand. With every stroke of her tongue and every tiny moan that escaped her, he allowed himself to believe.

"Stay with me." This begging was getting old, but he sure as hell would keep doing it if it meant keeping her near. "I know I'm crazy. I *know* it, and I don't care. I'm not strong. I'm not okay. Please don't take these visions of you from me."

"I will never leave you," she whispered, breathless from their kiss. He recognized it was an odd state for a hallucination to be in, but he wasn't about to argue. Having her like this, with her lips swollen and her face flushed, reminded him of their first kiss in the middle of a hurricane. "Remember, we have a deal. You stay, and I wait. It sucks for both of us, but the years will become nothing, and then we'll be together."

She was growing entirely too serious, and he couldn't stand it. He needed to see her smile again. "Why in the hell would you think I'd ever want to dance with someone else?" He tickled her ribs, holding on tight as she squealed and squirmed in his arms. "I'm offended."

"Because women throw themselves at you, and some are very pretty!" She popped up on her toes, trying to meet him face-to-face. "I can't blame them. You are the most beautiful man to walk the earth—"

"Oh, you are so full of shit."

"For certain, but I can still have that opinion."

He chuckled and continued their dance. Whatever beer he'd been drinking, he was going to bring home cases of it. "I'm doing better, but you know I'll have to tell that doctor about this."

"I'm so proud of your progress." She leaned her cheek against his chest. "And yes, tell him. It's okay to talk to people, Ben."

"People are overrated."

She poked a finger in his side. "What I'm trying to say is that it's okay to talk about me."

"I do talk about you. I talk about you all the time with Jamison. I tell her stories so she knows her mother. I do it with Evie, too, so she won't forget, but I include Albie."

"Don't let anyone make you think you're not a good man, Benjamin Fairweather. You're the best man. And I can't thank you enough for caring for my girls."

"Our girls." He rested his chin on the top of her head. "If Evie weren't an adult, I'd change her name to Fairweather. I should have done it already, but I've just been so... *lost*."

"Don't worry. She'll be a Fairweather one day."

"Dad!" Jamison shouted from the living room. "I'm off the phone. Is the popcorn ready?"

He dropped a kiss on Laura Jean's head before turning just enough to yell over his shoulder. He wanted to make sure Jamison could hear him or else she might come running in to investigate what was taking so long. "Almost. Two more seconds."

But when he turned back, his arms were empty. The dark kitchen, with its beautiful floral tiles and white curtains dancing in the night wind, sat completely vacant. Laura Jean was gone once more, leaving him alone to deal with this long life without her.

He knew none of it was real. It never was. His brain might have faulty wiring after losing so much, but he at least could keep a level head. He understood that these ghostly visits were his way of coping. They felt good. They allowed him to breathe again.

But it was time to admit the truth.

It was time to let Laura Jean go.

At least, that's what his shrink would have said.

When she was alive, Laura Jean taught him to believe in the impossible, and it would be a disservice to her memory if he stopped now. He would remain Benjamin Fairweather on the outside, but on the inside, he would always be her Ben—the man tamed and conquered by a fierce woman who would forever hold his heart.

Grabbing the popcorn off the counter, he grinned as their song continued to play on the radio. It didn't hurt to hear it like it once did, and as he passed the countertop jukebox on his way out of the kitchen, he cranked the volume higher, thinking he might ask his daughter to dance.

Chapter 43

Jamison

"**C**an we leave now?"

Damon must have asked the same question at least a dozen times. Snuggled in Liam's lap as they sat on a small corner hospital room chair, Jamison sincerely hoped the nurses would finally give him a straight answer.

"The doctor will be making his rounds momentarily," the nurse said as she wheeled out her blood pressure cart. "He'll let us know."

"Has anyone checked on Holden lately?" Claudia asked from the second chair, Madison still asleep on her chest. "I thought I heard he was awake."

"He has a concussion," Liam told her. "But he's being discharged into my dad's care, and they're getting ready to head back to the staging area."

The phrase complete devastation had been uttered repeatedly. The fireball that swept over the land during Michael's grand finale had taken out much of the forest and was still burning even now, hours later. Liam wanted to go with his father and Holden, but he refused to leave her, and neither she nor her dad felt comfortable leaving Damon and his sisters alone.

"If they let you out," Ben said to Damon from his designated corner spot near the door, "do you want to get a hotel here for the night? Or do you want to take the plane with Claudia back to North Carolina? We have a second jet here, and it's ready whenever you are. It can drop Emily in Houston first and then get you three back to Raleigh."

Claudia paled at the mention of North Carolina. "Um, I mean... it would be good for Madi to sleep in her own bed, but..."

But she didn't want to face returning to the home she shared with Parker. Wrapping her mind around what Claudia must be going through felt mentally impossible for Jamison. The entire world Claudia knew had been a lie.

"I don't need to go to Houston," Emily said, moving to Claudia's side and taking her sister's hand. "I'm going with Claudia and Madi to help them do whatever it is that you do after something like this."

Jamison remembered those days and snuggled closer to Liam. It wouldn't be overnight. Normalcy wouldn't come in a week or even a month from now. After Toby, she could easily recall how it had taken them so long to process the full extent of the trauma they'd dealt with on that horrible day.

"Liam's mom is pretty amazing," Jamison told Claudia. "She's a family therapist and is used to dealing with various cases. Some basic day-to-day things, and some—many, actually—more serious things as well. If you ever want to talk to her, just say the word, and I know Bernie will be more than happy to step in and help."

Claudia rested her cheek on top of Madi's head. "I think that sounds good," she replied, openly crying as she spoke. "For me and Madi, and for..."

And for the baby.

The doctors had checked Claudia thoroughly. Bruce hadn't lied—everything she'd been given while captive had been safe. The baby was strong and healthy, with an early summer due date in place.

Through quiet tears, Claudia smiled up at her sister. "And I think spending time with my bratty little sister sounds fantastic."

"Who are you calling a brat?" Emily lifted Claudia's hand and pressed a kiss to the back of it, the move shocking everyone. The sisters never showed any type of affection. Ever. "Maybe this Dr. Bernie can fix us both."

"Christ, Liam." Damon reclined back on the hospital bed. "I hope your mom's a miracle worker."

"Howdy!" The young nurse who had been overly eager to treat Damon came into the room, her hips holding a little more sway to them and her lips a little more color after she'd applied some gloss. "Doc says you're free to go. All the blood tests are coming back clear or on the decline. He wants you to take it easy for the next few days, and then you should start to feel normal."

Damon smiled at the woman, a canine snagging his bottom lip. His hair had fallen forward into his eyes, and he knocked it back with a jerk of his head. "Thank you for taking such good care of me."

"A-a-anytime." The nurse didn't move, simply staring at Damon until snapping out of her trance when an alarm down the hall went off. "Uh, excuse me. I'll be back with your paperwork in just a sec."

"Stop flirting with the nurses," Claudia admonished with a whisper.

"I wasn't flirting." Damon kicked off the covers, swinging his long legs over the edge of the bed. "All I did was smile."

"Same thing," Emily mumbled. "And you know it."

Heather and Trevor chose that moment to sweep into the room.

"Get up. All of you." Heather snapped her fingers at her daughters, waking Madison in the process. "We're leaving."

Not many people intimidated Jamison Fairweather, but Heather always had to some degree. To call her a terror was an understatement, and Jamison now partially understood why Claudia had been the way she'd been for so many years.

A monster of her mother's making.

"We're waiting on Damon's paperwork," Emily said calmly, placing a hand on Claudia's shoulder when she tried to rise. "They think the drugs are almost out of his system."

Decked out in a beautiful cream ankle-length skirt with a simple cashmere top and a pair of absurdly high heels, Heather stuck her nose in the air as she surveyed everyone present. "Why is he on drugs?"

"Because those people had to drug me, or else I would have killed them for kidnapping us." The usual icy indifference Damon held returned, dripping from every word as he spoke. "And hello, Mother. It's nice to see you again."

Damon wasn't one to back down, and Jamison was starting to realize the trait wasn't the usual innate stubbornness most Fairweathers held, but likely a survival tactic developed in the years he lived under Trevor and Heather's roof.

Mother and son stared at each other across the cramped hospital room. Or Jamison assumed they did. Heather refused to take off her ridiculously oversized sunglasses, so it was hard to tell.

"It's good to see you're doing well," Trevor said, his words muffled as he addressed the floor instead of his son. "We didn't know what we were walking into."

"I'm not doing well." Damon's glare shifted from Heather to Trevor, softening just a fraction. "You're walking into a moment where your children have just escaped being kidnapped by a group of deranged luna—"

"*Shhhh*!" Heather flailed both hands up and down, her diamond ring large enough to feed a small country sparkling under the fluorescents. "The entire hospital doesn't need to hear all the sordid details."

Jamison swore Damon would break his jaw by how tight he was clenching it. The extremely uncanny resemblance to her father was always there, but pissed off? Yeah, he most definitely took after their branch of the family tree.

The same could be said for Emily. "Oh, gee, Mom. Sorry. We wouldn't want the world to know that those crazies are actually crazy and came after us. We wouldn't want anyone to know that they kept Claudia in a dog crate and me bound while they drugged Damon to the point where we had to drag him out of that place."

"We should give them a minute," Liam whispered in Jamison's ear. "I think they need a little privacy."

Being nosy to a fault, Jamison didn't move off his lap. "You reopened your stitches," she whispered back to him. And he had, although mildly. The nurse patched him up in no time. "You really shouldn't move yet."

Liam pinched her butt, but she stayed in her place, listening so she could tell Simone everything later. Her father didn't move either, too busy staring daggers at Heather.

"You had to drag him out?" Heather sounded appalled, following up her outrage in true Heather fashion. "What kind of man gets rescued by women? A weak one, sure, but you, Damon? I thought we raised you better than that."

"Obviously not." Damon attempted to stand, but his legs couldn't hold him, and he grabbed onto the bedside railing before he fell. "Son of a bitch."

Liam didn't give her a choice then and moved her off him so he could help Damon. "Em and Claudia said they only fed you broth, so your system is likely in need of nutrients."

"We'll get you a big steak dinner," Trevor said, attempting to smile at Madison, but it only made her whimper. "I'm sure there's a decent place around here to eat."

"Nonsense. We're leaving for Raleigh immediately, and Madison, cease your crying. I will not listen to it for the entire plane ride home." Heather snapped her fingers again. "Let's go."

Jamison stepped back when she saw her father's eyes darken. The look encompassing his face meant only one thing. Benjamin Fairweather had heard enough.

"Heather, I'd like to see you in the hall."

Heather lifted her chin defiantly. "No."

"That wasn't a question."

Jamison pressed her lips together as her father closed the distance between himself and Heather. Holding his hand out, he gestured for the door. "Shall we?"

As Heather's heels clicked out into the hall, the tension in Trevor's body lessened, and he crouched down to speak to Madison. "Hey, sweetie. How's Grandpa's best girl doing?"

Madison's eyes filled with fresh tears. "Why was my daddy being bad?"

Stiffening, Claudia drew into herself and stared at the wall as her father tried to smooth over the situation.

"Oh." Trevor cleared his throat and thought for a moment. "Uh...well."

Her uncle was indeed stepping away from his duties at Fairweather, telling people that retirement suited him, but there were also whispers of something more happening. A mental decline. An unknown illness keeping him in its grips. Jamison thought there were too many rumors for any of them to be true, office gossip, and nothing more, but she hadn't seen him in a long time. The difference was staggering.

"Sometimes... sometimes people we love do bad things," Trevor continued. "It's not our fault."

"But why?" Madison whispered. She reached for him, and Trevor looked startled for a moment, but then extracted the little girl from Claudia's arms.

Settling her on his hip, Trevor gave a lengthy pause before answering. "Because the world is a bad place, and it has bad people in it, and sometimes those people are supposed to be our family. They're supposed to love us, but they don't. They love the badness in them more, and you know what, Madi? That's not your fault. You have to keep being good and not think about the bad people anymore."

The hospital door creaked open again.

"How are we doing in here?"

Holden sauntered in as if he hadn't been knocked unconscious by a flying projectile during the explosion. A line of stitches cut across his forehead, and he shot a smirk at Emily.

"Hey there, Speed Racer."

Emily hadn't hesitated. Hopping onto Holden's lap after he took a hit to the head, she'd gotten them the hell out of there.

A small blush tinted Emily's pale face, but she mirrored Holden's smirk. "That truck handled pretty well. It was smart of you to steal it."

Holden wiggled his eyebrows. "Stealing trucks and saving the day is kind of my job."

Talking on the phone, Will came in behind Holden, looking as tired as they all felt.

"Yeah, okay. I'll tell them. Yes, Evie. I will properly yell at everyone involved, but please calm down. Okay, okay, okay. Bye."

Putting his phone in his pocket, Will took a cleansing breath. "We are all in trouble from now until the end of time because we didn't tell Evie what was happening."

Albie had just been born, but it felt as if it had been months. Dizzy all of a sudden, Jamison placed a hand on the wall, and after settling Damon on the bed, Liam returned to her.

"I'm ready to go home," she whispered. "But I want to know what the authorities have learned."

"Are you sure?"

"I need to know."

"Me too." He pressed his forehead to hers. "Tell me you're okay."

She closed her eyes and breathed him in.

"I'm okay."

"Well, that makes one of us."

Liam peered out the window of the taxi as they pulled into the staging area. Spotlights flooded the scene while dozens of men and women moved around in various groups.

"Looks like Anderson made it."

They exited the cab and approached a cluster of feds holding Agent Anderson at its center. "Has anyone heard how Carter is doing?" Jamison asked.

"My dad said Carter isn't leaving Evie's side," Liam replied over the noise. "Carter tried to send Izzy home to get some rest, but they started arguing since Iz refused to leave her post."

"Who won?"

"Carter ended up winning when Abe said they should consider the girls and Josie, who all needed to get some sleep in a real bed." Liam took her hand as they entered a thicker crowd of people. "But then Samuel and Evie got upset over the idea of being separated from the girls, and now they're all camped out in Evie's hospital room having a giant sleepover, from what it sounds like."

Smiling felt wrong, but the image in her head left her with no choice. She was ready to be home and meet her new nephew, but first, they had to deal with the aftermath of Michael.

She squeezed his hand. "Dad said he was taking me back, but that you were staying?"

Being the partner of a man who served the public, she was familiar with the job's requirements. And while he worked in the private sector now, his internal need to do what was right would have him stay, even if the entire thing wasn't a very up close and personal incident for their family.

"I want you secured at Haven until I know for sure."

"Know what, for sure?"

"That they're all dead."

Michael and Taylor had been close to the blast, but those coordinates... she'd looked them up. Liam showed her how. They pinpointed a spot on the lake's edge where she imagined the view was spectacular without the fog. A perfect place to propose. Sinclair probably killed Taylor almost immediately, or so Liam thought, and the final shot they heard was him ending his own life before the explosion.

But Liam wasn't referring to Michael and Taylor. He wanted to know if any Zanmi members had escaped. "Do you think Emmett is alive?"

"Perhaps, but I highly doubt it."

They made it to Anderson and found not only him, but also Klausen.

"Ms. Fairweather." Klausen nodded in greeting. "It would appear that I have been correct all these years. You are one extraordinarily tough woman."

She would take time later to think about why that particular statement had tears springing forth, but for now, they needed to focus on getting the details. "Klausen, don't start being nice to me, or I'll start being nice to you, and then where will our relationship go?"

"Good to see you, Ms. Fairweather." Anderson held up a hand to halt the chatter coming from the group. "Thanks for making my last days at the Bureau interesting."

"Glad to be of service."

Will and Holden's cab pulled up next, and Liam waved them over. Her father was off securing hotel rooms, or he was coordinating the effort to find hotel rooms. In truth, it was probably Hillary helping him, since her father no longer had an assistant.

It turned her stomach, thinking of all the private details Taylor had access to during her time under Samuel and their father. She would have known every little detail of their lives, twisting the information into some warped narrative she could use on the people who followed her and Toby.

Toby.

She'd heard Liam quietly talking to what sounded like Rowan on the phone. He wanted a message sent without delay to Killian McIntyre. The first part of it was a stand down order, and that was to be expected. Liam was always good on his word, and one day, he would see that the hasty decision made by him and her brother came from a need to protect and nothing more. They were honorable at their core, and no one, no monster or man, would ever change that.

But the second part of his conversation, well, she did take a small amount of pleasure there. It jarred a sick satisfaction in her that she had no right to feel. The PR plan was that there would be no plan. Anyone could ask whatever they wanted. They weren't going to hide any details.

Not anymore. From here until eternity, the Fairweathers would operate with a *come one, come all* attitude. Come look at their highs. Come gasp at their lows. Come see the freaks that call themselves a family when they're made up of nothing but thin connections and poorly kept secrets. Come see the Fairweathers and how they are so very *flawed.*

Just like everyone else in the world.

So when Liam gave his second request, it was for something simple. Something that sent a message.

Turn on the news.

That was it.

Turn on the news and let Toby see what Michael had done.

Liam and Samuel might be honorable men, but they were vindictive as well. Jamison loved them a little more for it.

Moving around Anderson, Liam examined the map laid out on the hood of an unmarked car. "Has the site been cleared?"

"Bomb investigators are in there," Anderson replied. "Sinclair kept it neat for the most part."

Liam pointed to a spot on the map. "Sinclair's body should be here, and Taylor's probably not far off."

"They've already located something here." Anderson's finger slid down the map, stopping not far from the coordinates Michael had given her. "Might be Taylor. Hard to tell at this point. We're thinking he used some sort of phosphorus bomb on her, so there's not much left."

Holden approached and handed over a holster and Glock to Liam. "Thought you'd want this."

"Thanks, man."

Liam buckled in with practiced ease, not missing a beat in the briefing. Jamison watched him, sighing over the calm focus he held and the way he wore violence and honor like armor. She was being ridiculous and would need to snap out of it, but for just one second, she allowed herself to be a lovesick idiot fawning over her man.

And when he caught her looking, he winked.

"Behave," she whispered.

"You're the one staring."

Thankfully, the agents and cops were busy talking among themselves. Only Holden was paying attention. "You guys know we almost died, right?" he asked sarcastically. "Like you do you and all that, but can you hold it together until we're done here?"

"Holden, let me tell you something. When you love someone, show them every chance you can, regardless of the circumstances." Adjusting the holster to his body, Liam kissed her soundly to prove his point. "And we won't be done here for a long time."

The minuscule smile on her face fled. "What do you mean, a long time? I thought I was returning in a couple of hours, and you were coming home tomorrow or the next day."

A few heads turned their way, but Liam was already checking his gun and returning to his interrogation of Anderson. "Has the team made it to the house yet? That'll be where most of the casualties are."

"They have," Anderson confirmed. "But there's no way to tell anything at this time since there's nothing left."

Will was already in deep conversation with a couple of men who looked like feds, but paused to speak up. "So, we don't know who was in there, and who might have escaped the blast?"

"The blast field was incredibly wide," a man next to Anderson started to say.

"Yeah, we know that," Holden interjected, pointing to the angry gash on his forehead. "But has no one checked the area around the lake? Someone could have reached it in time to take cover."

"When Sinclair led us downstairs, everyone was asleep. Eugene Gilbert knocked them out using some sort of injection." Liam swiped a marker out of Klausen's hand. "But if anyone came to, and realized something was happening, they could have gained enough distance," he scribbled a line on the map, "if they ran this way."

"Do you have reason to believe that anyone could have made it?" Anderson asked, his head tilting out of curiosity.

"Michael let one guy go. Emmett Watson. He was headed in a northeasterly direction, and if he continued that way, he would have made it out." Liam drew an arrow on the map to show Emmett's path. "Did you pick up Gilbert yet?"

Anderson nodded. "About an hour ago."

"That's a start." Liam tossed the marker at Klausen, who fumbled the catch. "So, let's get to work."

Chapter 44

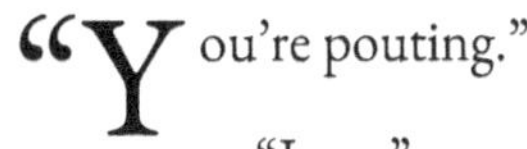

"**Y**ou're pouting."

"I am."

"You're cute when you pout."

Jamison dropped her forehead to Liam's chest, thumping it a few times in playful frustration. "Do you really think this is going to take a week?"

Alone in the private airstrip's waiting area, he pulled her into his arms. "I'll finish as soon as I can. But you know I have to do this."

She did know.

She just didn't have to like it.

"Hey. Look at me."

Tilting her head up, she slumped against him, becoming deadweight. "What?"

"I love you." He glanced around and, seeing no one, dipped his head. "Kiss me goodbye."

She melted a little further at the husky rasp of his voice. "If you want a kiss, come and get it."

His lips crashed into hers, and the power behind the kiss revealed how starved he was for contact. It was as if he had been holding back for as long as he could and had finally reached his limits. Walking her backward, he groaned deep in his chest, but when she felt the cold wall pressing against her back, the same sense of desperation came over her.

Slanting her mouth beneath his, she opened for him, shivering as his tongue swept in, all promise and possession. He kissed her like a vow, like a claim, and when he dragged his mouth down to the slope of her neck, running his tongue along the tender skin, her knees nearly buckled.

"It's really over?" she whispered.

"Yes. And if it's not, I'm making sure it is before I leave here." His teeth grazed her collarbone. "Then I'm coming home to marry you."

"Maybe now we can have our beach wedding after all."

His hands gripped her ass roughly as he kissed her again. "You can have anything you want as long as you'll be my wife."

"Jamison Cohen, at your service, sir."

Liam sucked in a sharp breath and froze, the color draining from his face.

"Did that scare you?" she asked half-jokingly. "Does hearing me call myself Jamison Cohen freak you out?"

He didn't answer right away. He just stared at her, all seriousness in his expression. "I thought I lost you. On that long drive, I really thought... I'd lost you."

"Hey. I'm here." She cupped his face in her hands, allowing him to be vulnerable while no one else could see. "Look at me, Liam. I'm here. I'm safe. You saved me."

His throat worked as he swallowed, and she was engulfed in his arms once more. "Just expect me to be overprotective for an extremely long time."

"How long are we talking?"

"I might be good once we reach our eighties. I figured most of my memory will be gone by then."

⁓⁓⁓ ⁂ ⁓⁓⁓

She dozed off on the plane, and the sun was already up when she woke. "Are we almost there?"

"Yeah," her father replied softly beside her. "How are you feeling?"

It should've been her asking him that question. He looked rough as hell. "Good," she lied, not wanting him to worry. "I'm ready to be home and see my new nephew."

"Here." He handed her his phone. "Selah and his crew have arrived and just sent photos."

Taking her time, she marveled at each one. "He's such a pretty baby. Most babies look all squished those first few days, but not Albie."

"Samuel looked like that when he was born."

Jamison snorted. "I highly doubt it. Samuel's ugly."

"Hey, don't insult my kid." Taking the phone back, her father chuckled. "Although I will say that you were the prettiest newborn out of all of them."

"Duh." She leaned her head against his shoulder. "Did you hear from Liam while I was asleep?"

"I heard from Will. They've cleared the site and are preparing to go in."

"But Liam is okay?"

"I would say he's staying focused."

"Which means no."

"It means that he's smart enough to know this isn't the time to let fear take over."

Chapter 45

Jamison

They were waiting for her.

With Simone at the front and the rest of them fanned out across
the porch, her *family* was waiting for her.

The wind chimes hanging from the eaves jingled softly as she stepped
out of her father's car, their melody so familiar it resonated deep in
her bones, as steady and constant as her own heartbeat. She ran up the
stone walkway, past the twin oaks standing guard, and past the rainbow
blooms in Ty's Garden.

And only when she stumbled up the steps to fall into Simone's open
arms did she believe she was home.

Her family surrounded her, holding her close and telling her
everything would be okay. She cried in their arms, hysterically relaying
the entire ordeal from the start. She told them about Michael. She told
Simone that CeCe had been loved and how that love had been twisted
into something unrecognizable after her death. She told them about
Taylor and those horrible people. She told them about her cousins and
the things they had endured.

They listened. They asked questions. They cried with her. And when
she finally began to quiet, they moved her into the parlor.

Abe held Izzy's hand; the two of them hadn't let go of each other since
she'd walked through the door. Lenora kept a tight grip on Xavier, while
Selah stood behind his wife with both hands on her shoulders. Simone

and Annabeth sat on either side of her on the parlor sofa, with her father and Rowan flanking them in quiet solidarity.

"Tell us what you need, Jamison," Abe said when the silence turned too heavy to bear. "Whatever you need, we'll make it happen."

She needed Liam. But since that wasn't possible, she asked for the next best thing.

"I'd like to see my sister."

Bernie suggested she take a shower first, but Simone was a little more forceful about the matter, even going after her father. "You are wrinkled, Benjamin, and that is no way to greet your grandson."

Once she and her dad were ready, they rode to the hospital together, a caravan of chaos descending on the maternity wing. Samuel heard them coming and was already in the hallway when they turned the corner.

Seeing him had Jamison getting emotional again, and she didn't resist when her big brother pulled her in for a hug.

"Just let me hold you, brat."

Unable to breathe and perfectly fine being in such a state, she hugged Samuel back.

"Okay, you big jerk."

Carter waited at the door, looking better than when she'd last seen him, and she hugged him next.

"Thank you for protecting them. I hope you haven't been too bored."

A little startled, Carter returned the hug. "The word boring will never cross my lips again."

Everyone stayed in the hall while she and her father slipped quietly into Evie's room. Upon entering, they both grinned at the girls sprawled out asleep on the hospital room's pullout sofa.

And Evie promptly burst into tears when she caught sight of them.

Not caring about propriety or hospital rules, Jamison crawled into the bed with her sister and snuggled close. "Let me see my nephew."

Still sniffling, Evie turned the bundle in her arms. "He's hungry all the time and is already so demanding."

Albert Benjamin Fairweather was perfect, and Jamison sighed over his beautiful face. "He is a Fairweather, you know."

"I know." Evie swiped at her tears. "Ben, would you like to hold him?"

"Absolutely." With his hands out, Benjamin Fairweather was already a goner over the kid. "Give me my new grandson."

Jamison grinned at his eagerness. But then the dark thoughts that would likely forever creep around in the back of her mind edged closer. They whispered the truth, reminding her that the excitement and complete adoration coming from her father as he gazed down at Albie would be something she could never give him. The soft maternal glow Evie exuded was something she would never experience. The firsts. The failures. The fun of being a parent... she would never have it.

It hurt. Especially now, when she needed Liam at her side, but it would be okay. One day. It would be okay.

Evie shifted to face her, their foreheads nearly touching.

"Talk to me."

"Not yet." Jamison shook her head. "This is a place of happiness, and I don't want to bring all that in here today."

"Liam?"

Jamison wrinkled her nose. "Working."

"For how long?"

"Too long."

Evie stroked her cheek. "You can take care of me in the meantime."

"I think that sounds like a great idea."

And it was too long.

Evie went home from the hospital a few days later, and Jamison stayed busy helping her. She talked to Liam every chance she could, which was at least twice a day. They were making progress. The smoke had cleared, so to speak, and body retrieval had begun. Excluding Michael and Taylor, they were up to—they thought—thirty-six. It was hard to tell, of course. Liam had kept the details limited for her sanity's sake, and she was thankful for it.

And while the news coming from Liam was in short supply, Agent Anderson was a little more forthcoming about how they could proceed with their lives. The buzz of activity surrounding Zanmi's highest members died off on the day of the bombing, and he assured them the threat to their safety had likely been neutralized.

She didn't want to ask Liam about Michael's body. He would do what he thought was best. The promise to try talking with Simone about it hung heavy in her heart, and one afternoon, she got brave enough to broach the subject.

But she made Annabeth come with her.

Which meant Rowan was there, too. He was keeping the security around them high, but allowing for less monitoring inside the homes. Most of his days were spent figuring out security details for a full return to the offices and running background checks on the new security personnel hires. They were increasing their numbers every day, vetting men and women who would keep their employees and themselves safe.

Annabeth, naturally, was right in the thick of it. Working alongside Rowan day and night, Jamison watched in awe as her friend found her footing amidst the paperwork. She kept Rowan organized, and when he didn't need her, she filled in as the personal assistant to the CEO of Fairweather Holdings.

The bookstore wouldn't reopen until closer to Christmas, which was just around the corner, yet Annabeth was taking her new temporary job seriously. "Ben, you need to keep better records. Samuel is up all night helping Evie with feedings, and you're over here messing up his project notes for next Tuesday's meeting!"

Jamison thought her father almost looked relieved when she stuck her head into the dining room and asked to borrow Annabeth for her dreaded chat with Simone. "Take as long as you need, girls."

"What are we doing?" Annabeth asked.

"Talking to your mom about something," Jamison explained as they went to corner Simone in the parlor. "Michael Sinclair had a request, and I promised him I would honor it if he released us."

Annabeth stopped dead in her tracks. "Whatever it is, the answer is no."

"I get that, but I still feel like I need to do my part and leave it up to Simone."

Surprising them both, Simone listened. She didn't shut it down. She wanted details—much more than Jamison had shared before—about her time with Michael. They talked for hours, going back and forth between the information she'd learned and the details Rowan had pieced together through his search.

Halfway through the conversation, Rowan slipped into the room and took a quiet seat in the corner. When Jamison reached the part where Parker knocked her out, she realized her father had joined them, too. He sat silently in the second wingback, listening to it all.

"Keep going," her father told her when she paused. "I want to hear it."

Recalling as many details as possible, Jamison stared at the floor as she spoke, not wanting to be distracted by their expressions. "He said he would only lead us out if I made the request to Simone personally."

"And now you've done just that." Simone turned in her seat to face Rowan. "What would you do?"

Rowan appeared mildly surprised. "Me?"

"Yes. I know what Ben would do. So, I'm asking you, Rowan McIntyre. What would you do?"

Rowan thought for a moment, clearly weighing his words. "He loved CeCe, obviously. But to bury him here, at Haven House? That doesn't feel right—"

"That wasn't the question," Simone said, lifting a hand, effectively cutting him off. "I asked what you would have done if you were in Michael Sinclair's shoes. What if Annabeth had been hurt the way CeCe had been hurt? What if she had been forced into a situation where she thought it was better to kill herself than go on living without you? What would you have done then?"

The confused expression on Rowan's face faded, his gaze darting between Simone and Ben. "You've made your point."

"She didn't make any point," Annabeth scoffed. "And I think you're all being ridiculous."

Simone regarded her daughter for a moment and then told Jamison she would think on the matter. "I'll let you know as soon as I decide."

CHAPTER 46

Jamison

"She said she would think about it and let me know."

Liam grunted under his breath, which told her nothing of his thoughts. "Sinclair's remains will go to his parents. My dad has already been in contact with them. Apparently, Sinclair left a note expressing his wishes to be laid to rest with CeCe."

"And they're okay with that?"

"The Sinclairs have lost a son. Their daughter has disappeared with their grandsons. I don't think they're *okay* with anything. But my dad said they seemed like decent people."

Jamison adjusted the phone and rolled onto her back. It was late, and she had waited up for his phone call, needing to hear his voice. It was almost time for him to come home now that things were winding down in Arkansas.

"When I was over at Evie and Samuel's place today, I looked at some of the Georgia designs."

"Did you find one that suits us?"

She loved that he was completely on board with moving to Georgia. Neither of them had enjoyed their time in Houston. It was their beginning, but it was time to leave it behind. "The small one would work. Three bedrooms, open layout."

"We'll need more than three bedrooms."

"Not really." She moved to get off the bed, too full of energy to rest. "Our bedroom, and then we each get a home office. The shared spaces are huge."

"Four bedrooms. Maybe five," he countered. "Minimum."

She laughed. "You're acting like we have all the money in the world. I'll have you know, Fairweather doesn't build cheap crap."

"I'll ask for a raise."

"How's that going to work?" She wandered into her closet and turned on the light, her shoulders slumping at the mess still hanging around. "I've never even asked if this head of Fairweather security position will require you to travel."

"For the first few months, yeah. After that... wait, what are you doing?"

"Cleaning up the shoes." She bent to grab one of his sneakers. "I can't sleep, and this place is a mess. Keep talking while I work. What did you learn today?"

"We got the journals."

She froze. "You're kidding! Tell me what they say."

Every day, it was something new. A new piece of truth in this bizarre puzzle, which, when lined up with the others, made perfect sense.

They had Michael to thank for that.

Not only did Michael Sinclair make his disposal of Zanmi tidy and neat, but he'd also written detailed notes revealing his motives along with an extremely helpful timeline. Left behind to carry out his wishes, Bruce sent Michael's parents five journals from wherever he and Kristina had run off to, and the Sinclairs called the police the second they realized what they had in their possession.

"I'm a civilian now," Liam said, and she rolled her eyes at the way he deadpanned the statement. "They don't allow regular people access to that kind of information."

"Cut the crap."

"I'm serious. They restricted my access once we reached the part where Sinclair admitted to doing unsanctioned jobs for his superiors under the guise of serving his country."

She should have been surprised. She wasn't. "No way."

"And he continued after his discharge. Every bombing that was labeled as a domestic terror strike was actually a hit put out by someone with a bunch of power in our government. The first one was an utter shitshow because he was feeling guilty about CeCe's death and didn't think she would have approved of him taking that route in life."

When he didn't continue, Jamison chucked his tennis shoe to the back of the closet, unable to find the second one. "What else?"

"I told you. We weren't allowed to read anything after that. Homeland is already on the ground and in the Bureau's face now that they know Michael Sinclair was involved in the bombing, so this news shot them into overdrive." Liam chuckled. "Then the DOD showed up, and Anderson got into a screaming match with what I think was a General. It was total pandemonium for a few hours."

"But that sucks." She decided to work on her clothes and went for her wedding dress first. It wouldn't hurt to look it over. "We'll never know what was in them. Or we won't know for a long time."

"Jamison, love of my life and my future wife, who do you think you're talking to?" Liam huffed as if truly offended. "It hurts my feelings that you would think I'm just going to let something like this go."

"William, what did you do?"

"While everyone was distracted and arguing over who was in charge of what, Holden and I nabbed the journals we hadn't read yet and made copies."

Halting mid-unzipping of the wedding gown's garment bag, she gasped. "Liam, if your dad found out—"

"My dad worked as the lookout while we got the job done."

Her eyes slowly closed. "Because, of course, he did."

"You sound like you're mad."

"I'm not mad. I'm just trying to figure out where to hide you when Homeland Security or the Department of Defense kicks down our door."

"I'm sure you'll figure it out."

She rolled her eyes and unzipped the garment bag fully. "Are you going to tell me what the journals say or not?"

"The first couple focus on his time in the service and how he met CeCe. He didn't lie. They met in a coffee shop in Miami, and he fell hard for her. He also states how when he met Toby and Taylor, he knew right away what he was dealing with and began to extract CeCe from the situation immediately. Missouri was a long shot, but he convinced her, and they moved."

"But did she help Toby kill?"

"Yes and no. Toby mainly killed when Taylor pushed him. She liked to watch, acting as the puppet master controlling the monster in a way. The ritualism behind the later murders stemmed from her obsession with the massacre that took place at Haven. Toby told her about it when they were young, and she became absolutely fascinated. Michael wrote that Toby exhibited dissociative behaviors seen in all impulse killers, but that he felt Taylor was the push Toby needed to act on those impulses. Sinclair thought that if she hadn't remained in his life, he would have never moved past the sexual sadism Taylor started him off on."

"Michael told me she was obsessed with my mother's death… but wait." She dropped to sit cross-legged on the floor, trying to remember everything Michael had told her. The drugs made her memories hazy, and the frustration was nearly unbearable. "He said Toby developed those sadistic kinks before college."

"He did. According to the journals, Toby and Taylor were tag-teaming young men and women in St. Thomas as far back as their teen years. But they didn't kill anyone except Charlie Fairweather. Their other killing didn't happen until Toby went to college and made friends. Marcus, Richard, and Eugene were just as we thought. Disgusting humans. But they weren't into murder. Maiming, sure, but not murder. Taylor got jealous of Toby connecting with others, and when the three of them pointed out how fucked up she was, Taylor set out to prove a point and convinced Toby to kill an island girl while his friends were with him."

"They were into it, weren't they? They might not have participated before that, but after it happened, they wanted more?"

"Eugene Gilbert was the only one with real reservations, but once Taylor figured out his pressure point—female children—she helped, again in Michael's words, feed his needs so he would stay loyal."

Jamison laid a hand on her stomach, suddenly nauseous. "What will they do with Eugene now that he's in custody?"

"Nothing. He's dead."

"How?"

"Heart attack."

Wherever Bruce and Michael's sister ran off to with her two boys, Jamison sincerely hoped they lived a long and peaceful life. Bryan Carroll's body had been found on the bathroom floor of his hotel room. The official cause of death was heart failure.

"Fancy that," she whispered, needing to lie down, and decided the bed was too far away, so she spread out on the carpeted floor of her closet. "Keep talking."

"There's so much to tell. What do you want to know?"

"Tell me about CeCe's life with him."

"They were happy, Jamison," Liam said simply. "They lived a quiet life, both craving normalcy. Michael was still bouncing in and out of war zones, and CeCe came from a life with her brother and the world of Bryan Carroll. Oh, and we were kind of right on one thing. Michael and his sister worked for Carroll at one point. As a bargaining chip for CeCe, Michael did a few off-the-books jobs for him while Kristina functioned as the brains, covering Carroll's digital footprints, which included erasing pictures of his daughter."

"So that's why Rowan couldn't find any photos of Taylor."

"Exactly. Kristina Scherer is one of the best, and Rowan is still pissed."

"But why would they work for Carroll at all if Michael wanted to pull CeCe away from that world?"

"Because CeCe refused to cut contact with them. Toby was her brother. Taylor was her friend. When Charlie started using and staying out drunk all the time, Taylor and Bryan stepped in to take care of a young CeCe and Toby. You have to understand that CeCe didn't have the usual upbringing, so hanging around a drug lord and his psycho daughter felt normal."

Jamison exhaled slowly. "Then she goes off to fall in love with a man who later becomes a domestic terrorist."

"Michael was already in the picture when Toby started sniffing around your family. Once CeCe found out Taylor was working at Fairweather Holdings, she was done. That sealed her decision to leave with Sinclair."

"But, when her big brother comes to town and starts killing women connected to CeCe, Michael gets pissed."

"They fight. He leaves," Liam continued. "And the rest is how we know it."

"He built CeCe that house."

"*After* she died. He built it when he refused to do any more black ops jobs, and not long after the house was complete, the headaches started. The doctors found the tumor almost immediately."

"That's so sad," she sighed. "I mean, it's sad, but it's not sad? I don't know what I'm trying to say, honestly."

Liam didn't reply, and she knew he was waiting for her to catch up. "Okay, tell me. You never go quiet unless you're getting to the meat of it."

"Sinclair was told he had ten to twelve months to live. Surgery was an option, but he wasn't sure that was the path he wanted. Living without CeCe wasn't worth it, so he came to Haven House and sat in the graveyard to feel close to her while he made his decision."

"He told me he did that a lot," she whispered.

"He wrote about it in the journals, too. But on this particular visit, he claims he saw CeCe's ghost. She told him the truth about how she died."

Jamison's eyebrows lifted. "Did he know then that the brain tumor was causing hallucinations?"

She might have been out of it on the night Michael tried to kidnap her, but she could remember how he screamed at the ball of light and almost begged her to admit she saw it, too. Perhaps one day, she would stop and reflect on her own experiences. Perhaps even find a rational explanation for them. But for now, she didn't have the time to dwell on her weird encounters or odd dreams.

And she certainly didn't want to think about how the dreams had tapered off into nothing.

Since they escaped, there had been no more nightly visions. Not of her mother or CeCe. She mourned the loss of her mother, but not CeCe. As far as she was concerned, CeCe Miller could rest in peace quietly.

"So, he understands that he has a brain tumor and knows they cause hallucinations, yet he thinks CeCe's ghost talked to him?"

"Not just talked to him. This ghost supposedly told him that Taylor was involved with CeCe's death and that she had only killed herself because she was terrified of what Toby would do once Taylor worked him into a frenzy."

She heard the shuffle of papers being shifted around. Liam and Holden were in the car, driving back to their hotel, which was quite a distance from the staging site.

"Everyone knows CeCe ate that manchineel fruit," he muttered, sounding like he was looking for something. "Toxicology confirmed it. Toby claimed it was suicide, which it was."

Jamison pressed her fingertips to her temples, massaging in circles as if it would help shove all this information into her head. "And what does that have to do with him hallucinating about CeCe?"

"The hallucination said he needed to go see Taylor and have a chat about the night CeCe died. The original story Taylor told Sinclair was that Toby never wanted to hurt his sister and had taken CeCe out into the swamp so she would have a nice view of Haven House from the water while he convinced her to reconnect with their family. That made complete sense to Sinclair. Hell, he was planning to build her a near replica of the place and knew how much Haven House meant to CeCe."

"So, ghost CeCe tells him Taylor did something bad, and to go talk to her, which he obviously did."

"Hold on, I want to read this part to you." He shuffled around more, sorting through something in the car. "Can you still hear me?"

"I can hear you."

"Okay, I'm going to read you some passages, but Jamison—don't repeat this to your dad. Or Simone. Or anyone, really. It'll probably never make it into any official file. And I think that might be for the best."

She didn't like the sound of that, but her curiosity was too great. "Let's hear it."

"Cecilia and I visited Haven House plenty, walking the trails and peeking up at the house through the trees. We would stop and visit with her sister and mother, who are buried in the graveyard. Cecilia never remembered much about her mother, but she remembered her sister. She would call her memories of Livy her sunshine memories because thinking of her always filled Cecilia with a sense of peace and happiness. Cecilia would complain how no one ever took care of the tombstones, and part of me wanted to believe the Fairweathers started cleaning up the graveyard after her death because Cecilia had finally come home."

Since she was lying on her back, the tears welling slid sideways out of the corner of her eyes. "That was a good way to describe Livy. I have about as many memories of her as I do of my mom, which is next to nothing, but I can remember very clearly the way Livy laughed. It was sweet and comforting, and thinking of it now tickles the edge of my brain."

He listened as she sniffled. "You're tired. We can talk about this tomorrow."

"No, keep reading. I'm fine."

"Before the day I saw her ghost, I'd made several trips to that graveyard. The first was right before Christmas, on the anniversary of her death. Ben and Evie Fairweather were there, talking and placing flowers on the markers. Cecilia has a nice marker, Mom. It's pretty and something I would've picked for her myself. Maybe they'll let you see it someday."

"These journals are written to his mother?" Jamison asked.

"Yeah, book one is almost an open confessional to her with things like, 'I'm sorry I never bathed the dog when I said I would,' or 'Sorry, I always told you I was at Bobby's when we were actually getting drunk behind the gas station.'"

It struck her how different CeCe and Michael's lives had been. Where CeCe hadn't lived in a world that could be called normal, Michael Sinclair's life had been the epitome of the word, at least in the beginning. Will had described Michael's life as the American dream gone wrong, and she was starting to see why.

"Let me hear more."

"When I first saw Cecilia's ghost (and yes, I am saying ghost), I thought I was insane. And maybe I am. People can call me whatever they want. I don't care. It was her. I would know the other half of my soul anywhere. I was sitting on the bench when she appeared, and the late afternoon sunlight shot through the trees, illuminating her perfectly. She was wearing her favorite dress and shaking out her hair in that way she always did. Her body would shimmer and fade in the light, and, Mom, I'm not at all embarrassed to say that I screamed. It wasn't manly in any way, shape, or form. Tell Dad if you want, and hopefully, you guys can have a laugh at my expense after I'm gone."

"The recognizing his soul part hurts. I didn't peg him as a romantic," she said, trying to break up this melancholy that had come over her suddenly. "But what section do you not want my dad to hear?"

"I'm getting there."

"Cecilia smiled and said hello, then proceeded to lecture me on taking care of myself and to stop the work Hayes kept arranging. I know what I

did was wrong, and I wouldn't have done it if I didn't believe the people who died weren't worth killing. I hope you and Dad can forgive me for the kids. I hate myself enough, but it's okay if you hate me a little, too."

Liam paused for a second to speak to Holden in the background, then came back on. "Okay. Where was I? Oh, here we go. *I cried while Cecilia yelled at me. She was so beautiful, but so angry. Other ghost people were watching and listening, all urging her to make me understand something, but I couldn't get exactly what it was. They stood on graves and weren't as solid as Cecilia, but I knew they were there. Some not from our time. Previous generations of Fairweathers, perhaps? A couple holding hands. Lots of women and children. One woman had a freckled face and wore a dress with embroidered flowers all over it. It reminded me of something grandma would sew."*

"That's not creepy at all," Jamison noted sarcastically. "I mean, we've always known the forest was a little spooky, but I don't know that I wanted to hear all those details."

"Oh, it gets better," Liam told her. "*Some of the apparitions were more modern. One girl had curly hair. Another was a blonde woman in all white, wearing something glowing green around her neck. I think that was Laura Jean Fairweather."*

A full-body chill rolled over Jamison.

"Laura Jean Fairweather?" she whispered. "No one has ever referred to my mother that way. And how would he know about the necklace? We kept that out of the media. We didn't want any more Zanmi members trying to steal it after Toby used it to freak us out."

"Sinclair probably saw a picture of it—"

"No. I had Rowan scrub every trace of it. I didn't tell you, but he wiped it from the police reports, too."

Liam made a soft *tsk* noise. "I'm so ashamed."

"No, you're not. Now keep reading!"

"Some ghosts stood by the fence looking out over Shepherd's Bayou. They felt more like shadows, with anger and hate radiating off them. Cecilia begged me to let go of my rage, or my fate would be the same. I'm sorry to say, that's when I lost it. She was dead and had come back to do what? Lecture me? She was the one who gave up on us. She gave up on me over an argument. I told her as much. She cried. I didn't know ghosts could cry. But

I told her I should have put Toby down long ago. It would have saved lives, including her own."

"In all fairness, Michael's not wrong."

Liam snickered in her ear. *"And Cecilia agreed with me and apologized. I hated when she did that. She always apologized for other people's bad behavior, and it was just one more symptom of the abuse she suffered for years. But when it came to Toby, it made me sick to think that she felt even the tiniest bit of responsibility for his actions."*

Jamison was quiet for a moment, then asked, "Do you think my mom's mother and brother ever met Taylor?"

"I was thinking about that. Do you remember the photo they gave us? The one of Toby standing with Judy and Nick in front of the Christmas tree? Who took the photo? I always assumed it was Judy's nurse, but she looked way too healthy in the picture. What if it was Taylor? They said Toby was a lady's man. Maybe Taylor's presence is what gave them that idea."

"I don't know how you remember all that."

"I have a big brain."

"And a big—"

Liam swiftly cut her off. "My phone is connected to the car's Bluetooth, Jamison."

Jamison winced. "Oh. Hey, Holden."

Will's chuckle carried through the background. "Maybe take her off speaker."

The connection clicked, and Liam's suppressed laughter was all she heard. "Hey."

"The gang's all there, huh? Try to warn me next time."

His laughter grew louder, and the sound warmed her from the inside out. "I didn't know you were going to toss out comments on my male anatomy."

"Maybe I was talking about your butt," she shot back, smirking. "So, keep reading to me, my big booty man."

"Yeah, I do have a nice ass. Okay, let me find my spot again." He adjusted the phone. *"Taylor's real name is Brandy Carroll. She uses her middle name and is not really married to Toby. They had some bullshit thing on a beach right after they killed Charlie Fairweather, but it's not legal. They made Cecilia stand as a witness with her father's blood still on* her. *The whole thing messed her up for years. But don't worry, Taylor will be dead by the time you read this. If she gets away from me, I have people in play who will finish the job. Our family is safe.*"

"His family is safe, but not ours," Jamison mumbled. "Is that it?"

"Not even close," Liam replied, and she could hear the excitement in his voice. "*Taylor's father is Bryan Carroll. I know you don't know who that is, but he's a very bad guy. I'm telling you this so you can protect yourself. We're going to handle him, too, but if we don't, call Hayes. He owes me.*"

"Hayes is the guy who was Michael's superior?"

"From what I understand, yeah."

Too keyed up to continue sitting on the ground, she stood with a sudden urge to try on her wedding dress. No one would know, and she could see if it still fit while she worked out all this new information in her head. "Get back to the ghost stuff."

"Alright, this is what I was looking for. *Cecilia's spirit said that when Toby showed up at our apartment, she told him about the fight we'd had, and Toby tried to use it as an opportunity to sway Cecilia to come with him. He had already made the move to Hollingsdale and was working at the hospital there with plans to reintroduce himself. Cecilia was pissed and asked how they were going to handle the whole Taylor thing. You see, Taylor works at Fairweather. She claimed it was so she could scope out the family, but Cecilia and I always thought that was bullshit.*"

"This sounds like most of what Michael told me in his room," Jamison said, trying to recall specifics. "But I thought he knew this information as facts and not something he made up."

"Patience, beautiful."

"Patience is not my strong suit."

"Don't I know it," Liam shot back before continuing to read. "*Toby then explained to Cecilia how he not only wanted to go home again, but how he wanted to be with Evie Fairweather. He was devoted to Taylor yet needed Evie to love him. I don't know why. He had basically accumulated a harem. Men and women. We've talked about this several times, Mom, but I want to reiterate to you, and to whomever else might one day read this, that Cecilia and I never participated or had anything to do with that weird ass shit.*"

"That's a very Michael thing to say. At least, I think it is after witnessing the type of personality he exhibited when it was just the two of us," she tried to explain. "Is there anything about the baby stuff?"

"Yeah, I'm just getting to that part," he murmured. *"Taylor worked for Samuel Fairweather, and when he moved north for a new project, she signed on to go with him. This was also around the same time she and Toby discovered that children were off the table. Taylor blamed Toby because nothing is ever her fault, and Cecilia was sympathetic. Taylor was Cecilia's rock for a big part of her life. They were best friends growing up together in the confined space of St. Thomas, and Cecilia felt as if she had no one else. Between all the shit she went through as a kid, then to have Toby as a brother and Taylor as a friend, I have no idea how my beautiful girl came out as sane as she did."*

Facing her wedding gown, Jamison smoothed the garment bag back from the dress. "But why all the insane drama to have a kid?"

"To put it bluntly, there was insane drama because Taylor is insane. If given the chance to study her, I bet we would have found not only narcissistic personality disorder, but probably a multitude of other mental health diagnoses."

Jamison thought of Albie and his perfect little face, with his perfect little toes and his perfect little everything. Taylor would have robbed them of him. She would have robbed them of the kids in the family, including Claudia's unborn baby. "Poor Claudia. Does Michael talk about Parker?"

"He does, and it's pretty much what Bruce told you. Parker was one of their lackeys and wanted to impress Taylor."

"I can't even imagine what's going through Claudia's head."

"Do you know how lucky we are with Madison?" Liam asked with a dark edge in his tone. "We're so fucking lucky judging by the timeline, and the only reason Taylor didn't try to run off with her is because she didn't deem Parker worthy enough in the beginning, making him constantly prove himself. But if Madison had been a boy? That would have been it. Sinclair goes on and on about how Taylor was never satisfied and wanted to have a mini-Toby."

Pausing in extracting the wedding gown's train, Jamison screwed her mouth tight. She had promised to be more forgiving in the future, hoping the new attitude might displace all the bad karma that continued to chase them.

But screw it. The universe could make an exception here.

"I'm glad that bitch is dead." Her bottom lip trembled, but she refused to cry over Taylor. "I hope Michael made her suffer."

And the beautiful thing about Liam was that he didn't judge her. Ever. "He did."

She gave a small, satisfied nod, as if he could see her. "Go on with the rest. Tell me about CeCe's ghost. Hearing it makes me feel less insane."

"In the journal, Sinclair goes on to claim that ghost CeCe tells him how Taylor is planning something awful and that he has to be the one to stop it. CeCe doesn't want people to get hurt, and it's right about then that Sinclair starts to realize what's happening isn't real. He freaks out, but when he tries to leave, CeCe stops him with a request. She says he needs to meet with Taylor and ask her a single question, and if Taylor gives him the answer that CeCe's supplies, then it would prove what he was hearing from her was true."

"What was the question?"

"CeCe wanted him to bring up Taylor having a Fairweather baby and ask her what she would name it. She then told him what Taylor would say."

"And Michael went and met with Taylor?"

"He was in the area, so yeah, he met her the next day."

"And he asked her the question?"

"Yes."

"Oh my God, William. You better tell me."

"Taylor said she loved the name Rachel for a girl and thought Dane would be a perfect name for a boy."

Remembering her talk with Taylor on the same subject, Jamison thought that perhaps she should sit back down. "He could have heard Taylor talking about kids' names before this. You said he and CeCe kept in touch, and if Taylor ran her mouth like we know she does, Michael could have already heard her say what baby names she liked."

"I think you're right," Liam replied. "It's easy to romanticize these journal entries, but really, there's nothing supernatural here. The tumor was distorting his reasoning, twisting his memories. The man was sick, and that's all there is to it."

She grinned at how pragmatic he could be at times. "I love it when you talk dirty to me."

"Just wait until I get back."

He yawned, and she almost said something since he'd been giving her grief for staying up late, yet he was doing the exact same thing every night, pacing the hotel hallways like a ghost himself.

"Sinclair was the one who leaked the blueprints to the guy who then sent them to your dad. Only he changed the large room on the second-floor to state that it was a nursery as a way to give a hint to what Taylor was planning."

"CeCe's library."

"What?"

"The room that's labeled on the blueprints as a nursery is actually a library he designed for CeCe." She sighed wistfully. "He said she had always wanted one."

"Hey, I thought we weren't romanticizing this. He would have let us die in that house."

"But do you have any idea why he would want to warn us if he didn't care?"

"He empathized with your dad," Liam admitted. "He'd studied what happened at Haven House back when CeCe was alive. And then there was Simone and Annabeth. He knew CeCe would never forgive him if they were hurt. Like on the night they tried the first kidnapping. Sinclair would have killed that Zanmi woman who attacked them if the forest hadn't done it first."

Michael had allowed Denise to die in the forest, whether it was by an animal or something else when he permitted her to lead the way through the dark trails. From what Jamison could recall, it had been horrific, but like with Taylor, she wasn't particularly upset about the woman's untimely death.

"Anything else good in the journal?"

"I wouldn't say good, exactly. I'm starting to think of these journals as the strangest example of hearsay in legal history."

Her heart fluttered as she traced a finger over her wedding gown's bodice. She loved this dress, and seeing it again helped diffuse her anger. "Can I just say that Taylor turning out to be the total evil bitch in this story proves how my intuition is always right?"

"I've never doubted you."

"Because you're brilliant. Now keep reading to me."

"Are you sure? It's late."

She chewed on her bottom lip and decided to give in to the impulse to try on the gown. "I'm in the closet playing dress up."

"Wedding gown?"

"You know me well."

"That I do."

She smiled, sliding her hands behind the satin train to free it from the bag. "Why us, though?" she asked. "Why was Taylor so weirdly freaking desperate to have a Fairweather baby?"

"Oh, you're going to love this. *With Toby's blessing, Taylor attempted to seduce Samuel so she could have a baby who would share DNA with Toby. Taylor is a disgusting monster that will allow anyone to do whatever they want with her body, but when it comes to things like having children, only someone with a worthy bloodline will do. Yes, Mom. I know you just snickered, but that's what I said. A worthy bloodline. This woman's father was spat out the back of a Roxbury alley, yet she feels the need to pretend like she comes from royalty. She's delusional, and so mentally unstable someone should have committed her a long time ago.*"

"Taylor thought the Fairweathers had a worthy bloodline? That's a joke, right?" Jamison's hands stilled as she worked on extracting her wedding dress from the garment bag. "And do you know how many criminals we have? Swindlers and thieves and God knows what else hanging on the branches of our family tree?"

"And let's not forget Carter's great-great-great grandmother, who was once a Fairweather and a murderess."

"Leave that poor woman out of this. I'm sure she had her reasons."

Chapter 47

Jamison

"**Y**ou went quiet on me."

"My dad took over driving, and I'm trying to read," Liam said. "But the old man is making me sick."

"I drive better than you," Will muttered in the background. "Not everything is a race, Liam."

Jamison grinned as she struggled with the zipper on her wedding dress. It was a little snug, but it fit. "Hold on, I'm putting you on speaker."

Setting the phone on the dresser, she zipped the gown the rest of the way and turned toward the full-length mirror on the closet door. It was hard to see everything in the tight space, but what she could see made her want to cry.

It was perfect.

"Are you there?" Liam asked.

She cleared her throat. "Yeah, I'm here."

"Did you put on the dress?"

"I did."

"I bet you're beautiful."

Shaking her hips, she danced around as much as she could, finding herself getting giggly at three o'clock in the morning. "I'm so ready to marry you."

"I'm holding you to it."

It was almost as if they were standing at the starting line of a new life. The years since Toby's return had been hell, and coming out the other side, she was starting to realize how truly awful it had been.

"When will you come home?"

Her father and Rowan both thought they could start easing back into regular life by the end of next week, which meant returning to Texas for her. But she didn't want to go without Liam.

Of course, Simone had been quick to point out that Christmas was right around the corner and that everyone should just stay at Haven House until the New Year.

"Sooner rather than later," Liam replied absently, his thoughts obviously occupied with the journals. "Listen to this. *Even though he was devoted to Taylor and hated Samuel, the truth is that Toby was fine with Taylor pursuing Samuel because he wanted Evangeline Fairweather. Obsessed isn't even a strong enough word. Cecilia always said Taylor tried to play it off like Toby was just nostalgic over his first love, but there was more to it, and looking back, I wouldn't be surprised if Toby had planned to keep Evie and get rid of Taylor.*"

"I don't think we'll ever know exactly what happened, will we?"

"All the players in the game are dead, and out of all of them, I would have wanted to talk to CeCe the most," Liam grumbled. "Sinclair said he started writing these journals because of her. Apparently, she journaled as a form of stress release, writing absolutely everything down. Her past, her present, and what she hoped for in the future. She was also very open with Sinclair and allowed him to read the entries. God, I'd love to get my hands on those."

Jamison thought of the closet full of CeCe's clothes. "CeCe's stuff was in the house, so I guess her journals went up in the blast?"

"Probably." Liam sighed with a laugh, drunk off his exhaustion. "Hey, do you think we could do a séance?"

He wanted answers. Liam needed a clear map in his mind of what exactly happened, and he would chip away at the information they had until he found it. She had a feeling these journals were going to become his new "hobby," and Jamison realized this must be what Bernie felt like when Will became fixated on a cold case.

"Very funny. I've had enough nightmares starring CeCe. Trust me, you don't want to talk to her," she replied, only half serious. "Does Michael talk about how he got into the group and his plans?"

Liam blew out a long exhale. "He wanted to do more than stop them. He wanted to burn the whole damn thing to the ground. When Sinclair met with Taylor, he told her he was sick and offered to help. They were basically family, after all, and her people had no organization. So he planned the wave of attempted kidnappings but used only his own men and made the operations deliberately sloppy to get Zanmi members caught. He was the one who sent the women to the houses. He tricked them into thinking it was a scare tactic—like they were putting on a show—before they were meant to grab you or Evie."

"But then, why did he warn us at the doctor's office?"

"Taylor planted the ultrasound tech. Sinclair had no idea until it was happening. He didn't care if Taylor snatched you, since your presence would only draw the other Zanmi members in. But Evie? Taking her would've been game over."

"Why did Taylor not go after Harper and Theo?" she asked, the thought of those people touching her nieces making her feel weak. "Oh my God. She did. The woman at Harper's school!"

"Without her father's full support, Taylor didn't have the means to pull off a full kidnapping. Her people were sexual deviants, not criminal masterminds. But yeah, I would assume that was one attempt. However, think about how Taylor was always doting on the girls. She was overly familiar with them, and since she once worked for Samuel, no one questioned it."

"You think she was grooming the girls to be comfortable with her, so when she tried to run off with them, they wouldn't put up much of a fight?"

"If the whole having a Fairweather boy thing didn't work out? Maybe." Liam released the groan he always made when stretching. "We're going off a bunch of assumptions here. We'll know more once Dad and I sit down and dissect these journals."

"Sinclair states several times how CeCe found peace in her writing, and that makes me feel that he wouldn't have allowed her journals to be destroyed," Will said in the background. "I bet we'll find them, eventually."

"Check the last few pages," Jamison suggested. "Every good story has a twist right at the end."

"Okay, hold on. Let me get the next journal." Liam's chin rubbed against the phone as he moved around. "This is the last section. *We didn't want to tell you, but Kris has wanted to leave Mark for a long time. The jackass got their secretary pregnant last year, and Kris has been hiding it from you and Dad. But then, somewhere in the middle of all that, she and Bruce came together. You know I love him like a brother. He'll take care of her and the boys.*"

"So, Sinclair family gossip. Got it." Jamison found her veil and fluffed the delicate material to secure it in her hair. "What else?"

"*I can't begin to tell you how much I love you and how sorry I am for everything. I wish I were a better man and a better son. I wish I could have been a husband and a father. That was how I convinced Taylor I wanted to help her in the first place. We talked about how much Cecilia and I wanted kids, and since she was gone and I was on my way out, I would help her with this one last thing to see that pieces of us lived on. Taylor already knew we wanted nothing except each other and a simple, quiet life in our own part of the world. I guess hearing me show my vulnerable side was all the convincing she needed.*"

Utterly still, Jamison stared at her reflection in the mirror, her heart breaking for a man who probably didn't deserve any sympathy. "That's so sad. Simone needs to hear this."

"*I would have made Cecilia happy, and I would have never stopped. I would have spent every day doing whatever I could to see her smile. And she loved you guys, Mom. Cecilia said you made her feel normal and at ease, which I can attest was not an easy thing to do. Her writings weren't confined to journals. She wrote letters of gratitude as well, and there are at least two dozen addressed to you. If you want to read them...*"

Liam paused, reading ahead again. "Son of a bitch," he hissed. "Son. Of. A. *Bitch*. He did save CeCe's journals."

"Where?" she shouted, along with Will and Holden.

"*If you want to read the letters, you can find them in a storage unit in Eureka Springs, along with some personal things I want you to have. The code to get in is the date I met Cecilia. If you can't remember it, you'll be able to find the information in a set of her personal journals that chronicled the years until she met me. I left them at Haven House. I thought it was fitting to keep them there.*"

The reflection before her gaped in shock. "Here? Where would he hide them here?"

"He doesn't say, but this is Sinclair," Liam replied. "I'm sure he's telling the truth, and we'll probably find them in the attic or library someday."

The urge to search nearly had her bolting from the closet. However, running around Haven House in the middle of the night while upending possible hiding spots was a sure way to piss off Simone.

"How does he close the final page?" Will asked. "Jamison is right. There's always a twist, and he would have provided his mother with a general idea of where to look."

"Let's not forget that Michael Sinclair has proven he has a flair for the dramatic," Holden added, sounding half asleep. "I bet the guy was an ass all the way up until the end."

Liam stayed silent, and Jamison, with the very limited patience granted to her, felt like she was about to burst as she waited. "Tell us, Liam! I know you're trying to analyze what you're reading before you say anything."

"This guy is dead, and he's still pissing me off," Liam growled. "It's just gibberish. *You can find the journals at the edge of the stone. Look for the shadows in the flower beds, and the beasts in the wilderness. Our secrets are with the ghosts who remain in the river.*"

"Graveyard? Or the mill?" she said, thinking aloud. "It's obviously outside, and I can go look—"

"No. You're not going anywhere near it," Liam ordered, and she heard a car door slam shut. "It's too dangerous, and Sinclair could have rigged the place."

"But then, why would he have sent his mother to retrieve them?"

Will grumbled loud enough for her to hear. "I agree with Liam. You need to wait until we can get someone in to take a look."

"Rowan and Selah are here. They can help. And Abe has some fancy equipment where he can find stuff underground—"

"No, Jamison. I want you to wait for me."

"But when will that be?"

"Soon."

Her eyes narrowed as she listened to the increased rate of his breathing. It almost sounded as if he were running. "What are you doing?"

There was a pause.

"Are you still in your wedding dress?"

"Well, yeah."

"I hope you're not overly superstitious." The closet door swung open, and Liam was there, his phone to his ear and a grin on his face. "Surprise."

She gasped, stumbling back a step. "You."

"Me." He smiled, his gaze sweeping over the dress. "I'm here."

Crying and stumbling through the mess, she reached him in seconds. They crashed together, lips colliding as the two of them tumbled out of the closet. Liam lifted her, and she wrapped her legs around his waist, burying her fingers in his hair.

"Did you drive all night?"

"Yes." He dropped onto the oversized corner chair with her still in his arms. "Door is locked."

Straddling him, she swept her hair over one shoulder so he could kiss down her neck. "And the cameras are off in the bedrooms."

Their mouths collided again, all teeth and tongue and need. She rocked against him, the movement wringing a growl from his chest. God, she craved more of that sound—so she did it again. And again, until they were both groaning from the friction.

He broke the kiss first, his ragged breathing matching her own. "Can I fuck you?"

Pulling his shirt off and then going for his pants next, she tossed his belt aside. "That's the general idea here."

"No." A grin edged the corner of his mouth. "I want to fuck you in the dress, but I don't want to mess it u—"

"Now, Liam."

Reaching under her skirt, he tore her panties clean off. "Now, works for me."

She nearly laughed, but then his mouth was back on hers—hot, consuming, unrelenting—and she forgot everything except the sharp burn of need between them and the maddening feel of his hands roaming over her waist.

"Jesus, baby," Liam groaned, leaning back to lift his hips as she shoved his pants and underwear down. "Come up here and sit on my face. Let me get you ready."

Back in position, she grinded against him, letting his cock slide along her soaked entrance. Arching her spine, she moaned, her body begging to be filled. "I can take it."

Since the wedding dress was short, they could both watch as she lined him up, inch by inch, sinking deeper with a controlled glide. Liam's grip on her hips flexed, the veins in his arms and hands popping.

"*Fuck.*" Lips parted, and eyes locked on the way her body took him so perfectly, he groaned in a way that had a shiver running through her. "You're so tight, baby. I don't want to hurt you. Go slow."

She whimpered, already moving. "I think not."

Bracing her hands on his shoulders, she rode him in a hungry, relentless rhythm. The wide seat of the reading chair gave her the leverage needed, and Liam didn't make her do it alone. His hands clamped onto her hips, thrusting upward in hard, controlled bursts that made the whole chair rock.

He was beautiful beneath her, the muscles of his body straining to give her what she needed. "Such a greedy fucking girl," he rasped, his words punctuated by the brutal pump of his cock when she picked up her pace. "Is this what you wanted?".

She moaned, her cries building with the orgasm that felt like fire under her skin. Releasing his grip on one hip, he pressed his hand against her lower stomach, allowing the pad of his thumb to rub circles on her clit until she was bucking uncontrollably.

And when the pleasure struck with an unparalleled intensity, she shook against him, clenching hard and fast. "Oh my God—*Liam*—"

"There it is." He growled against her neck when she bowed forward to scream against his skin. "That's what I want. That's all I fucking want."

Still panting, still trembling, she didn't resist when he stood with her in his arms and turned to lay her on her back on the plush rug. Her legs opened for him instinctively, and he kneeled between them, his hands rough on her thighs as he pulled her closer.

"My wife," Liam breathed, sinking back into her in one long, heavy roll of his hips. "Forever, Jamison. You're going to stand under that oak tree and swear to be—*fuck*," his breath caught as he filled her completely, *"you feel so good."*

Absolutely wild for him, she held on tight when he pumped into her like a man possessed—sharp, fast, feral—he took her savagely. All control lost, his moans filled the room, the sound holding a whisper of agony as he truly let himself go.

"I'm going to come so fucking hard." His voice shook from the heavy pounding he was giving her, the limits to his sanity snapping one by one. "Are you going to take it?"

She opened her legs wider, allowing him to do whatever he wanted—take her as hard as he wanted. She was completely his, deliciously at his mercy. "Yes."

"Are you going to be my wife?" He never paused in his rhythm, his gaze locked on her parted lips. "Today?"

"Yes." She was already crying again, her body bouncing hard under him. "Yes!"

"Right *fucking* no—" His voice broke, the words cut off by a shout. Pushing up on one arm, he pressed her thigh aside so he could watch her squeeze around him as he spilled into her. "You take me so fucking good. God, *too* good... too *fucking* good."

She couldn't form words, not when her whole body was convulsing again with a second orgasm, not when he was falling apart above her, swearing and filling her with everything he had.

"I'm marrying you right now. Right *fucking* now," he whispered, his body shaking from the pleasure rolling through him. "I will not greet another sunrise without you as my wife."

She pulled him down on top of her, needing his warmth. When his thrusts turned shallow, they kissed—slow, lingering kisses, messy from tears and sheer exhaustion. His hand cupped her face, his thumb stroking her bottom lip. "I meant what I said," he whispered. "Today, Jamison."

"Hmm?" She was melting into him, boneless and dazed. "Today?"

"Not another sunrise." His fingers trailed from her jaw to the neckline of her gown. "I hope the dress isn't too wrinkled, but, really, who cares? Let's go."

"Go wher—" She didn't finish. He was already up, leaving her empty and sprawled on the floor as he tugged on his pants. "Liam?"

"I have one rule," he said, snatching up his phone. "No underwear. I want you completely naked under that dress."

She snorted. "That's kind of kinky, and I like it, but you can't be serious about this whole before sunrise thing."

He was already dialing. "Hey, Abe. You're up? No? Well, you're up now. Do you still have the ceremony you wrote for me and Jamison? Yes, our wedding ceremony. Can you print it and meet us under the Marriage Oak? Yep, right now. Cool. I'll start waking everyone up."

"Waking everyone..." She scrambled to a sitting position. "Liam!"

He smirked as he made another call. "Hey, fucker. Get over here. I'm marrying your sister in half an hour and need a best man. No, I don't care what time it is. You'll survive. See, Evie's up, and I hear the girls. Yep, that's right, Theo. Unc is going to be Uncle, so get your dad up."

She stared at him, the shock and excitement growing. "Really? Right this very second?"

"You should probably pull your skirt down first, but yeah." He crossed the room and dropped to one knee, his grin softer now. "Jamison Scarlett Fairweather, will you marry me right this very second?"

"It won't be legal."

"It will be when we march our asses down to the licensing office the second they open."

She laughed through her tears. "Are you sure?"

"Why not?" He stood and took her hands in his. "Life is about to go back to normal, and when it does, we'll have to work around everyone's schedules, which will delay the wedding, and we'll have to wait again.

"I don't want to wait."

"I don't either. I'm done waiting. I feel like I've been waiting my whole life to make you mine, and I'm not going to wait any longer."

"Okay." She nodded, then threw her arms around him, giddy and glowing. "Let's get married."

CHAPTER 48

Rowan

“They really stole the journals?”

“It’s more like they borrowed them, made copies, and ran.” Lying on her side, with him wrapped tightly around her, Annabeth sighed. “So, they should be here soon?”

Rowan’s phone buzzed—a motion alert triggered from the highway turnoff leading to Haven House. There were still a few local and federal agents stationed along the gravel drive and at the gate, but not many. Most of the official security presence had pulled out once Anderson gave the all-clear.

“Liam wanted to surprise Jamison, and I think this is them.” Rowan angled the phone so she could see the live feed. “Yep. Look.”

Will was behind the wheel of the car Liam had stolen from the hospital. The cops had found it, and the Cohens had promised to return it to the distraught woman, even though Ben had thrown enough money at her she could have bought two cars by now.

Talking on his phone, a tired Liam sat in the passenger seat, and Holden appeared to be half asleep in the back. The three of them had taken turns driving, with both Will and Liam in a rush to return.

They would need to finalize which Fairweather guards would be assigned to which areas in the morning. With Anderson giving the signal that there was no longer a great enough threat to merit a federal detail, the local PD agreed. But needing extra support, for the time being, Rowan had borrowed a few temporary security personnel from his brother.

McIntyre Industries had plenty to spare, and Killian offered his best. Men who had been with their family for over two decades.

Rowan sent the McIntyre men to watch over Emily, Claudia, and Damon until suitable Fairweather security people could be found to fill the permanent position.

And it would be permanent.

Carter was with Evie and Samuel until Holden returned. Even though he was new, Carter was getting along with the family—including Samuel—but the girls missed "Holden the Hero."

Izzy had stuck close to Jamison. She and Abe moved into one of the downstairs bedrooms to stay nearby. Judging by how things were progressing in that relationship, it would seem that Haven House might be Izzy's permanent spot.

During one of his late-night chats with Simone, she confessed how much she liked Izzy. And yes, Rowan was proud to say he had moved up in the world and was now having nightly chats with Simone. They would sit in the kitchen alone while she sipped tea before bed. She claimed the chamomile and conversation soothed her nerves, and he'd been more than happy to have the chance to get to know her better. They talked about his life and growing up at Adare Hall. She wanted to know every detail regarding his parents and siblings.

"From what I've surmised, your brother is the muscle, you are the brains, and your sister is the fire that keeps both you boys in line," she had said just last night. "Am I correct?"

He'd never considered it, but the description was accurate. Sipping at his lemon and ginger tea, the flavor he'd learned he enjoyed the most, Rowan had nodded. "Killian is both brains and brawn, technically. But yeah. I'm smarter. And if you love me like I know you do, you'll tell him as much when he comes to visit next week."

Rowan yawned and closed out the security app once Liam and the rest of them were inside Haven House. "Let's get some sleep. The sun will be up soon."

Annabeth wiggled her naked butt against him. "Or we could do something else."

"Sweetheart, you have to let me rest." He pulled her around to face him, willing his gaze not to drop to her breasts. Their power held no limits, and he did actually need sleep. "Just for an hour. Tops."

Running her hands along his chest, she kissed him, her tongue teasing his lips. "Fine, but I want three more orgasms before sunrise."

"You've had seven since we came upstairs."

"Eight, actually." She sucked his bottom lip between her teeth. "You were too busy having your own in the shower to notice."

He couldn't stop his grin. "I think we have a problem. This can't be normal."

"Who the hell wants normal?"

Not him. Not ever. Not with her.

He pulled her across his chest, content to feel her heartbeat against his ribs. "I was looking at some dog rescue sites today."

From the cat bed in the corner, curled around his own female companion for the night, Colonel Brandon let off an offended growl.

"You have no say in this," Rowan told the cat. "And frankly, I think you need a new room to sleep in. It creeps me out that you watch me fuck your mom."

Annabeth giggled into his neck, laying kisses there as he continued to have a glaring contest with The Colonel. "And did you see any dogs that interested you?" she asked.

"As a matter of fact, I did. A golden retriever mix was surrendered yesterday when its elderly owner died. She's about two years old and trained."

"Let me see her."

His glare at Colonel Brandon morphed into an evil smirk, and Rowan grabbed the phone again to show Annabeth the website. The kennel staff had placed pink bows on the dog's ears, and he knew that alone would convince her.

Annabeth squealed. "Look at her! She is so ours. Can we go tomorrow? Wait—what if someone beats us there?" She hugged the phone to her chest. "Should we call and leave a message so when they open, they'll know we're her parents?"

Dog parents.

Yeah, he could go with that.

"The staff said she loves playing dress up."

Annabeth's eyes went wide. "Shut. Up."

"Her name is Beatrice, but they call her Bea."

"Beatrice McIntyre sounds very distinguished." She held the phone in the air so they could both see her picture. "We can call her our little Busy Bea."

"I've got a bigger Harley in storage down in Texas and was planning on bringing it here once things quieted." He took the phone from her to sit on the nightstand once more, sneaking himself a kiss in the process. "We can buy one of those sidecars specifically made for dogs to take her riding."

"That sounds perfect," she sighed, placing a hand on his cheek as their kiss deepened. "And you will eventually have to marry her mother."

"Her mother isn't interested in marriage." He smiled against her lips. "She's told me so. In many ways, and on multiple occasions."

The hand on his cheek slid down, diving beneath the blanket until she literally held him by the balls. "I said I'm allowed to change my mind."

"Are you?" Risking the lives of their possible future children, he arched an eyebrow. "That nonsense sounded pretty convincing out there in the cottage, and I could chalk up your quick change of heart to the excitement and stress brought on by the rescue."

"I will hurt you, Randall."

"Randall?" He rolled on top of her as she squealed. "Oh, now you've done it."

"That was easy." Opening her legs, Annabeth smirked in victory. "You may give me my orgasms now." She clapped her hands twice. "Post haste."

He had never seen anything more beautiful. Staring down at her, he knew without a doubt that the end of his line was here. Until his dying day, he would never know a moment without this woman in his heart, and it made him believe that perhaps there was a higher power, a cosmic force linking them together in some grand scheme.

"I'm going to make you so happy, Annabeth Howard."

"You better," she whispered, rubbing her nose against his. "Or I'll sic my mama on you."

"That's actually fucking terrifying."

Lowering his head, they kissed with laughter and the promise of happiness in their future. But the longer they lingered, the more fevered the strokes of their tongues became until—

"Annabeth?" A loud knock rattled the door, followed by Liam's voice: "Get out here. Jamison needs her bridesmaid."

Disentangling himself from Annabeth's arms, Rowan marched across the room butt ass naked, thinking he might just swing the door open wide to teach Liam a lesson about knocking on doors in the middle of the night.

But he held the urge back, cracking the door open to see a shirtless, grinning Liam with Jamison slung over his shoulder and wearing a wedding gown so short, Rowan could see all the way up to the backs of her upper thighs.

"We need Annabeth."

Already up and in her closet, Annabeth hustled into some clothes. "What's going on?"

"We're getting married." Jamison lifted her upper body to wave at Annabeth. "Can you help me find a few things?"

Running over, Annabeth frowned. "What are you going on about?"

She opened the door further, and Rowan had just enough time to step aside and grab a giant stuffed bear propped in a corner to cover his crotch. Colonel Brandon watched him struggle with evil glee, his tail waving when Rowan flipped the beast off.

"We're getting married," Liam told Annabeth. "Abe is meeting us under the oak in a few minutes, and Samuel is on his way with his brood."

"I need my lanterns," Jamison said, tapping Liam's shoulder. "Let me down?"

"Sure thing." Liam lowered her to stand. "I should probably put on a shirt."

Jamison smacked a kiss on his mouth. "Or don't. I'm cool with marrying a hot, shirtless man."

"Whatever the lady wants, she gets. I need to go wake everyone up." Liam planted another kiss on Jamison's lips before backing away. "I'll meet you under the oak."

He disappeared down the stairs, eyes on Jamison the whole time, who was watching him go with a sigh. "I'm so ready for this."

"Could you be ready during—oh, I don't know—the daylight hours?" Annabeth asked, pulling Jamison into the room. "Are you serious about this?"

"One hundred percent."

Annabeth huffed in disapproval and straightened the lopsided veil hanging precariously from Jamison's hair. "Fine. But you're letting me fix your hair, and we're doing the ceremony like we planned, or you'll regret it."

"I knew I could count on you." Jamison hugged her while Annabeth continued to work. "I love you."

"I love you too, you ridiculous woman." Giving up on the veil, Annabeth hugged her back. "Rowan, I'm going to need you to go into the guest room at the end of the hall. We have some lanterns in there with small, tapered candles. Can you grab them and take them to the kitchen?"

With his brain catching up, Rowan cleared his throat. "As soon as I put some clothes on."

Both women turned to him, and Jamison smirked. "Sorry, Rowan. I guess we can count this as my bachelorette party."

"Give me some privacy," he deadpanned. "Or I'm dropping the bear."

"We're good with that." Jamison tucked herself under Annabeth's arm. "Nice thigh tat, by the way."

"Come on." Annabeth dragged her into the hall. "We've got work to do."

Once the door shut, Rowan shook his head and pulled on a pair of black joggers and a T-shirt. If he needed to wear anything else, Annabeth would tell him.

And that thought alone made him pause to smile like a complete idiot. He and Annabeth would be doing this one day, and their happiness would make them act just as ridiculous as Jamison and Liam were acting now.

Only they'd have the decency to have a wedding ceremony in the afternoon.

Dressed, he stepped into the hallway, where Annabeth and Jamison were in full planning mode.

"Is what I'm wearing good?" he asked.

"It works because you're my muscle." Totally in her element, Annabeth pointed down the hall. "I also need the four candelabras that are stored in the second to last bedroom and the box of candles on the bed. Oh, and do you know when sunrise should start?"

Pulling his phone from his pocket, Rowan checked. "In about an hour and a half."

"Perfect!" Annabeth took Jamison's hand and led her back into her bedroom. "We can begin when it's dark to have that candlelight ambiance, and then—*bam*—the sun rises over the bayou and illuminates the Marriage Oak from behind while you say your wedding vows."

"Oh my God, you're a genius," Jamison gushed, one hand on the poor veil as they ran off. "What would I do without you?"

"Ruin everything," Annabeth said matter-of-factly. "I'm the visionary in this family."

The bedroom door slammed shut, and Rowan stood there for a second. Lanterns. He needed to start with the lanterns, and heading into the guest room, he found four of them easily enough. The candelabras were there also, but between them, the box of candles and the lanterns, it would take two trips.

When he returned to the hall, the sounds of feminine laughter were coming through the closed door of Annabeth's room, and he allowed himself a second to listen. It was good to hear. This house had held enough of this family's pain, and he imagined it was nice for Haven House to finally experience their joy once again.

And he would see to it that happiness would always be the way of things here. His Annabeth deserved nothing less.

Halfway to the stairs, he froze when a herd of women came barreling up. Wisely, he stepped aside, letting Lenora, Izzy, and Bernie pass. Moving at a slower pace, Simone brought up the rear, stopping to speak to him while the others went ahead into Annabeth's room.

"Lanterns? Her sharp gaze took in his clothing. "Four total?"

He held them up. "And the candles, but I still have to go back for the candelabras."

"In the jewelry box on my dresser is a small platinum ring with diamonds spread across the band. Jamison will wear it for her something borrowed," Simone told him, hurrying through what needed to be done. "Ben is going to his house for a bracelet that belonged to Laura Jean. That'll be the something old. Will's trying to find something of Bernie's to work as the something blue. The dress is the something new. I think that's everything. Isn't it?"

"Simone?"

She snapped out of her thoughts to blink up at him. "Yes, Rowan?"

"You're an amazing woman, and the best mother to these girls."

Her fingers fluttered to her throat. "What's gotten into you?"

"Nothing," he said, giving her a wink as he continued down the stairs. "Just thought you should know."

❧❧❧❧❧ ❧❧❧❧❧

"Put on a shirt." Samuel tossed a dark blue button-up at Liam. "You look like an idiot standing there in nothing but your jeans."

Yet to stop smiling, Liam swiped the shirt over his head. "Are my abs too much for you this morning?"

"I have best man privileges." Samuel glared at his friend, still pissy about being woken up in the middle of the night. "I'm allowed to punch you without repercussions."

"I don't think that's how it works," Holden drawled, snacking on an apple in the corner. "And let's be honest. His abs are spectacular. I'd marry him."

"Good to know I've got backup." Liam searched for something on the floor near the back door. "I probably should put some shoes on."

After setting everything up outside, Rowan returned to find the men gathered in the kitchen. Abe was flipping through his ceremony notes while the rest gave Liam a hard time over the impulsive decision. No one except Liam was in actual clothes. Everyone had on what would be considered their pajamas, the entire group running around in sweatpants and T-shirts.

Jamison was still upstairs, but if the plan was to hit sunrise, they needed to get moving.

"Okay, does everyone know what they're supposed to do?" Will held up his hands to silence the room. "Abe and I will go out first."

Abe glanced up, his leg bouncing nervously. "I'll need help with my chair, Will. It gets stuck on this one section of exposed root."

"I can handle it," Will replied. "Xavier, you can come with us in case I need extra muscle."

Still in his favorite Spider-Man pajamas, Xavier saluted him. "Yes, sir!"

"Liam, you'll come too and bring your mom across the yard." Will pointed at Samuel. "You'll follow and stand next to Liam while we wait for the girls to come down."

Samuel shook his head. "No. I need to wait for Evie and help her walk. There's a chair for her, right? I don't want her standing long."

"I set up a few folding chairs," Carter told them. "I've also directed the guards to spread out and stay at the front of the house to give a little privacy. I'll hang back by the path next to the side porch to watch as you guys do your thing."

"Thank you, Carter." Ben didn't look up, too busy working on the latch of a diamond tennis bracelet Jamison was to wear. "We appreciate the help and watchful eye."

The tiny bundle sighed in his arms, and Rowan snuggled a sleeping Albie against his chest. After coming back inside, he'd been assigned baby duty and didn't mind in the slightest. "Who's taking pictures?" he asked.

Will glanced at Selah, but Samuel quickly spoke up. "Oh, no. Selah is in charge of the music. Abe, where's that Bluetooth speaker you use when working in the front garden? The big circular one?"

"In the library." Abe closed his notebook and secured it in his lap. "But it's loud with lots of bass. We can use something smaller."

Samuel and Selah fist bumped with twin smirks on their faces. "Perfect," Samuel said. "We want it loud."

"Do we even need music?" Liam asked, now slipping into someone else's sneakers. "Jamison and I never really settled on a song."

"Don't worry about it." Selah shared a grin with Samuel. "Sammy and I have got this."

Ben stopped what he was doing to frown at them. "What does that mean?"

"Nothing," the brothers said in unison.

Ben didn't look convinced.

"Nothing she didn't ask for," Selah clarified.

"Let's just say we're good brothers," Samuel added. "And we always keep our promises."

"I don't trust your dad," Rowan whispered to Albie. "He's kind of shady."

Albie didn't respond, only giving him another sweet sigh. Rowan traced a finger along his cheek, careful not to wake him. Kids had never been on his radar, but thinking about having them with Annabeth had him not hating the idea.

The soft shuffle of Simone's house shoes came from the hallway, and all the men went quiet when she entered the kitchen. Somehow, she was already more put-together than she had been minutes earlier.

"We're ready," she announced, surveying the room like a general preparing for battle. "Liam, tuck in your shirt. Xavier, get a jacket. Ben, you're wearing two different shoes. Samuel, do something about that hair—it's sticking up in the back. Selah, find better pants. Spider-Man is fine for your son, but not for you."

As they all scrambled to obey, Simone turned to Will. "I've been instructed to make sure you have your glasses. I see that you do not. Please fix that."

"Oh, yeah." Will hurried off to the guest rooms to find his glasses and returned in seconds wearing them. "That is better."

Simone turned next to Carter. "Thank you for setting up the chairs."

"You're welcome, ma'am." Carter straightened under her approval. "I'm going to head out to make sure all the candles are lit."

Carter slipped out the back kitchen door, slapping a hand on Liam's shoulder as he left. Rowan didn't know the exact history between them, but it was clear their families went way back.

Simone turned to him. "My grandson is swaddled tight and warm?"

"Yes, ma'am."

"And you're sure you're fine holding him? Josie has Harper, I have Theo, Lenora's with Xavier. If you're not comfortable, we can switch things up."

Rowan grinned down at Albie. "We're friends now. I've got this."

With a nod, Simone turned her attention to Holden. "Josie said you're taking pictures?"

"Yes, ma'am." Holden smiled around a bite of apple. "I'm your guy."

"Well, then I guess we're ready." Simone clapped her hands together once. "Get into position. Ben, you're with me. It's time to bring the bride down."

As everyone left to go either outside or upstairs, Samuel came over to check on Albie. "Let me see if he's warm enough." He fiddled with the baby blankets. "Wait until the last minute to bring him out. If it's too cold, come back in. Or signal me, and I'll take him."

"We're going to be fine." Rowan scanned the kitchen for a diaper bag. "If he gets hungry, though... do I have like a bottle or something?"

"I'm the bottle," Evie said, coming into the kitchen and looking radiant in a lavender halter dress. "And there's a chair for me, right?"

"There is," Samuel mumbled, having frozen when his wife walked in. "That color... *uh*, looks really good on you."

Evie fluffed her long, wavy hair to fan out across her shoulders, smirking at her husband. "You're staring at my boobs, Samuel."

He was, and Samuel didn't bother to deny it. "Sorry."

"No, you're not."

"You're right," Samuel sighed, now openly staring. "I'm definitely not."

Josie entered with Harper in tow, and Simone followed with Theo. "Let's go, you two," Josie ordered Samuel and Evie before turning to Rowan. "You sure you're good with Albie?"

"If I'm not, I'll hand him to one of you."

Albie's grandmothers, parents, and sisters hesitated for a second, but then the group must have collectively decided he was going to be fine with the newest Fairweather and left.

Lenora and Izzy came rushing through next, with Lenora pausing to check on Albie. "I can take him if you need me to?"

Rowan smiled. "I've got him."

"Is Abe already outside?" Izzy asked. "There's a massive root under the oak that catches his wheel. I want to make sure he doesn't have any issues setting up."

"All the guys are out there already. I'm sure they've got it."

Izzy made a noise, and Rowan couldn't tell if what he had said was okay with her or not, but the two women were out the door, rushing off to see if they could help.

Annabeth came in last, wearing the same dress as Evie, and Rowan's jaw dropped.

"Good God."

"Jamison knows how to pick out a dress." Doing a quick glance down the hall to make sure no one was there, Annabeth shimmied for him. "I forgot how good my boobs look in this."

"Jesus, Annabeth," Rowan whispered, utterly mesmerized. "Not in front of the baby."

She squeezed his butt, knowing he couldn't reciprocate due to being the responsible baby-holding adult in the room. "You're keeping that dress on until I take it off you," he growled when she arched up on her toes for a kiss. "Understand?"

Her teeth grazed his bottom lip. "I understand. Are the lanterns outside?"

"They are." He tried to deepen the kiss, but she stayed just out of reach. "Oh, it's like that, huh?"

"It is." She smacked his ass on the way out. "I'm going to check the setup. See you outside."

The woman had the nerve to swish her full hips as she left, and Rowan exhaled slowly, trying to will his thoughts into more respectable territory.

But when this was over, she was getting bent right the fuck over while wearing that dress.

Ben escorted Jamison into the kitchen not long after Annabeth left. Bernie was behind them, still wrestling with the veil that just wouldn't stay put. The wedding dress was like nothing Rowan had ever seen, but, to be fair, he wasn't exactly well-versed in bridal fashion.

He grinned. "You clean up nice."

Jamison practically glowed. She was already a stunning woman, but like this? Poor Liam didn't stand a chance.

"And you look good holding a baby," she pointed out. "Are we ready?"

Bernie winced at the veil. "I'll go check."

The back door had been left partially open, and Bernie slipped through it, letting the screen door creak softly behind her. When things had calmed down, bringing back the screen door had been Simone's first demand, and Rowan had hung it back up just that morning.

"You look beautiful, Princess."

"Thank you, Daddy."

Ben had tears in his eyes, and as soon as Rowan realized this, he made his way across the kitchen to allow father and daughter some privacy.

"I'm going to find a spot near Evie, so I can hand off this little guy when it's time."

He was careful not to let the screen door slam on his exit. It was about time to replace the thing, and he made a note to see if Annabeth wanted to try going to a hardware store with him later in the week. One of the sinks upstairs also needed an updated faucet since it was beginning to drip. He could easily fix it; he only needed a few parts and some tools.

Then there was that cracked board on the side porch, and some of the stucco around a column looked like it was about to go, so he should get supplies for that, too.

Thinking through the to-do list, he paused on the walkway leading to the Marriage Oak. The candelabras lit the way, but sunrise was readying itself to begin, and Rowan turned to face Haven House, an idea striking.

"Yeah," he said to himself and Albie, who was now staring at him as if trying to figure out just who the hell was holding him. "That would work."

Haven House deserved to be loved. It deserved a long life where those who lived within her walls felt safe. It deserved laughter and peace where children could play, and dogs ran around in the yard. An existence where there were always one too many books on the library shelves and where you could spend stormy afternoons in the conservatory watching the rain fall. Cats should forever be sunbathing in the windows, and plants should always fill every empty corner.

Haven House deserved to be lived in again. Its fate should be one filled with happiness.

And maybe it shouldn't be the Fairweathers who held it any longer. Maybe their time here had come and gone. Sure, Simone owned Haven House in name, but the Fairweathers financially maintained it, and maybe that shouldn't be the case.

Maybe it was time for a changing of the guard.

Bernie hustled past him. "We're bringing Jamison down now."

Rowan nodded, eyes still on Haven. "Come on, Albie. Let's go get your aunt married."

Albie was asleep again by the time they reached the gathering spot under the oak. Rowan found a place on the direct opposite side of the aisle from Lenora and Selah, who stood with Xavier as he held up a speaker. Not far from them, Annabeth and Evie waited with glowing lanterns while Holden moved around the group, snapping photos with his phone.

Theo and Harper also held matching lanterns, with Theo dancing to music only she could hear. Simone sat with Josie—in the front row, of course—and Will sat in one of the two chairs on what Rowan would guess was the groom's side.

And there, beneath the branches of the Marriage Oak, stood Liam. Samuel and Abe flanked him, but his attention was fixed solely on Ben escorting Jamison across the lawn.

"Wait! Let me start the music," Selah shouted loud enough for his father and sister to hear several yards away. "X-Man, hold it up!"

Xavier raised the speaker high, and the quiet night was filled with music. The song choice made Rowan snort. "Is that the Twilight soundtrack?" he whispered to Albie. "Yeah, that's it. My little sister went through a vampire phase, and I would know that song anywhere."

Even in the partial dark, Rowan could see Ben cracking up and Selah beaming with pride at his musical selection. Samuel wasn't much better, swaying weirdly as he yelled across the yard at his sister. "A promise is a promise, Jamison."

"I love it!" she shouted back.

Theo and Harper went first, their metal lantern clanging loudly. Rowan noticed neither had an actual candle, but rather fake ones that banged around behind the glass. In their pockets were fake flower petals, which the girls sprinkled as they went, creating a crooked path for others to follow.

Once Harper and Theo completed their task, Xavier sat the speaker on the ground and made his way down to stand next to Samuel. Annabeth and Evie were next, walking side by side with their lanterns, and even though the setting probably wasn't exactly what Jamison likely had planned out in her mind with a beach wedding, the whole thing was coming off pretty nice in Rowan's opinion.

"Okay, little man," he whispered to Albie when Evie sat in her chair next to Josie. "It's time to go back to your mom."

Sneaking over, Rowan handed Albie off to Evie, carefully moving around Holden taking pictures and Izzy filming the entire thing. Evie mouthed her thanks, and he returned to his spot just as Jamison reached the point where their makeshift aisle of candelabras and petals thrown about by Theo began.

The music switched to a slower tune—still from the Twilight soundtrack—and while he'd been to plenty of weddings in his life, Rowan had to admit he had never seen a bride and groom stare at each other as intensely as Liam and Jamison were currently staring at one another now.

Above them, an easy gust of wind tangled with the moss dangling from the oak's branches, and Rowan noticed how the air suddenly held a particular scent he couldn't quite place. Something floral for sure, and maybe with a hint of vanilla as well. In her chair, Evie closed her eyes briefly and lifted her face to the breeze, allowing it to sweep through her hair before moving through the crowd to Jamison, where it caught her veil and lifted it to flow behind her.

Rowan smiled at how the moment came off as enchanting.

Enchanting.

That was it.

Enchanting was the word he'd been looking for this whole time. Annabeth had once called Haven House magical, but that wasn't it. Magic wasn't real. Magic belonged to fairy tales and bedtime stories, but this wasn't a fairy tale. This was the real world.

But enchanting? He glanced back at Haven House. Yeah, that was more like it. Haven House was enchanting, even with all her faults. She beguiled any who entered, leaving them with the memory of her to carry through life.

For better or for worse.

Ben stepped aside when he and Jamison reached Liam and took a seat, his own hair becoming ruffled in the dancing breeze. He wasn't hiding his tears, swiping at them as Simone leaned in, resting her head on his shoulder.

Jamison didn't have a bouquet, immediately taking Liam's hands once Abe began his speech. And when it came time for the vows, neither the bride nor the groom needed notes, both obviously having memorized what they wanted to say.

Liam spoke first, his voice rough with emotion. "Jamison, too many years ago, I walked through the door of Haven House not expecting to find the most beautiful woman ever to exist waiting there. From the moment I tripped my way over to you, I knew you were meant to be mine. You are the other half of me, the piece that makes me whole, and I will never allow a day to pass where I don't show you how much I love you."

Bouncing on her toes with excitement, Jamison smiled through her tears. "Liam, from the moment you came to Haven House, I knew you were made only for me. You might have tripped, but I was the one who tumbled. I tumbled straight off a cliff and into love with you. You're my best friend, the love of my life, and my always. The years will pass, and we'll change and grow old together, but at our core... we'll always be us. Soulmates."

Abe took a deep breath, his ceremony notes at the ready. "Okay, repeat after me. I, William, take you, Jamison, to be my wife—to have and to hold from this day forward, for better, for worse, for richer, for poorer, in sickness and in health, until death do us part. This is my solemn vow."

Samuel passed the ring into Liam's waiting palm, and with his eyes never leaving his bride, Liam repeated the vow as he slid the band onto Jamison's finger. "I, William, take you, Jamison, to be my wife—to have and to hold from this day forward, for better, for worse, for richer, for poorer, in sickness and in health..."

Abe's eyes went wide. "You forgot a part," he whispered loudly. "Say until death do us part. This is my solemn vow."

The first rays of sunrise lit the horizon behind them, casting shades of pink and purple with just a smidge of burnt orange through the trees. The growing light illuminated the Marriage Oak, giving it an otherworldly glow that seemed to rise from the giant tree's roots.

"I didn't forget it." Liam shook his head. "I've been waiting far too long to make this woman mine, and death sure as hell isn't going to keep me from her." His grin widened when Jamison's bottom lip began to tremble. "This is my solemn vow."

"Uh, okay." Abe shifted to face Jamison. "It's your turn, Jamison."

Abe ran through the vows for Jamison to repeat, and just as Liam had, she omitted the until death do us part line. Crying when finished, she spoke the last part loud and clear.

"This is my solemn vow."

"Then by the power vested in me as soon as the County Clerk's office opens," Abe said, closing his notebook. "I now pronounce you husband and wife. You may now kiss the... *oh, my God*, Jamison. Let me finish!"

Falling into Liam's arms, Jamison kissed her husband like they'd already lived a thousand lives together. Like this moment was just the next chapter in a story they would never stop writing.

Applause broke out, and as everyone cheered, Rowan caught Annabeth's gaze. They would be the next to stand under the Marriage Oak. The next to swear their eternal love for one another right here at Haven House.

Life with her would never be dull. It would be a loud existence mixed with soft moments just for the two of them to enjoy. It would be tackling the tough days together, battling frustrations and roadblocks they might never see coming. It would be loving each other without an end in sight.

But for the most part, it would be enchanting.

With Annabeth Howard—here in the world of Haven House—life would forever be *enchanting*.

And he couldn't wait for their story to start.

CHAPTER 49

Jamison

"Can you pass me my coffee, Mrs. Cohen?"

Perched on the hood of her father's Range Rover, Jamison handed Liam the coffee they had picked up in the drive-thru on their way to the courthouse. "Here you go, my dearly beloved husband."

Eating a bacon, egg, and cheese sandwich, her father groaned. The County Clerk's office wouldn't open for another half hour, and they were having breakfast in the parking lot while they waited. "In a week, no one's going to want to be around you two if you keep this up."

"A week? Try an hour," Carter scoffed as he scanned the empty parking lot behind a pair of sunglasses. "Never thought I'd see the day."

Crossing her legs, Jamison smoothed the short skirt of her wedding dress down on her thighs. She didn't want to flash anyone after all. Well, no one except Liam. "What do you mean?"

"Liam. Married." Carter shrugged. "Back in the day, he was a known—"

"Nice guy who only dated a few girls." Liam interrupted before taking another sip of his coffee. "Swear to God."

Jamison was already well aware of his dating history, but figured this show of chastity was for the benefit of her father. "Sure, okay."

"Promise." He kissed her, tasting like caffeine. "I was an angel."

"Not to change the subject," her father said, brushing crumbs from his shirt, "but Will told me about Sinclair's journals. I'd like to read them."

Liam's smile faded, his dark gaze dropping to the pavement. "There's a lot in there, Ben. Not all of it is hard to hear, but some passages are... disturbing. The loss of CeCe broke Michael Sinclair in ways we're still trying to understand. And, of course, the tumor didn't help."

"He saw Mama," Jamison blurted out, unable to keep it in. She and her father didn't hide from the tough stuff. That was their lifetime deal. "Sinclair would come to Haven's graveyard and hallucinate while there. He said he saw CeCe and other... *people*. One of them was Mama, and he called her Laura Jean Fairweather."

Not saying anything for a long minute, her father surprised them all and smiled. A real smile, where his dimples popped out and everything. "He called her Laura Jean Fairweather? I can't recall anyone ever," he shook his head as he laughed, "using Fairweather as her last name, but it sounds good."

"Michael knew about the necklace." She might not have told Liam when she scrubbed the mentioning of her mother's emerald necklace from public record, but her father knew. Benjamin Fairweather made a point of knowing every last detail about the people he loved. "Michael said when Mama appeared to him, she wore all white and had a glowing green thing around her neck."

"*Hmm.*" Her father's gaze shifted to a distant point behind her. "Any other interesting things in the journals?"

Liam went over the details they had obtained, and his frustration at not having the full picture began to show again. "CeCe's journals will probably fill in the gaps, and Sinclair left them in a storage unit we can easily break into, but, according to his final journal, he left a few of CeCe's early journals hidden at Haven House. I'm sure they're outside the house and probably in the graveyard, but we can't just start digging up graves."

The mention of the graveyard got Carter's attention. "Why do you think the graveyard? I saw the file, Liam. Sinclair would've gone wherever he wanted on that property."

Jamison carefully sipped from her coffee, not wanting to spill anything on the dress. "CeCe is there, and his clues point there."

"Let me find it." Pulling out his phone, Liam rested a hand on her exposed thigh as he flipped through photos. "Here it is. *The code to get in is the date I met Cecilia. If you can't remember it, you'll be able to find the information in a set of her personal journals that chronicled the years until she met me. I left them at Haven House. I thought it was fitting to keep them there. You can find the journals at the edge of the stone. Look for the shadows in the flower beds, and the beasts in the wilderness. Our secrets are with the ghosts who remain in the river."*

"The ghosts who remain in the river?" Carter frowned and leaned over Liam's shoulder to read. "Sinclair could have considered that bayou behind the house as a river, and didn't you guys have some ancestor who committed suicide there? My Great-Uncle George is obsessed with genealogy and has our whole family mapped out. He likes to show it off, especially after everything with Toby, and I swear there's a Fairweather on there who committed suicide by drowning herself. I can call Uncle George and get more details if you want me to."

"You know, I vaguely remember hearing something like that." Her father rubbed his jaw as he tried to remember the details. "When I was a kid, the locals used to say Haven House was haunted, but no one could agree on who exactly was doing the haunting. One option was a legend that claimed a couple had died in the bayou. When I moved Simone and Ty into Haven, she said weird shit started happening, so she had Ty paint the awnings blue as if that would help."

"If a couple drowned behind Haven, they had to be part of our family," Jamison said, then turned to Carter. "And our family is your family, too. So, your uncle might have some details."

Carter removed his sunglasses, looking less than amused. The man always seemed so serious, which solidified the fact in Jamison's mind that he indeed had Fairweather blood running through his veins.

"You don't have to keep bringing that up."

Liam smirked at his friend. "Wait. Are we related now?"

"Do you want me to call my uncle or not?"

"Go ahead," Jamison said, finding Carter's total disdain for Liam's teasing hilarious. "It's not like we're going anywhere."

Making the call, Carter nearly hung up on the fourth ring, but a sleepy elderly man finally answered. "Carter? Is everything okay? Your grandpa isn't hurt, is he?"

"No, Uncle Georgie. Sorry to wake you. We're all good, and Grandpa is still up in Arkansas, but I'm down in Florida," Carter replied. "I was wondering if you could do me a favor. Whenever you have a chance,

could you look at the information you have on the Fairweathers? I want
to clarify something that I thought I saw in your notes."

Carter's uncle groaned as he moved around. "Hold on, let me go into
my study."

"You don't have to do it now—"

"Don't be silly, kiddo," George said, cutting him off. "I'm retired and
can take a nap later."

Jamison swore Carter blushed at being called kiddo and bit her lip to
keep from smiling.

"Thank you, Mr. Anderson, for looking this up for us." Her father
leaned forward so he could be heard. "We're having an early morning
discussion regarding ghosts, and Carter tells us you might be able to
answer a few questions."

"Carter, who is that person?" George asked in a whisper.

"That's Ben Fairweather," Carter told his uncle. "He's here with me."

There was a long pause. "Holy Moley," George breathed. "It's nice to
meet you, sir. I'm a big fan. Well, not a big fan. You know what I mean.
I've followed this whole nasty business like everyone else in the world,
and it's kind of exciting to know that we're connected."

Jamison nudged her father's shoulder, knowing how much he disliked
the word *fan*. "It's nice to meet you, too, Mr. Anderson," he replied. "I'm
going to pass the phone to my son-in-law so he can ask his questions."

Son-in-law.

Her heart swelled when she caught the way Liam straightened at
hearing the phrase son-in-law come out of her father's mouth. "Hi, Mr.
Anderson. My name is Liam Cohen, and I'm wondering if you can tell
me anything about the bayou behind Haven House."

"What do you want to know?" George asked. "It was used for
transporting lumber—"

"No, not that," Liam cut in politely. "I mean, are you aware of any
deaths in or near the bayou?"

"Oh, yes!" George cleared his throat. "But, *uh*, Mr. Fairweather? I
want to clear one thing up first. My brother told me your family was led
to believe Wilhelmina Anderson murdered her father at Haven House,
but she didn't. Wilhelmina was my mother's grandmother, and Mom
said that her Nana told her all about the Fairweathers after they went
down to Florida for a visit. Wilhelmina told her how she escaped from

Haven House at Christmas. Her sister escaped too, though I can't recall her name—Lucinda, maybe? I'll check my notes."

Carter dipped his head so George could hear him. "Escaped what, Uncle George?"

"Willa escaped the men! The Fairweather men!" George yelled into the phone excitedly. "According to my mother, Willa said she got out just in time because the Fairweather men were evil to their core. No offense, Mr. Fairweather, but it was a whole sordid story."

Jamison winced as all eyes shifted to her dad, who merely shrugged. "You know what? Calling them evil is probably fair at this point."

"When all that mess came out about Tobias Miller, and we found out Haven House was real and the whole unbelievable story unraveled... my brother and I kind of thought maybe our mom was telling the truth about her grandmother. Maybe the men in that family were actually crazy." George gasped. "I'm sorry. I didn't mean to say that."

"It's fine," her father continued to assure the man, and Jamison patted his shoulder in silent thanks. "But are you aware of any deaths that might have occurred in or by the water?"

"Specifically, near the graveyard?" Liam added.

"Well, there's Stephen Fairweather. He would be your direct ancestor, Mr. Fairweather. Shot by either his lover, his son, or his wife—no one was really sure. My mother said her grandmother never found out who pulled the trigger." George let out a sharp yelp. "Sorry, my books fell over."

"Uncle George's study is cluttered with books and maps—" Carter began, but was interrupted by his Great-Uncle's shout.

"Maps! Yes, that's it!" George shouted, shuffling around. He let out an *oof* as if he'd tripped. "I wrote everything down on a survey map I procured of Haven House. Let me find it."

While they waited, Jamison whispered to Carter, "I think we should invite your Great-Uncle George over for dinner."

"Please don't," Carter mumbled. "He'd never leave. He's already mad that both me and his brother have been to Haven without him."

"Okay, here we go," George said, slightly out of breath. "Right, I already mentioned Stephen Fairweather. Then there was Calvin Fairweather's lover. I've got the name Jennie written down, so I'm guessing that's what Wilhelmina said, although I'm not sure. I gathered all this information years ago when my mother was in the end stages of heart failure. Anyway, Calvin Fairweather shot his lover, who I think is this Jennie, and then he buried her with his father. Isn't Calvin your grandfather, Ben?"

"No, my grandfather was Malcolm Fairweather."

Jamison's eyes widened when George whooped with excitement. "Malcolm was Calvin Fairweather's son! Okay, so we have Stephen and Jennie. Then there's Grace Fairweather, and she drowned with her lover. Maybe that's who you're looking for? I can barely read my handwriting, but I think that's what it says."

"How many freaking murderers are in this family?" Liam arched an eyebrow, smirking sarcastically as he went to sip from his to-go cup. "Maybe I need to rethink this whole marriage thing."

"No take backs." Jamison straightened her spine, sitting primly as she lifted her nose in the air. "Simone has a strict no-return policy."

"Well, then." Liam kissed her again. "Guess I'll just have to deal with it."

"I'm sorry you had to hear all that, Mr. Anderson. We're in the presence of newlyweds," her father remarked, giving them a look. "May I ask how you received all this information? You said your mother told you?"

George chuckled. "My mother was a wonderful woman. She was a photographer who loved to tell stories with her camera and played witness to many things in her life. But when she got older and slowed down, I asked her to tell me her life story—and she did. It was good for her and good for us. She was what we called 'the keeper' in our family. The keeper of stories, if you will. She loved to sit and listen to the tales of other people's lives and then photograph them to put a face to the story. Here, let me show you something."

A beat passed, and then Carter's phone buzzed. "Show them the pictures," George instructed. "I think you'll really get a kick out of them."

Carter swiped through each photo as they gathered around to look at his screen. Haven House. The images, from decades ago, captured what appeared to be a renovation. The framed shells of the cottages were out on the shore of the bayou, prepped and ready for completion. There were images of the interior. The dining hall. The conservatory. The library.

And the final picture showed an elderly couple. Tall and thin, they held each other on a white sandy beach, laughing wildly as the wind tugged at their clothes and hair.

"That's my mother's grandparents," George said. "Dr. Noah Anderson and his wife, Willa Anderson—formerly Wilhelmina Fairweather."

"They look happy," her father said, taking off his sunglasses to see the screen. "We were told she was sickly, and that's why they built the conservatory for her at Haven House."

"She did have a breathing condition. Noah specialized in pulmonary disorders and gave her a good life," George replied. "My mother adored her grandparents and spent every summer with them. She often said they taught her the value of stopping and listening to others instead of barreling through life and making everything about oneself."

"That's lovely," Jamison said into the phone. "Hi, I'm Jamison Fa—Cohen. I'm Jamison Cohen, Ben Fairweather's daughter."

"Hello, Jamison. It's nice to meet you."

"Can you tell us more about Grace and her lover? The ones who drowned?"

George moved about as he mumbled to himself. "I don't know much, only that they died in the bayou. Grace committed suicide after the man she loved died. I think his name was Tommy—or Thomas. He was a worker at the mill and was killed when Stephen Fairweather discovered them trying to run away."

"Are you saying Stephen Fairweather killed him?" Jamison asked. "And they're buried in the graveyard?"

"Hold on, let me read," George said, and went quiet for a beat. "Yes, here it is. According to what my mother learned, both Grace Fairweather and her lover drowned in the bayou."

Cars were beginning to pull into the parking lot, and Jamison straightened her dress. "What do you want to do?" she asked Liam, already seeing the excitement building in his eyes. "Are we making this official, or are we going back to hunt for some journals?"

"Oh, I'm marrying you today." He took her hand, tugging her toward the courthouse while Carter and her father lingered by the Rover, still talking to George. "But we're starting our honeymoon off with a hunt."

"I'm getting really tired of running around in wedding dresses!" Jamison shouted when Liam picked up the pace. "And why are we even running in the first place?"

The entire time they filled out the paperwork, Liam bounced theories off her, and she volleyed them back, sorting through his wild rush of ideas. It was their way, and it would always be the way of Mr. and Mrs. Cohen.

"Ben, tell Abe we're going to need shovels," Liam yelled back at her father, who they had left standing by the Rover, shaking his head as they darted across Haven's lawn toward the forest. "Oh, and get my dad!"

Carter jogged to keep up with them. "Why the hell does it always sound like someone is singing out here?"

Holding her veil with one hand, Jamison listened. She might not enjoy wearing wedding dresses in high-stakes situations, but at least this time, she'd had the foresight to put on tennis shoes before they left to get their marriage license. "Still don't hear anything, Carter."

"It's there. I swear, it's there."

They were nearing the tree line, with the wide yawning entrance to the forest trails dead ahead. "I know you want to hurry, but maybe we should pause and think about this. I mean, how would Michael know about Haven's past?" she asked, slightly winded. "How would he know anything about Grace and Tommy?"

"It doesn't matter. *The edge of the stone* finally makes sense. I've just been too tired to see it." Liam squeezed her hand tightly as they ran. "I guess I just needed my wife to help me work through it."

She would not giggle at hearing him say *my wife*. She wanted to. She wanted to go out and meet strangers, saying, 'Hello, my name is Jamison Cohen, and this is my husband.'

And she would.

Later.

Right now, they had a graveyard to dig up.

Hitting the forest trail, Carter skidded to a stop when they reached the fork in the path. "What the fuck?" His head spun around in every direction. "What the hell is out there?"

Liam slowed to a stop. "The first time I came here, the energy in this section hit me so hard I almost drew my weapon."

"It was cute," Jamison told Carter. "He tried to protect me and everything."

"Yeah." Carter rested his hand on the gun holstered on his hip. "I can understand why people think this place is haunted."

"You ain't seen nothing yet." Liam trudged ahead, the temperature dropping the deeper they walked into the forest. The thick canopy above blocked all sunlight, making the entire section feel suffocating with its eerie stillness. Everything would be different once they rounded the curve ahead, and the trees thinned to reveal the graveyard and the bayou beyond. "The graveyard is like nothing you've ever seen."

"So, are we just picking a spot and digging?" Jamison asked as they neared the curve. "Or what?"

"My guess is that he buried the journals under the stone bench Abe placed near the front corner when he overhauled the site. It's got the best view of the entire graveyard, and you can see the bayou."

"You can also see the spot where CeCe died if you think about it." Turning the corner, they stopped, the graveyard waiting on the right and up a small incline. Jamison shivered, unable to stop herself. "Michael probably sat there when he came to see her."

"Holy. Shit," Carter exhaled. "This is just here? In what is basically the backyard? A freaking massive graveyard with those creepy spikes and statues and—"

"Dead people," Liam finished with a pat on Carter's shoulder. "Welcome to Haven House."

They walked side-by-side up the slope, the trees groaning around them in the wind. At the tall wrought-iron gates, Carter tilted his head back to take it all in.

"Uncle George would lose his damn mind if he saw this."

"I don't know how old the graves are," Jamison said, weaving through the headstones toward her mother's. She kneeled and gently brushed the pine needles and moss from the top of Laura Jean's marker. "But Liam's right. If he buried them, it's probably by the bench."

While Liam and Carter examined the ground near the corner seat, Jamison took a moment to have a long overdue talk with her mother.

"Hi, Mama," she whispered. "I got married today."

Smiling softly, she ran her fingertips over the smooth marble. "It wasn't a beach wedding like we planned, but it was perfect. Daddy cried, and Simone made fun of him. Everyone was able to be there, and I think... I think you were there, too."

A light breeze gently lifted her veil, teasing it in the air before settling it again against her shoulders.

"I think you'd like him. Liam. He's steady. Kind. He's the other half of my soul and never lets me down. Not even with the tough stuff."

A hush settled over the graveyard, bringing with it the kind of quiet that felt less like absence and more like attention. Like something—or someone—might be truly listening.

"You have a new grandson. His name is Albert Benjamin Fairweather, and he has gray eyes like Evie, but she thinks they'll turn brown like Samuel's before too long. I don't know anything about babies, so maybe Evie's right."

The wind blew a little harder, spreading her hair from her face, and when she caught that familiar floral scent that always seemed to come in moments like this, Jamison closed her eyes and allowed herself to believe in the magic of Laura Jean.

"I won't ever know anything about babies, Mama. Not my own, at least."

She suddenly felt small and let the words tumble from her, wanting her mother to understand what she was going through. "It hurts, but I'm okay. Liam and I will be okay. I won't take anything for granted. There won't be a second of my life with him where I won't appreciate all I have and what we'll build together."

"What is going on?" Simone's sharp tone had Jamison popping up to stand. "Y'all can't wait two seconds for us to bring a shovel?"

Liam and Carter had started digging near the bench with their hands, convinced they'd found the right spot, but Simone didn't appear impressed with their work when she and Bernie came through the entrance.

Abe rolled in behind them, the hum of his motorized chair faint beneath the rustling trees. He often worked alone in the graveyard and knew every corner of it better than anyone. "I have equipment for this," he said dryly. "And don't you touch those flower beds, Liam."

Flower beds.

Jamison's head turned, her gaze taking in the entire rear of the graveyard. "Shadows in the flower beds," she murmured. "That's what he meant."

She waved to get Liam's attention and pointed toward the flower beds Abe had designed at the end of each section of headstones. Layer after layer, the neat rows were laid out to guide visitors through.

And from the bench, the trees overhead cast long shadows across them.

"Are you seeing what I'm seeing?"

Liam sat down on the bench, his legs spread as he postured himself as Michael would. It never failed to amaze her how observant he was around people, picking up on the small nuances that crafted personality and behavior.

"What is Liam doing?" Selah whispered to their father when they arrived with Lenora and Xavier.

"I have no idea," their father replied. "Abe's remodel is fantastic, but this place is still a maze of the unknown. Half the tombstones and markers don't have names on them."

"Liam, give me some guidance here." Izzy rushed up the incline with Will in tow and headed to the opposite side of the graveyard. "Are we looking for something in particular?"

Will went over to sit with Liam, the two of them in quiet conversation for a moment. "Look for a grave marked with the name Grace. It's impossible even to entertain this idea, but Sinclair said the lovers who remain in the river. According to Carter's great-uncle, two people drowned in the bayou. One of them was named Grace."

"Carter's uncle?" Simone's brows snapped together. "Someone better start explaining."

Jamison did her best to run through the whole thing. Rowan and Annabeth joined them halfway through, both looking rumpled as if they'd been taking a mid-morning nap. "And now we think the journals might be buried out here."

"This is insane," Annabeth muttered. "But okay, let's do this."

Xavier held up a tiny plastic beach shovel. "I'm gonna help dig!"

"Give Uncle Liam a sec, X-man," Lenora said. "Watch him work it out first. It's creepy, but it's kind of cool to see the Cohens do their thing."

"It is creepy, but my boys know what they're doing." Bernie stood with Simone, the two women seeking the small shot of sunshine breaking through the trees. "If those journals are here, they'll find them."

Will spoke quietly to Liam, who nodded. "I agree with that, but how?"

"Sometimes, the truth is bigger than us," Will replied. "And we have to learn to go with it."

Staring off at the rear corner of the graveyard, where the incline began to drop and slide into the bayou, Liam's dark eyes narrowed on something. "Hey, X-man, pass me that shovel."

Happily, Xavier obliged, and Liam continued to stare at the spot, his head tilting to the side. "Jamison, those two stones back there on the ground. Right by your left? What do they say?"

She hurried to the two stones close to the fence line. "Nothing. They're unmarked like half the graves here."

But she saw it then. The two markers. They were perfectly lined up together.

"Wait, these stones are... even? I guess that's the best way to say it. They're not haphazardly in a spot like the rest of the older stones."

Liam jogged over with Xavier's shovel. "This is it."

"But the bench?"

"I thought that at first, but something is telling me to look here." They crouched together on the ground, with Liam grinning at her. "I don't understand it either, but here we go."

"When you have eliminated all which is impossible, then whatever remains, however improbable, must be the truth," Will said, helping Simone and Bernie traverse the thick roots protruding from the ground. "Or, as I like to say, go with your gut no matter what, even if it's telling you, you're crazy."

Everyone converged around them, with nothing but the occasional creak of branches or the rustling of leaves filling the silence while Liam worked. Jamison went to help him, but almost toppled over when her veil caught on a nearby fallen branch.

"Here, let me help you." Working to set her free, her father extracted the veil from the gnarled branch. "There we go."

"Thanks, Daddy."

"Sure thing, Princess."

"Are we really digging up graves?" Lenora asked with concern. "Because if so, I might need to take Xavier back to the house."

"Of course we are. This is Jamison's wedding day." Annabeth dropped to her knees next to Jamison and nudged her shoulder. "What else would we be doing?"

"It'll be shallow," Abe said, watching Liam intently. "If Sinclair buried something, I'd have noticed. I come out here every week, and it would have caught my attention if the earth had been disturbed by a large hole."

Carter stepped away from the group to stand at the fence line. His head tilted as he stared out over the bayou. "I thought I was crazy, but listen. There's something out there, and it sounds like singing." He pointed to the pilings protruding from the water. "Those pilings have some sort of metal on them, and it's creating a sound when the wind blows."

Everyone stopped and listened, and sure enough, Jamison could finally hear what Carter had been going on about. "I've never noticed it before, but I hear it."

Her father frowned. "It does sound like a woman singing. Those pilings are from the old mill and were once part of the loading area, I think?"

"I don't hear anything." Rowan joined Carter at the black wrought-iron fence. "Nope. Nothing."

"Yeah, there is. It's like a lullaby," Selah argued, pulling Xavier up to settle on his shoulders. "Can you hear it, big guy?"

"I hear it!" Xavier swayed as he listened. "It sounds pretty."

Liam carefully shoveled dirt from around the two small stones. "Must be a Fairweather thing because I don't hear it." He paused and nodded at a spot to the left of the markers. "Abe, look at this. We're missing grass here, and the dirt is more compacted.

Abe narrowed his eyes, nodding. "Yeah, you're right. The surface looks normal, but it's loose around the edges. Dig deeper, but do it slowly so you don't damage anything buried."

Liam worked the dirt loose around the missing patch of grass, and—perhaps an inch below the surface—a box began to take shape.

"Oh my God," Jamison whispered. "My husband is a genius."

Liam paused to flash her a grin. "You just called me your husband."

"Do we need to be worried about bombs?" her father interrupted. "I know you're excited, but we're dealing with Michael Sinclair here."

"No," Liam replied softly and returned to his digging. "CeCe is here. He would never destroy this place."

Will nodded in agreement. "The tone in the journals showed how much he loved her, and those were simple words on paper. I can't imagine him ever hurting CeCe, even after death."

Extracting the box from the ground took less than five minutes. Metal and with no lock to keep anyone out, Liam placed it in the center of the group. "Selah, step back with Xavier. Just in case."

They waited while Selah and Lenora moved Xavier out to wait on the trail.

"Here we go." Liam flipped up the latch, and everyone leaned in when he lifted the lid. Cradled at the bottom of the box were books wrapped in cloth, and he gently pulled each one out. "Thank you for not killing us, Sinclair."

The soft leather bound journals were labeled numerically on their spines, and as Liam opened the first one, he snapped it closed again when he read the first page. "This isn't for me to do."

About to burst with anticipation, Jamison fought the urge to snatch the journal from him and read it herself. "What do you mean?"

"Michael Sinclair wrote his journals to his mother, and CeCe did the same." Holding the book out, Liam nodded for Simone to take it. "These are written to you, Simone. CeCe considered you her mother even up until the end."

Simone stared at the offering, tears welling in her eyes. With a shaking hand, she took the book and flipped to the first page, her bottom lip quivering as she read. *"Sometimes the family you're given isn't the one you're meant to keep. My name is Cecilia Miller, and when I was born, I had mothers and sisters and brothers who weren't mine by blood, but were mine, nevertheless. We lived in a place called Haven House, where every day was an adventure. This is my story."*

Annabeth went to her mother's side, wrapping an arm around her to keep Simone steady. "Oh, my." Simone ran her fingertips over the page. "Oh, my baby. Look at you still making those curls on the tips of your letter T." She tilted the book to proudly show Bernie. "CeCe always had a problem with writing the uppercase T because she just wanted it to be a lowercase, but Devon taught her how to make it fancy so she would get excited to write it correctly."

Annabeth pointed at the next passage. *"If you have somehow found these and cannot return them to me, please forward my journals to a woman named Simone Howard. She was my mother in the truest sense of the word, and I want her to know I never forgot her and always held her in my heart,"* she read and then laughed through her tears. *"And if you cannot locate Simone Howard, please send them to her daughter, Annabeth. My sister, and forever twin to my soul."*

Rowan came up behind Annabeth to look at the book, but Jamison had a sneaky suspicion he was doing it to remain close in case she needed him. The same could be said for Izzy, who had taken Abe's hand while he pretended not to cry.

"CeCe dedicated her life to keeping everyone safe from Toby, and when she tried to fight back, and find her happiness, they killed her for it," Jamison told everyone. "I know he wasn't a good person, but you should have seen that house. Michael built CeCe her version of Haven House and would have given her the happily ever after she deserved."

Simone remained quiet, reading to herself, and when she finally lifted her head, she stared directly at the man she had spent a lifetime traveling on the long road of grief with, neither of them ever able to escape it.

"Benjamin, he needs to be here with CeCe."

The late morning breeze coming in off the water teased the tips of her father's hair, ruffling it about. Jamison thought it made him look young again, and when his gaze dropped to Laura Jean's marker, everyone waited to hear him deny Simone's request.

But he didn't.

"If that's what you want, SiSi." With a bittersweet smile, Benjamin Fairweather nodded. "We'll bring him home to Haven House."

CHAPTER 50

LIAM

Once upon a time, Samuel Fairweather said that north wasn't always the right direction when following one's moral compass, and that bent principles on a crooked path would forever be the destiny of men like them.

Liam hadn't wanted to admit it at the time, but Samuel was right, and any lingering regret over choosing to take that crooked path with him had long faded with the years. North was no longer an option. Their broken moral compasses knew only one direction, guiding them to make decisions based on what was important.

Their women.

Their children.

Their family.

The rest of the world, including themselves, could go to hell as long as they were safe.

Yet, when he and Samuel decided to kill Tobias Miller, there had been that initial hesitation. It caused the orienting arrow on their compasses to spin out of control, but deep down, they knew it had to be done. It was the only way to know peace and balance the scales.

But then Michael Sinclair entered the picture.

"Any news?"

Sitting astride their boards, the horizon still pink with the rising sun in the distance, he and Samuel had thought they could release a little tension in their waiting game by catching a wave or two. But the Gulf of Mexico wasn't behaving this morning, annoying them both with low swells breaking a few feet off the shore.

"BOP should alert Klausen around seven," Liam replied, unzipping his wetsuit to slide it off his upper body. December or not, the heat was heavy, and he couldn't tell if it was the humidity or his nerves making him sweat. "Bruce's message was vague, but for sure, we'll hear something today, as will the rest of the world."

"Killian said he's still got a man inside, but the guy has orders only to confirm it's done."

Without the possibility of someone listening, they could talk openly out here on the emerald water. "We got lucky with the transfer. Toby being moved to a low-security transport facility made everything easier."

Samuel grunted in agreement. "I'm assuming Killian's man also made sure Toby was aware of what happened in Arkansas?"

"Oh, yeah."

That was the single thing Samuel had wanted. Sinclair's man could have the kill, but Samuel wanted—needed—Toby to know the fate of Taylor's gruesome end. In the first few days of sweeping the grounds, the assembled investigative teams had quickly found Taylor's body.

Well, what was left of her body.

Obliterated by the phosphorus bomb Sinclair had shoved in her mouth, Taylor's pretty face had been melted into indistinguishable piles of waste. Fragments of the rest of her remains were not far off, scattered across the now scorched lawn. The cleanup crew had spent an extensive amount of time ensuring that they collected every piece of her, leaving no bone or leftover body parts behind.

When they learned the full details, Samuel had no outward reaction, but he did make another call to Killian, asking for a second favor. Not only was his man on the inside to inform Toby about what happened to Taylor, but Samuel also wanted him to pass along a very special message to his cousin.

I win.

It might have been evil, but those two little words made Liam smile even now, and while he admired many things about his friend, Samuel's pettiness was his favorite trait in the man.

"The bastard won't care about Zanmi, but when he finds out it was Sinclair behind their deaths and that Sinclair had been the one to end Taylor's life, he'll lose his mind," Samuel said. "The piece of shit will know she suffered."

"And you're good with that? Taylor worked for you for years, Samuel. The betrayal—"

"I'm good with it," Samuel cut him off. "Sinclair was pressed for time. I get it, but what he gave her was an easy death, in my opinion."

"An easy death? Sinclair put a bomb in her mouth and taped it shut. Have you ever seen what phosphorus does to human flesh?" Liam raised an eyebrow when Samuel nodded. "You know, I think you might be getting vicious in your old age."

"Fuck you. I'm not old." Samuel lifted his leg out of the water and tried to knock Liam off his board with the flat of his foot. "And you're only a few years younger than me."

Keeping his balance, Liam waved at Jamison when she came out of the back door of their townhouse. Already in her bathing suit, she looked good enough to eat, and he thought he might do just that once he finished talking to Samuel.

A few houses down, Evie appeared on the rear pool patio of their home, settling into one of the loungers to nurse Albie. Outright sighing, Samuel watched his wife. "God, don't let me fuck this up."

As Samuel's closest friend, Liam figured it was only fair that he told him the truth. "You probably will."

Peeling off the top half of his own wetsuit, Samuel scooped up some cool water to drop on his overheated body. "Stop me if I do, and I'll do the same for you. Marriage and kids—"

"Gilbert told Jamison kids weren't possible."

Liam let those words sit between them, the low roll of waves causing their boards to rise and fall.

"Do you believe him?"

"Yes."

"Does Jamison?"

"Yes."

Samuel finally took his eyes off his wife. "And how is she processing it?"

They had spent these past few days hiding away at the townhouse, doing what honeymooners do. After the new year, Liam thought he would take her back to Paris for a real honeymoon, or maybe somewhere tropical, so she could wear that thong bathing suit for him again.

But between the sex and the laughter were the tears. They tackled the tough stuff, discussing a future that would have a piece missing in it. It was true that having kids scared him, but he still wanted them. Lots of them, and with her. Jamison would make a fantastic mother, giving their children adventures and fun filled days. On the other hand, he was aware he would make only an okay-ish dad. The type who would freak out if a kid sneezed wrong or burped too loudly after eating.

They would be loved, though. Any child who came into their lives with either too much gas or anything else thrown into the mix would have been given an insurmountable amount of love.

"She's taking it one day at a time, but I don't think it's settled into her brain completely yet." It hadn't settled into his brain either if he was honest. Gilbert might have been a sick pervert, but he was an expert in his field and had no reason to lie to them. "We discussed other avenues to eventually take."

"Blood doesn't make a family, Cohen."

Liam met the gaze of the man who had become a brother to him. "So I've learned."

"You know we've got your back, whatever you two decide."

He knew the Fairweathers would support them, as would his parents. Will and Bernie Cohen as grandparents would be an awesome thing to see.

"And listen, while it's just you and me out here, I want to say one thing." The water's surface had gone nearly flat, and Samuel placed his hands behind him to lean back on the board. "Thank you for being willing to risk it all for what I wanted. Toby isn't your fight, and I should have ended him in the graveyard."

"Yeah, maybe follow through next time."

"Kiss my ass." Samuel nodded at Jamison, who was stretching out on a lounger. "And thanks for taking on that, even after everything. I know she put you through hell there for a few months, and yet you never gave up on her."

That made Liam laugh. "Imagine what you would do if Evie pushed you away? Sit down and say no thanks the second she opened herself back up to you?"

Samuel snorted, getting the point. "My wife could set me on fire and dance around my burning carcass, and I would still find a way to crawl back to her."

"Exactly my point."

The sun peeked over the houses, and without a cloud in the sky, the day was readying to begin with an unobstructed burst of light. They promised Simone they would come over and decorate for Christmas this afternoon. Selah had already slipped off back to Atlanta to avoid the task, but the rest of them remained, including Ben, and everyone was expected to participate.

"I'm glad we didn't pull Rowan in any deeper," Liam said, bending forward to stretch his back. "We'll owe Killian for years after this."

"Years?" Samuel shook his head. "This is a life debt. Killian will hold us by the balls until we're dead, since he knows what we were really planning. Had Sinclair not come along, you and I both know we would have followed through on the favor, and McIntyres take this shit seriously."

Unfortunately, Samuel was speaking the truth, but Liam would never give up a chance to argue with him. "Rowan knows."

"Rowan knows enough, but not everything," Samuel countered as expected. "And we stick to Killian's request. Rowan is to keep his nose clean. It's to his benefit and ours. If we ever did have to run, we would need someone to stay behind."

Someone to stay behind and care for everyone. Simone. Annabeth. Abe. Ben would need support the most if he never saw two out of his three kids again, let alone his grandkids and Evie.

"Well, let's not make planning a murder common practice, and we should be fine."

"Christ, what have we become? We only wanted to protect them, but everything spiraled into this." Samuel mimicked his position, bending forward and gripping the board. "I don't recognize myself anymore."

"We're not good men. We know this. We've accepted this. We would do awful things for them—horrible things to protect our girls and Albie. But what you're feeling now? It's the future pressing in. A soul for an empire, Samuel."

It was all Liam could say, recognizing the twisted darkness growing in them both. It wanted the pain and suffering. It wanted their enemies and those who would dare threaten them to die horrible deaths.

"I remember the past, Cohen. I remember everything, and the pain never goes away." Samuel turned his haunted gaze to meet his, and Liam wasn't sure if he'd ever seen Samuel showing such vulnerability. "I won't allow my family to suffer ever again, and Evie... I still don't regret making that call to Killian. Maybe I never will. But you're right. I have to think about the fact that one day, it's all going to fall on my shoulders."

"Which is not something you want."

This wasn't a new discussion. Samuel didn't hate the idea of becoming the head of Fairweather Holdings, but he wasn't thrilled with it, either. He wanted to be there for his wife and kids, unwilling to miss life's big and little moments.

"My dad, whether he knows it or not, is a great man." Samuel nodded at Ben's house, sitting at the farthest end of the beach—a sprawling castle built for Laura Jean. "But when he lost Laura Jean, he threw himself into making Fairweather this massive thing, and I honestly don't think I can fill his shoes. I'm selfish. I want time with my wife. I want to see my kids grow up. The Fairweather Holdings empire might as well be a pile of dirt if I miss out on their lives."

Liam straightened into a sitting position. "But you're scared that if you step too far back, you'll let everyone down."

"There will be so many people relying on me, and I'm going to be tackling it alone."

Giving Jamison a thumbs up when she pointed at her coffee mug to ask if he was ready for a caffeine fix, Liam could only tell Samuel the one thing he knew for certain. "You're not alone. I'm here. I'll always be here. I don't know shit about corporations, but I'll handle my end of things, so you don't have to concern yourself with their safety. I'll protect them while you do the rest."

"I know you will, fucker."

"And we have Rowan."

That made Samuel grin. "Yeah, we do. Annabeth's not letting him go."

"Yep. McIntyre or not, he's stuck with us."

They went silent, but knew they couldn't linger. The minutes were ticking. Paddling to shore, they carried their boards to where they had left a few belongings on the sand and sat in the two low beach chairs they had set up before going out.

Eyes on the horizon, Samuel released a nervous exhale. "How much longer?"

"Soon."

And as they admired the sunrise, with their families waiting for them in the distance, the call that would change everything finally came. It was from his father, and Liam mentally prepared himself to give the performance of a lifetime.

"Hey, you're up early."

"Tobias Miller is dead," his father said by way of greeting. "Heart attack."

Liam waited for the appropriate number of shocked seconds to pass. "Heart attack? I'm with Samuel. Hold on, let me put you on speaker." Hitting the button, he repeated the news so Samuel could act out his part along with him. "Tell us what you know."

"The guards found Toby unresponsive in his cell around three this morning. Sinclair got to him somehow."

Liam shared a look with Samuel. They had assumed Toby's death would be a clean kill, with no signature left to determine who might have been responsible.

"How do you know it was Sinclair?" Liam asked.

"A manchineel." Nothing upset Dr. William Cohen more than the unexpected, and he grumbled under his breath. "Someone shoved a manchineel down Toby's throat. It was jammed in there tight, and the initial reports are saying its toxins are likely what triggered the heart attack."

A manchineel shoved into Toby's throat? Liam grinned at the same time as Samuel, both of them again impressed with Sinclair's genius.

"Holy shit," Liam whispered with just the right inflection of surprise. "When can we have access? Is Anderson or Klausen en route? They won't let me in, but they might let you in?"

Liam and his father tossed information back and forth, with Samuel leaving them to return to his family. He would need to be with Evie when the networks broke the news, not wanting his wife to hear the details alone.

"Listen to me," his father said once he finished relaying all the information. "I know you want to go, but maybe it's best that we sit this one out and get the details from Anderson or Klausen this time. Remember, we're still hunting Emmett Watson."

Emmett Watson's body hadn't been found around the blast, so they could only assume the slippery snake made it out alive.

"I guess you have a point." Liam pretended to think about it. "I am technically on my honeymoon."

"That's right," his father replied. "Go enjoy your wife and *try* to remember you're a private citizen."

Jamison had traveled down the three steps to the sand and was currently walking toward him in all her glory. God, she was beautiful with every curve—every fucking inch—of her luscious body and brilliant mind bound to his for eternity.

"I think I can do that."

He dropped the phone onto the stack of towels next to him, not even bothering to hang up since he was too distracted by his beautiful wife when she reached him. "Good morning, Mrs. Cohen. Wanna join me for a swim?"

Passing him without answering, she smirked over her shoulder, her hips swishing in a way that had his brain short-circuiting. When he gave chase, she squealed as the two of them ran into the waves that had now decided to appear.

"Gotcha." He caught her easily, lifting her so her legs wrapped around his waist. "What do you want to do this morning, wife? We can swim, surf... or do anything you want."

Clutching his neck, she gasped as a cold wave crashed against her back. "Well, husband, I want to do something that starts with the letter S—but it has nothing to do with water."

He kissed her, dropping low in the surf. "But that S word can be done in the water."

"Don't you dare." She tried to wiggle free, her slippery skin driving him crazier. "People could see!"

"We would just be giving the residents of Firewater Beach entertainment while they have breakfast."

She whooped with laughter, throwing her head back, completely and totally uninhibited. It was what he loved most about her. Jamison was unapologetic about who she was as a person. She loved with her whole heart, living out loud without a care of what anyone else might think.

"You're incredibly scandalous, Mr. Cohen."

"I guess you're just going to have to keep me in line, Mrs. Cohen."

Pressing her breasts against his chest, she squirmed in the most intoxicating way. "I think I can do that," she said, her expression turning serious. "Was that the call?"

"It was."

"And it's done?"

"It is."

Her throat worked as she swallowed, another wave flowing over them. "So, we're...free?"

"We're free, baby." He kissed her, never able to get enough. "Now and forever."

Ben

Reclining on the pool deck's sofa, Ben grinned as he watched his grandkids play in the sand. From one year to the next, Christmas weather was never a guarantee, but much like last year, it was pleasantly warm, allowing them to enjoy the beach as the sun bid farewell to the day.

"Look at those colors." Sitting next to him, Laura Jean rested her head on his shoulder. "I wish I could capture this on canvas."

"You would do it justice," he told her, wincing when Theo tackled Xavier, knocking the poor kid straight into the enormous sandcastle the group had constructed. Holden watched from a safe distance, settled in a beach chair and grinning. "Maybe leave that Theo part out, though."

"Our girls are all fire," she said proudly. "Theo and Harper know how to hold their own. But I bet Xavier and Albie will be the ones who surprise us."

"I'm looking forward to Albie giving Samuel hell."

Theo climbed onto the ruined sandcastle and roared, flexing her muscles like some kind of tiny beast. The move made Laura Jean giggle with pride. "I don't think Albie is the one he should be worried about."

While the day was giving them a healthy dose of sunshine, the wind was still pretty fierce, and the absurd urge to offer Laura Jean his coat so she wouldn't be cold hit.

Which was ridiculous.

"Get out of your head, Ben."

"I see you in my head, so I think it's a pretty nice place to be."

She snuggled closer, her body pressing solidly against his side. Some days, she was hardly here. A shadow on the edge of his vision, waiting and watching them all. But then other days were like now, where he could almost feel her warmth.

"Well, you think too loudly."

"Well, you're too beautiful for your own good."

She snorted, resting her hand on his chest. "I love that we're hosting Christmas Eve at our house this year."

"Hopefully, it becomes a tradition. Simone didn't even fight me on it when I asked."

"SiSi is tired," Laura Jean said on the edge of a sigh. "And it's time to prepare for the end."

He frowned. "What are you saying?"

There was no reply, his woman taken by the wind when it rolled off the gulf in their direction. He didn't need to look up to know someone was approaching. His warped mind at least had the decency to make Laura Jean vanish when others were nearby.

"Are the kids behaving?"

Ben scooted over to give Simone room on the patio sofa. Inside the house, their brood remained busy crafting holiday cheer for the kids. He glanced at the glass wall behind him to check for any new arrivals. "No one's lost a tooth this time, so I'm calling it a win."

Simone grunted in agreement. "A win is a win."

"Is everyone here?"

"Will and Bernie are on their way. I can't believe they wanted to drive all the way from Virginia."

Ben could. Like Will, he was learning to slow down. It was hard initially, but it was time, or else he'd find himself in an early grave, and he couldn't allow that to happen.

He'd made a deal.

Simone settled on the cushions with him, bundling the cardigan she wore around her. "Is it done?"

"Rowan and I signed the paperwork this morning." He leaned back so their shoulders touched. "The Fairweathers hold Haven House no more. She's a McIntyre now. Rowan is taking full financial responsibility with fifty-fifty ownership listed to Annabeth and Abraham Howard. We only need the twins to sign off on it."

"Rowan said he's proposing tonight," Simone said. "I swear if she says no…"

"Annabeth's been dropping hints about what kind of ring she wants for weeks. She knows it's coming, Simone."

"He's so good to my baby."

"And he's good to you. We're lucky to have him," Ben huffed. "But damn, I never thought I would say that about a McIntyre."

Down at the far end of the deck, the double sliding glass door opened, and Ben grinned when Diego popped his head out. "Hey, Diego. Going down there to play?"

Eleven years old and smart as hell, the kid was as adventurous as he was clever. Diego Martinez had come into Jamison and Liam's lives not long after they finished the home build in the new Fairweather Georgia development, and already having briefly cared for two others temporarily before him, they had quickly been approved for long-term placement.

On the beach, Theo body slammed Xavier again, and Diego rolled his eyes with a laugh. "I think Xavier could use my help."

"Theo!" Simone was up and at the railing, snapping her fingers at the children on the beach. "Theodora, look at me."

Everyone froze. Ben included. Simone was a better disciplinarian than him, but sometimes, she was downright terrifying.

"Was that nice?" Simone didn't give Theo a chance to answer. "No, it was not. And we're not going to do it again. Got me?"

The chorus of *yes, ma'ams* made Ben smile. They were good kids—the best, in his opinion—but he was biased and damn well knew it.

Diego trudged past him with his hands shoved in his pockets and a grin on his face as he made his way to the steps leading to the sand.

"Good luck," Ben whispered before he left. "It's wild down there."

The poor kid's entire family had passed away in a fire, leaving him alone in the world. Jamison said she and Diego often had long discussions about his parents, but with Liam, he really opened up and always wanted to talk about his siblings. He had been the eldest of five children and missed his brothers and sisters horribly.

Diego gave him a serious nod. "I can handle Theo."

"Famous last words."

Evie emerged next, already narrowing her gaze on the children. "Is Samuel's daughter misbehaving again?"

"Oh, I love how she's my daughter when she's being bad and yours when she's an angel," Samuel said as he joined her, smacking Evie's butt before moving around her to stand with Simone, and yell down at his middle child. "Theo, no more. If you want to wrestle, come inside and wrestle me."

Theo put her hands on her hips like she had something to say—but caught Simone's look and promptly changed course. "Okay, Daddy."

Evie leaned into Samuel's side. Pregnant again, she swore this would be the last one. "Harper, you're supposed to watch her."

"Watching Theo is an incredibly large request," Harper said, pushing her new glasses up her nose. "She doesn't listen."

"What's going on out here?" Selah boomed as he came out of the back door, eating a sandwich with an annoyed look on his face. "Xavier, are you trying to convince everyone to jump off the roof again?"

"Nah, it's ours this time," Evie said, grinning. "Theo thinks she's twice her size and keeps plowing into Xavier—who, by the way, is *letting* her do it."

"I was just showing my moves!" Theo argued. "See, watch me."

Theo went for Diego, and the kid relaxed in time, taking the hit like a champ. With an *oof*, he landed on his back, laughing along with Theo as she shouted a victory cry.

Carrying Albie on her hip, Josie came out just in time to see the whole thing. "Theo!"

"He's okay, Nana!" Theo scrambled to her feet, her brand-new Christmas dress now covered in sand. "Promise!"

Flat on his back, Diego waved a hand in the air. "I'm good. Honest."

The kids resumed their game of Conquer the Castle, and Diego joined in as the designated referee.

"Annabeth and I have the food ready," Izzy called from inside. She and Annabeth had been in the kitchen all day and were eager for everyone to try the food. "Adults come eat first while the kids are still distracted. We'll bring the crazies in after."

Ben stayed seated, content to watch the mayhem a little longer. Soon, they'd all scatter back to their own corners of the world, and he wanted to soak up every second of this.

"Here." Josie passed Albie into his arms. "Take a kid so I can eat."

Gray eyes blinked in his direction, and Ben grinned. Albie looked so much like his namesake that the emotions never failed to hit. "Hey there, big guy."

As everyone except Simone took off to eat, Liam and Jamison slipped outside to watch the kids play. Jamison had a worried look on her face, but before Ben could ask what was wrong, Simone beat him to it.

"What is with you two?" Simone demanded, returning to her spot on the sofa. She reached for Albie, but Ben shifted away, not yet ready to let go. "Y'all have been whispering to each other all day."

Jamison exchanged a glance with Liam. "You tell them."

"We're planning to talk to Diego tomorrow," Liam said, coming closer. "We're asking him how he would feel about staying with us permanently. Not adoption—not yet. We think he needs more time to heal before we even bring that up."

"I've been practicing my speech," Jamison rushed out. "Simone, can I go over it with you later, and you can tell me if I'm being too pushy? I don't want to be pushy. He can choose us or...not. But I know you'll tell me the truth."

Simone nodded, eyes softer than usual. "Of course, baby."

"You're going to do just fine," Ben assured her, hating how nervous she looked. "And Diego is a great kid."

Jamison positively bloomed with happiness. "He really is."

Albie giggled at a row of pelicans flying low over the water, and Jamison crouched next to him. "Quick, count them, Albie." She counted them down as Albie released grunts and oohs in time with the numbers. "Eight! That was eight."

"Boo!" Albie squealed his nickname for Jamison and held out his arms for her. Ben let him go without hesitation, knowing Albie adored his aunt. "Boooo!"

"Yep, boo!" Jamison nuzzled his nose, making him laugh even harder. "I'm taking him in while Liam switches out with Holden so he can eat."

"Simone and I can watch the kids," Ben insisted. "All of you go in and get some food."

He spoke too loudly.

"Food?" Xavier shouted from the beach. "The food's ready!"

The kids charged up the steps, with Xavier leading the herd and Holden taking up the rear. The group passed in a flurry of cheers, invading the house with their demands to be fed. A crash and excited voices echoed off the high ceilings, bouncing around the space and coming outside.

"Yeesh, I guess they were hungry," Holden said, walking by them on his way in. "I hope nothing's broken."

"I built this house to withstand hurricanes and children," Ben told him, very much proud of that fact. "They could run amok anywhere and still be completely safe."

As everyone went inside, he and Simone relaxed again on the sofa. But their peace was short-lived. Seconds later, Annabeth darted outside, tiptoe running over to them. "Now?"

Meeting her daughter's excited gaze, Simone showed no reaction. "Now what?"

"Is he proposing today?" Annabeth propped her hands on her hips. "Tell me, Mother."

"I don't know why you'd think I'd know."

Clucking her tongue, Annabeth aimed her stare at Ben. He hated when she did that. She looked so much like Simone when she was younger, and it felt like stepping back in time. "Ben. Do you know?"

He reminded himself to treat this like a negotiation. After all, Annabeth was the daughter of Simone and Devon Howard. She was the niece to Ty. There was no out-bullshitting this woman.

"I know..." He paused. "That you should probably be prepared."

"Prepared?" She cocked her head to the side. "Should I paint my nails, Ben?"

Ah, hell.

"Yes?"

Annabeth did a little dance and dropped a kiss on his cheek before running back inside. "Thanks, Ben."

Simone barely had enough time to give him a death glare before Rowan was coming their way. The dog he and Annabeth adopted trailed after him, and while Ben wasn't much for dogs, he liked Bea and thought she looked damn cute dressed in her Christmas tutu.

"Did you tell her?" Rowan asked Simone. "She came in and kissed me so hard that Bea started barking because she thought I was getting assaulted."

"How could you think that I would tell her?" Schooling her features, Simone rested her fingertips on her throat. "Of course, I didn't say anything."

Rowan physically relaxed, and Bea even wagged her tail. "Thanks, Simone." He turned to go back inside, whispering to Bea as they left. "See, I told you GiGi wouldn't say anything."

"I cannot believe you," Simone whispered when they were alone. "We promised not to say anything."

"You promised," Ben pointed out. "Not me."

Simone planted her sharp elbow directly into his ribs. "You better not be pulling this crap when I'm gone, or I'll make you sorry."

Comments like this were coming more and more from her lately, and it was really pissing him off. Something was going on, and she was being very Simone about the whole thing.

"Cut the shit and tell me." His tone surprised even him, but that was the fear taking over. "You keep talking about when you're gone. You're not going fucking anywhere."

"Watch your mouth." Simone stiffened, like she was bracing herself. "My heart. It's not working like it should."

He waited, and when she took too long, he nudged her. "Don't be ridiculous. You don't have a heart."

Wiping at a tear, she leaned into his side when he wrapped an arm around her. "Last year, when that Zanmi woman gave me the injection, the doctors at the hospital noticed the irregularity then. I've been to see a cardiologist several times since, and I'm doing what they say to do, but it's still on the decline."

"Decline?" The word stuck in his throat. "Give me the details."

"They say it's a mix of age and stress-related wear and tear." She rested her hand on his chest, right where his own heart beat strong. "It'll get me, eventually."

"Just don't let it be soon, okay?" Taking a deep breath, Ben laced his fingers with hers. He hated how his voice trembled, but Simone wouldn't judge. Well, she would, but he was fine with it. "We have grandkids to watch over."

"I'll do my best." She kept her eyes on the sunset, smiling softly at the few people on the beach. "And you'll do the same, Benjamin."

"We have a deal," he murmured. "And I keep my deals. Remember?"

"That I do." She nodded. "And speaking of deals… thank you for letting us bring him home to her."

Michael Sinclair. The day CeCe's journals were found, they had both agreed he should be with her, but that didn't mean there wasn't a lot of soul searching to do as they waited for information. And once they knew it could finally happen, it had been one hell of a fight with the government. They'd won, and in the end, Sinclair's ashes had come to rest in Haven's graveyard, allowing him to spend eternity with CeCe.

"I'm sorry I wasn't there for the burial."

"Rowan handled it."

Unable to sit still for very long, Simone rose to stand, and he joined her, knowing that's what she wanted. "Michael's parents are nice, normal people, Ben. I told them they could come and visit him whenever they wanted."

"That was good of you." He braced his hands on the cool metal railing, looking out over Firewater Beach in all its glory. "Especially considering that, as of tomorrow, you'll no longer own Haven House."

She smiled at that. "They're going to argue when we tell them."

"The proposal will distract Annabeth, and I'll talk to Abe."

"Abraham is so much like Ty," she sighed. "But with Izzy… Ben, they've been together a year."

"We might actually marry him off."

"And I like her," Simone said, as if shocked by the fact. "I really and honestly like her as much as I like Lenora, and I think that between those two and Rowan, my babies will be okay without me."

Without me. She'd already accepted her fate, and he hated that she had gone through this alone.

"Promise me something," he said, pulling her close again. "You keep doing what you're doing, keep listening to the doctors, and I'll never let you go through anything alone."

She felt so small in his arms, and he wondered how he hadn't noticed the weight loss or the way her eyes no longer held the same glimmer in them as they once did.

But he noticed it now and was already making plans to find the best damn cardiologist in the country to treat her.

"This isn't a threat—or maybe it is—but you know that if you leave me, I get to tell the grandkids a bunch of wild stories about you," he said, resting his chin on the top of her head. "And I've got plenty."

"You do not."

"Try me."

Slipping from his hold, she returned to the railing. A light breeze teased the ends of her short hair, and she closed her eyes, her lips curving at the departing warmth of the day. "It doesn't matter."

"Doesn't it?"

"No. It doesn't matter." She opened her eyes, and for a moment, that mischievous twinkle he thought might be lost forever shone brightly once again. "Because when it comes down to it, everything we do is just another story. Devon. Laura Jean. Miranda. Livy. CeCe. Ty. Albie... They're nothing but stories now, their lives reduced to tall tales we hope to remember as the years pass."

Abe's hearty laugh carried from the open door, and Ben turned with Simone to watch their family—the very best pieces of them—enjoy the holiday. In the corner, Annabeth waved mistletoe over Rowan's head while Bea barked at their feet. Selah and Lenora were curled up on the floor, deep in some animated debate with Abe and Izzy. Liam and Samuel had Theo and Harper hoisted on their shoulders, helping rearrange ornaments on the massive, twenty-foot Christmas tree that no one could agree on how to decorate.

Snuggled on the couch with Albie in her lap, Josie chatted with Holden while Diego and Xavier played video games.

And in the kitchen, Evie and Jamison worked side by side, setting up the food. They scrunched their noses at the same time, the resemblance to Laura Jean striking Ben directly in the heart.

"We'll all become tall tales one day," Simone said, almost too quietly to hear over the happy sounds pouring from the home he'd purposely built for times like this. "Take those Fairweathers in the graveyard. One day, we'll be just like them. One day, no one will know that any of this was real, and we'll become just another story until we're forgotten altogether."

"We won't be forgotten." A tear slid down Ben's cheek, and he let it fall, too lost in the moment to care. "Because when it comes down to it, SiSi... we gave them one hell of a story."

Simone smiled at the scene inside the house, watching as their family created memories that would last long after the two of them were gone. "Yeah," she whispered. "I think maybe we did."

Chloe I. Miller loves to write spooky, spicy stories that tend to make her readers cry. She lives on the beach with her husband, two children, and a dog that doesn't realize she's a dog. For more information on upcoming projects regarding Haven House, you can visit www.chloeimiller.com.

Acknowledgements

Caitlin... we did it. I can't begin to express my gratitude. Haven House would have remained an obscure thought in my crazy brain if you hadn't encouraged me to actually write the damn thing and put it out in the world. Five years later, and here we are with four books and a novella. You've helped craft these characters and their stories over the years, leaving pieces of yourself in the passages. You keep me on track, talk me down from the ledge at least once a week, and will forever and always be my bestie.

Pam, I bet you never thought you would be stuck reading manuscripts and listening to me ramble for hours on end. Thank you for your endless input and help with these books. The manchineel shoved into Toby's throat? That's Pam's genius, folks. She keeps me on track every single day.

Jan, thank you for your expert eyes and, of course, your faith in me. This last book would never have seen the light of day without you.

Sam, thank you for your guidance through the years. This is the last one, and I can safely say we made it to the other side with mostly every character intact.

My dear BETA readers: Chastity, Brandy, & Kristina. Thank you for tackling my messy manuscript! I am so happy all three of you made an appearance in our last hurrah at Haven House. I hope you've had fun spending time there.

A huge thank you to R.S. Crawford for pushing me to increase the carnage when it came to Michael's revenge. It took me a minute, but I finally did put the duct tape all the way *around* her head. I cannot wait to see you shine in your new writing path. Seriously, people. She's going to blow your mind.

Thank you to Combat Medic Matthew Crawford for teaching me how to melt a human. I thought my Google search history was bad before, but your suggestions have taken it to the next level.

Thank you, Emmy Wade, for swooping in to give last minute feedback. You have a long writing career ahead of you, and it's going to be phenomenal to watch.

Thank you, Leslie Vincent, for writing & performing an impromptu song about a serial killer. I know you probably will never see this, but that little melody pushed me through a severe bout of writer's block, and I can't wait to listen to it on Spotify one day.

Thank you to my ARC Team!!! You're an amazing group of people who always come through. Maybe we're not quite done with Haven House?

Rachel Dane! (*I swear, every time I say your name out loud, I sound like I'm announcing John Cena*) Thank you for the hype and for introducing new readers to Haven House. Your ability to bring characters to life is such a talent, and I hope to be listening to you narrate for years to come. Never give up, my darling.

Thank you, Holly & Hillary, for taking on that ARC sneak peek to analyze. I'm so happy to have brought you two into the family. (*and Holly, I told you I would get your whoo-whoo van in this book one way or another*)

Last but certainly never least, thank you to my husband and kids. Without your patience and understanding, none of this would be possible. Logan, you're such an amazing person, and I'm so proud to call you my son. Ella, that beautiful soul of yours will one day change the world. I'm so proud of you and have no doubt that you're going to rule the world someday. Ivan, thank you for the support. We all know I wouldn't be able to dedicate my time to writing without you.

And thank you, dear readers. Thank you for coming along on this journey. I hope you found a home here at Haven House, if only for a little while.